MORRIS WEST

MORRIS WEST

THE DEVIL'S ADVOCATE
THE SALAMANDER

CHANCELLOR
PRESS

The Devil's Advocate first published in Great Britain by
William Heinemann Ltd in 1959
The Salamander first published in Great Britain by William
Heinemann Ltd in 1973

This collected volume first published in Great Britain
in1992 by Chancellor Press
an imprint of
Reed International Books Ltd
Michelin House
81 Fulham Road
London SW3 6RB

ISBN 1 85152 187 9

Printed in Great Britain by The Bath Press

CONTENTS

THE DEVIL'S ADVOCATE

I

It was his profession to prepare other men for death; it shocked him to be so unready for his own.

He was a reasonable man and reason told him that a man's death sentence is written on his palm the day he is born; he was a cold man, little troubled by passion, irked not at all by discipline, yet his first impulse had been a wild clinging to the illusion of immortality.

It was part of the decency of Death that he should come unheralded with face covered and hands concealed, at the hour when he was least expected. He should come slowly, softly, like his brother Sleep—or swiftly and violently like the consummation of the act of love, so that the moment of surrender would be a stillness and a satiety instead of a wrenching separation of spirit and flesh.

The decency of Death. It was the thing men hoped for vaguely, prayed for if they were disposed to pray, regretted bitterly when they knew it would be denied them. Blaise Meredith was regretting it now, as he sat in the thin spring sunshine, watching the slow, processional swans on the Serpentine, the courting couples on the grass, the leashed poodles trotting fastidiously along the paths at the flirting skirts of their owners.

In the midst of all this life—the thrusting grass, the trees bursting with new sap, the nodding of crocus and daffodil, the languid love-play of youth, the vigour of the elderly strollers—he alone, it seemed, had been marked to die. There was no mistaking the urgency or the finality of the mandate. It was written, for all to read, not in the lines of his palm, but in the square sheet of photographic negative where a small grey blur spelt out his sentence.

'Carcinoma!' The blunt finger of the surgeon had lingered a moment on the centre of the grey blur, then moved outwards tracing the diffusion of the tumour. 'Slow-growing but well established. I've seen too many to be mistaken in this one.'

As he watched the small translucent screen, and the spatulate finger moving across it, Blaise Meredith had been struck by the irony of the situation. All his life had been spent confronting others with the truth about themselves, the guilts that harried them, the lusts that debased them, the follies that diminished them. Now he was looking into his own guts where a small malignancy was growing like a mandrake root towards the day when it would destroy him.

He asked calmly enough.

'Is it operable?'

The surgeon switched off the light behind the viewing screen so that the small grey death faded into opacity; then he sat down, adjusting the desk lamp so that his own face was in shadow and that of his patient was lit like a marble head in a museum.

Blaise Meredith noted the small contrivance and understood it. They were both professional. Each in his own calling dealt with human animals. Each must preserve a clinical detachment, lest he spend too much of himself and be left as weak and fearful as his patients.

The surgeon leaned back in his chair, picked up a paper-knife and held it poised as delicately as a scalpel. He waited a moment, gathering the words, choosing this one, discarding that, then laying them down in a pattern of meticulous accuracy.

'I can operate, yes. If I do, you'll be dead in three months.'

'If you don't?'

'You'll live a little longer and die a little more painfully.'

'How much longer?'

'Six months. Twelve at the outside.'

'It's a grim choice.'

'You must make it yourself.'

'I understand that.'

The surgeon relaxed in his chair. The worst was over now. He had not been mistaken in his man. He was intelligent, ascetic, self-contained. He would survive the shock and accommodate himself to the inevitable. When the agony began he would wear it with a certain dignity. His Church would guarantee him against want and bury him with honour when he died; and, if there were none to mourn him, this too might be counted the final reward for celibacy, to slip out of life without regret for its pleasures or fear of its unfulfilled obligations.

Blaise Meredith's calm, dry voice cut across his thought:

'I'll think about what you've told me. In case I should decide not to have an operation—go back to my work—would you be good enough to write me a report to my local doctor? A full prognosis, a prescription, perhaps?'

'With pleasure, Monsignor Meredith. You work in Rome, I believe? Unfortunately I don't write Italian.'

Blaise Meredith permitted himself a small wintry smile.

'I'll translate it myself. It should make an interesting exercise.'

'I admire your courage, Monsignor. I don't subscribe to the Roman faith, or to any faith for that matter, but I imagine you find it a great consolation at a time like this.'

'I hope I may, Doctor,' said Blaise Meredith simply, 'but I've been a priest too long to expect it.'

Now he was sitting on a park bench in the sun, with the air full of spring and the future a brief, empty prospect spilling over into eternity. Once, in his student days, he had heard an old missioner preach on the raising of Lazarus from the dead: how Christ had stood before the sealed vault and ordered it to be opened, so that the smell of corruption issued on the still, dry air of summer; how Lazarus at the summons had come out, stumbling in the cerecloths, to stand blinking in the sun. What had he felt at that moment, the old man asked? What price had he paid for this return to the world of the living? Did he go maimed ever afterwards, so that every rose smelled of decay and every golden girl was a shambling skeleton? Or did he walk in a dazzle of wonder at the newness of things, his heart tender with pity and love for the human family?

The speculation had interested Meredith for years. Once he had toyed with the idea of writing a novel about it. Now, at last, he had the answer. Nothing was so sweet to man as life; nothing was more precious than time; nothing more reassuring than the touch of earth and grass, the whisper of moving air, the smell of new blossoms, the sound of voices and traffic and high bird-songs.

This was the thing that troubled him. He had been twenty years a priest, vowed to the affirmation that life was a transient imperfection, the earth a pale symbol of its maker, the soul an immortal in mortal clay, beating itself weary for release into the ambient arms of the Almighty. Now that his own release was promised, the date of it set, why could he not accept it—if not with joy, at least with confidence?

What did he cling to that he had not long since rejected? A woman? A child? A family? There was no one living who belonged to him. Possessions? They were few enough—a small apartment near the Porta Angelica, a few ornaments, a roomful of books, a modest stipend from the Congregation of Rites, an annuity left to him by his mother. Nothing there to tempt a man back from the threshold of the great revelation. Career? Something in that maybe—Auditor to the Sacred Congregation of Rites, personal assistant to the Prefect himself, Eugenio Cardinal Marotta. It was a position of influence, of flattering confidence. One sat in the shadow of the Pontiff. One watched the intricate, subtle workings of a great theocracy. One lived in simple comfort. One had time to study, liberty to act freely within the limits of policy and discretion. Something in that ... but not enough—not half enough for a man who hungered for the Perfect Union which he preached.

Perhaps that was the core of it. He had never been hungry for anything. He had always had everything he wanted, and he had never wanted more than was available to him. He had accepted the discipline of the Church, and the Church had given him security, comfort and scope for his talents. More than most men he had achieved contentment—and if he had never asked for happiness it was because he had never been unhappy. Until now ... until this bleak moment in the sun, the first of spring, the last spring ever for Blaise Meredith.

The last spring, the last summer. The butt end of life chewed and sucked dry like a sugar stick, then tossed on to the rubbish heap. There was the bitterness, the sour taste of failure and disillusion. What of merit could he tally and take with him to the judgment? What would he leave behind for which men would want to remember him?

He had never fathered a child nor planted a tree, nor set one stone on another for house or monument. He had spent no anger, dispensed no charity. His work would moulder anonymously in the archives of the Vatican. Whatever virtue had flowered out of his ministry was sacramental and not personal. No poor would bless him for their bread, no sick for their courage, no sinners for their salvation. He had done everything that was demanded of him, yet he would die empty and within a month his name would be a blown dust on the desert of the centuries.

Suddenly he was terrified. A cold sweat broke out on his body. His hands began to tremble and a group of children bouncing a ball near a bench edged away from the gaunt, grey-faced cleric who sat staring with blind eyes across the shimmering water of the pond.

The rigors passed slowly. The terror abated and he was calm again. Reason took hold of him and he began to think how he should order his life for the time left to him.

When he had become ill in Rome, when the Italian physicians had made their first, tentative diagnosis, his instinctive decision had been to return to London. If he must be condemned, he preferred to have the sentence read in his own tongue. If his time must be shortened, then he wanted to spend the last of it in the soft air of England, to walk the downs and the beechwoods and hear the elegiac song of the nightingales in the shadow of old churches, where Death was more familiar and more friendly because the English had spent centuries teaching him politeness.

In Italy, death was harsh, dramatic—a grand-opera exit, with wailing chorus and tossing plumes and black baroque hearses trundling past stucco palaces to the marble vaults of the Campo Santo. Here in England it had a gentler aspect—the obits murmured discreetly in a Norman nave, the grave opened in mown grass among weathered headstones, the libations poured in the oak-beamed pub which stood opposite the lych-gate.

Now this, too, was proved an illusion, a pathetic fallacy, no armour at all against the grey insidious enemy entrenched in his own belly. He could not escape it, any more than he could flee the conviction of his own failure as a priest and as a man.

What then? Submit to the knife? Cut short the agony, truncate the fear and the loneliness to a manageable limit? Would not this be a new failure, a kind of suicide that the moralists might justify, but conscience could never quite condone? He had enough debts already to bring to the reckoning; this last might make him altogether bankrupt.

Go back to work? Sit at the old desk under the coffered ceiling in the Palace of Congregations in Rome. Open up the vast folios where the lives and works and writings of long-dead candidates for canonisation were recorded in the script of a thousand clerks. Examine them, dissect them, analyse and notate. Call their virtues in question and cast new doubts on the wonders attributed to them. Make new notes in a new script. To what end? That one more candidate for canonical honours might be rejected because he had been less than heroic, or less than wise in his virtues; or that half a century hence, two centuries maybe, a new Pope might proclaim in St Peter's that a new saint had been added to the Calendar.

Did they care, these dead ones, what he wrote of them? Did they care whether a new statue were permitted to wear an aureole, or whether the printers circulated a million little cards with their faces on the front and their virtues listed on the back? Did they smile on their bland biographers or frown on their official detractors? They had died and been judged long since, as he must die and soon be judged. The rest was all addendum, postscript and dispensable. A new cultus, a new pilgrimage, a new mass in the liturgy would touch them not at all. Blaise Meredith, priest, philosopher, canonist, might work twelve months or twelve years on their records without adding a jot to their felicity, or a single pain to their damnation.

Yet this was his work and he must do it, because it lay ready to his hand—and because he was too tired and too ill to begin any other. He would say Mass each day, work out his daily stint at the Palace of Congregations, preach occasionally in the English Church, hear confessions for a colleague on vacation, go back each night to his small apartment at the Porta Angelica, read a little, say his office, then struggle through the restless nights to the sour morning. For twelve months. Then he would be dead. For a week they would name him in the Masses . . . 'our brother Blaise Meredith': then he would join the anonymous and the forgotten in the general remembrance . . . 'all the faithful departed.'

It was cold in the park now. The lovers were brushing the grass off their coats and the girls were smoothing down their skirts. The children were dragging listlessly down the paths in the wake of scolding parents. The swans were ruffling back to the shelter of the islets, to the peak-hour drone of London traffic.

Time to go. Time for Monsignor Blaise Meredith to pack his troubled thoughts and compose his thin features into a courteous smile for the Administrator's tea at Westminster. The English were a civil and tolerant people. They expected a man to work out his salvation soberly or damn himself with discretion, to hold his liquor like a gentleman and keep his troubles to himself. They were suspicious of saints and chary of mystics, and they more than half-believed that God Almighty felt the same way. Even in the hour of his private Gethsemane, Meredith was glad of the convention that would force him to forget himself and attend to the chatter of his colleagues.

He got up stiffly from the bench, stood a long moment as if unsure of his own tenancy in the body, then walked steadily down towards Brompton Road.

Doctor Aldo Meyer had his own preoccupations this mild Mediterranean evening. He was trying to get drunk—as quickly and painlessly as possible.

All the odds were against him. The place where he drank was a low stone room with an earthen floor that stank of stale wine. His company was a brutish peasant proprietor and a stocky mountain girl with the neck and buttocks of an ox and melon breasts straining out of a greasy black dress. The drink was a fiery *grappa*, guaranteed to drown the stubbornest sorrow—but Aldo Meyer was too temperate and too intelligent to enjoy it.

He sat hunched forward over the rough bench, with a guttering candle beside him, staring into his cup and tracing monotonous patterns in the spilt liquor that flowed sluggishly in the wake of his finger. The *padrone* leaned on the bar, picking his teeth with a twig and sucking the remnants of his supper noisily through the gaps. The girl sat in the shadows waiting to fill the cup as soon as the doctor had emptied it. He had drunk swiftly at first, gulping on each mouthful, then more slowly as the raw spirit took hold of him. For the last ten minutes he had not drunk at all. It was as if he were waiting for something to happen before making the final surrender to forgetfulness.

He was a year short of fifty, but he looked like an old man. His hair was white, the skin of his fine Jewish face was drawn tight and spare over the bones. His hands were long and supple, but horned like a labourer's. He wore a townsman's suit of unfashionable cut, with frayed cuffs and shiny lapels, but his shoes were polished and his linen clean, save for the fresh stains where the *grappa* had splashed. There was an air of faded distinction about him which matched oddly with the crudeness of his surroundings and the coarse vitality of the girl and the *padrone*.

Gemello Minore was a long way from Rome, longer still from London. The dingy wine-shop bore no resemblance at all to the Palace of Congregations. Yet Doctor Aldo Meyer was concerned with death like Blaise Meredith and, sceptic though he was, he too found himself embroiled with Beatitude.

Late in the afternoon he had been called to the house of Pietro Rossi, whose wife had been in labour for ten hours. The midwife was in despair and the room was full of women chattering like hens, while Maria Rossi groaned and writhed in her spasms, then relapsed into weak moaning when they left her. Outside the hovel the men were grouped, talking in low voices and passing a wine bottle from hand to hand.

When he came they fell silent, watching him with oblique, speculative eyes, while Pietro Rossi led him inside. He had lived among them for twenty years, yet he was still a foreigner; in these moments of their tribal life he might be necessary to them, but he was never welcome.

In the room with the women, it was the same story: silence, suspicion, hostility. When he bent over the great brass bed, palpating and probing the swollen body, the midwife and the girl's mother stood close beside him, and when a new spasm came, there was a shocked murmur, as if he were the cause of it.

Within three minutes he knew there was no hope of normal birth. He would have to do a Caesarean. He was not unduly perturbed at the prospect. He had done them before, by candlelight and lamplight, on kitchen tables and plank benches. Given boiling water and anaesthetic and the tough bodies of the mountain women, the odds were loaded in the patient's favour.

He expected protests. These people were thick-headed as mules and twice as panicky—but he was unprepared for an outburst. It was the girl's mother who began it—a stout, muscular shrew, with lank hair and gapped teeth and black snake eyes. She rounded on him, yelling in thick dialect:

'I'll have no knives in my girl's belly. I want live grandchildren, not dead ones! You doctors are all the same. If you can't cure people you cut 'em up and bury 'em. Not my daughter! Give her time and she'll pop this one out like a pea. I've had twelve of 'em. I ought to know. Not all of 'em were easy, but I had 'em—and I didn't need a horse-butcher to gouge 'em out either!'

A burst of shrill laughter drowned the moaning of the girl. Aldo Meyer stood watching her, ignoring the women. He said simply:

'If I don't operate, she'll be dead by midnight.'

It had worked before—the bald professional pronouncement, the contempt for their ignorance—but this time it failed utterly. The woman laughed in his face.

'Not this time, Jew-man! Do you know why?' She plunged her hand inside her dress and brought up a small object wrapped in faded red silk. Her fingers closed over it and she thrust it under his nose. 'You know what that is? You wouldn't of course—you being an infidel and Christ-killer. We've got a saint of our own now. A real one! They're fixing to have him canonised in Rome any minute. That's a piece of his shirt. A real live relic, stained with his blood. He's worked miracles too. Real ones. They're all written down. They've been sent on to the Pope. Do you think you can do more than he can? Do you? Which do we choose, folks? Our own Saint Giacomo Nerone—or this fellow!'

The girl on the bed screamed in sudden agony and the women fell silent, while the mother bent over the bed making little soothing noises and rubbing the dingy relic round and round on the swollen belly under the coverlets. Aldo Meyer waited a moment, searching for the right words. Then, when the girl was quiet again, he told them soberly:

'Even an infidel knows that to expect miracles without trying to help ourselves is a sin. You can't throw away medicines and expect the saints to cure you. Besides, this Giacomo Nerone isn't a saint yet. It will be a long time before they even start to discuss his case in Rome. Pray to him if you want, but ask him to give me a steady hand, and the girl a strong heart. Now stop being silly and get me boiling water and clean linen. I haven't much time.'

No one moved. The mother barred his way to the bed. The women stood ranged in a tight semicircle, shepherding him in the direction of the door, where Pietro Rossi stood, blank-faced, watching the drama. Meyer swung round to challenge him.

'You, Pietro! Do you want a child? Do you want your wife? Then for God's sake listen to me. Unless I operate quickly, she will die and the child will die with her. You know what I can do—there are twenty people in the village to tell you. But you don't know what this Giacomo Nerone can do—even if he is a saint . . . which I very much doubt.'

Pietro Rossi shook his head stubbornly.

''Tisn't natural to rip out a child like a sheep's gut. Besides, this isn't an ordinary saint. He's ours. He belongs to us. He'll look after us. You'd better go, Doctor.'

'If I do, your wife won't see out the night.'

The matt peasant face was blank as a wall. Meyer looked round at them, the dark secret people of the South, and thought despairingly how little he knew of them, how little power he had over them. He made a shrugging gesture of resignation, picked up his bag and walked towards the door. At the threshold he stopped and turned to face them.

'You'd better call Father Anselmo. She hasn't much time.'

The mother spat contemptuously on the floor, then bent down again to rub the little silk bundle on the twitching belly of the girl, mumbling prayers in dialect. The other women watched him, stony-faced and silent. When he walked out and down the cobbled road, he felt the eyes of the men like knives at his back. It was then that he decided to get drunk.

For Aldo Meyer, the old liberal, the man who believed in man, it was the final gesture of defeat. There was no hope for these people. They were rapacious as hawks. They would eat your heart out and let you rot in a ditch. He had suffered for them, fought for them, lived with them and tried to educate them, but they took everything and learned nothing. They made a mockery of the most elementary knowledge, yet lapped up legends and superstitions as greedily as children.

Only the Church could control them, though it could not better them. It plagued them with demons, obsessed them with saints, cajoled them with weeping madonnas and fat-bottomed bambini. It could bleed them white for a new candelabrum, but it could not—or would not—bring them to a clinic for typhoid injections. Their mothers wasted away with TB and their bambini had swollen spleens from recurrent malaria. Yet they would as soon put a devil in their mouths as an Atabrine tablet—even though the doctor paid for it himself.

They lived in hovels where a good farmer would not house his cattle. They ate olives and pasta and bread dipped in oil, and goat meat on feast days, if they could get it. Their hills were bare of trees and their terraces held a niggardly soil, from which the nourishment leached out with the first rains and was lost on the stony slopes. Their wine was thin and their corn was meagre and they moved with the sluggish gait of folk who eat too little and work too hard.

Their landlords exploited them, yet they clung to their coat-tails like children. Their priests lapsed often into liquor and concubinage, yet they fed them out of their poverty and treated them with tolerant contempt. If the summer was late or the winter was harsh, the frost burned the olives and there was hunger in the hills. They had no schools for their children, and what the State would not supply they would not make for themselves. They would not sacrifice their idle hours to build a school-house. They could not pay a teacher, yet they would dig into their tiny hoards of lire to finance the canonisation of a new saint for a Calendar that was already overloaded with them.

Aldo Meyer stared into the dark lees, of his *grappa* to read futility, disillusion and despair. He lifted the cup and tossed off the dregs at a gulp. They were bitter as wormwood and there was no warmth in them at all.

He had come here first as an exile, when the Fascisti had rounded up the Semites and the left-wing intellectuals and the too vocal liberals, and presented them the curt alternative of rustication in Calabria or hard labour on Lipari. They had given him the ironic title of Medical Officer, but no salary, no drugs, and no anaesthetics. He had arrived with the clothes he stood up in, a bag of instruments, a bottle of aspirin tablets and a medical compendium. For six years he battled and intrigued, cajoled and blackmailed to build up a sketchy medical service in an area of constant malnutrition, endemic malaria and epidemic typhoid.

He lived in a crumbling farmhouse which he restored with his own hands. He farmed a stony two acres, with the help of a cretinous labourer. His hospital was one room in his house. His theatre was his kitchen. The peasants paid him in kind, when they paid at all, and he exacted from the local officials a tribute in drugs and surgical instruments, and protection from a hostile Government. It had been a bitter servitude, but there had been moments of triumph, days when he seemed at last to be entering into the closed circle of the primitive mountain life.

When the Allies straddled the Strait of Messina and began their slow bloody progress up the peninsula, he had fled and joined the Partisans, and after the armistice he had spent a brief while in Rome. But he had been away too long. Old friends were dead. New ones were hard to make, and the small triumphs of the locust years challenged him to greater ones. With freedom and money, and the impetus to reform, a man of good will might work miracles in the South.

So he had come back—to the old house, in the old town, with a new dream and a sense of renewed youth in himself. He would become a teacher as well as a doctor. He would lay down a prototype organisation for co-operative effort, an organisation that would attract development money from Rome and aid money from overseas foundations. He would teach them hygiene and the conservation of soil and water. He would train young men who would carry his message to outlying districts. He would be a missioner of progress in a land where progress had stopped three centuries before.

It had been a fine, fresh dream twelve years ago. He knew it now for a bleak illusion. He had fallen into the error of all liberals: the belief that men are prepared to reform themselves, that good will attracts good will, that truth has a leavening virtue of its own. His plans had made shipwreck on the venality of officials, the conservatism of a feudal Church, the rapacity and mistrust of a primitive, ignorant people.

Even through the thick fumes of the liquor he saw all too clearly. They had beaten him. He had beaten himself. And now it was too late to mend.

From the dusk outside came a long, wailing cry of women's voices. The girl and the *padrone* looked at each other and crossed themselves. The doctor stood up and and walked unsteadily to the door to stand looking out into the cool spring twilight.

'She's dead,' said the *padrone* in his thick, husky voice.

'Tell the saint about it,' said Aldo Meyer. 'I'm going to bed.'

As he lurched out into the roadway the girl put out her tongue at him and made the sign against the evil eye.

The dirge-cry rose and fell, whining like a wind over the sleeping mountain. It followed him down the cobbled street and into his house. It battered on his door and searched at his shutters and haunted him through the night of restless, muttering sleep.

In the fall of the same spring dusk, Eugenio Cardinal Marotta walked in the garden of his villa on Parioli. Far below him the city was wakening from the torpor of afternoon and settling back to business with screaming horns and clattering motor-scooters and chaffering shopkeepers. The tourists were trudging remorsefully back from St Peter's and St John Lateran and the Colosseum. The flower sellers were spraying their blooms for the last assault on the lovers of the Spanish Steps. The sunset spilled over the hills and down on to the roof-tops, but down in the alleys the dust-haze hung thickly, and the walls of the buildings were grey and tired.

Up on Parioli, however, the air was clear and the avenues were quiet, and His Eminence walked under drooping palms to the scent of jasmine flowers. There were high walls about him and grilled gates to keep him private, and armorial bronzes on the lintels to remind the visitor of the rank and titles of Eugenio Cardinal Marotta, Archbishop of Acropolis, Titular of St Clement, Prefect of the Sacred Congregation of Rites, Proprefect of the Supreme Tribunal of the Apostolic Signature, Commissioner for the Interpretation of Canon Law, Protector of the Sons of St Joseph and the Daughters of Mary Immaculate and twenty other religious bodies great and small in the Holy Roman Church.

The titles were ample, the power that lay behind them was ample too; but His Eminence wore it with a bland good-humour that masked a subtle intelligence and a dominating will.

He was a short, round man, with small hands and feet and a dewlapped face, and a high domed head, bald as an egg under the scarlet skullcap. His grey eyes twinkled with benevolence and his mouth was small and scarlet as a woman's against the matt olive of his complexion. He was sixty-three years of age, which is young for a man to reach the red hat. He worked hard, though without apparent effort, and still had energy left for the devious diplomacies and manipulations of power inside the closed City of the Vatican.

There were those who favoured him for election to the papacy itself, but there were others, more numerous, who held that the next Pontiff should be a more saintly man, less concerned with diplomacy than with the reform of morals among clergy and laity alike. Eugenio Marotta was content to wait on the outcome, knowing that he who goes into the conclave a Pope is likely to leave it a Cardinal. Besides, the Pontiff might be old, but he was still a long way from dead, and he looked with small favour on those who coveted his shoes.

So His Eminence walked in his villa garden on Parioli, watching the sun decline over the Alban hills and pondering the day's questions in the relaxed attitude of a man who knew he would answer them all in the end.

He could afford to relax. He had come by steady progression to the high plateau of preferment from which neither malice nor disfavour could unseat him. He would remain a Cardinal till the day he died, a Prince by protocol, a Bishop by irrevocable consecration, citizen of the smallest and least vulnerable State in the world. It was much for a man in his vigorous sixties. It was much more, because he was untramelled by a wife, unplagued by sons and daughters, set far beyond the pricks of passion. He had come as far as talent and ambition could drive him.

The next step was the Chair of Peter; but this was a high leap, halfway out of the world and into a vestibule of divinity. The man who wore the Fisherman's ring and the triple tiara carried also the sins of the world like a leaden cope on his shoulders. He stood on a windy pinnacle, alone, with the spread carpet of the nations below him, and above, the naked face of the Almighty. Only a fool would envy him the power and the glory and the terror of such a principality. And Eugenio Cardinal Marotta was very far from being a fool.

In this hour of dusk and jasmine he had problems enough of his own.

Two days before, a letter had been laid on his desk from the Bishop of Valenta, a small diocese in a run-down area of Calabria. The Bishop was known to him vaguely as a rigid reformer with a taste for politics. He had caused a stir two years previously by unfrocking a couple of country curates for concubinage and pensioning off some of his elderly pastors on the grounds of incompetence. The election figures from his diocese had shown a marked swing towards the Christian Democrats, and this had earned him a Pontifical letter of commendation. It was only the more subtle observers like Marotta who had noted that the increase had come from the Monarchist Party and not from the Communists, who had also registered a slight gain. The Bishop's letter was simple and explicit–too simple to be guileless and too explicit not to rouse suspicion in a seasoned campaigner like Eugenio Cardinal Marotta.

It began with salutations, florid and deferential, from a humble bishop to a princely one. It went on to say that a petition had been received from the parish priest and the faithful of the villages of Gemelli dei Monti for the introduction of the Cause for Beatification of the Servant of God, Giacomo Nerone.

This Giacomo Nerone had been murdered by Communist Partisans in circumstances which might well be called martyrdom. Since his death, spontaneous veneration had been paid to him in the villages and the surrounding countryside, and several cures of a miraculous nature were attributed to his influence. Preliminary investigations had confirmed the reputation for sanctity and the apparently miraculous nature of the cures, and the Bishop was disposed to grant the petition and admit the case to juridical investigation. Before doing so, however, he sought counsel of His Eminence, as Prefect of the Congregation of Rites, and his assistance in appointing, from Rome itself, two wise and godly men–one as the Postulator of the Cause, to organise the investigation and carry it forward, the other as the Promoter of the Faith, or Devil's Advocate, to submit the evidence and the witnesses to the severest scrutiny in accordance with the appropriate provisions of canon law.

There was more, much more, but this was the core of the apple. The Bishop might have a saint in his territory–a convenient saint, too, martyred by the Communists. The only way he could prove the sanctity was by a judicial investigation, first in his own diocese and then in Rome, under the authority of the Congregation of Rites. But the first investigation would be made in his own See and under his own authority, with officials appointed by himself. Local bishops were normally jealous of their autonomy. Why then this deferential appeal to Rome?

Eugenio Cardinal Marotta walked the trim lawns of his villa garden and pondered the proposition.

Gemelli dei Monti lay deep in Midday Italy, where cults proliferate and die as quickly, where the Faith is overlaid with a thick patina of superstition, where the peasants make with the same hand the sign of the Cross and the sign against the evil eye, where the picture of the Bambino is hung over the bed and the pagan horns are nailed over the barn door. The Bishop was a canny man who wanted a saint for the good of his diocese, but declined to put his own reputation on trial with that of the Servant of God.

If the investigation went well, he would have not only a *beato*, but a rod to beat the Communists. If it went ill, the wise and godly men from Rome could bear some of the blame. His Eminence chuckled at the subtlety of it. Scratch a Southerner and you found a fox, who smelled out traps a mile away, and trotted around them to the chicken-run.

But there was more at stake than the reputation of a provincial bishop. There was politics involved, and Italian elections were only twelve months away. Public opinion was sensitive to the influence of the Vatican in civil affairs. The anti-clericals would welcome a chance to discredit the Church, and they had enough weapons without putting another into their hands.

There were deeper issues yet, matters less relevant to time than to eternity. To name a man Blessed was to declare him a heroic servant of God, to hold him up as an exemplar and an intercessor for the faithful. To accept his miracles was to admit beyond all doubt the divine power working through him to suspend or cancel the laws of nature. Error in such a matter was unthinkable. The whole massive machinery of the Congregation of Rites was designed to prevent it. But premature action, a botched investigation, could cause grave scandal and weaken the faith of millions in an infallible Church which claimed the direct guidance of the Holy Ghost.

His Eminence shivered as the first chill darkness came down on Parioli. He was a man hardened by power and sceptical of devotion, but he too carried on his shoulders the burden of belief and in his heart the fear of the noonday devil.

He could afford less than others the luxury of error. Much more depended on him. The penalty of failure would be so much more rigorous. In spite of the pomp of his title and the secular dignity which attended it, his prime mission was spiritual. It related to souls—their salvation and damnation. The curse of the millstones could fall equally upon an erring Cardinal and a faithless curate. So he walked and pondered soberly while the faint harmony of bells drifted up from the city and the crickets in the garden began their shrill chorus.

He would grant the Bishop of Valenta his small triumph. He would find the men for him—a Postulator to build the case and present it, a Devil's Advocate to destroy it if he could. Of the two, the Devil's Advocate was the more important. His official title described him accurately: Promoter of the Faith. The man who kept the Faith pure at any cost of broken lives and broken hearts. He must be learned, meticulous, passionless. He must be cold in judgment, ruthless in condemnation. He might lack charity or piety, but he could not lack precision. Such men were rare, and those at his disposal were already occupied on other causes.

Then he remembered Blaise Meredith, the spare, sober man with the greyness of death on him. He had the qualities. He was English, which would remove the taint of political involvement. But whether he had the will or the time left to him was another matter. If the medical verdict were unfavourable he might not feel disposed to accept so heavy an assignment.

Still, it was the beginning of an answer. His Eminence was not unsatisfied. He made one more leisurely circuit of the darkened garden, then walked back to the villa to say vespers with his household.

2

Two days later Eugenio Cardinal Marotta sat in his study chair behind the great buhl desk and talked with Monsignor Blaise Meredith. His Eminence had slept well and breakfasted lightly and his round, good-humoured face was fresh and shining from the razor. In the lofty room, with its coffered ceiling and its Aubusson carpets and its noble portraits in gilded frames, he was invested with the unconscious dignity of possession.

By contrast, the Englishman seemed small and grey and shrunken. His soutane hung loosely on his thin body and the scarlet piping only emphasised the unhealthy pallor of his face. His eyes were clouded with fatigue and there were deep furrows of pain at the corners of his mouth. Even in the brisk, Romanesque Italian his voice was flat and expressionless.

'There it is, Eminence. I have at best, twelve months. Half of that, perhaps, for active work.'

The Cardinal waited a few moments, watching him with detached pity. Then he said gently:

'I grieve for you, my friend. It comes to all of us, of course; but it is always a shock.'

'Yet we of all people should be prepared for it.' The drooping mouth twitched upward into a wry smile.

'No!' Marotta's small hands fluttered in deprecation. 'We mustn't overrate ourselves. We are men like all the others. We are priests by choice and calling. We are celibates by canonical legislation. It is a career, a profession. The powers we exercise, the grace we dispense, are independent of our own worthiness. It is better for us to be saints than sinners—but like our brothers outside the ministry we are generally something in-between.'

'Small comfort, Eminence, when one stands in the shadow of the judgment seat.'

'It is still the truth.' The Cardinal reminded him coolly, 'I've been in the Church a long time, my friend. The higher one climbs the more one sees—and the more clearly. It's a pious legend that the priesthood sanctifies a man, or that celibacy ennobles him. If a priest can keep his hands out of his pockets and his legs out of a woman's bed till he's forty-five, he stands a reasonable chance of doing it till he dies. There are plenty of professional bachelors in the world too. But we are all still subject to pride, ambition, sloth, negligence, avarice. Often it's harder for us to save our souls than it is for others. A man with a family must make sacrifices, impose a discipline on his desires, practise love and patience. We may sin less, yet have less merit in us at the end.'

'I am very empty,' said Blaise Meredith. 'There is no evil that I repent and no good that I count. I have had nothing to fight. I cannot show even scars.'

The Cardinal leaned back in his chair, toying with the big yellow stone on his episcopal ring. The only sound in the room was the soft ticking of an ormolu clock on the marble mantel. After a while he said thoughtfully:

'I can release you now if you wish, I can provide you with a pension from the funds of the Congregation. You could live quietly. . . .'

Blaise Meredith shook his head.

'It's a great kindness, Eminence, but I have no talent for contemplation. I should prefer to go on working.'

'You will have to stop one day. After that?'

'I shall go into hospital. I understand I shall suffer a good deal. Then . . .' He spread his hands in a gesture of defeat. '*Finita la commedia.* If it were not too much to ask, I should like to be buried in Your Eminence's church.'

In spite of himself Marotta was touched by the bleak courage of the man. He was tired and sick. The worst of his Calvary was yet to come, yet he was walking towards it with a desolate dignity that was typically English. Before the Cardinal had time to comment, Meredith went on.

'In all this, of course, I assume that Your Eminence wants to use me. I . . . I'm afraid I can't guarantee the best of service.'

'You have always done better than you knew, my friend,' said Marotta gently, 'you have always given more than you promised. Besides there is a matter in which you can help me greatly—and perhaps—' he paused as if struck by an odd afterthought–'perhaps help yourself too.'

Then, without waiting for an answer, he told him of the petition of the Bishop of Valenta, and his need of a Devil's Advocate in the cause of Giacomo Nerone.

Meredith listened, intent as a lawyer on the details of a new brief. A new life seemed to take possession of him. His eyes brightened, he straightened in his chair and a small tinge of colour crept into his faded cheeks. Eugenio Marotta noted it but made no comment. When he had finished his outline of the situation he asked:

'Well, what do you think of it?'

'An indiscretion,' said Meredith precisely. 'It's a political move and I distrust it.'

'Everything in the Church is political,' Marotta reminded him mildly. 'Man is a political animal who has an immortal soul. You cannot divide him—any more than you can divide the Church into separate and unrelated functions. Everything the Church does is designed to give a spiritual character to a material development. We name a saint as patron of television. What does it mean? A new symbol of an old truth: that every lawful activity is conducive to good or can be perverted to evil.'

'Too many symbols can cloud the face of reality,' said Blaise Meredith dryly. 'Too many saints can bring sanctity into disrepute. I've always thought that was our function at the Congregation of Rites—not to put them into the Calendar, but to keep them out of it.'

The Cardinal nodded soberly.

'In a sense that's true. But, in this as in all cases, the first motion doesn't come from us. The Bishop begins it in his own diocese. Only afterwards the papers are forwarded to us. We have no direct authority to forbid the investigation.'

'We might counsel against it.'

'On what grounds?'

'Discretion. The timing is bad. We are on the eve of elections. Giacomo Nerone was murdered by Communist Partisans in the last year of the war. What do we want to do? Use him to win a provincial seat—or as an example of heroic charity?'

The Cardinal's red lips twitched into a small ironic smile.

'I imagine our brother Bishop would like to have it both ways. And up to a point he's likely to get it. Miracles have been claimed. An apparently spontaneous cult has sprung up among the people. Both must be judicially investigated. The first investigation has been made and the verdict leans towards approval. The next stage follows almost automatically . . . the introduction of the Cause for Beatification to the Bishop's own court.'

'Once that happens, every newspaper in Italy will run the story. The travel agencies will start organising unofficial tours. The local merchants will start shouting from the housetops. You can't avoid it.'

'But we may be able to control it. That's why I've decided to give His Lordship what he wants. That's why I'd like you to become the Devil's Advocate.'

Blaise Meredith pursed his thin, bloodless lips, considering the offer. Then after a moment he shook his head.

'I'm a sick man, Eminence. I could not do you justice.'

'You must let me judge that.' Marotta reproved him coolly. 'Besides, as I said, I believe it may help you too.'

'I don't understand.'

The Cardinal pushed back his high, carved chair and stood up. He walked across the room to the window and drew back the thick curtains so that the morning sun flooded into the room, lighting the scarlet and the gilt, making the rich patterns on the carpet leap into life like flowers. Blaise Meredith blinked at the raw brilliance and shaded his eyes with his hand. The Cardinal stood looking out into the garden. His face was hidden from Meredith, but when he spoke his voice was touched with a rare compassion.

'What I have to say to you, Monsignor, is probably a presumption. I am not your confessor. I cannot look into your conscience; but I believe you have reached a crisis. You, like many of us here in Rome, are a professional priest—a career churchman. There is no stigma in that. It is much already to be a good professional. There are many who fall far short even of this limited perfection. Suddenly you have discovered it is not enough. You are puzzled, afraid. Yet you do not know what you should do to restore the lack. Part of the problem is that you and I and others like us have been removed too long from pastoral duty. We have lost touch with the people who keep us in touch with God. We have reduced the Faith to an intellectual conception, an arid assent of the will, because we have not seen it working in the lives of common folk. We have lost pity and fear and love. We are the guardians of mysteries, but we have lost the awe of them. We work by canon, not by charity. Like all administrators we believe that the world would topple into chaos without us, that we carry even the Church of God on our backs. It is not true, but some of us believe it till the day we die. You are fortunate that even at this late hour you have been touched with dissatisfaction ... yes, even doubt, because I believe that you are now in the desert of temptation. ... That is why I believe this investigation may help you. It will take you out of Rome, to one of the most depressed areas of Italy. You will rebuild the life of a dead man from the evidence of those who lived with him—the poor, the ignorant, the dispossessed. Be he sinner or saint, it makes no difference in the end. You will live and talk with simple people. Among them perhaps you will find the cure for your own sickness of spirit.'

'What is my sickness, Eminence?' The pathetic weariness of the voice, the desolate puzzlement of the question, touched the old churchman to pity. He turned back from the window to see Meredith slumped forward in his chair, his face buried in his hands. He waited a moment, weighing his answer; then he gave it, gravely.

'There is no passion in your life, my son. You have never loved a woman, nor hated a man, nor pitied a child. You have withdrawn yourself too long and you are a stranger in the human family. You have asked nothing and given nothing. You have never known the dignity of need nor gratitude for a suffering shared. This is your sickness. This is the cross you have fashioned for your own shoulders. This is where your doubts begin and your fears too—because a man who cannot love his fellows cannot love God either.'

'How does one begin to love?'

'From need,' said Marotta firmly. 'From the need of the flesh and the need of the spirit. A man hungers for his first kiss, and his first real prayer is made when he hungers for the lost Paradise.'

'I am so very tired,' said Blaise Meredith.

'Go home and rest,' said the Cardinal briskly. 'In the morning you can leave for Calabria. Present your credentials to the Bishop of Valenta and begin work.'

'You are a hard man, Eminence.'

'Men die every day,' Eugenio Marotta told him bluntly. 'Some are damned, some achieve salvation; but the work of the Church continues. Go, my son—in peace and in the name of God!'

At eleven o'clock the following morning Blaise Meredith left Rome for Calabria. His luggage was one small suitcase of clothes, a brief-case containing his breviary and his notebooks, and a letter of authority from the Prefect of the Congregation of Rites to His Lordship the Bishop of Valenta. There was a ten-hour journey ahead of him and the *rapido* was hot, dusty and crowded with Calabresi returning from an organised pilgrimage to the Holy City.

The poorer folk were herded like cattle into the second-class coaches, while their betters spilled over into first-class and spread themselves and their belongings over the seats and the luggage-racks. Meredith found himself anchored firmly between a stout matron in a silk frock and a swarthy-faced cleric chewing noisily through a packet of peppermints. The seat opposite was occupied by a country man and his wife and four children who squalled like cicadas and tangled themselves in everyone's feet. All the windows were closed and the air was sour and stifling.

He took out his breviary and settled down with grim concentration to read his office. Ten minutes out of Rome Central he gave up in disgust. The foul air nauseated him and his head throbbed with the chatter of the train and the shrilling of the children. He tried to doze, but the stout woman shifted uneasily in her tight dress and the noisy mastications of the priest fretted him to screaming point. Defeated and dyspeptic, he struggled out of the seat and into the corridor, where he stood, propped against the panelling, looking out on the countryside.

It was green now, with the first flush of spring. The scars of erosion and tillage were covered with new grass, the stucco of the house-fronts had been washed clean by the rains and bleached by the sun, and even the ruins of the aqueducts and the old Roman villas were flecked with fresh moss and weeds that sprouted out of their weathered stones. The cyclic miracle of rebirth was more vivid here than in any other country of the world. Here was a tired land, raped ruinously for centuries, its hills eroded, its trees cut down, its rivers dry, its soil bled into dust; yet somehow every year it made this brief, brave show of leaf and grass and flower. Even in the mountains, on the ragged tufa slopes, too poor for goat-cropping, there was still a faint dapple of green for a reminder of past fruitfulness.

If one could leave the land a while, thought Meredith, if one could empty it of its proliferating tribes for half a century, it might come into heart again. But it would never happen. They would breed while the land died under their feet—slowly indeed, yet too fast for the technicians and agronomists to restore it.

The moving sunlit vistas began to weary his eyes, and he looked up and down the corridor at the others who had been driven out of the compartments by cigar smoke and stale salami and garlic and the smell of unbathed bodies. There was a Neapolitan business man with stovepipe trousers and short-tailed coat and a flashing zircon on one pudgy finger, a German tourist with thick shoes and an expensive Leica, a pair of flat-chested Frenchwomen, an American student with cropped hair and a freckled face, and a pair of provincial lovers holding hands near the toilet.

It was the lovers who held Meredith's attention. The youth was a nuggety peasant from the South, dark as an Arab, with flashing eyes and voluble hands. His thin cotton trousers were moulded over his flanks and his sweat-shirt clung to his chest so that the whole, compact maleness of him was suggestively visible. The girl was short and dark as he was, thick of waist and ankle, but her breasts were full and firm and they strained against the low-cut bodice of her dress. They stood facing one another across the narrow corridor, their locked hands a barrier against intrusion, their eyes blind to all but themselves, their bodies relaxed and swaying to the rhythm of the train. Their passion was plain, yet it gave no impression of urgency. The boy was preened like a cock, yet confident of his possession. The girl was content with him and with herself, in the small private eternity of new love.

Looking at them, Blaise Meredith was touched with a vague nostalgia for a past that had never belonged to him. What did he know of love but a theological definition and a muttered guilt in the confessional? What meaning had his counsel in the face of this frank, erotic communion, which by divine dispensation was the beginning of life and the guarantee of the human continuum? Soon, this very night perhaps, these two would lie together in the little death out of which a new life would spring—a new body, a new soul. But Blaise Meredith would sleep solitary, with all the mysteries of the universe reduced to a scholastic syllogism inside his skull-case. Who was right—he or they? Who came nearer to the perfection of the divine design? There was only one answer. Eugenio Marotta was right. He had withdrawn himself from the human family. These two were thrusting forward to renew it and perpetuate it.

His feet began to burn. His back ached. The small nagging pain started again in the pit of his belly. He would have to sit down and rest awhile. As he made his way back to his seat he found the Calabrian cleric launched on a full-scale sermon:

'. . . A wonderful man, the Holy Father. A saint in his own right. I was very near him in St Peter's. I could have stretched out my hand to touch him. One could feel the power going out from him. Wonderful . . . wonderful. . . ! We should thank God all the days of our lives for the privilege we have enjoyed on this pilgrimage.'

A wave of peppermint wafted through the compartment. Blaise Meredith closed his eyes and prayed for a respite, but the thick Calabrese voice droned on and on:

'. . . To have come to Rome, to have trodden in the footprints of the martyrs and knelt at the tomb of Peter, what other experience could match this? Here one sees the Church as it really is—an army of priests and monks and nuns preparing themselves to conquer the world for Christ. . . .'

If this is the way we conquer it, thought Blaise Meredith irritably, God help the world. This sort of mummery never did anyone any good. The fellow talks like a travelling salesman. If only he would shut up and think a little.

But the Calabrese was well launched now and the presence of a brother cleric only urged him to greater efforts.

'They are right when they call Rome the Holy City. The spirit of the great Pontiff broods over it night and day. Mind you, not all the saints of the Church are in Rome. Oh no! Even in our own small province we have a saint—not an official one yet—but real. Ah yes! Very real!'

Blaise Meredith was instantly alert. His irritation vanished, and he waited intently for the rest of it.

'Already the Cause of his Beatification has been opened. Giacomo Nerone. You have heard of him perhaps? No? A strange and wonderful story. No one knows where he came from, but he appeared one day in the village, like a man sent by God. He built a little hermitage with his own hands and gave himself over to prayer and good works. When the Communists moved in to take over the village after the war they murdered him. He died a martyr in defence of the Faith. And since his death miracle after miracle has been performed at his tomb. The sick have been cured; sinners brought to penance: sure marks of the favour of the Almighty.'

Blaise Meredith opened his eyes and asked innocently:

'Did you know him, Father?'

The Calabrese shot him a swift, suspicious glance.

'Know him? Er, well, not personally. Though, of course, I know a lot about him. I'm from Cosenza myself. The next diocese.'

'Thank you,' said Blaise Meredith politely, and closed his eyes again. The Calabrian shifted uncomfortably in his seat and then got up to relieve himself in the toilet. Meredith took advantage of his absence to stretch his legs and ease his aching head against the padded back-rest. He felt no compunction for what he had done. More than ever now, this sort of claptrap was distasteful to him. It was a kind of ecclesiastical jargon, a debased rhetoric that explained nothing but brought the truth into disrepute. It begged all the questions and answered none. The massive structure of reason and revelation on which the Church was founded was reduced to a ritual incantation, formless, fruitless and essentially false. Peppermint piety. It deceived no one but the man who peddled it. It satisfied no one but the old ladies and girls in green-sickness; yet it flourished most rankly where the Church was most firmly entrenched in the established order. It was the mark of accommodation, compromise, laxity among the clergy, who found it easier to preach devotion than to affront the moral and social problems of their time. It covered fatuity and lack of education. It left the people naked and unarmed in the face of terrifying mysteries: pain, passion, death, the great 'perhaps' of the hereafter.

The swarthy Calabrian came back, fumbling with the buttons of his cassock, and determined to re-establish himself with his audience and with his lean-jowled Monsignor. He sat down, blew his nose noisily and then tapped Meredith confidentially on the knee.

'You are from Rome, Monsignor?'

'From Rome, yes.' He was nettled by this intrusion on his rest, and his tone was terse; but the Calabrese was a hardhead, blind to all obstacles.

'But you are not Italian?'

'No. I'm English.'

'Ah, a visitor to the Vatican? A pilgrim?'

'I work there,' said Meredith coldly.

The Calabrese gave him a fraternal smile that showed a mouth full of carious teeth.

'You are fortunate, Monsignor. You have opportunities denied to us poor country folk. We work the stony acres while you till the lush pastures of the City of Saints.'

'I don't till anything,' Meredith told him baldly. 'I'm an official of the Congregation of Rites, and Rome isn't the City of Saints any more than Paris or Berlin. It's a place that's kept fairly orderly because the Pope insists on his rights under the Concordat to preserve its sacred character as the centre of Christendom. That's all.'

The Calabrese was as canny as a badger. He sidestepped the snub and seized swiftly on the new topic presented to him.

'You interest me very much, Monsignor. You live of course in a bigger world than I. You have much more experience of affairs. But I have always said that the simple country life is much more conducive to sanctity than the worldly bustle of a great city. You work with the Congregation of Rites. You deal possibly, with the causes of saints and *beati*. Wouldn't you agree?'

He was trapped and he knew it. He would be plagued into conversation in the end. It would save time and energy to submit now—and try to change his seat at Formio or Naples. He answered dryly:

'All my experience is that saints are found in the most unlikely places—at the most unpromising times.'

'Exactly! This is what has interested me so much about our own Servant of God, Giacomo Nerone. You know the place where he lived, Gemelli dei Monti?'

'I've never been there.'

'But you know what the name means?'

'What it says, I imagine . . . the mountain twins.'

'Precisely. Twin villages set on the horns of a hill in some of the most desolate country in Calabria. Gemello Minore the little town. Gemello Maggiore the greater. They're about sixty kilometres from Valenta, and the road is a nightmare. The villagers are as poor and depressed as any in our province. At least they were, until the fame of the servant of God began to spread.'

'And then?' In spite of himself, Meredith found his interest quickening.

'Ah, then!' One stubby hand was raised in a preacher's gesture. 'Then a strange thing happened. Giacomo Nerone had lived and worked in Gemello Minore. It was in this village that he was betrayed and murdered. His body was taken secretly to a grotto near Gemello Maggiore and buried there. Since that time Gemello Minore has sunk deeper and deeper into ruin and poverty, while Gemello Maggiore grows more prosperous every day. There is a new church, a hospital, an inn for tourists and pilgrims. It is as if God were visiting punishment on the betrayers and reward on those who sheltered the body of the Servant of God. Don't you agree?'

'It's a dubious proposition,' Meredith told him, with thin irony. 'Prosperity isn't always a mark of divine favour. It could be the result of some shrewd promotion by the Mayor and the citizens—even the parish priest. These things have happened.'

The Calabrese flushed angrily at the imputation and burst into an impassioned rebuttal.

'You presume too much, Monsignor. Wise and godly men have looked into this matter—men who understand our people. Do you set yourself in opposition to them?'

'I'm not in opposition to anyone,' said Meredith mildly. 'I simply disapprove of rash judgment and doubtful doctrine. Saints are not made by popular verdict but by canonical decision. That's why I'm going to Calabria now, to act as Promoter of the Faith in the cause of Giacomo Nerone. If you have any firsthand evidence to offer, I'll be happy to receive it, in the proper form.'

The priest gaped at him a moment; then his confidence collapsed in mumbled apologies, cut mercifully short by their arrival at Formio.

They had twenty minutes to wait for the north-bound train, which gave Blaise Meredith the opportunity to stretch his legs—and the grace to be ashamed of himself.

What had he gained by this cheap, dialectic victory over a country cleric? The Calabrese was a bore—and, worse, a pious bore—but Blaise Meredith was a dyspeptic intellectual with no charity in him at all. He had gained nothing and given nothing—and he had missed the first opportunity of learning a little about the man whose life he was charged to investigate.

As he paced the sunlit platform, watching the peasant travellers pressing about the drink vendor, he asked himself for the hundredth time what was the lack that cut him off from free communication with his fellows. Other priests, he knew, found an intense pleasure in the raw, salty dialect of peasant conversation. They picked up pearls of wisdom and experience over a farmhouse table or a cup of wine in a workman's kitchen. They talked with equal familiarity to the rough-tongued whores of Trastevere and the polished *signori* of Parioli. They enjoyed the ribald humour of the fish market as much as the wit of a Cardinal's dinner table. They were good priests, too, and they did much for their people, with a singular satisfaction to themselves.

What was the difference between him and them? Passion, Marotta had told him. The capacity to love and to desire, to feel with another's pain, to share another's joy. Christ ate and drank wine with touts and tavern-girls, but Monsignor Meredith, his professional follower, had lived alone amid dusty tomes in the library of the Palace of Congregations. And now, in this last year of his life, he was still alone, with a small grey death growing in his belly—and no soul in the world to bear him company.

The guard blew his whistle and Meredith climbed aboard again, to sweat out the long, humid voyage—Naples, Nocera, Salerno, Eboli, Cassano, Cosenza and, in the late evening, Valenta, where the Bishop was waiting to welcome him.

Aurelio, Bishop of Valenta, was a surprise, in more ways than one. He was a tall, spare man, still in his vigorous forties.

His iron-grey hair was meticulously brushed and his fine aquiline features were bright with intelligence and humour. He was a Trentino, which seemed an odd choice for a Southern diocese, and before his translation he had been an auxiliary in the Patriarchate of Venice. He was waiting at the station with his own car and instead of driving into the town he took Meredith a dozen kilometres into the country to a handsome villa, set in acres of oranges and olives, and looking down into a valley where a narrow stream glowed faintly under the moon.

'An experiment,' he explained in clear metallic English. 'An experiment in practical education. These people imagine that the clergy are born in cassocks, and that their only talent is for Paters and Aves and swinging censers in the cathedral. I was born in the North. My people were mountain farmers—good ones. I bought this place from a local landowner who was up to his eyes in debt, and I'm farming it with half a dozen lads, to whom I'm trying to teach the rudiments of modern agriculture. It's a battle; but I think I'm winning. I've also made it my official residence. The old one was hopelessly antiquated ... right in the middle of the town, next to the cathedral. I've handed it over to my Vicar General. He's one of the old school—loves it!'

Meredith chuckled, caught by the infectious good-humour of the man. The Bishop shot him a quick, shrewd look.

'You are surprised, Monsignor?'

'Pleasantly,' said Blaise Meredith. 'I expected something quite different.'

'Bourbon baroque? Velvet and brocade and gilt cherubs with the paint peeling off their backsides?'

'Something like that, yes.'

The Bishop brought the car to a stop in front of the stuccoed portico of the villa and sat a moment behind the wheel, looking over the fall of the land, where the moonlight touched the treetops with silver. He said quietly:

'You will find more than enough of it here in the South ... formalism, feudalism reaction, old men following old ways because the old ways seem safer, and they are unprepared for the new. They see poverty and ignorance as crosses to be borne and not injustices to be remedied. They believe that the more priests and monks and nuns there are, the better for the world. I'd like to see fewer and better ones. I'd prefer to have fewer churches and more people going to them.'

'Fewer saints too?' asked Meredith blandly.

The Bishop looked up sharply, then burst out laughing.

'Thank God for the English! A little tramontane scepticism would do us all a lot of good at this moment. You wonder why a man like me should take up the cause of Giacomo Nerone?'

'Frankly, yes.'

'Let's keep it for the fruit and the cheese,' said His Lordship without malice.

A servant in a white coat opened the car door and ushered them into the house.

'Dinner in thirty minutes,' said His Lordship. 'I hope you'll find your room comfortable. In the morning you can look right down over the valley and see what we've done.'

He took his leave, and the servant led Meredith upstairs to a large guest-room with french doors that opened on to a narrow balcony. Meredith was struck by the clean, modern lines of the furniture, the ascetic strength of the wooden crucifix over the prie-dieu in the corner. There was a shelf of new books in French, Italian and English, and a copy of the *Imitation of Christ* on the bedside table. A door opened from the bedroom into a freshly tiled bathroom, with a toilet and a shower recess. His Lordship had the instincts of a builder and the good taste of an artist. He also had a sense of humour, a virtue all too rare in the Italian Church.

As he bathed and changed, Meredith felt the weariness and frustration of the journey falling away from him like a sloughed skin. Even the nagging pain of his illness seemed to subside, and he found himself looking forward with pleasure and curiosity to dinner with His Lordship. It was a simple meal—*antipasto, zuppa di verdura*, a roast of chicken, local fruit and a sharp country cheese—but it was cooked with distinction and meticulously served, and the wine was a full-bodied Barolo from the vineyards of the North. The talk that went with it was much more subtle; a fencing match between experts, with the Bishop making the first probing thrusts.

'Until you came, my dear Meredith, I was beginning to feel I had made a mistake.'

'A mistake?'

'In appealing to Rome for assistance. It involved a concession, you see—a certain sacrifice of my autonomy.'

'Did it cost Your Lordship so much?'

The Bishop nodded gravely.

'It could have, yes. Modernisers and reformers are always suspect, especially here in the South. If they succeed they become a reproach to their more conservative colleagues. If they fail, they become an example. They have tried to do too much, too fast. So I've always found it wiser to go my own way and keep my affairs to myself—and leave the critics to make the first move.'

'Do you have many critics?'

'Some, yes. The landowners don't like me—and they have strong voices in Rome. The clergy find me too rigid in matters of morals, and too indifferent to local ritual and tradition. My metropolitan is a Monarchist. I'm a moderate socialiser. The politicos mistrust me, because I preach that the party is less important than the individual who represents it. They make promises. I like to see that they are kept. When they're not, I protest.'

'Do you find support in Rome?'

His Lordship's thin mouth relaxed into a smile.

'You know Rome better than I do, my friend. They wait for the results—and the results of a policy like mine in an area like this may not be seen for ten years. If I succeed, well and good. If I fail—or make the wrong mistake at the wrong time—they'll nod their heads wisely and say they've been expecting it for years. So I prefer to keep them guessing. The less they know, the freer I am.'

'Then why did you write to Cardinal Marotta? Why did you ask for Roman priests as Postulator and Promoter of the Faith?'

His Lordship toyed with his wineglass, twirling the stem between his long, sensitive fingers, watching the light refract through the red liquid on to the snowy tablecloth. He said carefully:

'Because this is new ground to me. I understand goodness, but I am unfamiliar with sanctity. I believe in mysticism, but I've had no experience of mystics. I'm a northerner, a pragmatist by nature and education. I believe in miracles, but I've never expected to find them performed on my own doorstep. That's why I applied to the Congregation of Rites.' He smiled disarmingly. 'You are the experts in these matters.'

'Was this the only reason?'

'You talk like an inquisitor,' said His Lordship, with wry good-humour. 'What other reason should there be?'

'Politics,' said Meredith flatly. 'Election politics.'

To his surprise, the Bishop threw back his head and laughed heartily.

'So that's it. I wondered why His Eminence was so co-operative. I wondered why he'd sent an Englishman instead of an Italian—and a secular priest instead of a long-faced Barnabite. Clever of him! But I'm afraid he's wrong.' The laugh died suddenly on his lips and he was as serious again. He set down his wineglass and spread his hands in an eloquent gesture of explanation. 'He's quite wrong, Meredith. That's what happens in Rome. The stupid get stupider still and the clever fellows like Marotta get too clever for everyone else's good. There are two reasons why I'm interested in this case. The first is simple and official. It's an unauthorised cultus. I have to investigate it, for approval or condemnation. The second isn't half so simple—and the officials wouldn't understand it.'

'Marotta might,' said Meredith quietly. 'I might too.'

'Why should you two be different?'

'Because Marotta's a wise old humanist—and because I'm due to die of a carcinoma in twelve months.'

Aurelio, Bishop of Valenta, leaned back in his chair and studied the pale, drawn face of his visitor. After a long moment he said softly:

'I've been wondering about you. Now I begin to understand. Very well, I'll try to explain. A man in the shadow of death should be beyond scandal, even from a bishop. I believe that the Church in this country is in drastic need of reform. I think we have too many saints and not enough sanctity, too many cults and not enough catechism, too many medals and not enough medicine, too many churches and not enough schools. We have three million workless men and three million women living by prostitution. We control the State through the Christian Democratic Party and the Vatican Bank; yet we countenance a dichotomy which gives prosperity to half the country and lets the other half rot in penury. Our clergy are under-educated and insecure and yet we rail against anti-clericals and Communists. A tree is known by its fruits—and I believe that it's better to proclaim a new deal in social justice than a new attribute of the Blessed Virgin. The first is a necessary application of a moral principle, the second is simply a definition of a traditional belief. We clergy are more jealous of our rights under the Concordat than the rights of our people under the natural and divine law. . . . Do I shock you, Monsignor?'

'You encourage me,' said Blaise Meredith. 'But why do you want a new saint?'

'I don't,' said the Bishop, with surprising emphasis. 'I'm committed to the case, but I hope, with all my heart, it fails. The Mayor of Gemello Maggiore has collected fifteen million lire to advance the cause, but I can't get a thousand out of him for a diocesan orphanage. If Giacomo Nerone is beatified, they'll want a new church to house him—and I want nursing nuns and an agricultural adviser and twenty thousand fruit trees from California.'

'Then why did you ask His Eminence for help?'

'It's a principle in Rome, my dear Meredith. You always get the opposite of what you ask for.'

Blaise Meredith did not smile. A new and disturbing thought was shaping itself in his mind. He paused a little, trying to find words to frame it.

'But if the case is proved? If Giacomo Nerone is really a saint and a wonder-worker?'

'I'm a pragmatist, as I told you,' said His Lordship with side-long humour. 'I'll wait on the facts. When would you like to begin work?'

'Immediately,' said Meredith. 'I'm living on borrowed time. I'd like to spend a few days studying the documents. Then I'll move out to Gemelli dei Monti to begin taking depositions.'

'I'll have the records delivered to your room in the morning. I hope you will regard this house as your home and myself as your friend.'

'I am grateful to Your Lordship, more grateful than I can say.'

'There is nothing to be grateful for.' The Bishop smiled in deprecation. 'I shall be glad of your company. I feel we have much in common. Oh . . . there is a small counsel I would give you.'

'Yes?'

'It's my private opinion that you will not find the truth about Giacomo Nerone in Gemello Maggiore. They venerate him there. They make profit from his memory. In Gemello Minore, it's quite another story—provided you can get them to tell it. So far none of my people has succeeded.'

'Is there any reason?'

'Better you ask the reasons for yourself, my friend. As you see, I'm rather prejudiced.' He pushed back his chair and stood up. 'It's late and you must be tired. I suggest you rest late in the morning. I'll have breakfast sent to your room.'

Blaise Meredith was touched by the patrician politeness of the man. He was chary of confidences, jealous of his own privacy, but he said very humbly:

'I am a sick man, Your Lordship. I am suddenly very lonely. You have made me feel at home. Thank you.'

'We are brothers in a big family,' said the Bishop gently. 'But being bachelors we grow selfish and singular. I'm glad to be of service. Good-night—and golden dreams.'

Alone in the big guest-room with the moonlight streaming through the open casements, Blaise Meredith prepared himself for another night. Its course was familiar to him now, but none the less frightening. He would lie wakeful till midnight, then sleep would come, shallow and restless. Before the cocks began to screech at the false dawn he would start up, his belly cramped with pain, his mouth full of the sour taste of bile and blood. He would struggle to the toilet, weak and retching, then cram himself with opiate and go back to bed. Just before sunrise he would sleep again—one hour, two at most—not enough to refresh him, but enough to keep the sluggish, diminishing life-stream flowing in his arteries.

It was a strange compound of terrors: the fear of death, the shame of slow dissolution, the eerie solitude of the believer in the presence of a faceless God whom he acknowledged unseen but must soon meet unveiled and splendid in judgment. He could not escape them into sleep and he could not exorcise them by prayer, since prayer had become an arid act of the will which could neither stifle pain nor set a balm to it.

So tonight, in spite of his fatigue, he tried to defer the purgatory. He undressed, put on pyjamas, slippers and dressing-gown and walked out on the balcony.

The moon was high over the valley—a ship of antique silver, placid on a luminous sea. The orange groves glowed coldly and the olive leaves were bright as dagger-tips out of a twisted mass of shadows. Below them the water lay flat and full of stars, behind a barricade of logs and piled rubble, while the arms of the mountains encircled it all like ramparts, shutting out the chaos of the centuries.

Blaise Meredith looked at it and found it good. Good in itself, good in the man who had made it. Man did not live by bread alone—but he could not live without it. The old monks had had the same idea. They planted the Cross in the middle of a desert—and then planted corn and fruit trees, so that the barren symbol flowered into a green reality. They knew, better than most, that man was a creature of flesh and spirit; but that the spirit could not function except in and through the flesh. When the body was sick, the moral responsibility of man was reduced. Man was a thinking reed, but the reed must be anchored firmly in black earth, watered at the roots, warmed by the sun.

Aurelio, Bishop of Valenta, was a pragmatist, but a Christian pragmatist. He was the inheritor of the oldest and most orthodox tradition in the Church: that earth and grass and tree and animal were the issue of the same creative act that produced a man. They were good in themselves, perfect in their nature and in the laws that governed their growth and decay. Only Man's misuse could debase them to instruments of evil. To plant a tree was therefore a godly act. To make barren earth flourish was to share in the act of creation. To teach other men these things was to make them, too, participate in a divine plan. . . . Yet Aurelio, Bishop of Valenta, was suspect to many of his own colleagues.

This was the mystery of the Church: that it should hold in organic unity humanists like Marotta and formalists like Blaise Meredith and fools like the Calabrian, reformers, rebels and puritan conformists, political Popes, and nursing nuns, worldly priests and devout anti-clericals. It demanded an unwavering assent to defined doctrine and permitted an extraordinary divergence of discipline.

It imposed poverty on its religious, yet played the stock markets of the world through the Vatican Bank. It preached detachment from the world, yet collected real estate like any public company. It forgave adulterers and excommunicated heretics. It was harsh with its own reformers, yet signed concordats with those who wanted to destroy it. It was the hardest community in the world to live in—yet all its members wanted to die in it, the Pope, Cardinal or washerwoman, they would take their viaticum with gratitude from the lowest country priest.

It was a mystery and a paradox, yet Blaise Meredith was further from understanding it, further from accepting it than he had been for twenty years. This was what troubled him. When he had been well, his mind had bent naturally to accept the idea of a divine intervention in human affairs. Now that the life was bleeding out of him, slowly, he found himself clinging desperately to the simplest manifestation of physical continuity—a tree, a flower, lake water quiet under an eternal moonlight.

A faint breeze stirred along the valley, rattling the crisp leaves, ruffling the stars in the water. Meredith shivered in the sudden chill and went inside, closing the french door behind him. He knelt down on the prie-dieu under the wooden figure of the Christus and began to pray . . .

'*Pater Noster qui es in Coelis . . .*'

But heaven, if heaven there were, was shut blank against him, and there was no answer from the faceless Father to his dying son.

3

Doctor Aldo Meyer stood at the doorway of his house and watched the village wake sluggishly to a new day.

First, old Nonna Patucci opened her door, peered up and down the cobbled street, then tottered across the road and emptied her chamber-pot over the wall and on to the vine-terrace below. Then she went inside, furtive as a witch, and closed the door with a resounding slam. As if at a signal, Felici the cobbler came out, in singlet and trousers and wooden pattens, to stand yawning and scratching his armpits and watch the sun light up the roof of the new hospital in Gemello Maggiore, two miles across the valley. After a minute of contemplation, he hawked noisily, spat on the ground and proceeded to unbolt his shutters.

Then the door of the priest's house opened and Rosa Benzoni waddled out, fat and shapeless in a black dress, to draw water from the cistern. As soon as she had gone the upstairs window opened and Father Anselmo's tousled grey head appeared, tentative as a tortoise making its first cautious exploration of the day.

Martino the smith came next, squat, barrel-chested, brown as a nut, to open the door of his shed and start the bellows working. By the time the first strokes of his hammer began to sound on the anvil, the whole village was stirring—women emptying slop-pails, barelegged girls wandering down to the cistern with great green bottles on their heads, half-naked children piddling against the road-wall, the first labourers moving off to the terraces and the garden patches, with ragged coats slung over their shoulders and their bread and olives wrapped in cotton handkerchiefs.

Aldo Meyer watched it all, without curiosity, without resentment, even when they passed him with averted heads or made the sign of the evil eye in the direction of his door. It was the measure of his disillusionment that he could ignore their hostility and yet cling like an animal to familiar sights and sounds: the rhythmic clang of the hammer, the trundle of a donkey cart on the stones, the shrill cries of children, the scolding of housewives; the vines and the olive groves, climbing down the hillside towards the valley fields, the straggle of crumbling houses up the road towards the big villa that crowned the hill-top, the gleam of sunrise on the prosperous town on the farther hill where the saint worked wonders for the tourists while Maria Rossi died in child-bed with his relic on her swollen body.

Each day he promised himself that tomorrow he would pack and go—to a new place with a new future—and leave this graceless tribe to its folly. But each night the resolution drained out of him and he sat down to drink himself into bed. The comfortless truth was that he had no place to go and no future to build. The best of himself was here—faith, hope and charity poured out to exhaustion, sucked up and wasted in a barren earth, trodden by a thankless, ignorant people.

From far down in the valley he heard the muted clatter of a motor-cycle and, when he turned towards it, he saw a small Vespa with a pillion passenger jolting up the track in a cloud of grey dust. The spectacle was banal enough but it moved Aldo Meyer to wintry amusement. The Vespa and the Contessa's automobile were the only motor vehicles in Gemello Minore. The Vespa had caused a minor riot and a gaping wonder that went on for weeks. Its rider was an oddity, too—an English painter, house-guest of the Contessa who lived in the villa on the hill-top and who owned all of the farmland and most of Gemello Minore as well. The painter's name was Nicholas Black, his pillion passenger was a local youth, Paolo Sanduzzi, who had attached himself to Black as guide, baggage animal and instructor in local dialect and customs.

To the villagers, the Englishman was *matto*—a crazy fellow who ambled about with a sketch book or sat for hours in the sun painting olive trees and tumbled rocks and angles of ruinous buildings. His dress was as crazy as his habits, a bright red shirt, faded denims, rope sandals, and a battered straw hat, under whose brim a faun-like face grinned crookedly at the world about him. He had not even the excuse of youth—he was past thirty—and when the girls gave up sighing after him, the elders began to make crude gossip about his association with the Contessa, who lived in solitary splendour behind the grilled gates of the villa.

Aldo Meyer heard the rumours and discounted them. He knew too much about the Contessa, and in his Roman days he had met too many artists, and quite enough Englishmen like Nicholas Black. He wondered more about Paolo Sanduzzi, with his slim, Arab body and his smooth face and his bright, shrewd eyes and his tyranny over his eccentric master. He wondered the more because he had seen the boy into the world and he knew that his father was Giacomo Nerone, whom folk were beginning to call the Saint . . .

At the lower end of the village the Vespa stopped, the youth got off and Meyer watched him scrambling down the hill-side towards his mother's house, a rough stone hut set in the middle of a small garden patch and sheltered by a clump of ilex. The Vespa started off again with a clatter and a few moments later came to a halt outside Meyer's cottage. The painter eased himself stiffly out of the saddle and threw out his arm in a theatrical salutation:

'*Coméva, Dottore?* How goes it this morning? I'd like some coffee if you've got any.'

'There's always coffee,' said Meyer, with a grin. 'How else would I face the sunrise?'

'Hangover?' asked the painter with malicious innocence.

Meyer shrugged wryly and led the way through the house and out into a small walled garden, where an old grey fig tree made a canopy against the sun. A rough table was covered with a checked cloth and set with cups and dishes of Calabrese pottery. A woman was bending over it, laying out new bread, a cut of white cheese, and a bowl of the small local fruit.

Her legs and feet were bare in the peasant fashion, and she wore a black cotton dress and a black head-scarf, both meticulously clean. Her back was straight, her breasts deep and firm, and her face was pure Greek, as if some ancient colonist from the coast had wandered into the mountains and mated with a woman of the tribes, to begin this new hybrid strain. She was perhaps thirty-six years of age. She had borne a child, yet she had not coarsened like the mountain women, and her mouth and eyes were curiously serene. When she saw the visitor, she gave a small start of surprise and looked inquiringly at Meyer. He said nothing, but made a cautionary gesture of dismissal. As she walked back into the house the painter's eyes followed her and he grinned like a knowing goat.

'You surprise me, Doctor. Where did you find her? I've never seen her before.'

'She belongs here,' said Meyer coolly. 'She has a house of her own and she keeps pretty much to herself. She comes up each day to clean and cook for me.'

'I'd like to paint her.'

'I don't advise it,' Meyer told him curtly.

'Why not?'

'She's the mother of Paolo Sanduzzi.'

'Oh.' Black flushed and let the subject drop. They sat down at the table and Meyer poured the coffee. There was silence for a few moments; then Black began to talk, volubly and dramatically.

'Big news from Valenta, Dottore! I was down there yesterday to pick up canvases and paints. The place is humming with it.'

'What sort of news?'

'This saint of yours, Giacomo Nerone. They're going to beatify him, it seems.'

Meyer shrugged indifferently and sipped his coffee.

'That's not news. They've been talking about it for twelve months.'

'Ah, but it is!' The sharp faun's face lit up with sardonic amusement. 'They've stopped talking and started an official process. They're circulating the notices now—tacking them up in all the churches, and calling for any person who has evidence to give. The Bishop's got a house-guest, a Monsignor from Rome who has been appointed to open the case. He'll be coming up here within a few days.'

'The devil he will!' Meyer set down his cup with a clatter. 'Are you sure of that?'

'Certain of it. It's all over town. I saw the fellow myself driving in His Lordship's car—grey and pinched like a Vatican mouse. He's English, it seems, so I took it on myself to offer an invitation from the Contessa to lodge him. She's a godly woman and lonely, as you know.' He chuckled and reached out to pour himself another cup of coffee. 'This place will be famous, Dottore. You'll be famous too.'

'That's what I'm afraid of,' said Meyer sombrely.

'Afraid?' The painter's eyes brightened with interest. 'Why should you be afraid? You're not even a Catholic. It's no concern of yours.'

'You don't understand,' Meyer told him irritably. 'You don't understand anything.'

'On the contrary, my dear fellow!' The long artist's hands gestured emphatically. 'On the contrary I understand everything. I understand what you have tried to do here and why you have failed. I know what the Church is trying to do, and why it will succeeed, at least for a while. What I don't know—and what I'm dying to see—is what will happen when they start digging up the real truth about Giacomo Nerone. I'd intended to leave next week; but now I think I'll stay. It should be quite a comedy.'

'Why did you come here in the first place?' There was an edge of anger in Meyer's voice and Nicholas Black was quick to notice it. He grinned and fluttered an airy hand.

'It's very simple. I had an exhibition in Rome—quite successful, too, even though it was on the fringe of.the season. The Contessa was one of my clients. She bought three canvases. Then she invited me to come down here and paint for a while. I'm hoping she'll finance another show in the near future. It's as simple as that.'

'Nothing is ever as simple as that,' said the doctor mildly. 'And the Contessa is not a simple person. Neither are you. What you see as a provincial comedy may well turn into a grand tragedy. I advise you not to become involved in it.'

The Englishman threw back his head and laughed.

'But I am involved, my dear Doctor. I'm an artist, an observer and recorder of the beauty and the folly of mankind. Imagine what Goya could have made out of a situation like this one. Fortunately he's been dead a long time, so now it's my turn. There's a whole gallery of pictures here—and the title's ready made: "Beatification", by Nicolas Black! A one-man show on a single theme. A village saint, the village sinners, and all the clergy, right up to the Bishop himself. What do you think of that?'

Aldo Meyer looked down at the backs of his hands, studying the brown liver spots and the rough slack skin that told him more clearly than words how old he was getting. Without lifting his eyes, he said quietly:

'I think you are a very unhappy man, Nicholas Black. You are looking for something you will never find. I think you should go away immediately. Leave the Contessa. Leave Paolo Sanduzzi. Leave us all to deal with our problems in our own way. You don't belong here. You speak our language, but you don't understand us.'

'But I do, Doctor!' The handsome, epicene face was lit with malice. 'I do indeed. I know that you've all been hiding something for fifteen years, and now it's going to be dug up. The Church wants a saint and you want to keep a secret that discredits you. That's true, isn't it?'

'It's half a truth; which is always more than half a lie.'

'You knew Giacomo Nerone, didn't you?'

'I knew him, yes.'

'Was he a saint?'

'I know nothing about saints,' said Aldo Meyer gravely. 'I only know men.'

'And Nerone . . .?'

'. . . was a man.'

'What about his miracles?'

'I have never seen a miracle.'

'Do you believe in them?'

'No.'

The bright sardonic eyes were fixed on his drawn face.

'Then why, my dear Doctor, are you afraid of this investigation?'

Aldo Meyer pushed back his chair and stood up. The shadow of the fig tree fell across his face, deepening the hollows of his cheeks, hiding the stark pain in his eyes. After a moment he answered:

'Have you ever been ashamed of yourself, my friend?'

'Never,' said the painter cheerfully. 'Never in my life.'

'That's what I mean,' said the doctor softly. 'You will never understand. But I tell you again, you should go—and go quickly.'

His only answer was a smile of rueful mockery as Black stood up to take his leave. They did not shake hands and Meyer made no attempt to accompany him out of the garden. Halfway to the house, the painter stopped and turned back.

'I'd almost forgotten. There's a message for you from the Contessa. She would like you to dine with her tomorrow evening.'

'My thanks to the Contessa,' said Meyer dryly. 'I'll be happy to come. Good day, my friend.'

'*Ci vedremo*,' said Nicholas Black casually. 'We'll see each other again—quite soon.'

Then he was gone, a slim, faintly clownish figure, too jaunty for the years that were beginning to show themselves in his intelligent, unhappy face. Aldo Meyer sat down again at the table and stared unseeingly at the broken crusts and the brown, muddy dregs in the coffee cups. After a while the woman came out of the house and stood looking down at him, with gentleness and pity in her calm eyes. When he looked up and saw her standing there, he said curtly:

'You can clear the table, Nina.'

She made no move to obey him, but asked:

'What did he want, that one who looks like a goat?'

'He brought me news,' said Meyer, lapsing into dialect to match the woman's. 'They are starting a new investigation into the life of Giacomo Nerone. A priest has come down from Rome to assist the Bishop's court. He will be coming here shortly.'

'He will ask questions, like the others?'

'More than the others, Nina.'

'Then he will get the same answer—nothing!'

Meyer shook his head slowly

'Not this time, Nina. It has gone too far. Rome is interested. The press will be interested. Better they get the truth this time.'

She stared at him in shocked surprise.

'You say that? You!'

Meyer shrugged defeatedly and quoted an old country proverb.

'Who can fight the wind? Who can drown the shouting they make on the other side of the valley? Even in Rome they have heard it—and this is the result. Let's tell them what they want and be done with it. Maybe then they will leave us in peace.'

'But why do they want it?' There was anger now in her eyes and in her voice. 'What difference does it make? They called him all sorts of names in his life—now they want to call him a *beato*. It's just another name. It doesn't change what he was—a good man, my man.'

'They don't want a man, Nina,' said Meyer wearily. 'They want a plaster saint with a gold plate on top of his head. The Church wants it because it gives them another hold on the people—a new cult, a new promise of miracles to make them forget their belly-aches. The people want it because they can get down on their knees and beg for favours instead of rolling up their sleeves and working for them—or fighting for them. It's the way of the Church—sugar for old sour wine.'

'Then why do you want me to help them?'

'Because if we tell them the truth, they'll drop the case. They'll have to. Giacomo was a remarkable man, but he was no more a saint than I am.'

'Is that what you believe?'

'Don't you, Nina?'

Her answer shocked him like a blow in the face.

'I know he was a saint,' she told him softly. 'I know he did miracles, because I saw them.'

Meyer gaped at her; then he shouted.

'God Almighty, woman! Even you? He slept in your bed. He gave you a bastard child, but never married you. And you can stand there and tell me he was a saint who did miracles. Why didn't you tell the priests that the first time? Why didn't you join our friend across the way and go shouting to have him beatified?'

'Because he would never have wanted it,' said Nina Sanduzzi calmly. 'Because it was the one thing he asked—that I should never tell what I knew about him.'

He was beaten and he knew it, but there was one more weapon left and he struck with it viciously.

'What will you answer, Nina, when they point to your boy and say, "There is a saint's son, and he makes himself a *feminella* for the Englishman?"'

There was no hint of shame in the calm, classic face as she replied:

'What do I say when they point to me in the street and whisper: "There is the one who was a saint's whore?" Nothing, nothing at all! Do you know why, Dottore? Because before Giacomo died, he made me a promise, in return for mine. "No matter what happens, *cara*, I shall look after you and the boy. They can kill me, but they can't stop me caring for you from now to eternity!" I believed him then, I believe him now. The boy is foolish but he is not lost yet.'

'Then he damned soon will be,' said Meyer brutally. 'Go home now, for God's sake, and leave me in peace.'

But even after she was gone there was no peace; and he knew there never would be until the inquisitors came and dragged the truth out into the daylight.

No hint of morning had yet entered the high, baroque room in the villa where the Countess Anne Louise de Sanctis slept behind velvet curtains. No premonition of trouble could penetrate the barbituric haze beyond which she dreamed.

Later, much later, a servant would come in and open the curtains to let the sun flow over the worn carpet and the rusted velvet and the dull patina of the carved walnut. It would not reach as far as the bed, which was a kindness, because the Contessa in the morning was an unpleasing spectacle.

Later still, she would wake, dry-mouthed, grey, puffy-eyed and discontented with the advent of a new day exactly like the old. She would wake, and doze, then wake again and thrust the first cigarette of the day into her pale, down-drawn lips. The cigarette finished, she would pull the bell-cord and the servant would return, smiling in anxious good-humour and carrying a breakfast tray. Since the Contessa disliked eating alone at any time, the servant would remain in the room, folding the scattered clothes, laying out fresh ones, bustling back and forth to the bathroom, while her mistress kept up a flow of waspish comment on the household and its shortcomings.

Breakfast finished, the servant would take away the tray, the Contessa would smoke one more cigarette before beginning the small intimate ritual of the toilet. It was the one important ceremony of her unimportant day, and she performed it in rigid secrecy.

She stubbed out her cigarette in the silver ashtray, then got out of bed, walked to the door and locked it. Next she made a circuit of the room, standing at each of the windows and looking out on the terraces and over the gardens to make sure no one was near. Once an inquisitive gardener had stood staring through the casements, and he had been instantly dismissed for this sacrilegious intrusion into the mysteries.

Assured at last of her privacy the Contessa went to the bathroom, undressed and stepped into the great marble bath with its gilt taps and its array of soaps and sponges and bottles of bath-salts. There was no pleasure now to be compared with this first solitary immersion in steaming water that soaked away the effusions of a drugged sleep and brought back the illusion of youth to an ageing body. Unlike other pleasures this one could be renewed at will, prolonged to satiation. It demanded no partner, involved neither dependence nor surrender; and the Contessa clung to it with the passion of a devotee.

As she lay back in the steaming water, she surveyed herself: the lines of the flanks, still slim and youthful, the belly flat and unmarked by childbearing, the waist, thickening a little, but not too much, the breasts massaged to firmness, small but round and still youthful. If there were lines about her neck, there was no mirror yet to tell her, and the tell-tale creases at mouth and eyes could still be massaged into subjection. Youth had not yet dried out of her and age could be held a little longer at bay with a weekly consignment of compounds from a discreet salon on the Via Veneto.

But the bath was only the beginning. There was the drying with soft warm towels, the rubbing with rough ones, the perfuming with sharp, astringent lotion, the powder dusted on and whisked gently away, the first combing of the hair—no grey in it yet, though the gold was fading—the ribbon to tie it back from the scrubbed and shining cheeks. Finally, she was ready for the processional climax of the ritual.

Naked and glowing from the new illusion, she walked back into the bedroom, crossed to the dressing table and took from the top drawer the photograph of a man in the uniform of a colonel of Alpini and set it up facing the room. Then, self-conscious as a mannequin, she began to dress herself in front of it, carefully, coquettishly, as if to charm him out of the frame and into her expectant arms.

When she was clothed, she laid the photograph back in the drawer, closed it, locked it, then, quite calmly, sat down in front of the mirror and began to make up her face.

Twenty minutes later, dressed in a modish summer frock, she walked out of the bedroom, down the stairs and into the bright garden, where Nicholas

Black, stripped to the waist, was working on a new canvas.

He turned at her footfall and came to greet her with theatrical pleasure, kissing her hands and then spinning her round to display her frock, while he chattered like a happy parrot:

'Magnificent, *cara*! I don't know how you do it! Every morning is like a new revelation. In Rome you were beautiful but rather terrifying. Here you're a country beauty reserved for my private admiration. I must paint you in that frock. Here, sit down and let me look at you.'

She bridled happily at the compliments and let him lead her to a small stone seat shaded by a blossoming almond tree. He made a great show of settling her to his satisfaction, fanning out her frock along the bench, tilting her head upward to the flowers and settling her hands in her lap. Then he snatched up a sketch-block and, with swift, bravura strokes, began to draw, talking all the time.

'I had coffee with our doctor friend this morning. He had his usual hangover, but he brightened up when I told him of your invitation to dinner. I had the idea he's more than half in love with you. . . . No, no! don't talk, you'll spoil the pose. I don't suppose the poor fellow can help it. He's lived so long among the peasants, you must seem like the fairy princess up here in your castle. . . . Oh, and another thing: the Bishop of Valenta is starting a full-scale investigation into the life and virtues of Giacomo Nerone. He's imported an English Monsignor from Rome to act as Devil's Advocate. He'll be coming up here in a few days. I took the liberty of telling His Lordship you'd be happy to have him as a guest.'

'No!' It was a panic cry. All her composure fell away and she stared at him, angry and afraid.

'But, *cara*!' He was instantly penitent. He put down the sketch-block and went to her, with solicitous hands and voice. 'I thought that's what you'd want me to do. I couldn't consult you, but I knew you were friendly with the Bishop and I knew there was really no other place for the visitor to lodge. He couldn't sleep with the peasants, now could he? Or under the counter in the wine-shop? Besides, he's a countryman of yours—and mine. I thought it would give you pleasure. If I've offended you, I'll never forgive myself.'

He went down on his knees beside her and buried his face in her lap, like a penitent child.

It was an old, old trick to charm the dowagers, and it worked again. She ran her fingers caressingly through his hair and said gently:

'Of course you haven't offended me, Nicki. It was surprise, that's all. I . . . I'm not prepared for them now as I used to be. Of course you did right. I'll be happy to have this Monsignor.'

'I knew you would be!' Instantly he was gay again. 'His Lordship was grateful—and I don't think our visitor will be too stuffy. Besides . . .' A small smiling malice shone again in his eyes. 'We'll be able to follow the investigation from the inside, won't we?'

'I suppose so.' Her face clouded again and she began to pluck nervously at the folds of her frock. 'But what will he do here?'

Nicholas Black gestured airily.

'What they all do. Ask questions, take notes, examine witnesses. Come to think of it, you'll probably be one yourself. You knew Nerone, didn't you?'

She shifted uneasily and refused to meet his eyes.

'Only slightly. I . . . I couldn't tell anything worth knowing.'

'Then what are you worrying about, *cara*? You'll have a box seat at the village comedy–and some Roman gossip as well. Come on now, settle yourself again and let me get this sketch done.'

But for all his care, he could not charm the fear out of her, and when he came to draw her face, every stroke was a lie. But all women were fools. They saw only what they wanted to see–and Nicholas Black had been making a profit from their follies for the best part of his life.

When the sketch was done, he handed it to her with a flourish and grinned inwardly at her expression of relief and pleasure. Then with calculated casualness he kissed her hand and dismissed her:

'You disturb me, darling. You're a beautiful nuisance. Go and pick me some flowers for the bedroom and let me finish my picture.'

As he watched her walking uncertainly across the lawn he chuckled to himself. She had been kind to him, and he bore her no personal malice. But he too had his secret pleasures, and the most subtle of all was to humble by intrigue what he could never subdue by possession–the hungry, hateful flesh of womankind.

For Anne Louise de Sanctis the moment had far other meanings. She was neither stupid nor vicious, though she consented equally to the follies of middle age and the vices that a still lively body imposed on her. When she submitted herself to the small tyrannies of the painter, it was because they piqued her vanity, and because she knew that she still held the balance of power. He wanted her to finance a new exhibition in Rome. She could do it–or she could send him packing tomorrow, back to the catch-penny life of a mediocre artist, and the sedulous pursuit of complaisant dowagers.

It pleased her to see that he, too, was getting old, and that each new conquest was a little more difficult. His malice was like the malice of a child, hurtful sometimes, but always joined with an unacknowledged need of her. And it was a long time since she had been needed by anyone. She had her own needs, too, but though he understood them and played on them, he was powerless to use them against her. He played on her fears and her loneliness, but the real terror he had not yet discovered.

It was this terror that walked with her now in the dappled garden on the hill-top, where wealth and cheap labour had planted an oasis in the raw, parched land of Calabria. The earth for the lawns and flower-beds had been brought up the hill in baskets on the shoulders of village women. The stone had been hacked out of the hill-side by local masons, the olives and the pines and the orange groves planted by tenant farmers as their tribute to the family that had held them in fee for centuries. Neapolitan artists had painted the walls and the coffered ceilings, and a dozen connoisseurs had bid for the pictures and the statuary and the porcelain demanded by Count Gabriele de Sanctis for his English bride.

The circling wall had been built, and the crested gates forged, to give her privacy. The staff had been chosen by the Count himself to serve her solicitously. The house and the land and everything in it were his wedding gift to her; a provincial retreat after the hectic season of Rome, where Gabriele de Sanctis was rising high in the service of the Duce. For the daughter of a minor diplomat, fresh from her first season in London, it was like an Arabian night's enchantment, but the terror had come in with her at the gates and it had stayed with her all the years since.

Gabriele de Sanctis had begun it–but he was dead long ago, a discredited suicide in the Libyan desert. A dozen other men had come and gone in the intervening years, but none of them had been able to rid her of it.

Then there was Giacomo Nerone. In this same garden, on a morning such as this, she had humbled herself and begged him to exorcise her, but he had refused. She had revenged herself in the end, but the revenge had brought new furies to torment her—nightmares in the big baroque bed, ghosts haunting the olive groves and grinning like satyrs through the orange-blossom. Lately they had plagued her less. There were drugs to bring sleep, and Nicholas Black to divert her in the daytime.

But now a man was coming: a grey-faced cleric from Rome commissioned to dig into the past, to tally old debts and record buried guilts, no matter what pain might follow the revelation. He would lodge in her house and eat at her table. He would pry and probe and even the locked door of her bedroom would keep no secrets from him.

Suddenly the life she had drawn in from the morning bath seemed to drain out of her, leaving her slack and tired. She made her way with slow, dragging steps to a small arbour on the fringe of the olive plantation where a small statue of a dancing faun was poised on a weathered stone pedestal. In front of the faun was a rustic bench over which honeysuckle drooped, languid and cloying. She sat down, lit a cigarette and inhaled greedily, drawing the smoke down into her lungs and feeling the tension in her relax slowly.

She understood now. She had been running too long. There was no escape from the fear which she carried like a tenant in her own body. There must be an end to it, else she would topple over into the black madness that threatens all women who come to the climacteric unhappy and unprepared. But how to end it? Break down all doors, humble herself to the inquisitors, submit to a confessional purging? She had tried it before, and it had failed utterly.

There was one alternative, bleak, perhaps, but sure: the small bottle full of gelatine capsules that seduced her nightly into sleep. The little more—and so little more—and it would be finished, once for all. In a sense it would be the completion of her revenge on Giacomo Nerone, and a revenge on the body which had betrayed her to him, and him to her.

But not yet. There was still a little time. Let the priest come, and if he did not press her too hard it would be a favourable omen—a promise of other solutions. If he did . . . why, then it would be simple, ironic and final; and when they found her she would still be beautiful as she was each morning from the perfumed bath.

4

For Blaise Meredith, the days he spent in the Bishop's house were the happiest of his life. A cold man by nature, he had begun to understand the meaning of fellowship. Withdrawn and self-sufficient, he saw, for the first time, the dignity of dependence, the grace of a shared confidence. Aurelio, Bishop of Valenta, was a man with a gift of understanding and a rare talent for friendship. The loneliness and the wintry courage of his guest had touched him deeply, and with tact and sympathy he set about establishing an intimacy between them.

Early the first morning he came to Meredith's room carrying the bulky volume of records on the first investigation of Giacomo Nerone. He found the priest, pale and fatigued, sitting in bed with the breakfast tray on his knees. He put the volume down on the table and then came, solicitously, to sit on the edge of the bed.

'A bad night, my friend?'

Meredith nodded wanly.

'A little worse than usual. The travel perhaps, and the excitement. I must apologise. I had hoped to serve Your Lordship's mass.'

The Bishop shook his head, smiling.

'No, Monsignor. Now you are under my jurisdiction. You are forbidden all but the Sunday Mass. You will sleep late and retire early, and if I find you working too hard, I may have to withdraw you from the case. You're in the country now. Take time for yourself. Smell the earth and the orange-blossom. Get the dust of the libraries out of your lungs.'

'Your Lordship is kind,' said Meredith gravely. 'But there is all too little time.'

'All the more reason to spend some of it on yourself,' the Bishop told him. 'And a little on me as well. I'm a stranger here too, remember. My colleagues are good men, most of them, but very dull company. There are things I should like to show you, talk I should like to hear from you. As for this—' he pointed to the bulky, leather-bound volume—'you can read it in the garden. Half of it is repetition and rhetoric. The rest you can digest in a couple of days. The people you want to see are only an hour away by car . . . and mine is at your disposal at any time, with a driver to look after you!'

A slow, puzzled smile dawned on Meredith's pallid face.

'You are kind to me and I find it strange. I wonder why?'

A youthful grin brightened the face of the Bishop.

'You have lived too long in Rome, my friend. You have forgotten that the Church is a family of the faithful, not simply a bureaucracy of believers. It's a sign of the times—one of the less hopeful signs. This is the century of the machine and the Church has conceded too much to it. They have time-clocks in the Vatican now and adding machines and ticker tape to tally the stock market.'

In spite of his weariness, Meredith threw back his head and laughed heartily. The Bishop nodded approvingly.

'That's better. A little honest laughter would do us all good. We need a satirist or two to give us back a sense of proportion.'

'We'd probably prosecute them for libel,' said Meredith wryly, 'or indict them for heresy.'

'*Inter faeces et urinam nascimur*,' the Bishop quoted quietly. 'It was a Saint who said it—and it applies equally to Popes and priests and the prostitutes of Reggio di Calabria. A little more laughter at our comic estate, a few honest tears for the pity of things—and we'd all be better Christians. Now finish your breakfast and then take a walk in the garden. I've spent a lot of time on it; and I'd hate an Englishman to ignore it!'

An hour later, bathed, shaved and refreshed, he walked out into the garden, taking with him the volume of depositions of Giacomo Nerone. It had rained during the night and the sky was clear, while the air was full of the smell of damp earth and washed leaves and new blossom. The bees were bumbling round the orange-flowers and the scarlet hibiscus, and the yellow gillyflowers stood straight and strident round the stone borders of the paths. Again Meredith was touched with hunger for a permanence on this thrusting earth whose beauty he was seeing for the first time. If only he could stay with it longer, root himself like a tree, to be weathered and blown, but still survive for the rain and the sun and the renewal of spring. But no. He had lived in the dust of the libraries too long and when the time came they would bury him in it. No flowers would grow out of his mouth as they did from the mouths of humbler men, no roots would twine themselves round the moult of his heart and his loins. They would screw him down in a leaden box and carry him to a vault in the Cardinal's church, where he would moulder, barren as he had lived, until Judgment Day.

Round the trunks of the olive trees the grass was green and the air was warm and still. He took off his cassock and his stock and opened his shirt to let the warmth fall on his thin chest: then he sat down, leaning against the bole of a tree, opened the big leather volume, and began to read:

'Preliminary depositions on the life, virtues and alleged miracles of the Servant of God, Giacomo Nerone. Collected at the instance and under the authority of His Lordship, Aurelio, Titular of Valenta in the Province of Calabria, by Geronimo Battista and Luigi Saltarello, priests of the same Diocese.'

Then followed the careful disclaimer:

'The following depositions and information are of a non-judicial character, since to this date no court has been set up and no authorities promulgated to examine officially the cause of the Servant of God. Though every effort has been made to arrive at the truth, witnesses were not sworn, nor placed under canonical sanction to reveal any matters known to them. None of the processes of a diocesan court have been observed either as to secrecy or the method of recording. Witnesses have, however, been warned that they may be called to give evidence under oath at such a court, when and if constituted.'

Blaise Meredith nodded and pursed his thin lips with satisfaction. So far so good. This was the bureaucracy of the Church in action – Roman legality applied to the affairs of the spirit. The sceptics might sneer at it, believers might chuckle at its excess, but in essence it was sound. It was the same genius that had given to the West the civilising code under which, in part at least, it still lived. He turned the page and read on:

'*De non cultu. (Decree of Urban VIII, 1634)*

'In view of the reports about the visits of pilgrims and the veneration paid by certain members of the faithful at the resting place of the Servant of God, we deemed it our first duty to inquire whether the decrees of the Pontiff Urban VIII prohibiting public cultus have been observed. We found that many members of the faithful, both visitors and local people, do visit the tomb of Giacomo Nerone and pray there. Some of them claim spiritual and temporal favours through his intercession. The civil authorities and, in particular, the Mayor of Gemello Maggiore have organised certain press publicity and improved transport facilities to encourage the flow of visitors. While this may constitute an indiscretion, it does not contravene the canons. No public worship is permitted in the canonical sense. The Servant of God is not invoked in liturgical ceremonies. No pictures or images are exposed for public veneration and, apart from garbled press accounts, no books or leaflets containing accounts of miracles have so far been circulated. Certain relics of the Servant of God are in private circulation among the faithful but no public veneration has been permitted to be paid to them. It is our view therefore that the canons prohibiting public cultus have been observed. . . .'

Blaise Meredith drowsed lightly over the formal phrases. This was old ground to him—familiar but reassuring. It was the function of the Church not merely to impose belief, but to limit it as well, to encourage piety but discourage pietists. The laws were there, however much they were obscured by ignorance, and their cool reason was a curb on the excesses of devotees and the harsh demands of the puritans. But he was still a long way from the heart of the problem—the life and virtues and alleged miracles of Giacomo Nerone. The next paragraph brought him no closer. It was headed:

'De scriptis

'No writings of any kind attributable to the Servant of God have been found. Certain references, noted later in the depositions, point to the possible existence of a body of manuscript which has been either lost, destroyed or is being deliberately concealed by interested persons. Until a judicial process has begun and it is possible to bring moral pressure to bear on witnesses, we are unlikely to get further information on this important point.'

Blaise Meredith frowned with dissatisfaction. No writings. A pity. From a judicial point of view the things a man wrote were the only sure indication of his beliefs and intentions, and, in the rigorous logic of Rome, these were even more important than his acts. A man might murder his wife or seduce his daughter and still remain a member of the Church; but let him reject one jot of defined truth and he set himself immediately outside it. He might spend himself in lifelong charities, yet have no merit in him at the end. The moral value of an act depended on the intention with which it was performed. But when a man was dead, who was to speak the secrets of his heart?

It was a discouraging beginning and what followed was even less reassuring:

'Biographical Summary

'*Name:* Giacomo Nerone. There is reason—noted later in the depositions—to assume that this was a pseudonym.

'*Date of Birth:* Unknown. Physical descriptions by witnesses vary considerably, but there is general agreement that he was from 30 to 35 years of age.

'*Place of Birth:* Unknown.

'*Nationality:* Unknown. There is evidence that Giacomo Nerone was at first accepted as an Italian, but that, later, doubts were cast on his identity. He was described as tall, dark and brown-skinned. He spoke Italian fluently and correctly though with a Northern accent. He did not at first speak dialect, but later learned it and spoke it constantly. During the period covered by his life in Gemelli dei Monti, there were units of German, American, British and Canadian troops operating in the province of Calabria. Various guesses have been made at his nationality, but the evidence advanced in support of them is, in our view, inconclusive.

'We are of the opinion, however, for reasons not yet clear that he did make a deliberate effort to conceal his true identity. We are also of the opinion that certain persons knew his identity and are still attempting to hide it.

'*Date of Arrival in Gemelli dei Monti:* The exact date is uncertain, but there is general agreement that it was towards the end of August, 1943. This date corresponds roughly with the Allied conquest of Sicily and the operations of the British Eighth Army in the Calabrian province.

'*Period of Residence in Gemelli dei Monti:* August, 1943, to 30th June, 1944. The whole of the testimony refers to this period of less than twelve months and any claims to heroic sanctity must be judged on the available records of this unusually short time.

'*Date of Death:* June 30th, 1944. 3 p.m. Giacomo Nerone was executed by a firing squad of Partisans under the leadership of a man known as Il Lupo, the Wolf. Both the date and the time are specific and confirmed by eye-witnesses. The circumstances are also confirmed by unanimous testimony.

'*Burial:* The burial took place at 10.30 p.m. on June 30th. The body of Giacomo Nerone was removed from the place of execution by six persons and buried in the place known as Grotta del Fauno, where it now lies. Both the identification of the body and the circumstances of the burial are confirmed by the unanimous testimony of those who took part in the interment.'

Blaise Meredith closed the thick volume and laid it down on the grass beside him. He leaned his head back against the rough bole of the olive tree and thought about what he had just read. True, it was only a beginning, but from the point of view of the Devil's Advocate it was a dubious one.

There were too many unknowns and the imputation of deliberate secrecy was disturbing. All that was known and covered by testimony was a period of eleven months, out of a lifetime of thirty to thirty-five years. There were no writings available for scrutiny. None of these things precluded sanctity, but they might well preclude proven sanctity, which was the matter of Meredith's investigation and the judicial process of the Bishop's court.

Always, in cases like this, one was forced back to the cool logic of the theologians.

It began with the premise of a personal God, self-continuing, self-sufficient, omnipotent. Man was the issue of a creative act of the divine will. The relationship between the Creator and His creature was defined first by the natural law, whose workings were visible and apprehensible by human reason, then by a series of divine relations, culminating in the Incarnation, the Teaching, Death and Resurrection of God-made-Man, Jesus Christ.

The perfection of man and his ultimate union with the Creator depended on his conformity to the relationship between them, his salvation depended on his being in a state of conformity at the moment of death. He was aided to this conformity by divine help, called grace, which was always available to him in sufficient measure to guarantee salvation, provided he co-operated with it by the use of free will. Salvation implied perfection, but a limited perfection.

But sanctity, heroic sanctity, implied a special call to a greater perfection, through the use of special graces—to none of which a man could attain by his own power. Every age has produced its crop of saints, not all of them were known, and not all known were officially proclaimed.

Official proclamation involved something else again: the implication that the Divinity wished to make known the virtues of the saint by calling attention to them through miracles—acts beyond human power—divine suspensions of the law of nature.

It was this implication that troubled Meredith at the outset of the case of Giacomo Nerone. It was a simple axiom of every theologian that an omnipotent Being could not, of his nature, lend himself either to triviality or to trivial secrecy.

There was nothing trivial in the birth of a man, since it involved the projection of a new soul into the dimensions of the flesh. There was nothing trivial in the progression of his life, since every act conditioned him for the last moment of it. And his death was the moment when the spirit was thrust out of the body in the irrevocable attitude of conformity or rejection.

So, whatever the gaps in the personal history of Giacomo Nerone, they must be filled. If facts were concealed, Blaise Meredith must ferret them out, because he, too, must soon be called to judgment.

But what a man must do and what his strength permits him are often two different things. The air was warm, the bourdon of the insects were deceptively soothing and the weariness of a sleepless night crept back insidiously. Blaise Meredith surrendered himself to it and slept on the soft grass until lunch-time.

His lordship chuckled delightedly when Meredith made rueful confession of his morning's slackness.

'Good! Good! We'll make a countryman of you yet. Did you dream pleasantly?'

'I didn't dream,' said Meredith with dry good-humour. 'And that was as big a mercy as sleep. But I didn't get much work done. I glanced through a few of the testimonies just before lunch, but I'm afraid I find them rather unsatisfactory.'

'How?'

'It's hard to define. They're in the normal form. They're obviously the result of careful cross-examination. But—how shall I put it?—they give no clear picture either of Giacomo Nerone, or of the witnesses themselves. And for our purposes both are important. The picture may grow, of course, as I go further, but just now there are no clear outlines.'

The Bishop nodded agreement.

'It was my own impression, too. It is one of the reasons for my doubts about the matter. The depositions are all of one piece. There are no elements of conflict or controversy. And saints are generally very controversial people.'

'But there are elements of secrecy.' Meredith put it to him quietly.

'Precisely.' The Bishop sipped his wine and considered his explanation. 'It is almost as if one section of the population had convinced itself that this man was a saint and wanted to prove it at all costs.

'And the other section?'

'Was determined to have nothing to say—either for or against.'

'It's too early for me to judge that,' said Meredith carefully. 'I haven't read enough or studied enough. But the tone of the statements I have read so far is stilted and strangely unreal, as if the witnesses were speaking a new language.'

'They are!' said the Bishop with sharp interest. 'Oddly enough, my friend, you have put your finger on a problem that has exercised me for a long time: the difficulty of accurate communication between the clergy and the laity. It is a difficulty which grows greater, instead of less, and which inhibits even the healing intimacy of the confessional. The root of it, I think, is this: the Church is a theocracy, ruled by a priestly caste, of which you and I are members. We have a language of our own—a hieratic language if you like—formal, stylised, admirably adapted to legal and theological definition. Unfortunately we have also a rhetoric of our own, which, like the rhetoric of the politician, says much and conveys little. But we are not politicians. We are teachers—teachers of a truth which we claim to be essential to man's salvation. Yet how do we preach it? We talk roundly of faith and hope as if we were making a fetishist's incantation. What is faith? A blind leap into the hands of God. An inspired act of will which is our only answer to the terrible mystery of where we came from and where we are going. What is hope? A child's trust in the hand that will lead it out of the terrors that reach from the dark. We preach love and fidelity, as if these were teacup tales—and not bodies writhing on a bed and hot words in dark places, and souls tormented by loneliness and driven to the momentary communion of a kiss. We preach charity and compassion but rarely say what they mean—hands dabbling in sick-room messes, wiping infection from syphilitic sores. We talk to the people every Sunday, but our words do not reach them, because we have forgotten our mother tongue. It wasn't always like this. The sermons of St Bernardine of Siena are almost unprintable today, but they reached hearts, because the truth in them was sharp as a sword, and as painful. . . .' He broke off and smiled, as if in deprecation of his own intensity. Then, after a moment, he said gently, 'That's the trouble with our witnesses, Monsignor. We don't understand them because they are talking to us as we talk to them. And it means as little either way.'

'Then how do I, of all people, come near them?' asked Meredith, with wry humility.

'The mother tongue,' said Aurelio, Bishop of Valenta. 'You were born, like them, *inter faeces et urinam*, and they will be surprised to know that you have not forgotten it—surprised enough, maybe, to tell you the truth.'

Later that afternoon, while the sun blazed outside the closed shutters and the wise folk of the South dozed away the heat, Blaise Meredith lay on his bed and pondered the words of the Bishop. They were true and he knew it. But the habit of years was strong on him; the careful euphemism, the priestly prudery, as though his tongue should be shamed by mention of the body that bore him and the sublime act that gave him being.

And yet Christ himself had dealt in such common coinage. He had talked in the vulgar tongue of vulgar symbols: a woman screaming in labour, the fat eunuchs waddling through the bazaars, the woman whom many husbands could not satisfy and who turned to a man who was not her husband. He had invoked no convention to shield himself from the men He had himself created. He ate with tax-farmers and drank with public women, and He did not shrink from the anointing hands that had caressed the bodies of men in the passion of a thousand nights.

And Giacomo Nerone? If he were a saint, he would be like his Master. If he were not, he would still be a man and the truth about him would be told in the simple language of the bedroom and the wine-shop.

As the afternoon wore on and the first chill of evening filtered into the room, Blaise Meredith began, slowly, to understand the task that lay ahead of him.

His first problem was a tactical one. Although the notices had been published, and the two major officials appointed, the court itself had not yet been constituted. Since all court testimony would be sworn and secret—and since there was no point in wasting its time with frivolous or unco-operative people—it was necessary to test them first in private and unsworn interviews, in the same fashion as a civil lawyer tests his witnesses before presenting them.

They had already been interviewed once by Battista and Saltarello, whose records were in his hands. But these were local priests, and by presumption impartial—if not actually in favour of the candidate. His own position was vastly different. He was a foreigner, a Vatican official, the crown prosecutor. He was suspect by the very nature of his office, and if worldly interests were involved—as they undoubtedly were—he could count on active and powerful opposition.

Those who were promoting the Cause of the Saint would be careful to steer him clear of any contentious information. If they had given testimony in favour of Giacomo Nerone, they would not change it for the Devil's Advocate—though they might break down if he could find grounds on which to challenge them. It was folly, of course, to make intrigues about the Almighty, but there was as much folly and intrigue inside the Church as there was outside. The Church was a family of men and women, none of them guaranteed impeccable even by the Holy Ghost.

His best chance therefore seemed to lie with those who had refused to give evidence at all. It might not be easy to find out why some people didn't believe in saints and regarded their cults as a noxious superstition. These might well be willing to reveal anything that pointed to clay feet on a popular idol. Some folk believed in saints but wanted no truck with them at all. They found them uncomfortable company, their virtues a perpetual reproach. There was no one so stubborn as a Catholic at odds with his conscience. Finally there might be those who hesitated to reveal facts creditable to the candidate because they were discreditable to themselves.

The next problem was where to find such people. According to the records of Battista and Saltarello, all the positive information came from Gemello Maggiore, the prosperous village, and all the refusals from the depressed twin across the valley. The distinction was too obvious to be ignored and too artificial to be accepted without question. Meredith decided to discuss it with the Bishop at their next meal together.

His Lordship approached the question with more than usual caution.

'For me, too, this has been one of the most puzzling features of the situation. Let me try to put it into perspective for you. Here are two villages, twins by name and twins by nature, perched on the horns of the same mountain. Before the war, what were they? Typical Calabrian hamlets–small depressed places, inhabited by tenant farmers of absentee landlords. In their outward aspect and in their standard of living there was no perceptible difference between them; except that in Gemello Minore there was a resident *padrona,* the Contessa de Sanctis. . . .' The Bishop leaned ironically on the parenthesis. 'An interesting woman, the Contessa. I'll be curious to know what you think of her. You'll be her house-guest when you go to Gemello Minore. However, her presence, then as now, made no difference to the state of the local population. . . . Then came the war. The young men were taken for the Army, the old ones and the women were left to farm the land. It is poor land at best, as you will see, and it got poorer and poorer as the years went on. There was a State levy on the crops, and by the time the landlords had taken their share, there was little enough left for the peasants, and often there was real starvation in the mountains. Now . . .' His Lordship's long, sensitive hands gestured emphatically. 'Into this situation comes a man, a stranger, who calls himself Giacomo Nerone. What do we know about him?'

'Little enough,' said Blaise Meredith. 'He arrives from nowhere dressed in peasant rags. He is wounded and sick with malaria. He claims to be a deserter from the fighting in the South. The villagers accept him at face value. They have sons of their own who are far away. They have no sympathy with a lost cause. A young widow named Nina Sanduzzi takes him into her house and cares for him. He enters into a liaison with her which is later broken off . . . right in the middle of her pregnancy.'

'And then?' The Bishop prompted him shrewdly.

Blaise Meredith shrugged in puzzled fashion.

'Then I find myself at a loss. The record is unclear. The witnesses are vague. There is talk of a conversion, a turning to God. Nerone leaves the house of Nina Sanduzzi and builds himself a small hut in the most desolate corner of the valley. He plants a garden. He spends hours in solitude and contemplation. He appears in church on Sundays and takes the Sacraments. At the same time–the same time, mark you–he appears to have taken over the leadership of the villages.'

'How does he lead them, and to what? I'm quizzing you, Meredith, because I want to see what you, the newcomer, have made of this story. I myself know it by heart, but I am still puzzled by it.'

'As I read the evidence,' said Meredith carefully, 'he began by going from house to house offering his services to anyone who needed them–an old man whose land was getting away from him, a grandmother, feeble and alone, a sick farmer who wanted someone to hoe his tomato patch. From those who could afford it he demanded a payment in kind–goat milk, olives, wine, cheese–which he passed on to those who were in need of these things. Later, when winter came, he organised a pooling of labour and resources, and enforced it rigorously, sometimes violently.'

'An unsaintly proceeding, surely?' suggested the Bishop, with a thin smile.

'That was my own feeling,' admitted Meredith.

'But even Christ whipped the money-changers out of the Temple, did he not? And when you know our Calabresi, you'll agree that they have the hardest heads and the tightest fists in Italy.'

Meredith was forced to smile at the trap the Bishop had set for him.

He conceded the point, smiling:

'We mark it then to the credit of Giacomo Nerone. The next thing is in his favour too. He nurses the sick and appears to have given some kind of rough medical service in collaboration with a certain doctor, Aldo Meyer, a political exile, who curiously enough refused to give any testimony in the case.'

'That point, too, has been much in my mind,' the Bishop told him. 'It is the more interesting since, before and after the war, Meyer himself had tried to organise these people for their own benefit, but failed completely. He's a man of singular humanity, but handicapped by being a Jew in a Catholic country–perhaps by other things too. You should try to get close to him. You may be surprised. . . . Go on, please.'

'Next we find evidence of more religious activity. Nerone prays with the sick, comforts the dying. He makes journeys in the snow to bring the priest with the Last Sacrament. When there is no priest he himself waits out the death-watch. Now there's an odd thing . . .' Meredith paused for an uncertain moment. 'Two of the witnesses say: "When Father Anselmo refused to come . . ." What would that mean?'

'What it says, I imagine,' His Lordship told him coolly. 'There has been much scandal about this man. I have thought often of removing him, but so far I have decided against it.'

'You have a reputation for rigid discipline. You have removed others. Why not this one?'

'He is an old man,' said the Bishop softly. 'Old and, I think, very near to despair, I should hate to think I was the one who drove him into it.'

'I'm sorry.' Meredith was instantly apologetic.

'Not at all. We're friends. You have a right to ask. But I'm a Bishop, not a bureaucrat. I carry the shepherd's crook and the stray sheep are mine, too. Go on. Read me more of Giacomo Nerone.'

Meredith ran a hand through his thinning hair. He was getting tired. It was an effort to keep his thoughts in order.

'Somewhere about March, 1944, the Germans came–a small detachment at first, then a larger one–garrison reinforcements for those fighting against the British Eighth Army, which had crossed the Strait of Messina and was fighting its way up the toe of Calabria. Giacomo Nerone is the one who negotiates with them, successfully, it seems. The peasants will supply a guaranteed minimum of fresh food in return for medicines and winter clothing. The garrison commander will discipline his troops and protect the women whose husbands and brothers are away. The bargain is kept reasonably well, and Nerone establishes himself as a respected mediator. This association with the Germans was later alleged as a reason for his execution by the Partisans. When the Allies broke through and began pushing up towards Naples, they bypassed the villages and left the local Partisans to deal with the scattered and retreating German forces. Giacomo Nerone stayed on . . .'

The Bishop checked him with a slim, upraised hand.

'Stop there a moment. What do you see, so far?'

'Ignotus!' said Meredith calmly. 'The unknown. The man from nowhere. The lost one, who suddenly becomes the godly one. He has a sense of gratitude, a touch of compassion, a talent, and perhaps a taste, for leadership. But who is he? Where does he come from, or why does he act as he does?'

'You see no saint in him?'

Meredith shook his head.

'Not yet. Godliness perhaps, but not sanctity. I have not yet examined the evidence for the alleged miracles, so I leave this out of consideration. But I make one point. There is a pattern in sanctity, a great reasonableness. As yet I see no reason here, only secrecy and mystery.'

'Perhaps there is no mystery—just ignorance and misunderstanding. Tell me, my friend, what do you know of conditions here in the South at that time?'

'Little enough,' Meredith admitted frankly. 'For all of the war I was locked inside Vatican City. I only knew what I heard and read—and that was garbled enough, God knows.'

'Then let me explain them to you.' He got up and walked to the window, to stand looking out on the garden, where the wind stirred faintly through the shrubbery and the shadows were deep because there was still no moon over the hill-tops. When he spoke his voice was tinged with an old sadness. 'I am an Italian, and I understand this story better than most though I do not yet understand the people in it. First you must realise that a defeated people has no loyalties. Their leaders have failed them. Their sons have died in a lost cause. They believe in no one—not even in themselves. When our conquerors came in, shouting democracy and freedom we did not believe them either. We looked only at the loaf of bread in their hands and calculated exactly the price they would ask us to pay for it. Hungry people don't even believe in the loaf until it is safely swallowed and they can feel it aching in their unaccustomed stomachs. That's the way it was here in the South. The people were defeated, leaderless, hungry. Worse than that, they were forgotten; and they knew it.'

'But Nerone hadn't forgotten them,' Meredith objected. 'He was still with them. He was still a leader.'

'Not any more. There were new barons in the land. Men with new guns and full bandoliers and a rough rescript of authority from the conquerors to clean out the mountains and hold them tidy until a new and amenable Government was established. Their names and their faces were familiar—Michele, Gabriele, Luigi, Beppi. They had bread to bargain with and meat in tin cans and bars of chocolate, and old scores to settle as well: political scores and personal ones. They saluted with the clenched fist of comradeship, and with the same fist beat the faces of those who dared to differ from them. They were many and they were strong, because your Mr Churchill had said that he would do business with anybody who could help him to clean up the mess in Italy and let him get on with the invasion of France. What could Giacomo Nerone do against them—your Ignotus from nowhere?'

'What did he try to do? That's what interests me. Why did some folk cling to him as the holy one and others reject him and betray him to the executioners? Why were the Partisans against him in the first place?'

'It's in the record,' said His Lordship with a tired smile.

'They called him a collaborator. They accused him of profitable commerce with the Germans.'

Meredith rejected the suggestion emphatically.

'It's not enough! It's not enough to explain the hate and the violence and the division and why one village prospers and the other lapses deeper into depression. It's not enough for us either. The people claim a martyrdom—death in defence of the Faith and moral principles. All you've shown me is a political execution—unjust and cruel maybe—but still only that. We're not concerned with politics, but with sanctity, the direct relationship of a man with the God who made him.'

'Perhaps that's all it was—a good man caught up in politics.'

'Does Your Lordship believe that?'

'Does it matter what I believe, Monsignor?'

The shrewd patrician face was turned towards him. The thin lips smiled in irony.

Then, quite suddenly, the truth hit him, cold water in the face. This man too had a cross to bear. Bishop he might be, but there were still doubts to plague him and fears to harry him on the high peak of temptation. A rare compassion stirred in the dry heart of Blaise Meredith and he answered quietly:

'Does it matter? I think it matters much.'

'Why, Monsignor?' The deep, wise eyes challenged him.

'Because I think that you, like me, are afraid of the finger of God.'

5

Nicholas Black, the painter, was making a new picture.

It was a simple composition but oddly dramatic: a tumble of bare rocks, pitted and weathered, stained by fungus and mottled like the sloughed skin of a snake; out of the rocks grew a solitary olive tree, dead and bare of leaves, whose naked arms were outflung like a cross against the clear blue of the sky.

He had been working on it for an hour now, in the bright solitude of a small plateau behind the shoulder of the hill, with the chequer-board valley below him, and above, the heave of the tufted mountain, splashed with noon sun.

The sun was warm on his brown, stringy torso. The air was languid and dry but noisy with cicadas, and Paolo Sanduzzi dozed a yard from his feet, relaxed as a lizard on a grey rock.

Nicholas Black was a stranger to contentment, and full satisfaction came to him rarely; but in this quiet place and hour, in the company of the sleeping boy, with a picture growing strongly under his hand, he was as close to it as he had ever been.

He painted steadily, contentedly, his thoughts turned outwards on the canvas and on the grey, writhing tree, which was like a gallows on a miniature Golgotha. There was a strength in it that appealed to him—a sinew in the wood, muscle and bone under the rough, grey bark, as if one day it might split asunder and a man emerge shining and new to a kind of resurrection in the dawn.

He admired strength—the more because there was so little in himself—yet he was rarely able to translate it into works. The critics had noted the lack long ago. They admired the charm of his pictures, the bravura, the dramatic brilliance, but deplored the soft bone and the pale blood beneath their sleek skin. Later they called him *raté*—the man who would never quite make it, because of some fundamental weakness in his own personality. After that, of course, they were kind to him, in the condescending style they reserve for amiable mediocrities and hardy perennials. They always noticed his shows. They gave him praise enough to keep the dowagers buying and the smaller dealers mildly interesed. But they never took him seriously.

Now and again one of the young bloods sharpened his teeth on a Nicholas Black exhibition, and it was one of these who had written the brutal epitaph that set London laughing for a week and drove Black across the Channel to Rome and Anne Louise de Sanctis.

'One of the eunuchs of the profession,' said the clever young critic. 'Doomed to live forever in the contemplation of beauty, but never, never to possess it.'

In the Bag O' Nails and the Stag and the B.B.C. Club they chuckled into their beer. In the Georgian sitting-rooms of Knightsbridge they giggled over the cocktails. Under the mansards of Chelsea they made a bawdy lyric about it; and the one who shared his flat and more than half his love chanted it to his face at the end of a quarrelsome evening.

It was the bitterest moment in his life, and even now, two thousand miles and six months away from it, the memory was vivid and shameful. It was a special terror, this one; a very particular hell reserved for those poor devils who, by oversight or irony of the Creator, come into the world defective in those attributes which define a man. Their more normal fellows disdain them, as poetasters disdain a parody which points to the pomposities of their own work, as honest wives disdain a prostitute who sells for money what they refuse for love. So they make a kingdom among themselves, a half-world of lost lovers, of furtive encounters and strange marriages. There is loyalty in the half-world, but not enough of it for armour against the intriguers inside and the mockers at the flimsy gates. And when a man like Nicholas Black leaves it he becomes the lone pilgrim of a secret cult, whose symbols are the *graffiti* on toilet walls, the phallic gesture and the brushing touch in an assembly of strangers.

But now he had come to an oasis on the pilgrim road. He was painting a tree as strong and alive as a man. And a boy, berry-brown and languid, was sleeping at his feet in the sun. He made one last careful stroke, then laid down his brush and palette and stood looking down at Paolo Sanduzzi.

He was lying on his back, one knee drawn up, one arm pillowed under his head, the other lying slack on the warm grey rock. His only clothing was a pair of stained shorts and worn leather sandals. In the dry, warm air his skin shone like oiled wood and his smooth boyish face wore, in repose, an air of curious innocence.

Nicholas Black had long been a stranger to innocence. He had joined too often in the mockery and seduction of it. But he could still recognise it, still be jealous of it—and here, remote from the mockery, he could still regret the loss of it.

He sat down on the warm rock a few paces from the boy and smoked a pensive cigarette, caught in the rare syncope of contentment between the accusing past and the dubious future.

Suddenly the boy sat up and looked at him with shrewd, speculative eyes.

'Why do you always look at me like that?'

Black smiled calmly and said:

'You are beautiful, Paolino. Like the Young David whom Michelangelo carved out of a piece of marble. I am an artist—a lover of beauty. So I like to look at you.'

'I want to piss,' said the boy, grinning.

He leapt up and walked to the edge of the plateau and stood straddle-legged, easing himself in full view of Nicholas Black, who saw the mockery in it but made no protest. The boy came lounging back and squatted down beside him. He was still smiling, but there was a sidelong calculation in his dark eyes. He asked bluntly:

'Will you take me to Rome when you go?'

Black shrugged in the manner of the South.

'Who knows? Rome is a long way and expensive. I can get plenty of servants here. But a friend—that might be different.'

'But you told me I was your friend!' The eagerness was so bright and childish that it might have deceived him, but the truth was in the boy's eyes, dark as onyx.

'A friend must prove himself,' said the painter, with careful indifference. 'There's time yet. We'll see.'

'But I'm a good friend. A true one,' Paolo pleaded childishly. 'Look, I'll show you!'

He flung his arms round Black's neck, embraced him quickly, and then leapt away, shy as an animal, out of reach. The painter wiped his mouth with the back of his hand and then got up slowly, with the salt taste of disillusion on his tongue. He did not look at the boy who stood, arms akimbo, on a rock ledge ten feet away. He walked to the easel, picked up his brush and palette and said over his shoulder:

'Take off your clothes!' The boy stared at him.

Black yelled at him harshly.

'Go on! Take them off. I want to use you as a model. That's what you're paid for, among other things.'

After a moment's uneasy pause, the boy obeyed, and Black smiled with sardonic satisfaction when he saw how the boldness and the challenge was stripped from him with the tattered breeches. He was just a child now—scared, uncertain, in the presence of a temperamental employer.

'Stretch out your arms. Like this.'

The boy raised his arms slowly to the level of his shoulders.

'Now hold them there.'

With swift sure strokes Nicholas Black began to paint a crucified figure on the writhing shape of the olive tree: no tormented Christus, but a youth in full puberty with the face and body of Paolo Sanduzzi, nailed to the tree bark through hands and feet, with the red spear thrust in his breast, but smiling even while the life bled out of him.

The boy was weary long before it was finished, but he kept him standing there and cursed him whenever he dropped his arms. Then when it was done he called him over and showed him the picture. The effect was startling. The boy's face crumpled into a mask of terror, his mouth dropped open and he stood shivering and gibbering and pointing at the canvas.

'What's the matter? What are you trying to tell me?'

Black's voice was high and harsh but it made no impression on Paolo Sanduzzi. He was like someone at the beginning of an epileptic fit. Black walked up to him and slapped him sharply on both cheeks. The boy cried out in pain and then began to weep, squatting on the ground and covering his face with his hands, while Black knelt beside him trying to soothe him. After a while he asked him again:

'What's the matter? What frightened you?'

The boy's voice was almost a whisper.

'The picture!'

'What's the matter with it?'

'That's my father's tree!'

The painter gaped at him.

'What do you mean?'

'That's how they killed my father. On that same tree. They stretched him out on it, like on a cross, tied him up—and then shot him.'

'O God!' Nicholas Black swore softly. 'Sweet angels, what a story! What a sweet, sweet story.'

Then after a while he began to laugh, and the boy slunk away, frightened and subdued, carrying his trousers and sandals in his hand.

The same noontide saw Doctor Aldo Meyer restored to temporary favour in Gemello Minore.

Martino the smith had suffered a stroke while working at the anvil. He had fallen against the forge and been badly burned on the breast and face. They had carried him down the road to Meyer's cottage and the doctor was working on him now, assisted by Nina Sanduzzi, while Martino's wife watched nervously from the corner of the room and the villagers crowded outside the cottage chattering like starlings over this crumb of drama.

The thick barrel body of the smith was wrapped in blankets and laid on the plank table in Meyer's kitchen. One side of him was completely paralysed—the leg and arm useless, the face wrenched sideways into a rictus of surprise and fear. His eyes were closed and his breathing was shallow and noisy. As Meyer probed and swabbed the burns on his cheeks, a low, mumbling cry issued from his twisted mouth. When they had finished dressing the face, they unrolled the blankets and Meyer gave a low, thoughtful whistle as he saw the extent and the depth of the body burns. Nina Sanduzzi stood impassive as a statue, holding the bowl of boiling water and the swabs. When Martino's wife started forward, she laid down the bowl quite calmly and led her back to the corner, soothing and chiding her in a low confident voice. Then she came back to Meyer and, attentive as any nurse, helped him to pick the charcoal from the burns, cleanse them and dab them with gentian violet and the last small stock of Merthiolate.

When the dressings were done, Meyer made another auscultation and a pulse count, wrapped the blankets back again, and turned to talk to the weeping woman in the corner. He told her gently:

'You'd better leave him here for a couple of hours. Then I'll have him taken home to you.'

She pleaded with him, plaintive as an animal.

'He won't die, will he, Doctor? You won't let him die?'

'He's as strong as an ox,' said Meyer calmly. 'He won't die.'

She caught at his hands, kissing them and calling on the saints to bless the good doctor. Meyer disengaged himself brusquely.

'Go home now, like a good woman, and get your children fed. I'll send for you, if I want you—and later you'll get your husband home.'

Nina Sanduzzi took her by the arm and led her out of the room, and when he turned back to his patient he heard her at the door, shouting at the bystanders and urging them off about their business. When she came back she asked bluntly:

'Did you mean what you told her? He will live?'

'He'll live,' Meyer told her, shrugging. 'But he'll never be any good to himself or to her.'

'He's got six children.'

'Too many,' said Meyer with thin humour.

'But he has them,' she persisted stubbornly. 'Who is to feed them now that he cannot work?'

Meyer shrugged.

'There's public relief. They won't starve.'

'Public relief!' She flung it back at him scornfully. 'A dozen interviews and a hundred printed forms for a kilo of pasta! What sort of answer is that?'

'It's the only one I know these days,' Meyer told her with cool bitterness. 'I used to have lots of others, but no one would listen. They wanted to go on in the old way. Well . . . this is the old way!'

Nina Sanduzzi stared at him. There were pity and contempt in her dark, intelligent eyes.

'You know what Giacomo would have done, don't you? He'd have gone into the forge himself and worked. He'd have knocked on every door and begged or bullied people into helping. He'd have gone up to the villa and talked to the Contessa for money and work for Martino's wife. He'd have prised some poor-box money out of Father Anselmo. He understood this sort of thing. He knew how scared people get. He could never bear to hear a child crying . . .'

'He was a remarkable man, your Giacomo,' said Meyer tersely. 'That's why they killed him. Martino, as I remember, was one of those who fired the volley.'

'And you signed a paper saying that he had been legally executed after a proper trial.' There was no anger in her voice, only a quiet recollection of familiar facts. 'But none of you ever told the true reason why he was killed.'

'What was it, then?' he challenged her harshly.

'There was not one reason. There were twenty. There was Martino's reason and the Contessa's and Father Anselmo's and Battista's and Lupo's and yours, too, *dottore mio*. But you couldn't admit them, even to one another, so you found one that suited you all–Giacomo was a collaborator, a lover of Fascists and Germans! You were the liberators, the friends of freedom, the little brothers of all the world. You brought us democracy. All Giacomo ever brought was a crust of bread and a bowl of soup and a pair of hands to work when the man of the house was sick.'

Her calm indictment goaded him and he blazed back:

'That's the whole damn trouble with this country. That's why we're still fifty years behind the rest of Europe. We won't organise, we won't discipline ourselves. We won't co-operate. You can't build a better world on a bowl of pasta and a bucket of holy water.'

'You can't build it on bullets, either, Dottore. You got what you wanted. You killed Giacomo. Now what's to show for it? Martino can't work any more. Who's to feed his wife and six children?'

There was no answer to this brutal logic and he turned away, shamed and impotent, and walked to the door that gave on to the hot, bright garden. After a moment Nina Sanduzzi followed him and laid a tentative hand on his sleeve.

'You think I hate you, Dottore. I don't. Giacomo didn't hate you either. Before he died, he came to see me. He knew what was going to happen. He knew you were concerned in it. But do you know what he said to me? "This is a good man, Nina. He has tried to do too much, but he is unhappy because he has never really understood what it is to love and to be loved. He wants to organise and reform, but he does not see that these are barren things without loving. I'm lucky, because I had you to teach me in the beginning. He has been alone too long. When I am dead, go to him and he will be kind to you. If a time should come when you find that a man is necessary to you again—this would be one who would be good to you and to the boy." He wrote a letter to you and put it among his papers. I was to deliver it to you, after he died.'

Meyer swung round to stare at her.

'A letter! Where is it, woman? Where, for God's sake?'

Nina Sanduzzi spread her hands in despair.

'I had all his papers in my cupboard. When Paolo was little, one day he got to them and jumbled them together. Some he tore, others he crumpled, and when I gathered them up again, I could not tell one from the other. . . .' She blushed as if at a shameful revelation. 'I—I've never learned to read!'

His hands reached out and grasped her roughly by the shoulders.

'I must see the papers, Nina. I must see them. You don't know how important it is.'

'Six children are important,' said Nina Sanduzzi quietly. 'And a woman whose man cannot work any more.'

'If I help them, you'll show me the papers?'

She shook her head in outright refusal.

'That was something else Giacomo said: "One should never bargain with people's bodies." If you want to help them you will do it, without asking to be paid. Later we can talk about the papers.'

He was beaten and he knew it. There was a granite strength in this woman who could not read, an inviolable reserve of wisdom which he, the lifetime student, could not match. What puzzled him was that there were no roots for it in her peasant origins and he would not admit she had acquired it from Giacomo Nerone. Yet she, like Nerone, held the key to a mystery that had eluded Aldo Meyer for twenty years: why some men with talent, good will and compassion never achieve full human contact and raise only contention and ridicule among those they try to help; and why others, with no apparent effort, walk straight into intimacy and are remembered with love long after their death.

In Nerone's papers he might read the answer which he lacked the courage to ask from Nina Sanduzzi. But he could not get them on her terms. So he shrugged in resignation and told her:

'I'm dining tonight with the Contessa. I'll tell her about Martino and see what we can do.'

A smile lightened her calm, classic face. With an impulsive gesture, she caught up his hand and kissed it.

'You are a good man, Dottore. I'll tell Martino's wife. No one should be left afraid too long.'

'You can tell me something too, Nina.'

'Yes, Dottore?'

'What would you say if I asked you to marry me?'

Her dark, deep eyes showed neither surprise nor pleasure.

'I would tell you what I told you the first time, Dottore. Better you didn't ask.'

The she left him quickly and Aldo Meyer returned to his patient to feel the fluttering, uncertain pulse and hear the hardy peasant heart battling for life inside the scarred breast.

Paolo Sanduzzi stood on the edge of the stream, bouncing pebbles off the water and watching them skip into the bushes on the opposite side. The stream had one name and three faces. Its name was Torrente del Fauno–the torrent of the faun–because in the old days, long before Christ came down from Rome with St Peter, the fauns used to play here, chuckling goat boys, chasing the tree girls who were called dryads. After the church was built, they all went away; which was rather a pity, because the valley was dull without them. But the name persisted and sometimes the boys and girls of the village met here secretly to play the old pagan games.

The face of the stream changed with the seasons. In winter it was dark, cold and sinister, fringed sometimes with the white rime of frost and piled snow. In spring it was brown and boisterous, roaring so loud with thaw water that one could hear it right up in the village. By summer it had dwindled to a thin, clear runnel singing softly over the stones, lying in quiet pools under the overhang of the banks. Before autumn came, it was dry again–a parched bed full of bleached stones. Now it wore its gentle face, and Paolo Sanduzzi, who was like a faun himself, was glad to be here away from the dead gallows-tree and the Englishman whose laughter was like water bubbling in a black pot.

He had never been so frightened in his life; and he was still frightened. It was as if the painter held the key to his life: to the past which shamed him and to the future which he could see only dimly as a vision of Rome with its churches and palaces, its streets full of shiny automobiles and its pavements crowded with girls who dressed like princesses.

The vision laid a spell on him–half-pleasant, half-sinister–like the charms old Nonna Patucci gave to the girls to draw their lover to them. He could feel it working now, an itch under his skin, an oppressive image behind his eyeballs. Sooner or later it would draw him back to the Englishman, whose mocking smile sometimes made him feel awkward as a child and sometimes woke strange, disturbing passions in him, without even a word or a hand's touch.

He tossed a last negligent stone into the water, thrust his hands into his pockets and began to walk downstream. As he rounded a bend in the bank, a shrill voice hailed him.

'Eh, Paoluccio!'

He looked up and saw Rosetta, the daughter of Martino the smith, sitting on a rock and dangling her legs in the water. She was a thin, elfin child, a year younger than himself, with lank hair and a small, pert face and budding breasts under the faded cotton shift which was her only clothing. In the village he ignored her studiously, but now he was glad to see her. He waved an indifferent hand.

'Eh, Rosetta!'

Then he went and sat beside her on the rock.

'My father's sick. He fell down in a fit and burned himself on the forge. He's in the doctor's house.'

'Is he dying?'

'No. The doctor says he'll live. Mother's crying. She gave us all bread and cheese and sent us out to play. Want some?'

She held up a hunk of rough bread and a cut of goat cheese.

'I'm hungry,' said Paolo.

She broke the bread and the cheese carefully into equal pieces and handed him his share. They sat there munching silently in the sun, cooling their feet in the water. After a while she asked him:

'Where have you been, Paoluccio?'

'With the Englishman.'

'What doing?'

He shrugged indifferently, as a man does with inquisitive women.

'Working.'

'What sort of work?'

'I carry his things. When he paints, I watch. Sometimes he asks me to model for him.'

'What's model?'

'I just stand there and he paints me.'

'Teresina says there are girls in Naples who take off their clothes for men to paint them.'

'I know,' he nodded wisely.

'Do you take your clothes off, too?'

The question caught him unawares and he answered it roughly.

'That's my business.'

'But you do, don't you? If you're a model, that is.'

'It's a secret, Rosetta,' he told her seriously. 'Don't tell anyone; they wouldn't understand.'

'I won't tell. I promise.' She put her thin arm round him and leaned her head on his bare shoulder. The gesture embarrassed him, but pleased him, too. He let her stay there and because he was pleased, he said:

'The Englishman says I'm beautiful, like the statue that Michelangelo carved out of marble.'

'That's silly. Only women are beautiful. Boys are nice or nasty. Not beautiful.'

'That's what he said anyway,' he answered defensively. 'He said I was beautiful and he loved beauty and liked to look at me!'

In her odd elfin way she was angry with him. She took her arm away from him and slewed around to face him.

'Now I know you're making it up. Men don't say things like that. Only women!'

She put her arms round his neck and pressed her lips on his, and when he tried to resist, she held him more tightly; and when he felt her breasts against him through the shirt, he decided that it was pleasant after all. And he began to kiss her, too.

Later she took his face in her small hands and said gravely:

'I love you, Paoluccio. I love you really. Not like a statue.'

'I love you, too, Rosetta!'

'I'm glad.' She leaped up and stood holding her hand out to him. 'Now take me for a walk!'

'Why?'

'Because we love each other, silly, and that's what lovers do. Besides, I've got a secret.'

'What secret?'

'Take me for a walk and I'll show you.'

In spite of himself, he reached up his hand to her. She caught it and dragged him to his feet, and they walked upstream, through the clear water and under the green bushes, to share the old secrets that the dryads told to the dancing fauns.

From his high, plateau eyrie behind the shoulder of the mountain, Nicholas Black looked down on the spread pattern of his past. For the first time in his life, its form was clear to him—and how the future grew out of it, inevitable and identical, as the new shoots on a tree.

From the beginning, he had been cheated: the hidden foetal beginning when the determinant elements were doled out by whatever power decided that, out of the blind coupling of man and wife, there should grow a parody of a man.

He had been born a twin—identical in face and form with the brother who preceded him by an hour out of the womb. He had been born a Catholic, to one of the old Fenland families who had kept the Faith whole from the time of the first Elizabeth to that of the last George. He had been baptized with his brother and blessed with the same blessing, in the manor chapel from whose steps the lawns flowed down broad and green to the reed fringe and the grey fen-water.

But here the identity ended and the slow division began. The first-born grew swart and strong, the second was wan and sickly. They were like Esau and Jacob—but Esau enjoyed the birthright: the field sports, the fishing, the long rides in the dappled summer; while Jacob clung to the shelter of the house and the safe harbour of the sewing-room and the library. At school he lagged behind, was a year late at Oxford; and while his twin went off with a gunnery commission in the Western Desert, he was confined to a hospital bed with rheumatic fever. All the strength was in the one; all the weakness in the other. All the maleness belonged to the first-born, and in Nicholas Black there was only an epicene beauty, the soft subtlety of a mind turned back too long upon itself.

While his brother lived, there was a hope for him that he might borrow strength and find dignity in affection. Afterwards, when the word came through, 'Missing, believed killed', the last hope died and the hidden bitterness began to grow. He had been cheated: by God, by life, by his dead twin, by his father, who after a hushed scandal in London had warned him out of the house and given him a small annuity to keep him away from it.

He had been solitary ever since. His belief had been shipwrecked on the most difficult mystery of all: that a just God can make monsters and still expect them to live like men. His heart had been hardened by the brief loves of the half-world. And now, suddenly, power was put in his hands—power to make another what he had failed to make himself: a man, noble in nature, talent and execution. In the making he might reframe his own life—to dignity, to understanding, to a purer love than any he had yet experienced.

He was getting old. Passion woke more slowly and was easier to control, except when it was piqued by vanity and competition. With the boy as his ward, he would achieve a kind of paternity, which would give to his own life a discipline and a direction it had always lacked.

It was a dizzy moment, a god-like elevation.

This youth was the son of a reputed saint, begotten on the body of a village whore. His life was as predictable as that of a million others in the workless villages of Midday Italy. He would mature in idleness, marry too young and breed too often and live aimlessly on the extreme margin of poverty. Whatever talent he had would be stifled by the brute struggle for existence. The Church would censure him while he lived and absolve him before he died. The State would be saddled with a dozen reproductions of him, fecund and hungry as rabbits, eating out the last green of an impoverished land.

But take him out of the village, give him opportunity and education, and he might well grow to greatness, justifying himself and his teacher as well. Where his father had failed, and the Church had failed, Nicholas Black might yet succeed—and his success would be a splendid negation of the beliefs he had long rejected.

To the critics, Nicholas Black was a mediocre artist. If out of this peasant clay he could mould a perfect man, it would be a triumph beyond cavil, a masterwork beyond the reach of malice.

It was a strange ambition, and yet, in its own idiom, no stranger than the triumphs and revenges that other men dreamed for themselves—financial empires strong enough to crush all opposition, power in the press to make men or bury them in obscurity, woman dreams and opium dreams and the dream of standing one day at the dispatch box to hear one's enemies say . . . 'The Right Honourable the Prime Minister . . .'

Each man to his own damnation, and nobler men have dreamed more basely in their nightshirts than Nicholas Black on his sunlit plateau in Calabria.

It was late and he had not eaten, but he was drunk on the heady wine of anticipation and he did not care. The village would be settling down to siesta. The Contessa would be locked in her baroque room and he could bring his picture into the villa without exciting too much attention.

He was counting much on this canvas. He wondered how Anne Louise de Sanctis would react to it—and Aldo Meyer, and the grey cleric who was coming to research into the past of Giacomo Nerone. He smiled as he pictured them gaping at it for the first time, their secrets written in their eyes and on their faces.

He cast about for a title, and found one almost immediately—'The Sign of Contradiction'. The more he thought of it, the more he liked it. It reminded him of the old *graffito* in which an ass is crucified to represent the Christus, a bawdy joke by a bumpkin comedian. But for Nicholas Black the symbol had a new significance: youth nailed to the cross of ignorance, superstition and poverty, half-dead and damned already, but smiling still, a drugged, ecstatic victim of time and its tyrannies.

6

Monsignor Blaise Meredith and Aurelio, Bishop of Valenta, were concerned with another contradiction: the alleged miracles of Giacomo Nerone.

They were standing on the broad, flagged terrace of the villa looking down into the valley, where workmen were moving slowly up and down the plantation, spraying the young trees from new shoulder-packs of American pattern. On the wall of the small dam others were working to instal new sluice-gates that would control the flow of water to farms outside the

Bishop's domain. Beyond the spillway, on a grey, untilled hill-side, women with baskets on their backs were carrying stones to build new vine-terraces, and earth to pack behind them.

They were like ants, small and industrious, and Meredith was moved to the ironic reflection that this was as great a miracle as any in his leather folio: barren land being built back slowly to fruitfulness by the creative will of one man. He said as much to the Bishop, whose lean, intelligent face puckered into a smile.

'It's bad theology, my friend; but a pleasant compliment. To these people, it is a kind of miracle. Suddenly there is work and bread on the table and an extra litre of oil for the cook-pot. They cannot understand how it has happened, and, even now, they have a shrewd suspicion that there's a catch in it somewhere. Those sprays for instance . . .' He pointed to the humped figures threading their way between the orange trees. 'I had to buy them with my own money, but they were worth every lira. It is only a year or two since these people were washing their trees from a spit bucket–a pail of water set in the middle of the floor, into which the men of the house spat tobacco juice as they smoked or chewed. Some of the old ones still refuse to see that my method is better than theirs. The only thing that will convince them is when I get three oranges to their one, and sell them for twice the price because they are full of juice. But we'll show them in the end.'

'You puzzle me,' said Meredith frankly.

'Why?'

'What have oranges got to do with the human soul?'

'Everything,' said the Bishop flatly. 'You can't cut a man in two and polish up his soul while you throw his body on the rubbish heap. If the Almighty had designed him in that way, he would have made him a biped who carried his soul in a bag round his neck. If reason and revelation mean anything they mean that a man works out his salvation in the body by the use of material things. A neglected tree, a second-rate fruit, are defects in the divine scheme of things. Unnecessary misery is an even greater defect because it is an impediment to salvation. When you don't know where your next meal is coming from, how can you think or care about the state of your soul? Hunger has no morals, my friend.'

Meredith nodded thoughtfully.

'I've often wondered why missionaries are usually better priests than their brothers in the centres of Christendom.'

His Lordship shrugged and gestured with expressive hands.

'Paul was a tentmaker and he worked at his trade so as not to be a burden on his people. Christ himself was a carpenter in Galilee of the Gentiles–I imagine he was a good one. When I am dead, I should like to be remembered as a good priest and a good farmer.'

'It is enough,' said Meredith gravely. 'Enough for you, enough for me. I imagine the Almighty Himself would hardly quarrel with it. But is it enough for everybody?'

'What do you mean?'

'There are miracles all around us: the miracle of an orange tree, the miracle of design that holds the fidget wheels of the universe spinning on their axes. But still people want a sign–a new sign. If they don't get it from the Almighty they turn to palmists and astrologers and table-rappers. What does all this mean—' he tapped the heavy volume of depositions–'But that folk demand wonders in the sky and miracles on earth?'

'And get them sometimes,' the Bishop reminded him tartly.

'And sometimes make them for themselves,' said Blaise Meredith.

'You're not satisfied with the miracles of Giacomo Nerone?'

'I'm the Devil's Advocate. It's my business to be dissatisfied.' He smiled ruefully. 'It's a curious assignment, when you come to think of it. To test by reason the alleged operations of Omnipotence, to apply the code of canon law to the Lawgiver who framed the universe.'

His Lordship nodded a grave assent and said quietly:

'It may be less disturbing to think about Giacomo Nerone.' Blaise Meredith put on again his prim, pedant's manner.

'It's the problem with all new Causes–to apply to alleged miracles the medico-legal methods of the twentieth century. In the case of Lourdes, for example, it's fairly easy. A medical bureau has been established and a series of tests laid down which conform to both medical knowledge and the rigid demands of the Church. A sufferer arrives with a complete medical history. The bureau examines the patient in the approved fashion–X-rays, clinical and pathological tests. All diseases of neurological or hysterical origin are discounted as grounds for a miraculous claim. Only deep-seated organic disorders whose prognoses are familiar are accepted. If a cure is claimed, the bureau examines the patient again and makes an interim certification of the cure. But it is not finally certified until two years afterwards, and then on new medical evidence.

'So far as it goes, it is a sound method. It enables us to say that, in the present state of medical knowledge, this cure has taken place in defiance of, or by a suspension of, the known laws of nature. Now . . . in the case of a new thaumaturge, in a new place, these tests cannot be applied. At best we have eye-witness accounts, a garbled medical history, with perhaps a certification from a local doctor. It may well be a miracle. But in the legal sense, demanded by canon law, we find it very hard to prove. We may accept it on the sheer weight of non-expert evidence, but generally we don't.'

'And the evidence in the case of Giacomo Nerone?'

'Of the forty-three depositions I have read, only three show any conformity to the canonical demands. One is the cure of an elderly woman certified as suffering from multiple sclerosis, the second is that of the Mayor of Gemello Maggiore, who claims to have been cured of a spinal injury incurred during the war, and the third is that of a child in the last stages of meningitis who recovered after an application of a relic of Giacomo Nerone. But even these . . .' He paused and went on in his emphatic advocate's voice. 'Even these will require a much more rigid examination before we go half-way to accepting them.'

To his surprise the Bishop smiled, as if at some private joke. Meredith was nettled.

'Have I said something amusing to Your Lordship?'

'I was asking myself what happened in the old days when medical knowledge was limited and the rules of evidence were less stringent. Is it not possible that many miracles then accepted were not miracles at all?'

'Very probable, I should say.'

'And that certain saints are venerated whose records are so obscure that their very existence is doubtful?'

'That's true. But I don't see where Your Lordship is leading me.'

'I've been reading recently,' said His Lordship coolly, 'that certain theologians are again advancing the opinion that the canonisation of a saint constitutes an infallible declaration by the Pope, binding on all the faithful. In my view it's a dubious proposition. Canonisation is generally based on biography and the historical record of miracles. Both are open to error—and the Pope is only infallible in the interpretation of the deposit of Faith. He can't add to it. And every new saint is an addition to the Calendar.'

'I agree with Your Lordship,' said Meredith with a puzzled frown. 'But I don't see that a minority theological opinion matters very much.'

'It's not the opinion that worries me, Meredith. It's the tendency: the tendency to elaborate so much by commentary, glossary and hypothesis that the rigid simplicity of the essential Faith is obscured, not only for the faithful but for honest inquirers outside it. I deplore this. I deplore it greatly because I find it raises barriers between the pastor and the souls he is trying to reach.'

'Do you believe in saints, Your Lordship?'

'I believe in saints as I believe in sanctity. I believe in miracles as I believe in God, who can suspend the laws of His own making. But I believe, too, that the hand of God writes plainly and simply, for all men of good will to read. I am doubtful of His presence in confusion and conflicting voices.'

'As I am doubtful of the miracles of Giacomo Nerone?'

The Bishop did not answer him immediately, but walked away from him to stand looking out across the peace of the valley, at the grey olives and the green orange trees and the flat water where the men were working on the sluices, stripped to the waist in the sun. His face was clouded as if he were absorbed in an inner struggle. Meredith watched him with puzzlement and anxiety, afraid of having offended him. After a while the Bishop came back. His face was still sombre, but his eyes were full of a grave gentleness. He said slowly:

'I have thought much these last days, Meredith. I have prayed too. You have come into my life at a moment of crisis. I am a Bishop of the Church, yet I find myself in opposition to much that is currently being said and done by my colleagues in Rome, not in matters of faith, but in discipline, policy, attitude. I believe that I am right, but I know there is danger that in following my own path I may tumble into pride and ruin all I hope to do. You were right when you told me that I am afraid of the finger of God. I am ... I sit on a high pinnacle. I am subject only to the Pontiff. I am lonely and often puzzled ... as I am by this matter of Giacomo Nerone. I told you I do not want a saint. But what if God wants him? This is only one thing. There are many others. Now you come, a man in the shadow of death. You too are puzzled and afraid of the finger of God. I find in you a brother, whom I have come to love and trust with my heart. Both of us at this moment are looking for a sign ... a light in the darkness that besets us.'

'I lie awake at night,' said Meredith. 'I feel the life slipping out of me. When the pain comes, I cry out, but there is no prayer in it, only fear. I kneel and recite my Office and the Rosary but the words are empty—dry gourds rattling in the silence. The dark is terrible and I feel so alone. I see no signs but the symbols of contradiction. I try to dispose myself to faith, hope and charity, but my will is a blown reed in the winds of despair ... I am glad that Your Lordship prays for me.'

'I pray for both of us,' said Aurelio, Bishop of Valenta. 'And, out of the prayer, I have come to a decision. We should ask for a sign.'

'What sign?'

The Bishop paused, and then, very solemnly, he told him.

'We should make this prayer, both of us. "If it is your will, O God, to show the virtue of your servant Giacomo Nerone, show it in the body of Blaise Meredith. Restore him to health and hold him longer from the hands of death, through Jesus Christ our Lord!'

'No!' The word was wrung from Meredith like a cry. 'I can't do it! I daren't!'

'If not for yourself, then for me!'

'No! No! No!' The desperation of the man was pitiful, but the Bishop pressed him brutally.

'Why not? Do you deny omnipotence?'

'I believe in it!'

'And mercy?'

'That too!'

'But none for yourself?'

'I've done nothing to earn it.'

'Mercy is given, not earned! Bestowed on beggars, not bought with virtue!'

'I dare not ask for it.' His voice rose higher in fear. 'I dare not!'

'You will ask for it,' the Bishop told him gently. 'Not for yourself, but for me and all poor devils like me. You will say the words even if they mean nothing, because I, your friend, ask you.'

'And if they fail. . . .' Meredith lifted a ravaged face at last. 'If they fail, I am in greater darkness yet, not knowing whether I have presumed too much or believed too little. Your Lordship lays a new cross on my back.'

'It is a strong back, my friend—stronger than you know. And you may yet carry Christ on it across the river.'

But Meredith stood like a stone man, staring out across the sunlit land, and after a while the Bishop left him, to talk with the gardeners who were spraying the orange trees.

It was the moment he had long dreaded, but never quite understood: the moment when the harsh consequences of belief became finally clear.

For a man born into the Church there is a singular comfort in the close-knit logic of the Faith. Its axioms are easy of acceptance. Its syllogisms are piled one on top of the other, firm as the bricks in a well-built house. Its disciplines are rigid, but one moves freely inside them, as one does in the confines of a well-bred family. Its promises are reassuring: that if one submits to the logic and the discipline, one walks naturally in the way of salvation. The complex, terrifying relationship of Creator and Creature is reduced to a formula of faith and a code of manners.

For priests and monks and nuns, the logic is more meticulous, the disciplines more rigid, but the security of body and spirit is commensurately greater. So that if a man can surrender himself completely to the Will of the Creator, as expressed by the Will of the Church, he can live and die in peace—either a cabbage or a saint!

Blaise Meredith was by temperament a conformist. He had kept the rules all his life; all the rules—except one: that sooner or later he must step beyond the forms and the conventions and enter into a direct, personal relationship with his fellows and with his God. A relationship of charity—which is a debased Latin word for love. And love in all its forms and degrees is a surrender of bodies in the small death of the bed, the surrender of the spirit in the great death which is the moment of union between God and Man.

Never in his life had Blaise Meredith surrendered himself to anyone. He had asked favours of none—because to ask a favour is to surrender one's pride and independence. Now, no matter what name he put to it, he could not bring himself to ask a favour of the Almighty, in whom he professed belief, to whom, according to the same belief, he stood in the relationship of son and father.

And this was the reason for his terror. If he did not come to submission he would remain for ever what he was now: lonely, barren, friendless, to eternity.

Aurelio, the Bishop, sat in his cool, austere study, writing letters. It was an activity he distrusted, even when his office forced it upon him. He had been bred a farmer, and he would rather watch a tree grow than write a treatise on it. He had been trained to diplomacy and he knew that a thing, once written, is beyond recantation. Many a hapless fellow has been damned for heresy simply because he was weak in grammar or discretion.

So, when he wrote officially, over the seal of his bishopric, he kept to the conventions for his clergy, a blunt message thinly coated with Southern rhetoric; for Rome, a studied circumlocution, a careful qualification, a slightly florid style. Those who knew him well chuckled at his shrewdness. Those who knew him little—even acute fellows like Marotta—were apt to be misled by it. They regarded him as a somewhat stuffy provincial who would be very good for the locals, but a bumbling nuisance in Rome. Which was precisely the Bishop's intention. Too many new men had been abruptly translated to Rome, just when they were getting things done in their own diocese. It was the Vatican's way of kicking them upstairs: a bishop in his own See is a power to be reckoned with; in the city of the popes he is very small beer indeed.

But this afternoon's letters were private ones, and His Lordship composed them with more than usual care. To Anne Louise de Sanctis he wrote:

> ... I am more grateful than I can say for your offer to receive Monsignor Meredith as a house-guest during his stay in Gemello Minore. We clerics are often a burden to our flock—and sometimes an embarrassment; but I am sure you will fird in Monsignor Meredith an agreeable and witty compatriot. He is a sick man who is marked, unfortunately, for an early death; and whatever you can do for him I shall count as a personal favour.
>
> You are much in my mind these days. I am not unaware of the loneliness which afflicts you as the châtelaine of a poor and primitive community. It is my hope that you will find in Monsignor Meredith a confidant for your problems and a counsellor in the affairs of your conscience.
>> Believe me, my dear Contessa,
>> Yours affectionately in Christ Jesus
>>> Aurelio +
>>> Bishop of Valenta

He signed his name with a flourish and sat awhile scanning the letter, wondering whether he should have said less or more—and whether there were words to touch the heart of a woman like this one.

Women were the perennial problem of the priesthood. More women than men knelt at the Judas-window of the confessional. Their outpourings were franker and more disturbing to the celibate who sat behind it. Often they tried to use him as the replacement for an unresponsive husband and what they dared not whisper in the marriage-bed they talked freely and often grossly in the coffin-box at the side of the church. The men could be reached through the women–the children too. But often the old Adam who slept under the cassock was wakened dangerously by the murmured confidences of an adolescent girl or a dissatisfied matron.

Aurelio, Bishop of Valenta, was very much a man, and he was quick to see the passion that stirred behind the polished gentility of the Contessa de Sanctis. She, too, was one of his sheep, but discretion put her beyond the reach of his shepherd's crook and he asked himself whether Blaise Meredith, the cold, suffering man, might come any closer to her.

To Doctor Aldo Meyer he wrote in far different terms:

> . . . Monsignor Blaise Meredith is a sensitive and liberal man whom I have come to cherish as a brother.
>
> His commission to investigate the life of Giacomo Nerone is a difficult one, and I have hopes that you may be willing to place your considerable local knowledge at his disposal. You may feel, however, that, as a non-Catholic, you prefer not to embroil yourself in this delicate affair. Let me assure you then that neither Monsignor Meredith nor I would wish to embarrass you with inquiries.
>
> I have, however, a personal favour to ask you. Monsignor Meredith is a very ill man. He is suffering from carcinoma of the stomach and, in the normal course of events, will die very soon. He is reserved, as the English are, but he has considerable courage, and I am concerned lest he overwork himself and endure more pain than is necessary.
>
> It would please me greatly, therefore, if you would consent to act as his medical adviser during his stay in Gemello Minore, and do your best to look after him. I shall make it my business to procure for you whatever drugs you may need and I shall be personally responsible for all the expenses of consultation and treatment.
>
> I commend him most warmly to your charity and your professional care. . . .

Basta! thought His Lordship. Enough. One does not make homilies to the Sephardim. They understand us as well as we understand them. They are theocrats as we are–absolutists as we are. They know the meaning of charity and fraternity; and often they practise them better than we do. They have been persecuted as we have. They have had their Pharisees as we–God help us–have ours, even in the highest places. Meredith my brother will be in good hands.

The third letter was the most difficult of all, and His Lordship pondered it a long time before he wrote, in a fine cursive hand, the superscription:

> The Very Reverend Don Anselmo Benincasa,
> Pastor of the Church of the Madonna of the Seven Dolours,
> Gemello Minore, Diocese of Valenta.

> Dear Reverend Father,
>
> We write to inform you of the arrival in your Parish of the Right Reverend Monsignor Blaise Meredith, Auditor of the Sacred Congregation of Rites, who has been appointed Promoter of the Faith in the Ordinary Cause for the Beatification of the Servant of God, Giacomo Nerone. We beg that you will extend to him a fraternal hospitality and render him every assistance to carry out his canonical commission.
>
> We are aware of your poverty and the straitness of your accommodation and we have, therefore, accepted an invitation from the Contessa de Sanctis to lodge him during his stay in the parish. We know, however, that you will not deem

yourself dispensed on this account from the courtesies owed to a brother priest, who is also a commissioner of the Diocesan Court.

We have been long exercised, Reverend Father, by reports reaching us of the low state of spiritual affairs in your parish, and of certain scandals touching your own private life. Not the least of these scandals is your long association with the widow Rosa Benzoni, who acts as your housekeeper.

Normally such an association would have caused us to institute a canonical process against you, but we have refrained from this drastic step in the hope that God may give you grace to see your error and reform it, so that the last years of your priesthood may be spent in penitence and dignity and the proper service of your flock.

It may well be—God grant it so!—that because of your advanced years, this association may have lost its carnal character and that we may be disposed to permit you to retain this woman in your employment in discharge of the debts you have contracted towards her. But such lenience on our part would not dispense you from the moral duty of repairing the scandal and of devoting yourself with renewed vigour to the interests of your people.

We suggest that the presence of a visiting priest in your parish may give you the opportunity of taking counsel with him and setting your conscience in order without too much embarrassment.

Our patience has been long and we have great care for you as our son in Christ, but we cannot ignore the sorry state of the souls in your charge. One cannot tempt God too long. You are already old and time grows dangerously short.

We remember you daily in our prayers and we commend you to the patron of your church, the Madonna of the Dolours.

> Yours fraternally in Christ,
> Aurelio +
> Bishop of Valenta

He laid down the pen and sat a long time staring at the thick crested notepaper and the script that flowed across it in urgent disciplined lines.

The case of Father Anselmo was a symbol of all the ills of the Mediterranean Church. It was not an isolated case. It was common enough to have become a cliché in the depressed area of the South—and it was none too rare in the North either. In its local context, it was a small scandal—the Church was founded on the idea of sin, and its oldest maxim was that the habit did not make a monk, nor the tonsure a religious man. But in the context of a national Church, of a country in which Catholicism was the dominating influence, it pointed to grave defects, to a singular need of reform.

A man like Anselmo Benincasa was the product of a seminary ill-staffed and dispensing an outdated system of education. He came to ordination half-educated, half-disciplined, and with his vocation wholly untested. He emerged another priest in a country where there were too many priests and, not enough priestliness—and immediately he became a charge on another depressed community. His stipend from the diocese was purely nominal. With the swift debasement of modern currency, it would not buy him a loaf of bread. And the Hierarchy still clung to the comfortable fiction that those who preached the gospel should live by the gospel—without caring to define too clearly how they were to do it. He had no pension, and there was no institution to receive him when he lapsed into senility: so that he was plagued by the constant fear of age, and the constant temptation of avarice.

When he came to a village like Gemello Minore, he represented another mouth to feed. And if he opened his mouth too wide, he was liable to go hungry. So he was forced to accommodate himself: to submit to the patronage of the local landowner, or make an unhappy compromise with his depressed flock. In many Calabrian communities there was a shortage of men. Pre-war emigration and war-time levies had denuded them, and women lived for years separated from their husbands, while marriageable girls were forced to take temporary lovers, or husbands years older than themselves. But the priest was there. The priest was poor and dependent on the poor to get his washing done and his food cooked and his house cleaned and his collection plate full enough to buy next week's pasta.

Small wonder that he lapsed often and that his bishop preferred to deplore the lapse as fornication, rather than haul him to court for the canonical scandal of public concubinage.

It was the system that was to blame as much as the man, and reformers like Aurelio, Bishop of Valenta, were hard put to change it, saddled as they were with the historic sins of a feudal Church. The answer was fewer priests and better ones, money to provide at least a basic living independent of the contributions of the faithful, pensions for old age and sickness, better seminary training, more rigid screening of aspirants to Holy Orders. But money was short and prejudice was strong and men like Anselmo Benincasa took a long time to die, and the youths who grew up in the villages were uneducated and unsuitable.

A bishopric like Valenta was poor and obscure. Rome was rich, remote and preoccupied—and requests for special funds to make tendentious reforms were greeted coldly by the Cardinals who were the stewards of the Patrimony of Peter.

So Anselmo Benincasa stayed on in Gemello Minore and His Lordship of Valenta was left with the problem of what to do with him, and how, at least, to salvage his immortal soul.

He folded the letters, put them in envelopes, sealed them with red wax and the arms of his bishopric, then rang for a messenger to arrange their immediate delivery, by motor-cycle to Gemello Minore. He had no illusions about their importance. He had been a long time in the priesthood and he understood that the truth can lie barren for a hundred years until it strikes root in the heart of a man.

On the eve of his departure for Gemello Minore, Blaise Meredith was lonelier than he had ever been in his life.

The brief, brotherly communion between himself and the Bishop was about to be broken. He must go out among strangers, a sedulous inquisitor digging up unpopular facts. His night-time terrors he must bear alone. He could give no more confidences, only try to worm them out of others. He must exchange the trim privacy of the Bishop's domain for the poverty and depression of a mountain village, where there was little privacy even for birth, death and the act of love.

He would be the house-guest of a woman—and, unlike many of his colleagues, he had small talent for dealing with the opposite sex. He was a celibate by profession and a bachelor by disposition; and he resented the effort he would have to make for small-talk over the coffee cups. His strength was running out swiftly and he could not bear to waste it on the trivia of domestic intercourse.

So, while the labourers slept under the olive trees and His Lordship wrote in his study, he surrendered himself to the final indulgence of a walk round the plantations. He took off his cassock and stock, rolled up his sleeves to let the sun shine on his thin, pale arms, and then headed down the narrow path that led to the dam and the outer fringe of the domain.

Under the trees the air was cool and the path was dappled with sunshine, but when he broke out into the valley, where the dam lay shining between the grey walls of the hill, the heat hit him like an oven-blast. When he looked about him he could see it rising in shimmering waves from the tufa rock. He hesitated a moment, regretting the shelter of the plantations, but then, ashamed of his weakness, walked steadily forward round the fringe of the dam and towards the retaining wall.

On the slope above the path the labourers were sleeping, heads pillowed on their jackets, in the shadow of jutting rocks. Their short brown bodies were sprawled, slack as rag dolls, and Meredith, who had long been a stranger to sleep, was moved to envy of their good fortune.

They were poor, but not so poor as many. They had work with a benevolent master. Their clothes were stained and dusty and they wore wooden sandals instead of shoes, but they could sleep quietly and walk home with dignity, because they had work, and pasta for the table and wine and oil to go with it. In a poor land with three million workless it was very much indeed.

At the edge of the spillway the path forked into two goat tracks, one leading down to the bed of the stream, the other heading up towards the saddle of the hill. Meredith chose the upward path, hoping vaguely that from the top he might get a view of the surrounding countryside. The track was rough and covered with sharp stones, but he trudged on with dull determination, as if to defy the weakness of his wasting body and affirm that he was still a man.

Halfway up, he found himself on a small plateau, invisible from the valley, where the rock walls folded back into a shallow re-entrant like a cave. There was a shadow here and he sat down gratefully to rest a few moments. As his eyes rested themselves from the glare, he saw near the base of the wall a few courses of rough stonework, reticulated in the old Roman manner, and above them the toolmarks on the walls where other courses had once been keyed to the natural stone. He stood up and began to examine them more closely, and followed the lines of the stonework back towards the rear of the re-entrant.

The shadows were deeper here, and it was a moment or two before he noticed a small shelf cut back into the rock on which lay a few withered marigolds and crumbling vine leaves. Behind the offerings was a piece of marble, so old and weathered and stained that at first he could not make out what it was. Then he saw that it was part of the base of an old statue, roughly cubic in shape, out of which jutted the crude shape of a phallus.

In antique days, when the hills were covered with forests before the hungry tribes had denuded them for fuel and building, this cave must have been the shrine of a wood god. Now all that was left of him was the symbol of fertility; but the flowers were of the twentieth century—the first offering of spring to an old discredited god.

Meredith had heard, often enough, of the superstitions that still persisted among the mountain people—of charms and spells and love philtres and odd rites—but this was the first time he had seen the evidence with his own eyes. The marble block was stained and discoloured, but the phallus was white and polished as if by frequent contact. Did the women come here, as they used to in old times, for an assurance against barrenness? Did the males still worship the symbol of their dominance? Was there yet in these mountain folk a half-conscious hope that Pan might do what the new god had not done: make the raped land virgin again and fruitful with grass and trees?

The worship of the male principle was rooted deep among these people. The young men stood arrogant as preened cockerels while the girls came in at least putative virginity to present themselves for inspection and admiration. When they were married they bred their women into exhaustion and coddled their sons to precocious maleness while they beat their daughters into chastity. In a barren land they were the last symbols of fruitfulness and the first symbols of joy to a woman whose end would be a joyless servitude in a tumbling hovel in the hills.

Perhaps this was why the correlative Christian symbol was not the agonised Christus, but the fruitful Madonna with the Bambino suckling at her peasant breast.

Blaise Meredith found himself curiously fascinated by the crude stone symbol and its active survival not half a mile from the Bishop's domain. Perhaps this was the explanation of much of the anomaly of the Mediterranean Church: the strong belief in the supernatural, the thick overlay of superstition, the fierce zeal of the Latin saints and the equally fierce rejection of the Communists and the anti-clericals. Perhaps this was the reason why cool liberals and urbane sceptics made so little impact on these people; why an exalted mysticism was the only answer to the Bacchic frenzy that woke in their brown, undernourished bodies. Was this the real explanation of the death of Giacomo Nerone, that he had been trampled under the hoofs of the goat-god?

And how could Blaise Meredith, the legalist from Rome, enter into the mind of this secret people who were old when Rome was young, and who had once made alliance with the black, fiery god of Hannibal's Carthage?

In spite of the heat he felt suddenly cold. He turned away from the obscene little image and walked out into the sunlight.

An old woman, bent almost in two under a load of twigs and driftwood from the stream, was struggling up the path, towards the saddle. When she came abreast of him he raised his hand and called a greeting in his precise Roman Italian. She turned her head and stared at him with blank rheumy eyes, then passed by without a word.

Blaise Meredith stood a moment looking after her, then turned his face towards the valley. He felt old and tired and strangely afraid of going to Gemello Minore.

7

Anne Louise de Sanctis woke from her siesta in a mood of black depression. When she remembered that Aldo Meyer was coming to dinner her mood became blacker still; and when His Lordship's letter was delivered into her hands by the messenger, her temper was frayed to screaming point. It was all too much. She could not cope with these intrusions on her privacy. Even boredom was preferable to the effort she would have to make to be agreeable.

When they met for tea in the afternoon, Nicholas Black was quick to notice her ill-temper, and subtle enough to suggest an immediate remedy.

'You're tired, *cara*,' he told her solicitously. 'It's the heat—spring fever. Why not let me charm it out of you?'

'I wish you could, Nicki.'

'Will you let me?'

'How? I still have to cope with Meyer. And tomorrow this cleric arrives.' Her voice took on the petulant tone of a child's. 'I wish they'd leave me alone.'

'You have me, *cara*,' he said gently. 'I'll keep them amused. I shan't let them bother you. Now, why don't you let me give you a face massage and do your hair for dinner?'

She brightened immediately.

'I'd love that, Nicki. It's the thing I miss most here. I feel I'm getting to be an old hag.'

'Never, *cara*! But a new hat and a new hair-do are the best cures for the megrims. Where shall we do it?'

She hesitated a moment, then answered with affected casualness:

'I suppose the bedroom's the place. I've got everything there.'

'Come on, then! Let's start. Give me an hour and I'll have you ravishing as any Roman beauty.'

He took her hand with stagey gallantry and led her upstairs to the baroque bedroom, chuckling inwardly at the easy victory. If there were secrets to be learned about the Contessa he would find them here, given time, patience and the sedulous skill of his own soft hands.

When the door closed behind them he made a sexless little ceremony of helping her off with her dress and wrapping the negligée about her and settling her in a brocaded chair opposite the dressing-table with its rows of toiletries in crystal jars. She bridled dutifully and made coquettish remarks intended to underline the intimacy of the occasion. The painter smiled and flourished his towels and let her prattle contentedly. He had a chameleon talent for identifying himself with every situation even while his thoughts and plans ran contrariwise. Now he was the *parrucchiere*—my lady's confidant, witness of things denied even to lovers, teller of scabrous little tales for which my lady had no need to blush, since valets are impervious to the best pretended virtue.

He laid her head back, cleansed the face of make-up, creamed it carefully and then began to massage with firm but gentle fingers, upward from the slack throat and the corners of the discontented mouth. She was stiff and cautious with him at first, but she surrendered quickly to the rhythmic, hypnotic touch and after a while he could feel the slow sensuality waking in her. It gave him a special satisfaction to coax her while he himself remained unmoved; and, while he worked, he began to talk in the devious idiom of the salon:

'You have beautiful skin, *cara*; supple as a girl's. Some women lose that very quickly. You're one of the fortunate ones . . . like Ninon de L'Enclos, who kept the secret of eternal youth . . . That was a strange story. When she was still the rage of Paris, at sixty, her own son came to pay court to her without knowing who she was. He fell in love with her, and committed suicide when he found out the truth . . .' He chuckled lightly. '. . . You're lucky you have no sons!'

She gave a small complacent sigh.

'I've always wanted children, Nicki. But . . . perhaps it's just as well I didn't have them.'

'You could still have them, couldn't you?'

She giggled girlishly.

'I'd need some help, wouldn't I?'

'I've often wondered why you never married again; why an attractive woman chose to bury herself in the wilds of Calabria. You're not poor. You could live anywhere you liked–London, Rome, Paris . . .'

'I've been there, Nicki. I still go regularly to Rome, as you know. But this is my home. I always come back.'

'You haven't answered my question, *cara*.' His deft hands covered the malice in the query. As he massaged her cheeks and the fine network of lines about her eyes, he could feel the tension gathering in her as she fumbled for an answer.

'I've been married, Nicki. I've been in love. I've had affairs too and I've had proposals. None of them really satisfied me. It's as simple as that.'

But it wasn't simple, and he knew it; she was more complex than any other woman he had known–and she was shrewd enough to turn the tables on him immediately.

'You've never married either, darling. Why?'

'I've never needed marriage,' he told her lightly. 'I've always managed to get what I want outside it.'

'You gay bachelors!'

'If there weren't gay bachelors, *cara,* there wouldn't be merry widows–only frustrated dowagers.'

'Do you ever get frustrated, Nicki?'

He smiled secretly at the new plaintive note in her voice. Odd, he thought, how the word brings them every time; how they use the Freudian jargon as if it were the answer to the ultimate riddle of the universe. They're never spoilt. They're never hot for a man they can't have. They're never scared of getting too old for a tumble in the hay. They're frustrated. I am too, for that matter, but I'm damned if I'll let her know it.

'With you, *cara*, how could any man be frustrated?'

As if in gratitude for the compliment she reached up and took his hand, still greasy from the cream, and pressed it to her lips. Then, without warning, she drew it down and laid it on the naked curve of her breast under the negligée. The action took him by surprise and he reacted sharply.

'Don't do that!'

Then, surprisingly, she laughed.

'Poor Nicki! Didn't you think I knew?'

'I don't know what you're talking about!' His voice was high with irritation, but Anne Louise de Sanctis was still laughing.

'That you're different, darling. That you don't really care for women at all. That you're head over heels and gone for young Paolo Sanduzzi. It's true, isn't it?'

He was almost weeping with anger as he stood there with the towel in his hands, staring over her head at the gilt *amorini* on the ceiling. Her hand reached out for him again and held him. She stopped laughing and her voice was low, almost caressing.

'You don't have to be angry, Nicki. You don't have to have secrets from me!'

He wrenched away from her fiercely.

'There's no secret, Anne. I like the boy. I think I could do a great deal for him. I'd like to get him out of the village and have him educated and give him a decent start in life. I haven't much money, God knows, but I'd be willing to lay out every penny on that.'

'And what would you want in return?' Her voice was still soft, but edged with irony.

He gave the answer with an odd pathetic dignity.

'Nothing. Nothing at all. But I don't expect you to believe that.'

For a long moment she stared at him with bright, speculative eyes. Then she told him:

'I do believe you, Nicki. And I think I might help you to get him.'

Wondering, he raised his head and looked at her, trying vainly to decipher the thoughts behind her subtle, smiling lips.

'I have my own reasons, Nicki. But I mean what I say. You help me handle this priest and I'll help you with Paolo Sanduzzi. Is that a bargain?'

He bent and kissed her hand in abject gratitude, and she rumpled his hair with the half-maternal, half-contemptuous gesture she used towards him.

It was an alliance of interest, and each of them knew it. But even enemies smile at one another across the treaty table. So, when Doctor Aldo Meyer arrived for dinner, the Contessa was radiant and Nicholas Black was as deferential as a page in the service of a beloved mistress.

Meyer himself was tired and ill-disposed for society. He had spent the whole afternoon with Martino the smith, waiting for the second, and possibly fatal, seizure which might well follow the first one. It was nearly dark when he decided it was safe to move the patient to his own house, and then he had been forced to listen to the lamentations of the wife who had just become aware of the precarious situation of her family. He had had to give assurances that he was unconfident of fulfilling: that the illness would not last too long, that someone—the Countess perhaps—would see the family fed, that he himself would make arrangements for assistance from the commune, that he would try to find someone who would keep the smithy working and not charge too much.

By the time he made his escape he had mortgaged his soul and his reputation twenty times over, and was more convinced than ever of the hopelessness of reform among this ignorant people, bred for centuries to feudalism, who would kiss the hand of the meanest baron provided it held a loaf of bread and offered them an illusion of safety against acts of God and the politicians.

When he reached his house, he found the Bishop's letter waiting for him, and this was another straw added to the burden of the day's irritations. His Lordship asked nothing but a medical service, better paid than that which he normally performed, but he suggested much more: a courtesy that might grow into a heavy commitment. Aldo Meyer the liberal Jew had a healthy mistrust of the absolutist churchman whose predecessors had harried his people out of Spain and then given them uneasy refuge in the ghettos of the Trastevere. But willy-nilly, the Englishman would come, and under his Æsculapian oath Meyer would be bound to serve him. He hoped perversely that he would not be seduced into friendship.

There was no friendship in his relations with Anne Louise de Sanctis. He was her physician for want of a better one. He was her guest for want of other educated company to divert her dinner table. Occasionally he was the mouthpiece of the villagers in their pleas to the *padrona*. But beyond these narrow definitions, there was an area of unspoken mistrust and concealed animosity.

Both had known Giacomo Nerone. Each, for an opposite reason, had been involved in his death. Meyer knew only too well the nature of his patient's illness though he never put the diagnosis into words. Anne Louise de Sanctis knew her doctor's failures and she goaded him with them because he knew too much about her own. But, because they saw each other rarely, they rubbed along in reasonable politeness, and in a cross-grained fashion were grateful to each other—Meyer for good wine and a well-cooked meal, the Contessa for the chance to dress and dine with a man who was neither a clod nor a cleric.

But tonight there was something else in the wind. The presence of Nicholas Black and the coming of the Roman emissary lent a new and faintly sinister character to the occasion. As he shaved and dressed by the yellow light of a paraffin lamp, he prepared himself for a disagreeable evening.

At first meeting his fears seemed groundless. The Contessa was well groomed, relaxed and charming. She seemed genuinely glad to see him. The painter's smile was free of sardonic subtleties, and he talked well and amiably on whatever subject was started.

With the aperitif they talked weather and local customs and the decline of the Neapolitan school of painters. By the soup they were up to Rome, and Black was retailing the pleasanter scandals of the Via Margutta and the price the critics were charging for a favourable notice. When the fish was brought they were through the Vatican and out among the politicos, discussing the prospects for the forthcoming election. The wine had loosened the doctor's tongue and he was launched on a lively dissertation:

'. . . last time the Christian Democrats came in through the confessional box and the American dollar aid. The Church held damnation over the head of every Catholic who voted Communist, and Washington waved a bundle of dollar bills on the sideline. The people wanted peace and bread at any price, and the Vatican was still the only institution in Italy with stability and moral credit. So between them they carried the polls. But we still have the strongest Communist party outside of Russia, and a singular disunity of aim even among those who voted under the Vatican banner. What's going to happen this time? The Democrats will hold on, of course, but they'll lose votes in a general swing to the left. The Monarchists will gain somewhat in the South, and the Communists will stay about where they are—a hard core of discontent.'

'What will cause the losses in the Christian Democrats?' Nicholas Black put the question with sharp interest.

Meyer shrugged expressively.

'The record first. There are no spectacular reforms, no perceptible diminution in the pool of unemployed. There is an equilibrium in industry, held by the infusion of American money and aid from the Vatican Bank. There is a rise in the national income, which is reflected hardly at all in the living standards of vast numbers of the population. But it's enough to keep the financiers reasonably happy and the votes stable for another term. The second reason is that the Vatican itself has lost credit through its identification with a party. It's the trouble with a political Pope. He always wants it both ways—the kingdom of Heaven and the majority in the earthly parliament as well. In Italy he can get it—at a price, and the price is anti-clericalism among his own flock.'

'It interests me.' Black caught at the tag of the statement. 'All over Italy you meet women who communicate every day and men who wear the badges of half a dozen confraternities and they still quote the old phrase: *Tutti i preti sono falsi*—All priests are cheats. It's amusing, but damned illogical.'

Meyer laughed and spread his hands in mock despair.

'My dear fellow, it's the most logical thing in the world. The more priests you get, the more their faults show up. Clerical government is like petticoat government—bad for both sides. I don't believe all priests are liars. I've met some damned good ones in my time. But I'm an anti-clerical for all that. The Latin is a logician at heart. He's prepared to admit that the Holy Ghost guides the Pope on matters of faith and morals; but he chokes on the proposition that he fixes the bank rate as well.'

'Talking of priests,' said Anne Louise de Sanctis, 'I wonder what Monsignor Meredith will be like.'

It was as bland as butter, but Aldo Meyer understood the malice of it. They had herded him like a sheep from one topic to another—and now they had him penned and they watched him, grinning with subtle mockery, to see what he would do to escape. To hell with them, then. He wouldn't give them any satisfaction. He shrugged off the question.

'You mean our Roman inquisitor? He's no concern of mine. He comes and goes away. That's all. Just now I have problems of my own—which I wanted to discuss with the *padrona*.'

'What sort of problems?' the Contessa frowned at this check to her mockery.

'Martino, the smith, had a stroke today. He's paralysed and incapacitated. The family's going to need help. I wondered if you'd make some money available—and also take a couple of the girls into service here. Teresina and young Rosetta are old enough to begin work.'

To his surprise the Contessa took it quite casually.

'Of course. It's the least I can do. I've been thinking quite a lot lately about the young people. There's nothing for them here—and even if they try to migrate, they end up on the streets in Reggio or Naples. I thought we should begin to revive some of your plans, Doctor, and create work for them here.'

'A good idea,' said Meyer cautiously; and wondered where the devil she was leading him. Her next words showed him all too plainly.

'Paolo Sanduzzi, for instance. Nicki tells me the boy is intelligent and willing. It seems such a waste to have him lounging about so much. I'll bring him here and set him to work with the gardeners. No doubt his mother could use some extra money.'

Now he was really trapped. He had accepted a favour and he must take the sour portion that went with it. They sat there, smiling at him over the rims of their glasses, challenging him to protest and make a fool of himself. Instead he nodded and said indifferently:

'If you can use him, why not? You'd have to discuss it with his mother, of course.'

'Why?' asked Nicholas Black.

'Because he's under age,' said Meyer pointedly. 'His mother is still his legal guardian.'

The painter flushed and buried his nose in his glass, and Anne Louise permitted herself a small, secret smile at his discomfiture. She said simply:

'You might ask Nina Sanduzzi to call and see me tomorrow, Doctor.'

'I'll ask her, certainly. She may not care to come.'

'For barefoot peasants, we ride damned high!' Black commented sourly.

'We're an odd people,' Meyer told him mildly. 'It takes time to understand us.'

Anne Louise said nothing, but signalled to the servant to pour more wine and serve the roast. She had made her point. Meyer had taken it—and if Nicki cared to cross swords with the Jew, she might be amused, but she would not be embroiled. Meyer's next words drew her back into the argument.

'I had a letter from the Bishop today. He asks me to act as medical adviser to Monsignor Meredith. Apparently he's dying of carcinoma.'

'My God!' Nicholas Black swore softly. 'That's a damned nuisance.'

'You invited him, Nicki,' said the Contessa irritably. 'I don't see what you have to complain about.'

'I was thinking of you, *cara*. A sick man in the house is a big burden.'

'There's a room in my place,' said Meyer amiably. 'It's none too comfortable, but it's adequate.'

'I wouldn't hear of it.' She reacted sharply. 'He'll stay here. There are servants to look after him and you can visit him whenever he needs you.'

'I thought you'd say that,' said Meyer calmly and there was no hint of irony in his eyes.

The roast was brought and the wine was served and they ate for a while in silence, each totting up the score in the battle of interests that had gone on under the thin politeness of the talk. After a while the Contessa put down her fork and said:

'I've been thinking that, as a courtesy to His Lordship, we should arrange a welcome for this man.'

Nicholas Black choked suddenly over the chicken.

'What sort of welcome, *cara*? A procession of the Confraternity of the Dead and the Children of Mary and the Society of the Holy Name? Banners and candles and acolytes, and Father Anselmo trotting behind in a dirty surplice?'

'Nothing of the sort, Nicki!' Her tone was harsh and peremptory. 'A quiet dinner party, tomorrow night, with ourselves and the doctor and Father Anselmo. Nothing elaborate, but a simple occasion to meet the people in the village who are best able to help him.'

Aldo Meyer kept his eyes studiously fixed on his plate. How could you match a woman like this one? A simple dinner party!—with the *padrona* playing gracious lady to a country doctor and a cloddish priest who would fumble the cutlery and slop his wine and probably fall asleep over the fruit bowl while the Roman Monsignor looked on with tolerant good-humour. And when he came to take evidence, whom would he lean on, but this same gracious lady, who gave him such courteous house room? A simple party— how very, very simple!

'Well, Doctor, what do you think?'

He looked up, cool and unsmiling.

'It's your house, he's your guest.'

'But you'll come?'

'Certainly.'

He could see her relax, and he caught the furtive triumph dawning in her eyes. When he looked at Nicholas Black, he too was smiling and Aldo Meyer felt suddenly naked to the daggers of this oddly matched pair of intriguers.

'I wonder what he'll be like?' Black asked the question of no one in particular.

'Who?' queried the Contessa.

'Our Monsignor from Rome. When I saw him in Valenta he looked pinched and grey and rather like a mole.'

'He's dying,' said Meyer bluntly. 'That tends to spoil a man's complexion.'

The painter laughed.

'But not his temper, I hope. I hate people who are crotchety at meals. He's English, of course, which should make a difference. Probably dry and brilliant and dull as ditch-water in conversation. I wonder if he'll be stuffy. Some of the Roman clergy are very liberal. Others would like to see creation rearranged to have universal autogenesis. I'm anxious to see what this one makes of the love affair of Giacomo Nerone.'

Aldo Meyer turned sharply to face him.

'What do you know about it?'

The painter's smile was a bland insult.

'Not quite as much as you perhaps. But I do employ his son and you've got his mistress doing your housework. Of course that could be useful, too. The recent lists are full of virgins and confessors and beardless boys just out of novitiate. They could use a good penitent like Augustine or Margaret of Cortona. It helps them to cope with the sinners. You know . . . "There's always a way to come back to God!" They're great opportunists, these clerics. Don't you agree, Doctor?'

'I'm a Jew,' said Meyer with tart finality. 'I have small taste for Catholicism, but even less for blasphemy. I'd like to change the subject.'

The Contessa added her own abrupt warning:

'You're drinking too much, Nicki!'

The painter flushed angrily, pushed back his chair and marched out of the room. At a sign from the Contessa the servant left too, and Anne Louise de Sanctis was alone with her medical adviser.

She took a cigarette, pushed the box across the table to Meyer and waited while he lit up for both of them. Then she leaned forward and blew a cloud of smoke full in his face.

'Now then, *dottore mio*, stop fencing and say what you have to say.'

Meyer shook his head.

'You wouldn't thank me, Anne. And you wouldn't believe me.'

'Try me. I'm in a receptive mood tonight.' She laughed lightly and held out her hand to him across the table. 'You're an obstinate fellow, Aldo *mio*, and when you look down that damn Jewish nose at me, you make me obstinate too. Come on now, tell me, and tell me nicely—what's wrong with me, and what's your prescription?'

For a moment he sat silent, staring at the face which had once been beautiful—the fine bones of it, the slack sagging muscles, the crowsfeet round the eyes, the dragging lines of discontent, the tired skin under the careful make-up. Then with clinical bluntness he answered her.

'I'll give you the prescription first. Stop stuffing yourself with barbiturates. Stop collecting oddities like Black who fill you up with dirty stories and give you no joy at the end of it. Sell up this place—or put a steward in–and get yourself a flat in Rome. Then get yourself married to a man who'll keep you happy in bed and make you keep him happy afterwards.'

'You've got a dirty mind, Doctor,' she told him with a smile.

Aldo Meyer went on, unsmiling:

'It gets dirtier yet. You missed satisfaction in marriage because you were too young and your husband too careless to worry. You've never had it since because, every time you tried, you failed yourself and the man. It's common enough and curable enough, provided you face up to what you want and what you need to prepare yourself to get it. But you've never done that. You've retired into your own private little world, and filled it with a kind of mental pornography that drives you crazy with desire and leaves you still unsatisfied. You're the wrong age for that, my dear. It's dangerous. You end up with gigolos and fellows like Nicholas Black and an overdose of sedatives at the end of it. You can still be a lover. But you may make yourself a bawd–as you're doing with Paolo Sanduzzi.'

She ignored that last thrust, and asked him, smiling:

'And how do I get myself a husband, Doctor? Buy one?'

'You might do worse,' said Aldo Meyer soberly. 'Given the elements, you'll probably do better with an honest bargain than a dishonest love. That's why you like to tyrannise over your painter, because you're under the tyranny of an unsatisfied body.'

'Anything else, Doctor?'

'Only one thing,' said Meyer calmly. 'Get Giacomo Nerone off your mind. Stop trying to strike at him through Nina and the boy. You aren't the first woman who destroyed a man because he rejected her. But if you can't look that one in the face, you'll end by destroying yourself.'

'You've forgotten the most important thing, Doctor.'

Meyer looked at her with sharp interest.

'What's that?'

'I've always wanted a child, needed one more than you know. My husband couldn't give me one. Giacomo Nerone refused me and bred himself a boy out of a barefoot peasant. I hated him for that. But I don't hate him any more. If you didn't stand between me and his mother, I could do something for the boy . . . give him a good start in life, save him from running to seed like the rest of the lads in the village.'

'What would you do with him, Anne?' asked Meyer coldly. 'Hand him to your painter?'

Without a word, she picked up a half-empty wineglass and dashed the contents in his face. Then she laid her head down on her arms and sobbed convulsively. Aldo Meyer wiped the wine from his thin cheeks, got up from the table and rang for a servant to show him out.

When he reached his house, he was surprised to find the lamp lit and Nina Sanduzzi sitting at the table with a pile of mending in front of her. Her presence at this late hour was sufficiently rare to make him comment on it. Her answer was quite simple.

'I spent the evening with Martino's wife. She's a fool, but kind, and she just begins to see what trouble she is in. When I got the family bedded down and made Martino comfortable, I thought I would wait here and see what news you had from the Contessa.'

For a moment he was tempted to vent his feelings in an ironic outburst; then he remembered that she did not understand irony and would only be troubled by it. So he answered her baldly:

'It's good news for Martino. The Contessa will make a gift of money and also take Teresina and Rosetta into service with her. With their wages and the bit of help from public assistance, they won't be too badly off.'

'Good!' She gave him one of her rare, calm smiles. 'It's a beginning. Later, perhaps, we can improve it. Would you like coffee?'

'Yes, please.' Meyer slumped heavily into a chair and began unlacing his shoes. Instantly she was at his feet, helping him. This, too, was new; she had never before assumed the functions of a body servant. Meyer said nothing, but sat watching her thoughtfully as she crossed the room to light the small primus under the coffee-pot. He said, without emphasis:

'The Contessa would like to see you tomorrow, too.'

'Why would she want to see me?'

'She wants to offer Paolo a job helping the gardeners.'

'Is that the only reason?' She was still bending over the primus.

'For you, yes. For Paolo, there could be other reasons!'

Slowly she turned to face him across the shadowy room. She asked: 'What sort of reasons?'

'The English painter has a fondness for him. The Contessa wishes to use him in a way that is not yet clear. Also I think she wants the boy to be there when this priest comes from Valenta to inquire about Giacomo.'

'They are like dogs rutting on a dung heap,' said Nina Sanduzzi softly. 'There is no love in anything they do. I won't go. The boy won't go, either.'

Meyer nodded agreement.

'I promised only that I would tell you. For the rest, I think you're wise. It's a house with a touch of madness in it.'

'They practise on us, as if we were animals.' She threw out her arms in an angry gesture. 'This is a child—a boy with his first manhood stirring in him—and they want to use him like that.'

'I warned you,' he reminded her soberly.

'I know.' She began to lay out the coffee cups on the table, talking as she moved. 'And this is another reason I came here tonight. Paolo told me he had been walking by the Torrente del Fauno, with young Rosetta. I was glad of it. They are both young, and this is a good time for love to begin, provided it begins the right way. I think Paolo was glad too. I know he wanted to talk, but he did not know how to put it into words. I wanted to help, but . . . you understand how it is with a boy. He would never believe his mother might know the words, too. It's hard when there's no man in the house, and I wondered whether—whether you might help him a little.'

The coffee-pot boiled over, and as she hurried to rescue it Meyer had time to consider his answer. He gave it to her gently and haltingly.

'A boy in his first waking is like a strange country, Nina. There are no maps, no signposts. Even the language is different. I could make mistakes and do him harm. What he feels for the Englishman I don't know. What has happened between them I don't know. But whatever it is there will be shame in it for the boy; just as there is a shame in his first want for a girl. This is what makes him furtive like a fox, timid like a bird. You understand?'

'I understand, surely. But I understand his need too. It is a strange world for him. His father was someone they call a saint. His mother is someone they call a whore. I will not justify myself or his father to him. But how do I explain the wonderful thing there was between us? And how it should be wonderful for him too?'

'How can I explain it—' Meyer grinned ruefully–'when I didn't understand it myself?'

Her next question shocked him out of his weariness.

'Do you hate the boy?'

'God Almighty, no! What makes you say that?'

'He might have been yours–before Giacomo came.'

Meyer's face clouded with old memories.

'That's true. But I never hated the child.'

'Do you hate me?'

'No. There was a time when I hated Giacomo and when he died I was glad–but only for a while. Now I am sorry.'

'Enough to help his son?'

'And you, too, if I could. Send him to me and I'll try to talk to him.'

'I've always known you were a good man.'

And that for the moment was all the thanks she gave him. She went to the stove, picked up the coffee-pot and brought it back to the table. She poured a cup for him and one for herself, and stood watching him while he sipped tentatively at the bitter scalding liquid. Her own cup she tossed off at a gulp and then crossed to the corner of the room to gather up her wooden sandals and the battered basket which held her day's purchases: a bundle of charcoal, pasta and a few vegetables.

Then she came back to the table and held out to him a thick parcel wrapped in cotton cloth and tied with a faded ribbon.

'Take it,' she told him firmly. 'I don't want it any more.'

'What is it?' His eyes searched her calm face.

'Giacomo's papers. Somewhere in there is his letter to you. They may help you to understand him and me. They may help you to help the boy.'

Wondering, he took the soiled package and held it between his hands as he had once held the lolling, lifeless head of Giacomo Nerone. Memories flooded back, vivid and oppressive–old fears, old hates, old loves, small triumphs and monstrous failures. His eyes misted and he felt his stomach knot up and a small nerve begin twitching at the corner of his mouth.

When he raised his eyes at last he saw that Nina Sanduzzi was gone and that he was left alone in the lamplight with the soul of a dead man, held between his own trembling fingers.

Nina Sanduzzi walked back to her house in the peace of spring moonlight. The harsh outlines of the hills were soft, under the stars; the crumbling village was no longer drab but silvered to an antique beauty and down in the valley the torrent ran, a ribbon of grey light through the shadows. The air was crisp and clean and her wooden sandals clattered sharply on the stones above the intermittent voices of the crickets and the distant muted sound of the water.

But Nina Sanduzzi was blind to the beauty and deaf to the night-music. She was a peasant, rooted in the countryside as a tree is rooted, tough, persistent, insentient to the pathetic fallacy which is at best a sentimental diversion for the literate. The landscape was a place in which she lived.

Only the figures in it were important. The beauty she saw–and she saw much of it–was in faces and hands and eyes, smiles and tears and the laughter of children, and the memories treasured like water in a cistern. Spring was a sensation in her own strong body. Summer was a warmth on the skin and dust under her bare feet, and winter was a cold hibernation and a careful husbanding of twigs and charcoal.

She could neither read nor write, yet she understood peace, because she had known conflict, and she was receptive to harmony, because it built slowly but perceptibly out of the dissonances of the life about her.

Tonight she was at peace. She could see the beginning of fulfilment to the promise of Giacomo Nerone, that even after his death there would be care of herself and the boy. They were poor, but poverty was their natural state and Giacomo had never let them want too much or too long. Now in their greater need there was Aldo Meyer, ready to pay, out of his own need, a debt to a dead man.

There was harmony in her life, too–a slow concordance building between her and the villagers. They needed her. They were grateful, like Martino's wife, for her help in their troubles; and, when they called her the old crude names–'the whore', 'the woman who slept with a saint'–there was no longer much malice in it; only a dim memory of old jealousies. They were a harsh people and they used harsh words, because they had few others. Their symbols were vulgar, because their life was brutish–and belly hunger cannot be satisfied with dreams.

So tonight as she walked home to the small hut among the ilex trees she was grateful, and all her gratitude centred on Giacomo Nerone, dead long since and buried in the Grotto of the Faun, where folk came to pray and went away cured of their infirmities of body and spirit.

Everything else in her life was blotted out by the memory of this man: her parents, who had died of malaria when she was sixteen and left her the hut, a few sticks of furniture and a small dowry chest; her husband, a brown, turbulent boy who had married her in the Church and slept with her for a month and then been taken by the Army to die in the first Libyan campaign. After his death she had lived, as the other women did, alone in her small hut, hiring herself out for farm labour and occasional house service when one of the maids fell sick in the Contessa's villa.

Then, Giacomo Nerone had come . . .

It was a summer's night, hot and heavy with thunder. She was lying naked on the big brass bed, tossing restlessly with the heat and the mosquitoes and the need that woke often in her strong body for a man's arms and the feel of him in the bed beside her. It was long past midnight, and even after a gruelling day on the vine-terraces sleep would not come.

Then she heard the knocking–weak and furtive on the barred door. She sat up in sudden terror, drawing the bedclothes about her breasts. The knocking came again, and she called out:

'Who is it?'

A man's voice answered her in Italian.

'A friend. I'm sick. Let me in, for the love of God!'

The weak urgency of the voice touched her. She got out of bed, pulled on her dress and went to the door. When she unbarred it and opened it cautiously, he tumbled forward on to the earthen floor–a big, dark man with blood on his face and a glutinous stain seeping into the shoulder of his ragged shirt. His hands were bramble-scratched and his boots were broken and gaping, and when he tried to get up, he crawled two paces and then pitched forward on his face.

It took all her peasant strength to drag him and lever him on to the bed. While he was still unconscious, she bathed the cuts on his face and cut his shirt away from the wound in his shoulder and washed that too. Then she took off his boots and drew the bedclothes over him and let him sleep until the first dawn brightened the eastern sky. He woke in the sudden panic of the hunted, staring about him with wide, scared eyes; but when he saw her he smiled and relaxed again, grimacing ruefully at the pain of his shoulder wound.

She brought him wine and black bread and cheese, and marvelled that he wolfed it so greedily. He drank three cups of wine, but would take no more food because, he said, folk were hungry and he had a right only to the traveller's share. He smiled again, as he said it, a wide, boyish smile that charmed the last fears out of her and brought her to sit on the edge of the bed and ask who he was and what had brought him to Gemello Minore and how he had come by the wound in his shoulder.

His accent was strange to her and he had difficulty in understanding her thick Calabrese dialect, but the lines of his story were clear enough. He was a soldier, he said, a garrison gunner based at Reggio at the tip of the boot of Italy. The Allies had taken Sicily and the British Army had crossed the Strait of Messina and was working its way up the peninsula. Reggio had fallen. His unit had broken and he was on the run. If he rejoined his own army they would patch him up and send him back into the line. If the British got him they would make him a prisoner of war. So he was trying to make his way back to Rome, to his own family. He had been hiding by day and travelling by night, living on what he could steal. Last night he had been flushed by a British patrol and they had fired at him. The bullet was still in his shoulder. It would have to be taken out, or he would die.

Because she was a simple peasant, she accepted his story at face value. Because she liked him and because she was lonely for a man, she was willing to hide him and care for him until his wound was better. Her hut was away from the village and no one ever came there. That was the beginning of it: simple and unimportant as a hundred other war-time tales of lonely widows and soldiers on the run. But the richness that grew out of it and the tragedy that ended it, and the peace that followed it, were her daily wonder and her nightly remembrance . . .

When she reached the house, she found the lamp burning low, and Paolo curled up, apparently asleep, on the rough truckle bed on the opposite side of the room from the big brass *letto matrimonio* in which he had been begotten and born. Until the onset of puberty he had slept with her, in the custom of the South, where whole families sleep in the one great bed, husbands and wives and babes and maturing boys and girls growing into womanhood. But for a lone woman and her son it was a bad thing, so she had bought another bed and each of them slept alone.

She closed the door, barred and bolted it, then put down her basket and kicked off her sandals. The boy on the bed watched her through veiled eyes, feigning sleep. Every detail of the ritual that followed was familiar to him though, for a long time now, he had refused to take part in it.

Nina Sanduzzi crossed the room to the rough dower chest that stood at the head of her bed. From the inside of her dress she unpinned a small key with which she unlocked it. Then she took out a flat parcel wrapped in white paper. She unwrapped it carefully and took out a man's shirt, old and tattered and stained in many places as if with rust. She held it a moment to her lips and then unfolded it and spread it over the back of a chair so that the tatters were seen as old bullet holes and the stains were the marks of blood. Then she knelt down awkwardly, buried her face in her hands on the seat of the chair and began to pray in a low muttering voice.

Try as he might the boy had never been able to catch the words. When he had knelt there with his mother she had told him simply to say Paters and Aves as he did in church, because his father was a saint who had great power with God–like San Giuseppe, who was the foster-father of the Bambino. But she would never admit him to the privacy of her own communion with his father and, in an odd way, he was jealous of it. Now he looked on the whole thing as a piece of woman's nonsense.

Her prayers over, Nina Sanduzzi re-wrapped the parcel and locked it away in the dower chest. Then she came over to her son's bed, bent to kiss him and turned away. Paolo Sanduzzi kept his eyes closed and breathed steadily because, although he wanted often to kiss her and have her hold him as she did in the old days, there was now a revulsion in him that he could not explain. It was the same thing that made him close his eyes and turn away his head when she undressed her thickening body or got up to relieve herself in the night. He was ashamed of her and he was ashamed of himself.

So he lay still until his mother blew out the lamp and climbed into the creaking brass bed. Then he too settled himself and lapsed slowly into sleep. While he slept, he dreamed–of Rosetta standing on the rock ledge by the torrent and calling him to her. He went to her running and scrambling, seeing her lips parted and her eyes laughing and her arms outflung to welcome him. But before the arms closed round him, they changed to the arms of Nicholas Black, and instead of the girl's face there was the pale goat visage of the painter.

Paolo Sanduzzi stirred and groaned and opened his eyes in the half-sweet, half-shameful moment when the sap of youth runs over, and a boy is not sure whether he sleeps or wakes.

8

It was Blaise Meredith's last night in Valenta: his last in the company of Aurelio the Bishop. They dined, as they always did, comfortably and well. They talked without nostalgia of a variety of subjects, and, when the meal was over, His Lordship suggested that they take coffee in his study.

It was a big, airy room, lined from floor to ceiling with books but sparsely finished with a desk, a prie-dieu, a set of steel cabinets and a grouping of leather chairs near a big majolica stove. Yet somehow it reflected accurately the character of the man who worked in it: learned, ascetic, practical, with a taste for modest comfort.

The coffee was brought and with it a bottle of old brandy, dusty from the cellar, with the seals still intact. His Lordship insisted on opening it and pouring it himself.

'A libation,' he told Meredith, smiling. 'The last cup of the *agape*.' He raised his glass. 'To friendship! And to you, my friend!'

'To friendship,' said Blaise Meredith. 'I'm sorry I've come to it so late.'

They drank, as good men should, of an old and precious liquor, slowly and with savour.

'I shall miss you, Monsignor,' said the Bishop gently. 'But you will come back. If you're ill, send me word immediately and I'll have you brought back here.'

'I'll do that.' Meredith's eyes were fixed studiously on his glass to hide the pain in them. 'I hope I may do well for Your Lordship.'

'I have a small gift for you, my friend.' The Bishop put his hand into his breast pocket and brought out a small box of tooled Florentine leather, which he handed to Meredith.

'Go on, open it!'

Meredith pressed the catch and the lid flew open to reveal, bedded in satin, a small *bulla,* a bubble of antique gold, about the size of his thumb-pad, attached to a fine gold chain. He took it out and held it in the palm of his hand.

'Open the *bulla*,' said His Lordship.

But Meredith's fingers trembled and the Bishop took the ornament from him, opened the bubble, and held it out to him. Meredith gave a small gasp of surprise and pleasure.

Set inside the curve of the gold was a large amethyst, carved with the most ancient symbol of the Christian Church, the fish, with the loaves on its back, whose name was the anagram of the Christus.

'It is very old,' said His Lordship. 'Probably early second century. It was found during the excavations in the catacomb of San Callisto and presented to me on the occasion of my consecration. The *bulla* was a common Roman ornament, as you know, and this must have belonged to one of the very early Christians—possibly a martyr, I don't know. I'd like you to have it—for friendship's sake.'

Blaise Meredith, the cold man, was moved as he had not been moved for twenty years. Tears pricked at his eyelids and his voice was unsteady.

'What can I say, but "Thank you." I shall keep it till I die.'

'There's a price on it, I'm afraid. You'll have to listen to a final sermon.'

'This will be my charm against boredom,' Meredith told him with wry humour.

The Bishop leaned back in his chair and sipped his brandy. His opening gambit seemed curiously irrelevant.

'I've been thinking, Meredith, about the little phallic shrine. What do you think I should do about it?'

'I don't know. . . . Destroy it, I suppose.'

'Why?'

Meredith shrugged.

'We-ell . . . it's a link with paganism, a symbol of idolatry, an obscene one at that. Someone obviously pays some sort of homage to it.'

'I wonder if that's right,' His Lordship queried thoughtfully. 'Or is it something very much simpler?'

'What, for instance?'

'A good-humoured piece of vulgarity—a genial superstition like throwing coins in the Trevi fountain.'

'I'd hardly have thought genial was the word,' said Meredith. 'Bawdy perhaps. Even sinister.'

'All primitive peoples are bawdy, my dear Meredith. They live so familiarly with the grosser natural functions that their humour becomes very earthy indeed. Listen to the chatter and the songs at a village wedding and—if you can translate the dialect and the allusions—you'll blush to your reverend ears. But such people have their own modesties too, which, if they seem less logical, are often more sincere than the false modesties of evolved communities. . . . As for "sinister"—yes, it could be sinister. Vestigial paganism does exist here. You'll find a woman selling charms and love philtres in Gemello Minore. . . . But what do I do about it? Make a big song and ceremony? Hold an exorcism and break the marble to bits? They can draw a dirty picture on any wall in town if they really want to—and they would probably put my face on top of it. You see?'

In spite of himself, Meredith laughed heartily and the Bishop smiled approvingly.

'My sermon goes well, Meredith. And you've got the text of it already—*"Piano, Piano!"*—walk softly and talk gently. You're an official, remember, and they mistrust officials—Church officials most of all. You've also got the official point of view. Which is a handicap. Look!' He waved an expressive hand at the book-lined walls. 'All the Fathers from Augustine to Aquinas. All the great historians, all the great commentators. All the encyclicals of the last five pontiffs—and a selection of the more important mystics as well. The mind of the Church, inside these four walls. The man who wore that *bulla* had never heard of one of them—yet he was as much a Catholic as you or I. He had the same faith, though much of it was implicit and not explicit as it is now. He was close to the Apostles, who taught what they had learned from the lips of Christ and what they had received from the infusion of the Holy Ghost at Pentecost. The mind of the Church is like the mind of a man, expanding itself to new consequences of old beliefs, to new knowledge flowering out of the old, as leaves spring from a tree. . . . Who among my flock can digest all this? Can you or I? This is the mind of the Church, complex and subtle. But the heart of it is simple, as these people are simple. So when you go to them, you must work with your heart and not your head.'

'I know,' said Blaise Meredith; and the words sounded very like a sigh. 'The trouble is I don't know how to work that way. I confess it frankly, it is only with Your Lordship that I have come to any warmth at all. I'm defective in sympathy, I suppose. I regret it, but I don't see how I can mend it. I don't know the words. The gestures are awkward and theatrical.'

'It's a matter of attitude, my friend. If you feel pity and compassion you are not far from love. These things communicate themselves even through the most stumbling words. The way to these people is through their needs and through their children. Try filling your pockets with sweets and strolling down the street. Try taking a gift of oil or a kilo of pasta when you go into the houses of the poor. Find out where the sick are and visit them with a flask of *grappa* on your hip. . . . And that, my friend, is the end of my sermon!'

He leaned forward and poured another dram of brandy into their glasses. Meredith sipped the smooth, fragrant liquor and looked down at the small golden *bulla* in its satin bed. Aurelio the Bishop was a good pastor. Everything he preached he practised himself. And Blaise Meredith had not yet performed the one thing asked of him in friendship. He confessed it gravely:

'I've tried several times to bring myself to pray for this miracle, but I can't do it. I'm sorry.'

His Lordship shrugged as if the delay were of no consequence.

'You will come to it in the end. *Piano . . . Piano . . .*! Now I think you should go to bed. Tomorrow will be a long day, and possibly a troubling one for you.'

He stood up, and, moved by a sudden impulse, Blaise Meredith knelt to kiss the big Episcopal ring on his finger.

'Will Your Lordship bless me for the journey?'

Aurelio, Bishop of Valenta, raised a slim hand in the ritual gesture.

Benedicat te Omnipotens Deus. . . . May God bless you, my son, and keep you from the noonday devil—and from the terror of the long night . . . in the name of the Father and of the Son and of the Holy Ghost . . .'

'Amen,' said Blaise Meredith.

But the blessing had no virtue against the pain which took him that night: the worst of his illness, a retching agony that drained him of all strength, so that when he left in the morning he looked like a man riding to his own funeral.

From Valenta to Gemello Minore the survey distance is sixty kilometres, but the road is so winding, the surface so poor and rutted, the climb so steep, that it takes two full hours by car.

Immediately after he left the town, Meredith lapsed into an uneasy doze, but soon the jolting and wrenching wakened him, and he began to take a forced interest in the landscape. The hills were not high by alpine standards, but they were steep and scarped and folded one upon the other so that the road seemed to cling precariously to their flanks, now crawling upwards, now plunging downwards out of a hair-pin bend towards a rickety bridge that looked as if it would hardly support a mule-cart.

The valleys were green where the peasants farmed the silt-wash, but the hills were sparsely grown, hardly fit for goat pasture. It was hard to believe that in the old days the Romans had cut pines here to build their galleys and burned charcoal for the armourers' forges. All that was left now was a rare plantation encircling a villa whose owner or steward was a better farmer than his fellows.

Some of the villages were built on the saddles of the hills, a huddle of rusty buildings round a crumbling church, built perhaps by some old Angevin mercenary who had trailed his pike and his petty title round this roistering, southern kingdom. Others were simply a line of peasant huts lower down in the valleys, where the water was nearer and the soil less sparse. But all of them were poor, shambling and depressed. Their inhabitants had the weathered, used-up look of the mountains themselves. Their children were draggled and spindly as their goats and chickens and cage-ribbed cows.

This was poverty as Meredith had not seen it, even in the baser alleys of Rome. This was what Aurelio the Bishop had meant when he pointed out the folly of coming here with a textbook in one hand and a missioner's cross in the other. These people understood the Cross . . . they had endured their own crucifixion for a long time; but they could not eat ideas, and the Christ of Calabria would need to announce himself with a new miracle of the loaves and fishes, and the old compassion for the maimed and the unclean.

They lived in houses that were no better than cow byres. Some of them were still troglodytes, inhabiting caverns in the rocks, where the damp festered on the walls. They had no gas, no electricity, no sewage, no safe water supply. Their children died of malaria and tubercular infections and pneumonia. Their women died of septicaemia and puerperal fever. Their men were twisted with arthritis before they were forty. Typhoid could wipe out a whole community in a month. Yet somehow they survived. Somehow they clung to a belief in God and the hereafter, in prayer and the ministrations of the Church–clung to it with a fierce logic because in this belief were the roots of human dignity. Without it they would become what they seemed to most of the world, animals in form and habit.

Blaise Meredith's heart sank as they drove farther·and farther into the mountain reaches. A deep depression had settled on him after his night's ordeal, and he pictured himself wasting helplessly among these people and begging for death to release him from their company. If he must die out of due time, then at least let him die in dignity, with clean sheets and a clean smell and sunlight coming through the windows. It was a childish thought and he tried to put it away, but the depression stayed with him, until, suddenly, at the top of a steep rise, the driver halted and pointed across the valley:

'*Ecco, Monsignore!* Look! There they are, *Gemelli dei Monti*–the Mountain Twins!'

Meredith got out of the car and walked to the edge of the road to get a better view. Below him the road ran steeply into a valley on the other side of which a single mountain reared itself up against the clear sky. For more than half its height it was a solid mass; then it parted into twin peaks, separated by a broad cleft, about two miles across. On each peak was a village, girt by a crumbling wall, below which the cultivation began and spread itself into the hollow between them. Out of this hollow a stream flowed, tumbling down the solid flank of the mountain into the valley at Meredith's feet.

What struck him most sharply was the difference between the two peaks. One of them was in full sunlight; the other shadowed darkly by its twin. The sunlit village seemed larger, less ruinous; and right in the centre of it, under the campanile of the church, a large white building shone in bright contrast to the burned tiles of the surrounding roofs. The road which forked up to it was black and shining with new bitumen and at the top of it, just outside the walls, a large flat parking space had been made, on which half a dozen cars were standing, their windscreens gleaming in the sun.

'Gemello Maggiore,' said the driver at his shoulder. 'You see what the saint has done for it. The new building is the hospital for pilgrims.'

'He's not a saint yet,' said Meredith coolly.

The driver spread his hands in disgust and moved away. One could not reason with a priest who had a belly-ache. Blaise Meredith frowned and turned to took at the darker twin, Gemello Minore.

There were no cars on the dusty goat track that led up to it, only a tiny donkey-cart with an old peasant padding beside its wheels. The walls were breached in many places, and on some of the taller buildings he could see the naked roof-trees where the tiles had been blown off and never been replaced. The roof line was gapped and ragged in contrast to the compact security of Gemello Maggiore. Meredith knew only too well what it would be like inside the walls–a single main street, a tiny piazza in front of the church, a warren of narrow lanes with washing strung between the walls and filth running over the cobbles and ragged children squalling among the refuse. For a moment his heart failed him and he was half-inclined to head for Gemello Maggiore and make his headquarters there, in the new hostel or even with the Mayor, who would be happy to welcome an official of the Bishop's court. But he knew that he would never outlive the shame of such a surrender, so he got back into the car and told the driver:

'Gemello Minore. *Subito!*'

The labourers in the lower fields saw him first, as the car lurched over the pot-holes and skidded in patches of loose gravel. The leaned on their hoes and watched it pass, and some of the younger ones waved derisively, but the old ones simply wiped the sweat from their faces and rubbed their hands on their breeches and began work again. A car or a coach-and-four–or a rocket from the moon–it was all one. You weeded one line and you began another. The women piled the weeds for compost and gleaned the twigs for fuel. And when the last row was weeded there was water to be hauled from the stream and poured avariciously at the roots of the plants. There were stones to be carried too for the storm-breaches in the terraces, and sods to be turned in the fallow. . . . You couldn't make pasta from engine oil, nor get milk from a priest's tit. So to hell with them both–and back to the hoeing!

Paolo and Rosetta saw him as they squatted under a clump of bushes where Paolo swore he had seen quail, and where there was nothing but the droppings of the hare which nibbled the cabbage plants, and an old grey lizard dozing in a patch of sun. Rosetta clapped and shouted and hopped from one leg to another–a brown elf in a ragged frock; but Paolo stood, arms akimbo, staring after the car. The time would come when this fellow would want to talk to him about his father, and he was determined to meet him as a man, not a snot-nosed urchin to be coaxed first and beaten afterwards. Besides, the affair was important to him and if Rosetta was to be his girl she must understand that. And if he was a little afraid of a black ferret rooting into his mother's life and his own, nuzzling the village into an ants' nest of curiosity, this, after all, was his own business, and his girl should be the last one to know it. So, after the car had passed, he took her by the hand and, in spite of all her protests, hurried her through the bushes and down to the secret stretch of the torrent where no one ever came in the daytime.

Aldo Meyer saw him when the car slowed just outside his doorway and began nosing its way slowly through a mob of yelling children. He saw the grey, pinched face and the lips drawn back in a painful smile, and the hand up-raised in a half-hearted greeting to the children. Here, if ever he knew one, was a man with the sign of death on him. He wondered what tortuous reasoning had induced the Bishop to accept an official like this and send him to be harried and badgered by all the conflicting interests in the affair of Giacomo Nerone. He wondered what manner of man he was and what the pain and the daily familiarity with death were making of him: what he would make of the Contessa and her dinner guests and how he would react to the tangled stories he must hear. Then he remembered that he would be taking the butt end of this life into his own hands, and he was ashamed that he had not even saluted the visitor as he passed.

By the time the car had reached the piazza the whole village was out. Even old Father Anselmo had stood peering furtively through his shutters, with the Contessa's summons in his hand, wondering vaguely how he was to show the 'courtesies to a brother priest' which the Bishop demanded of him. His most urgent problem, however, was what to wear to dinner at the villa; and, as soon as the car had passed, he waddled into the kitchen, shouting for old Rosa Benzoni to wash him a collar and sponge the sauce stains off his best soutane.

Only Nina Sanduzzi refused to make herself a spectator of this inauspicious arrival. She was sitting on the bed in the house of Martino the smith, spooning broth into the big man's twisted mouth, and when they beckoned her to the door she would not come. She had her own dignity, and if the priest wanted to see her he would come and she would know what to answer him.

As for Blaise Meredith, he saw them all, yet saw none of them. They were a blur of faces and a clamour of alien voices and a pervasive smell of dust and bodies and refuse rotting in the sun. He was glad when the car pulled out of the village and roared up the last steep incline to the villa, where the porter stood at the great iron gates to let him in and the Contessa was waiting to greet him, fresh as a flower on the cropped lawn.

'My dear Monsignor Meredith! So nice to see you!'

The smile was warm; the eyes unclouded; the hand soft but firm in greeting. After the clatter of village dialect, Meredith was comforted by the sound of an English voice. His pinched face brightened into a smile.

'My dear Contessa! Thank you for having me here!'

'Did you have a good journey?'

'Fair enough. The roads are rough and I'm not a good traveller these days. But I'm here in one piece.'

'You poor man! You must be quite exhausted. I'll have Pietro show you your room, then you can wash and rest a little before lunch.'

'I'd like that,' said Meredith. And he thought gratefully: Thank God for the English. They understand these things better than anyone else in the world! They don't fuss and they know that when a man is tired his first need is privacy and hot water!

At a sign from the Contessa the servant picked up the bags and led Meredith into the house. The Contessa stood on the edge of the lawn watching his stooped, retreating back until the shadow of the doorway swallowed him up.

A moment later, Nicholas Black walked out from the shrubbery and joined her. He was grinning all over his lean satyr's face.

'Well, well, well! So that's what we're in for! He looks like a seedy edition of John Henry Newman. Oxford, I'd say. Magdalen probably, with a dash of the English College—and a Vatican veneer to top it off. . . . You did it beautifully, *cara*. Not too little, not too much. The charming châtelaine welcoming the Church, the expatriate *Inglesa* doing the honours to a fellow countryman. You're quite an actress!'

She ignored his irony and said thoughtfully:

'He looks very ill.'

'Prayer and fasting will do that too, darling. I wonder if he wears a hair shirt.'

'Oh, for God's sake, Nicki!'

He shrugged irritably and demanded:

'What do you expect me to do? Kiss his clerical backside and ask him to bless my medals? What's happening to you, anyway? Don't tell me you're in the full flush of conversion!'

She rounded on him with low, fierce invective.

'Listen, Nicki! You're a nice enough little man and a middling good painter. You're doing very well out of me and I'm helping you to get some things you want very badly. But I've got my own problems with this priest and I'm not having you make bigger ones just to show how clever you are. If you're not prepared to behave, you can pack your bags and I'll have Pietro drive you down to Valenta to catch the next train to Rome! I hope that's clear.'

He wanted to scream at her and strike her in the face and call her all the bawdy names he could think of; but, as always, he was afraid. So he caught at her hand and kissed it and said in his penitent boyish fashion:

'I always do it, *cara*, don't I? I'm sorry. I don't know what gets into me. I'll behave. I promise! Please, please forgive me.' Anne Louise de Sanctis smiled. She had made her point. She had tasted again the sour pleasure of flagellation and she could afford to be generous. She rumpled his thin hair and patted his cheek and said:

'All right, darling. We'll forget it this time. But be a good boy in future.'

Then she made him take her arm and walk her around the garden, gossiping about Roman scandals. But, clever as she was, she never quite understood how much he hated her.

Alone in his high room, with the shutters drawn against the noonday heat, Blaise Meredith washed and changed and lay down on the big walnut bed.

Once again, it seemed, he had reason for gratitude. His lodging was comfortable; his hostess was charming; the servants were attentive. Whatever the squalor of the village he could come back here and forget it. Whatever his problems, he could count on the good will of the Contessa to help him unravel them. When he was ill he would not be alone, and, with a full staff, he would not be too much of a burden.

He reminded himself that he should write to the Bishop and tell him of his satisfaction with the arrangements made for him. Then, relaxed and resting, he thought about his work and how he should go about it.

A talk with the Contessa first, he decided: a survey of the village and its characters, an indication of the most likely sources of information on Giacomo Nerone. She would know much. She would have a certain valuable authority. As a feudal châtelaine she would stand *in loco parentis* with the peasants, and a word from her might loosen many tongues.

Then he should call on the parish priest to present his letter of authority and request his official co-operation. Whatever the reputation of the pastor, he still had canonical status in the matter. He had also a long and apparently contentious acquaintance with Nerone. There was a problem here, of course. If he had been, even for a while, Nerone's confessor, he could not be called on for evidence. Even if his penitent had released him from the seal, his evidence could not be admitted in the court. It was a wise provision of the law; but it was also a useful bolt-hole for a man who had something to conceal. He could sit pat and refuse even to indicate sources of information and the canonists would uphold his discretion. On all counts it looked as if Father Anselmo might prove a problem to the Devil's Advocate.

Who next? The doctor, perhaps, Aldo Meyer, who was a Jew and a disappointed liberal. There were problems here too. He would know too much. His evidence was admissible, since even infidels and heretics might give testimony for or against the Cause. But he could not be forced to give it, as a Catholic could, by moral sanctions. One could only depend on his good will. For the present, at least, Doctor Aldo Meyer must be put down as doubtful.

Then there was Nina Sanduzzi, who had been the mistress of Giacomo Nerone and had borne his child. According to the records of Battista and

Saltarello, she had refused to give any information at all. It seemed unlikely that a foreign priest would have any greater success with her. But even if he had, the inquiry promised to be most distasteful of all. It would entail a confessional probing into the deepest intimacies of their relationship: their mutual confidences, their moral attitudes, the reasons for their separation, even the nature of their sexual commerce. And all this between a priest who spoke only Roman Italian and a woman whose tongue was the bastard dialect of Calabria with its polyglot elements of Greek, Phoenician, Levantine Arab and Angevin French. . . .

Blaise Meredith was still wrestling with this problem when a servant entered and announced that luncheon was served and that the Contessa was waiting for him downstairs.

Luncheon began well: a pleasant conversation piece between people of taste and breeding, oddly met in a strange land. The Contessa steered the talk carefully. Nicholas Black seemed to enjoy his role as the urbane cosmopolite, and Blaise Meredith, relaxed after his rest, talked with a rare charm and considerable knowledge of books and music and the politics of Europe and the Church.

By the time they came to the cheese and the fruit, the Contessa had begun to feel comfortable again. This was a man she could understand. She had met many like him, in the old days in London and Rome. He had polish and discretion and, what was more important, he understood the English idiom of allusion and understatement. With a little care she could bring him to lean on her to interpret the provincial crudities. Provided Nicki continued to behave himself, there would be no trouble at all. She felt confident enough to put the first probing questions to Meredith.

'You must forgive my ignorance, Monsignor; but how do you usually begin work in a case like this?'

Meredith made a small, rueful gesture.

'I'm afraid there aren't any rules at all. It's a question of talking to as many people as possible and then collating and comparing their information. Later, when the Bishop's court is set up, one can question and cross-examine them under oath—and in secrecy, of course.'

'And where do you think you'll start now?'

'I had hoped that you might be able to help me first. You've lived here a long time. You're the *padrona*. Your knowledge of local conditions would be a very good preparation for me.'

Nicholas Black shot a swift, ironic glance at the Contessa, but she was smiling calmly.

'I'm happy to do anything I can of course, but I think there's a danger in referring to me. I'm the *padrona*, as you say, and I'm English as well. I live a different life. I think differently from these people. I could be quite wrong in my ideas. I've been proved so many times. But I do want to help, for your sake and for the Bishop's. He's an old friend of mine, as you know.'

'Of course.' Meredith nodded and did not press the point.

The Contessa went on:

'After His Lordship wrote to me, I thought that the most helpful thing would be to have you meet the doctor and the parish priest. They both know much more about the village than I do. I've asked them both to come to dinner tonight. Then we can all four of us exchange views. I'll feel more confident then, that you are getting a balanced opinion. Nicki agrees with me, don't you, Nicki?'

'Of course, *cara*. This is a strange country. Quite different from Rome. I'm sure your idea is the right one. Don't you agree, Monsignor?'

'You're the experts,' said Meredith deprecatingly. 'I appreciate the trouble you're taking for me.'

The Contessa pushed back her chair.

'I don't usually take coffee in the afternoon. I find it spoils my siesta. Pietro will serve yours on the terrace, and afterwards Nicki will show you the gardens. Will you excuse me, Monsignor? A woman's beauty sleep, you know. . . .'

The two men stood up as she left the table, and when she was gone, Nicholas Black led the way out on to the terrace, where the coffee service was laid under the shade of a striped awning. The painter offered Meredith a cigarette from a slim gold case.

'Smoke?'

'No, thank you. It's a luxury I've had to give up since my illness.'

'The Contessa tells me you've been very ill.'

'Very,' said Meredith flatly. He was feeling warm and at ease and he did not want to be reminded of death.

The servant came out and poured the coffee and Black smoked a few moments in silence, pondering his next gambit. For all his charm, this fellow was acute and intelligent. A mistake with him might be irreparable. After a while he said, casually:

'While you are here, Monsignor, I hope you will let me paint you. You have an interesting face and expressive hands.'

Meredith shrugged disarmingly.

'You must have twenty better subjects than I, Mr Black.'

'Let's say you provide the contrast,' said the painter with a grin. 'The courtly Roman among the provincials. Besides, I'm hoping to make a pictorial record of the whole case of Giacomo Nerone. It could be a wonderful basis for a one-man show. I've thought of calling it "Beatification".'

'It may never come to beatification,' said Meredith carefully. 'Even if it does, it may take years.'

'From an artistic point of view that hardly matters. It's the characters that count—and there's a fantastic gallery of them here. I'm wondering what you'll make of them, Monsignor.'

'I'm wondering, too,' Meredith told him frankly.

'The thing that interests me, of course, is the love affair. I don't really understand how one could possibly consider beatifying a man who seduces a village girl, gives her a bastard boy and then leaves her. He was here long enough to marry her.'

Meredith nodded thoughtfully.

'It raises problems, of course—problems of fact and motive. But it doesn't necessarily put the case out of court. There's the classic example of Augustine of Hippo, who lived with many women and had, himself, an illegitimate son. Yet he became in the end a great Servant of God.'

'After a much longer life than Nerone's.'

'That's true, too. I'll admit candidly the circumstances are puzzling. I'm hoping to find out the full story while I'm here. But, in strict theology, one cannot ignore the possibility of sudden and miraculous conversion.'

'If one believes in miracles, of course,' said the painter dryly.

'If one believes in God, one believes necessarily in miracles.'

'I don't believe in God,' said Nicholas Black.

'It's a pointless world without Him,' said Blaise Meredith. 'And it's rough enough with Him. But . . . one can't argue a man into faith. So let's agree to differ, shall we?'

But the painter was not to be put off so easily. He was too anxious to see what sort of man lay under the black soutane. He returned to the argument.

'I'd like to believe. But there's so much professional mumbo-jumbo. So many mysteries.'

'There are always mysteries, my dear fellow. If there were none, there would be no need of faith.'

'But you're not taking Giacomo Nerone on faith,' said Black pointedly. 'You're investigating him legally.'

'That's a matter of fact and not of faith,' said Meredith.

The painter chuckled happily.

'But you'll still find lots of mysteries, Monsignor. More than you bargain for, I think. And the biggest mystery of all is why nobody in Gemello Minore wants to talk about him . . . not even the Contessa.'

'Did she know him, then?' A new interest quickened in Meredith's voice.

'Of course she knew him. She's trying to get his son to come and work for her. She was here when he was alive. She was here when he died. All the others were too. They're not all amnesiacs. But they're as close as oysters just the same. You'll see, at dinner tonight.'

'And what's your interest in the case?' There was an undertone of irritation in the question.

'A village comedy,' said Black blandly. 'And a one-man show growing out of it. It's really quite simple. Anyway, you're involved in the case. I'm not. I'm just giving you a friendly tip. . . . If you're finished with your coffee, I'll show you the garden.'

'I'll sit awhile if you don't mind. Then I may take a siesta.'

'Just as you like. I'm a painter. I don't like wasting light. I'll see you at dinner, Monsignor.'

Meredith sat and watched him go, a tall, slim figure lounging across the lawn and into the shrubbery. He had met men like this before, some few of them, even in the cloth. He wondered what was the root of the malice he bore towards the Contessa and why she continued to give him house room. He wondered also why the Contessa had fobbed off his own request for help with the promise of a country dinner party.

Doctor Aldo Meyer sat in his kitchen and watched while Nina Sanduzzi polished his shoes and pressed his shirt and sponged the lapels of his last respectable suit. He, too, was preoccupied with the Contessa's dinner party. After the scene of the night before, he had been tempted to cut it altogether, but the more he thought, the more sure he was that he should go. It was as if a battle had been joined, and he could not afford to surrender a single advantage to the Contessa and her intriguing cavalier, Nicholas Black.

The real difficulty was that he could not be sure what he was fighting for—unless it were the interests of Nina and Paolo Sanduzzi. But this was too limited a goal to explain his anxiety to meet the English priest, and his complete involvement in the affair of Giacomo Nerone.

He was looking for a key to the mystery of his own failure, and for a signpost in the waste of his future. He had the curious conviction that Blaise Meredith might supply him with both. Part of his answer lay in the papers of Giacomo Nerone, which were still in the drawer of his bureau, but so far he had not found courage to open them.

Several times he had held them in his hands and fumbled with the wrappings; but each time he had drawn back, afraid of the hurt and shame they might hold for him. They were like the letters of a rejected lover, which, once reopened, would remind him of the times when he had been less than a man. Sooner or later he would have to face the revelation: but not now, not yet.

Nina Sanduzzi looked up from her ironing and said calmly:

'I've been thinking about Paolo. I've decided he should work for the Contessa after all.'

Meyer stared at her open-mouthed.

'Good God, woman! Why?'

'First, because Rosetta will be there, and I think she is good for him. She is near to being a woman, and she will fight for what she wants. Also she will talk and I will know what is going on at the villa. Once she starts to work, Paolo will have nothing to do but idle and wander the hills—and the painter will get him anyway.'

'The Contessa will be there, too,' Meyer cautioned her gravely. 'And she is a woman also—older and cleverer than Rosetta.'

'I've thought of that,' she admitted quietly. 'But I have thought also that there will be the priest in the house. He will come to see me, like the others did, and I will tell him what goes on there. I will ask him to look after Paolo.'

'He might not believe you.'

'If I tell him all the others things—about Giacomo—I think he will believe me.'

Meyer looked at her with puzzled, brooding eyes.

'Yesterday you were decided to tell him nothing at all. What made you change your mind? What about your promise to Giacomo?'

'The boy is more important than a promise. And besides—' there was a strange conviction in her voice—'I prayed last night as I always do, to Giacomo. I don't see him, I don't hear him—there is just the shirt he wore when he was killed, with the bullet holes round his heart. But I know what he wants, and this is what I shall do.'

'I didn't think people changed their minds when they were dead,' said Meyer with wintry humour, but there was no answering smile on the calm face of the woman. She said simply:

'It is not changing his mind. It is just that the time was not right before—and now it is right. The priest will come to me when he is ready. Then I shall tell him.'

Meyer shrugged and spread his arms in a small despair.

'Whatever I say, you will do what you want. But before the boy goes to the villa have him talk with me.'

'I'll do that. Have you read Giacomo's papers yet?'

'Not yet.'

'You should not be afraid,' she told him, with singular gentleness. 'He did not hate you, even at the end. Why should he shame you now?'

'I'm ashamed of myself,' said Aldo Meyer curtly, and he walked out into the garden, where the cicadas were shrilling in the blaze of the afternoon, and the dust clung to the green leaves of the fig trees.

9

When Meredith came down to dinner that night, he found the Contessa and her guests already assembled, taking drinks in the salon.

The contrast between them was startling. The Contessa was groomed as if for a Roman evening and Nicholas Black was immaculate in a black dinner jacket. Meyer was dressed in a shabby lounge suit, much cleaned and shiny with long wear. His shirt was clean and newly pressed, but the collar and the cuffs were beginning to fray, and his tie was faded and old-fashioned. Yet he carried himself with dignity and his worn, intelligent face was calm. Meredith was drawn to him immediately and his greeting was less reserved than usual.

'I'm happy to meet my medical adviser. I'm going to be in good hands.'

'Better reserve judgment, Monsignor,' said Meyer, with cool humour. 'I have a bad reputation.'

And there they left it, while the Contessa drew Father Anselmo out of his corner and presented him to his Roman colleague.

He was a short man, on the wrong side of sixty. His face was lined and weathered like that of a peasant and his lank grey hair was long and brushed down over his collar. The shoulders of his soutane were speckled with dandruff and the front of it was spotted with old wine stains and sauce droppings. His hands were knotted with arthritis and he kept twining and untwining them as he talked. When he greeted Meredith his Italian had the thick, coarse accent of the province.

'I'm glad to see you, Monsignor. We don't get many Romans down this way. Too far and too rough for 'em, I suppose.'

Meredith smiled uneasily and murmured a banal remark, but the old man was garrulous and would not be put off.

'That's a trouble we have in this part of the world. The Vatican doesn't even know what's going on. They've got more money than you could poke a stick at, but we never get a smell of it. I remember when I was in Rome . . .'

He would have gone on talking for an hour, had not the Contessa signalled to the servant, who put a glass of sherry into his hands and edged him gently away from the visitor. Meredith was embarrassed. Seedy clerics were distasteful to him at the best of times, but the prospect of a longish association with this one was daunting in the extreme. Then he remembered Aurelio, Bishop of Valenta, and his care for the lost one of his flock, and he was instantly ashamed of himself. Ignoring the shepherding servant, he moved back to the old man and said in a friendly fashion:

'His Lordship sends you his greeting and hopes that I won't be too much trouble to you. But I'm afraid I'll have to lean on your judgment a good deal.'

Father Anselmo took a long swallow of sherry and fixed him with a rheumy eye. He shook his head and said querulously:

'His Lordship sends his greetings! Nice of him! I'm a flea in his ear and he'd like to get rid of me. But he can't do it without a court case. That's the way it is. We might as well understand each other.'

Like most polite people, Meredith had no armour against the grossness of others. It pained him, but he lacked the brutality to administer a frank snub. He said, genially enough:

'I'm the visitor, I'm not up on local politics. There's no reason why we shouldn't get along.'

Then he turned back to make small talk with Anne Louise de Sanctis.

Aldo Meyer had been quick to notice the brusque little exchange and mark it as a credit to Blaise Meredith. The man had breeding and discretion. There was hope that later he might reveal a heart as well.

Nicholas Black had noticed it too, and he grinned slyly at the Contessa, whose answering eyebrow lift told him plainer than words: This goes as I planned it—crookedly and well. And because his interest was common with hers in this moment, he was prepared to co-operate and forget his hatred of her. While Meredith talked with his hostess and Father Anselmo stood a little apart, with one eye on the sherry and one ear on the talk, he drew Meyer aside and said, grinning:

'Well, *dottore mio*, what do you think of our Devil's Advocate?'

'I'm sorry for him. He has the mark of death on him. Already he must be suffering a good deal.'

The painter shivered involuntarily, as if a goose had walked over his grave. He answered plaintively:

'Let's not have death at the dinner table, my dear chap. I was thinking of something else. How do you think he'll work? Pleasantly or . . .?'

He let the question hang, a suspended chord of irony; but Meyer made no move to resolve it.

'Why should we care, you and I?'

'Why indeed,' said Nicholas Black tartly, and dropped the subject.

Meyer sipped his sherry and watched Meredith's face as he talked to the Contessa and Father Anselmo. He noted the leanness of it, the sallow transparency of the skin, the lines of pain etched deeper and deeper round the mouth, the tired, injected eyes that slept too little and saw too much of the tears of things. Men reacted variously to pain and fear. This one seemed to be bearing both with courage, but it was too early to see what else was happening to him.

A few moments later dinner was announced and they filed into the dining-room. The Contessa took the head of the table, with Meredith on her right, Meyer on her left and Father Anselmo and Nicholas Black in the lower places. Before they were seated, she turned to Meredith.

'Will you give us a grace, please, Monsignor?'

As he stood with bowed head through the brief Latin formula, the painter chuckled to himself. What an actress the woman was! Not one piece of business forgotten! He was so absorbed in his amusement that, without thinking, he made the Sign of the Cross after the grace and spent an uncomfortable five minutes wondering whether Meredith had noticed it. As a confirmed atheist, the priest would leave him to the mercy of God; but as a lapsed Catholic he would probably come fishing for his soul, which could be an embarrassment in his plans for Paolo Sanduzzi.

As if on cue, the Contessa repeated the name to Aldo Meyer.

'About young Paolo, Doctor? Is he coming to work for me?'

'I believe so,' said Meyer cautiously. 'His mother will probably come to see you tomorrow.'

'I'm glad.' She bent to explain it to Meredith. 'This will probably interest you, Monsignor. Young Paolo Sanduzzi is, of course, the son of Giacomo Nerone. He was baptised with his mother's name. He's rather wild, but we—that is, Doctor Meyer and I—thought it would do him good to begin work. I've offered him a job as assistant gardener.'

'That seems a kind thought,' said Meredith casually. 'How does his mother live?'

'She works for me,' Meyer told him.

'Oh.'

'She used to be a very pretty woman,' said Father Anselmo, with his mouth full of fish. 'She's thickened up now, of course. I remember her when she made her First Communion. Lovely child!'

He washed the fish down with a draught of wine and wiped his lips with a crumpled napkin. Then, as nobody answered, he bent over his plate again. Meredith turned to Meyer.

'You knew Giacomo Nerone, I believe, Doctor?'

'Yes, I knew him,' Meyer answered with easy frankness. 'I was the first person who saw him after Nina Sanduzzi. She called me in to pick a bullet out of his shoulder.'

'She must have trusted you, Doctor,' said Nicholas Black blandly.

Meyer shrugged the thrust aside.

'There was no reason why she shouldn't. I was a political exile. My sympathies were known to be against the Administration.'

The painter grinned and waited for the next question. His face clouded with disappointment when Meredith said simply:

'You're probably aware, Doctor, that in a Cause for Beatification even the evidence of non-Catholics is admitted, provided they're willing to give. I'd like to talk to you about that, at your convenience.'

'Any time, Monsignor.'

And he thought gratefully: He measures bigger than I thought. They won't snare him too easily.

Anne Louise de Sanctis cut quickly into the small following silence.

'Father Anselmo can probably help you a good deal too, Monsignor. He's very close to all our people. You knew Nerone too, didn't you, Father?'

Anselmo put down his fork with a clatter and took another draught of wine. His voice was thickening noticeably and his accent was broader than ever.

'I never thought much of the man. He interfered too much. Anyone would have thought he was a priest himself. Used to come battering on my door as soon as anyone had a belly-ache. Wanted me to come racing out with the Sacraments. One night he nearly had me shot by the Germans. After that I wouldn't go out after curfew.'

'I'd forgotten,' said Meredith easily. 'You had the Germans here, of course. That must have been uncomfortable.'

'They took over the villa,' said the Contessa quickly. 'I was under open arrest most of the time. It was terrible. I've never been so afraid in my life.'

Nicholas Black wiped his thin lips and smiled behind the napkin. He pictured her walking the lawns with the conquerors, making her coquetries on the arm of a blond captain, bedding with him in the big baroque room behind the velvet curtains, while the peasantry starved outside the iron gates and the stone wall. House arrest? There might be other names for it. A little patience and he would have the whole story of Anne Louise de Sanctis.

Blaise Meredith seemed unconscious of the irony and went on:

'The first evidence seemed to indicate that Giacomo Nerone acted as a kind of mediator between the peasants and the occupying troops. What would you think of that, Contessa?'

'I think that's probably an exaggeration. Most if not all of the mediation was done by myself. When relations became strained in the village my servants would tell me, and I would approach the commander.... On a very official basis, of course. Usually he was co-operative. I think perhaps Nerone exaggerated his influence to build up his credit with the people.'

At that moment the servants began moving round the table clearing the dishes and laying out the next course. Meredith seemed in no hurry to pursue the question. Nicholas Black took advantage of the lull to pose his own barbed query:

'Has anyone ever established definitely who this man was and where he came from?'

Anne Louise de Sanctis was busy with the manservant. Meyer was quizzically silent. Father Anselmo was busy with another glass of wine and, after a moment's awkward pause, Meredith answered him:

'It's never been clearly established. At first he was accepted as an Italian. Later, it seemed, there was an opinion that he might have been a member of one of the Allied units in the South—English, perhaps, or Canadian.'

'Interesting,' said the painter dryly. 'There were quite a few thousand deserters in the Italian theatre.'

'That's possible too,' said Meredith. 'It's something I hope to find out more definitely.'

'If he were a deserter, he couldn't be a saint, could he?'

'Why not?' asked Meyer with sudden interest.

The painter spread his hands in mock humility.

'I'm no theologian, of course; but every soldier takes an oath of service. To break a lawful oath would be a sin, wouldn't it? And a deserter would be living in a constant state of sin.'

'For a non-believer you have a very Christian logic,' said Meredith, with mild humour. A small chuckle went round the table and the painter flushed uncomfortably.

'It seems a logical proposition.'

'Perfectly logical,' said Meredith. 'But there may be other facts. A man cannot bind himself by oath to commit sin. If a sin is required of him under an oath of service, he is obliged to refuse it.'

'How do you establish the fact, Monsignor? And the motive?'

'We must rely on the sworn testimony of those who knew him intimately. Then the court must examine the value of the testimony.' He smiled disarmingly. 'It's a long job.'

'Trouble with you Romans,' said Father Anselmo suddenly, 'you don't see the simplest things—even when they stick up under your noses . . .' His voice was so blurred and unsteady that the guests looked at one another in sharp uneasiness and then at the Contessa, sitting rigid at the head of the table. The old man stumbled on . . . 'Everybody's talking as though they knew nothing. We all knew who he was. I knew. The doctor knew. The . . .'

'He's drunk,' said the Contessa, in a clear hard voice. 'I'm sorry for this exhibition, Monsignor, but he should be got home immediately.'

'He's old,' said Meyer quietly. 'His liver's packing up and it takes very little to put him under the table. I'll get him home.'

The old man stared hazily round the table, fumbling for the thread of his thought. His grey head nodded and a small runnel of wine dribbled down from his slack lips.

'Pietro can go with you,' said the Contessa curtly.

'I'll go,' said Nicholas Black.

Meredith pushed back his chair and stood up. There was a new ring in his flat precise voice.

'He's a brother priest. I'll get him home, with the doctor.'

'Take my car,' said Anne Louise de Sanctis.

'Better he walks,' Aldo Meyer told her quietly. 'The air will sober him up a little. It isn't far. Give me a hand with him, Monsignor.'

Together they got him out of the chair and manoeuvred him past the servant at the door and out on to the gravelled drive.

Nicholas Black and the Contessa sat still at the table, staring at one another. After a while the painter said softly:

'A near thing, *cara*, a very near thing, wasn't it?'

'Go to hell!' said the Contessa and left him alone, grinning like a satyr at the wreckage of my lady's dinner party.

As they walked down the rough road towards the village with Father Anselmo hanging from their shoulders, his feet trotting aimlessly in rhythm with their own, Meredith was astonished to feel how light he was. In the salon and at the dinner table he had seemed bloated and gross; now he was just a frail old man with a pot-belly and a lolling, greasy head, who mumbled and dribbled and clung to them, helpless as a sick child.

Meredith, who had rarely come near a drunk and had never seen a drunken priest, was at first disgusted and then touched with a sharp compassion. This was what happened to some men when the terror of life caught up with them. This was what they became when age weakened the faculties and decay crept in among the tissues and the will faltered under the burden of time and memory. Who could love this shambling old wreck? Who now could care whether he lived or died and whether his soul was damned to eternity–if indeed a soul was left after the long wasting of the years?

Meyer cared–enough at least to whisk him quickly away from further indignities, to make dignified apology for him, to lend him a shoulder and walk him home on his two feet. Meyer cared: the shabby Semite with the tarnished reputation, who understood what happens when a man's liver packs up and his prostate fails him and he can't hold his spoon straight because of the arthritis in his joints. And Blaise Meredith? Did he care too? Or was he so preoccupied with his own belly-ache that he could not see that there were meaner ways of dying, and sharper torments than his own?

He was still chewing on this tasteless cud when they came to the door of the priest's house. They eased him off their shoulders and propped him against the wall, and Meyer hammered loudly on the front door. A few moments later they heard shuffling footsteps inside, and then the door was opened by a fat old woman in a shapeless black shift with a soiled nightcap askew on her tousled hair. She peered at them sleepily.

'Well! What's the matter? Can't you let a body sleep? If you want the priest, he's not here, he's . . .'

'He's drunk,' said Meyer amiably. 'We brought him home. You'd better get him to bed, Rosa.'

She turned on him angrily.

'I knew it would happen. I warned him. Why can't they leave him alone? He's not made for hobnobbing with the quality. He's just an old man—and a big baby who doesn't know how to look after himself.' She took Anselmo's hand and tried to lead him into the house. 'Come on, crazy one. Rosa will get you to bed and look after you . . .'

But the old man lurched and stumbled and would have fallen unless Meyer had caught him. He said curtly:

'Come on, Monsignor. We'd better carry him to bed. The woman's almost as old as he is.'

They lifted him head and feet and carried him into the house and up a flight of rickety stairs, with Rosa Benzoni lighting the way ahead with a tallow candle. The house smelt stale and musty as a mouse-hole, and when they came to the bedroom Meredith saw that it held a large double bed covered with greasy blankets, and that one side of it was already in disorder. They carried the old man over to it and laid him down. Meyer began to loosen his collar and his shoes.

The old woman bustled him away, grumbling.

'Leave him! Leave him for pity's sake! You've done enough damage tonight. I can look after him. I've been doing it long enough.'

After a moment's hesitation, Meyer shrugged and walked out of the room. Meredith followed him, feeling his way down the creaking stairs, through the fusty air, and out into the grateful freshness of the moonlight.

Meyer put a cigar between his thin lips, lit it and inhaled deeply. Then he gave Meredith a sidelong speculative look and said coolly:

'Are you shocked, Monsignor?'

'I'm sorry for him,' Meredith answered in a low voice. 'Deeply sorry.'

Meyer shrugged.

'The Church is to blame for half of it, my friend. They send a poor devil like Anselmo out to a place like this, with half an education and no stipend and no security at all—and expect him to stay celibate for forty years. He's just a peasant and not very intelligent at that. He's damned lucky to have found a woman like Rosa Benzoni, to bully him and keep his socks clean.'

'I know,' said Meredith absently. 'That's what touched me most of all. She was like a wife to him. She—she loves him.'

'Does that surprise you, Monsignor?'

'It shames me . . .' He shook his head as if to chase away a haunting nightmare. 'I've spent all my life in the priesthood and I think . . . I think I've wasted it.'

'That makes two of us,' said Aldo Meyer softly. 'Come down to my place and I'll make you a cup of coffee.'

In the low, dimly lit room of Meyer's cottage, with its peasant furniture and its rows of copper vessels, polished by the careful hands of Nina Sanduzzi, Meredith felt the same relaxation and intimacy that he had experienced in the house of Aurelio the Bishop. He was grateful for it, as he had been before, but this time he warmed to it more quickly and less consciously. He knew now how much he needed friendship, and he was prepared to go more than halfway to the making of it. As Meyer moved about the room laying out the cups, spooning out coffee, and slicing the last of a loaf to go with the cheese, he asked him bluntly:

'What was the meaning of the dinner party tonight? Everything seemed very pointed; but I couldn't see what it was pointing at.'

'It's a long story,' Meyer told him. 'It will take some time to put it in order for you. The party was the Contessa's idea. She wanted to show you the type of people you'd be dealing with–and how much better it would be to lean on her, not on a couple of country bumpkins like Anselmo and me.'

'I had the idea she was afraid of what might be said.'

'That too.' Meyer nodded. 'We've all been afraid, for a long time.'

'Of me?' Meredith looked at him in surprise.

'Of ourselves,' said Meyer with a crooked grin. 'All of us there tonight were involved one way and another with the life and death of Giacomo Nerone. None of us came out of it very creditably.'

'Does that include the Englishman–the painter fellow?'

'He's a late involvement. He's an odd one–and he's taken a fancy to young Paolo Sanduzzi. He's enlisted the Contessa's help to seduce him.'

Meredith was shocked.

'But that's monstrous!'

'It's human,' Meyer told him quietly. 'It sounds better if it's a girl and not a boy. But the idea's the same.'

'But the Contessa said you had agreed the boy should work at the villa.'

'She was lying. She's a very accomplished liar. Which makes it difficult to help her.'

He brought the coffee-pot to the table and poured the steaming contents into the earthenware cups. Then he sat down opposite Meredith, who looked at him with puzzlement in his eyes.

'You're very frank, Doctor–why?'

'I've learned something, very late in life,' said Meyer firmly. 'You can never bury the truth so deep that it can't be dug up. We've been trying to bury the truth about Giacomo Nerone, and now it's festering round our feet. You'll get it sooner or later–and it's my view you ought to get it now. Then you can go back to Rome and leave us in peace.'

'Does this mean you're prepared to give evidence as well?'

'It does.'

'And this is your only motive–truth?'

Meyer looked up quickly and saw, for the first time, the inquisitor who lived in the skin of Blaise Meredith. He said cautiously:

'Does my motive matter, Monsignor?'

'It colours the evidence,' Meredith told him. 'It may obscure the truth–which is the truth about a man's soul.'

Meyer nodded gravely. He saw the point. He respected the man who made it. After a pause he answered:

'So far as any man can be honest about his motives, this is mine. I've made a mess of my life. I'm not quite sure why. I had a part, too, in the death of Giacomo Nerone. I was wrong in that. But I don't believe I was wrong in my other estimates of him. I want to talk all this out; have another set it in perspective for me. Otherwise I'm going to end like old Anselmo giving myself cirrhosis of the liver because I can't face my nightmares. . . . That's why I was afraid of you, like the others. If I couldn't trust you I couldn't talk to you.'

A gleam of amusement showed in Meredith's eyes. He asked quizzically:

'And what makes you think you can trust me, Doctor?'

'Because you have the grace to be ashamed of yourself,' said Meyer

baldly. 'And that's rare enough in the Church or out of it. . . . Now drink
your coffee and we'll talk awhile before I send you to bed!'

But there was no more talk for Meredith that night. The first mouthful of
coffee choked him; the pain in his stomach took him again and Meyer led
him stumbling out into the garden to void the bile and the blood that choked
him. Then, when the spasm had passed, he laid him down on his own bed
and began palpating the shrunken belly, pressing down to the hard, deadly
mass growing against the wall of it.

'Is it like this often, Monsignor?'

'It's getting more frequent,' Meredith told him painfully. 'The nights are
the worst.'

'How long did they give you?'

'Twelve months, possibly less.'

'Halve it!' Meyer told him flatly. 'Halve it again and you'll be nearer to
the truth.'

'As soon as that?'

Meyer nodded.

'By rights you should be in hospital now.'

'I want to stay on my feet as long as I can.'

'I'll try to keep you there,' said Meyer with grudging admiration. 'But too
much of this, and it'll take a miracle!'

'That's what the Bishop wanted me to ask for—a miracle.' He said it
humorously to make a joke out of the new pain that was coming on him. But
Meyer seized on the tag like a terrier.

'Say that again!'

'The Bishop wanted me to ask for a sign—a tangible proof of the sanctity
of Giacomo Nerone. Some of the reported cures could be miracles, but I
doubt we'll prove any of them judicially . . . so I could be the one provable
one.'

'And you, Monsignor? What did you say to that?'

'I didn't have the courage to agree.'

'You would rather bear the pain you have now—and what is still to come?'

Meredith nodded.

'Are you so afraid of your God, my friend?'

'I'm not sure what I'm afraid of. . . . It's—it's as if I were being asked to
make a leap through a paper hoop, on the other side of which is either
darkness or a shattering revelation. The only way I can find out, is to leap.
And I . . . I haven't the courage to do it. Does that sound strange to you,
Doctor?'

'Strange—and yet not so strange,' Meyer said thoughtfully. 'Strange from
a man like you; but for me, easy enough to understand.'

He was thinking of the papers of Giacomo Nerone that still lay untouched
in his bureau: and he was thinking of the fear that came on him every time
he tried to open them.

But Meredith did not ask for explanations. He closed his eyes and lay
back, pale and exhausted, on the pillow. Meyer let him doze till midnight
and, when he woke again, walked him back to the villa and had the
gatekeeper take him up to his bedroom.

At midnight Nicholas Black was wakeful, too. He was sitting up in bed,
smoking a cigarette and contemplating with deep satisfaction the picture of
Paolo Sanduzzi, which was propped on the easel in front of the drawn

curtains. He had chosen the position with some care, so that the light fell on it from the correct angle and the white figure of the boy seemed to thrust itself forward from the dark wood of the gallows tree. The scarlet lips smiled at the man who had painted them, and the eyes were bright in contemplation of the veiled, deceptive future.

Narcissus in his pool saw himself no more beautiful than Nicholas Black in his solitary contemplation of his own creation. Yet even this pleasure could not blind him to the pity of his situation: that this was the nearest he could come to what other men had by natural right—sons of their own to love, cherish and train towards the maturity of manhood. Would there never be an end to the pursuit, the panic grasping, the sour humiliation of defeat?

Sometime, with someone, there must be a term to it. Other rakes married their virgins who bred them children and warmed their slippers, while they repented happily in their Indian summer. Soon, soon, he must come to his own harbour, before the winter winds began to blow and the dead leaves rattle around the garden walks.

Then he remembered the dinner talk and hope began to wake again. Tomorrow, Meyer had said, the boy would come. His mother would speak with Anne Louise de Sanctis and he would be signed into service with the gardeners. Morning and afternoon he would be there—a raw peasant to be drawn towards gentility, a servant to be attracted into sonship. It would need tact and gentleness, firmness, too, sometimes, so that from the first the nature of the relationship should be clearly established. Nicholas Black was shrewdly aware of the attraction he had for the boy, equally aware of the boy's capacity to attract him, to their mutual ruin. The boy must be brought to see that all his hopes lay in a disciplined association, and that any attempt to exploit his patron would wreck them utterly. Still, given time and the casual intimacy of the villa, he felt confident that he could do it.

What troubled him still was that he could see only half the motive of the Contessa in helping him to the conquest. The half he saw was simple enough. She wanted his co-operation in handling the priest. She needed an understanding ally to bolster her courage. But the reasons which she still held back were of much deeper concern to him.

The world of lost lovers is a jungle where it is rutting season all the time. There is no mercy in the desperate, headlong flight from loneliness.

The race is to the swift, possession is for the strong. The wild urge to couple and forget colours the most civilised gestures. The simplest words take on a colour of passion and intrigue.

Nicholas Black had lived a long time in the jungle, and he had no illusions left. If Anne de Sanctis helped him, it would be to compass her own designs in the end. What were they? Passion, perhaps? Every season brought its crop of dowagers who hoisted their skirts and played hot cockles with the boys in the Mediterranean spring. The dowagers paid and the boys acted out the cold comedy with Latin cynicism and went back to marry their girls on the profits. But the Contessa was too experienced to make a fool of herself in her own village. Capri was just round the corner. Rome was distant and more discreet. She had money and freedom to pleasure herself where she chose.

So there must be another reason. Her fear of Meredith pointed to a personal involvement with Giacomo Nerone. Potiphar's wife, perhaps? My lady bountiful turned bitch when Joseph fled from her, leaving his cloak in her hands—and taking his fun with a peasant wench instead of the *padrona* of the villa.

Jealousy took freakish forms at times. Paolo Sanduzzi, the stripling boy, would be a perpetual reproach to her failure as a woman and a lover. To seduce him from his mother would be an oblique revenge on his father . . . and a consummate insult to Nicholas Black.

A slow heat of anger grew in him and he lay back on the pillows staring at the picture of Paolo Sanduzzi, loathing the woman who for house room and the promise of an exhibition had thought to buy him into so brutal a bondage.

Anne Louise de Sanctis lay back in her marble bath and felt the soft water move over her skin like a symbol of absolution. The perfumed steam rose gratefully, blurring the harsh edges of reality and blending with the euphoric haze of the barbiturates which would soon coax her downwards into forgetfulness.

This narrow room, with its crystal bottles and its misted mirror, was the womb from which she issued, new, each morning, into which she retreated each night from the howling confusion of loneliness. Suspended in the foetal fluid, within the warm, veined walls of marble, she could float self-absorbed, self-justified, irresponsible, lapped in an illusion of eternity.

But the illusion became more tenuous each night. The impact of each morning became more brutal. Invading hands reached forward into her privacy: voices challenged her out of the twilight into the bitter day and she knew she could not shut them out much longer.

Meyer was the first of her adversaries: the down-at-heel doctor with the disappointed face and the frayed cuffs, the shoe-string reformer, the penny philosopher, the man who knew everything and did nothing, who was the enemy of illusions because he had none himself. Once she might have commanded his alliance against Giacomo Nerone, but now all his care was for Nina Sanduzzi, who had borne Nerone's child. He had refused even the pity she had pleaded from him, and with one brutal sentence had laid bare her self-deceit.

She wanted a child. There was truth in that. She wanted Paolo Sanduzzi. There was truth in that, too. But she wanted him for herself. He was Nerone's boy, flesh of his flesh, bone of his bone. She had love to spend on him—money, too. Love that Nerone had tossed back in her face. Money to ransom him out of the sordid life to which his father had condemned him. But Meyer stood in her way. Meyer and Nina Sanduzzi, and even the grey cleric from Rome.

She had lived a long time in Italy and she understood the subtle workings of the Church in its southern vineyard. Its princes played politics with Machiavellian skill, but they were rigid in the enforcement of the public moralities, through which they ruled a passionate and recalcitrant people. They did not hesitate to invoke the civil statute as a sanction for the ten commandments. As an ally, Meredith could help her greatly; as an enemy he would be implacable and unconquerable.

So, by twisting roads, she came back to Nicholas Black. She had small faith in his stability; but she needed an ally, and this one was already bought and easy to manage. She did not for a moment believe his protestation of pure affection for the boy. She saw it simply as a calculated gambit of seduction; and her promise of help was equally calculated.

She would give the painter time and opportunity to work on Paolo, tempting him with friendship and the promise of a gentleman's life in Rome. The boy would respond quickly, being touched already with the discontents of adolescence. The small scandal of their association would grow to a larger one. Nina Sanduzzi's maternal control would be called in question. Then . . . then the Contessa would step in, the solicitous *padrona*, the châtelaine careful of the interests of her people. She would offer to remove the boy from an occasion of corruption, to educate him, in Rome first and later in England.

Even the Church would see merit in such a course. If Giacomo Nerone were to be raised to the altars, they would not want his son whoring round the villages like so many other country youths. Let Nicholas Black play to his heart's content the role of petty intriguer, she would still win the game in the end. She would walk down the Via Veneto with Paolo Sanduzzi, proud and complete, as though Nerone had fathered him on her own barren body.

She got out of the bath, dried and perfumed herself and dressed for bed. Then she lay down under the great brocaded canopy and let herself drift into a drugged sleep, dreaming of a dark smiling youth whose hand was clasped firmly in her own. And when he changed from youth to man, from son to passionate lover, this was, after all, a delusion of the night, with no guilt in it at all. . . .

IO

Early the following morning, while Nina Sanduzzi swept and polished his cottage, Aldo Meyer sat under the fig tree and talked with Paolo.

The interview began awkwardly. The boy was sullen and withdrawn and Meyer's first fumbling queries did nothing to gain his confidence. He kept his eyes fixed on the tabletop, chewed nervously at a twig and gave his answers in a mumbling undertone, so that Meyer was forced to fight down his irritation and keep a proper friendliness in his voice.

'Your mother has spoken to you about working for the Contessa?'

'Yes.'

'You know young Rosetta's going to the villa too?'

'Yes.'

'How do you feel about it?'

'I s'pose it's all right.'

'Do you want to go, or not?'

'I don't mind.'

'The pay's not bad. You'll be able to help your mother and still have something for yourself.'

'Yes, I know.'

'This means you're getting to be a man, Paolo.'

The boy shrugged and picked his teeth with the twig. Meyer took a sip of coffee and lit a cigarette. The next gambit was the important one. He hoped he would not spoil it. After a moment he said, as gently as he could:

'The beginning of a man's life is the most important part of it. It's usually a father's job to set his son on the right road. You haven't a father, so . . . I'd like to help instead.'

For the first time the boy raised his eyes and looked at him squarely. There was a challenge in the look and a faint hostility. His question was blunt and unfriendly.

'Why should you care?'

'I'll try to tell you,' said Meyer equably. 'If I don't satisfy you, ask me anything you like. The first thing is that I haven't a son of my own. I'd like to have one. You could have been my son, because once upon a time I was in love with your mother. I'm still very fond of her. However, she chose your father—and that was that. I knew your father. For a while we were friends, then . . . we were enemies. I had a hand in his death. I'm sorry for that now. If I can help you, I'll be paying a debt to him.'

'I don't need your help,' the boy told him roughly.

'We all need help,' said Meyer quietly. 'You need it because you're involved with the Englishman and you don't quite know what to do about it.'

Paolo Sanduzzi was silent, staring down at the mangled twig in his fingers. Meyer went on:

'I want to explain something to you, Paolo. You know what men are, and women. You know how they come to kiss and caress and what passes between them when they make love. You know what you feel when you look at a girl whose breasts are grown and who begins to walk like a woman. But what you don't understand is how you can feel this for Rosetta, and at the same time feel it when the Englishman touches you.'

Again the boy's head jerked up, defensively.

'There is nothing between me and the Englishman. He has never touched me!'

'Good!' said Meyer calmly. 'Then there is nothing to shame you. Still, you should know that when a man's heart wakes and his body, too, they can be bent this way or that, as the wind bends a sapling. But after a while the sapling stiffens and grows hard as a tree. Then it cannot be bent any more, but grows to its own shape. The proper way for a man to grow is towards a woman—not towards a *feminella*. That is why you cannot stay with the painter. You see that, don't you?'

'Then why are you sending me to work at the villa? He'll be there all the time. He frightens me. He makes me feel that I don't know what I want.'

'Which do you want—him or Rosetta?'

'I want to get out of Gemello!' said the boy savagely. 'I want to go somewhere else, where people don't know about me or my mother or my father. Do you think I like to be called a saint's bastard—the son of a whore? That's why I want to stay with the Englishman. He can do that much for me. He can take me to Rome, give me a new start. . . .'

'And in Rome they'll put a dirtier label on you—and you'll never shake it off wherever you go! Listen, boy . . .' He pleaded with him in a low, passionate voice. 'Try to be patient with me. Try to understand what I'm going to tell you. Your mother is a good woman—ten times better than those who put this name on her. Whatever she did, she did for love—and a whore is one who sells herself for money. Your father was one with a touch of greatness in him . . . and I say that—the man who helped to kill him.'

'Then why didn't he marry my mother and give me his name? Was he ashamed of it? Or of us?'

'Have you ever asked your mother that?'

'No–how could I?'

'Then I think we should ask her now,' said Aldo Meyer. Without waiting for an answer, he called loudly: 'Nina! Come here a moment, please.'

Nina Sanduzzi came out of the house and the boy watched her approach with frightened eyes.

'Sit down, Nina.'

She sat down between them, looking from one to the other with grave, questioning eyes. Meyer told her soberly:

'There is a question the boy has asked, Nina. I think he has a right to the answer. You are the only one to give it. He wants to know why his father didn't marry you.'

'Will you believe me if I tell you, son?'

The boy looked up, troubled and ashamed, and nodded dumbly. Nina Sanduzzi waited a moment, gathering her strength and her words; then, in a steady voice, she told him.

Blaise Meredith too was stirring early on this fine spring morning. After his attack in the doctor's house, he had slept less restlessly than usual, and when the servant came to bring his coffee and draw back the curtains on the new day, he decided to get up and begin work.

He drank his coffee, ate a little of the new bread and the salt country butter, bathed and shaved, and went downstairs to read his Office in the sunshine. With this liturgical duty behind him, he would be free to begin his interviews with the witnesses. Meyer's warning was still vivid in his mind. His time was running out faster than he had hoped and he could not afford to waste a minute of it. He was glad that the Contessa and Black were still in bed so that he would be spared the rituals of greeting and breakfast small talk.

He had finished Matins and was halfway through Lauds when he heard the sounds of footsteps on the gravel path and looked up. A woman and a boy were walking towards the rear of the house. The woman was dressed peasant-fashion in shapeless black, with a bandanna tied round her head. The boy had on a striped shirt and a pair of patched trousers, and his feet were thrust into worn leather sandals.

He walked uncertainly, looking this way and that, as if overcome by the splendour of his surroundings after the barren harshness of the village. The woman walked proudly, head erect, eyes straight ahead of her, as if determined to discharge an uncomfortable duty with dignity. Meredith was struck by the classic serenity of her face, rounding with middle age, but still touched with a youthful beauty.

This would be Nina Sanduzzi, he decided. The boy would be the son of Giacomo Nerone, who, Meyer had told him, was the subject of the conspiracy of seduction between the Contessa and Nicholas Black. They would have a long time to wait before the Contessa was up and ready to see them.

Moved by a sudden impulse, he put down his book and called:

'Signora Sanduzzi!'

They stopped in their tracks and turned to look at him. He called again:

'Can you come here a moment, please?'

They looked at one another uncertainly; then the woman walked across the lawn with the boy a couple of paces behind her. Meredith stood up to greet her.

'I'm Monsignor Meredith, from Rome!'

'I know,' said the woman calmly. 'You came yesterday. This is my son, Paolo.'

'I'm happy to know you, Paolo.'

Meredith held out his hand, and after a nudge from his mother the boy took it, limply.

'You know why I'm here, signora?'

'Yes, I know.'

'I'd like to have a talk with you as soon as possible.'

'You'll find me at the doctor's place—or at home.'

'I thought perhaps we could talk a little now.'

Nina Sanduzzi shook her head.

'We have to see the Contessa. Paolo begins work today.'

Meredith smiled.

'You'll have a long wait. The Contessa isn't up yet.'

'We're used to waiting,' she told him gravely. 'Besides, I will not talk to you here.'

'Just as you like.'

'But when Paolo is working here you can talk to him. That would be different.'

'Of course. May I come and see you today?'

'If you want. In the afternoon I'm at home. Now we must go. Come, Paolo.'

Without another word she turned away. The boy followed her, and Meredith watched their retreating backs until they disappeared round the rear corner of the villa.

Brief as their encounter had been, the woman had impressed him deeply. There was an air about her—an air of serenity, containment, wisdom perhaps. She walked and talked like one who knew where she was going and how she intended to get there. She had neither the thrusting impudence of some peasant women, nor the practised humility which centuries of dependence had imposed on others. Her tongue was the roughest dialect in Italy, yet her voice was soft and strangely gentle even in her blunt refusal. If Giacomo Nerone had taught her these things, then he, in his time, must have been a greater man than most.

Meredith found his attention wandering from the Latin cadences of the Psalms to the consideration of two important elements in the sketchy life of Giacomo Nerone.

The first was the element of conflict. It was an axiom in the Church that one of the first marks of sanctity was the opposition it raised, even among good people. Christ himself had been the sign of contradiction. His promise was not peace, but the sword. No saint in the Calendar had ever done good unopposed. None had ever been without detractors and calumniators. The absence of this element from the records of Battista and Saltarello had troubled him. Now he was beginning to be aware of its existence and of its strength and complexity.

The second element was equally important: the tangible good or evil that sprang from the life, works and wonders of a candidate for saintly honours. There was an axiom here too: the Biblical axiom that a tree is known by its fruits. Sanctity in one man leaves its imprint like a seal on the hearts of others. A good work reproduces itself as the seed of one fruit grows into another. A miracle that produces no good in a human heart is a pointless conjuring trick unworthy of omnipotence.

If there was good in Nina Sanduzzi, and if this good had sprung from her association with Giacomo Nerone, then it must be weighed in the meticulous reckoning of the Devil's Advocate.

He bent again to his breviary, his lips moving in the familiar strophes of the poet-king. Then, when he had finished, he closed the book, thrust it into the pocket of his cassock and walked out of the villa to talk with Father Anselmo.

Old Rosa Benzoni met him at the door and, after a grumbling parley, let him into the house, where he found the old priest, in shirt-sleeves and braces, shaving awkwardly in front of a cracked mirror tacked to the wall of the kitchen. His eyes were blearier than usual and his knotted hands trembled as he scraped at his stubbled chin. He was using an old blade razor and Meredith marvelled that he had not yet cut his throat with it. His greeting was less than cordial.

'Hullo! What do you want?'

'I'd like to talk to you,' said Meredith mildly.

'I'll listen. I don't promise to answer, though.'

'Better we were private, don't you think?' suggested Meredith.

The old man chuckled and then swore as he nicked himself.

'You mean Rosa? She's half-deaf and I doubt she'd understand a word when you talk with a Roman grape in your mouth. Besides, she's got a bad temper—and I've got to live with her. Go ahead, man, and say what you've got to say.'

Meredith shrugged and went on.

'It's about Giacomo Nerone. I notice from the first reports that you refused to give any evidence about him. Is that because you were his confessor?'

'No. I didn't like the fellows they sent round. Long-nosed humbugs the pair of 'em. Read me a long lecture about doomsday and damnation. I sent 'em off with a flea in the ear. Besides, who the hell cares what I say? I'm the scandal of the diocese.'

'I'm not interested in scandals,' said Meredith coolly.

The old man put down the razor and daubed at his face with a soiled towel. He said roughly:

'Then you're the first one I've met who isn't. God, how they love 'em! Give 'em a piece of dirt and they'll chew on it like dogs on a ham-bone. I had a letter from the Bishop hoping my association with Rosa had lost its carnal character. . . .' He gave a high, harsh laugh. 'How long does he think a man keeps going at that sort of thing? At my age the best you can hope for is to keep warm at night.'

'At your age,' suggested Meredith gently, 'most married couples sleep in separate beds.'

'In Rome, maybe,' growled Father Anselmo. 'But down here we haven't enough money to buy a new bed—let alone two sets of blankets. Look . . .' He flung down the towel with a gesture of impatience. 'We're not children, Monsignor. I don't like the position I'm in, any more than the Bishop. But at my age, how do I get out of it? I can't toss Rosa out into the street. She's an old woman. She's been good to me—when a lot of my damned brothers in the cloth couldn't have cared whether I lived or died. I've got little enough, God knows, but she's entitled to half of it. Does His Lordship have any answer to that one?'

Meredith was moved. The naked dilemma of the man was frightening. For the first time in his priestly life he began to understand the real problem of repentance, which is not the sin itself, but the consequences which proliferate from it, like parasites on a tree. The tree has no remedy but must go on lending its life to the parasite, borrowing beauty from it, but dying slowly all the time, for want of a knowledgeable gardener. It was a stark thought that a man might lapse into despair and damnation because he couldn't afford a pair of blankets. Suddenly the case of Giacomo Nerone seemed small and insignificant beside the case of Father Anselmo. If Giacomo was a saint he was lucky—he had finished with the long fight. All else was glossary and of little moment. A sudden thought struck Meredith but he hesitated to give it voice. After a moment he said carefully:

'His Lordship's a surprising man. He'd like to help you. I think—I'm sure—if you were to move Rosa to another bed in another room, he'd accept that and let the rest of it drop.'

The old man shook his head stubbornly.

'Who pays for the bed and bedclothes? You don't seem to understand. We live down to the knuckle-bone here. It's a matter of eating.'

'I'll tell you something,' said Meredith with a wry smile. 'I'll pay for them. I'll give you and Rosa enough to set yourselves up with some new clothes and I'll put a hundred thousand lire in the Banco di Calabria for you. Would that help?'

Father Anselmo shot him a swift suspicious glance.

'And why should you care so much, Monsignor?'

Meredith shrugged.

'I'm due to die in three months. I can't take it with me.'

The rheumy eyes stared at him in unbelief. The rough peasant voice questioned him again.

'What else do I have to do?'

'Nothing. If you want me to confess you, I'll do it gladly. You can't tell me much I don't know already, so it shouldn't be too hard. There's no point in going halfway. You've got to set your conscience in order some time.'

'The Bishop talked about repairing the scandal.' There was still doubt in his voice, but the stubborn harshness had gone out of it.

Meredith gave him one of his rare, humorous smiles.

'The Bishop's a character in his own right. I think he knows that most people make their own scandals. Good Christians keep their mouths shut and pray for their brothers in distress. It'll soon get around the village that you're sleeping apart. The rest will grow out of what you do from then on. . . . Well, what do you say?'

Anselmo rubbed a knotted hand across his badly shaven chin. His slack mouth twisted into a grin.

'I—I suppose it's a way out. I've been worried a long time, but I love the old girl in a way and I'd hate to hurt her.'

'I don't think the loving does any harm. I could use some of it myself just now.' The voice seemed to belong to another man, not Blaise Meredith, the cold fellow from the Congregation of Rites.

'All right!' said the old man brusquely. 'I'll think about it. I'll talk to Rosa and explain things to her. But you can't do things like that in a rush. Women are sensitive—and when they're old they get stupid as well. . . .' His old eyes gleamed shrewdly. 'And when do we see the colour of *your* money, Monsignor?'

Meredith took out his wallet and laid thirty one-thousand lire notes on the table.

'That's the beginning of it. You can buy the blankets and the bed. The rest I'll have to fix in Valenta. Will that do?'

'It'll have to,' the old man told him grudgingly. 'We'd like something fixed before you die. Once the lawyers get their hands on an estate—finish! All that's left is birdseed! Now, what else did you want?'

'Giacomo Nerone. . . . What can you tell me about him?'

'What happens if I do tell you?'

'I'll make notes and then you'll be examined under oath at the Bishop's court.'

'Tell you what, Monsignor. Wait till you hear my confession. Then I'll give you the full story. Will that do?'

'A confessional secret is no good for the court record.'

The old man threw back his head and laughed in his high harsh fashion.

'That's what I mean, friend! They've had enough scandals out of me already. Damned if I'm going to give 'em another one.'

'Just as you say,' said Meredith wearily. 'I'll call and see you in a few days.'

'And don't forget what you have to do in Valenta.'

'I won't forget.'

He got up and walked to the door. There was no farewell, no word of thanks, and as he walked down the hill towards the doctor's cottage, he had the uncomfortable feeling that he had made a fool of himself.

Meyer greeted him good-humouredly, led him into the garden and poured him a cup of country wine from an earthenware pitcher, cooling in the sun. Meredith was quick to notice the change in him: his eyes were clear, his drawn face was relaxed, and he had the comfortable air of a man who has come to terms with himself and his situation. Meredith commented on it quizzically.

'You look better this morning, Doctor.'

Meyer grinned into his wine-cup.

'A good beginning to my day, Monsignor. I've talked to a boy like a father; and heard wise things from his mother.'

'Nina Sanduzzi?'

'Yes. Between us I hope we have done something for the boy.'

'I saw them at the villa—spoke to them for a few moments. I'm calling on Nina Sanduzzi this afternoon. She's prepared to talk.'

'Good.' Meyer nodded with satisfaction. 'I'll give you a tip, my friend. Walk gently and you will go a long way with her. She is disposed now to be frank. And she wants you to keep an eye on the boy while he's at the villa.'

'I'll do my best. She impressed me deeply.'

'And Paolo?'

'Is like any other adolescent.'

'Not quite like . . .' Meyer cautioned him. 'He is in the dangerous years. He is attracted to the Englishman and he is afraid of him as well. Also he is curious about his mother and father. Not quite so curious now that Nina and I have spoken to him. But when you're old, you never know how much a young man understands—or what bees he has buzzing in his bonnet. And what now, Monsignor?'

'I'd like to talk with you, Doctor.'

'About Nerone?'

'Yes.'

Aldo Meyer took a long draught of wine and then wiped his thin lips with the back of his hand. He said with bleak humour:

'Isn't it usual to put on a stole when you hear confessions?'

'I'll take off my shoes instead,' said Blaise Meredith.

'It's a long story, Monsignor. When it gets dry, you help yourself to a drink. . . .

. . . It was full summer in a world without men. Hot mornings and blazing noons, and nights when the clouds rolled in, sweating, over the valley and then moved on unspent of rain. Tempers were high, and vitality was low, because the armies were like locusts, eating out the land, and there were no men in the beds—except the old ones, who were a nuisance, and occasional visitors, like the *polizia* and the *carabinieri* and the agricultural inspector and the requisitioning officers from the Army. These were a nuisance, too, because when they were gone there were quarrels in the houses and bloody faces and torn skirts in the fields.

The valley was like a nest of cats, musky and hot and languid for coupling, then breaking suddenly into screams and violence. Meyer lived in it, because he was a Jew and an exile and every second day he must tramp across the valley to Gemello Maggiore to assure the *quaestura* that he was neither sick nor dead. They were indifferent either way, but they cursed him when he came and threatened him if he missed a day—and then gave him wine and cheese and cigarettes if their children were sick or their girls pregnant or they themselves went down with malaria. They made coarse jokes about his being a Jew and circumcised and warned him about polluting the pure blood of the women, who, being good Calabrese, were part Greek, part Phoenician, part French and Spanish and Italian and Levantine Arab—anything and everything but Jew.

Meyer swallowed it all, and digested it in secret and kept his ears open to the rumours that bumbled like bees in and out of the valley. The Allies were in Sicily, there were beach-heads in other places. Partisans were arming in the hills, deserters were holing up in caves and friendly beds. The Germans were rushing reinforcements south. Sooner or later the end would come and he wanted to be alive to see it.

He worked his rough acres, made his rounds of the sick, dozed at siesta time and in the night sat late over his books and his bottle.

If he kept himself free of the village women, it was because he was a fastidious man, and also because he did not want to face the dawning future with a village shrew at his coat-tails. He had waited a long time. He could afford to wait a little longer.

It was in the night time, late, that Nina Sanduzzi came to see him. She came barefooted lest the sound of her wooden sandals be heard in the sleeping village; and she climbed the garden wall from the valley side, in case some late busybody saw her knocking on the doctor's door. She was right inside the pool of lamplight before he woke from his reverie and saw her. He was startled and angry.

'Nina! What the devil are you doing here?'

She put her finger to her lips to silence him and then explained in low, rattling dialect:

'There's a man in my house. He's a deserter and wounded. There's a bullet hole in his shoulder all red and swollen, and he tosses and mutters as if he had the fever. Will you come and see him, please? I've brought money.'

She fished into the neck of her dress and brought up a small bundle of greasy notes. Meyer waved it away impatiently.

'Keep it, for God's sake! Does anyone else know he's there?'

'No one. He came last night. I gave him breakfast and he stayed inside all day. When I got back from work he was like this.'

'All right, I'll come.'

He closed his book, turned down the lamp and gathered up his bag of instruments and his small stock of antiseptic, and followed her out from the back of the house, over the wall and down to the small hut hidden in the ilexes.

He found his patient delirious on the big brass bed, a long dark fellow with days of stubble on his shrunken cheeks, and staring eyes and a drooling, muttering mouth, from which issued broken words and phrases that he recognised as English. A pretty situation! Deserters were bad enough, but an English soldier was sudden death. He made no comment to the girl, but bent over the bed and began cutting the sodden bandages from the shoulder wound.

When he saw it, he gave a low whistle of surprise. It was pulpy and swollen, and a slow yellow suppuration had already begun. An awkward job and a dirty one. It would hurt like hell without an anaesthetic and the fellow might well die in a matter of days.

He turned back to Nina Sanduzzi.

'Get the fire going. Boil me a pot of hot water. Then you'll have to hold him down for me.'

The girl's white teeth showed in a smile.

'It's a long time since I've had a man in my arms, Dottore. It'll be a pleasure.'

But the pleasure soon went out of it, even for her. The bullet had struck the shoulder blade and slanted downward against the bone, and Meyer had to probe for it for twenty minutes, while the sick man shouted vainly against the gag they thrust in his mouth, and Nina Sanduzzi had to use all her strength to hold him.

Then when it was over and the worst of the pain was finished they tucked him into the bed, and Nina and Meyer sat down to drink wine and break a crust together.

'You can't keep him here. You know that, Nina. If anyone finds out, you're as good as dead.'

She stared at him in astonishment.

'You want me to throw him out. A sick man like that?'

'Afterwards,' said Meyer wearily. 'When he's better.'

'Let's wait for afterwards, then,' said Nina Sanduzzi with a smile.

Looking at her then by lamplight in the low room, he had felt his first real temptation in years. Her face was pure Greek. Her body was slimmer than those of her peasant fellows. Her breasts were full and firm and there was a thrusting animal vitality under her olive skin. She had intelligence, too, and courage. She did not wait and scream like the others. She knew what was needed and she did it, calmly and competently. It amazed him that he had passed her a hundred times and never noticed her.

But he was a cautious fellow and accustomed to continence, so he finished his wine quickly and made to go.

'Understand something, Nina. He's very sick and he could die. Make some soup and see if he can hold it down. When you go to work, lock the door and leave him wine and food. I daren't come here in the daytime, but I'll come again in the night after the village has settled down.'

'You're a good one,' said Nina Sanduzzi softly. 'In a place full of pigs you stand up like a man.' She snatched up his hand and kissed it quickly. 'Now go, *dottore mio*! I'm not used to men around the place!'

As he trudged up the rocky slope, avoiding the roadway, he wondered whether continence was not, like all his other sacrifices, a pointless waste–and whether this might be a woman with whom he could be happy. It was the thing he had been afraid of all his exile–the thing his enemies wanted him to do–go slack, go native, hit the bottle and the country whores, and forget to wash his shirts and use a knife and fork with his dinner. So far he had managed to avoid it. With Nina Sanduzzi he might still avoid it. . . . But the risk was there–and there were faint trumpets sounding in the hills. Better forget it and go home to sleep.

It took him more than a week to nurse the patient out of danger. The wound was deep and new infections broke out, and he had to keep draining the wound with the primitive means at his disposal. More than one night he sat up, with Nina, watching the fever rise and break, until the false dawn lightened in the east and it was time to go home before the village was astir.

Each night he came, he felt the need of her. Each time he left, he felt a pang of jealousy at leaving her alone with the sick man, who now had begun to eat and talk a little between the fever bouts and the long intervals of restless sleep.

At first he was cautious with them; but when he understood Meyer's position as a political exile, and the risks the girl was taking for him, he relaxed a little, but still refused to tell them anything but the story he had first told Nina Sanduzzi.

'Better you don't know any more than that. If you're questioned, you can answer truthfully. Though I hope to God you won't be. I'm Giacomo Nerone, a gunner from Reggio. I'm trying to get back to Rome to my family. When do you think I'll be strong enough to travel, Doctor?'

Meyer shrugged.

'A fortnight, three weeks, maybe–unless you get another infection. But where do you aim to go? There's talk that the Allies have landed north of here, and that they're advancing up the toe from Reggio. But this place is a pocket in the hills. With our chaps pulling back and the Germans moving down, you'll have trouble getting very far. Your accent doesn't belong to Calabria. Sooner or later someone's going to ask questions . . . unless you're going into hiding again–and then how do you eat?'

Nerone smiled ruefully and they saw how the humour transfigured him, into a boy again.

'What else do you expect? I can't stay here.'

'Why not? demanded Nina Sanduzzi. 'There's a house and a bed and food. It's not much, but it's better than dying in a ditch with another bullet in you.'

The two men looked at each other. After a pause Meyer nodded dubiously.

'She could be right. Besides . . .' He made the point cautiously. 'When things change here, you might be in a position to help.'

The dark fellow shook his head.

'Not in the way you think, Doctor.'

Meyer frowned, then said bluntly:

'You don't understand me. I heard you talking in your sleep. You have other loyalties, it seems. These might be useful to us later.'

Now it was the girl's turn to stare. She demanded sharply:

'What do you mean, other loyalties?'

'I'm English,' said Nerone. 'And now that it's said, forget it.'

'English!' Nina Sanduzzi's eyes widened.

'Forget it!' said Meyer harshly.

'It's forgotten.' But she smiled as she said it and then put another proposition which left them momentarily speechless. 'If you stay here, there's no reason why you can't work for your living. . . . Don't look so surprised! There are half a dozen lads doing it this very minute. They've given the war away too. Two of them are locals and the others come from God knows where. But we're short of men, and there's a lot to be done before winter—and nobody wants to make a fuss about it. If there's anybody suspicious hanging around, the boys go to cover, but most of the time they work out in the open. . . .' She laughed cheerfully. 'And they're never short of a bed! I could get you a job with old Enzo Gozzoli. He's the foreman of my crowd. He's lost two sons in the war and he hates the Fascisti like poison. When you're better, I'll talk to him. . . . If you want to, that is.'

'I'll think about it,' said Giacomo Nerone. 'I'm very grateful but I'll have to think about it.'

He lay back on the pillow and closed his eyes, and a few moments later he lapsed into sleep.

The girl poured Meyer another cup of wine, and he drank it, thoughtfully, watching her as she bent over the bed, settling the dark head on the pillow, drawing the bedclothes carefully round the wounded shoulder, standing a moment in silent comtemplation of the sleeping guest.

When she came back, Meyer stood up, took her in his arms, and tried to kiss her. She pushed him away, gently.

'No, *dottore mio*. Not now.'

'I want you, Nina!'

'You don't want me really, *cara*,' she told him softly. 'Otherwise you'd have taken me long before now—and I'd have been glad of it. It's summer and you're lonely, and we've spent some evenings together. But I'm not for you and you know it. . . . Afterwards you would hate me. I want a man, God knows! But I want all of him.'

Meyer turned away and picked up his bag. He made a quick gesture towards the bed.

'Maybe you've got him!' he said dryly.

'Maybe,' said Nina Sanduzzi. Then she walked to the door and held it open for him, and as he walked up the hillside he heard it shut—a dry, sharp sound in the languid air.

. . . 'And that was the beginning of it?' asked Blaise Meredith.

'The beginning.' Meyer reached for the pitcher of wine. 'In three weeks he was out and about, working for Enzo Gozzoli. At night he went back to Nina's house and they were lovers.'

'And, beyond the fact that he was English, you still had no idea who he was?'

'No.' Meyer took a long swallow of wine and wiped his lips with a soiled handkerchief. 'There were three things he might have been: an escaped prisoner, a British agent sent to make contact with the first Partisan groups, a deserter.'

'And which did he look like to you?'

'I took them in turn and tried to fit him into the mould. An escaped prisoner? Yes. Except that he showed no inclination to do what such a man should do—try to rejoin his unit. An agent? This too. He spoke good Italian—not the *argot* of the cookhouse and the military brothel. He was an educated man. He was alive to the local colour. But when I threw out hints about joining me in an attempt to contact the Partisans, he refused.'

'Did he give any reason?'

'No. He refused politely, but quite definitely.'

'A deserter, then?'

Meyer pursed his thin lips thoughtfully.

'It seemed the most likely category. But a deserter is a man who is afraid. He has the fugitive look. He lives with the conviction that one day he must be caught. Nerone had none of that. Once he was well, he walked and talked and laughed like a free man.'

'Was he an officer?'

'I thought so. As I say, he was a cultivated man. He had the habit of decision, a talent for getting things done. But he carried no identification at all. I pointed out that if he were caught like this by the Germans or the Italians, he could be shot as a spy. He just laughed and said Giacomo Nerone was a good Italian who saw no reason in the war. . . . More wine, Monsignor?'

Meredith nodded vaguely, and as Meyer filled his glass he asked:

'What estimate did you form of his character at this first period?'

'Part of it, I've already given you,' said Meyer. 'Courage, good-humour, a capacity for getting things done. The rest? I wasn't quite sure. I was jealous of him, you see.'

'Because of Nina Sanduzzi?'

'That and other things. I had lived among these people, served them, too, for years. I had never arrived at intimacy with them. Nerone was at home in a week. The men trusted him. The women loved him. He could make them laugh by twitching his black eyebrows. They told him all the scandals and taught him dialect and shared their wine with him. I was still the outsider—the Jew from Rome.'

'I know how you felt,' said Meredith gently. 'I've been like that all my life. Except that I've never served anyone.'

Aldo Meyer shot him a quick appraising glance, but Meredith was staring absently at the dark wine in his cup. He went on.

'The thing that irritated me about him was that he seemed to take everything for granted and for permanent. As if the present were the only thing that mattered. For him it was natural enough, I suppose. He had had his war. He was content with the day. I had been waiting so long that I cried for action and for change.'

'So you were at odds with each other?'

Meyer shook his head.

'That's the queer part. When I didn't see him, I disliked him. But when we met in passing—or when, later, he used to come to my place in the evening to talk or borrow a book, he charmed me. There was a calm about him—a gentleness. The same sort of thing you find now in Nina Sanduzzi.'

'What did you talk about?'

'Everything–except Nerone. He refused any topic that might give me a clue to his identity. What interested him most was the place itself, the people, their history, their customs, their relationships with one another. It was as if he were trying to forget all that had belonged to him and absorb himself into the life of the mountains.'

'Was he concerned for them?'

'At first, no. He seemed to regard himself as one of them. But he had no plans as I had. No schemes for their betterment.'

'What were his relations with Nina Sanduzzi?'

Meyer grinned wryly and spread his hands in deprecation.

'They were happy together. One saw it in their faces. That was all I knew. More than I wanted to know. For the rest you'll have to talk to Nina.'

Meredith nodded.

'I'm sorry to press you like this, Doctor. But you understand what I am commissioned to do.'

'I understand. I'm not hedging. I'm trying to keep my evidence first-hand.'

'Please go on.'

'The next stage begins about the end of October . . . the middle of autumn. Nerone called me in to examine Nina. She was two months' pregnant.'

'What was his reaction to that?'

'He was glad of it. They both were. I think I was never more jealous of him than at that moment. He had come from nowhere and he had achieved what had eluded me all my life: acceptance, love, a promise of purpose and continuity.'

'Yet he made no move to marry Nina?'

'No.'

'Did she want it?'

'I put it to them both,' said Meyer carefully, 'not because I was concerned–in a country without men, there is no shame in a fatherless child–but because I wanted to see what sort of man this was.'

'What did he say?'

'Nothing. It was Nina who answered. She said: "Time enough for wedding bells, Dottore, when we know what is going to happen."'

'And Nerone?'

Meyer looked down at the backs of his hands, spread like spiders on the warm wood of the table. He hesitated a moment, then said:

'I remember the next part very well. Just when it seemed I had measured Nerone for what he was–a fly-by-night who would be on his way before the dawn showed–he surprised me again.'

'How?'

'He said, quite simply, apropos of nothing at all: "It's going to be a bad winter, Doctor. You and I had better start preparing for it now!"'

. . . In the old days, before the men were taken, before the war had started to go wrong, when there was still an authority and a purpose in the land, the winter had been bearable–if never a happy time.

There was charcoal in store and wine laid down and oil in the big green bottles. The onions hung in strings from the rafters and the corncobs were piled in the corner and there were potatoes buried in straw. There was cheese to be bought, and salami and smoked ham and lentils, and the millers had flour to sell for the pasta. The food was there, even if you had to scratch a hole in your breeches to find the money to buy it. Before the snows closed in, there was always a traffic of barter between the villages; and when work in the fields slowed down to a dead stop, the commune paid out a small dole to have the roads cleared and gravel spread on the ice patches.

It was a life—not much of a life, to be sure—but if you hung on to it long enough, you would hear the torrent roaring and smell the first warm winds from the south and feel the ice thawing out of your bones with the coming of spring.

But now there were no men and the crops were poor and the Quartermaster's levies took the best of them. The barter was a nothing, because who would take his donkey-cart to market and risk the thieves and deserters and patrols on the way? Better to stay at home and live on your own fat as long as you could. Besides, the boys were straggling back, leaderless, disillusioned and belly-hungry—new mouths to feed out of the diminished stores.

There was no government any more. Those officials who had been reasonable fellows stayed on, hoping their pay packets might arrive and, if they didn't, hoping for a small return for their kindness. Those who had been bastards were moving out, tagging themselves on to still active units, or selling themselves and their local knowledge to the German detachments moving south to engage the Allied Eighth Army.

And in Gemelli dei Monti they smelt the wind, and felt the first rain squalls, and counted the first frosts, and said: 'It's going to be a bad winter.'

Giacomo Nerone said it too, coolly and emphatically. But he added a rider or two of his own.

'You and I are the only people round here with any brains or any influence. We'll have to run the organisation.'

Meyer gaped at him, thunderstruck.

'For God's sake, man! You don't know what you're talking about. You're on the run! I'm a political exile. The moment we stick out our necks, they'll drop the axe on them.'

'Who's they, Doctor?' Nerone grinned at him.

'The authorities. The police. The *carabinieri*. The Mayor of Gemello Maggiore.'

Nerone threw back his head and laughed as heartily as if it were a washerwoman's joke down by the torrent.

'My dear doctor! These fellows are so scared just now, they're only interested in saving their own hides. We haven't seen any of 'em round here for weeks. Besides, this is our business, not theirs. We handle it ourselves.'

'Handle what, for God's sake?'

'The elementary problem of survival for three months. We've got to see that everyone gets enough food and fuel to keep alive during the winter. We've got to get you some more medicines and try to find some more blankets. We've got to set up a central store and see that rations are doled out fairly. . .'

'You're mad!' Meyer told him flatly. 'You don't understand these people. They're close-fisted at the best of times, but in famine they're like carrion birds. They'll eat out one another's livers before they'll let a crust of bread pass from one house to another. The family's the only thing that counts. The rest can rot in a ditch.'

'Then we'll teach 'em the next step,' said Nerone calmly. 'We'll make 'em a tribe.'

'You can't do it.'

'I've already started.'

'The hell you have!'

'I've got ten families to agree to put a quarter of their food stocks into a common store for the winter. Each of these families is going to try to bring in one more. Then you and I will go round and try to beat some sense into those who are still standing out.'

'I don't understand how you did it.'

Giacomo Nerone smiled and shrugged.

'I talked to them. I pointed out that there are still more levies to come: Italian, German, Allied. When things get tough—as they will in the winter—there'll be house searches for hoarded stocks. No, while the going's good, we'd better co-operate and build up a common store in a secret place. I told them Nina and I would make our own contribution first, as evidence of good faith; and then we'd set up a committee to administer it. You, me, and three others. Two men and a woman. It took a little time, but they agreed in the end.'

'I've been here all this time,' said Meyer sombrely, 'and I've never been able to do anything like that.'

'You have to pay a price for it, of course.'

Meyer stared at him puzzled.

'What sort of price?'

'I don't know yet,' said Nerone thoughtfully, 'but I think it will come very high in the end....'

... 'Did he explain what he meant?' asked Blaise Meredith.

'No.'

'Did you ask him to explain it?'

'Yes.' Meyer made a rueful mouth. 'But once again it was Nina who answered for him. She was standing behind him, I remember, and she bent down and kissed his hair and then held his face between her hands. Then she said: "I love this man, *dottore mio*. He's afraid of nothing—and he always pays his debts!"'

'Did that satisfy you?'

Meyer chuckled and thrust himself back in his chair to reach for the wine.

'You miss the point, Monsignor. When you see a man and a woman like that—and when you are in love with the woman yourself—there's only one satisfaction. And you can't have it. I got up and went home. Next day Nerone and I met again and began to prepare for winter.'

'And you succeeded?'

'Yes. Before the first snows came, everybody in Gemello Minore had agreed, and we had nearly three tons of supplies sealed up in the Grotta del Fauno.'

Recollections stirred sharply behind the thoughtful eyes of Blaise Meredith.

'The Grotto of the Faun. ... That's where they buried him, wasn't it?'

'That's where they buried him,' said Aldo Meyer.

II

While Blaise Meredith talked under the fig tree with Doctor Aldo Meyer, Anne Louise de Sanctis sat in the ornate salon at the villa and interviewed Nina Sanduzzi.

She had risen late, but less ill-tempered than usual, and when the servant informed her that Nina Sanduzzi was waiting to see her with the boy, she had taken a little longer with her breakfast and her toilet. She had chatted for ten minutes with Nicholas Black, who was off to the garden with his paint-box; she had looked over the household accounts and the menu for the evening meal; then she had settled herself in the salon and sent a servant to fetch Nina Sanduzzi.

Now they were alone while Paolo scuffed his feet on the path outside and watched the gardeners moving up and down the flower-beds and the flight of a yellow butterfly, lazy among the shrubbery.

The Contessa was seated in a high-backed chair, freshly groomed, faintly triumphant, her hands placid in her lap, her eyes searching the blank face of the peasant who stood before her, dusty from the road, feet bare in wooden sandals, but straight and proud as a tree waiting for the wind to blow.

'You understand,' said Anne Louise de Sanctis, 'this is a great opportunity for the boy.' She used the familiar *thou* to indicate the vast gulf that lay between the châtelaine and the servant.

'It is work,' said Nina Sanduzzi calmly. 'That is good for the boy. If he works well, it is good for you, too.'

'How does he feel about it? Is he glad to come?'

'Who can say how a boy feels? He is here. He is ready to start work.'

'We haven't yet discussed payment.'

Nina Sanduzzi shrugged indifferently.

'The *dottore* said you would pay what was usual.'

Anne Louise de Sanctis smiled benevolently.

'We'll do better than that. Signore Black tells me he is intelligent and willing. We'll pay him a man's wage.'

'For a man's work—good! So long as it is a man's work!'

The reply was barbed, but the Contessa, being weak in dialect, missed the sharpness of it. She went on, genial and condescending.

'If the boy works well and shows promise, we may be able to do much for him—give him an education, help him to make a career—send him to Rome, perhaps.'

Nina Sanduzzi nodded thoughtfully, but her eyes were veiled and expressionless as a bird's. She said simply:

'His father was an educated man. He used to say, one should educate the heart first and the head later.'

'Of course,' said the Contessa with unnatural brightness. 'His father! Giacomo Nerone was your lover, wasn't he?'

'He was the man I loved,' said Nina Sanduzzi. 'He loved me and he loved the boy.'

'Strange that he never married you.'

There was no flicker of emotion in the blank eyes and the calm face. The sentence hung suspended in the silence between them. Anne Louise de Sanctis was irritated. She wanted to strike out and see the marks of her fingers rise in weals on the other's olive cheeks. But this was an indulgence she could not afford, being committed to diplomacy and an alliance of smiles and concealment. She said briskly:

'The boy will lodge here, of course. He'll be well fed and comfortable. You can have him home with you on Sundays.'

'I've spoken to the Monsignor from Rome,' said Nina Sanduzzi quietly. 'I've asked him to talk with the boy and help him. These are awkward years in his life.'

'You shouldn't have bothered Monsignor Meredith,' the Contessa snapped at her. 'He's a sick man and busy with important affairs!'

'He is busy with my Giacomo, Signora. And what could be more important than Giacomo's son? Besides, the Monsignor said he would be happy to help.'

'You may go,' said the Contessa. 'Leave the boy here and the gardener will set him to work.'

Nina Sanduzzi made no move to go. Instead she stooped and picked up the straw bag she always carried. She fumbled inside it, brought up a small package neatly wrapped in paper and held it out to the Contessa.

'What's this?'

'My boy is coming into your house. He should not come empty-handed. It's a gift.'

The simple grace of the gesture embarrassed her. She took the package in her hands and said awkwardly:

'Thank you. May I ask what it is?'

'We are poor people,' said Nina Sanduzzi carefully. 'We give from our hearts and not from our wealth. One day Giacomo may be made a *beato*, and then this will be precious to you. It is part of what he wore when they killed him. His blood is on it. I would like you to have it—from his son!'

Anne Louise de Sanctis said nothing, but sat there, staring like a hypnotic at the package, her face dead white, her lips moving in a soundless murmur. When, after a long time, she looked up, Nina Sanduzzi was gone, and there was only the sunlight slanting in through dust motes, and a vista of green lawn where a boy walked side by side with a gardener—a boy who might have been her own son.

Aldo Meyer and Monsignor Blaise Meredith had got up from the table and were walking, side by side, up and down the flagged path that ran the full width of the garden. They passed alternately from sunlight into shadow and their shoes made a dry, crisp sound on the stones.

'To this point,' said Meredith, in his precise, legal fashion, 'what have we? A man in flight, a man in love, a man assuming leadership and responsibility in the community which has given him refuge. His past is a mystery. His future, a doubt in his own mind. His present . . . what you have told me. We have no indication of his religious belief or his moral attitude. On the face of it, he is living in sin. His acts, good in themselves, have no spiritual value. Now . . .' He kicked at a small pebble and watched it bound away towards the rough stone wall. 'Now, according to my records, he comes to a crisis, a moment of conversion, in which, or as a result of which, he turns away from this woman and surrenders himself to God. What do you know about this?'

'Less than I should, perhaps,' said Meyer deliberately. 'Certainly much less than Nina, to whom you will be talking this afternoon. But I do know something. I give it to you for what it's worth. . . .'

. . . The winter was harder than they had ever dreamed possible. The snows came down in blinding blizzards from the high peaks to the west; they piled in drifts along the roads and in the hollows. They choked the mountain tracks and broke the olive branches and heaped themselves against the doors of the houses. They froze hard, and the winds whipped the powder off them, leaving exposed ridges of ice like ripples on a dead white sea. Then came new calms and new downfalls so that a soft layer was laid on the hard rime underneath.

In the south the engaged armies dug themselves in and waited for the thaw. The patrols bivouacking in the hills lost men from exposure and frostbite. The stragglers and deserters hammered on barred doors in the night and, if they were not opened, died in the snow before morning.

Inside the houses, the families clung together for warmth in the big brass beds, rising only to relieve themselves or to seek food and brew coffee, because charcoal stock had to be conserved, and the earthen floors were frozen and the wind searched keenly through the cracked doors and the crazy window frames stuffed with mud and old newspapers. The old ones coughed and grumbled with the rheumatic cold in their joints; the young ones fretted with flushed cheeks and sore throats and congested chests; and when any of them died, as many did, they were carried out into the snow and buried there until the thaw—because who would make coffins in this bleak weather and who could turn a sod in the Campo Santo when the ground was frozen hard as granite?

They lived like hibernating animals, each litter an island in a sea of snow, drawing warmth from each other's bodies, familiar with each other's stench, munching blindly on the common crust, wondering bleakly how long they would last and whether there would ever be another spring.

If a knock came on the door, they ignored it. Who but thieves or crazy men or starving ones would be abroad at this time? If the knock was persistent, they cursed in chorus, until finally it stopped and they heard the crackling footsteps retreat across the frozen snow. There was only one knock they knew and one voice to which they answered—Giacomo Nerone's.

Every day and all day he was about, making the rounds of the houses—a black-jowled, smiling giant, with his boots wrapped in sacking and his body padded in layers of scarecrow garments and his head muffled in a cap made of one of Nina's stockings. On his back he carried an old army knapsack, filled with rations, and his pockets were stuffed with aspirin tablets and a bottle of cod-liver oil and odds and ends of medicine.

When he came into a house, he stayed as long as they needed him and no longer. He checked their food stocks, looked at the sick, dosed them when he could, cooked a broth for those who were incapable, cleaned up the accumulated messes and then moved on. But before he went there were always five minutes for news and greetings, and a couple of minutes for a joke to leave them laughing when he trudged out again into the waste. If they needed Meyer, he would bring him back. If they were ready for a priest, he tried to get one—though this was a rather more chancy proceeding since Father Anselmo was old and cold, and disinclined to stir, and the young curate from Gemello Maggiore often had his hands too full with his own dying.

Always his last call of the day was on Aldo Meyer. They would drink a thimbleful of *grappa*, exchange notes, and then Nerone would plunge off down the hill to Nina's hut.

At first he was cheerful, exulting in the challenge to his strength and vitality. Then, as December wore on into January and there was still no break in the weather, he began to get edgy, preoccupied, like a man who slept too little and thought too much. Meyer urged him to rest, give himself a couple of days at home with Nina, but he refused curtly, and afterwards seemed to drive himself even harder.

Then one evening when it was late and bitter with a new wind, he came in, dumped his pack on Meyer's floor, tossed off the *grappa* at one gulp and said abruptly:

'Meyer! I want to talk to you!'

'You always do,' said Meyer mildly. 'What's so different about tonight?'

Nerone ignored the irony and plunged on.

'I never told you why I came here, did I?'

'It's your own business. You didn't have to tell me.'

'I'd like to tell you now.'

'Why?'

'I need to.'

'It's a good reason,' said Meyer with a grin.

'Tell me . . . do you believe in God, Meyer?'

'I was brought up to believe in Him,' said Meyer guardedly. 'My friends the Fascisti have done their best to persuade me otherwise. Let's say I have an open mind in the matter. Why do you ask?'

'I could be talking nonsense to you.'

'It's a man's right to talk nonsense when he has a need.'

'All right. You make what you like of it. I'm English, you know that. I'm an officer, which you didn't know.'

'I guessed it.'

'I'm also a deserter.'

'What do you want me to say?' asked Meyer with dry humour. 'How much I despise you?'

'Say nothing, for God's sake. Just listen. I was in the advance guard for the assault on Messina. It was the last toe-hold in Sicily. For us, nothing to it. Your people were beaten. The Germans were pulling out fast. Just a mopping-up operation. My company was assigned to clean out a half-mile square of tenements leading down to the docks. Scattered snipers, a couple of machine-gun posts . . . nothing. There was a blind alley, with windows facing down towards us and a sniper in the top window. He had us pinned down for ten minutes at the mouth of the alley. Then, we thought we might have got him. We moved in. When we got to the house, I followed the usual routine, and shouted a surrender warning. There was another shot—from the lower window this time. It got one of my boys. I pitched a grenade through the window, waited for the burst and then went in. I found the sniper—an old fisherman, with a woman and a nursing child. All dead. The baby had taken the full burst. . . .'

'It happens in war,' said Meyer coolly. 'It's the human element. It has nothing to do with God.'

'I know,' said Giacomo Nerone. 'But I was the human element. Can you understand that?'

'Yes, I can understand it. So you decided this was the end for you. You had done what you'd been paid to do. You were dispensed from all the rest. Your war was over. Is that right?'

'More or less.'

'You went on the run. But where did you expect to go?'

'I didn't know.'

'Why did you come here?'

'I don't know that either. Call it an accident if you want.'

'Do *you* believe in God, Nerone?'

'I used to. Then for a long time I didn't.'

'And now?'

'Don't press me, man! Let me talk it out!'

Meyer shrugged and poured an extravagant measure of *grappa* into Nerone's glass. When Nerone protested, he said with wintry humour:

'*In vino veritas*. Drink it.'

Nerone held the glass with two shaky hands and drank it greedily, then wiped his chapped mouth with the back of his hand. He said moodily:

'When I met Nina, she was a refuge. When we fell in love it was more–a kind of absolution. When she became pregnant, I felt as if I was undoing what had been done; putting a new life back in the place of the one I'd destroyed. When we started to do something for these people, it was my kind of reparation to the old fisherman and the dead woman. . . . It wasn't enough. It still isn't enough.'

'It never is,' said Aldo Meyer. 'But where does God come in?'

'If He doesn't, it's all a monstrous folly. The death means nothing, the reparation means less. We're ants on the carcass of the world, spawned out of nothing, going busily nowhere. One of us dies, the others crawl over us to the pickings. This whole valley could freeze to death and it would mean nothing–nothing at all. . . . But if there is a God . . . everything becomes enormously important . . . every life, every death. . . .'

'And the reparation?'

'Means nothing at all,' said Nerone sombrely, 'unless you give yourself as part of it.'

'You're in deep water, my friend,' said Aldo Meyer gently.

'I know,' Nerone told him in a dead voice. 'I'm damn near drowning in it.'

He leaned his head on his hands and began running his fingers through his hair. Meyer came and sat on the edge of the table and said good-humouredly:

'Let me give a piece of advice, my friend–medical advice. You're running yourself ragged with fatigue and undernourishment. You've never been quite sure whether you were right or wrong to walk away from your war; and, because you're fatigued, you're beginning to worry about it. You've done a good job for all of us here and you're still doing it. Now, all of a sudden, you're preoccupied with God. If you'll forgive my saying so–half the shoddy mysticism in the world comes from bad digestion, overwork, lack of sleep or lack of sexual satisfaction. If you want a doctor's advice, stay at home and play honeymooners with Nina for a few days. Vote yourselves an extra day's ration and give yourselves a *festa*.'

Nerone looked up and his dark, stubbled face relaxed into a grin.

'You know, Meyer, that's where all you liberals make your mistake. That's why there's no place for you any more in the twentieth century. There are only two things you can do about God: affirm Him like the Catholics or deny Him like the Communists. You want to reduce Him to a belly-ache or a hot flush, or a comforting speculation for the coffee and cigars. You're a Jew. You should know better.'

'And what are you?' Meyer was nettled.

'I used to be a Catholic.'

'That's your trouble,' said Meyer definitely. 'You might make a good Communist, but you'll never make a good liberal. You're an absolutist at heart. You've got religion like an itch in the crutch, and you'll carry it till the day you die. . . . But my prescription still stands.'

'I'll think about it, Doctor. I've got to think about it—very carefully.'

. . . Meredith stopped walking and stood a moment in the shade of the fig tree, absently shredding one of the thick, tough leaves and feeling the white sap glutinous on his fingers. After a while, he said:

'This is the first glimmer I've seen of the thing one looks for in every case history: the entry of God into a man's calculations, the beginning of acceptance of the consequence of belief, the start of a personal relationship between Creator and Creature. If this theme continues. . .'

'It recurs,' said Meyer slowly. 'But there are gaps in my story. You'll have to fill them in from other witnesses, like Nina Sanduzzi.'

'If there were writings,' said Meredith thoughtfully, 'they would help immensely. One might be able to follow a personal attitude that would explain the external relationships.'

'There are writings, Monsignor. I have them.'

Meredith stared at him in surprise.

'Is there much of them?'

'There's a large packet. I haven't opened it yet. Nina gave them to me.'

'Could I see them?'

'If you don't mind waiting a while,' Meyer agreed awkwardly. 'I haven't read them myself yet. I've been afraid of them—in much the same way as you have been afraid of your request for a miracle. Somewhere in them may be the answer to a lot of questions that have plagued me for a long time. Till now I haven't been sure I wanted the answer. I'd like to read them this afternoon while you're talking to Nina. Then tomorrow I'll hand them over—with the rest of my own evidence. Would that satisfy you?'

'Certainly. Take longer if you want.'

'It's enough,' said Meyer with a wry smile. 'You're a good confessor, Meredith. I'm glad to talk with you.'

A grave pleasure dawned in the eyes of Blaise Meredith. He said:

'If only you knew how glad I am to hear that.'

Meyer looked at him quizzically.

'Why, Monsignor?'

'For the first time in my life, I think, I am beginning to be close to people. It terrifies me to think how much time I've wasted—and how little there is left.'

'Afterwards,' said Meyer soberly. 'You will be close to God.'

'That terrifies me most of all,' said Blaise Meredith.

In a far corner of the villa grounds, Paolo Sanduzzi was at work, sawing a fallen olive tree into firewood. The head gardener, a taciturn fellow, himself gnarled and dark as a tree, had left him there with a curt direction to keep his hands out of his pockets and work off his puppy fat, and have the whole tree cut and corded by sundown.

He was glad to be alone. The place was new and strange. This was his first man's work and his hands were clumsy and inexpert. To be laughed at would be an agony, and he needed time to learn the rhythm of the tool he was using, and the idioms of this life among the *signori*.

He had stripped off his shirt because the sun was hot, and after lopping away the twigs with a hatchet, had set to work sawing off the main branches. The wood was dry and easy enough to cut, but he was too eager and the saw jammed and twanged in his hand until, little by little, he fell into the knack of it, and the teeth bit cleanly into the wood while the sawdust spilled on to the leaves at his feet. He liked the sound of it and the smell of it and the salt taste of the sweat trickling down his face to the corners of his mouth.

It would have been pleasant to have Rosetta here to sit and talk with him and admire his skill, but she was not coming till tomorrow and then she would be in the kitchen with the cook, or dusting and polishing about the villa with the other maids. She would sleep in the women's quarters, sharing a bed with one of the young girls, while he would have his own place—a narrow cubbyhole next to the tool shed, with a straw mattress and a chair and a box with a candle on it. But they would meet at meals and walk out on Sundays, and perhaps at siesta time they might steal an hour together. He would feel better when she was there; less raw and less afraid of the Contessa, whom he had not met, and of the Englishman, whom he had met all too often.

Now that his secret was out and shared with the doctor, now that he knew more of his father, he felt safer, more his own man. To be a bastard was no longer a terrifying mystery, and to be attracted by the Englishman was not, it seemed, so strange a thing at all.

Perhaps even a way might be found to do the thing he wanted most of all: shake the dust of the village off his sandals and go to Rome, where the Pope lived and the President, and the streets were full of fountains and everyone had a car and the girls wore smart clothes and shoes and every house had running water and, sometimes, even a bath and a toilet. These were wonders about which the painter had spoken to him often, and their magic was still strong on him. He had made the first step. He had left the village and entered the green, enclosed world of the villa. Rome was so much nearer, so much more possible.

Thinking of Rome, he thought naturally of Nicholas Black, with his mocking eyes and his mouth twisted up in the smile that could make you feel either a man or a child, and could promise all kinds of revelations without a word spoken. The impression was so vivid that when a dry twig cracked behind him, he spun round, startled, expecting to see the Englishman behind him.

Instead it was the Contessa who stood there, bright as a butterfly, in a new spring frock, with a scarlet beach hat shading her face from the sun.

Not knowing what to do or say, he stood gape-mouthed, arms hanging slackly at his sides, feeling the sweat running down his face and chest, yet not daring to move and brush it away. Then she smiled at him and the smile was in her eyes, too.

'Did I startle you, Paolo?'

'A little,' he mumbled awkwardly.

The Contessa came closer and looked around at the sawn wood.

'You've been working hard, I see. That's good. If you work well for me, Paolo, you'll never be sorry.'

'I'll try, signora.'

Her smile gave him confidence, and when she drew her skirts aside to sit down on the fallen trunk of the olive, he acted on a sudden impulse and spread his shirt on the rough bark.

'The tree's dirty, signora. You'd spoil your dress.'

'Charming boy!' murmured Anne Louise de Sanctis. 'That was the sort of thing your father would do. Did you know I knew your father?'

'Did my father work for you, too, signora?'

'Dear me, no!' She gave a high, tinkling laugh. 'Your father was a friend of mine. He used to come here sometimes to visit me. He was a *signore—a gran' signore*!'

He felt a sudden pang of shame that he should be standing here, a servant, where his father had once walked as a guest of the house. Before he had time to answer, the Contessa went on.

'That's why I brought you here, for your father's sake. Mr Black tells me you're bright and learn things quickly. If that's true, we may be able to make you into a gentleman like your father.'

There was no mention of his mother, he noticed, and once again he was ashamed of her, with her rough dialect and her coarse clothes and her bare dusty feet. He said quickly:

'I'd like that, signora. I'll work well, I promise.' Then, made bold by her approving smile, he told her: 'I don't know very much about my father. What was he like?'

'He was English,' said the Contessa. 'Like me, like Signor Black and the Monsignor from Rome.'

'English!' He seemed not to believe the sound of his own voice. 'That means I'm half-English too!'

'That's right, Paolo. Didn't your mother ever tell you?'

He shook his head.

'Didn't she ever say how much you were like him?'

'Sometimes. But not very often.'

'That's another reason why I want you to do well here. I'll see that you go to school at Valenta, learn to read and write and speak properly, wear the right clothes. Then, perhaps, you can be my friend, too. Would you like that?'

'And could I go to Rome?'

'Of course!' She smiled at him. 'You want that very much, don't you?'

'So much, signora!'

'I might ask Signor Black to take you there for a visit.' She was still smiling at him but there was an odd warning in her eyes. Without quite knowing why, Paolo said quickly:

'I'd much rather go with you.'

As he flung out his arms in the Southern gesture of appeal, she caught his hands and drew him down so that he was half-kneeling, half-squatting, at her feet. Her perfume was all about him and he could see her breasts rising and falling under the thin frock. She took his face in her hands and tilted it up towards her and said softly:

'Before I could do that, Paolo, I'd have to trust you. You'd have to know how to keep secrets. Not to gossip to the village people—not even to the Monsignor or Signor Black.'

'I would, signora. I promise.'

'Then we'll think about it, Paolo. But not a word—even to your mother.'

'Not a word.'

Her hands were soft and perfumed on his cheeks and he had the odd feeling that she wanted to bend down and kiss him; but at the same moment there was the sound of a footfall behind them and the bland voice of Nicholas Black said:

'Really, *cara*! You're quite shameless. The boy hasn't lost his milk teeth and you're trying to seduce him already.'

'You're a fine one to talk about seduction, Nicki!'

The words were English and Paolo did not understand them; but when he looked up at the thin satyr's face of the painter and the flushed angry one of the Contessa, he felt trapped—like a mouse in a corner with two cats ready to pounce.

Shortly after noon, Blaise Meredith returned to the villa to wash and rest awhile before luncheon. He was not unpleased with his morning's work. Meyer was a good witness and his recollections were dispassionate but vivid; so that, for the first time since his assignment began, Meredith was beginning to see Giacomo Nerone as a man and not a legend.

He would have preferred to lunch with Meyer, to have gone on talking about the next critical period in Nerone's life. But Meyer had not invited him, and Meredith sensed that he needed time to recover himself and privacy to begin his reading of the papers of the dead man.

As he lay back, resting on the bed, feeling the familiar ache in the pit of his belly, he wondered how he should comport himself at the meal with the Contessa and Nicholas Black. Now that he knew the Contessa for a liar and the pair of them for conspirators, his position was vastly distasteful to him. As a house-guest he was bound by discretion and courtesy. As a priest, he could not make himself, even by silence, a partner in the corruption of a child. As Devil's Advocate he came in search of evidence and he needed co-operation from his witnesses.

Once again, as it had done in the house of Father Anselmo, the case of Giacomo Nerone faded into unimportance. There were souls at stake, and if priesthood meant anything it meant the care of souls. A simple statement but a complex proposition. One solved nothing by waving the commandments like a bludgeon at people's heads. There was no point in shouting damnation at a man who was already walking himself to hell on his own two feet. One had to pray for the Grace of God and then go probing like a good psychologist for the fear that might condition him to repentance or the love that might draw him towards it. Even then one had to wait for the place and the propitious moment—and one could still fail in the end. When one's own body was sick and one's mind preoccupied, the difficulty doubled itself.

When lunch-time came, he got up, combed his hair, put on a light summer cassock and walked down to the terrace under the striped awning. Nicholas Black was already seated alone at the table. He waved an airy greeting and said:

'The Contessa sends her apologies. She has a migraine. She'll lunch in her room. She hopes to see us both at dinner.'

Meredith nodded and sat down, and immediately a servant spread his napkin and poured wine and iced water into the glasses before him.

'A good morning, Monsignor?' asked the painter.

'Very good. Very informative. Doctor Meyer's an excellent witness.'

'A clever fellow. I'm amazed he hasn't done better for himself.'

Meredith shrugged off the insinuation. He had no wish to be drawn into an argument with the *antipasto*. Black dug into his plate and sipped his wine and they ate in silence for a while. Then the painter asked again:

'How is your health, Monsignor?'

'Indifferent, I'm afraid. Meyer gives me a worse prognosis than I expected. Three months, he says.'

'Do you have much pain?'

'Quite a lot.'

'In three months,' said the painter, 'you'll hardly finish your case.'

Meredith smiled ruefully.

'I'm afraid not. Fortunately the Church doesn't care to hurry these things. A century or two is neither here nor there.'

'And yet I have the impression that you are anxious to get through with it.'

'The witnesses are available,' Meredith told him coolly. 'Some of them are co-operative. The more testimony I can collect now the better for everybody. Besides ...' He wiped a crumb from the corner of his pale mouth. 'When your term has been set, you suddenly become aware of the shortness of it. "The night comes, when no man can work."'

'Are you afraid of death, Monsignor?'

'Who isn't?'

'At least you're frank about it. Many of your colleagues aren't, you know.'

'Many of them haven't yet had to face the reality,' said Meredith tartly. 'Have you?'

Black chuckled and took a long swallow of wine, then leaned back in his chair while the servant changed the dishes in front of him. He said in mock apology:

'I'm teasing you, Monsignor. Forgive me.'

Meredith bent over his fish and said nothing. A few moments later, Paolo Sanduzzi came out of the shrubbery and walked across the lawn in the direction of the kitchen. The painter watched him, and Meredith watched the painter with a sidelong speculative eye. When the boy had disappeared round the angle of the house, Black turned back to the table and said casually:

'Charming boy. A classic David. Pity to think he'll go to seed in a village like this. I wonder the Church doesn't do something for him. You can't have the son of a *beato* chasing the girls and getting into trouble with the police like any other youth, can you?'

The bland effrontery of the man was too much for Meredith. He put down his knife and fork with a clatter, and said, with cold precision:

'If the boy is corrupted, Mr Black, you will be the one to do it. Why don't you go away and leave him alone?'

To his surprise the painter threw back his head and laughed.

'Meyer must have been a very good witness indeed, Monsignor. What else did he tell you about me?'

'Isn't that enough?' asked Meredith quietly. 'You are doing a detestable thing. Your private vices are a matter between you and the Almighty. But when you are set out to corrupt this boy, you are committing a crime against nature.... '

The words were hardly out of his mouth before Black cut him short.

'You've judged me already, haven't you, Meredith? You've picked up every shred of filthy gossip round the village and damned me with it, before you've heard a word in my defence.'

Meredith flushed. The accusation was uncomfortably close to the truth. He said quietly:

'If I've misjudged you, Mr Black, I'm deeply sorry. I'd be more than happy to hear you deny these—these rumours.'

The painter laughed bitterly.

'You want me to defend myself to you? Damned if I'll do it, Monsignor. I'll take you on your own ground instead. Let's say I am what everybody calls me—an unnatural man, a corrupter of youth. What does the Church offer me by way of faith, hope or charity?' He stabbed a lean, accusing finger at the priest. 'Let's understand each other, Meredith. You can bluff your penitents and charm your Sunday congregations, but you can't fool me! I've been a Catholic myself and I know the whole shoddy routine. You know why I left the Church? Because it answers every damn question in the book—except the one you need answering. ... "Why?" You tell me I'm committing a sin against nature because you think I'm fond of this boy and intend to get him. Let's examine that. If you can give me a satisfactory answer, I'll make you a promise. I'll pack my bags and leave here on the first available transport. Do you agree to that?'

'I can't bargain with you,' said Meredith sharply. 'I'll listen and I'll try to answer. That's all.'

Nicholas Black laughed harshly.

'You're hedging already, you see. But I'll take you all the same. I know your whole argument on the question of the use and misuse of the body. God made it first for the procreation of children and then for the commerce of love between man and woman. That's the end. All its acts must conform to the end and all else is sin. The sin according to nature is an act in excess of the natural instinct ... like sleeping with a girl before you marry her, or lusting after another man's wife. To want a boy, in the same fashion, is a sin against nature. ... ' He grinned sardonically at the pale, intent face of the priest. 'Do I surprise you, Meredith? I was stuffed full of Aquinas, too. But there's a catch, and here's what I want you to tell me. What about my nature? I was born the way I am. I was a twin. See my brother before he died and you'd have seen the perfect male—the excessive male, if you want. Me? ... It wasn't quite clear what I was to be. But I knew soon enough. It was my nature to be drawn more to men than to women. I wasn't seduced in the shower-room or blackmailed in the bar. This is what I am. I can't change it. I didn't ask to be born. I didn't ask to be born like this—God knows I've suffered enough because of it. But who made me? According to you—God! What I want and what I do is according to the nature He gave me.... '

In the passion of the argument his attitude had changed from a sardonic insult to a plea for understanding. He himself was unconscious of it, but Meredith was quick to see it, and he was again ashamed of his own obtuseness. Here was the place and the moment made ready for him, but again, it seemed, for lack of wisdom and sympathy he had misused them. The painter plunged on, the words tumbling out of him in a bitter spate.

'. . . Look at yourself! You're a priest. You know damn well that if I were setting out to seduce a girl at this moment instead of young Paolo, you'd take an entirely different view. You'd disapprove, certainly! You'd read me a lecture on fornication and all the rest. But you wouldn't be too unhappy. I'd be normal . . . according to nature! But I am not made like that. God didn't make me like that. But do I need love the less? Do I need satisfaction less? Have I less right to live in contentment because somewhere along the line the Almighty slipped a cog in creation? . . . What's your answer to that, Meredith? What's your answer for *me*? Tie a knot in myself and take up badminton and wait till they make me an angel in Heaven, where they don't need this sort of thing anymore? . . . I'm lonely! I need love like the next man! My sort of love! Do I live in a padded cell till I die? You're the Church and the Church has all the answers! Give me this one!'

He broke off and sat, waiting, his silence a greater challenge to Meredith than the rush of his invective. Meredith stared down at the small chaos of crumbs on his plate and picked over the words to frame his answer. He tried to make a silent prayer for this soul, naked in front of him—but the prayer, like the argument he gave, seemed strangely arid and impotent. After a moment, he answered gravely:

'You tell me you've been a Catholic. Even if you weren't you'd understand the words and what they mean. To your problem—and to lots of others—there's no answer that doesn't involve a mystery and an Act of Faith. I can't tell you why God made you the way you are any more than I can tell you why he's planted a carcinoma in my stomach to make me die painfully while other men die peacefully in their sleep. The cogs of creation seem to slip all the time. Babies are born with two heads, mothers of families run crazy with carving knives, men die in plague, famine and thunderstorms. Why? Only God knows.'

'If there is a God.'

'I'll accept the "if",' said Meredith, with quiet concern. 'If there is no God, then the universe is a chaos with no meaning. You live in it as long and as pleasantly as you can, for the best you can get out of it. You take your Paolo and enjoy him—the police and social custom permitting. I can't quarrel with you. But if there is a God—and I believe there is—then. . .'

'Don't tell me the rest of it, Monsignor,' said the painter bitterly. 'I know it by heart. No matter what a bloody mess Creation gets into, you take it and like it; because that's a cross God lays on your back. If you take it long enough, they'll make you a saint like Giacomo Nerone. That's no answer, Meredith.'

'Have you got a better one, Mr Black?'

'I have indeed. You keep your cross and your hair-shirt, Meredith. I'll take the cash in hand and waive the rest!'

He pushed back his chair, got up from the table, and without another word walked into the house. Blaise Meredith wiped his clammy hands on his napkin and took a sip of wine to moisten his dry lips. He was surprised to find it suddenly sour, like vinegar on a sponge.

12

Early the same afternoon, in the small hut between the ilexes, Nina Sanduzzi talked with the Monsignor from Rome. They sat, one on either side of the rough scrubbed table, halfway between the open door and the big brass bed where Giacomo Nerone had slept and where his son had been born. After the blaze outside, the room was cool and shadowy and even the chatter of the cicadas was muted to a half-heard monotone.

The tramp down the hill had tired Meredith quickly; his face was grey and his lips bloodless, and a small knot of pain tightened in the pit of his stomach. Nina Sanduzzi looked at him with faint pity. She had small experience of priests and those she knew, like Father Anselmo, had little to recommend them. But this one was different; he would have understanding and delicacy. He would not trespass too roughly on the privacy of her past with Giacomo. Still, she was cautious, and when he began to question her she answered briefly and without embellishment. Meredith for his own part was sedulously delicate.

'I want you to understand something first: there are questions that must be asked. Some of them may seem strange—even brutal. I ask them, not because I think ill of Giacomo Nerone, but because we must try to know everything, good and bad, about this man. Do you understand that, signora?'

She nodded calmly.

'Better you should call me by my name, Nina. The doctor does and you are a friend of his.'

'Thank you. Now, Nina, my information is that shortly after his arrival in Gemello you and Giacomo Nerone began to live together.'

'We were lovers,' said Nina Sanduzzi. 'It's not quite the same thing.'

Meredith, the legalist, smiled, where once he might have frowned. He went on.

'You were a Catholic, Nina. So was Giacomo. Didn't you think this was a sin against God?'

'When you are lonely, Monsignor, when there is fear just outside the door, and the winter is coming and tomorrow you may not be alive, you think of these things and you forget about sin.'

'You can never quite forget.'

'Not quite. But when these things happen so often—even to priests—they do not look so bad.'

Meredith nodded. A week ago, he might have understood less and said more. Now he knew that the heart had deeper reasons than most preachers ever knew. He asked again:

'Your relations with this man—your physical relations—were they normal? Did he ever ask you for what should not be done between men and women?'

She stared at him in momentary puzzlement. Then her head went up proudly.

'We loved each other, Monsignor. We did what lovers do and were glad of each other. What else could there be?'

'Nothing,' said Meredith hastily. 'But if you loved each other so much, why didn't you marry? You were having a child. Did you owe nothing to him? What did Giacomo think?'

For the first time since he had known her, he saw a smile brighten on her lips and in her eyes. It was like an echo of the old Nina—the one who had wanted a man to hold in her arms and was prepared to face the executioner to get him. She told him in vivid, slangy dialect:

'You all ask the same question—as if it were big and important instead of a wart on a green melon. You don't understand how it was in those days. Only today was certain. Tomorrow the police might come or the Germans or the English. We could all die of the *tifo* or of malaria. A ring on your finger meant nothing. I had a ring, but I had no man to go with it.'

'Did Giacomo refuse to marry you?'

'I never asked him. More than once he told me he would marry me if I wanted it.'

'And you didn't want it?'

Once again the old fire flickered in her eyes, and the proud Greek smile twitched at the corners of her mouth.

'You still don't see it, Monsignor. I had a husband once. I wanted to hold him and the Army took him away to be killed. Now I had a man. If he wanted to go—he would go and no ring would keep him. If the police took him or the soldiers, he would still be lost to me. Marriage might come later, if ever it were important enough. Besides, there was another thing Giacomo talked about often....'

'What was that?'

'He had it fixed in his head that one day, soon, something would happen to him. He was a deserter and if the English won the war they would take him. The Fascisti were active still and they might take him. Or the Germans. If they did, I would never know whether he was alive or dead. He wanted me to be free to marry again. Free to disown him so that they could not punish me and the child.'

'Was that important to you, Nina?'

'To me, no. But to him, yes. If it made him happy to feel that, I was happy too. Nothing else mattered. Have you never been in love, Monsignor?'

'Never, I'm afraid.' Meredith's thin lips puckered into a smile. 'You'll have to be patient with me. . . . Tell me, when you were living together, what sort of a man was Giacomo? Was he good to you?'

It was almost eerie to see how memory flooded back on her and how her whole body seemed to come alive like a flower in the rain. Even in her voice there was a kind of splendour.

'What sort of man? . . . How do you expect me to answer that, Monsignor? Everything a woman wants was in this man. He was strong in bed and yet gentle as a babe. He could be angry so that you trembled at the silence of him and yet he never lifted his hand or raised his voice. When I served him, he was grateful and thanked me as if I were a princess. When I was afraid, he would make me laugh and when he laughed it was like the sun coming up in the morning. He was afraid of nobody and nothing except that I should be hurt. . . .'

'And yet,' said Meredith, with calculated bluntness, 'he left you in your pregnancy and never lived with you again.'

Her head came up, proud as a marble goddess in the sun.

'We lived in love and we parted in love – and there was never a day afterwards that I did not love him. . . .'

. . . Winter fretted itself out in a long alternation of storms and frozen calms. In the village and in the mountains there was much sickness. Some died and some recovered – but slowly, because of the damp and the foulness of the closed hovels and because food was getting scarcer every day.

Once there was an epidemic in which people came out in spots and had sore eyes and fever. Nina herself fell sick of it, and she remembered the doctor and Giacomo talking gravely in the corner about something they called *rubella*. But she got better soon and thought no more of it.

Even Giacomo Nerone was showing the strain of the long, cold time. The flesh was being honed off his big frame; his dark, stubbled cheeks were hollow and his eyes were sunken and burning when he trudged home from a day in the hills.

Nina, with the constant nausea and tiredness that comes to some women in early pregnancy, found the monotony of the food revolted her, and as her body thickened slowly, she was even disinclined for the love-making in which formerly she had taken so much and such frank delight. Both these things troubled her. A man was a man and he demanded to be soothed and satisfied, however his woman felt. But Giacomo was different from the men of her own people. He was gentle with her when she was sick. He made, with his own hands, food to tempt her. If she was unready for him, he would not force himself on her, and in the long mourning nights of the storm he would distract her with stories of strange places and people and cities piled like blocks almost to the sky.

She loved him the more for his attentions because she knew he had his own troubles: problems that kept him wakeful at night and preoccupied in the daytime. Sometimes he would talk them out with her, fumbling for the right phrase in dialect to explain his meaning. In this, too, he was different from her own menfolk, who took their counsel in the wineshop and not from their wives, because a woman was supposed to know nothing but the house and the bed and the simpler aspects of religion. But Giacomo talked freely, so that she felt strong and wise with him.

'Listen, Nina *mia*, you know how it is sometimes, that a man does a thing and his woman hates him, because she doesn't understand why?'

'I know, *caro mio*, but I understand you. So why should you worry?'

'Whatever I did, you would still love me?'

'Always.'

'Then listen now, Nina. Don't stop me talking, because this is hard to say. When I'm finished tell me if you don't understand. For a long time now I've been a lost man. I've been like a Calabrese standing in the middle of Rome and asking everyone: "Who am I? Where did I come from? Where am I going?" No one answers him, of course, because they don't understand him. . . . And even if they did, he wouldn't understand because he doesn't speak with a Roman tongue. It wasn't always like this. There was a time when I was like you. I knew that I came from God and would go back to Him in the end, that I could talk to Him in the Church and take Him to myself in Communion. I could do wrong and still be forgiven. I could stray a little and still come back to the straight road. . . . Then, suddenly, there was no road. There was darkness and voices shouting at me: This way! That way! I followed the voices into a deeper darkness and then there were other voices. But no road—I was lost. There was no God, no Church, no place to go in the end. I was your Calabrese shouting in a city of strangers. . . . When this thing happened to me in Messina I could not be like other men and say: "This is war! This is the price of peace! I will forget about it and go on fighting for what I believe." I didn't believe in anything—in war, in peace, in anything at all! There was just a child, a woman and an old man whom I had killed for no good reason at all. . . . Then I began to run, and suddenly, without knowing why or how, I am here with you—home again. But nothing is quite the same. I am changed. It is not dark any more but misty, like the valley in the first grey of morning. I see you and I know you and love you, because you are near and you love me, too. But outside the door there is the mist and the strangeness. Even the people are different. They look at me with wondering eyes. For no reason that I know, I am a big fellow to them. They depend on me. I am their Calabrese who has been to the big city and seen it all, who knows the Pope and the President and the way to get things done. I am their man of confidence. I should be proud of this, but I am not, because I am walking in the mist, still uncertain where I came from and where I am going and what I should do. . . . Can you understand me, Nina? Or am I talking like a crazy man?'

'You are talking to me with love, *caro mio*, and my heart understands.'

'Will you understand what I am going to ask you?'

'When you hold me like this and I can feel the love in your hands and in your voice, nothing is hard.'

'It is hard for me to tell you. . . . When the spring comes and life is easier, I want to leave you—go away for a while.'

'No, *caro mio*!'

'Not from the valley. From this house.'

'But why, *caro mio*? Why?'

'There are two reasons and the first is mine. I want to find myself a small secret place—build it, if I must, with my own two hands. I want to live there alone with this God whose face I cannot see any more. I want to say to him: Look, I am lost. It's my own fault, but I am lost. If You are there, speak to me clearly. Show me who I am, where I come from, where I am going. These people of Yours who know You—why do they turn to me and not to You to help them? Is there a mark on my forehead I cannot read? If there is, tell me what it means. . . .' I must do this, *cara*.'

'And what about me and your child?'

'I will be here all the time. I will see you often and if God speaks to me, I will speak to Him for you—because if He knows anything at all, He knows I love you.'

'And yet you go away?'

'There is love in this, too, Nina—more love than you know. And there is great reason in it, too. When spring comes the armies will be on the move again. The Germans will come first and there will be fighting south of here. The Partisans will move in to harry the Germans, and the Allies must in the end push them back. Some of these or all of them will come, in their turns, to Gemello. I will come under their notice because of what I am—Giacomo Nerone, the man of confidence, the big, black one. If I am lucky, they will accept me and I can help the people. If I am not, one or other of them will take me—and possibly kill me.'

'*Dio!* No!'

'It may happen, Nina. It may be this is what lies behind the mists and that I will see at the one time the face of God and the face of the executioner. I don't know. But, whatever happens, when spring comes we must be separate. You cannot be involved with me, because there is the child. If I am taken, Meyer will look after you. If not, I shall be here to look after you. And if it falls well, I shall marry you and give the boy my name. You are both mine and I love you and I will not let you suffer for me or the people.'

'I will suffer anyway, when you are not here.'

'Less that way than the other, Nina. There will be so much hate, you will not believe it possible. I've seen it all before and it is very terrible.'

'Hold me, *caro mio*! Hold me, I'm afraid.'

'Lie on my arm, *carissima*, and hear my heart beating. I'm your man of confidence, too, and you can sleep safe.'

'Now, perhaps–but when you are gone?'

'I shall never be wholly gone, Nina *mia*. Never, till eternity.... '

... The Biblical simplicity of her narrative was more compelling than any rhetoric, and Blaise Meredith, the dry man from the Congregations, found himself hurried along by it like a twig in a torrent. Even through the harsh dialect the dialogue rang like a poet's lines in the mouth of a lover–long cherished and long remembered. Behind them the face of Giacomo Nerone took shape and hardened into reality–a lean, dark, suffering face, with a tender mouth and deep eyes suffused with gentleness. The face of a searcher–one of those on whom is laid the burden of mysteries and who come sometimes to a great holiness.

But this was not enough for the grey lawyers at the Congregation of Rites, the inquisitors at the Holy Office. They must see more than this, and Blaise Meredith must give it to them. So, more gently, but no less persistently, he questioned Nina Sanduzzi again:

'When did he leave you?'

'After the thaw, when the spring was breaking.'

'And up till the time he left, he slept with you–made love to you?'

'Yes. Why?'

'Nothing. It is a question that must be asked.' But what he did not say to her was what it proved to him. This was still a man in the dark, a searcher, perhaps, but one who had not yet found his God, nor made the act of abandonment to His will. There was love in him, but it was yet a defaced symbol of the love which is the beginning of sanctity.

'And when he left, what then?'

'He went up into the neck of the valley where the caves are and began to build his hut. While it was building, he slept in a cave and cooked his own food and in the daytime did what he had done in the winter–travelled the valley, working for those who could not work, looking after the sick, bringing food to those who needed it.'

'Did you see him during this time?'

'He came every day, as he promised.'

'Was he changed at all?'

'To me? No. Except that he was more gentle and more careful of me.'

'Did he make love to you?'

Once again she smiled at him with that faint pity for his clerical ignorance.

'I was big with the child, Monsignor. I was calm and content . . . and he did not ask it.'

'Had he changed in himself?'

'Yes. He was thinner than I had ever seen him. His eyes were sunk right back in his head and his skin was stretched tight over the bones of his face. But he was always smiling and much happier than I had known him.'

'Did he say why?'

'At first, no. Then one day he took my hands in his and said: 'I'm home, Nina. I'm home again.' He had been over to Gemello Maggiore to make his confession to young Father Mario and on the Sunday he told me he was going to Communion. He asked if I would go to church the same day.'

'And did you?'

'No. On the Saturday the Germans arrived and made their headquarters in the villa. . . .'

. . . They came, early in the morning, while the village was still rubbing the sleep out of its eyes. There was an armoured car, with a sergeant driver and a worried-looking captain sitting in the back. There were two truckloads of troops and a fourth vehicle loaded with ammunition and supplies. They churned up the dusty road with engines roaring, checked a little in the narrow street of the village with a clatter of gears and some strange cursing, then headed straight up the last hill to the villa of the Contessa de Sanctis.

Nina Sanduzzi heard them come, but paid small attention. She was still heavy with sleep, wrapped in the remote contemplation of a woman who feels the first life stirring inside her. She did not wake fully until she heard the urgent knocking on the door and Aldo Meyer's voice calling her to open it.

When she let him in, she was surprised to see him dressed for the road, with heavy boots and a sheepskin jacket and a pack hitched on to his shoulders. First he asked her to feed him, and while she bustled to do it he talked to her in swift, terse sentences—half-fearful, half-elated.

'When you see Giacomo tell him I've pulled out. The Germans are here and it won't be long before they hear there's a Jew in the valley. If they catch me, I'll be shipped north to the concentration camps. I'm taking my instruments and some medicines, but I've left a stock for Giacomo in the big box under my bed.'

'But where are you going, Dottore?'

'Farther east, into the hills, towards San Bernardino. It's a Partisan hideout and I've been in contact with them for some time. Their leader's a man who calls himself Il Lupo. I think he came from the North especially for this job. He has the look of a trained man. He has guns and ammunition and a good system of communication. If Giacomo wants to get in touch with me, tell him to go out along the San Bernardino road for about ten kilometres, then turn off at the place they call Satan's Rock. That's where the first Partisan sentries are. He's to climb to the top of the rock, sit down and light a cigarette—then take his handkerchief and knot it round his neck. Someone will come out to make contact with him. Have you got that? It's important. If he forgets, he's liable to get shot.'

'I won't forget.'

She laid coffee and bread and cheese in front of him, and while he ate she made a parcel of food and stuffed it into his knapsack. It was only when she saw the pistol and felt the hard shapes of the ammunition clips that she understood what Giacomo had told her. The war was coming to Gemello Minore and all the hate and killing, too.

With his mouth full of bread and cheese, Meyer said to her:

'I tried to get Giacomo to come with me and bring you too. The Germans won't be much kinder to him than to me. He could be shot as a spy.'

'What did Giacomo say to that?'

'Just laughed and told me he knew the Germans better than I did. I hope he's right. What time do you usually see him?'

She shrugged and made a vague gesture with her hands.

'It changes. Sometimes early in the day, sometimes late. But he always comes.'

Meyer looked at her quizzically over the rim of his cup.

'Are you happy with this arrangement, Nina?'

'I'm happy with Giacomo. There was never another man like this.'

Meyer smiled sourly.

'You could be right at that. Do you know what he does up there in his hut?'

'He prays. He thinks. He works in his garden . . . when he isn't working for someone else or out among the hills. Why do you ask?'

'I went up there the other night to look for him and talk about this thing. I called to him, but there was no answer although his lamp was burning. I went inside and found him kneeling in the middle of the floor with his arms stretched out. His eyes were closed and his head was thrown back and his lips were moving. I spoke to him and he didn't hear me. I went up and shook him, but his body was quite rigid. I couldn't budge him. After a while I went away.'

There was no surprise in her dark eyes. She nodded and answered quite casually:

'He told me he prays a lot.'

'And doesn't eat very much either,' said Meyer with faint irritation.

'That, too. He's got very thin. But he says the praying gives him what strength he needs.'

'He should take more care of himself. Lots of people depend on him. They're going to depend more now that the Germans are here. This prayer business is all right in its way—but men go crazy with too much of it.'

'Do you think Giacomo's crazy?'

'I didn't say that. He's strange, that's all.'

'Perhaps it's because there aren't so many good men around. We've forgotten what they look like.'

Meyer chuckled and wiped his lips with the back of his hand.

'You could be right, Nina *mia*.' He stood up and hoisted his pack on to his shoulders. 'Well, I must be moving. Thanks for the breakfast and the other stuff. Tell Giacomo what I said.'

'I'll tell him.'

He put his hands on her shoulders and kissed her on the lips. She did not resist because she liked him and he was a man going off to his own private war.

'Good luck, Dottore!'

'Good luck, Nina *mia*. You deserve it!'

She stood at the door and watched him scrambling down the valley. She thought he had never looked so young nor so alive, and she wondered idly what would have happened if Giacomo had not come to Gemello Minore.

But Giacomo was there and his presence filled all her life, and when he came just before lunch-time she clung to him desperately, crying on his shoulder. He held her there until the strain went out of her; then he disengaged her gently and listened while she told him about Aldo Meyer and his message. He listened gravely and then said:

'I tried to talk him out of it. These Germans are nothing—a patrol detachment, nothing more. They won't bother anyone very much. But Meyer's been waiting so long for his own war he can't see what he's in for.'

'It will probably be good for him, *caro mia*. I saw him go and he was happy as a boy going to hunt.'

Nerone shook his head gravely and his face clouded.

'Meyer is the wrong man for this company. I've heard about Il Lupo and I can guess where he comes from. He's a professional and he's been trained in Russia. He wants more than a victory. He wants a Communist State in Italy. When the Germans are pushed out and the Allies move in, he'll bid for control of the civil administration. On their record, he'll probably get it. Meyer's in the wrong boat. He thinks Il Lupo wants another gun. What he wants is a man to use afterwards. I wonder what will happen when Meyer finds out.' He shrugged and smiled and spread his hands palm-downwards on the table. 'Anyway, it's done now. We've got our own work to do here.'

She brought a big bowl of pasta to the table and stood over him while he ate it, noting how sparing he was, and how little relish he took in the spicy sauce.

'And what are you going to do, Giacomo?'

'What I'm doing now—except that I've had to bring the Germans into my calculations. I went up to see the Contessa a couple of days ago.'

It was something he had not told her and she felt a sharp pang of jealousy. It was as if she saw him stepping back into a world he had left—a world where he had been lost and where she could never reach him. But she said nothing and waited for him to tell her the rest of it.

'I told her I was English. I didn't tell her but I let her think I was an agent, moved in here to prepare the way for the Allies. She was glad to see me. She's in an awkward position. I suggested she nominate me steward of her estate so that I can talk on fairly equal terms with the German commander. She's given me a room in the servants' quarters.'

'You're going to live at the villa?'

'I have a room there. I'll sleep there when I must. But I'll get a pass from the commander and I'll be free to come and go. I'll need that. The whole villa has been turned into an armed camp.'

'Nice for the Contessa!' she told him with sudden viciousness. 'She'll be able to have a new man every night.'

Nerone's face clouded. He reached out and took her hands and drew her gently towards him.

'Let's not say that, *carissima*. She's a strange, lonely woman, with a fire in the blood that no man has yet been able to put out. That's a torment and not a joke. Why should we cock our fingers at her when we have so much?'

'She eats men, *caro mio*. And I don't want her to eat you.'

'She'll get indigestion if she tries it,' he told her with a smile.

But when he was gone the fear was still with her, and often she would wake in the night, dreaming that Giacomo had left her and was married to the woman on top of the hill with her flat childless belly and her pinched mouth and her predatory eyes. . . .

... 'There is another thing I must ask,' said Blaise Meredith, in his dry voice. 'During this time, did Giacomo perform any religious duties? Did he go to Mass and the Sacraments?'

Nina Sanduzzi nodded.

'Whenever he could—except when there were sick in the mountains, or lost men to be hidden away from the Germans. He used to go to the Mass here on Sundays and I would see him, though it was an arrangement that we would not sit together nor greet each other, because some of the Germans were there. They came it seems, from a part of Germany where there are many Catholics. When he wanted to go to confession he would walk across the valley to young Father Mario.'

'But not Father Anselmo.'

She shook her head.

'Father Anselmo didn't like him. Sometimes there were angry words between them, when Father Anselmo refused to go out to the sick, after curfew.'

'And what did Giacomo say about Father Anselmo?'

'That he was to be pitied and prayed for—but that the men who sent him here would have a heavy judgment. He used to say that *Gesù* had built the Church like a house for his family to live in, but that some men—even priests—used it like a market and a wineshop. He said they made trade out of it and filled it with quarrels and shouting and even fouled the floor like drunken men do. He said if it were not for the love of *Gesù* and the care of the Holy Spirit, it would fall into ruin in a generation. He said that was what every house needed—much love and little argument. And he was right.'

'I know he was,' said Meredith. And wondered that his voice sounded so vehement. 'Now tell me, what did Giacomo say and feel about the Germans?'

For the first time, the question seemed to give her pause. She thought about it a long moment and then she said:

'This was a thing he talked about often, and sometimes I found it hard to understand him. He would say that countries are like men and women and that people take the character of the country they live in. Each country has its own special sin and its special virtue. The English were a sentimental people, but tough and selfish with it, because they lived on an island and wanted to keep it for themselves as they had always done. They were polite. They had much justice, but little charity. When they fought, they fought stubbornly and bravely, but they always forgot that many of their wars had sprung from their own selfishness and indifference. The Americans were different. They were sentimental and tough, too, but they were simpler than the English, because they were younger and richer. They liked to possess things, even though they often did not know how to enjoy them. They were, like all young men, inclined to violence. They could easily be deceived by loud voices and magnificence. And they often deceived themselves, because they like the sound of words, even if they did not understand their meaning. The Germans were something else again. They were hard workers, lovers of order and efficiency and very proud. But there was a grossness in them and a violence that was released by liquor and big speeches and the need to assert themselves. Giacomo used to laugh and say that they liked to feel God rumbling in their bellies when a big music played. . . .'

'Was that all?'

'No. Giacomo liked to talk like that. He said you had to skim the grease off the soup or it would go sour. But he always came back to the same thing: no matter what people were like–or countries–they had to live together like a family. This was how God made them; and if a brother waved a gun at his brother, they would end by destroying each other. There were times when each had to swallow his pride and give way–be polite when he felt like spitting in someone's eye. And that was how he tried to live with the Germans here.'

'Did he succeed?'

'I think so. We lived in peace. We were not robbed. A girl could walk safely to the cistern and home again. Sometimes there were killings when the Partisans met a German patrol–but that was always away from Gemello. There was a curfew and we stayed inside at night. If there were quarrels, Giacomo talked to the commander and the thing was worked out. After a while, the Germans went away, moving down to the south, and the Partisans followed them, as wolves follow the sheep in the Abruzzi.'

'And afterwards?'

'In May we heard the news that Rome had fallen to the Allies, and early in June Paolo was born–and he was born blind. . . .'

. . . The first warnings came late one morning while Giacomo was with her. They were light and uncertain, but Giacomo was so concerned that he insisted on calling Carla Carese, the midwife, and Serafina Gambinelli and Linda Tesoriero. They came running and clamouring because he was so urgent with them; but when they saw that she was still on her feet and in no trouble at all, they all stood around with their hands on their hips and laughed at him. Nina laughed too, and was surprised to see the cloud of anger that darkened his face. His voice was angry too and he snapped at them.

'You're fools–all of you! Stay with her and don't leave her. I'm going to get Doctor Meyer.'

They gaped at him then, and even Nina was amazed, because this business of bearing a child was a woman's affair. Doctors were for sick people and they knew that, if everything went well, childbirth was a simple if noisy business, with a lot of joy to follow it. But before they had time to tell him all this, Giacomo was gone, a lean, ominous figure, thrusting up the track towards the San Bernardino road.

Nina was concerned for him because of the long distance; but the women soon laughed her out of it. The child would arrive before he got back, they told her; and he and the doctor could get drunk together as good friends should when one of them has fathered a bouncing *bambino*.

They were half-right at least. The babe was born and washed, wrapped and laid in her arms an hour before Giacomo arrived with Aldo Meyer. But they did not act like other men at a birth. Giacomo kissed her and held her in his arms for a long time. Aldo Meyer kissed her, too, lightly, like a brother. Then Giacomo lifted the child from her arms and carried him over to the table and held the lamp while Meyer sounded the heart and peered into the ears and lifted the tiny eyelids and bent closer and closer to examine them.

The midwife and the women stood in a small group by the bed, and Nina hoisted herself up on to the pillows to ask fearfully:

'What's the matter with him? What are you looking for?'

'Tell her,' said Aldo Meyer.

'He's blind, *cara*,' said Giacomo Nerone gently. 'He was born with cataracts growing on his eyes. It was the fever you had, the illness with the spots, which is called *rubella*. A woman who gets it the second or third month sometimes bears a blind child or a deaf one.'

It was perhaps half a minute before his meaning reached her. Then she screamed like an animal and buried her face in the pillow while the women huddled about her like hens, clucking to comfort her. After a time, Giacomo came to her and put the child in her arms and tried to talk to her, but she turned her face away from him, because she was ashamed to have given a maimed child to the man she loved so much.

Then a long while later the women went away and Giacomo came back to her with Aldo Meyer. She was calmer now and Meyer talked to her soberly.

'This is a sad thing, Nina; but it has happened and, for the present, it cannot be altered. If things were different, I could take you down to the hospital at Valenta and then, maybe, to Naples to see a specialist and find out if anything can be done. But the war is not over yet. There is still fighting and the roads are cluttered with refugees. Broken German units are fighting their way home and the Partisans are out after them. Naples is a shambles and you would be just another peasant with no one to help her. Giacomo is a wanted man and I am committed to my band in the mountains. So, for the present, there is nothing to do but wait. When there is peace again, we shall see what can be done.'

'But the boy is blind!' It was all she could think or say.

'The maimed ones need much love,' said Aldo Meyer.

Giacomo Nerone said nothing at all; but her heart almost broke at the grief and the pity in his eyes. Meyer went on talking to her in his gentle, professional fashion, showing her the growths on the child's eyes, making some kind of reason out of the first terror. Giacomo poured wine for them all and then set about preparing a meal. The two men ate it at the table, while Nina held the bowl on her lap and talked to them from the bed. When the child whimpered, she put it to the breast, and when the small, blind bundle nuzzled against her, she found herself weeping silently.

Meyer left before midnight to sleep in his own house, safe at last from the threat of the concentration camp. When Giacomo took him to the door, Nina was dozing, but she heard Giacomo's voice say sharply:

'You're a friend of mine, Meyer, and I understand, even if I don't agree. But keep Lupo away from the village. Keep him away from me.'

And Meyer's voice in the terse reply:

'This is history, man! You can't stop it. I can't either! Someone's got to start organising...'

The rest of it was lost as they moved to the door and into the clear night. A few minutes later Giacomo came back and bolted the door behind him. He said quietly:

'You can't be alone tonight, *cara*. I'll stay with you.'

Then all the disappointment welled up like a spring inside her and she clung to him, sobbing as if her heart were broken, as indeed it nearly was.

Then, when she was calm again, Giacomo settled her on the pillows and turned the lamp low, and through half-closed eyes she saw him do a strange thing. Quite unselfconsciously, he knelt down on the earthen floor, closed his eyes and stretched out his arms like the arms of *Gesú* on the cross, while his lips moved in soundless prayer. There was a moment when his whole body seemed to become rigid, like a tree, and when she called out in fright he did not hear her. She lay back watching him until exhaustion overcame her, and she slid into sleep.

When she woke, the room was full of sunlight and the baby was bawling lustily and Giacomo was boiling the coffee-pot for breakfast. He came and kissed her and lifted the child in his arms and said gravely:

'I want to tell you something, Nina *mia*.'

'Tell me.'

'We will name the boy Paolo.'

'He's your son, Giacomo. You must name him—but why Paolo?'

'Because Paolo, the Apostle, was a stranger to God, and, like me, found Him on the road to Damascus. Because, like this boy, Paolo was blind but saw again, through the mercy of God.'

She stared at him in disbelief.

'But the doctor said...'

'I am telling you, *cara*.' His voice was strong and deep as a bell. 'The boy will see. The cataracts will disappear in three weeks; when a baby should begin to see the light, our Paolo will see too. You will hold the lamp in front of his eyes and watch how he blinks and begins to follow it. I promise you, in the name of God.'

'Don't tell me that just to comfort me, *cara*. I could not bear to hope and be cheated at the end.' There was agony in her voice, but he only smiled at her.

'It's not a hope, Nina *mia*. It's a promise. Believe it.'

'But how do you know? How can you be sure?'

All he said was:

'When it happens, Nina, let it appear like news to you, too. Tell nobody about this morning. Will you promise me?'

She nodded dumbly, wondering how she could bear the waiting and hide the doubt she felt.

Three weeks later, to the day and the hour, she took the child from his cradle and wakened him. When he opened his eyes, they were clear and shining like his father's, and when she held him to the light he blinked. She shaded it with her hand and his eyes stared steadily, then blinked again when she took her hand away.

The wonder of the moment was like a revelation. She wanted to shout and sing and go calling down the village street to tell them all that Giacomo's promise had come true.

But Giacomo was already dead and buried. The village folk turned away in shame as she passed. Even Aldo Meyer had gone to Rome, and she thought he would never come back....

... 'I should go home now,' said Monsignor Blaise Meredith. 'It's late and you've given me a lot to think about.'

'Do you believe what I have told you, Monsignor?'

Her voice and her eyes challenged him, calmly. He looked at her for a long moment, and then he said, with a curious finality:

'Yes, Nina. I don't know what it means yet. But I do believe you.'

'Then you will look after Giacomo's boy, and keep him safe?'

'I'll look after him.' But even as he said it, his conscience challenged him: How? In God's name, how?

13

For Doctor Aldo Meyer, evening was closing in on an afternoon of strange calm.

Immediately after luncheon he had sat down to read the papers of Giacomo Nerone. He had come to them hesitant and afraid, as if to a moment of crisis or revelation. But when he opened them and set them in order and began to read the bold cursive hand, it was like hearing the old challenging arguments of Giacomo himself.

There were moments of shame at his own failures, moments of poignant recollection, of nostalgia for a relationship that had begun in conflict, had come at times close to friendship and was soon to end in tragedy. But there was no bitterness in the record—as there had never been bitterness in Giacomo himself. There were passages of child-like simplicity that touched Meyer almost to tears, and phrases of mystical exaltation that left him groping, as Giacomo had often done, for the explanation of his own bankruptcy.

But at the end there was peace and calm and certainty, which communicated itself to the reader even after the lapse of years. And in the last writing of all, the letter to Aldo Meyer, there was a great gentleness and a singular grace of forgiveness. The rest of the papers were in English, but the letter was in Italian and this, too, was a delicacy not to be lightly forgotten:

My dear Aldo,

I am at home and it is late. Nina is asleep at last and the boy is sleeping, too. Before I go in the morning, I shall leave this note with her, among my other papers, and, when it is all over and the first grief has passed, perhaps it will come safely into your hands.

We shall be meeting tomorrow, you and I, but as strangers, each committed to an opposite belief and an opposite practice. You will sit with my judges and walk with my executioners, and sign the certificate of my death, when it is all done.

I blame you for none of this. Each of us can walk only the path he sees at his own feet. Each of us is subject to the consequences of his own belief—though I think one day you will come to believe differently. If you do, you will hate what has been done, and you may be tempted to hate yourself for your part in it, the more because there will be no one to whom you can say you are sorry.

So I want to tell you now I do not hate you. You have been my friend and a friend of Nina and the child. I hope you will always lean to them and care for them. I know you have loved Nina. I think you still do. And this will be another cross on your back, because you will never be sure whether, in joining yourself to my condemnation, you have done it from belief or jealousy. But I know and I tell you now that I shall die still counting you my friend.

Now there is a service I want to lay on you. When you get this letter, will you go to Father Anselmo and to Anne de Sanctis and tell each of them that I bear them no grudge for what they have done and that, when I come to God, as I hope I may, I shall remember them both.

So, *dottore mio*, I leave you. It is not long till the dawn and I am cold and afraid. I know what must happen and my flesh crawls with terror at the thought of it. I have no strength left and I must pray awhile. It is a thing I have always desired, the grace to die with dignity, but never, till now, have I understood how hard it is.

Good-bye, my friend. God keep us both in the dark time.

Giacomo Nerone

When Meyer read the letter for the third time, he had been moved to rare tears, but when he had walked awhile and pondered it and read it again, the charity of it lay on him like an absolution. If he had failed in all else—and his failures were written large on the calendar of fifteen years—he would not die unloved or unforgiven. And this was the answer to the question that had plagued him so long: why great men die and drop out of creation without a ripple of care for them, and the memory of others is cherished in the secret hearts of the humble.

The thought lingered with him through the fall of the afternoon, and it was still expanding itself when the knock came at the door and he opened it to find Blaise Meredith standing outside.

The priest's appearance shocked him. His face was ashen, his lips bloodless, and small beads of sweat stood out on his forehead and on his upper lip. His hands were shaky and his voice husky and trembling.

'I'm sorry to bother you, Doctor. I wonder if I could rest awhile with you.'

'Of course, man! Come in, for God's sake! What's happened to you?'

Meredith smiled wanly.

'Nothing's happened. I'm on my way back from Nina's place. But it's a long scramble before you get to the road, and it was just a little too much. I'll be all right in a minute!'

Meyer led him into the house, made him lie down on the bed and then brought him a stiff tot of *grappa*.

'Drink that. It's foul stuff, but it will put some life into you.'

Meredith choked on the raw spirit, but he got it down and after a few moments he began to feel the warmth spreading out and the strength returning to his limbs. Meyer stood looking down at him with grave eyes.

'You worry me, Meredith. This sort of thing can't go on. I'm half-inclined to get in touch with the Bishop and have you sent to hospital.'

'Give me a few more days, Doctor. After that, it won't matter so much.'

'You're a very sick man. Why drive yourself like this?'

'I'll be a long time dead. Better to burn out than rust out.'

Meyer shrugged despairingly.

'It's your life, Monsignor. Tell me—how did you get on with Nina?'

'Very well. I'm deeply impressed by what she's told me. But there are a couple of questions I'd like to clear up with you—if you don't mind, that is.'

'Ask what you like, my friend. I've gone too far to draw back now.'

'Thank you. Here's the first one. Was there an outbreak of German measles here in the winter of 1943? And was Paolo Sanduzzi born blind because of it?'

'Yes.'

'How long was it before you saw the child again?'

'Three years—no, nearer to four. I went away to Rome, you see.'

'When you came back, the boy could see?'

'Yes. The cataracts had disappeared.'

'Medically speaking, was this strange?'

'Quite abnormal. I'd never know another case.'

'Did you remark on it to Nina Sanduzzi?'

'Yes. I asked her how and when it had happened.'

'What did she say?'

'She just shrugged and said, the way the peasants do . . . "It just happened." Our relations then weren't as good as they are now. I didn't press the point. But it puzzled me. It still does. Why do you ask, Monsignor?'

'Nina told me that, on the day of the birth, after you had left, Giacomo had prayed all night—and that, in the morning, he had promised her that the baby would see normally, when other children did—three weeks later. According to her that's just what happened. The cataracts were gone. The child could distinguish light and shadow. And afterwards the sight developed as it did in other children. What would be your opinion of that, Doctor?'

But Meyer did not answer him immediately. He seemed lost in a new thought of his own. When he spoke it was as if to himself:

'So that's what she meant when she said Giacomo had done miracles and that she had seen them.'

'When did she say that?' Meredith prompted him sharply.

'When we were discussing your arrival, and I was trying to persuade her to talk to you.'

'Would you say she was telling the truth?'

'If she said it,' Meyer answered him sombrely, 'it was the truth. She would not lie to save her life.'

'What would be your medical opinion?'

'At first blush I would say it couldn't happen.'

'But it did. The boy is seeing today.'

Meyer gave him a long, searching look; then smiled and shook his head.

'I know what you want me to say, Meredith, but I can't say it. I don't believe in miracles, only in unexplained facts. All I can admit is that this doesn't normally happen. I might go further and say I've never heard of another case like it, that I don't know of any medical explanation for it. But I'm not prepared to make a leap in the dark and tell you this is a miracle caused by divine intervention.'

'I'm not asking you to say that,' said Meredith good-humouredly. 'I'm asking you whether you can explain it medically.'

'I can't. Others might.'

'If they could, could they explain Giacomo Nerone's foreknowledge of the cure?'

'Clairvoyance is an established, if unexplained, phenomenon. But you can't ask anyone to judge a second-hand report of something that happened fifteen years ago.'

'But you accept the truth of the report?'

'Yes.'

'You would record it as unexplained and, possibly, unexplainable in the present state of medical knowledge?'

'. . . Of my medical knowledge,' Meyer corrected him, smiling.

'And you would testify in these terms at the Bishop's court?'

'I would.'

'That's all,' said Meredith with gentle irony. 'I'll put it on record in my notes.'

'What's your own opinion, Monsignor?' Meyer quizzed him pointedly.

'I've an open mind,' said Meredith precisely. 'I shall try, and so will my successor, to prove by every possible means that this is not a miracle, but simply a rare physical phenomenon. As it rests only on one witness and your later testimony, we shall probably end by refusing to accept it as a miracle–though in fact it may be one. Where you and I differ, my dear Doctor, is that you reject the possibility of miracles and I accept it. It's a long argument but I suggest my position is rather more tenable than yours.'

'You'd have made a good lawyer, Monsignor.' Meyer tacked away from the supposition. 'What's your next question?'

Meredith gave it to him baldly.

'Who was Il Lupo? And why did Nerone tell you to keep him away from the village?'

Meyer looked at him in swift surprise.

'Who told you that?'

'Nina. She was half-asleep but she heard you and Nerone talking at the door.'

'What else did she hear?'

'You said ... "This is history! You can't stop it. Neither can I. Someone's got to start organising. . ."'

'That was all?'

'Yes. I thought you could tell me what it meant.'

'It had many meanings, Monsignor. I can only try to give its meaning for me. . . .'

. . . Their camp was a shallow basin, high up in the spine of eastern hills. Æons ago it might have been the crater of a volcano. The lip of it was jagged as a saw, and the outer slopes were barren and scree-covered; but inside there was a small lake into which the water drained, and beside it there were copses and a stretch of tough, wiry grass. Their tents were hidden under the bushes, and the goats and the cow they had levied from the local peasants cropped safely on the inside of the saucer, while their look-outs swept the countryside from the shelter of the high sawteeth.

There was only one way in–the goat track that began at Satan's Rock, where the first sentry was posted. The watchers on the rim could see him all day–and if a visitor were admitted they could keep him in their sights every step of the way. When he reached the lip of the crater he would be met and searched and two men would walk him down through the tussocks to the tent of Il Lupo, who was their leader.

Meyer remembered him vividly–a short, fair man, with clear eyes and a chubby face and a smiling mouth, from which a placid voice spoke, now in the purest Tuscan, now in the roughest provincial dialect. His dress was rough like that of his men, but his hands and teeth were immaculate and he shaved, carefully, every day. He talked little about his past, but Meyer gathered that he had fought in Spain and then gone to Russia and then returned to Italy before the outbreak of war. He had worked in Milan and Turin and later still in Rome, though how or at what was never quite clear. He had admitted to being a party man, and he discussed policy with authority and expertness.

The day Giacomo Nerone was brought in from Satan's Rock, Meyer was in Il Lupo's tent discussing a new patrol operation. The guards gave his name and his business and Il Lupo stood up and held out his hand.

'So you're Nerone! I'm happy to know you. I've heard a great deal about you. I'd like to talk with you.'

Nerone returned the greeting but said briskly:

'Could we leave it? My wife's in labour. I'd like the doctor to see her as soon as possible. It's a long walk back.'

'She's had *rubella*,' Meyer explained hastily. 'We're afraid of complications.'

The clear eyes clouded with immediate concern. Il Lupo clucked sympathetically.

'A pity. A great pity. That's where a State Medical Service is such a help. One can start inoculations at the first hint of an outbreak. You had no serum, Meyer, of course.'

'No. We can only wait and see how the child is born.'

'The midwives are with her?'

Nerone nodded.

'Then she's being looked after, at least. Ten minutes won't make any difference one way or the other. Let's have a cup of coffee and talk a while.'

'Relax, Giacomo,' Meyer told him genially. 'Nina's as strong as an ox. We'll make up the time on the downhill walk.'

'Very well.'

They sat down on torn canvas chairs. Il Lupo offered cigarettes and shouted for coffee, and after a few moments of polite fencing he came to the point.

'Meyer's told me about you, Nerone. I understand you're an English officer.'

'That's right.'

'And a deserter.'

'That's right, too.'

Il Lupo shrugged and blew a cloud of smoke up towards the canvas roof.

'It's immaterial to us, of course. The capitalist armies have served their purpose in winning the war. It's our job to establish the peace we want. So your personal history is no disadvantage. On the contrary, it could even help you—with us.'

Nerone said nothing, but sat waiting calmly.

Il Lupo went on in his quiet, educated voice.

'Meyer's also told me of the work you've done in Gemello. The confidence you've built up with the people. That's excellent ... as a temporary measure.'

'Why temporary?' asked Nerone quietly.

'Because your own position is temporary—and equivocal. Because when the war ends—as it soon must—this country will need a strong and united Government to organise it and run it.'

'That means a Communist Government?'

'Yes. We're the only people who have a clear platform and the strength to carry it into practice.'

'You need a charter too, don't you? A mandate?'

Il Lupo nodded amiably.

'We've got it now. The British have made it clear that they'll play ball with anyone who can help them run the country. They've armed us and given us at least a reasonable scope for military operations. The Americans have other ideas, but they're politically immature and we can discount them for a while. That's the first half of the mandate. The second we must win for ourselves.'

'How?'

'How does any party win confidence? By showing results. By establishing order out of chaos. By getting rid of dissenting elements and building unity on strength.'

'That's what the Fascisti tried to do,' Nerone told him evenly.

'Their mistake was to build their dictatorship on one man. Ours will be the dictatorship of the proletariat.'

'And you'd like me to join you in that?'

'As Meyer has done,' Il Lupo pointed out calmly. 'He's a liberal by nature but he's seen the failure of liberalism. It's not enough to hold out promises of work and education and prosperity as the rewards of co-operation. People aren't built like that. They're naturally stupid, naturally selfish. They need the disciplines of strength and fear. Take yourself, for instance. You've done a good job, but where has it led you? You'll be running round with a basket of eggs on your arm playing Lady Bountiful till the day you die. . . . And they'll let you do it. What's the future in that?'

For the first time since his coming, Meyer saw Nerone relax. His lean, dark face split into a grin of genuine amusement.

'There's no future at all. I know that.'

'Why do it, then?'

'The world's a grim place without it,' said Nerone lightly.

'Agreed,' said Il Lupo. 'But in the world we build there won't be any need of it.'

'That's what I'm afraid of,' said Giacomo Nerone. He stood up. 'We understand each other, I think.'

'I understand you very well,' said Il Lupo, without resentment. 'I'm not sure if you understand me. We're moving into the villages one by one and setting up our own administration. Gemello is next on the list. What do you propose to do about it?'

Nerone smiled, denying the proposition before he uttered it.

'I could rally the people and fight you.'

Il Lupo shook his head.

'You're too good a soldier for that. We have the guns, the bullets and the training to use them. We'd cut you up in an afternoon. What's the profit in that?'

'None,' Nerone told him calmly. 'So I'll pass the word around to the people to wait it out without violence until the first free elections.'

A ghost of a grin twitched Il Lupo's thin lips.

'By that time they'll have forgotten the guns. They'll remember only the bread and the pasta and the bars of American chocolate.'

'And the boys you've shot in the ditches!' Sudden anger rang in Nerone's voice. 'The old men beaten, and the girls with shaven heads! The new tyranny built on the old–the liberty pawned again for an illusion of peace. They'll submit now, because they're lost and afraid. Later they'll rise in judgment and throw you out!'

'Give a man a day's work, a full belly at night and a woman in his bed, and he'll never think of Judgment Day.' Il Lupo stood up. His lean figure seemed to grow in stature, filling the tent. 'Another thing, Nerone. . .'

'Yes?'

'There's no room for two of us in Gemello. You'll have to get out.'

Surprisingly, Nerone threw back his head and laughed heartily.

'You want the meat without the mustard. You want me discredited and running like a rabbit while you march in as the Saviour of Italy. You're too greedy, man!'

'If you stay,' said Il Lupo with cool deliberation, 'I'll have to kill you.'

'I know,' said Giacomo Nerone.

'You want to make yourself a martyr, is that it?'

'That would be a folly and a presumption,' Nerone told him simply. 'I don't want to die any more than the next man. But I stand on land that I've tilled with my own hands, in a place where I've found love and hope and belief. I refuse to be hunted out of it to give you a cheap victory.'

'Very well,' said Il Lupo without resentment. 'We know where we stand.'

'Do you mind if Meyer comes now?'

'Not at all. If you'll wait outside a second, we'll just tidy up our business.'

When he had gone, Il Lupo said, without emphasis:

'He's a zealot. He'll have to go.'

Meyer shrugged uneasily.

'He's a good fellow. He does a lot of good and no harm at all. Why not let him be?'

'You're soft, Meyer,' said Il Lupo genially. 'We'll be taking over Gemello in ten days. You've got that long to talk some sense into him.'

'I wash my hands of it,' said Meyer tersely.

'That's Pilate's line, my dear doctor. The Jews have another one—"It is expedient that one man should die for the people."'

He was still smiling when Meyer turned and went out to join Giacomo Nerone....

. . . Blaise Meredith lay back on the bed, relaxed in body but active in mind, listening to the cool, clinical narration of the doctor. When Meyer paused awhile, he asked:

'It's a personal question, Doctor. Did you actually join the Communist Party?'

'I never held a party ticket. But that's irrelevant. There weren't any tickets in the mountains. The important thing was that I had committed myself to Il Lupo and to what he stood for: the dictatorship of the proletariat, order imposed by strength.'

'May I ask why?'

'It's quite simple.' Meyer's hands gestured eloquently in exposition. 'For me it was the most natural development. I'd seen the breakdown of liberalism. I'd seen the drawbacks of clericalism. I'd been the victim of a one-man dictatorship. I understood the need for equality and order and a redistribution of capital. I'd also seen the stupidity and stubbornness of depressed people. Il Lupo's answer seemed to me the only one.'

'And his threat to Giacomo Nerone?'

'Was also logical.'

'But you disagreed with it?'

'I disliked it. I didn't disagree.'

'Did you talk to Giacomo about it?'

'Yes.'

'What did he say?'

'Surprisingly enough, Monsignor, he agreed with Il Lupo.' Meyer's face clouded at the recollection of it. 'He said quite plainly: "You can't believe one way and act another. Il Lupo's right. If you want to build a perfect political mechanism, you must toss out the parts that don't work. Il Lupo doesn't believe in God. He believes in man only as a political entity, so he's quite logical. You're the illogical one, Meyer. You want omelettes for breakfast, but you don't want to crack the eggs."'

'Did you have any answer to that?'

'Not a very good one, I'm afraid. It was too close to the truth. But I did ask him how he squared up his own admission that there was no future in the work with the fact that he was prepared to die for it.'

'What did he say?'

'He pointed out that he, too, had his own logic. He believed that God was perfect and man, since the fall, was imperfect, and that there would always be disorder and evil and injustice in the world. You couldn't create a system that would destroy these things, because the men who ran it would be imperfect, too. The only thing that dignified man and held him back from self-destruction was his sonship with God and his brotherhood in the human family. Giacomo's own service was an expression of this relationship. Between him and Il Lupo conflict was inevitable, because their beliefs were opposed and contradictory.'

'And Il Lupo, being the man with the guns, must destroy him?'

'That's right.'

'Why didn't he go away?'

'I put that to him, too,' said Meyer wearily. 'I suggested he take Nina and the boy and move out to another place. He refused. He said Nina would come to no harm—and he himself had stopped running long ago.'

'So he stayed in Gemello?'

'Yes. I returned to the mountains. The day before Il Lupo was due to move in and set up his administration, I came back. They were going to use my house as headquarters and I had to get it ready. Also, I had been told to have a last talk with Giacomo Nerone to get him to change his mind....'

... It was early afternoon, warm with the late spring, noisy with the first cicadas. They walked together in the garden under the fig tree, and talked as soberly as lawyer and client about what would happen when Il Lupo came down with his men. There was no argument between them. Nerone was firm in his refusal to quit, and Meyer's words were a flat recitation of the inevitable.

'Il Lupo's quite clear on what will be done. You're to be discredited first and then executed.'

'How does he propose to discredit me?'

'Their arrival is timed for sunrise. You'll be arrested round about nine and brought here for summary trial.'

'On what charges?'

'Desertion from the Allied cause and co-operation with the Germans.'

Nerone smiled thinly.

'He shouldn't have much difficulty proving those. What then?'

'You'll be sentenced and taken out for immediate and public execution.'

'How?'

'The firing squad. This will be a military court. Il Lupo is careful about the formalities.'

'And Nina and the boy?'

'Nothing will be done to them at all. Lupo was quite definite on that. He sees no benefit in raising sympathy by punishing a woman and a child.'

'He's a clever man. I admire him.'

'He asks me to point out that this leaves you nearly eighteen hours to clear out, if you want to. I'm carrying enough money to keep you and Nina and the baby for two months. I'm authorised to give it to you on your assurance that you'll be clear of the area by sunrise.'

'I'm staying. Nothing will change that.'

'Then there's nothing more to be said, is there?'

'Nothing. I'm grateful to you for trying. Meyer. We've been good friends. I appreciate it.'

'There's one thing—I'd almost forgotten it.'

'What's that?'

'Where will you be at nine in the morning?'

'I'll save Il Lupo the trouble. I'll come here.'

'That wouldn't do. I'm afraid. He wants a public arrest.'

'He can't have everything. I'll walk here on my own two feet at nine o'clock.'

'I'll tell him what you say.'

'Thank you.'

Then, because everything was said that needed to be put into words and because neither quite knew how to say good-bye, they walked in silence up and down the flagged path under the fig tree until Meyer said, awkwardly:

'I'm sorry it's ending like this. It's not my business any more, but what are you going to do now?'

Nerone answered him quietly and frankly:

'I'm going down to have Father Anselmo hear my confession. I'll call at the hut to collect a few things and hand them to Nina. Then, I'll walk up to the villa to ask the Contessa if she'll have Nina and the boy there till it's all over. She's British by birth and Il Lupo's too clever to fall foul of the people who are giving him his guns. Then . . .' His dark, hollow face broke into a smile. 'Then I'm going to say my prayers. I'm lucky to have time to prepare. It isn't every man who knows the time and place of his death.' He stopped pacing and held out his hand. 'Good-bye, Meyer. Don't blame yourself too much. I'll remember you in eternity.'

'Good-bye, Nerone. I'll have a care for Nina and the boy.'

He wanted to use the old, familiar formula and say 'God keep you'. But he remembered in time that, in Il Lupo's new world, which was now his own, there would be no God any more. The farewell was therefore pointless, and he did not say it. . . .

. . . Blaise Meredith asked:

'What happened with Father Anselmo?'

Meyer made a gesture of indifference.

'Nothing much. The old man didn't like him. They'd quarrelled often, as you know. He refused to hear his confession. I heard about it later in the village.'

'And the Contessa?'

'This isn't first-hand. I gathered it from Pietro, the manservant, who's a patient of mine. Giacomo went up to the villa to ask a refuge for Nina and the boy. Also, I gathered, he wanted to sleep there the night, so that Il Lupo would not know where he was and would have to forgo the value of a public arrest. Anne de Sanctis was willing enough, it seems, but she wanted a price for it.'

'What price?'

'She's a strange woman,' said Meyer, obliquely. 'I've known her a long time, but I would not claim to understand her fully. She is passionate by nature and she has great need of a man—a greater one now that she faces the terror of the middle years. Her husband disappointed her. Her other lovers came and went away as soldiers do in war-time. She was always too proud to satisfy herself with a man from the village. Nerone might have matched her, but he was already in love with Nina Sanduzzi. From the beginning she was jealous of that. So her whole emotional life has taken on a colour of perversion. Her price was that Nina sign over the boy as her ward and Giacomo Nerone sleep with her that night.'

'A man on the eve of execution?' Meredith was shocked.

'I told you,' said Meyer evenly, 'everything is coloured for her. That's why this painter fellow has so much influence at the villa. He panders to her. Anyway, as you might expect, Giacomo refused. Apparently she was shrewd enough to guess that he would spend the night at Nina's place. She sent a man down with the message to Il Lupo. Giacomo was arrested two hours after sunrise.'

'So that's why she hates his son.'

'I don't think she hates the boy,' said Meyer, with grim humour. 'If anything, she's probably attracted to him. But she is still jealous of Nina and she hates herself, but doesn't know it.'

Blaise Meredith swung his legs off the bed and sat up, running his fingers through his thin hair in a pathetic gesture of weariness and puzzlement. In a voice that was very like a sigh, he said:

'It's late. I'd better get back for dinner. Though, God knows, I don't feel like facing them both tonight.'

'Why not dine here?' said Meyer impulsively. 'You'll eat worse, but at least you won't have to be polite. I'm nearly at the end of my evidence and you might as well get the rest of it tonight. I'll send a lad up to the villa to make your apologies.'

'I'd be grateful, I assure you.'

'I'm grateful to you,' said Meyer with a grin. 'And from a Jew to an inquisitor, that's a big compliment.'

In the ornate room at the villa, the Contessa and Nicholas Black dined by candlelight, in the uneasy intimacy of conspirators. The Contessa was irritable and snappish. She was beginning to understand how far the situation had passed out of her control—with Nicholas Black holding her to ransom and Meredith picking up God knows what information from Meyer and Nina Sanduzzi and old Anselmo. Very soon now he must come to her with his dry, pedantic questions and his sunken, probing eyes. Whether she answered or remained silent, she stood to be discredited while the painter walked off, grinning, with the prize.

Nicholas Black was edgy, too. Meredith had forced his hand at lunch-time and things had been said which could never be recalled. Now they were in open opposition and, for all his mockery, Black had a healthy respect for the temporal influence of the Church in a Latin country. If Meredith took it into his head to invoke the help of the Bishop, all sorts of influences might be set in motion–influences reaching back to Rome itself–and the end might be a discreet call from the police and the revocation of his sojourn permit. It had happened before. The Christian Democrats were in power and behind them was the Vatican, old and subtle and ruthless.

So he was quick to seize on the Contessa's fear and exploit it to his own advantage.

'The priest's a damn nuisance, I agree, *cara*. I feel it's my fault for bringing him here. You're in a mess. I'd like to help you get out of it.'

Her face brightened immediately.

'If you can do that, Nicki. . .'

'I'm sure we can, *cara*.' He leaned over and patted her hand in encouragement. 'Now listen! The priest is here. We're stuck with him. We can't get rid of him without a discourtesy, and you don't want that.'

'I know.' She nodded miserably. 'There's the Bishop, you see, and. . .'

Black cut in briskly:

'I know about the Bishop, too, *cara*. You've got to live here, so it pays to be friendly. Meredith must stay. We're agreed on that. But there's nothing to stop you going away, is there?'

'I–I don't understand.'

'It's simple, *cara*.' He waved an eloquent hand. 'You haven't been feeling well at all. Meredith himself knows you've been suffering with migraine and God knows what other feminine ills. You need to consult your doctor immediately. So you go to Rome. You've got an apartment there. You need staff to run it. You take your maid, and Pietro–and, as a special favour to Nina Sanduzzi, you take the boy. You want to buy him new clothes. You want him to be trained to service in polite society. You may even want to thinking about having him educated by the Jesuits. . . .' He chuckled sardonically. 'What mother could refuse an opportunity like that? And if she did? The boy's under a contract of service to you. Italian law is such a confounded muddle, I think you'd get away with it, provided the boy consents. The onus would be on his mother to show why she wanted him here and what work she could find for him. You'd cover that, too, by providing a weekly remittance of part of his wages through your major-domo here.'

Her eyes lit up at the new, encouraging thought, but immediately clouded again.

'It's a wonderful idea, Nicki. But what about you? Meredith knows what you want. He'd do his best to make trouble.'

'I've thought of that, too,' said the painter, with his satiric grin. 'I stay here–at least for a week. If Meredith asks any questions, you can tell him quite frankly you think I'm a bad influence on the boy. You want to act like a good Christian and get him away from me. Simple, isn't it?'

'Wonderful, Nicki! Wonderful!' Her eyes sparkled and she clapped her hands in delight. 'I'll make all the arrangements tomorrow and we'll leave the day after.'

'Why not tomorrow?'

'We can't, Nicki. The train for Rome leaves Valenta in the morning. There wouldn't be time to get everything done.'

'A pity,' said Black irritably. 'Still, it's only a day. I think we can keep our Monsignor at bay for that long. You'd better talk to the boy yourself. I mustn't seem to be involved.'

'I'll talk to him in the morning.' She reached out and filled his wineglass.

'Let's drink, darling! Then we'll open another bottle and make a celebration of it. What shall we drink to?'

He raised his glass and smiled at her over the rim.

'To love, *cara!*'

'To love!' said Anne Louise de Sanctis–then choked suddenly on the thought: But who loves me? And who will ever love me?

'I'll be frank with you, Doctor,' said Meredith, picking moodily at the last of his dinner. 'At this moment, I'm less concerned with Giacomo Nerone than with his son. Nerone's dead; and, we hope, among the blessed. His boy is in a grave moral crisis, in daily danger of seduction. I feel responsible for him. But how do I discharge the responsibility?'

'It's a problem,' said Meyer, with sober concern. 'The boy's more than half a man. He has free will and he's morally responsible–if inexperienced. He's certainly not ignorant of what's involved. Children mature early in the matrimonial beds. I think he's a sound lad; but Black's a very persuasive character.'

Meredith was toying absently with a broken crust, crumbling it on his plate and making small patterns of the grey particles.

'Even in the confessional it's hard to reach an adolescent. They're shy as rabbits and much more complex than adults. If I could get at either the Contessa or Black himself I might stand some chance.'

'Have you tried?'

'With Black, yes. But the man is fixed in bitterness and resentment. I couldn't find a common term of agreement. I haven't tried the Contessa yet.'

Meyer gave him a wintry smile.

'You may find that even harder, Monsignor. There's no logic in women at the best of times and this one has a sickness on her: the sickness of the middle years and an old love turned sour and shameful. There's a cure for one, but the other . . .' He paused a moment, frowning dubiously. '. . . One thing I'm sure of, Meredith. No priest can cure it.'

'How will she end, then?'

'Drugs, drink or suicide,' said Meyer flatly. 'Three words for the same thing.'

'And that's the only answer?'

'If you want me to say that God is the answer, Monsignor, I can't do it. There is another one, but it's a dirty word and you mightn't like it.'

To his surprise, Meredith lifted his grey face and smiled at him good-humouredly.

'You know, Meyer, that's the dilemma of the materialists. I wondered so few of them see it. They cut God out of the dictionary and their only answer to the riddle of the universe is a dirty word.'

'Damn you!' said Meyer, with a crooked grin. 'Damn you for a long-nosed inquisitor. Let's have some coffee and talk about Giacomo Nerone. . . .'

. . . At eight o'clock in the morning they arrested Nerone in Nina's house. They were not too rough with him, but they bloodied his face and tore his shirt, so that it would seem that he had put up a struggle. In fact he did not struggle at all, but stood there, silent, while two of them held his arms and a third battered him, and the others held Nina, who screamed and struggled like a wild thing–and, when they took him away, collapsed moaning on the bed. The child did not scream, but lay quietly in its cot, groping with tiny bunched hands at the folds of the pillow.

They then marched him up the hill and on to the road, and, to make a better spectacle, they twisted his arms behind his back and bent him almost double to walk through the village. The people stood at their doors, silent and staring, and even the children were hushed as he passed. No voice was raised in protest, no hand raised to help him. Il Lupo had calculated exactly. Hunger had no loyalties. These folk had seen too many conquerors come and go. Their allegiance was to the strong and not to the gentle. This was a harsh land with a harsh history. It was not the inheritance of the meek.

When they came to Meyer's house, they thrust him roughly inside and shut the door. The people came running like ants to stand outside, but the guards drove them back, cursing them into their houses. Il Lupo wanted an orderly trial, and no riots to disturb it.

Inside the room, Giacomo Nerone stood a moment flexing his cramped arms and wiping the blood from his face. Then he looked around him. The room was set like a court. Il Lupo and Meyer and three other men sat at the table, and behind them the guards were ranged–dark, stubble-faced men, in leather jackets and cocked berets, with pistols in their belts and automatic rifles held loosely in their hands. Two other guards stood between Nerone and the door, and between him and the table there was a clear space with a single chair.

All the faces were set and serious, as was becoming to men witnessing a historic act. Only Il Lupo was smiling, clear eyed and polite as a host at a dinner party. He said in his cool voice:

'I'm sorry we had to be rough with you, Nerone. You shouldn't have resisted arrest.'

Nerone said nothing.

'You have a right, of course, to know the charges against you.' He picked up a paper from the table and read from it in careful Tuscan: 'Giacomo Nerone, you are charged before this military court with desertion from the British Army and with active collaboration with German units operating in the area of Gemelli dei Monti.' He laid the paper down on the table and went on: 'Before you are brought to trial on these charges, you are at liberty to say anything you wish.'

Nerone looked at him with calm eyes.

'Will you put my remarks in the record?'

'Certainly.'

'On the charge of desertion, this court has no jurisdiction. Only a British Army court martial can try me for that. Your proper procedure is to hold me in custody and hand me over to the nearest British command.'

Il Lupo nodded placidly.

'We will note your objection, which seems to me well founded, in spite of the fact that you have no proof of your identity as a British soldier. You will, however, be brought to trial on the second charge.'

'I challenge your jurisdiction on that, too.'

'On what grounds?'

'This is not a proper court. Its officials hold no legal commission.'

'I disagree with you,' said Il Lupo placidly. 'Partisan groups are guerrillas operating in support of the Allies. They have a *de facto* identity as military units and a summary jurisdiction in local theatres of war. Their authority derives ultimately from the Allied High Command and from the Occupation Authority in Italy.'

'In that case, I have nothing to say.'

Il Lupo nodded politely.

'Good. We're anxious, of course, to see that justice is done. You will be given some time to prepare your defence. I propose to clear the room. You will be given coffee and something to eat. Doctor Meyer here is prepared to act as your defence counsel. As president of the court I am prepared to give full weight to any points you may care to raise with me. Is that clear?'

For the first time since his arrival, Nerone smiled.

'Quite clear. I'd enjoy the coffee.'

At a sign from Il Lupo, the guards went out into the garden and the three men were left alone. Meyer said nothing, but went to the stove and began making the coffee. Nerone sat down and Il Lupo offered him a cigarette and lit it for him. Then he sat on the edge of the table and said pleasantly:

'You were foolish to stay, you know.'

'It's done,' Nerone told him briefly. 'Why discuss it?'

'You interest me, that's why. I have a good deal of admiration for you. But I can't see you in the role of a martyr.'

'You cast me for it.'

'And you accepted it.'

'Yes.'

'Why?'

'I like the lines,' said Nerone, with grave humour. 'The last one most of all: "*Consummatum est.*"'

'You—and the work,' said Il Lupo.

Nerone shrugged.

'The work isn't important. A million men can do it better. You will probably do it better yourself. The work dies. How many men did Christ cure? And how many of them are alive today? The work is an expression of what a man is, what he feels, what he believes. If it lasts, if it develops, it's not because of the man who began it, but because other men think and feel and believe the same way. Your own party's an example of it. You'll die too, you know. What then?'

'The work will go on,' said Il Lupo. The clear eyes lit suddenly as if at a great revelation. 'The work will go on. The old systems will perish of their own corruption, and the people will come into their own. It's happened in Russia. It will happen in Asia. America will be isolated. Europe will be forced into line. It will happen. Nerone, I may not be here to see it, but I'm not important.'

'That's the difference between us,' said Giacomo Nerone softly. 'You say you're not important. I say I am. ... What happens to me is eternally important, because I was from eternity in the mind of God ... me! The blind, the futile, the fumbling, the failed. I was, I am, I shall be!'

'You believe that, really?' Il Lupo's eyes probed him like a scalpel.

'I do.'

'You'll die for it?'

'It seems so.'

Il Lupo stubbed out his cigarette and stood up. He said with flat conviction:

'It's a monstrous folly.'

'I know,' said Giacomo Nerone. 'And it's gone on for two thousand years.

I wonder whether yours will last so long.'

Il Lupo made no answer. He looked at his watch and then said briskly:

'We'll have coffee and then you can rest for the morning. We'll bring the trial on at one o'clock. How do you propose to plead?'

'Does it matter?'

'Not really. The finding's a matter of course. The execution is fixed for three o'clock.'

Nerone's face clouded momentarily and he said:

'Why so late? I'd like to get it over.'

'I'm sorry,' said Il Lupo politely. 'I'm not being cruel. It's just a matter of policy. There'll be less time for riots or demonstrations. By the time they get the gossip over and begin to think about it, they'll be ready for supper. You understand, I hope?'

'Perfectly,' said Giacomo Nerone.

Meyer brought the coffee and the breakfast things and they sat together at the table eating in silence, like a family. When they had finished, Il Lupo asked him:

'By the way, do you intend to make any speeches before the execution?' Nerone shook his head.

'I've never made a speech in my life. Why?'

'I'm glad,' Il Lupo told him genially. 'Otherwise I'd have to have you beaten before you went out. The one thing I can't afford is heroics.'

'I'm no hero,' said Giacomo Nerone.

For the first time since his arrival, Meyer spoke to him. Without raising his eyes from the table-top, he said gruffly:

'If you want to be private for a while, use the other room. No one will disturb you. I'll call you when we're ready to begin.'

Nerone looked at him with gratitude in his sombre eyes.

'Thank you, Meyer. You've been a good friend. I'll remember you.'

He got up from the table and walked into the other room, closing the door behind him. The two men looked at each other. After a moment, Il Lupo said, not ungently:

'I'll release you from service after the execution, Meyer. If you take my advice you'll cut loose and go away for a while. You're not made for this sort of thing.'

'I know,' said Aldo Meyer in a dead voice. 'I don't believe enough—either way.... '

. . . 'And the rest of it' asked Blaise Meredith.

Meyer's long hands made a gesture of finality.

'It was quite simple. He was tried and found guilty. They took him up the hill to the old olive tree, tied him to it, and shot him. Everyone was there, even the children.'

'And Nina?'

'She, too. She went up to him and kissed him and then stood back. Even when they shot him, she didn't say a word: but when all the others left, she stayed there. She was still there when the burial party came that night to take him away.'

'Who buried him?'

'Anselmo, the Contessa, two men from the villa, Nina—and myself.'

Blaise Meredith frowned in puzzlement.

'I don't understand that.'

'Simple enough. All three of us wanted to hate him—but at the end he shamed us into loving him.'

'And yet,' persisted Meredith, 'when I came you were all afraid of him.'

'I know,' said Meyer gruffly. 'Love is the most terrible thing in the world.'

It was after eleven when Blaise Meredith left the doctor's house to walk back to the villa. Before he went, Meyer showed him Nerone's last letter and handed him the package containing the rest of the papers. They said good-night to each other and Meredith began to stroll up the cobbled street in the grey moonlight.

A sense of remoteness and separation took hold of him, as if he were walking out of his own body, in a strange place and another time. There were no doubts any more, no storms, only a great tranquillity. The storms were all about him, roaring and restless, but he lay becalmed in the eye of the cyclone, in a wonder of silence and flat water.

Like Giacomo Nerone, he was near the end of his search. Like Nerone, he saw how his death must come in a flurry of violence, inevitable but brief as sunset. He was afraid of it, yet he walked towards it, on his own two feet, enveloped in the peace of a final decision.

He came to the iron gates of the villa and passed them, pressing onwards up the last steep incline to the place of Nerone's execution—the small plateau where the olive tree stood like a cross, black against the white moon. When he reached it, he laid down the package and leaned against the tree, feeling his heart pounding and the rough touch of the bark against his skin. He raised his arms slowly, so that they lay along the knotted branches and the dead twigs pricked the skin of his hands.

Giacomo Nerone had stood like this, with wrists and ankles bound and eyes covered, in the moment of final surrender. Now it was his turn—Blaise Meredith, the cold priest from the Palace of the Congregations. His body stiffened, his face knotted in the agony of decision as he struggled to gather his will to the act of submission. It seemed an age before the words wrenched themselves out of him, low and agonised:

'. . . Take me, O God! Make me what you want . . . a wonder or a mockery! But give me the boy—for his father's sake!'

It was over—done, finished! A man sold under the hammer to his Maker. Time to go home. To bed, but not to sleep. Time was running out. Before morning came, there were Giacomo Nerone's papers to be read, and a letter to be written to Aurelio, Bishop of Valenta.

14

To Blaise Meredith, the legalist—and even in this time of climax he could not lay aside the mental habit of a lifetime—the writings of Giacomo Nerone were, in many respects, a disappointment. They added nothing, except by inference, to the biography of his past, and little but glossary to the known details of his life, works and death in Gemello Minore.

What Aldo Meyer had found in them—a poignant recollection, a glimpse into the mind of a man once known, once hated, finally loved—presented itself under another aspect to the Devil's Advocate. Blaise Meredith had read the writing of a hundred saints, and all their agonies, all their revelations, all their passionate outpourings had for him the familiarity of old acquaintance.

They conformed to the same belief, to a basic pattern of penance and devotion, to the same progression from purgation to illumination, from illumination to a direct union with the Almighty in the act of prayer. It was the conformity he was looking for now, as each of the examiners and assessors would look for it, in each of the processes that must follow the first presentation of evidence in the Bishop's court.

To the biographer, to the dramatist, to the preacher, the personality of the man was important. His quirks and oddities and individual genius were the things that linked him to the commonalty of men and made them lean to him as patron and exemplar. But to the Church itself, to the delving theologians and inquisitors who represented it, the importance lay in his character as a Christian—his conformity to the prototype which was Christ.

So, in the slow hours of the night, Blaise Meredith bent himself to the scrutiny, coolly and analytically. But even he could not escape the personal impact—the living man thrusting himself out from the yellowed leaves and the strong, masculine hand-writing.

The writing was disjointed: the jottings of a man torn between contemplation and action, who still felt the need to clarify his thoughts and make his affirmations clear to himself. Meredith pictured him, sitting late at night in the small stone hut, cold, pinch-bellied, yet oddly content, writing a page or two before the time came to begin the long prayerful vigil which, more and more, became his substitute for sleep.

Yet, in spite of their random character, the writings had a rhythm and a unity of their own. They grew as the man grew. They ended as the man ended, in dignity and calm and a strange content.

. . . I write because of the common need of man to communicate himself, if only to a blank sheet of paper; because the knowledge of myself is a weight on me and I have no right to lay it all on the woman I love. She is simple and generous. She would bear it all and still be ready for more, but concealment is as much a part of love as surrender. A man must pay for his own sins and he cannot borrow another's absolution. . . .

. . . To be born into the Church—and I can only speak of my own Church, knowing no other—is at once a burden and a comfort. The burden is felt first. The burden of ordinance and prohibition and, later of belief. The comfort comes afterwards, when one begins to ask questions; and when one is presented with a key to every problem of existence. Make the first conscious act of faith, accept the first premise, and the whole logic falls into place. One may sin, but one sins inside a cosmos. One is constrained to repentance by the sheer order of it. One is free within a system, and the system is secure and consoling, so long as the will is fixed in the first act of faith. . . .

. . . When Catholics become jealous of unbelievers, as they often do, it is because the burden of belief lies heavy and the constraints of the cosmos begin to chafe. They begin to feel cheated, as I did. They ask why an accident of birth should make fornication a sin for one, and a week-end recreation for another. Faced with the consequences of belief, they begin to regret the belief itself. Some of them end by rejecting it, as I did when I came down from Oxford. . . .

. . . To be a Catholic in England is to submit to a narrow conformity instead of a loose, but no less rigid, one. If one belongs to the old families as I did, to the last Elizabethans, the last Stuarts, it is possible to wear the Faith like a historic eccentricity—as some families sport the bar sinister, or a Regency rakehell, or a gambling dowager. But in the clash of conformities this is not enough. Sooner or later one is forced back on the first act of faith. If one rejects this, one is lost. . . .

. . . I was lost a long time, without knowing it. Without the Faith, one is free, and that is a pleasant feeling at first. There are no questions of conscience, no constraints, except the constraints of custom, convention and the law, and these are flexible enough for most purposes. It is only later that the terror comes. One is free—but free in chaos, in an unexplained and unexplainable world. One is free in a desert, from which there is no retreat but inward, towards the hollow core of oneself. There is nothing to build on but the small rock of one's own pride, and this is a nothing, based on nothing . . . I think, therefore I am. But what am I? An accident of disorder, going nowhere. . . .

. . . I have examined myself a long time on the nature of my act of desertion. At the time, it had no moral significance. The oath of service ends with invocation of the Deity. But for me there was no Deity. If I chose to risk liberty and reputation and suffer the sanctions of the State, this was my business. If I escaped the sanctions, so much the better. But I did not reason like this at the time. My action was instinctive—an unreasoning reaction from something that did violence to my nature. But, by what I then believed, I had nothing that could be called a nature. I was cast in a common form, like a spark out of a furnace, but if one spark sputtered out, what did it matter? I was lost already . . . I could only plunge a little deeper into darkness. . . .

. . . Then there was Nina. I woke to her as one wakes to the first light of morning. The act of love is, like the act of faith, a surrender; and I believe that the one conditions the other. In my case, at least, it has done so. I cannot regret that I loved her, because love is independent of its expression—and it was only my expression of it that was contrary to the moral law. This I regret and have confessed and prayed to be forgiven. But even in sin the act of love—done with love—is shadowed with divinity. Its conformity may be at fault, but its nature is not altered, and its nature is creative, communicative, splendid in surrender. . . .

. . . It was in the splendour of my surrender to Nina, and hers to me, that I first understood how a man might surrender himself to God—if a God existed. The moment of love is a moment of union—of body and spirit—and the act of faith is mutual and implicit. . . .

. . . Nina has a God, but I had none. She was in sin, but within the cosmos. I was beyond in sin, in chaos. . . . But in her I saw all that I had rejected, all that I needed, and yet had thrown away. Our union was flawed because of it, and one day she would understand and might come to hate me. . . .

. . . How does one come back to belief, out of unbelief? Out of sin, it is easy; an act of repentance. An errant child returns to a Father because the Father is still there, the relationship is unbroken. But in unbelief there is no Father, no relationship. One comes from nowhere, goes nowhere. One's noblest acts are robbed of meaning. I tried to serve the people. I did serve them. But who were the people? Who was I? . . .

. . . I tried to reason myself back to a first cause and first motion, as a foundling might reason himself back to the existence of his father. He must have existed, all children have fathers. But who was he? What was his name? What did he look like? Did he love me–or had he forgotten me for ever? This was the real terror, and, as I look back on it now, from the security I have reached, I tremble and sweat and pray desperately: 'Hold me close. Never let me go again. Never hide Your face from me. It is terrible in the dark!' . . .

. . . How did I come to Him? He alone knows. I groped for Him and could not find Him. I prayed to Him unknown and He did not answer. I wept at night for the loss of Him. Lost tears and fruitless grief. Then, one day, He was there again. . . .

. . . It should be an occasion, I knew. One should be able to say: 'This was the time, the place, the manner of it. This was my conversion to religion. A good man spoke to me and I became good. I saw creation in the face of a child and I believed.' It was not like that at all. He was there. I knew He was there, and that He made me and that He still loved me. There are no words to record, no stones scored with a fiery finger, no thunders on Tabor. I had a Father and He knew me and the world was a house He had built for me. I was born a Catholic, but I had never understood till this moment the meaning of the words 'The gift of faith'. After that, what else could I do, but say: 'Here am I, lead me, do what you want with me. But please stay with me, always. . . .'

. . . I am afraid for Aldo. There is much merit in his sceptic honesty, but when the others get hold of him, I do not know what will happen. This is the difference between the two absolutes–the Church and Communism. The Church understands doubt and teaches that faith is a gift, not to be acquired by either reason or merit. Communism permits no doubt and says that belief can be implanted like a conditioned reflex. . . . To a point, it is right, but the conditioned reflex answers no questions–and the questions are always there–Whence? Where? Why? . . .

. . . The question of reparation worries me greatly at times. I am changed. I have changed. But I cannot change any of the things I have done. The hurts, the injustices, the lies, the fornications, the loves taken and tossed away. These things have changed and are still changing other people's lives. I am sorry for them now, but sorrow is not enough. I am bound to repair them as far as I can. But how? It is winter. The paths are closed before me and behind. I am a prisoner in this small world I have found. I can only say: When the way is clear, I will do what is asked of me. But the way is never clear. There is only the present moment in which one can live with certainty. Why do I fear so much? Because repentance is only the beginning. There is still a debt to pay. I ask for light, pray for submission, but the answer is unclear. I can only go on in the present. . . .

. . . Meyer laughs at me about good works. He points out that they have no continuity. The sick die and the hungry are hungry tomorrow. Yet Meyer himself does the same things instinctively. Why? Men like Meyer doubt the existence of God and therefore doubt any but a pragmatic relationship between man and man. Yet I have seen Meyer spend himself more freely than I have ever done. The man who does good in doubt must have so much more merit than one who does it in the bright certainty of belief. 'Other sheep I have which are not of this fold. . . .' A warning against the smugness of inherited Faith. . . .

. . . Nina tells me I am getting thin. I don't eat enough or sleep enough and pray too long at night. I try to explain how the need for food and sleep seems to get less, when one is absorbed in this new wonder of God. She seems to understand it better when I point out that she does not feel the need of me, physically, because of the child filling her womb. . . . I ask myself what must be done about this question of marriage. We are apart in body now, but close in heart and spirit. I have the feeling that things are being prepared for me over which I have no control and that, for this reason, marriage might be a greater injustice than those I have already done. I am ready to do what seems right. I have told her that she has the first claim to decide, but that I believe it wise to wait. . . . I have had so much these last months—of love, of happiness, of spiritual consolation. I must pay for it sometime. I do not know how the payment will be asked. I pray and try to make myself ready. . . .

. . . Father Anselmo worries me. I have quarrelled with him and I regret it. There is nothing solved by anger. I must understand that a priest is just a man with sacramental faculties. The faculties are independent of his personal worth. Anselmo is carrying his own cross, the load of one lapse, multiplied by its consequences. But even in the sin there is an element of love, and this, I know, is a goodness not to be despised. Celibacy of the clergy is an ancient discipline, but not an article of faith. One sees its value, but one must not judge too harshly when men stumble under the weight of it. Poverty is a state which some men accept to make themselves holy. It can be for others conducive to damnation. If there were a way to talk to Anselmo, as a friend . . . but this is another problem for a priest. He is trained to direct the faithful, but never to accept counsel from them. This is a defect in the system. . . .

. . . Today I met the man who calls himself Il Lupo. Strange how quickly and easily we understood each other. I believe in God. He believes in no-God. Yet the consequences of each belief are equally rigid and inescapable. He is honest in what he believes. He does not expect me to be less honest in my own faith. He knows that there can be no coexistence between us. One must destroy the other. He is the prince of this world and he has the power of life and death. What power have I against him? 'My kingdom is not of this world.' I could rally the people. I could make them follow me to resist Il Lupo's band. But to what end? Fratricide is not Christianity. Bullets breed no love. . . . Il Lupo would like me to argue and act. I must not argue. I must only accept. But I fear for Meyer. He is too gentle a man for this embroilment. I must try to make him see that I understand. Later, he will have much to suffer. The weight of doubt is heavy on honest men. . . .

. . . I have a son and the boy is blind. Nina's grief is harsh on me. I understand now how faith can stagger on the mystery of pain. I understand how the old Manichees could fall easily into their heresy—since it is hard to see how pain and evil come into a creation of which an omnipotent Goodness is the sole author. A black time for me. It seems I am back in darkness and I pray desperately and cling to the first act of faith and say: 'I cannot understand; but I believe. Help me to hold to it!' . . .

. . . If faith can move mountains, faith can open blind eyes. If God wills it. How do I know what He wills? Speak to me, O God, for Your Son's sake. . . . Amen. . . .

There was more, much more, and Blaise Meredith scanned it meticulously as a good advocate should, but he had found the core of it, and the core was sound and solid. The conformity was there, the conformity of mind and heart and will. And the surrender had been made by which a man cuts loose from every material support to rest in faith, hope and charity, in the hands that framed him.

On the last page of all, Giacomo Nerone had written his own *obit*.

. . . If there be any, after my death, to read what I have written let them know this of me:

I was born in the Faith; I lost it; I was led back to it by the hand of God.

What service I have done was prompted by Him. There is no merit in it of my own.

I have loved a woman and begotten a son, and I love them still in God and to all eternity.

Those I have injured, I beg to forgive me.

Those who will kill me, I commend to God, as brothers whom I love.

Those who forget me will do well. Those who remember me, I beg to pray for the soul of

> Giacomo Nerone,
> Who died in the Faith.

Blaise Meredith laid down the yellowed sheet on the counterpane, leaned back on the pillows and closed his eyes. He knew now with certainty that he had come to the end of his search. He had looked into the life of a man and seen the pattern of it—a long river winding slowly, but with certainty, homeward to the sea. He had looked into the soul of a man and seen it grow, like a tree, from the darkness of the earth, upward into the sun.

He had seen the fruit of the tree: the wisdom and the love of Nina Sanduzzi, the struggling humanity of Aldo Meyer, the reluctant repentance of Father Anselmo. It was good fruit, and in the bloom of it he saw the mark of the nurturing finger of God. But all the fruits was not yet mature. Some of it might wither on the branch, some of it might fall unripe and rot into extinction, because the gardener was careless. And he, Blaise Meredith, was the gardener.

He began to pray, slowly and desperately, for Anne de Sanctis and Paolo Sanduzzi and Nicholas Black, who had chosen the same desert to walk in as Giacomo Nerone. But before the prayer was finished, the old sickness took him, griping and wrenching so that he cried out in the agony of it, till the blood welled up, hot and choking in his throat.

A long time later, weak and dizzy, he dragged himself to the writing desk and, in a shaky hand, began to write. . . .

> My Lord Bishop,
>   I am very ill, and I believe that I may die before I have time to record fully the results of my investigations here. In spite of all the medical predictions, I feel that I am being hurried out of life and I am oppressed by the thought of the little time left to me. I want Your Lordship to know, however, that I have made my surrender, as you promised I would, and that I rest content, if not courageous, in the outcome.
>   First, let me tell you what I have found. I believe most firmly, on the evidence of those who knew him and on the writings which I have found, that Giacomo Nerone was a man of God, who died in the Faith and in the attitude of

martyrdom. What the Court will decide is another matter—a legality, based on the canonical rules of evidence, and irrelevant, it seems to me, to the fundamental facts, that the finger of God is here and that the leaven of goodness in this man is still working in the lives of his people.

Your Lordship's best witnesses will be Doctor Aldo Meyer and Nina Sanduzzi. This latter has produced evidence of a cure that may well be miraculous, though I doubt seriously whether it will pass the assessors. The writings of Nerone which I shall send you with this letter are authentic and definitive, and, in my view, sound corroboration of his claim to heroic sanctity.

I confess to you, My Lord, in friendship, that I am less concerned at this moment for the Cause of Beatification than for the welfare of certain souls here in Gemello Minore. I have spoken to Father Anselmo and presumed to suggest that if he separates physically from Rosa Benzoni, even while lodging her still in his house, and if he makes a sincere confession, Your Lordship will accept these as evidence of reform. I'm sorry for him. It is a question of money and security for a poverty-stricken and rather ignorant man. I have promised him a lump sum of a hundred thousand lire from my estate as well as money enough to buy bedding and other needs for a separate sleeping room for Rosa Benzoni. It seems now that I may not have time to arrange these things. May I count on Your Lordship to do them for me, and use this letter for a claim on my executors? To fail Anselmo now would be an intolerable thought.

The other matter touches the Contessa de Sanctis, Paolo Sanduzzi, who is the son of Giacomo Nerone, and an English painter, who is house-guest at the villa. It is too sordid to detail in this letter; and I fear there is little Your Lordship could do about it. I have commended them all to God and asked Him to accept my surrender as the price of their salvation. I hope tomorrow to be able to plan more active measures; but I am so weak and ill, I dare not count on anything.

I have two favours to ask, which I trust Your Lordship will not find burdensome. The first is that you write to His Eminence, Cardinal Marotta, explaining my position and making my apologies for what I count as a failure in my mission. Give him my greetings and beg him to remember me in his Mass. The second is that you will permit me to be buried here in Gemello Minore. I had once asked to be buried in His Eminences's church, but Rome is very far—and here, for the first time, I have found myself as a man and a priest.

It is very late, my Lord, and I am tired. I can write no more. Forgive me and, in your charity, pray for me.

I am Your Lordship's most obedient servant in Christ,

Blaise Meredith

He folded the letter, sealed it in an envelope and tossed it on the desk. Then he crawled back to bed and slept till the sun was high over the green lawns of the villa.

Paolo Sanduzzi was working on the rock garden at the back of the villa. The terraces had been breached in places where the mortar had weathered out, and the soil was spilling. When it rained, the soil would be lost and, in this rocky land, it was too precious for that. The old gardener had shown him how to mix lime with the black volcanic sand from the river, and how to work it into the crevices with a trowel, then trim and surface it.

It was a new thing learned, a new skill to be proud of, and he knelt there with the sun shining on his back, whistling contentedly. The lime burned his fingers and made his hands feel rough and sandy, but this was another small pride—his hands were hardening like a man's. The gardener was pleased with him, too. Sometimes he would stop and talk in his gruff chewing fashion, and tell him the names of the plants, and how they grew and why the grubs would eat one and not another.

At mealtimes, in the long flagged kitchen, the old man would protect him from the chaffing of the women, who made jokes about his young maleness and what the girls would do to him when they got hold of him. The only one who did not laugh at him was Agnese the cook, a waddling mountain of a woman, who fed him double portions of pasta and always had a lump of cheese or a piece of fruit to tuck in the pocket of his breeches.

He had no name to put to all this, but he understood that it was a good way to be. He had a place and work to do, and friendly people about him—and at the end of the month there would be lire to rustle in his pocket and take home to his mother. Even Rome was beginning to recede into a dimmer distance. The Contessa had not spoken to him again, and the painter had left him alone, except for a genial word or two in passing. His fear of them had begun to diminish and they wove themselves pleasantly into his daydream of fountains and girls with shoes, and streets full of shining automobiles.

He was dreaming now, to the rhythm of his own whistling and the scrape of his trowel on the grey stone, when suddenly the dream became a reality. The Contessa was standing behind him and saying in her gentlest voice:

'Paolo! I want to talk to you.'

He straightened immediately, dropped his trowel and scrambled down from the rockery to stand before her, acutely conscious of his sweating, naked torso and his grimy hands.

'Yes, signora. At your service.'

She looked around quickly as if to make sure they were alone. Then she told him:

'Tomorrow, Paolo, I'm going away to Rome. I'm not very well and I must see my doctor. I'm taking Zita and Pietro to look after my apartment and I thought of taking you, too.'

He gaped and stammered at the sudden wonder of it and the Contessa gave her high, tinkling laugh.

'Why are you so surprised? I promised you, didn't I? And you have worked well.'

'But . . . but . . .'

'But you didn't believe me? Well, it's true. The only thing is, you'll have to ask your mother. You'll tell her that you'll be away for a couple of months and that part of your money will be paid to her here each month. Is that clear?'

'Yes, signora!' It was clear and bright as summer.

'You will tell her that Pietro is going and Zita, too, and that Pietro will be training you all the time.'

'Yes, signora. But . . .'

'But what, Paolo?'

He did not know how to say it, but finally he got it out in a swift stumble of words.

'My . . . my mother doesn't like the Englishman, Signor Black. She may not let me go.'

Again she laughed and charmed all the fears out of him.

'You tell your mother, Paolo, that Signor Black is staying here to work. And that this is why I am taking you away, because it is better for you not to see him.'

'When—when can I tell her?'

'Now, if you like. Then come back and let me know what she says.'

'Thanks, signora. Thanks a thousand, thousand times.'

He snatched up his shirt, struggled into it so roughly that he tore it, and then went racing away down the gravelled path towards the iron gates. Anne Louise de Sanctis watched him go, smiling at the boyish eagerness of him. It was a good thing to see, a pleasantness to have near one in the house. This must be what other women found in their sons, in the autumn of marriage, when the sap of passion was drying out, and a husband was a companion perhaps, but no longer a youthful lover.

Suddenly, and quite clearly, she understood what she had done—the malice of it, the dirt of it, the stark damnation into which she had walked herself on the arm of Nicholas Black. Her blood ran cold at the thought. She shivered and turned away; and as she rounded the corner of the house, she walked almost into the arms of Blaise Meredith, who was stepping on to the lawn with a folder of papers in his hand.

When he greeted her, quietly, she was shocked by the look of him. His face seemed to have shrunken overnight. His eyes were like red coals set deep in his skull. His skin was the colour of old parchment and his lips were bloodless. His back was stooped as if he walked under a heavy load and his long hands were tremulous against the black fabric of his soutane.

For a moment she forgot her own thought and said:

'Monsignor! You're ill!'

'Very ill, I'm afraid,' he told her. 'I don't think I have much more time. Would you walk with me a little?'

She wanted to refuse outright, to run from him and hide herself in her bedroom within reach of the small bottle of oblivion, but he took her arm gently and she found herself falling into step beside him, listening to his voice and answering him in a voice that seemed not to belong to her.

'I saw young Paolo running down the path. He seemed to be excited about something.'

'He was—very excited. I'm taking him to Rome with me tomorrow, if his mother will let him come.'

'Is Mr Black going, too?'

'No. He's staying on here.'

'But joining you later, is that it?'

'I—I don't know what his plans are.'

'You do.' The voice was tired but gentle and it held her, hypnotically.

'You do, my dear Contessa, because you made the plans with him. Terrible plans. Terrible for you and him—and the boy. Why did you do it?'

Her feet were fixed to the treadmill rhythm of their pacing. In spite of herself, the words came out:

'I—I don't know.'

'Did you still want revenge on Giacomo Nerone?'

'So you know that, too?'

'Yes. I know.'

It didn't matter now. Nothing mattered. He could ask what he liked and she would answer, and when it was finished she would go upstairs and take a bath, and lie down to sleep and never wake again. This was the last terror. It would soon be over.

His next words shocked her back into reality. Meyer might have said them but not this priest with the mark of death on him. In Meyer's mouth, they would have lacked something—an intimacy, a gentleness, a love, perhaps? It was hard to say.

'You know, my dear Contessa, Italy is a bad country for a woman like you. It is a country of the sun, aggressive in its worship of the processes of generation. It is primitive and passionate. The male symbol is paramount. The woman unloved, unbedded, childless, is a sign of mockery to others and of torment to herself. You're a passionate woman. You have a great need of love–a need, too, of the sexual commerce that goes with it. The need has become a frenzy with you–and the frenzy betrays you into viciousness while it inhibits your own satisfaction. You're ashamed of it and you do worse things, because you don't know how to do better. . . . Is that right?'

'Yes.'

It was all she said–but she wanted to add: I know all this, know it more terribly than you. But knowing isn't enough. Where do I go? What do I do? How do I find what I need?

Meredith went on, his dry voice warming as he talked.

'I could tell you to pray about this–and that wouldn't be a bad thing, because the hand of God reaches down even into the private hells we make for ourselves. I could tell you to make a general confession–and that would be a better thing, because it would give you a free conscience, and set you in peace with your God and yourself. But it wouldn't be the whole answer. You would still be afraid, still unsatisfied, still lonely.'

'What do I do then? Tell me! For God's sake, tell me!'

The plea was wrung out of her at last. Meredith answered her, calmly.

'Leave this place for a while. Go away. Not to Rome, which is a small city and can be a vicious one. Go back to London and establish yourself there for a while. I'll give you a note to a friend of mine at Westminster, who will put you in touch with a specialist who deals with problems like yours–problems of the body and of the mind. Put yourself in his care. Don't expect too much too soon. Go to theatres, make some new friends, find yourself a charity that interests you. . . . Maybe, too, you will find a man, not to sleep with only, but to marry you and love you. You're still attractive–particularly when you smile.'

'But if I don't find him?' There was a note of panic in her voice.

'Let me tell you something very important,' said Meredith patiently. 'It is no new thing to be lonely. It comes to all of us sooner or later. Friends die, families die. Lovers and husbands, too. We get old, we get sick. And the last and greatest loneliness is death, which I am facing now. There are no pills to cure that. No formulas to charm it away. It's a condition of men that we can't escape. If we try to retreat from it, we end in a darker hell–ourselves. But if we face it, if we remember that there are a million others like us, if we try to reach out to comfort them and not ourselves, we find in the end that we are lonely no longer. We are in a new family, the family of man, whose Father is God Almighty. . . . Do you mind if we sit down now? I'm–I'm very tired.'

Now it was her turn to take his arm and help him to the small stone seat under the honeysuckle. Meredith sat down but she remained standing, looking down at him with slow wonder and a pity she had never felt for any but herself. After a moment, she asked him:

'How do you understand all this? I've never heard a priest talk like that before.'

His bloodless mouth twitched into a tired smile.

'People ask too much of us, my dear Contessa. We're human too. Some of us are very stupid, and it takes us a lifetime to learn the simplest lessons.'

'You're the first man in my life who's ever helped me.'

'You've been meeting the wrong men,' said Meredith, with dry irony.

She smiled at him then, and he saw, as if for the first time, how beautiful she had been.

'Would you—would you hear my confession, Father?'

Meredith shook his head.

'Not yet. I don't think you're ready for it.'

She stared at him, frowning, more than a little afraid. He went on, gravely:

'Confession is not the psychiatrist's couch, a device to encourage self-revelation, to promote well-being by a purge of memory. It is a judicial sacrament, in which pardon is given on an admission of guilt and a promise of repentance and reform. For you the first part is easy—it is already half-done. For the second, you must prepare yourself, by prayer and self-discipline—and by beginning to repair the evil you have already done.'

She looked at him with troubled eyes.

'You mean Nicki—Mr Black?'

'I mean you, my dear Contessa—your own desires, your jealousy of Nina Sanduzzi and her son. As for Mr Black . . .' He hesitated a moment; then his eyes clouded and his mouth set into a grim line. 'I'll talk to him myself. But I'm very much afraid he won't listen.'

15

Halfway through the village, Paolo Sanduzzi ran, full tilt, into his mother. She was standing outside the smithy, talking to Martino's wife. Rosetta was with them, dressed in her Sunday finery, ready to be taken to the villa for the first time. Nina stared at him in amazement.

'Where do you think you're going? You're supposed to be working. What's all the hurry?'

The words tumbled out of him in a torrent.

'I don't have to work today. The Contessa told me. I'm going to Rome. She said I was to ask you and tell you that Pietro's going and Zita and I'm going to be trained . . .'

'Wait a minute!' Nina Sanduzzi's voice was harsh. 'Start again! Who said you're going to Rome?'

'The Contessa. She's going up there to see her doctor. She'll be there for two months.'

'And she wants to take you?'

'Yes.'

'Why?'

'She needs servants, doesn't she?'

'You're a gardener, son. There are no gardens in Rome.'

The boy's mouth dropped sullenly.

'She wants me, anyway. She sent me down to ask you.'

The two women looked at each other significantly. Nina Sanduzzi said bluntly:

'Then you can go straight back and tell her you're not going. I know who wants you in Rome and it's not the Contessa.'

'But it isn't like that at all! She told me to tell you. The Englishman is staying on here.'

'For how long?' Slow anger began to build behind the classic face. 'A week–ten days, maybe! And then he'll be packing his bags for the big city–and for you, Paolo *mio*. That trick wouldn't fool a baby.' She caught at his arm roughly. 'You're not going and that's flat. I'm your mother and I won't allow it.'

'Then I'll go anyway.'

She lifted her hand and slapped him hard on the face.

'When you're a man and can pay your own fare, and find your own work–then you can talk like that. If the Contessa asks me, I'll tell her to her face. And if there's any nonsense I'll have the doctor get in touch with the police at Gemello Maggiore. That'll keep your Englishman quiet for a while. Now forget about it, like a good boy!'

'I won't forget about it! I won't! She asked me and I want to go. She's the *padrona* and you're nobody! You're just–just a saint's whore!'

Then he wrenched away from her and went running down the street, with his shirt-tails flapping over his rump. Nina Sanduzzi stared after him, her face a marble mask. Martino's wife scuffed the ground with her bare feet and said awkwardly:

'He didn't mean it. He's just a boy. They hear things. . . .'

'His father was a saint,' said Nina Sanduzzi bitterly. 'And his son wants to make himself a *feminella*.'

'He doesn't at all,' said Rosetta, in her high clear voice. 'He's just a baby. He doesn't know what he wants. I'll bring him back and make him say sorry.'

Before her mother could protest, she had started away, running swiftly in her Sunday shoes, and the last they saw of her was a flurry of skirts and a pair of brown legs up-ended over the wall that screened the torrent from the road.

In a sunlit corner of the garden, Nicholas Black was putting the final varnish on the picture of Paolo Sanduzzi crucified on the olive tree. At the sound of Meredith's footfall, he looked up and called ironic greeting.

'Good morning, Meredith. I trust you slept well.'

'Indifferently, I'm afraid. I hope I'm not disturbing you?'

'Not at all. I'm just finishing. Would you like to see it? I think it's my best work so far.'

'Thank you.'

Meredith walked round to the front of the easel and looked at the picture. The painter grinned when he saw the expression on his face.

'Do you like it, Meredith?'

'It's a blasphemy, Mr Black.' The priest's voice was cold.

'That depends on the point of view, of course. To me it's a symbol. I've called it "The Sign of Contradiction". An apt title, don't you think?'

'Very.' Meredith walked a pace or two away from the picture and then said, 'I've come to tell you, Mr Black, that neither the Contessa nor Paolo Sanduzzi will be going to Rome. The Contessa would be pleased if you would leave the villa as soon as possible.'

The painter flushed angrily.

'She might have had the politeness to tell me herself.'

'I offered to do it for her,' Meredith told him quietly. 'She's an unhappy woman who needs a great deal of help.'

'Which the Church is only too ready to give her. She's quite rich, I believe.'

'The Church would like to help you, too, Mr Black—and you are very poor indeed.'

'To hell with your help, Meredith. I want nothing from you. Now do you mind going? I'm busy.'

'I've brought you something that might interest you.'

'What is it—a tract from the Catholic Truth Society?'

'Not quite. They're the personal papers of Giacomo Nerone. Would you care to look at them?'

In spite of himself, the painter was interested. He wiped his hands on a scrap of cloth and, without a word, took the folder from Meredith. He turned back the manila cover and scanned a few pages in silence. Then he closed the folder and asked in an odd, strained voice:

'Why do you show me this?'

Meredith was puzzled by the strangeness of him, but he answered simply:

'They make a very moving document—the spiritual record of a man who had lost the Faith, as you have, and then came back to it. I felt they might help you.'

Nicholas Black stared at him a moment; then his lips drew back in a smile that looked more like a grimace of agony.

'Help me! You have a wonderful sense of humour, Meredith! You know what you've done, don't you? You've had me thrown out of the house. You've robbed me of the last chance to finance an exhibition that might have re-established my reputation as an artist. And you've dirtied the one decent thing I've ever tried to do in my life.'

Meredith gaped at him blankly.

'I don't understand you, Mr Black.'

'Then I'll explain it to you, Monsignor,' said the painter, in the same taut voice. 'Like everyone else in this damned village, you've convinced yourself that my only interest in Paolo Sanduzzi is to seduce him. That's true, isn't it?'

Meredith nodded but did not speak. The painter turned away and stood for a long time looking out across the sun-dappled lawns towards the villa. When he spoke at last, it was with a strange, remote gentleness.

'The irony is, Meredith, that any time in the last fifteen years you might have been right. But not now. I'm fond of this boy—yes. But not in the way you think. I've seen in him everything that's been lacking in my own nature. I wanted to take him and educate him and make him what I could never be—a full man, in body, intellect and spirit. If it meant denying every impulse to passion and every need I have for love and affection, I was prepared to do it. But you'd never believe that, would you?'

Then, without thinking, Meredith made the most brutal remark of his life. He said gravely:

'I might believe you, Mr Black, but you could never do it—not without a singular grace from God. And how could you ask it, not believing?'

Nicholas Black said nothing. He was staring at the picture of Paolo Sanduzzi, nailed to the dark olive tree. After a while he turned to Meredith and said, with bleak politeness:

'Will you please go, Monsignor? There is nothing you can do for me.'

Blaise Meredith walked slowly back to the house, sick with the cónsciousness of his own failure.

Luncheon was a dismal meal for him. His head buzzed, his hands were clammy and whenever he breathed deeply he could feel a sharp pain in the region of his ribs. His food had no taste, the wine had a sour edge to it. But he was forced to smile and make conversation with the Contessa, who, now that her fear of him was gone, was disposed to be talkative.

Nicholas Black did not appear at all. He sent a message by the manservant excusing himself and asking that a collation be sent to his room. The Contessa was curious to know what had passed between them, and Meredith was forced to fob her off with the courteous fiction that they had exchanged a few bad-tempered words and that Black was probably too embarrassed to join them.

When the meal was over, he went upstairs to rest through the hot hours. The climb up the stairs told him, more plainly than a doctor, how ill he was. Each step was an effort. Perspiration broke out on his face and his body, and the pain in his ribs was like a knife whenever he breathed deeply. He knew enough of medicine to understand that this was what happened to cancer patients. The growth and the haemorrhages weakened them so much that they lapsed into pneumonia, which killed them quickly. But, by all the norms, he was still a long way from this stage. He was still on his feet and he wanted to stay there as long as he could.

When he reached the landing at the top of the stairs, he did not go straight to his own room, but turned down the corridor to the one occupied by Nicholas Black. He could hear the painter moving about inside; but when he knocked there was no reply, and when he tried the handle he found that the door was locked. He knocked again, waited a moment and then went back to his own room.

Alone in his high room, with the sun slanting through the lattices on to the picture of Paolo Sanduzzi, Nicholas Black lapsed quietly into the final blankness of despair. There was no madness in the act, no wild ruin of reason under the impact of unexplainable terrors. It was a simple, final admission that life was a riddle without an answer, a game not worth the candle that guttered over its last, profitless gambits.

Those who won might surrender themselves a little longer to the gambler's illusion; but those who lost, as he had lost, had no recourse but to walk away with as much dignity as possible from the scattered cards and the spilt liquor, and the staling smoke of the last cigars.

He had staked everything on this last play—money, the patronage of the Contessa, the opportunity to re-establish his reputation as an artist, the hope to justify even the maimed and incomplete manhood with which nature had endowed him. But now he knew that he had been playing, as always, against marked cards and with every pack stacked against him. His own nature, society, the law, the Church, all conspired to shut him out from the simplest and most necessary satisfactions of existence. He was stripped clean—bankrupt even of hope. There was no place for him to go but back to the half-world, which had already laughed him out.

The Church would take him back, but it would exact a brutal price:

submission of intellect and will, repentance, and a lifelong bitter denial. The grey inquisitors like Meredith would purge him relentlessly, then coax him forward with the stale carrots of eternity. He could not face it and he would not. No man should be asked to pay for the freaks and whims of a sardonic Creator.

He got up, walked to the writing desk, pulled a sheet of notepaper towards him, scribbled three hasty lines and signed them. Then he picked up a palette knife, walked to the picture on the easel and began coolly and methodically, to cut the canvas to pieces.

Never in his life had Meredith felt so ashamed of himself. Whatever the past sins of Nicholas Black, whatever the follies of his thwarted nature, he had still been the subject of calumny, and he had revealed in himself a deep and not unnoble impulse to good. Kindness might have nurtured it, gentleness might have bent it to better purpose. Yet his only comment, his only offering as a priest, had been a cloddish and brutal indiscretion. There was no excuse for it. To invent one would be a hypocrisy. The charity he thought to have acquired through Giacomo Nerone was a monstrous sham, which had failed him when he needed it most. He was what he had been at the beginning: an empty man, devoid of humanity and godliness.

The thought haunted his shallow sleep and when he woke in the late cool, it was still with him. There was only one thing to do. He must make an apology for his grossness and try again to make a humane contact with Black, who must be suffering greatly.

He got up, washed and tidied himself and walked back along the corridor to the painter's room. The door was ajar this time, but when he knocked there was no answer. He pushed it open and looked in. There was no one there. The bed was unruffled. But the picture of Paolo Sanduzzi stood on its easel by the window, slashed to ribbons.

Meredith stepped into the room and walked over to look at it. As he passed the writing desk his eye was caught by a single sheet of paper lying on the green baize top. The superscription bore his own name:

My dear Meredith,
    I've taken the Almighty's jokes all my life. Yours is one too many. You'll be able to make the old sermon on me – Galilean, thou hast conquered. All the best preachers use it.

Yours,
Nicholas Black

Seconds ticked past unnoticed as he stood there, staring down at the paper in his pale hand. Then the full horror of it burst on him and he hurried from the room, down the stairs, along the gravelled path, shouting for the gatekeeper to open for him. The old man opened the grille, rubbed the sleep out of his eyes and then trotted out into the roadway to watch the crazy Monsignor pounding up the hill with his cassock flapping about his heels.

It was quite late when they were missed and later still when they were found – Nicholas Black swinging aimlessly from a branch of the olive tree and Blaise Meredith prone at the roots of it. At first it seemed they were both dead, but Aldo Meyer heard the faint beating of Meredith's heart and sent for Father Anselmo, while Pietro drove the Contessa's car like a madman to the Bishop's Palace in Valenta.

Now the thing he had feared most of all was come to pass. He was trying to explain himself—not to justify, because he knew that justification was impossible—but just to explain to God how it had happened, and how he had lapsed, without any intention of malice.

But there was no God, there was only a mist and silence and, out of the silence, the echo of his own voice.

'. . . I was sleeping, you see. I didn't know he was gone. I ran to find him and he was already hanging there. I couldn't get him down; I wasn't strong enough. I thought he might be alive and I tried to pray with him. I said the Acts of Contrition and of Love—of Faith and Charity, hoping he would hear and join me in them. But he didn't hear. After that I don't remember. . . .'

'But God would hear and God would remember.'

The voice came to him out of the mist, familiar, but far away.

'I failed him. I wanted to help, but I failed.'

'No one can judge failure but the Almighty.'

'A man must judge himself first.'

'And then commit himself to mercy.'

The mists cleared slowly and the voice came nearer; then he saw bending over him the face of Aurelio, Bishop of Valenta. He stretched out one emaciated hand and the Bishop held it between his own.

'I am dying, My Lord.'

Aurelio, the Bishop, smiled at him, the old, brotherly ironic smile.

'As a man should, my son. With dignity and among friends.'

He looked beyond the Bishop and saw them grouped at the foot of his bed. Anne de Sanctis, Aldo Meyer, Nina Sanduzzi, old Anselmo in his stained cassock with the sacramental stole round his neck. He asked weakly:

'Where is the boy?'

'With Rosetta,' said Nina in dialect. 'They are friends.'

'I'm glad of that,' said Blaise Meredith.

'You shouldn't talk too much,' said Meyer.

'It's my last chance, Doctor.' He rolled his head on the pillow and turned back to the Bishop. 'Nicholas Black . . . you'll give him a Christian burial?'

'Who am I to deny him?' said Aurelio, the Bishop.

'I . . . I wrote a letter to Your Lordship.'

'I have it. Everything will be done.'

'How are the oranges?'

'Ripening well.'

'You should . . . send some to His Eminence. . . . They might help him to understand. A present from me.'

'I'll do that.'

'Will Your Lordship confess me, please? I'm very tired.'

Aurelio, the Bishop, took the grubby stole from the neck of Father Anselmo and laid it on his own shoulders; and when the others had gone from the room, he bent forward to hear the last tally of the last sins of Monsignor Blaise Meredith. When he had absolved him, he called the others back and they knelt around the bed holding lighted tapers while old Anselmo gave him the Viaticum, which is the only food for the longest journey in the world.

When he received it, he lay back with closed eyes and folded hands, while the room filled slowly with the murmur of the old prayers for the departing spirit. A long time after, after they were finished, Meredith opened his eyes and said, quite clearly:

'I was afraid so long. Now, it's so very easy.'

A faint rigor shook him and his head lolled slackly on to the white pillow.

'He's dead,' said Aldo Meyer.

'He is with God,' said Aurelio, the Bishop.

Eugenio Cardinal Marotta sat in his high-backed chair, behind the buhl desk on which his secretary had just laid the day's papers. Beside him was a small box of polished wood, in which were six golden oranges, each nestling in a bed of cotton-wool. In his hands was a letter from His Lordship, the Bishop of Valenta. He was reading it, slowly, for the third time:

> ... I regret to inform Your Eminence that Monsignor Blaise Meredith died yesterday morning at nine o'clock in the full possession of his faculties and after receiving the full rites of our Holy Mother the Church.
>
> I regret him, as I regret few men. I mourn him as the brother he had become to me. He had great courage, a singular honesty of mind and a humanity of whose richness he was never fully aware. I know he will be a great loss to Your Eminence and to the Church.
>
> Before he died, he charged me to apologise to Your Eminence for what he termed the failure of his mission. It was not a failure. His researches have thrown great light on the life and character of the Servant of God, Giacomo Nerone, and have proved him, in the moral if not the canonical sense, a man of great sanctity. I am still doubtful whether any good will be served by advancing this Cause even as far as the Ordinary Court, but I have no doubt at all of the good that has already been done through the influence of Giacomo Nerone and the late Monsignor Meredith. An erring priest has returned to God, a child has been kept from great moral harm and a lost and unhappy woman has been given light enough to seek remedies for her condition.
>
> In the worldly sense, these are small and insignificant things. In the true sense of our Faith they are very great ones, and in them I, who am normally sceptical, have seen clearly the finger of God.
>
> The oranges which I send you are a last gift from Monsignor Meredith. They are from my own plantation—first fruits of a new strain which we have imported from California. Next year, God willing, we hope to have more of these trees to distribute on a co-operative basis to local growers. Monsignor Meredith was much interested in this work; and, had he lived, I think he would have liked to take part in it. His request to send this gift was made on his deathbed. He said—and I quote exactly: 'They might help him to understand.' Your Eminence will no doubt understand the allusion.
>
> The body of Monsignor Meredith is now lying in the Church of the Madonna at the Dolours in Gemello Minore, from whence it will be buried tomorrow, in newly consecrated ground, close to the tomb of Giacomo Nerone. I shall myself officiate at the Mass and the interment.
>
> The usual Masses will, of course, be said, and I myself shall make special, permanent remembrance in my own Masses—as Your Eminence will no doubt wish to do in yours.
>
> I understand that Monsignor Meredith once made a request to be buried in Your Eminence's church in Rome. The reason for his change of heart may be of some final interest. In his last letter to me written on the eve of his death, he says: 'Rome is very far—and here, for the first time, I have found myself as a man and a priest.'
>
> I am humbled by the thought that many of us have lived longer and done much less.
>
> Yours fraternally in Christ Jesus,
Aurelio +
Bishop of Valenta

His Eminence laid the letter down on his desk and leaned back in his chair, thinking about it. He was getting old, it seemed. Or perhaps he had lived too long in Rome. He could neither read a letter nor judge a man.

The man who had died was not the man he had sent away—a desiccated pedant with the dust of the libraries thick on his heart.

The Bishop who had written the first request for a Devil's Advocate was not this Aurelio, with his trenchant mind and his more than a hint of irony.

Or perhaps they were the same men, and only he was changed—another victim to the insidious temptations of princes: pride, power, blindness and coldness of heart. Christ had made bishops and a Pope—but never a cardinal. Even the name held more than a hint of illusion—*cardo*, a hinge—as if they were the hinges on which the gates of Heaven were hung. Hinges they might be, but the hinges were useless metal, unless anchored firmly into the living fabric of the Church, whose stones were the poor, the humble, the ignorant, the sinning and the loving, the forgotten of the princes, but never the forgotten of God.

It was a disturbing thought and he promised himself to return to it at the time of his evening examination of conscience. He was a methodical man and now he had other things to attend to. He took out of his pocket a small leather notebook and wrote, under the date for the following day, 'Remembrance in Mass . . . Meredith.'

Then he put the notebook back in his pocket, glanced quickly through his correspondence, and rang to have his car brought round to the entrance. The time was a quarter to eleven. It was the second Friday of the month, the day when the Prefect of the Sacred Congregation of Rites waited on His Holiness the Pope to discuss, among other things, the beatification and canonisation of Servants of God.

Scrupulous people are not suited to great affairs.

Turgot

Between midnight and dawn, while his fellow Romans were celebrating the end of Carnival, Massimo, Count Pantaleone, General of the Military Staff, died in his bed. A bachelor in his early sixties, a soldier of spartan habit, he died alone.

His servant, a retired sergeant of cavalry, brought the General's coffee at the accustomed hour of seven in the morning and found him lying on his back, fully clothed, gape-mouthed and staring at the coffered ceiling. The servant set down the coffee carefully, crossed himself, closed the dead eyes with two fifty-lire pieces, then telephoned the General's aide, Captain Girolamo Carpi.

Carpi telephoned the Director. The Director telephoned me. You will find my name on the Salamander dossier: Dante Alighieri Matucci, Colonel of Carabinieri, seconded for special duty to the Service of Defence Information.

The Service is usually called by its Italian initials, SID (Servizio Informazione Difesa). Like every other intelligence service, it spends a huge amount of taxpayers' money perpetuating itself, and somewhat less in scavenging information which hopefully will protect the Republic against invaders, traitors, spies, saboteurs and political terrorists. You will gather I am sceptical about its value. I have a right to be. I work in it; but every man who works in it becomes disillusioned in some fashion. The Service encourages the loss of innocence; it makes for pliable instruments of policy. However, that's a digression. . .

Massimo, Count Pantaleone, General of the Military Staff, was dead. I was appointed to stage a clean exit for the corpse. I needed help. The Army supplied it in the shape of a senior medical officer, rank of Colonel, and a military advocate, rank of Major. We drove together to the General's apartment. Captain Carpi received us. The General's servant was weeping over a glass of *grappa* in the kitchen. So far, so good. No confusion. No neighbours on the landing. No relatives yet informed. I had no great respect for Carpi, but I had to commend his discretion.

The medical officer made a cursory examination and decided that the General had died from an overdose of barbiturates, self-administered. He wrote a certificate, countersigned by the military advocate, which stated that the cause of death was cardiac arrest. It was not a false document; simply a convenient one. The General's heart had stopped. A pity it hadn't stopped years ago. A scandal would benefit no one. It might harm a great many innocent people.

At eight-thirty, a military ambulance arrived and removed the body. I remained in the apartment with Carpi and the servant. The servant made us coffee and while we drank it, I questioned him. His answers established a series of simple facts.

The General had dined out. He had returned twenty minutes before midnight and retired immediately to his bedroom. The servant had secured doors and windows, set the burglar alarm and gone to bed. He had risen at six-thirty and prepared the morning coffee. ... Visitors? None. ... Intruders? None. The alarms had not been triggered. Telephone calls, in or out? No way to know. The General would use the private line in his bedroom. Certainly the domestic telephone had not sounded. ... The General's demeanour? Normal. He was a taciturn man. Hard to know what he was thinking at any time. That was all. ... I gave him a pat on the shoulder and dismissed him to the kitchen.

Carpi closed the door behind him, poured two glasses of the General's whisky, presented one to me and asked a question:

'What do we tell his friends—and the Press?'

It was the sort of question he would ask: trivial and irrelevant.

'You saw the death certificate, signed and notarized: natural causes, cardiac arrest.'

'And the autopsy report?'

'My dear Captain, for an ambitious man you are very naïve. There will be no autopsy. The General's body has been taken to a mortuary where it will be prepared for a brief lying-in-state. We want him seen. We want him honoured. We want him mourned as a noble servant of the Republic—which in a certain sense he was.'

'And then?'

'Then we want him forgotten. You can help us there.'

'How?'

'Your patron is dead. You did well for us. You deserve a better appointment. I'd suggest something far away from Rome—the Alto Adige, perhaps Taranto, or even Sardinia. You will find promotion a lot quicker in places like that.'

'I'd like to think about it.'

'No time, Captain! You pick up your transfer papers this morning. You deliver them, completed and signed, by five o'clock this afternoon. I guarantee you will have a new posting immediately after the funeral. ... And, Captain?'

'Yes?'

'You will remember that you are in a very delicate position. You accepted to spy on a superior officer. We of SID are grateful; but your officer colleagues would despise you. The slightest indiscretion would therefore damage your career, and might well expose you to great personal danger. I trust you understand me?'

'I understand.'

'Good. You may go now. . . . Oh, a small matter.'

'Yes?'

'You have a key to the apartment. Leave it here please.'

'What happens next?'

'Oh, the usual routine. I examine papers and documents. I file a report. Please try to be sad at the funeral. . . . *Ciao!*'

Carpi went out, wrapping the rags of his dignity around him. He was one of those weak, handsome fellows, who always need, and generally attract, a patron: and who will always betray him to a more potent one. I had used him to report on Pantaleone's movements, contacts and political activities. Now he was a redundant nuisance. I poured myself another glass of whisky and tried to set my thoughts in order.

The Pantaleone affair had all the makings of a political time-bomb. The irony was that you could shout the name up and down the Corso and not one in a thousand of the citizens of the Republic would recognize it. Of those who did recognize it, not one in ten would understand its potency or the magnitude of the conspiracy which had been built around it. The Director understood; so did I. I had dossiers on all the principal participants. For a long time I had chafed at my impotence to do anything about them. They were not criminals—at least not yet. They were all high men—ministers, deputies, industrialists, service officers, bureaucrats—who looked to a day when the confusions of Italy—unstable government, industrial unrest, a faltering economy, an inept bureaucracy and a very frustrated people—would bring the country to the brink of revolution.

On that day, which was closer than many people imagined, the conspirators hoped to seize power and present themselves to a bewildered populace as the saviours of the Republic and the conservators of good order and human rights. Their hope was tolerably well-founded. If a Junta of Greek Colonels had done it, there was no good reason why a much larger and more powerful group of Italians could not do it better . . . especially if they had the support of the Army and the active co-operation of the Forces of Public Security.

Their figure-head had been named for a long time: that noble soldier, one-time junior aide to Marshal Badoglio, passionate patriot, friend of the common man, General Massimo Pantaleone. Now the General had removed himself from the scene. Why had he done it? Who, or what, had nudged him towards the final act; and why again? Was there a new man waiting in the wings? Who was he? When and how would he reveal himself? And was the day already at hand? I was commissioned to answer all these questions; and the margin for error was very slim indeed.

Even a hint that an investigation was in progress would split the country down the middle. If the Press got half an idea that a dubious document had been notarized and uttered by the Army, there would be headlines in every newspaper in the world.

Conspiracy is endemic to Italy, always has been, since Romulus and Remus began horse-trading from Tiber Island; but if the dimension of this plot were made known and the very real possibility that it might succeed . . . *Dio!* There would be barricades in the streets and blood on the tram-tracks within a day: one could not rule out even mutiny in the armed services, whose political loyalties were deeply divided between Left and Right. I had made no idle threat to Captain Carpi. If he tried to sell himself or his information to new masters, an accident would be speedily arranged for him. Meantime, I had my own work to do.

I drank the last of the whisky and began to comb the apartment for papers. I opened drawers and cupboards and tested each one for secret hiding-places. I went through the pockets of each garment in the wardrobe. I shook out every book in the library and removed the blotting paper from the desk-pad. I made no attempt to examine what I found; but simply piled it into a heap. There would be hours of work to sift and analyse it all—and very little value at the end. The General was too old a fox to have left dangerous documents lying about his house.

Still, I could not afford to take risks; so I moved pictures and mats in search of a concealed safe. Then I made a final circuit, lifting ornaments, upending cups and vases, prising up the felt beds of the jewel-cases which held the General's orders and decorations. Even so, I nearly missed the card.

It was lying on its edge against the skirting board, behind the bedside table; a small rectangle of stiff paste-board with a design on one side and an inscription on the other. Both the design and the inscription had been done by hand in black Indian ink. The design had been executed at a single stroke, in a series of intricate whorls and flourishes. It showed a salamander with a coronet on its head, couched in a bed of flames. The inscription was four words of perfect copperplate: '*Un bel domani, fratello*'.

'One fine tomorrow, brother' . . . It was a very Italian phrase, which could preface a variety of sentiments: a vain hope, a promise of reward, a threat of vengeance, a rallying cry. The word 'brother' was ambiguous, too, and the salamander made no sense at all, unless it were the symbol of a club or a fraternity. Yet there was no association with any sign or code-name in my dossiers. I decided to refer it to the specialists. I went back to the study, picked up a clean envelope, sealed the card inside it and put it in the pocket of my jacket.

Then I decided it was time for a private chat with the sergeant of cavalry. I found him in the kitchen, a dejected old man ruminating over an uncertain future. I consoled him with the thought that the General had probably remembered him in his will, and that, at least, he was entitled to severance pay from the deceased's estate. He brightened then and offered me wine and cheese. As we drank together, he became garrulous; and I was happy to let him ramble.

'. . . He didn't have to be a soldier, you know. The Pantaleone always had money running out of their ears. Not that they were free with it. Lord, no! They looked at both sides of a coin and wept before they spent it. Probably that's why they stayed rich. Lands in the Romagna, apartment buildings in Lazio, the old estate in Frascati, the villa on Ponza—of course, she's got that now.'

'Who has?'

'You know—the Polish woman. The one he had dinner with last night. What's her name? . . . Anders—that's it—Anders. She's been his girl-friend for years. Although, I must say, he was pretty close about it. He never brought her here. Funny that. . . . He didn't want people to think he was enjoying himself. Like we used to say in the Army, he was born with a ram-rod up his backside. I knew about her, of course. I used to take her calls. . . . Sometimes I went to her place to deliver things for the General. Good-looking woman, not over the hill yet, either. Which reminds me. . . . Someone ought to tell her what's happened.'

'I'll do that. Where does she live?'

The question was a blind. I knew the answer and a great deal more about Lili Anders.

'Parioli. The address is in the General's pocket book.'

'I'll find it.'

'Hey! Now that's a thing! You're not taking any of the General's stuff away are you? I'm responsible. I don't want any trouble.'

'I'm taking all his papers, and I'll borrow a valise to carry them.'

'But why?'

'A matter of security. We can't leave confidential documents lying around. So, we'll go through the lot, take out the ones that belong to the Army and return the private ones to his lawyer. You won't have any trouble, because I'll give you an official receipt before I leave. Clear?'

'If you say so. . . . Wait a moment! Who are you? I don't even know your name.'

'Matucci. Carabinieri.'

'Carabinieri! . . . There's nothing wrong is there?'

'Nothing at all. . . . Normal procedure with an important man like the General.'

'Who's going to make all the arrangements, tell his friends, that sort of thing?'

'The Army.'

'So, what do I do? Just sit around here?'

'There's one thing you could do. People will telephone. Take their names and numbers and we'll arrange for someone to call them back.'

'I'll still be paid?'

'Don't worry. You have to be paid. It's the law. . . . I meant to ask you something else. Where did the General dine last night?'

'At the Chess Club.'

'You're sure?'

'Of course, I'm sure. I had to know always where he was. Sometimes there were calls from Headquarters or from the Ministry. . . . Another drop?'

'No, thanks, I'll be on my way.'

'And you're sure about the money?'

'I'm sure. And you'll remember to record the telephone calls?'

'Trust me, friend. The General did. I never let him down. You know, he was as cold as a fish; but I'll miss the old bastard. I really will.'

The fellow was becoming maudlin now and I was ready to be quit of him. I scribbled a receipt, picked up the bag of documents and walked out into the thin spring sunshine. It was ten minutes after one. The shop-keepers were closing their shutters and the alleys were busy with Romans homing for lunch and siesta.

I have to tell you frankly I don't like the Romans. I'm a Tuscan born and these people are first cousins to the Hottentot. Their city is a midden; their countryside a vast rubbish tip. They are the worst cooks and the most dyspeptic feeders in Italy. They are rude, crass, cynical and devoid of the most elementary graces. Their faces are closed against compassion and their spirits are pinched and rancorous. They have seen everything and learned nothing, except the basest arts of survival. They have known imperial grandeur, papal pomp, war, famine, plague and spoliation; yet they will bow the knee to any tyrant who offers them an extra loaf of bread and a free ticket to the circus.

Yesterday, it was Benito Mussolini, drunk with rhetoric, haranguing them from the balcony in the Piazza Venezia. Tomorrow it might be another. And where was he now, at this very moment on Ash Wednesday, in this year of doubtful grace? . . . One thing was sure, he wouldn't be standing like Dante Alighieri Matucci, flat-footed in the middle of the Campo Marzio.

I shook myself out of the reverie, walked half a block to my car, tossed the documents on to the seat and drove back to the office. I might have saved myself the trouble. My two senior clerks were out at lunch; number three was flirting with the typist and the data bank was out of action because the power supply had been interrupted by a two-hour strike. There was a message from the Ministry of the Interior requesting 'immediate contact on a most urgent matter'. When I called, I was told that my contact was entertaining some foreign visitors and might possibly be back at four o'clock. Body of Bacchus! What an oafish lot! Judgment Day might come and go, the Maoists might even now be storming the Angelic Gate at Vatican City, but the Romans must finish siesta before they did anything about it.

I dumped the bag of documents on the desk and shouted for number three clerk to sort and collate them. Then, because the strike had put the elevator out of action, I climbed three flights of stairs to the forensic laboratory, where there had to be someone alive, even at lunch time. As usual, it was old Stefanelli who, according to local legend, slept every night in a bottle of formaldehyde and emerged fresh as a marmoset at sunrise every morning. He was a tiny wizened fellow, with wispy locks and yellow teeth and skin like old leather. He must have been ten years past retirement age, but still managed by a combination of patronage and sheer talent to hang on to his job.

What other technicians burst their brains to learn, Stefanelli knew. Sprinkle a peck of dust in his palm and he would name you the province and the region and even make a reasonable guess at the village from which it came. Hand him a swatch of fabric and he would fondle it for a moment, then tell you how much cotton was in it and how much polyester, and give you a list of the factories that might have made it. Give him a drop of blood, two nail clippings and a tress of hair and he would build you the girl who owned them. He was a genius in his own right, albeit a tetchy and troublesome one, who would spit in your eye if you crossed him, or slave twenty-four hours at a stretch for a man who trusted him. He read voluminously and would bet money on his technical knowledge. Only a very new or a very vain junior would bet against him. When I came in, puffing and sour-faced, he greeted me, exuberantly.

'Eh, Colonel! What have you got for Steffi today? I've got something for you. ... Death by suffocation ... green alkaloids in the blood ... no punctures, no abrasions, no apparent means of entry into the blood system. Five thousand lire if you can tell me what it is.'

'Put it that way, Steffi, and I know I'll lose my money. What is it?'

'It's a shell-fish. Comes from the South Pacific. They call it the Cloth of Gold. On contact, the fish injects microscopic needles full of alkalide which paralyse the central nervous system. Case in point—a marine biologist working with the Americans in the South Pacific. ... If you're interested, I'll send you a note on it.'

'Thanks, Steffi, but not today. I have troubles on my own doorstep.' I fished out the salamander card and handed it to him. 'I want a full reading on that: paper, penmanship, the meaning of the symbol and any prints you can lift. I want it fast.'

Stefanelli studied the card intently for a few moments, and then delivered himself of a peroration.

'The card itself is made from Japanese stock—fine quality bonded rice. I can tell you who imports it within a day. The penmanship–fantastic! So beautiful it makes you want to cry! I haven't seen anything like it since Aldo the Calligrapher died in 1935. You remember him, don't you? Of course, you wouldn't. You're too young. Used to have a studio over near the Cancelleria. Made a fortune forging stock certificates and engrossing patents of nobility for fellows who wanted to marry wealthy Americans. . . . Well, Aldo's dead, so he can't help you. We have to go to the files to find who's in practice now. . . . The design? Well . . . it's obviously a salamander, the beast that lives in the fire. What it means here, I don't know. It could be a trade-mark. It could be a *tessera*–a member's card for a club. It could be adapted from a coat-of-arms. I'll put it up to Solimbene. . . . You don't know him. Old friend of mine. Works in the Consulta Araldica. Knows every coat-of-arms in Europe. He can read them like another man would read a newspaper.

'Good idea. In fact, why don't you do some copies now, before the others get back from lunch. I'll need one for my own inquiries anyway.'

'Where did you get this, Colonel?'

'General Pantaleone died last night. I found it in his bedroom.'

'Pantaleone? The old *fascista*! What happened to him?'

'Natural causes, Steffi . . . and we've got a notarized certificate to prove it.'

'Very convenient!'

'Very necessary.'

'Suicide or murder?'

'Suicide.'

'Eh! That smells bad.'

'So, Steffi, for the present, this business is between you and me, and the Director. Keep the card in your own hands. No files, no discussion in the laboratory. Dead silence until I tell you.'

Stefanelli grinned and laid a bony forefinger on his nose–the gesture of knowing and agreeing a conspiracy.

'I don't like Fascists any more than you do, Colonel–and we've got our share of them in this Department. Sometimes I wonder if we've got any democrats left–or whether we ever had any in Italy–except you and me. If we don't get a stable government soon, we'll get a *colpo di stato,* with a Fascist in the saddle. The week after that there'll be civil war–or something very like it–Left against Right, North against South. I'm an old man. I can smell it in the wind. . . . And I'm scared, Colonel. I have sons and daughters and grandchildren. I don't want them to suffer as we did . . .'

'Nor I, Steffi. So we have to know who steps into the General's shoes. Get busy on the card. Call me day or night as soon as you have anything.'

'Good luck, Colonel.'

'I'll need it. . . . *Ciao,* Steffi.'

Now I was at a loose end. I could make no sense of the Pantaleone documents until they were listed and collated with the General's dossier. The Director was the only man to whom I could talk freely and he was out of the office. I could, of course, call on Francesca, the little model who was always available after midday. But that would leave me drugged and dozy for the rest of the afternoon. I settled for a cup of coffee in a bar and then drove out to Parioli to see Lili Anders.

Her apartment was on the third floor of a new condominium, all aluminium and glass, with a porter in livery and an elevator panelled in walnut. The place had cost, according to the lady's dossier, sixty million lire; the upkeep according to the contract was a hundred and twenty thousand a month. The fiscal records of the Comune di Roma showed that Lili Anders was taxed on a visible standard of living of a million lire a month. Since she paid the tax without demur, it was obvious she must be living at twice the scale assessed. I was keeping an apartment, a servant, a three-year-old Fiat and an occasional playmate on six hundred thousand a month less taxes and I thought Lili Anders was a very fortunate woman. By the time I came to ring the bell, therefore, I was feeling bad-tempered and resentful. An elderly house-keeper, dressed in black bombazine and starched white linen, confronted me like a true Roman, laconic and hostile:

'Yes?'

'Matucci. Carabinieri. I wish to see the Signora Anders.'

'You have an appointment?'

'No.'

'Then you'll have to come back later. The Signora is asleep.'

'I'm afraid I must ask you to wake her. My business is urgent.'

'Do you have any identification?'

'I offered my card; she took and read it slowly, line by line, then swept me into the hallway like a pile of dust, and left me.

I waited, grim and dyspeptic, but touched with a sour admiration for this ancient matron, whose ancestors had tossed rooftiles on popes and cardinals and puppet princelings. Then Lili Anders made her entrance. For a woman in her middle thirties, she was singularly well-preserved; a little plump for my taste, but still most definitely on the right side of the hill. For a woman who had just been sleeping, she was beautifully turned out; every blonde hair in place, no slur in the make-up, no wrinkle in skirt, blouse or stockings. Her greeting was polite but cool.

'You wished to see me?'

'Privately, if that is possible.'

She passed me into the salone and closed the door. She prayed me to be seated and then stood herself by the mantel under an equestrian portrait of Pantaleone.

'You are, I believe, from the Carabinieri.'

'I am Colonel Matucci.'

'And the reason for this visit?'

'A painful matter, I'm afraid.'

'Oh?'

'I regret to inform you that General Pantaleone died early this morning.'

She did not weep. She did not cry out. She stared at me, wide-eyed and trembling, holding on to the mantel for support. I moved towards her to steady her; but she waved me away. I crossed to the buffet, poured brandy into a goblet and handed it to her. She drank it at a gulp, then gagged on the raw spirit. I gave her the clean handkerchief from my breast pocket and she dabbed at her lips and the front of her blouse. I talked to her, quietly:

'It's always a shock, even in our business. If you want to cry, go ahead.'

'I will not cry. He was kind to me and gentle, but I have no tears for him.'

'There is something else you should know.'

'Yes?'

'He died by his own hand.'

She gave no sign of surprise. She simply shrugged and spread her hands in a gesture of defeat.

'With him it was always possible.'

'Why do you say that?'

'There were too many dark places in his life, Colonel; too many secrets; too many people lying in wait for him.'

'Did he tell you that?'

'No, I knew.'

'Then, perhaps, you know this. Why did he choose last night to kill himself? Why not a week ago, or next month?'

'I don't know. He had been moody for a long time, a month or more. I asked him more than once what was troubling him. He always put me off.'

'And last night?'

'One thing only. During dinner a waiter brought him a message. Don't ask me what it was. You know the Chess Club—it's like being in church, all whispers and incense. He left me at the table and went outside. He was away about five minutes. When he came back, he told me he had had a telephone call from a colleague. Nothing more was said. Later, when he brought me home, I invited him in. Sometimes he stayed the night, sometimes he didn't. This time he said he had work to finish at home. It was normal. I didn't argue. I was tired myself, anyway.'

I took out the photo-copy of the salamander card and handed it to her.

'Have you seen this before? Or anything like it?'

She studied it intently for a few moments and then shook her head.

'Never.'

'Do you recognize the animal?'

'Some kind of lizard . . . a dragon, perhaps.'

'The crown?'

'Nothing.'

'The words?'

'What they say . . . "One fine tomorrow, brother" . . . that's all.'

'Have you ever heard them before anywhere?'

'Not that I can remember. I'm sorry.'

'Please, dear lady! You must, in no sense, reproach yourself. You have had a grievous shock. You have lost a dear friend. And now. . . . How to say it! . . . I have to distress you still further. It is my duty to warn you that from this moment you stand in grave personal danger.'

'I don't understand.'

'Then permit me to explain. You have been for a long time the mistress of an important man, whom certain elements have considered an explosive man. A mistress is presumed to be a confidante, a repository of secrets. Even if the General told you nothing, others will believe he told you everything. Inevitably, therefore, you will come under surveillance, under pressure, possibly even under threat.'

'From whom?'

'From extremists of the Right and of the Left, persons who are trained to use violence as a political weapon; from foreign agents, operating within the confines of the Republic; even—though I blush to confess it—from officials of our own Public Security. As a foreigner, residing here on a sojourn permit, you are especially vulnerable.'

'But I have nothing to tell! I lived a woman's life with a man who needed comfort and affection. His other life, whatever it was, I did not share. When his door closed on us, the world was shut out. He wanted it so. You must believe that.'

She was shaken now. Her face seemed to crumple into the contours of middle-age. Her hands fumbled restlessly at the balled handkerchief. I leaned back in the chair and admonished her.

'I wish I could believe you. But, I know you Lili Anders. I know you chapter and verse, from your first birthday in Warsaw, to your latest despatch to one Colomba, who is a printer and book-binder in Milan. You identified yourself, as usual, by the code-word 'Falcone'. All the members of your network are called by bird-names, are they not? You are paid by Canarino from account number 68-Pilau at the Cantonal bank in Zurich. . . . You see, Lili, we Italians are not really as stupid or inefficient as we look. We are very good conspirators, because we love the game and we make the rules to suit ourselves. . . . Another brandy? I'll have one myself, if you don't mind. Relax now, I'm not going to eat you. I admire a good professional. But you are a problem, a real problem. . . . *Salute!* To your continued good health!'

She drank, clasping the glass in both hands as if it were a pillar that would support her.

'What happens to me now?'

'Eh! That's a very open question, Lili. As I see it at this moment there are two alternatives. I take you into custody on charges of conspiracy and espionage. That means a long interrogation, a stiff sentence and no hope even of provisory liberty. Or, I could leave you free, on certain conditions, to continue your comfortable life in Rome. Which would you prefer?'

'I'm tired of the game, Colonel. I'd like to be out of it. I'm getting too old.'

'That's the problem, Lili. You can't get out. You can only change sides.'

'Which means?'

'Full information on the network and all your activities, and a contract with us as a double-agent.'

'Can you protect me?'

'As long as you're useful, yes.'

'I was a good mistress, Colonel. I kept my man happy and gave value for money.'

'Let's try some more questions then. Who arranged your first meeting with the General?'

'The Marchesa Friuli.'

'What is her code-name?'

'Pappagallo.'

'It suits the old girl. She even looks like a parrot. What was your directive?'

'To give early warnings of any attempt at a *coup d'état* by neo-fascist groups, and of actions designed to provoke it.'

'Such as?'

'Acts of violence planned against police or Carabinieri during labour demonstrations, bomb attacks that could be attributed to Maoist or Marxist groups, the spread of disaffection among conscripts and new levies in the armed services, any contracts, secret or open, between the Greek regime and officials of the Republic of Italy, shifts of influence or changes of political groups in the Italian High Command.'

'Had there been any such changes recently?'

'No . . . at least not to my knowledge.'

'Then why was the General depressed?'

'I don't know. I was trying to find out.'

'Money problems?'

'I wouldn't think so. . . . He was never a lavish man—even to me.'

'Political pressures—blackmail?'

'I had the feeling that it was a personal and not a political matter.'

'What gave you that impression?'

'Things he said when he was relaxed here with me.'

'For example?'

'Oh, odd remarks. He had a habit of saying something—how would you call it?—something cryptic; then passing immediately to another subject. If I pressed him to explain, he would close up like a shell-fish. I learned, quickly to hold my tongue. . . . One night, for example, he said: "There is no simple future for me, Lili, because my past is too complicated." Another time he quoted from the Bible: "A man's enemies are those of his own household." . . . Things like that.'

'Anything else?'

'I'm trying to remember. . . . Oh, yes, about three weeks ago we met in Venice. He took me to the opera at the Phoenix Theatre. He talked about the history of the theatre and he explained the name to me. He said that the Phoenix was a fabulous bird that rose again, alive, from its own ashes; then he said that there was another animal more fabulous and more dangerous—the salamander that lived in fire and could survive the hottest flames. . . . Wait! That's your card . . . the Salamander!'

'So it is, Lili. You see how far we come when we talk like friends? What else did he say about the salamander?'

'Nothing. Nothing at all. Some friends joined us. The subject was dropped and forgotten.'

'Let's leave it then. There will be other times and other questions. From now on you will be under constant surveillance. There is my card with day and night numbers. You'll be notified of the date of the funeral. I'd like you to be there.'

'Please, no!'

'Please, yes! I want tears, Lili. I want deep grief and black mourning. You will not move back into society until I tell you. Naturally, you will have telephone calls from your masters and from friends of the General. Your house-keeper will want to know the reason for my visit. You will tell them all the same story. The General died of a heart attack. It would not hurt to confess that he had an ailment which sometimes interfered with his love-making. . . . One other thing. No new boy-friends until you are out of mourning. That would make an ugly figure. If you find a live one after that, I'd like to check him out before you adopt him.'

She managed a weak and watery smile.

'Him or me, Colonel?'

'I admire you, Lili, but I can't afford you. If you could make an old fossil like Pantaleone sit up and beg, God only knows what you'd do to a hungry fellow like me. Still, it's a thought to keep. One fine tomorrow, we just might play a little chamber music. Be good now. And there's a prize for every tear of the requiem. . . . Where's your telephone?'

Half an hour later I was seated in a glass booth on the Veneto, with a sandwich and a *cappuccino*, scanning the afternoon editions of the Roman and Milanese papers. The General's death was reported only in the stop press. The terms of each report were identical, a direct quotation of the

Army announcement. There were no obituaries, no editorial comments. There might be some in the final editions but the bloodhounds would not be in full cry until morning. By that time, the General would be safely embalmed and lying in state in the family chapel at Frascati, with the cadets of his old regiment standing the death watch.

The obsequies of Massimo Count Pantaleone, General of the Military Staff, made a splendid piece of theatre. The requiem was sung by the sub-urbicarian Bishop of Frascati, Cardinal Amleto Paolo Dadone, assisted by the choir of the monastery of Sant' Antonio della Valle. The panegyric was delivered in classic periods and ringing tones by the Secretary-General of the Society of Jesus, a former class-mate of the deceased. The Mass was attended by the President of the Republic, Ministers of the Council, Members of both Chambers, Prelates of the Roman Curia, Senior Officers of all Services, representatives of NATO and the Diplomatic Corps, relatives and friends of the deceased, family retainers, press-men, photographers and a motley of Romans, countrymen and casual tourists. Six field-officers carried the bier to the vault, where the regimental chaplain consigned it to rest until resurrection day, while a detachment of junior officers fired the last volley, and the Penitentiaries of Sant' Ambrogio recited the Sorrowful Mysteries of the Rosary. The door of the vault was closed and locked by the President himself, a gesture of respect, gratitude and national solidarity not lost upon the gentlemen of the Press. Lili Anders was there, heavily veiled and leaning on the arm of Captain Girolamo Carpi, who was visibly moved by the passing of his beloved patron.

I was among the mourners, too; but I was less concerned with the ceremonies than with the efforts of my camera crew to produce a clear photograph of every person at the funeral, from the Cardinal celebrant to the florist who laid the tributes. I hate funerals. They make me feel old, unwanted and disposed to sexual exercise which is a kind of defiance of my own imminent mortality. I was glad when the rites were over, so that I could drive down to see Francesca, while my colleagues were still guzzling spumante and sweet pastry at the Villa Pantaleone.

At three-thirty in the afternoon, I went back to the forensic laboratory to talk to Stefanelli. The old fellow was jumping like a grass-hopper.

'. . . I told you, Colonel! Bet with old Steffi and you have to win! I showed the card to Solimbene and he recognized it at first glance. The crowned salamander is the emblem of Francis the First. It recurs, with certain modifications, in arms derived from the House of Orleans, the Duchy of Angoulême and the Farmer family in England. I've retained Solimbene to get us a list of existing Italian families who use the symbol. You'll have to authorize the payment. The pen-work? We say it's based on Aldo the Calligrapher but probably executed by Carlo Metaponte who used to be a forger, made papers for the partisans during the war and has been going straight ever since. The card itself . . . I was wrong about that. It's not Japanese at all. It's a very passable Italian imitation made in Modena by the Casaroli Brothers. They're supplying us with a list of their principal customers in Europe. The inscription makes no sense yet; but we're coming to it. How's that, eh! Not bad for forty-eight hours. Tell me you're happy, Colonel, otherwise I'll drown myself in the toilet.'

'I'm happy, Steffi. But we need a lot more. Fingerprints for instance.'

'I'm sorry, Colonel. The only ones we've been able to lift belong to the late lamented General. You didn't expect anything else, surely?'

'I want miracles, Steffi. I want them yesterday.'

'Spare us a little pity, Colonel. Everything takes time. . . . How was the funeral?'

'Beautiful, Steffi. I cried all through it! And the eloquence! . . . "That noble spirit snatched untimely from among us, that dedicated servant of the Republic, that Christian patriot, that hero of many battles . . ." *Merda!*'

'*Requiescat in aeternum.*' Stefanelli crossed hands on his bony chest and rolled his eyes heavenwards. 'If he's in heaven, I hope never to go there. Amen! . . . Have you read today's papers?'

'Now, when have I had time to read, Steffi?'

'I've got them in my office. Come on! They're worth a look.'

The obituaries were, like the obsequies, an exercise in grandiloquence. The Right wing was fulsome; the centre was respectful and only mildly censorious of the General's Fascist period; the Left achieved a kind of poetry of abuse, culminating in a pasquinade, which for form's sake was attributed to some anonymous Roman:

'*Estirpato oggi,*	'*Uprooted today,*
L'ultimo della stirpe,	*The last of his line,*
Pantaleone,	*Pantaleone,*
Mascalzone.'	*The rogue.*'

I was not unhappy with the things I read. They were good reviews for a bad score and a book full of contradictions. Not one of them called in question the official version of the General's demise; which was not to say they believed it but only that it suited all parties to accept it. The pasquinade worried me a little. Take it at face value and it was a harmless squib. The General was the last of the Pantaleone line, and an old rogue to boot. Read it another way and it might mean that the Left had taken a hand in rooting him out and that happily no successor was in sight. If one were very subtle—and I was paid to read meaning even into blank pages—one might see it as the opening gambit of a campaign to vilify the General and bring all the skeletons out of his family vault. A pity if it happened, but there was nothing I could do about it. I was still drowsy and disinclined to exert myself, so I began leafing through the journals, while Stefanelli added a spicy commentary.

'. . . Now, here's a pretty thing: "The Principessa Faubiani presents her summer collection!" You know about her, don't you? Came from Argentina originally, married young Prince Faubiani, set him up with a boy-friend, and then petitioned for separation on the grounds of his impotence. That way she kept her freedom, the title and a right to maintenance. Since then, she's had a new protector every couple of years—old ones now, and all rich. They finance the collections and improve her standard of living as well. That last one was the banker, Castellani. . . . Wonder who it is this year? Funny thing, she still stays friends with them all. See, there's Castellani, next to the model in the bikini. Ah, there's the new one, in the front row, behind Faubiani and the Editor of Vogue. That's the place of honour. Ritual, you know. When the High Priestess gets tired of you, she hands you down to the models. Still, if you're sixty or over, who cares? The girls come cheaper than a whole summer collection, eh? . . . I must find out who the new one is.'

'And what's your interest in fashion, Steffi?'

'My wife has a boutique on the Via Sistina ... high mode for rich tourists.'

'You crafty old devil!'

'I'm a lucky man, Colonel. I married for love and got money for my old age as well. Also the staff is decorative and the gossip's always interesting. . . . Which reminds me. Pantaleone is supposed to have a brother floating around somewhere.'

'Not in my dossier, Steffi. The old count, Massimo, had two daughters in the first three years of his marriage and a son about ten years later. One daughter married a Contini and died in childbirth. The other married a Spanish diplomat and lives in Bolivia. She has three adult children who all have Spanish nationality. The son, our General, was the only male issue. He inherited the title and the bulk of the real estate. That's the record, verified at Central Registry, and from the baptismal files at Frascati.'

'Well, I agree she's not as official as the Central Registry, but the old Baroness Schwarzburg has been a client of my wife's for years. She's tottering on the edge of the grave, but she still spends a fortune on clothes. She claims she knew the General's father—which is very possible, because the old boy was chasing girls until the day he fell off his horse on the Pincio and broke his neck. According to her story, the Count bred himself a bastard from the girls' governess. He paid her off and she married someone else who gave the boy a name, though what the name was the Baroness couldn't remember. She's getting doddery, of course, so it could be nothing but scandalous rumour. You know what these old girls are. They've never got over their first waltz, and the time King Umberto showed them his coin collection. . . . Anyway, it's a note in the margin, if you're interested.'

'Not really, Steffi. Now, if you could find me a suicide note or a blackmail letter that would tell me why Pantaleone killed himself, I'd be much happier. . . . *Dio!* It's nearly five. The funeral photographs should be ready. If they're not, I'll send you three heads for pickling. See you later, Steffi. Keep in touch.'

Naturally enough, the photographs were not ready, and the Chief of Photographic Records was liverish and unhappy. Everyone understood the urgency, but I must be reasonable. Could I not see that the tanks were clogged with film, the enlargers were working overtime, and even with three photographers and two photo-file experts, it would take hours yet to identify all the personages. Even then there would be gaps. This was like an epic at Cinecitta, the whole set crowded with hundreds of extras—and how did one put names to farm-labourers and three bus-loads of tourists?

After ten minutes of snappish dialogue, I gave up in disgust and went back to my own office. Here, at least, there was a semblance of order and efficiency. The documents I had brought from the General's flat were all indexed and filed, and number one clerk had made some interesting discoveries.

'Brokers' advice notes, Colonel. All sales. The General has unloaded about eighty million lire worth of prime stock in the last four weeks. Covering letters from the Brokers, each one in the same terms . . . "We have remitted proceeds in accordance with your instructions". Question: Where did the proceeds go? Not into his bank, because there's his last statement, issued a week ago. Then there's a letter from the Agenzia Immobiliare della Romagna. They advise that though the Pantaleone property has been on open offer for more than two months, there has been no serious interest at the figure named. They recommend withdrawing the property until the credit situation in Europe eases a little, and the new agricultural agreements have been announced for the Common Market. . . . Now come to this little piece. It's a handwritten note from Emilio del Giudice in Florence. You know him; a big name, a heavy dealer in important art works. Here's what he says: "Strongly advise against any transactions which involve you personally in a commitment to export works from the Pantaleone collection. As vendor you offer the works for sale subject to the conditions of the laws in force. After that, full responsibility for export formalities rests on the purchaser" . . .'

'So, he was trying to sell up. Any indication why?'

'Not in these papers.'

'What else have we got?'

'Cheque stubs, household accounts, bank statements, correspondence with estate managers and renting agencies, desk directory, pocket address-book. I'm still checking those against the names in our dossiers and so far, no surprises. This is the General's key-ring with a key to a safe-deposit box at the Banco di Roma. I'd like to see the inside of that.'

'We will—as soon as the banks open in the morning.'

'His lawyer is howling for us to release the documents.'

'I'll worry about him later. I'll also have a chat with the General's brokers. I'd like to know where they remitted the sale money. . . . If you want me in the next hour, I'll be at the Chess Club. After that, at home.'

The Chess Club of Rome is an institution almost as sacred as the Hunt Club. You enter it, as you hope one day to enter Heaven, through a noble portico, and find yourself in a courtyard of classic dimension. You climb a flight of stairs to a series of ante rooms, where servants in livery receive you with cautious deference. You tread softly and speak in muted tones, so as not to disturb the ghosts who still inhabit the place, Kings and Princes, Dukes, Barons, Counts and all their consorts. In the salone, you are dwarfed by soaring pilasters and frescoed ceilings, and gilt furniture designed for the backsides of grandees. In the dining-room you are awed by an afflatus of whispers, the talk of men who deal with great affairs like money and statecraft and spheres of commercial influence. You are daunted by the cold eyes of dowagers, sour with the virtue of age. You are hounded by waiters so disciplined, that even a crumb upon the shirt-front seems a sacrilege. . . . And you will look in vain for chess players, although it is rumoured that they do exist, cloistered as Carmelites in some secret cell.

I was not coming to play chess. I was coming to wait upon the Secretary, who might condescend to present me to the head-waiter, who, might if the stars were in favourable conjunction, put me in touch with the steward who had served General Pantaleone on the eve of his death.

I did not relish the prospect. The Chess Club is one of those places that makes me despair of my countrymen. In the uplands of Sardinia, where I once served as a junior officer, there are shepherds who live a whole winter on corn-bread and black olives and goat-cheese, and turn to banditry to feed their families, while their landlords lobby senators and ministers over brandy in the Club. In the mortuary at Palermo, I have identified the body of a colleague murdered by the Mafia, while the man who ordered him killed was lunching with a Milanese banker—at the Chess Club, of course. The economists weep tears of blood over the flight of capital from Italy to Switzerland, but the men who put wings to the money, sit sober and respectable over lunch at the corner table. Here, the survivors of the old order and the exploiters of the new, make truce and treaty and marriages of convenience, while the people, poor, ill-educated, impotent, fume at the chicanery of politicians and the tyranny of petty bureaucrats.

Time was when I toyed with the idea of joining the Communists who promised at least a levelling and a purging and one law for all. My enthusiasm died on the day when I saw a high Party official sharing smoked salmon and fillet steak with the president of a large chemical corporation. The more things change in Italy, the more they are the same. The scion of an old house joins the Christian Democrats; the cadet is free to flirt with Left or Right; and no matter who wins the last race, the bets will still be settled in the Chess Club. . . . Eh! Philosophers are as big a curse on the country as politicos: and a muddled conscience is bad medicine for an investigator. Let's be done with the job and go home!

It was still only eight-thirty and the guests were sparse. The Secretary was unusually urbane and the head-waiter was disposed to be helpful. He installed me in the visitors' room, brought me an aperitif, and, five minutes later, reappeared with the head-porter and the steward who had served the General's last meal. I explained my mission with suitable vagueness. Sometime during dinner the General had been called to the telephone. For reasons connected with military security, I wished to trace the call and contact the person who had made it. Then I had my first surprise.

'No, Colonel.' The head-porter was very definite. 'You have been misinformed. The General was called from the dining-room, but not to the telephone. A senior member of the Club had asked to speak with him in private. He waited in the card-room. The steward conducted the General to him. They spoke for a few moments, the General returned to his table, the member collected his coat and left the Club. I saw him leave.'

'And who was this member?'

'A gentleman from Bologna. The Cavaliere Bruno Manzini. He's in the Club now. Came in about twenty minutes ago with the Principessa Faubiani.'

'La Faubiani, eh?' I permitted myself a small grin of satisfaction. At least I was one up on old Steffi. The head-porter coughed eloquently.

'Colonel . . .?'

'Could you tell me something about the Cavaliere?'

'I could, sir, but–with respect–that sort of request should be addressed to the Secretary.'

'Of course. My compliments on your discretion. Would you give the Cavaliere my card and ask him to spare me a few moments?'

In any company, the Cavaliere Manzini would have been an impressive figure. He must have been nearly seventy years old; his hair was snow-white, brushed back in a lion's mane over his coat-collar; but his back was straight as a pine, his skin was clear, his eyes bright and humorous. His clothes were modish, his linen immaculate and he carried himself with the air of a man accustomed to deference. He did not offer his hand but announced himself with calm formality.

'I am Manzini. I understand you wished to see me. May I see your official identification?'

I handed him the document. He read it carefully, passed it back and then sat down.

'Thank you, Colonel. Now, your question.'

'You were, I believe, a friend of General Pantaleone?'

'Not a friend, Colonel, an acquaintance. I had small respect for him, none at all for his politics.'

'How would you define his politics?'

'Fascist and opportunist.'

'And your own?'

'Are private to myself, Colonel.'

'On the night before he died, the General dined here with a lady. I understand you had a conversation with him.'

'I did.'

'May I know the substance of it?'

'Certainly. I am the client of an art-dealer in Florence. His name is del Giudice. He had told me that Pantaleone was about to sell the family collection. I was interested in certain items, an Andrea del Sarto and a Bosch. I told Pantaleone I would like to negotiate with him directly. It would save us both money.'

'And . . .?'

'He said he would think about it and write to me soon.'

'You didn't press him for a date?'

'No. I could always buy through del Giudice. May I know the reason for these inquiries?'

'At this moment, sir, I am not at liberty to disclose it. Another question. The Pantaleone collection is an old and important one. Why would the General want to disperse it?'

'I have no idea.'

'May I ask you to keep this conversation private?'

'No, you may not! I did not invite it. I gave no prior promise of secrecy. I stand upon my right to discuss it or not, as I please–and with whom I please.'

'Cavaliere, you know the organization which I represent?'

'The Service of Defence Information? I know of its existence. I am not familiar with its activities.'

'You know, at least, that we deal with highly sensitive matters, both political and military.'

'My dear Colonel, please! I'm an old man. I lost my milk teeth years ago. I have no taste for spies, provocateurs or those who treat with them. I know that intelligence services can become instruments of tyranny. I know that they tend to corrupt the people who work in them. If you have no more questions, I trust that you will excuse me. . . . Good evening!'

He stalked out of the room, stiff as a grenadier, and I let out a long exhalation of relief. This was a sturdy one for a change, hard to coax, impossible to frighten. He looked you straight in the eye and gave you clean answers crack-crack-crack, knowing that you dared not gainsay him. But there were important questions still open. Why would Pantaleone, with suicide on his mind, engage in the long and tedious business of selling an estate? If he did embark on it, why not complete it? And why promise a letter he knew he would never write?

Boh! It was enough for one day and more than enough. My head was full of cotton wool and my heart full of envy for a seventy-year-old Cavaliere who could afford expensive pets like the Principessa Faubiani. I walked out of the Club into a soft spring rain, prised my car out of the court-yard and drove reluctantly homeward, to a hot dinner, a tepid hour of television and a cold bed afterwards.

In fact, I had a very troubled night. Shortly after ten, a colleague from Milan telephoned with the news that a young Maoist, under questioning in a bomb case, had fallen to his death from the window of the interrogation room. There would be headlines in every morning paper. The Left would swear he had been pushed. The Right would affirm that he had jumped. Either way, they had a martyr on their hands. My colleague was evasive, but when he mentioned the name of the interrogator, I knew the truth. The man was a sadist, a rabid idiot who didn't care how he got his evidence, or where he made it stick. He also had friends in high places who would spray him with rosewater at any inquiry. This was the kind of madness that bedevilled the whole country and brought the police and the judicial system into disrepute. There would be troops on every street corner for a week and this, too, would heighten the tension and polarize the factions, the one crying tyranny and repression, the other shouting law and order and an end to anarchy. *Dio!* What a nightmare mess! If I had any sense I should pack my bags and take the next boat to Australia.

At eleven-thirty, Lili Anders telephoned in panic. Her network contact had called and summoned her to a rendezvous at the Osteria del Orso. She was due there at midnight. What should she do? I told her to keep the rendezvous, rehearsed her three times in her story and then spent an anxious fifteen minutes trying to regroup my surveillance team.

I was just about to crawl into bed, when the telephone rang again. This time it was Captain Carpi's shadow. The Captain was drunk and mumbling darkly to a bar-girl at the Tour Hassan. What did I want done about it? For God's sake! Let him drink himself silly on bad champagne. The girls at the Tour Hassan wouldn't leave anyway until four in the morning. After that, if Carpi was still on his feet—or even if he wasn't—bundle him into a taxi and take him home. . . . Expenses? Have them put the drinks on Carpi's bill. They'd be padding it anyway. Goodnight and the devil take the pair of you!

At nine-thirty next morning, I sat in conference with a senior official of the Banco di Roma. He was courteous but very firm. There could be no access to the late General's safe deposit until every juridical requirement was met. He understood perfectly my position. He was sensible that matters of national security were involved. However, they were equally involved in his own case. The bank was a national institution. Public confidence depended on the rigid performance of contracts between banker and client. The law demanded it. The Carabinieri were servants of the law. Besides—he paused before delivering the *coup de grâce*—the strong box was empty. The General's lawyer had taken possession of its contents under an existing authority. I acknowledged defeat and went to see the General's brokers.

The brokers, an affiliate of a large American house, were much more co-operative. They had indeed sold large parcels of stock for the late General. They had remitted the proceeds, under instruction, to the General's legal representative, Doctor Sergio Bandinelli. So far as they were concerned, the transaction was closed at that point. They had no information as to the ultimate disposition of the funds. They were brokers only. They offered market advice under the normal disclaimers. They bought and sold under instruction. They functioned rigidly within the prevailing laws. End of conference.

Back in my office, I signed an *invito* requesting Doctor Sergio Bandinelli to wait on me within forty-eight hours. Then I spread the funeral photographs on the desk and settled down to examine them minutely against the accompanying check-list. It was not the names or the personages which interested me so much as the juxtapositions: who was talking to whom, which group seemed the most cohesive and intimate. Sometimes, in a crush like that, public enemies were revealed as secret allies. Sometimes, by a thousand to one chance, one saw a sign given or a message passed from hand to hand. At the end of an hour, I was left with one small surprise.

The surprise was the Cavaliere Manzini, the old autocrat from the Chess Club. He appeared in three shots, once talking to Cardinal Dadone, once with the Minister of Finance and the third time, a little removed from the cemetery vault, standing beside an elderly peasant who was listed as employed at the Villa Pantaleone. For a man who had small respect for Pantaleone, who regarded him as a Fascist and an opportunist, it was a singular gesture. I wondered why he had troubled to make it. I made a telephone call to a colleague in Bologna and asked that a copy of the Cavaliere's dossier be sent post-haste to Rome. Then I called the laboratory and summoned Stefanelli for a private talk.

Old Steffi was bursting with news, little of it good. First, his wife had told him that the new protector of the Principessa Faubiani was one Bruno Manzini, a Bolognese, richer than any one had a right to be—big enterprises, textiles, electrics, steel, food processing. Eat any pie you liked, Manzini owned a slice of it.

'I know all that, Steffi.'

'The hell you do? How?'

I told him at length and in detail. Then I spread the photographs on the desk.

'Now, tell me, Steffi. What's he doing at the funeral of a man he disliked and despised?'

'Easy, my friend. The Club. Members may not like each other; but they don't insult each other either. You may not like me, but you'll come to bury me, won't you? How else can you be sure I'm dead?'

'Maybe . . . maybe. . . . What else have you got for me?'

'The Casaroli Brothers sell rice-paper to wholesalers only; one in each province of Italy. The wholesalers sell to retail printers and stationers. That's the list of the wholesalers. The retailers will run into hundreds, possibly thousands.'

'Body of Bacchus! Don't you have any good news, Steffi?'

'Solimbene called me from the Consulta Araldica. He'll have his list ready tomorrow morning. So far, he's found fifteen surviving families in Italy who use the salamander in their coat-of-arms. Another paper-chase, I'm afraid. . . . Did you read the headlines this morning?'

'I did.'

'I'm scared, Colonel. When the police look like gangsters . . .'

'Or are made to look like gangsters, Steffi.'

'Either way, there's trouble ahead. They had two thousand Carabinieri on the streets of Milan this morning. And there's another thousand on extra duty in Rome; to say nothing of Turin and down south in Reggio. Right now, we've got the country clamped down tight—but we're not curing anything, we're not reorganizing anything.'

'It's not our job, Steffi. We're an arm of government–but we're not the Government itself.'

'We don't have a Government, friend. We have parties, factions, warring interests; and the man in the street doesn't know where to turn. Who represents the Government to him? A cop who walks away from a traffic jam; some little clerk in the pensions office who slams a window in his face. If things don't change soon, our man in the street is going to start shouting for a leader . . . a new *Duce!*'

'And who would that be, Steffi? Go on, toss me names! Pantaleone's dead. He's off stage. Who enters next–and from where–left, right or centre? That's what I'm trying to find out.'

'And when you do?'

'Say it, Steffi . . .'

'You buried an embarrassing corpse yesterday–under orders. Suppose you stumble on another embarrassment, a live one this time–a man in our own service for example. Suppose you're ordered then to close the file and keep your mouth shut. What will you do? Tell me honestly, friend to friend.'

'Steffi, I'm damned if I know. Old Manzini was right. This trade corrupts people. I know it's corrupted me; I don't like to ask how much.'

'You may have to ask very soon, Colonel. Look! Last night in Milan a suspect under questioning jumped or was pushed from a window. He's dead now. He can't be brought to trial. Nobody else can, either. You and I are guardians of public security. What do we do? What does the whole service do? We absolve ourselves. Why? Because we can put ten, twenty thousand armed men in the streets to keep the people cowed and stifle the questions. Who are the real rulers of Milan at this very moment? The Government? Hell! We are–the Carabinieri and our colleagues of the police. That's a tempting blue-print, you know. Terribly tempting. We don't have to offer bread and circuses any more; just public order, peace in the streets and the buses running on time. I told you I'm scared. Now I'll tell you why. I'm a Jew, Colonel. You didn't know that? Well, here and now, it doesn't pay to advertise the fact. I live over behind the synagogue in the old Ghetto. In the synagogue we've got a list of names, three hundred men, eight hundred women and children. They were shipped out of Rome to Auschwitz on the Black Sabbath of 1943. After the war, fifteen came back. Fourteen men and a woman. Do you know why I joined the service? So that I'd know in advance if it were ever going to happen again. . . . How old are you, Colonel?'

'Forty-two. Why?'

'You were a boy when it happened. But every time I see an election poster now, I get nightmares. I'm sorry if I've offended you.'

'You haven't, Steffi. I'm glad you told me. Now, why don't you go play with your microscope, eh?'

When the old man had gone, I sat a long time staring at the littered desk, the photographs, the memoranda, the tapes recorded last night in the Osteria del Orso. Suddenly, it all seemed irrelevant, trivial to the point of absurdity. What was at issue was not politics, not power-games and the sordid ploys of espionage, but myself, Dante Alighieri Matucci, who I was, what I believed and what price I would accept for my soul–if indeed I had one.

To be a servant of the State was easy. The State was like God. You couldn't define it. Therefore, you didn't have to ask questions about it. You didn't even have to believe that it existed. You had only to act as if you did. This was the difference between the Anglo-Saxons and the Mediterraneans. For the Anglo-Saxon, the State was the people. Parliament was its voice. The bureaucracy was its executive. For the Latin, the State was the *res publica*—the public thing had little, if anything, to do with people. The Latin, therefore, was always in an attitude of defence against the State, of opposition to its directives, of compromise with its exactions. The policeman was not his servant, but the factor of his master. In England they called their bureaucrats 'public servants'. In Italy they were *'funzionari'*, functionaries of the impersonal State.

But I, Dante Alighieri Matucci, was a person—or hoped I was. How much of me did the State own? How far could it legitimately direct me? To toss a living man out of a window? To shoot a rioter? To stifle a citizen with papers so that he couldn't even piss without a permit? And then there was the other side of the coin: fifty million people locked in a narrow peninsula, poor in resources, rich only in sap and energy, turbulent in spirit, easy prey to demagogues and agitators. How did you stop them tearing each other to pieces if you didn't break a few heads from time to time? It was all too easy to live underground like a mole nibbling at the roots of other people's lives, never caring to stick your dirty snout into the sunlight. . . .

I was still chewing on that sour thought when the boys from the surveillance team presented themselves to report on Lili Anders. Their tapes of the night-club meeting were almost unintelligible. I wanted to know why.

'No time to plant anything effective, Colonel. A crowded night-club, haphazard table placement, half-an-hour's notice . . . no chance. Anyway, they only stayed half an hour. We followed them back to Anders' apartment. The contact dropped her there and drove off. Giorgio followed him. I stayed to get a report from the lady.'

'Who was the contact?'

'Picchio . . . the woodpecker.'

'What did sweet Lili have to say for herself?'

'I've got it here: Woodpecker asked what the General died of? She replied a heart attack. Had she known he was sick? No, but he did have occasional chest pains that he called indigestion.

'Good for Lili. Go on.'

'Who brought her the news? A Colonel of Carabinieri. What was his name? Matucci. Why a full Colonel? She didn't know. She'd been wondering. How long had he stayed? Twenty minutes, half-an-hour. She'd been upset. The Colonel had been kind. Had he asked any significant questions? Only about Pantaleone's movements and contacts on the night of his death. She had told him the truth, there was nothing to hide. Woodpecker asked who were the General's heirs. She didn't know. She had never seen his will. Did she know the General's lawyer? Yes. Was she friendly with him? Reasonably. Then she was ordered to cultivate his acquaintance and if possible his friendship; and find out all the things she could about the General's estate. Had she ever met a Major-General Leporello?'

'He's one of ours, for God's sake.'

'It shook me a little, too, Colonel.'

'What did Lili say?'

'She'd never met him. Had the General ever spoken of him? No. At least not that she remembered. What would her next assignment be? Sit tight, concentrate on the lawyer, await further contact and instructions. . . . Fade out, *fine*. That's it, Colonel. . . . And, by the way, I didn't get to bed until three in the morning.'

'Poor fellow! I hope you slept well and chastely. Anything from Lili's phone tap?'

'Nothing since her call to you, Colonel.'

'Good. . . . Now, let's hear about our little Captain Carpi.'

'Nothing to tell, Colonel. He passed out cold about three in the morning. I paid the girl and the drink bill from his wallet and then took him home. He's a bad drunk, Colonel.

'That's something new. Anyway, he's off to Sardinia tomorrow. That should sober him up. Thank you, gentlemen. You may now resume your sleep. Make sure you're fresh and sharp by eight this evening. You're still on night roster. . . .'

They slouched out, bleary-eyed and grumbling and I grinned at their discomfiture. This was what the Americans called the name of the game. You walked your feet off. You knocked on doors. You stood watch on street-corners and cruised round smoky clubs. You waded through reams and reams of useless information, until you came up with one fragment of fact, that began or completed a whole mosaic. I had one now: why was Woodpecker, a Polish agent, interested in Marcantonio Leporello, Major-General of the Carabinieri?'

As an investigator I have many shortcomings and two special talents. The first is a photographic memory. The second is that I know how to wait. Comes a moment in every investigation when there is nothing to do except wait, and let the chemistry of the case work itself out. If you try to hurry the process, to satisfy yourself or a superior, you make mistakes. You accept false premises, create a fictional logic. You harry your operatives so that they make myopic observations and give you half-answers to keep you happy. You snatch at facile solutions and come up with a handful of smoke.

The Italians love bustle and brouhaha. Sketch them a scene and they will build you an opera inside an hour. They are glib; they are dilatory; they are evasive. They hate to commit themselves either to an opinion or an alliance, lest tomorrow they be held to the consequences. They would rather lose a tooth than sign a binding document. I am a colonel at forty-two because I have learned to make a virtue out of the vices of my countrymen.

The Minister of the Interior wanted action? He got it, scored for brass and tympani. NATO needed a spy care to tighten up security? *Bene!* There were twenty scripts to choose from and authentic villains to fit them. There was a stink over a procurement contract? For that, too, there was a magic formula: sabotage by enemy agents, at source, in transit, or on delivery site. But when a big thing came up, the trick was to create a zone of quiet and sit there, visible but enigmatic, digesting the facts in hand, calm as a Buddha waiting for the next turn of the wheel of life. It was a tactic that disconcerted many of my colleagues and irritated some of my superiors: but, most times, it worked—with a little sleight of hand to help the illusion.

At that moment in time, the Pantaleone affair was in suspense. The meaning of the salamander card was not yet deciphered. The General's papers and his money were in the hands of his lawyer who would probably wait until the last moment before he answered the *invito* and then stand pat on legal privilege. The man at the funeral might mean nothing. The Cavaliere Manzini was simply a buyer of expensive art. There was nothing yet from the heraldic expert. Nothing . . . nothing . . . nothing. Except that a Polish agent, named Woodpecker, was interested in Major-General Leporello. It seemed an appropriate time to have a chat with the Director.

The Director of the Defence Information Service was a character in his own right. He was related on his mother's side to the Caraccioli of Naples and on his father's to the Morosini of Venice. In the Service they called him Volpone—the old fox. I had another name for him: Cameleonte, the chameleon. One moment you saw him plain, the next you had lost him against the political undergrowth. He had the manners of a prince and the mind of a chess-player. He had a sense of history and a conviction that it always repeated itself. He was an ironist in eight languages, and had made conquests in all of them. He played tennis, sailed a keel-boat, collected primitive art and was a devotee of chamber music in which he sometimes played viola. He was inordinately rich, generous to those he liked and ruthless as a public executioner to those he did not. He insisted that I, Dante Alighieri Matucci, was one of those he liked; one of the few he respected. We had clashed often. He had tempted me, more than once, but I had sniffed at the bait and turned away from it with a grin and a shrug. I made no secret of my weakness, but I was damned if I would be blackmailed with them, by the Director or anyone else. And if the Director wanted to play games, I had a few of my own, with rather complicated rules.

I was playing one now. Major-General Leporello was a big man in the Carabinieri. I wanted to know whether the Director was big enough to handle him if ever there were a need. So, without ceremony, I put the question:

'Woodpecker is interested in Leporello. Why?'

The Director was instantly alert, the old fox sniffing a hostile air. He said, evenly:

'Isn't it your job to tell me?'

'No, sir, not yet. Leporello's dossier is marked "Reserved to Director".'

'Forgive me, I'd forgotten. Let me see now. General Leporello has spent the last five months abroad.'

'Where?'

'Japan, Vietnam, South Africa, Brazil, the United States, Great Britain, Greece, France.'

'Who paid the fare?'

'The tour was official. The General was on a study mission.'

'Studying what?'

'Riot control and counter-insurgency.'

'Do you know the General personally, sir?'

'Yes. He's a sound man.'

'Vulnerable?'

'He's a patriot, a devout Catholic, a Christian Democrat and financially independent. I doubt he could be bought or frightened.'

'Attacked? Assassinated?'

'Possibly.'

'Seduced?'

'By what, Colonel?'

'The ultimate infirmity–ambition.'

'For example . . .?'

'The man who devises the strategy of counter-revolution might decide to put it into practice on his own account . . . or on account of a potent minority.'

'Any evidence?'

'Indications only. Woodpecker and his network have a commission which I quote: ". . . to give early warning of any attempt at a *colpo di stato* by neo-fascist groups, or of actions designed to provoke it." If Woodpecker is interested in Leporello, we have to be interested, too.'

'You're in unicorn country, Matucci.'

'Half our lives, we deal with fables. Sometimes the fables come true.'

'In Leporello's case, I think not. However, let me play with the idea. I'll come back to you. For the moment, no action.'

'Yes, sir.'

'Anything else?'

'No, sir.'

'Then, permit me to offer you a compliment. I like your attitude to your work, careful and open-minded. That's rare, necessary, too, in these times.'

'You are kind, sir. Thank you.'

'Until later then.'

I walked out a very pensive man. If the Director was scared, everybody else should be running for cover. If the Director was committed to a cause or a compromise, nothing would divert him but a bullet in the head. He was the perfect *cinquecento* man, with a confessor at his right hand and a poet on his left, while his enemies rotted, howling, in the dungeons beneath his feet. I was named after a poet and needed a confessor; but I had no slightest wish to end my days in the dungeons of official disfavour. And yet . . . and yet. . . . A man who could control rioters and urban guerrillas might, one fine tomorrow, control the country, especially if he were a patriot, a good Christian and didn't have to worry about his rent or his dinner.

I was hardly back in my office when my secretary announced that Doctor Sergio Bandinelli had answered my *invito* and was waiting to see me.

The advocate was short, fussy and very irascible. I debated for a moment whether to play the bureaucrat or the gentleman, and then decided to smother him with courtesy. I regretted the need to disturb a busy man. I was grateful for so prompt a response. I trusted to dispose quickly of the few matters in question. I understood the relationship between advocate and client. It was my duty to protect that relationship and to discourage any breach of it. However. . . .

'. . . In cases where national security is involved, Avvocato, we both need to be slightly more flexible. I am sure you understand that.'

'No, Colonel, I do not. I am here to protest the illegal seizure of my client's papers and to require their immediate delivery into my hands.'

'No problem at all. You may take the papers with you when you leave. As for the protest, what's the profit? The Defence Information Service works under presidential directive, and to rather special rules. Of course, if you wish to press a complaint . . .'

'Well . . . under the circumstances. . . .'

'Good! I am encouraged now to take you into our confidence, to solicit your assistance in a matter of importance.'

'I am happy to assist, Colonel, provided I may reserve my position in the event of conflict of interest.'

'Of course. Let us proceed then. General Pantaleone was an important man. His death has political consequences. I am directed to study those consequences. I am interested, therefore, in every aspect of the General's activities. He was, for example, engaged in liquidating his estate, selling shares, preparing to disperse his art collection. Why?'

'I am not at liberty to say.'

'His brokers inform us that the proceeds of his shares were transmitted to you. What were you directed to do with the money?'

'I cannot tell you that, either.'

'I am afraid you must.'

'No, Colonel. Legal privilege.'

'Before you invoke it, let me tell you something else. Your late client maintained relations with a member of a foreign espionage network.'

'I don't believe it.'

'It's true, nevertheless. You, yourself, are under surveillance by the same network.'

'Is this some kind of threat, Colonel?'

'No threat, Avvocato, a statement of fact. So ... when you refuse to disclose what has happened to large sums of money, you put yourself in some jeopardy. Crime is involved, a threat to the security of the State. Your client is dead. You are answerable for your part in his affairs. So, I ask you again. What happened to the money?'

'I was instructed to reinvest it.'

'Where?'

'Abroad. In Switzerland and in Brazil for the most part.'

'And if the art collection had been sold, and the land?'

'The same instruction applied.'

'Such exports of funds requires approval from the Ministry of Finance. Did you have it?'

'Well, no ... but the nature of the transaction. . . .'

'Don't tell me, Avvocato. The transaction would involve intermediaries who have safe channels for currency export. They charge five per cent for their services. For this, they guarantee immunity to the client. It's an old story. It doesn't hold water and you know it. You can be charged with conspiracy to circumvent the law. You're lucky I'm an intelligence investigator and not a policeman ... but I can change my hat any moment I choose. So talk, Avvocato! Don't play children's games! ... Why was Pantaleone exporting funds?'

'In sum, he was afraid. He had joined himself with the new Fascists as their military adviser and as commander-in-chief in case of a *colpo di stato*. Their provocative tactics worried him. He felt they were not strong enough to risk a *colpo di stato* and that, if they tried, it would lead to civil war. All the strength of the Movement is in the South. In the North, the Left is in control and far better organized. So the Movement began to lose faith in Pantaleone. They wanted to move him out in favour of a bolder man.'

'Who?'

'I don't know.'

'Did Pantaleone know?'

'No. All he knew was that it was someone who was not in the Movement but who might be attracted into it when the time was right.'

'A military man?'

'Obviously. If they were provoking a disturbance, they had to be able to offer military action to suppress it. That's the whole point of provocation, no?'

'So, the General was frightened. Of a rival or of something else?'

'Of action against himself.'

'What sort of action?'

'I don't know.'

'Then guess.'

'Damage to his reputation. Some kind of revelation of his past.'

'Blackmail, in fact?'

'Yes. He had a chequered career and many enemies.'

'Had he received any direct threats?'

'Well . . . in a legal sense, no.'

'In common sense, Avvocato?'

'About a week ago he received a communication by messenger.'

'What sort of communication?'

'It consisted of a very complete and accurate biography which, if it had ever been published, would have damaged his reputation beyond repair and banished him forever from public life.'

'He showed it to you?'

'Yes. He asked whether there might be any defence against publication or any means of tracing the author. I advised him there was not . . . at least not without risk of spreading the information dangerously.'

'But a threat of publication was made?'

'I read it so.'

'Read what?'

'A card, attached to the typescript.'

I laid the salamander card on the table before him.

'This card?'

The advocate picked it up, gingerly, examined it and agreed.

'Yes, that's the one. Where did you get it?'

'I found it in the General's bedroom. What happened to the biography?'

'He lodged it in his strong box at the bank.'

'Which you emptied yesterday.'

'Yes.'

'I want it. I want all his documents.'

'I'll give them to you, happily–on a judge's order. Without it, no.'

'This card, Avvocato, what does it signify?'

'To me, nothing.'

'What did it signify to the General?'

'I can only tell you what he said.'

'Yes?'

'He was a taciturn man, given to aphorisms. He said . . . "Well, Saint Martin's day at last."'

'And what the devil was that supposed to mean?'

'He wouldn't explain it. He never did. I puzzled over it for a long time; then I found the reference. It's in Don Quixote: "To every pig comes Saint Martin's day." In Spain, pigs are usually killed on the feast of St Martin.'

'Doctor Bandinelli, I am sure you are a very good advocate. You never tell a lie. You simply bury the part of the truth that really matters and the law protects you while you do it. However, you've stepped outside the law and put yourself and your privilege in jeopardy. You can fight me, of course.

You can delay me, by tactics and quibbles, but your St Martin's day will come in the end. If you want to avoid it, I'm prepared to make a bargain with you. I'll forget the currency question. I'll send a man with you now to assemble every paper you hold on the Pantaleone family. He will list the papers, then lock and seal them in your safe. Tomorrow I will come to your office and go through them with you. That way you keep your privilege and I get the information I want. Agreed?'

'I seem to have no choice.'

'Very little.'

'Then I agree.'

'Good. You can sign for the papers we hold and take them back with you. When you go home this evening, leave the key of your office with my man. He will spend the night there.'

'Why?'

'Protection, Avvocato. Politics is a risky business these days.'

I meant it as an irony. I was the old-line professional patronizing a civilian. I should have known better. In this trade, in this country, you are always standing on a trap-door with a hangman's noose around your neck.

The which being said, I agree an explanation is needed. This so-called Republic of Italy, we so-called Italians, are not a nation at all. We are provinces, cities, countrysides, tribes, factions, families, individuals–anything and everything but a unity. Ask that fellow over there, the street-cleaner, what he is. He will answer, "I am a Sard, a Calabrese, a Neapolitan, a Romagnolo." Never, never, will he tell you he is an Italian. That girl in the Ferrari, she's a Venetian, a Veronese, a Padovan. Wife, mistress, mother or rare virgin, she names herself for a place, a plot of separate earth. I, myself, as I have told you, am a Tuscan. I serve, because I am paid to serve, the nebulous public thing called the State; but my belonging is elsewhere–Florence and the Medici and the Arno and the pines planted over the graveyards of my ancestors. The consequence? A kind of anarchy, which the Anglo-Saxons will never understand; a kind of order which they understand even less. We know who we are, man by man, woman by woman. We despise the outlander because he is different. We respect him because he knows and we know who he is. So, my dilemma: I can never say, "This is the enemy, destroy him!" I must say, "This is the enemy of the moment, but he comes from my country, his sister is married to my cousin and tomorrow we may need to be friends. How must I comport myself so that the links are not broken even though the chain be stretched to breaking-point?'

There are many who say that, in this system, there is no place for patriots, only for pragmatists and opportunists. These are dirty words–or are they? We have to survive: a practical problem. We have one life, one opportunity to come to terms with it. So long as the terms are negotiable, we try to negotiate. If we are forced to a base bargain, we accept it and wait for a tomorrow when the contract may be annulled or varied by mutual consent. As you see, I know it all. So there is no excuse for the follies I began to commit that afternoon.

The first was my contemptuous bargain with Doctor Sergio Bandinelli. I judged him for a frightened and pliable man. I gave him for guardian a junior agent, one Giampiero Calvi. I issued a set of simple instructions. Calvi would accompany Bandinelli to his office. He would take possession of the Pantaleone papers, list them, lock them in the advocate's safe, seal the safe and remain in the office until I relieved him at nine the next morning. During the night, he would call the duty-officer at headquarters every hour on the hour. Calvi was a promising young man. I read him no lectures. I presumed on the training I, myself, had given him.

Then, because I was tired, I decided to mix business with pleasure. Because I was—and am—too arrogant for my own good, I elected to play out my little game against the Director. I telephoned my maid and told her that I would not be home for dinner and that I might have to spend the night outside Rome. Then I called Lili Anders and told her that, in line of duty, I would call on her at eight-thirty for a cocktail and take her out to dinner afterwards. Where? A discreet place, but elegant, where she could forget her grief and relax. My intentions? Dear Madam, those of a colleague and collaborator; no more, no less.

I walked down the corridor to chat with my associate Rigoli, who concerns himself with the movements and the security of public and not-so-public officials. Rigoli is a grey, mousey fellow with a card-index mind. What he does not know, he can guess with seventy per cent accuracy: where the Minister of Finance can be found at three on Friday morning, what First Secretary took what flight to Venice and who had the seat next to him. He told me that Major-General Leporello was presently in Rome, lodged at the Hassler, and engaged in a series of conferences with senior service officers. I called the hotel and, after a brief passage-at-arms with a junior aide, was put through to the General. The conversation was brief and terse.

'General, this is Colonel Matucci, SID.'

'Yes?'

'An urgent matter. I should like to see you.'

'How urgent?'

'Very.'

'I am busy until six. I can spare you half an hour after that. Call me from the lobby. Suite 10.'

'Thank you, sir.'

'The name again?'

'Matucci. Section E.'

I put down the telephone and waited. If I judged my man aright, he would check back either to me or to the Director. If he called the Director, I was in for an uncomfortable hour. I was gambling on the fact, well-known in the Service, that the Director was a very secretive fellow who refused casual contacts, even to senior officials. Sure enough, within three minutes my phone rang and Leporello came on the line.

'Who is this, please?'

'Matucci, Section E.'

'This is Leporello. We have an appointment I believe.'

'Yes, sir. Suite 10 at 1800 hours.'

'Please be punctual. Goodbye.'

Boh! I might well need a little relaxation after half an hour with this hard-head. I made one more call, this time to a curious little office on the Via Bissolati which feeds to the Press and to private subscribers news of the comings and goings of celebrities. I don't subscribe to it. I use it and pay my way by encouraging my colleagues at the Questura to overlook a few irregularities in procedure—German telephonists whose sojourn permits are out of date, English typists who don't pay social service contributions and the like. It's a kind of corruption, but there is a more historic name for it–*toleranza,* live and let live, but remember always that the law has a long memory and a heavy boot. My contact is a busty Dane, who lives, unhappily, with a Spanish journalist accredited to the Holy See. Her civil status is highly dubious, but her information is always accurate.

'Faubiani . . . ? Well, old Manzini's in town, so she's doing the rounds with him. Let's see. . . . Yesterday Valerio was showing knitwear. Tonight Fosco is displaying jewellery and they've tied in the Lavezzi who is launching a coffee-table book on Renaissance goldsmiths. Faubiani will probably be there. It's a buffet supper at Fosco's, eight-thirty until the champagne runs out. If you want a ticket, I can let you have mine. Claudio's working tonight and I only get envious when I look at all that expensive junk.'

'You're an angel, Inge.'

'Don't tell Claudio that. He's getting demonic again. . . . When am I going to see you, Dante?'

'When I pick up the card at seven-thirty. *Ciao, bambina!*'

And so, with my evening laid out, hour by shining hour, one small decision remained: what number should I leave with the night duty-officer? I gave him two–Lili Anders' and my house. Now I was ready for grooming; a change of clothes, a trim, a shave, a massage to tone up my sagging face muscles and half an hour of instructive gossip from my favourite manicurist.

At eighteen hundred hours precisely, I telephoned Major-General Leporello from the front desk of the Hassler. He commanded me to wait until his aide came to fetch me. The aide, I noted, was a muscular young blood with red hair and freckles and a Trentine accent. He was respectful but laconic, and he wanted to see my card before we moved from the lobby. I suspected that when he left me with the General, he posted himself just outside the door of the suite. Leporello, himself, was a surprise. He was a tall man, blond and ruddy, more German than Latin. His chest was broad, his belly flat. His gestures were restrained and his manner brisk and businesslike. He had no sense of humour at all.

'Your identification, please.'

I gave it to him. He studied it, line by line, and then handed it back to me.

'What do you wish to discuss, Colonel?'

'Matters arising out of the death of General Pantaleone.'

'Such as?'

'This card, sir. It was found in the General's room after his death.'

'What does it signify?'

'That's what I am trying to establish. It was attached to a set of records which were delivered to Pantaleone before his death.'

'What sort of records?'

'Incriminating documents of the General's past life.'

'Blackmail?'

'We believe so.'

'Where are they now?'

'In his lawyer's office, in custody of an officer of SID.'

'The card?'

'Is our only clue to the identity of the blackmailer.'

'The symbol?'

'A salamander.'

'That's odd.'

'Why, sir?'

'During the war, one of the most important partisan groups in the Valpadana was led by a man who called himself the Salamander.'

'What was his real name?'

'I don't know. He dropped out of sight about 1943. There was a rumour the Germans had got him.'

'Did he use a card like this?'

'My memory is vague, because all my information at the time was second or third hand; but I seem to remember some talk of a calling card pinned to the chest of victims of the band.'

'Was this a Marxist group?'

'Most groups in the North had real or imputed connections with the Marxists.'

'Did you ever work with such groups, General?'

'I? Never. My loyalties were to the Crown. I never changed them–even when it might have been convenient to do so. I disliked the Fascists, I loathed the Germans; but even for that I could not make myself a turncoat soldier. Today I am able to be both honest and proud.'

'I am sure you are, sir. You are also a natural target for the terrorists of the Left.'

'I must presume so.'

'Which brings me to the real purpose of my visit; which is to inform you that you are under surveillance by at least one network of foreign agents.'

He gave me a thin, humourless smile.

'That's hardly fresh news, Colonel. I have always assumed surveillance by all groups–foreign or local.'

'The news is, General, that this group regards you as a possible successor to General Pantaleone.'

'In what capacity?'

'As a military and political leader in the event of a right-wing coup.'

'Which is nonsense, of course . . .'

'Of course, sir. But it does make you vulnerable.'

'To what?'

'To blackmail or assassination.'

I had thought to shake him or at least to interest him. Impossible. He was hard and smooth as cemetery granite.

'Blackmail, Colonel? Quite impossible I assure you. My life is an open book. I am not ashamed of any single page. As for attempts on my life, these have been foreseen, and security measures arranged to protect me and my family. I am more concerned by the suggestion–even from hostile elements–that I might have political ambitions. I have none. I believe in hierarchy and order. I see myself only as a servant of duly constituted authority.'

'I understand perfectly, sir.'

'A question, Colonel.'

'Sir?'

'Have you discussed this matter with your Director?'

'I have.'

'His opinion?'

'That no action is required by SID. I have, in fact, exceeded my brief by seeking this interview with you.'

'Why did you seek it then?'

'We are colleagues, General, you and I. We are members of the same corps. I felt that a point of honour was involved. I decided to act on my own initiative and at my own risk.'

'What risk, Colonel?'

'Well . . . to put it gently, the Director is a very formidable character.'

'Are you afraid of him?'

'No, sir—but I have a healthy respect.'

'So, you would prefer I did not report our meeting to him?'

'I have not said that, sir. Nor would I say it. I have done my duty as I read it. I was, and am, prepared to accept all consequences.'

For the first time, Leporello relaxed. He offered me a cigarette from a gold case, and condescended to light it for me. He leaned back in his chair and surveyed me with grim approval.

'You impress me, Colonel. If you need a friend in the Service, you have one in me. I shall instruct my staff that you may have instant access to me at any time.'

'That is very generous, sir.'

'Not at all. We have a common aim: the security and stability of the Republic. We must co-operate whenever we can. Pantaleone was a dangerous fool and more than half a rogue. Today we need strong men who are prepared to risk themselves in public service. I judge that you are such a one. Your present experience is, of course, most valuable. If ever you felt an inclination to join my personal staff, I should be happy to have you.'

'That's a great compliment.'

'You deserve it. And, Colonel . . .?'

'Sir?'

'I have no intention of discussing this meeting with your Director.'

'Thank you, sir.'

He shook my hand and ushered me out, commending me to the care of his athletic aide, who escorted me downstairs with a trifle more grace and favoured me with a salute as I drove away.

In the gardens of the Pincio I stopped the car and sat for twenty minutes trying to make sense of Major-General Leporello. I have an instinctive fear of characters who act as if they were first cousins to God Almighty. Their virtue dazzles me. Their ruthlessness never ceases to amaze me. Their passion for order sets them beyond reason or pity. They have all the rectitude of a grand inquisitor, and a Jesuit skill in casuistry. They are dogmatists all, and they have no hesitation about rewriting the codex to suit themselves. They attract minions and satellites and suborners who feed their ambition and bloat their conscious virtue into a legend of impeccability. In short, I loathe their guts and I am more afraid of them than of all the venal villains I meet in my trade. They make me afraid of myself, too; because they provoke me to anger and misjudgment and savage reaction.

Still there was a tenuous profit. Leporello was tempting me into an alliance, first with a scrap of information, true or false, on the Salamander, then with a promise of friendship and advocacy. An alliance pointed to a strategy; a strategy pointed to a goal. What goal? What was the next ambition of a man who was appointed to control ant-heap cities and their millions of volatile humans? Even if he had not yet defined it for himself, there were others ready to prescribe it for him. Eh! It was too late and too early for Dante Alighieri Matucci to read the future. I started the car and drove through the dappled alleys of the gardens to drink cocktails with Lili Anders.

The apartment had changed since my last visit. The equestrian portrait of Pantaleone was gone from the mantel, and in its place was a bright surrealist piece of Spiro, a landscape of flowers with smiling human faces, and a procession of musical instruments playing them into a dance. The furniture had been rearranged, the ornaments culled to produce an air of undiluted feminity. Lili herself was changed in some subtle fashion that I could define only by details; the hair more softly swept, the clothes more modish and extravagant, her manner more relaxed and confident. Even the house-keeper was a shade less brusque, if still suspicious and unwelcoming. When I commented on the changes, Lili smiled and shrugged.

'I am my own woman now. Not as much as I would wish, but a little more anyway. What will you drink?'

'Whisky, please.'

'You are changed, too.'

'How?'

'More human, perhaps. Less professional. How am I to call you, Colonel?'

'My name is Dante Alighieri.'

'Dante was a very sombre man. You?'

'Sometimes. Not tonight.'

'What is different about tonight?'

'There is business to be done; but I would still like us to enjoy ourselves.'

'That's hardly possible is it?'

'Why not?'

'Because, Dante Alighieri, you own me. You direct me like a puppet. I have no choice of what or how I may enjoy. . . . Your drink, master.'

'Your health, Lili.'

'Where are we dining?'

'We are guests at an exhibition and a champagne supper afterwards. Fosco is displaying his new season's jewellery.'

'That should be interesting. Do you like jewellery, Dante?'

'I do—even though I can't afford it.'

'Would you like to see mine?'

'If you like.'

'I'll show it you when we come back. I presume you will bring me back after the supper.'

'You're being rough with me, Lili.'

'No. I want you to know that I understand our relationship. I promised value for money and protection.'

'I'm not a whore-master, Lili.'

'Then what are you?'

'Would you believe me if I told you?'

'I might.'

'It's very simple. I'm a self-indulgent bastard who likes pretty women.'

'Now tell me the rest of it.'

'I'm tired and I want to laugh. I'm puzzled and I want to stop thinking. I'm scared and I don't really want to ask why.'

'You, scared?'

'Yes. This is the age of the assassins, Lili—the age of the fanatics and the destructors. They want a new world. They'll tear down twenty centuries of civilization to achieve it. What they don't see is that when they're sitting in the ruins, the old gang will have to come back, the technocrats to build the factories, the financiers to create a new illusion of money, the police to bully people into order, even the city rat-catchers like me. It's a madness, Lili, and I'm at the centre of it. So are you. There's no escape for either of us, but I thought, just for an hour perhaps there might be a zone of quiet in the eye of the hurricane. I was a fool. Forget it. I'm not a sadist. So, for Christ's sake, don't be insulted! . . . Now, please, may I have another drink?'

She took the glass from me without a word, refilled it and brought it back. Then she laid a cool hand on my cheek and said, very calmly:

'Even if you mean only half of it, I'll believe you. And I'm not insulted.'

I wasn't sure I believed myself; but I wanted to feel less like a pimp and more, much more, like a man who could face the sunlight without shame. I drew her hand down to my lips and kissed it lightly.

'Now, let's start the scene again. Enter Dante Alighieri Matucci, who is welcomed by Lili Anders. Her greeting is formal but not unfriendly. . . .'

'Correction. Her greeting is friendly though not yet intimate.'

She bent and kissed me on the forehead and then moved away to pour herself another drink. Twenty minutes later we were driving down to Fosco's and we joined the gathering, hand in hand, like lovers.

I had not told Lili; but I knew a small something about Fosco, the jeweller. He was—still is for that matter—a phenomenon: a young and talented homosexual who leapt from a back-alley apprenticeship in Florence to establish himself in five years as one of the best private goldsmiths in Rome. He showed up once in our files as the friend of an Arab Embassy official; but the association lapsed quickly and we lost interest in him. We are very tolerant in moral matters but highly sensitive to Middle Eastern politics. Sometimes, because his shows attracted a motley group of titled somebodies and monied nobodies, I planted an observer among his guests or his security guards. But, though the exercise was profitable in minor ways, Fosco himself always showed clean: a good craftsman, with exquisite manners, and an iron-clad egotism that enabled him to impose his taste and his exorbitant price-list on a wide spectrum of Roman matrons, diplomatic wives, rising film-stars and vagrant notables.

The presentation of his spring collection was a gala occasion. The best titles in Rome staged a slow pavane round the show-cases. The most expensive models disposed themselves at strategic points in the gallery. A master chef presided over the buffet. An army of handsome young waiters distributed champagne and canapés; and even the security guards contrived to look like Milanese captains of industry. It was a sophisticated social ballet and Fosco directed it with considerable charm and only a hint of contempt for the performers.

We arrived in the middle of the first movement; the early diners who would come, be seen, drink a cocktail or two and leave. The serious ones, the friends of the Master, would come later, linger over the buffet and leave at midnight. Fosco received us with vague courtesy, and waved us into the concourse. We snared two glasses of champagne and a pair of catalogues and began our circuit of the exhibits. One fact was immediately clear: Fosco had made a killing. Half the items were already pre-empted, some marked 'sold' others 'reserved', optioned in advance to great houses—Bulgari, Cartier, Buccellati, Tiffany. Not that he did not deserve it. He was a master of every style, the baroque, the antique, the avant-garde. His designs were original, his craftsmanship superb. The poorest stones looked like gems of the first water. The best were set like sacred relics alive under the artful lights.

He was not modest about them either. He labelled every exhibit as if it were a museum piece, described the genesis of the design, the particulars of the stones and their setting, and whenever he could, the name and title of the person who had commissioned it. The older houses sniffed at such vulgarity, but Fosco demolished their snobbery at a stroke.

'I want my jewels to be talk-pieces. How can a woman talk about what she doesn't know. I explain my work and thus emphasize its value. Right or wrong? Look at the result! I carry no dead stock. I am liquid after every exhibition. . . .'

After this one, it seemed, he would have money running out of his ears. We were about half-way round the gathering when Lili tugged at my sleeve and pointed to the catalogue. The section she indicated was entitled, 'A Fantasy of Rare Beasts' and referred to a collection of jewelled butterflies, birds and animals to be worn as brooches, pendants, clasps, buckles, earrings and symbolic guardians of women's chastity. Lili was pointing to number 63 of which the description read:

> Salamander. Brooch in the form of an heraldic beast. Emeralds in pavé. Crowned with brilliants and ornamented with Burma rubies. Adapted from a calligraphic design. Commissioned by Cav. Bruno Manzini, Bologna.

The piece itself was twenty feet away, laid on a bed of black velvet, in a small show-case, mounted on a pillar of alabaster. It was not a gaudy jewel, but the craftsman had preserved the character and sweep of the original calligraphy, so that when I compared it with the card there was no shadow of doubt that the designs were identical.

I drew Lili away from the show-case into the crush of people round the buffet. At the same moment, the Cavaliere Bruno Manzini entered the gallery with the Principessa Faubiani at his side and a small retinue of friends in attendance. Fosco greeted them effusively, snapped fingers at his minions to bring them champagne and catalogues and then led them on his own personal tour of the masterworks.

Immediate problem: how to confront Manzini before he left the gallery. I had him under my hand here. Once he left, I could be chasing him all over the peninsula. On the other hand, with the Press and the gossips of the city turned out in force, I could not risk a scandal. Leaving Lili at the buffet, I made my way to the entrance where an agreeable young man was deputizing as host for Fosco. I flashed my card at him.

'Carabinieri. Who is in charge of your security guards?'

'Over there, by the stairwell, tall fellow with grey hair. There's no trouble, I hope?'

'None. Just routine.'

I drew the tall fellow into the shadows and showed him my card too, but this time I made sure he read it carefully before I instructed him.

'This is important. We can't afford a mistake. You will take me to Fosco's private office. I'll give you a note to the Cavaliere Bruno Manzini. You will escort him to the office, then leave us alone. Stay outside the door and let no one in while we're talking—clear?'

'Clear. There's no trouble, I hope.'

'No trouble. I've noted your security arrangements. First class.'

He was happy then. He led me to Fosco's office—a fairy bower done in Pompeian red. I scribbled a note to Manzini on the house note-paper. The text was respectful but cryptic:

Regret intrusion but have urgent and official communication. Please accompany messenger to office.

Matucci SID

He was with me in three minutes, cool and condescending as ever. He would not sit down. He had guests waiting. He demanded that I state my business and be done with it.

'My business is still the late General Pantaleone.'

'So?'

'Shortly before he died, he received a communication which was, in effect, a dossier of his past life.'

'And what has that to do with me?'

'Attached to the dossier was this card. You will note the design–a crowned salamander. We have established that the design corresponds exactly with exhibit No. 63 in the Fosco catalogue. We are confident you will wish to explain the connection.'

'Why should I wish to explain it, Colonel?'

'A matter of national security is involved.'

'Is that fact or opinion?'

'Fact.'

'And you could establish it as such to my satisfaction?'

'I believe so.'

'Is there any suggestion of criminal activity in this case?'

'As yet, none.'

'Then what do you want from me, Colonel?'

'At this stage an informal discussion.'

'When?'

'Now, Cavaliere.'

'Quite impossible. I am occupied with friends.'

'Afterwards then. At your hotel, perhaps?'

'My dear Colonel, I am seventy years old. By midnight I am near to dying. You would get no sense out of me at all. Say, nine in the morning at the Grand Hotel, and I'll do my best to enlighten you. Now, may I be excused?'

'Some questions before you go, Cavaliere.'

'Yes?'

'The salamander, what does it signify?'

'Survival. It was my code-name during the war. The rest is too long to tell you now.'

'The inscription?'

'That's a long story too.'

'The beginning of it then, if you please.'

'The beginning and the end, Colonel. Pantaleone was my half-brother. Only he happened to be conceived on the right side of the blanket.'

I stared at him, open-mouthed like an idiot. He smiled at my discomfiture and made a small gesture of deprecation.

'Please! I am not trying to make theatre, only to show you that we do need time to be clear with each other. Agreed?'

'Agreed.'

'Now, Colonel, will you answer one question for me?'

'If I can, yes.'

'Who killed Pantaleone?'

'The death certificate states that he died of a cardiac arrest.'

'But that's what kills us all, Colonel.'

'Exactly.'

'No other comment?'

'None. Until tomorrow, Cavaliere.'

'My compliments, Colonel. Goodnight.'

Why didn't I hold him? Why didn't I hammer him with questions while I had him off-balance? I told you before, this was a very special one, the best of the breed. Off-balance? Never for an instant. I was the unsure novice, groping for hand-hold and foot-hold on a bare mountain. Besides—let me make it plain to you—this is Italy, where the law goes back to Justinian, and half of it hasn't been dusted off for centuries, and the rules of the game are written in sand. Three people in Manzini's retinue could immobilize me for a month by lifting a telephone. Twenty names at Fosco's party could consign me forever to the limbo of the retired list. And if you've ever tried to collect a debt or enforce a claim against the Republic, then you'll know what I'm talking about. In China, they drowned their enemies in a bath of feathers. Here in Italy, they stifle them with silence and bury them under a tumulus of *carta bollata*.

It was still only ten-thirty. I rescued Lili from the crush at the buffet and carted her off to dinner at a place I knew in Trastevere, where the food was honest Tuscan, the wine was honourable and the waiters were proud to serve you, and there was a great open fire for the winter and an arbour of vines for the summer nights. There was music, too; a skinny, plaintive fellow with a guitar, who would come to your table, when you were ready for him, and sing the soul out of your body with the old songs of the South. I was known here, but not for my trade, only because I prized the cook, and sometimes drank enough to sing and strum a song or two while the sad fellow ate his supper.

I had friends there: Castiglione, who used to be a great locksmith until the arthritis got him; Monsignore Arnolfo Ardizzone of the Vatican Secretariat of State, a cleric, knowledgeable and discreet, who had renounced marriage to serve God and adopted the bottle as the only mistress acceptable to Mother Church; Giuffredi, the poet, who wrote satires in Romanesco which nobody read any more; and Maddalena, who sold yesterday's roses at five hundred lire a bloom and was said to own a whole apartment block on the Tuscolana. True or false? I had never cared to inquire. This was one place where I was myself—whoever that might be. I accepted everyone at face value. I used no one. I paid the score and was welcome in the house. Enough! Everyone needs a bolt-hole. This was mine.

I tried to explain all this to Lili as we walked the last hundred metres through lanes hung with laundry and came out into a tiny square guarded by a dusty virgin in a glass case. I wanted to explain, which in my trade is a weakness. She seemed happy to listen, holding close to me as we stepped over foul runnels and spilt refuse, while the cats of the quarter slunk back into the shadows. Sometimes, when the rare light fell on her face, she looked like a young girl. When she crossed herself at the shrine of the little virgin, she looked like a peasant woman, weary from a long day in the fields. You may not believe me, but I did not care. I was not hunting now, I was simply glad not to be alone.

When we were settled at the table, with bread and wine and a fresh candle, Lili leaned across to me and laid her hands on mine.

'You look different now, Dante Alighieri.'

'How?'

'At Fosco's you were tight, wary, like a fox. Now you are loose, free. You greet people like human beings. They, too, are glad to see you.'

'This is Trastevere, my love. Across the river. You know what these people call themselves? *Noantri*—we others. They refuse to belong to anyone but themselves.'

'I like that. For now, we, too, are *noantri*. Please, may I have some wine?'

'I may get drunk and sing.'

'I'll sing with you.'

'And who will drive us back across the river?'

'Perhaps we won't go back—ever again.'

It was a happy thought and we nursed it with all sorts of fantasies through the *zuppa* and the *pasta* and the *griglia* and the *dolci*. We embroidered it with the music of the plaintive one as he perched on the stool next to Lili, and played her the curiosities of his repertoire—The Song of the Washer-woman of Vomero; Friend Don't Trust the Spinster; The Undressing Song and the Tale of the Lecherous Clogseller.

Midnight came and we were still singing. At one-thirty in the morning we were vaguely drunk, and the waiters had begun to wilt; so we wandered into the square, said goodnight to the lonely virgin and strolled towards the riverside car-park. Lili said, drowsily:

'Do you know something?'

'What?'

'I want to go to bed with you; but I don't want to go home.'

'Why not?'

'Because home is yesterday. I want to forget it.'

'And tomorrow?'

'Tomorrow starts when the sun comes up, and this place will be ugly and smelly and full of sad people afraid of each other and you'll be all wise and wary again.'

'So let's drive out along the ring-road. There's a place I know. . . .'

'Anywhere you say, *caro mio*. Anywhere you say.'

'I have to make a phone call first.'

'Why?'

'I left your number with my duty officer. I'll have to check in and give him a new one.'

'There's no escape is there?'

'We escaped tonight.'

'So we did. But you still have to telephone. . . .'

'Please, Lili.'

'Please, just kiss me. . . .'

In case you're hoping—as I was—for a happy tale of love and lechery, forget it! The evening of liberty ended with that kiss. I called Headquarters from the corner phone booth. The time was 0210 hours. The duty-officer told me agent Calvi had not made his hourly call. What did I want done about it? I ordered two cars of our mobile squadron, one to pick up Stefanelli, one to meet me at the lawyer's office. I flagged a passing taxi, bundled Lili into it and sent her home. Then I climbed into my own car and drove like a madman across the sleeping city.

The office of Doctor Sergio Bandinelli was on the fifth floor of a large modern block on the Via Sicilia, only two hundred metres from the bustle of the Via Veneto. When I arrived, one car of the mobile squadron was already parked outside the entrance. The second, carrying Steffi and his little black bag, came hurtling round the corner a few seconds later. Before we entered the building, I gave a few sharp directions to the squadron leaders: this was a high security matter; no police, no Press, no curious sightseers; two men standing by the cars, one on guard with the concierge, three to accompany Steffi and myself to the fifth floor. Then we rang the bell.

The porter, bleary-eyed and grumbling opened the door, and immediately launched into a babble of questions. We flashed our cards, left him still babbling and took the elevator to the fifth floor. Bandinelli's office was in darkness, the door was closed but unlocked. I entered first and switched on the lights.

The scene was curiously tranquil. Doctor Bandinelli lay stretched on a leather settee. Agent Giampiero Calvi was seated in a chair behind the desk, head pillowed in his arms. On the desk beside him was a Moravia novel, a loaded pistol, two ham rolls, a hard-boiled egg and a flask of coffee. The coffee was warm. The two men were stone-cold. Old Steffi sniffed the air, made a brief examination of the bodies and pronounced his verdict.

'Dead. Cyanic acid gas. Pistol or pressure-pack.'

I examined the safe. The seals were broken, the door was open, the Pantaleone papers gone. The immediate temptation was to plunge into action; forensic procedure, interrogation of witnesses, all the rest of it. It was a temptation hard to resist for any man with police training, but in my work it could be fatal to a sensitive project. I picked up the phone and called the Director's private number. He answered with surprising promptness. I told him:

'. . . We're in trouble. Documents missing and two bundles of dirty linen for immediate disposal—one of them ours.'

'So . . .?'

'As soon as the situation is tidy, I'll report in person!'

'When might that be?'

'Before breakfast, I hope.'

'I'll expect you for breakfast then—the earlier the better.'

Steffi cocked his head and cackled at me, for all the world like an ancient scruffy parrot.

'When everything's tidy! Eh! So now we're in the miracle business!'

The boys from the mobile squadron were fidgeting on their feet, waiting for me to make some decisions. The problem was that every decision carried highly explosive consequences. If I made a big scene with police procedures and interrogations, the Press would come swarming like wasps to a honey-pot. Once they found the Pantaleone papers were involved, they would immediately start asking questions about Pantaleone's death and hasty burial. On the other hand, if we could not interrogate freely, we would be grievously handicapped in reconstructing the events of the evening, and, therefore, in our search for the Pantaleone documents. Besides, there were two bodies to be disposed of in a convincing, if not legal fashion. Steffi was right as usual. Willy-nilly, we were in the miracle business. So it was time to get the ritual started.

The first problem was to get the two bodies out of the building without fuss or comment. I sent Steffi down to question the porter in his own cubby-hole, out of view of the entrance. Steffi's talk would hypnotize a fighting-cock. I counted on having the porter so bemused that he would miss a herd of elephants six feet from his nose.

Next we emptied Bandinelli's pockets and Calvi's as well. The boys of the mobile squadron carried the bodies into the elevator, rode them to the ground floor and bundled them into the waiting cars like a pair of late drunks. One car drove Bandinelli's remains to the casualty department of the Policlinico; the other deposited Calvi at the hospital of the Blue Sisters. In each case the story was the same; the mobile squadron had found a man lying, apparently unconscious, in an alley. They were consigning him to hospital while they pursued inquiries as to his identity. Dead on arrival? Dear me! Then give us a receipt and hold him in the mortuary while we complete our inquiries!

It sounds naïve! Then let me explain that even if your grandmother, with all her documents in her purse, falls sick on the Corso and is carted off to a public hospital by some street samaritan, it may well take you the best part of a week to trace her. We have small talent for administration at the best of times; but our public health service is a mess beyond description. Unless you go to an expensive private clinic, you may find your blood report really belongs to a ballet-mistress and your urine was supplied by a fellow who caught clap in Fregene. So, by all the rules of the game, two unidentified bodies should stay unclaimed until we were ready to deal with them.

While Stefanelli was questioning the porter, I drank Calvi's coffee and ate one of his ham rolls, while I examined the entries in his notebook.

20.00 hrs.	Bandinelli's staff left.
20.30 „	Completed indexing of Pantaleone documents. Locked and sealed safe in presence Bandinelli. Signed receipt for papers and keys. Bandinelli left.
21.00 „	Telephoned duty-officer H.Q.
21.25 „	Office cleaners arrived.
21.55 „	Office cleaners left.
22.00 „	Telephoned duty-officer H.Q.
23.00 „	Telephoned duty-officer H.Q.
23.36 „	Made final check of fifth floor.
24.00 „	Telephoned duty-officer H.Q.
00.37 „	Bandinelli telephoned. He wished pass by office for late night conference with two clients. He explained it as a police matter. He would not disturb me, but would use outer office for conference. Since my instructions referred only to custody of safe and contents, I had no authority to refuse him access to his own office. I agreed.
01.00 „	Telephoned duty-officer. Asked him note Bandinelli's request and my decision.

The entries ended at that point. I called the duty-officer myself. He confirmed the entries from his own log. Which left me with a vital question: had Bandinelli come to the office under duress, or had he come as an accomplice who was liquidated when his usefulness was ended? I was still puzzling over it when Steffi came back, cross-grained and unhappy.

The porter knew nothing, had seen no one. He worked strictly by the book and the terms of his contract, which stated that he would remain awake and on duty until midnight or until the cleaners left, whichever was the later. After that he might go to bed. All tenants had pass-keys to the front door. They had free access to their offices at any hour. Non-tenants were refused admission outside office hours unless they were identified as cleaners or contractors.

'. . . So, in fact, Steffi, anyone with a pass-key could bring a whole army into the building after midnight, with no one any the wiser?'

'That's the size of it, Colonel.'

'Where was Bandinelli when he telephoned at thirty-seven minutes after twelve?'

'One way to find out, Colonel. Ring his house.'

I lifted the telephone again and called Bandinelli's villa on the Cassia. The phone rang for a long while and then a very surly male answered:

'Villa Bandinelli! Who is this?'

'Carabinieri. We wish to speak to the Advocate.'

'He's not here.'

'His wife then.'

'The Signora is in Naples.'

'Who are you?'

'De Muro, Major-domo.'

'Where can I find the Advocate?'

'At this hour, God knows!'

'What time did he go out?'

'He hasn't been home since yesterday morning. He telephoned in the evening to say he wouldn't be home for dinner.'

'No idea where he might be?'

'None at all.'

'Thank you. Good morning.'

He did not return the greeting. He hung up in my ear. Steffi grinned.

'No luck?'

'No. His wife's away. He didn't go home for dinner.'

'Which helps your little fiction about an unidentified body.'

'But it doesn't tell me who did the killing and took the documents.'

'Does it matter, Colonel?'

'For God's sake, Steffi! What sort of question is that?'

'A very good one I thought, Colonel. Look! This is a professional job, neat, tranquil, simple as walking. Which do you want? The liquidators or the people who paid them? This is not police work, friend; it's intelligence analysis, an exercise in pure reason. Start from the bottom and you'll be wandering round the sewers six months from now. Start from the top and you halve the work and double your chances—believe me!'

'I do believe you, Steffi. But sometime in the next three hours I have to face the Director. What do I offer him?'

'Human sacrifice! . . .' Steffi favoured me with a gallows grin. 'So why don't you pour me some coffee, Colonel, and let's discuss the candidates.'

The Director's apartment was the top floor of a sixteenth-century palace just off the Via della Scrofa. The revenues from the rest of the palace—dwellings and fashionable shops—would keep him in kingly state for a lifetime. His paintings, sculptures and objects of virtue were a fortune in themselves. His library was a minor treasure-house of rare editions, specialist studies and exotic poetry in a variety of languages. The Director was an exotic himself, resplendent in a brocaded dressing-gown, attended by a wiry Sicilian who was both butler and bodyguard. At six in the morning, grubby, unshaven and very unsure of myself, I was in no mood to appreciate the dramatic effect.

The Director offered me a cool welcome, and an English breakfast–tea, toast, scrambled eggs and marmalade. I asked for coffee and pastry. The Director conceded the point with a smile and then proceeded to make a few of his own.

'You knew the Pantaleone papers were important, Colonel. Why did you not take immediate possession of them?'

'I needed a judicial order. To get it, I would have had to appear against Bandinelli in the presence of a judge. I thought it unwise.'

'So, you made an arrangement which resulted in the death of agent Calvi and of Bandinelli himself?'

'Yes.'

'Any excuses?'

'No excuse. An explanation. I was trying to scare Bandinelli into further revelations. I thought the security risk was minimal. In the event, I was wrong.'

'Who else knows the facts at this moment?'

'Only SID. We had the bodies out and the place cleaned up by four this morning. We're in a holding situation for a few days at least.'

'But we don't know who has the Pantaleone papers?'

'No.'

'So, let's guess, Colonel. Local group or foreign?'

'Local, I think.'

'Right wing or Left?'

'Right.'

'Why?'

'The Left have a lot of dirt they haven't published yet. The Right have a lot of dirt they want to bury–I think last night was a funeral party.'

'You don't convince me, Colonel.'

'I'm not trying to convince you, sir. I'm telling you what I believe. If you're thinking of Woodpecker and his network, forget him. I had him pulled in at four this morning. I worked on him myself, for nearly two hours, before I came to see you. I know what his brief is. Assassination is not part of it. Besides, he's been under constant surveillance and he doesn't have the resources or contacts to set up a job like this in half a day. Now, let's look at the other side of the coin. Bandinelli was on the Right wing. He served Pantaleone. He could have sold out to a successor. . . .'

'And been killed for his pains?'

'That, too.'

'Name me a possible successor.'

'Major-General Marcantonio Leporello.'

For the first time, the Director was shaken and he showed it. He set down his tea-cup with a clatter and sat a long moment staring at me with bleak and hostile eyes. Then he said, quietly:

'I presume you have evidence in support, Colonel?'

'Some. I interviewed the General yesterday at the Hassler Hotel.'

'You what?'

'I interviewed Leporello.'

'In spite of my orders that no action was to be taken with that subject?'

'Yes, sir.'

'And what did you tell him?'

'That he was under surveillance by a foreign network who had tipped him as political candidate for the Right.'

'What else?'

'The whereabouts of the Pantaleone papers.'

'Oh . . . !'

'And the fact that I was acting against direct orders.'

'And what was his reaction to that?'

'He promised to keep the interview secret—and he offered me a job on his own staff.'

'I'm tempted to make you immediately available, Matucci.'

'That's your privilege, sir—and, even from the point of view of the Service, it mightn't be a bad idea.'

'You're bargaining with me, Matucci. I don't like that.'

'And you're threatening me, sir. I don't like that either.'

'You disobey orders and that's dangerous.'

'It was a risk. I took it. I think it paid dividends.'

'It gave you a convenient suspect, nothing more.'

'Something more.'

'What?'

'I've identified the Salamander.'

That brought him up short. He held a piece of buttered toast half-way between the plate and his thin lips. Then he popped it into his mouth and chewed on it pensively. Finally, he said:

'And do you propose to tell me who he is?'

'Yes, sir. If I'm still in the Service at nine o'clock this morning, I'll be keeping an appointment with him. He's the Cavaliere Bruno Manzini. He tells me, and I hope to confirm it from the records, that he is the bastard brother of General Pantaleone.'

'First Leporello, now Manzini. Leporello is your military superior. Manzini is one of the most powerful financiers in Italy. You're flying very high, my friend.'

'And you can shoot me down now, if you choose.'

'I mightn't need to do it. Whoever killed Calvi, could as easily kill you.'

'I know.'

'So, if I let you go on?'

'I want a free hand, and access to the Leporello file.'

'Can I trust you, Matucci?'

'You can, but you'd rather not.'

'Do you trust me?'

'With reservations, yes.'

'What reservations?'

'You're the Director. I know what you are commissioned to do. What I don't know is how you interpret your commission and to what secret ends you direct the activities of SID.'

'Do you have any right to know?'

'Legally, I suppose not. I'm a serving officer, I do as I'm told . . . *basta*! Personally? That's another matter. If you'd asked me the same question a week ago, I'd have given you a nice, complaisant answer: bless me father, lead me in the way of salvation and look after my pension rights! This morning, it's different. I'm middle-aged and tired and I haven't had a shave and I lost a good lad because I didn't think straight. So, I don't want to be manipulated any more. I want to know where I'm being directed and why—and if I don't like it, I'll resign my job with you and go back to desk duty or police work.'

The Director drank the last of his tea and dabbed at his lips with a linen napkin. He pushed back his chair, walked to the window and stood a long time looking out at the tumbled roof-tops of Rome, gold and umber and crimson in the early light. When he turned, the light was at his back and the contours of his face were in shadow. He began to talk, quietly at first, then with mounting passion and eloquence.

'You are a presumptuous fellow, Colonel. Yet, I can forgive you, because I, also, presume too much and too often. I presume on wealth and family and myself as a product of all the alliances and misalliances of our history. In a way, I am yesterday's man; but then Italy is yesterday's country as well as today's. We build our houses on tombs. We built our prosperity on ruins and papal monuments and the genius of our ancient dead. Our law is an idiot confusion of Justinian, the Codex Canonicus, Napoleon, Mussolini and the founding fathers of the United States. Our nobility is a hodge-podge of ancient families and the last upstarts ennobled by the House of Savoy. In politics, we are Marxists, Monarchists, Socialists, Liberals, Fascists, Christian Democrats—opportunists all! We have the best business men and the worst bureaucrats in the world. We're a nation of anti-clericals and we've manipulated the Catholic Church for centuries. We shout federal republican democracy—yet every province is a separate continent. A man's country is whatever miserable village he was born in. . . . Now you, my dear Colonel, demand that I should tell you to what I am committed and to what end I direct the Defence Information Service. . . . Let me turn the question then and ask you where you would walk if you were in my shoes—as you may be one day if you are cool enough and clever enough and understand the price to be paid? . . . No answer? Then, here is mine. Our problems will not be solved by an election, by a coalition of parties, by the victory of one system over another. We are Mediterranean men, Colonel. We are, whether we like it or not, a mongrel breed of Greek and Latin and Phoenician and Arab and Iberian Celt and Viking and Visigoth and the Huns of Attila. We live, as we have lived for centuries, in a precarious balance of tribal and family interests. When the balance tips, ever so slightly, we are plunged into disorder and civil strife. When the strife becomes too bloody for us all, we cry halt and beg to be delivered—by the Church, by a personal saviour—or, most pathetically of all, by politicians and bureaucrats who are as bloodied and confused as we are ourselves. The Spaniards and the Greeks and the Portuguese turned to dictators. The Arabs threw out the Colonial powers and replaced them with local autocrats. We Italians have tried one dictator and made a shambles of democracy. Now, we don't know what we want. Me? I don't know what the people want. I can't even judge what they will tolerate. So, I manipulate information and situations to hold things in balance as long as I can. I don't want dictatorship. I don't want Marxism. I'm sure the kind of democracy we have is too unstable to last. But, come one or the other, I'll try to make it as tolerable as I can. Politics is the art of the possible. Mediterranean politics is the art of the impossible and I understand it better than most. You're worried about Leporello, but you have no evidence against him and I'm not going to antagonize him just at a moment when we may need him. You're worried about your Salamander, who, I confess, makes no sense to me at all just now. You want a free investigation? I'll give it to you, but, understand me, Matucci, when I move, in whatever gambit, I am king of the board and you are a pawn. Take it or leave it.'

I gave him the answer without a second's hesitation.

'I'll take it. And I'll give you an honest report. If I don't like what you do, I'll argue it face to face. If we don't agree, I'll fight you; but I'll do it in the open.'

'It's a rash promise, Matucci. I won't hold you to it. If ever you fight me, you'll have to lie like a whore and cheat like a card-sharp, just to save your skin. . . . By the way, you can't meet Manzini looking like that. My valet will show you to the guest-room and find you a razor and a clean shirt.'

At eight o'clock on the same spring morning, with an hour to kill before my meeting with Manzini, I rejoined old Stefanelli as he strolled whistling down the Spanish Steps. The sun was bright; the air was crisp; every tread of the staircase blossomed with girls. I had been up all night, but I felt miraculously refreshed and I could see the sap rising even in Steffi's withered trunk.

This was the best of Rome: the smell of dust and women and new bread and fresh violets; the clatter of the gossips on their way to market, the honk of taxis, the solemn parade of tourists, pale from the mists of Denmark and High Germany; the tumble of cupolas and campaniles and russet roofs crowned with clothes-lines and television antennae. This was the fountain of youth that gave a man fantasies, put birds in his head and wings on his bunioned feet.

At the foot of the steps, we paused so that Steffi could buy himself a carnation for his button-hole, then we turned into Babington's Tea Rooms, where Steffi had promised to buy Solimbene tea and English muffins. Solimbene was a pedant but an amiable one, who affected small eccentricities—velvet smoking jackets, fin-de-siècle cravats, gold fob-seals and eyeglasses on a ribbon of watered silk. He also nourished a passion for red-headed women and English manners, though he had never in his life travelled further than Paris.

We found him enthroned in a corner of the tea-room, clasping the hand of a blonde waitress and pouring out his passion in execrable German. He let her go, reluctantly, and turned the flood of his eloquence on Steffi:

'My dear colleague! My brother in arms and in art! I have revelations for you, Steffi mine! Revelations, mysteries and scandals. Don't laugh! Your trade is horrible—blood and dust and excrement and clothing from the dead. Me? I live with fairy-tales—gryphons rampant and unicorns couchant, allocamels and lioncels and dancing dolphins and magical swords in disembodied hands. . . . But, when you need a simple little fact, who finds it? Me! Solimbene, the herald! . . . Yes, my love, my dove, tea, muffins and English marmalade. Coffee is a madman's drink. It produces dyspepsia and dries out the kidneys. . . . Now, my friends, we begin with this.' He laid the salamander card on the table and stabbed at it with a cake-fork. '. . . Which is not heraldry at all, but calligraphy, a monkish art. Even the crown is corrupted. However, notwithstanding, *mutatis mutandis*, I was prepared to accept an heraldic origin. Result? I found myself chasing salamanders across every escutcheon in Europe. Insanity! Total insanity! Finally, I reduced the number of possibles to five. Insanity again!' He spread a set of glossy photographs on the table and annotated them. 'These two families are extinct. The only survivor of this one is a monk in the Certosa of Florence. Which leaves us, my dear friends, with this last photograph. I found it listed in our files under *"curiosa* and *exotica"*. There is your salamander in the first and fourth quarterings; the supporters are lions rampant. It's beautifully executed, as you can see. Only one problem: it is not a coat of arms at all. It is an artist's conceit. It belongs to no known family.'

Stefanelli shrugged and spread his hands in a Levantine gesture.

'So, it's beautiful and it means nothing. Why show it to us?'

'Oh, it does mean something, dear colleague. It means a great deal—fraud, fakery and scandals juicy as a beefsteak. How old are you, Steffi?'

'None of your business.'

'Come now, don't be touchy. I'm doing you a favour.'

'No favour, you're being very well paid—provided the Cononel here authorizes the invoice. Now, let's see the meat in the sandwich.'

The waitress came back with tea and muffins and Solimbene detained her again with compliments and cajolery. Then, when she whisked herself away, he began another comedy with notebook and eyeglasses and a new flourish of rhetoric.

'In the year of Our Lord, nineteen hundred and ten, when Pius X was gloriously reigning, and you, dear Steffi, were still wet behind the ears, there lived not a stone's throw from here a very notable lady of fashion, who called herself the Countess Salamandra. She entertained only the noble and the wealthy—among them a certain opera singer, who, as he left her house early one morning, was shot and killed, presumably, by a jealous rival. There was, of course, a scandal. The lady, assisted by some of her clients, fled the country and went to live in Nice. Police inquiries revealed that the Countess Salamandra was not a countess at all, but a young Scots lady named Anne Mackenzie, who, having fallen from grace in a noble bed, decided to enrich herself by the same means. . . . How's that for a prelude, Colonel? Will you authorize the invoice now? Or are you bored already?'

'Go on! Go on, man!'

'This coat of arms was used by the Countess Salamandra. She had caused it to be forged for professional purposes.'

'Is that all?'

'All?' Solimbene was outraged. 'My dear Colonel, when I do a job, I do it properly. I have tramped this city in your service. I have burrowed like a badger into the files of Central Registry. I have spent hours of my life with withered old dowagers, who have almost, but not quite, cured me of concupiscence. Miss Anne Mackenzie was once in service with the Count Massimo Pantaleone, as nurse and governess to his daughters. She became pregnant to the old Count and left his service. In August 1900, she married one Luca Salamandra, described in the marrage certificate as a circus performer, who, two days after the wedding, fell from a high-wire and broke his neck. The child, a boy, was born a week after his demise and was baptized Massimo Salamandra in the Capuchin church in the Via delle Zoccolette. In proof of which I offer certificates of marriage and birth and baptism, all dated 1900. In October of the same year, a lady calling herself the Countess Salamandra set herself up in the Palazzo Cherubini, just down the road here, and began to prepare her entry into Roman society. It is a reasonable guess, supported by the gossip of my dowagers, that she was financed in her venture by a generous allowance paid by old Count Pantaleone.'

'And what happened to the boy?'

'His mother took him with her when she fled to Nice. After that, no record until 1923, when a young man named Massimo Salamandra presented himself before a tribunal in Rome and applied to change his name to Bruno Manzini. The tribunal approved the application and the transaction was entered at the Central Registry in Rome—which is where I found it yesterday. . . . Now, gentlemen, do I get my money?'

I didn't tell him; but at that moment he could have tripled the price without a murmur from me. When you are playing against the house it always pays to have a spare ace in your sleeve. Even that doesn't help, of course, when the rest of the deck is stacked against you.

The Cavaliere Bruno Manzini received me in a suite large enough to house a division of infantry and still leave room for the camp followers. His morning face was benign. His manners impeccable. He was even solicitous for my health.

'You look a little peaked this morning, Colonel. A late night?'

'A long one, Cavaliere. I haven't been to bed yet.'

'My dear fellow! Had I known, we could have made a later appointment.'

'Kind of you, but I need, desperately, whatever information you can give me.'

'Let's save time then. How much do you know already?'

'That your mother was one Anne Mackenzie, some-time nurse to the Pantaleone family. That you are the son of her union with the old Count. That you were baptized Massimo Salamandra in Rome in 1900. That your mother, for reasons of business, adopted a spurious title and a coat-of-arms to match it. The device of the salamander appears in that coat-of-arms. In 1923 you changed your name to Bruno Manzini . . .'

'And how did you come by all that information?'

'Some luck, some heraldry, and the Central Registry.'

'What else can you tell me?'

'That depends, Cavaliere, on how much you are prepared to tell me.'

'Anything you wish to know.'

'Do you mean that?'

'I would not say it otherwise.'

'Then, why were you blackmailing your brother?'

'Blackmail? My dear Matucci, since the war I have become inordinately rich. I could have bought and sold him twenty times over. I was threatening him with public disgrace! If he had persisted in these crazy politics of his, I should have exposed him without mercy.'

'Instead you killed him.'

'I beg your pardon?'

'He died of an overdose of drugs—self-administered.'

'A fact which was not made public. Why?'

'Bluntly, Cavaliere, for fear of a political scandal which might lead to civil disorder.'

'Now I could make the scandal.'

'Will you?'

'No. It would defeat my purpose; which is the same as yours. To avoid political disruption and civil violence.'

'Next question then. If the document you sent your brother fell into other hands, what use could be made of it?'

'Now that he is dead, very little. Oh a newspaper could publish it and make a ten-day wonder, but politically—in my view at least—it would be a damp fire-cracker. Why do you ask?'

'Because all the Pantaleone papers were stolen last night from the offices of Doctor Sergio Bandinelli. Bandinelli and one of our agents were murdered.'

'There was no news of this in the Press.'

'Nor will there be, unless you choose to release it.'

He stared at me in blank disbelief. Then he shook his head like a man waking from a dream and wondering where he was. He pieced out the next words, slowly, as if they were quite inadequate to express his thought.

'I do not believe . . . I cannot believe . . . that any intelligent man would . . . would be so rash as to commit himself to a stranger in this way. You have put an atomic bomb into my hands, Colonel. I could blow up the country with it. . . . My God, don't you see! You, a serving officer, have just admitted to falsifying the records of a suicide and . . . concealing two murders! How do you know that I will not lift this telephone and call the Press—some of which I own—and splash the news all over the world?'

'I don't know, Cavaliere. I'm gambling.'

'Then you're a madman.'

'Only if you lift the telephone. If you don't, if you place your knowledge at my disposal, then I'm the sanest man in Rome.'

'But you have no guarantees have you?'

'In this dog's world, Cavaliere, there are no guarantees and you know it. The law is no more than a thin crust over a nest of soldier ants. Even death is big business now—international business. You want someone dead in Israel, you fly the killers in from Japan. You want a murder in Venice, you phone London or Munich and your assassin arrives the next day. Hijack an airliner? Simple. You let the contract in New York, embark your people in Stockholm, fly the damn thing to Libya if it suits you. . . . I have to trust someone. Let's say I trust you because you despise the trade I'm in and make no secret of it. . . . Now, can we go on?'

'You'll check my answers, of course?'

'As if I were the Grand Inquisitor himself.'

'That's better. Please begin.'

'Cavaliere, what would you expect to find in the Pantaleone papers that would be worth two lives and the risk of the crime itself?'

He pondered that for a long while before he answered:

'In the family papers themselves, very little. There would be title-deeds, business transactions, wills, settlements, old correspondence, some of it scandalous perhaps, but of interest only to the social historian. In my brother's personal papers . . .? Well, let's think of him as a political soldier, playing a power-game. He would assemble dossiers on friends and enemies alike. Some of those might be very valuable either to the subjects themselves or to political rivals. But murder . . . ? Somehow I don't see it. You're an expert on dossiers. I use them, too, in business. But, truly, how important are they? Everybody in Italy knows a little dirt—or a lot—about the man next door. We're all gossips and scandalmongers, and what we don't know, we invent. It's a social disease, tolerable only because it's endemic—like syphilis among the Cossacks. Our sexual morals are special, our social ethics non-existent. After the Fascists and the war, and the occupation and the scrabble for world trade and the late history of the Vatican and all the chicanery of our recent politics, who has clean hands anyway? No matter what my brother wrote in his notebooks, you can safely wager twenty other people knew it before he did. I'm not saying the stuff couldn't be valuable. . . . But the murder of a lawyer and a Government agent . . . ? No, I can't see it. There must be something else.'

'For example . . . ?'

'Plans, more likely. The tactics and strategy of a *colpo di stato*. The political and military organization that must be ready to take over at a moment's notice. The list of participants, active and passive. The location of arms, the disposition of available forces in sympathy with the plotters. Even your own service might do murder for such things.'

'In this case they didn't.'

'So now, Matucci, we are at the heart of the artichoke. We have to decide whether or no we can trust each other. Who makes the next move?'

'It's your turn, Cavaliere!'

'Before you arrived your Director telephoned me.'

You know that strange sensation of disembodiment that comes in moments of shock. You are suddenly outside yourself, looking at the antics of a body that doesn't belong to you. I had it then. I watched myself tumbling into the trap which opened under my unwary feet. Then the hallucination passed and I was back in my own skin, writhing under the irony of my situation. Manzini watched me, grave and unsmiling. He went on:

'You are angry. You have a right to be. I know your Director very well. He is sometimes too clever for his own good and always as vain as Lucifer. He wanted to display his cleverness to me and also, I think, to teach you a lesson for some delinquency.'

'That's true, at least. Now what, Cavaliere?'

'Now I am going to give you a piece of information which your Director does not yet possess. At eight o'clock yesterday evening, I signed, on behalf of one of my companies, a procurement contract with the Government. The contract calls for the urgent supply of large quantities of riot-control equipment. The specifications were drawn up by Major-General Marcantonio Leporello; and the equipment will be used by troops under his command. . . . I have drawn certain conclusions from this situation. You may care to hear them.'

'Please . . . !'

'If I were a new Fascist or an old one, if I were looking for a new leader, I should be very ready to bargain with Marcantonio Leporello.'

'Perhaps the bargain has already been struck.'

'No, Colonel. Leporello was waiting on the contract which would put fire-power and bargaining power into his hands. He was waiting for something else, too.'

'What?'

'He would not commit himself until the Pantaleone papers were safe in his own hands.'

'And he has them now?'

'I believe so.'

'It seems to me, Cavaliere, you're something more than a business man.'

'I'm a salamander, Colonel–a perennial survivor. You?'

'A servant of the State. Except that I'm not sure what the State is today–and I'm scared of what it may be tomorrow.'

'That makes us allies.'

'In a lopsided league.'

'That frightens you?'

'Yes, Cavaliere, it frightens me.'

'Then, let me offer you a small reassurance. I shall write you a name and an address. If you go there you will hear part of the truth about me. If it satisfies you, you will come to see me in Bologna. If it doesn't, you will still be in profit.'

He took a business card from his wallet, wrote a name and address on the back of it and handed it to me. The name was Raquela Rabin; the address, a street near the Theatre of Marcellus. He made no explanation. I did not ask for one. We shook hands, he led me to the door and held it open for me.

'One other thing, Colonel. . . .'

'Yes?'

'Advice from an old campaigner. Always walk close to the wall, and sleep with one eye open. . . . I hope we meet again soon.'

'I hope so, too, Cavaliere. Good day!'

When I hit the street, it was exactly ten o'clock. The bells of Santa Susanna were tolling the hour; the traffic made a dramatic discord, the vast indifference of the city was a blow in the face. All of a sudden I was maudlin tired, rocking on my feet. I climbed into my car and drove, in a perilous daze, all the way to Parioli. I hammered on Lili's door and almost fell into her arms when she opened it herself. She asked no questions but led me by the hand into the bedroom and helped me to undress. I don't know what I said or tried to say; but she hushed me like a child and drew the covers over me and let me collapse into sleep.

That sleep was a journey into the underworld, so deep I could not hope to escape from the nightmares that beset me: I was harried by faceless huntsmen, bayed through dark tunnels, stood naked in a desert under the eyes of a hundred accusers, I was arraigned in a graveyard by dead men, I was hung by the thumbs in my own interrogation room, while a masked executioner held a vial of poison under my nose. I screamed as he crushed it in his giant fingers; and woke, sweating and trembling, with the sheets knotted about me like a shroud.

The smell of my own body offended me. It was the odour of fear, dammed up too long, souring the body juices, spilt like the voidings of an animal for the predators to follow. I was marked now–by the Director as an intransigent, by Leporello as a man who must be bought or seduced, by Manzini as a collaborator, useful one moment, dispensable at the twitch of an eyebrow. I was in danger because I knew too much. I was exposed because I could do too little. I was a silly goat tethered to attract the tiger–and if the tiger did not come, the marksman in the tree could pick me off at a whim.

Lili could be picked off, too: by her own people, if not mine. I had pulled in Woodpecker. His network was in disorder. Lili was compromised. In the code of the trade she was marked for liquidation. If the assassins did not get her, the Director would order her arrested, if only to teach me a lesson. I looked at my watch. Three o'clock. Siesta time still. I lifted the bedside phone and called Stefanelli's house.

'Steffi? Matucci!'

'Don't you ever sleep, for God's sake?'

'Steffi, the roof's falling in. Have you got a spare room?'

'For you?'

'No. To store a very sensitive package.'

'Now sensitive?'

'It has to be kept away from heat and light until other storage is arranged.'

'*Porca miseria!* I was up all night with you. I had breakfast with you. I've had two hours of bad sleep and I'm still in my pyjamas!'

'Steffi–the package may explode and blow my head off!'

'Eh-Eh-Eh . . . ! Where do I collect it?'

'I'll bring it to you. Go back to sleep.'

'Thank you for nothing, dear friend.'

I had just put the phone down when Lili came in, frowning and solicitous.

'I thought you were talking in your sleep. Earlier you were shouting and groaning.'

'I had bad dreams, Lili.'

'You look like a bad dream yourself. What happened after you left me last night?'

'Don't ask. Just listen to me.'

'But . . .'

'Lili, it's condition red for you. I want to try to get you out of the country into Switzerland. That needs time and planning. So, I'm taking you to a safe house. You stay there until I'm ready to move you. Yes or no?'

I felt the sudden tension in her hands; saw the suspicion in her eyes.

'If I say no . . . ?'

'You get killed by your own people or gaoled by mine.'

'I don't believe it. Last night . . .'

'Last night was a million years ago. While you and I were singing the Undressing Song, two men were murdered–one of them mine, the other Pantaleone's lawyer. It's not in the papers because we did some stage-management. I arrested Woodpecker at four this morning. The network is broken. You're compromised. I can't protect you more than a few days; and I'm putting myself at risk to do it.'

'Why?'

'Just to prove to myself I'm not a whore-master. Will that do? You've got fifteen minutes; which is about how long it will take me to shower and dress. After that, you're on your own.'

'Please . . . ! Hold me. I'm frightened.'

'I want you frightened, Lili. I want you to do exactly as I tell you and don't for Christ's sake try to make second guesses. Understand?'

'Yes.'

'Start now. Pack a small overnight bag. Take your jewellery, your cheque books, whatever cash you have in the house.'

At that moment, the doorbell chimed: four musical notes, ominous in the silence. I laid a finger on Lili's lips and whispered:

'The house-keeper?'

'Out. Her day off.'

I rolled out of bed, ridiculous in my nakedness, and crept from the bedroom, through the salon and into the hallway. A letter had been thrust through the letter-box and was lying about a foot from the door. I bent to pick it up and then drew back. This was siesta time. No self-respecting postman would be on the streets at the sacred hour. I went back into the bedroom.

'Lili, do you have a kitchen spatula or anything like that?'

'I think so, why?'

'Get it for me, please.'

While she was rummaging in the kitchen, I dressed. Then, incongruously armed with a fish-slice, I walked back into the hall, lifted the letter by sliding the fish-slice under it and carried it gingerly to the coffee-table in the centre of the salon. The address was typed. The stamp was Italian. But it had not been franked by a post office. I left it there, walked back into the bedroom, snapped at Lili to get the packing done, and telephoned a friend of mine in the security section of Posts and Telegraphs. He gave me the cheerful news that a normal letter-bomb contained enough explosive to kill the man who opened it and maim anyone else in a normal sized room. He promised to have an expert on the doorstep in thirty minutes. I told him I couldn't wait that long. He told me to call the police and put a man on guard until the expert arrived.

I hurried Lili through the packing. We locked the apartment and then, avoiding the elevators, walked down four flights of stairs to the lobby. The porter was sitting at his desk, his nose buried in the *Corriere dello Sport*. The street was lined on both sides with parked vehicles. My own car was jammed beautifully between a Mercedes and a Fiat 600.

I left Lili in the foyer and walked outside. The road was deserted except for a woman walking a dog, an old street cleaner, laboriously pushing a tin can on wheels, and the flower-seller dozing at her booth on the corner. I looked up at the buildings on the opposite side. All the windows were closed, some where shuttered. There was no place for a marksman. I walked back into the building and dialled *Pronto Soccorso,* the police emergency service of the Carabinieri.

Five minutes later a squad car pulled up at the entrance to the apartments and the two-man crew came in at a run. The *brigadiere* was cool and efficient. He would call the explosives squad to handle the letter and to check my car for booby traps. Meantime, if I would give him a deposition ... ? My card convinced him he could wait for it. I needed his car and his driver to deliver the lady and myself to the Excelsior Hotel.

Senz'altro! ... We took off at speed and he dropped us diagonally opposite the hotel. We waited five minutes window-shopping at Rizzoli's, then took a taxi to the Theatre of Marcellus and walked through the maze of alleys to Steffi's house.

Steffi received us with characteristic flourish. He clucked over Lili, showered her with compliments, insisted on settling her into her room himself and then stormed downstairs to give me the rough edge of his tongue.

'Matucci, you're a madman! That little baggage upstairs is dangerous! When the Director hears of this—and he will, sooner or later—you'll be cooked, screaming, like a lobster. God Almighty! It's a ready-made case to put you away for twenty years: SID Colonel sells out to Polish Agent! I could write the indictment myself, blindfolded. And all this other melodrama—letter-bombs and calling the Carabinieri to defuse your car. Wait till that paper-work starts going the rounds!'

'Steffi, have you got a whisky?'

'For you, hemlock and soda.'

'Then pour me a big one and shut up.'

'Shut up, he says! The next thing you'll be wanting to sleep with the woman under my roof.'

'I might at that, Steffi.'

'Oh, no you don't! This is a good Jewish house. If anybody's going to defile it, it won't be a dumb goy like you. There's your drink.'

'Chin-chin, Steffi.'

'I hope it rots your gullet! . . . Now, can we be serious a minute?'

'I'm serious, Steffi. I'm sweating blood.'

'Good! Sweat a little more for me.'

'Tell me. Who is Raquela Rabin?'

'Will you repeat the question, Colonel?'

'Who is Raquela Rabin?'

'Why do you want to know?'

'I have an introduction. I'd like to know something about her before we meet.'

For a moment he stared at me, blank-faced and hostile; then he sat down heavily on a chair, cupped his hands round the glass and sat staring into the liquor. An old man ravaged by time and history.

'. . . Fifteen came back from Auschwitz, Colonel. Raquela Rabin was the only woman. In the ghetto, when you say her name, you say it with respect—great respect. She did not have to go away; she had powerful protectors. But when the trucks came she was here, standing in the *piazza*, waiting like a daughter of David. She was an artist, Matucci, an angel voice, one of the greatest of her time. When you see her, you will say she is older than I, but she is still only sixty-six. Everything that should not happen to a woman happened to her; but she is still sane and splendid as the evening star. . . . You will be very gentle with her. What she tells you, you will believe without question. You will not mix her in this stinking business of ours. You will not mix her—understand that!'

'Easy, Steffi. . . . Easy!'

'I'll take you to her, because I want you clean when you go in—clean and humble, because this is a great woman. I've done you a favour, Colonel. Your woman—and she is your woman, no?—is under my roof, at my risk. Now you will tell me, who gave you this introduction?'

'Bruno Manzini.'

'Why?'

'He said that if Raquela Rabin spoke well of him I might be prepared to trust him. I need that, Steffi. You warned me once I would be put on the auction block. I'm there now, Steffi. Tomorrow or the next day someone's going to open the bids. They'll be high and tempting. I'm not sure I'll be able to resist them. . . . A wise friend would help. A strong one might lend me courage. I'm running out of it, Steffi, because I don't know what to believe any more. I don't even know who I am.'

He brightened at that, as if I had read him the best news in the world. He cocked his head with that old parrot pose and surveyed me with grudging approval.

'So! History is being made. The *Risorgimento* of Dante Aligheiri Matucci. So you don't know what you are? Who does? But sure as breathing, you'd better see what's being done to you.'

'I see it. I don't understand it.'

'Because you refuse to come to terms with yourself. You don't want to decide what you are—a patriot or a mercenary.'

'Hard words from a friend!'

'True words, because I am your friend.'

'I've seen too many rogues wearing too many bright labels, Steffi.'

'A simple question then. Today you might have been killed. Tomorrow the risk is bigger. Why do you take it? When you stake your life, what are you staking it for—or against?'

'Maybe for a dream, Steffi. . . . I don't know. Maybe against a madness I smell every day in the streets. The land is the centre of it somehow. The vines greening on the terraces, the white hills and the brown stubble and the river sedge with the mist on it. My land! I will not live in it by sufferance and privilege. The people? That's another thing. I hate the crowds that jostle me, the silly functionaries who bedevil me from dawn till dark; but then, I see a woman bursting like a grape with love; I am served by a peasant who says "*Salve!*" and offers me wine and bread and salt as if I were his brother. . . . These are the good things, Steffi, painted on the walls of Etruscan tombs, celebrated in the songs of fishermen. . . . Boh! This is home. And I don't want it trampled by jackboots, or desecrated by mindless mobs. . . . Now, let's leave it, eh?'

'I can leave it, friend. You can't. You're the man who knows the underside of politics, the cogs in the power machine. You have to decide how you will use that knowledge.'

'I'm not paid to use it—only to collect it.'

'You collect it, but you filter it, too. You suppress, you emphasize, you interpret. To what end?'

'For Christ's sake, what do we all want? A quiet life. Some dignity in our living and dying.'

'Not enough! Not half enough! Look . . . !'

'Be quiet, old man!' Lili challenged him from the doorway, cold and angry. 'Let him find his own answers in his own time.'

'He has no time.' Steffi was brusque and brutal. 'He robbed himself, when he gave it to you.'

'I am here to give it back. May I sit down, please?'

Steffi pointed to the chair and she sat down between us. She laid her palms flat on the table as if to hold herself erect and in command. She was silent for a few monents, gathering herself, then she told us:

'You are friends. I am the outsider. I accept to be here because I am afraid. I don't want to be killed. I don't want to spend the rest of my life in a Roman prison. But I am not a beggar. I can pay for what you give me.'

'You were not asked to pay.'

'No; but I will.' She turned to me and laid her hands on mine. 'You are going to be very angry with me, Dante Alighieri.'

'Am I?'

'There's something I haven't told you. I might have told you last night if . . . if things had been different. Then again . . . I might not. We were still bargaining then. This morning, you held my life in your hands. You did not bargain. Neither did your friend.'

'So . . . ?'

'Massimo Pantaleone did not leave all his documents in the bank.'

'Where are the rest?'

'In the villa on Ponza.'

'What are they, Lili?'

'Microfilms and maps.'

'How long have they been there?'

'He took them on our last visit to the villa—a week before he died.'

'But you didn't tell Woodpecker or any of your own people?'
'No.'
'Why not?'
'I had no control over what Woodpecker might do. If he stole the stuff, I was finished. Only Massimo and I could possibly know the hiding-place.'
'Could you describe it to me?'
'No. I would have to take you there.'
'That means new arrangements. You have to wait here while we make them. Steffi, you and I have a visit to make. Don't leave the house, Lili. If there are any callers, don't answer. We'll be back in an hour or so.'
'I may never come back,' said Steffi, mournfully. 'I may drown myself in the Tiber. I do not want to be alive when you try explaining this madness to the Director.'

He did not drown himself. He withdrew, quite deliberately, into his own yesterdays and forced me to withdraw with him, as if it were some rite of passage that I must undergo before I met Raquela Rabin. As we strolled–he would not let me hurry–through the alleys of the old ghetto, he conjured ghosts out of every doorway: old Marco the furniture-maker who whittled a piece of pine into the shape of a fearsome brigand and carved his name on the underside; Ruggiero, the pharmacist, who once made him privy to mysteries: a mummified hand and waters that changed colour when you mixed them; Blasio, the gunsmith, who showed him pistols which had killed five men in duels of honour.

As he talked, his narrative became more vivid, his gestures more ample and exotic. He swept away all traces of the present and planted me firmly in the city of his own childhood. Over there, for instance, was Salamone, called by the folk of the Quarter, Salamone Vecchione. He was so old that he looked like a twin brother to Methuselah, so shrunken that one more year must see him disappear altogether. He wore a long black caftan that was green when the sun shone on it, a little black cap perched on his wispy scalp and a silver chain with a star pendant on his wheezy, hollow bosom. He trundled a barrow from which he sold old prints and books with mildewed bindings and metal tubes with scrolls inside and clay tablets that looked as though birds had walked on them before they were fired in the oven.

The market people were afraid of Salamone and treated him with the exaggerated respect due to a magus or a caster of spells. When he passed they made the sign against the evil eye, and muttered, balefully, about the fire that would consume all Jews and pagans. But to the young Stefanelli, he was like the imp out of a bottle, with a wonder in every pocket.

Not all of Steffi's ghosts were friends. Some were sad traitors; some were nightmare enemies. Luca, the hunch-back, for instance, who sat on his stool outside the hairdresser's and allowed his hump to be touched for a coin. Luca was a police pimp who spied on the ghetto people for the Fascists. Balbo was a ruffian policeman who took tribute from every shopkeeper on his beat and Fra Patrizio was a shave-pate Franciscan who in every sermon railed against the perfidious Jews who crucified the Saviour every day. . . .

'Sometimes,' said Steffi, moodily, 'I would like to forget them all. But God is an ironist who keeps the key to memory in his own hands. . . . Here we are, Colonel. I will present you to Raquela Rabin and then leave. You will come directly to the point with her and not stay too long. She is very frail.'

She was frail indeed, white-haired, pale as milk, almost transparent, so that you felt the next *scirocco* might blow her away. Only her eyes were alive, dark and lustrous, and strangely pitying. She sat erect and calm, listening in silence while I explained who I was and why I had come. When I had finished, she seemed to lapse into meditation like an ancient pythoness waiting for the spirit of divination to animate her. I felt oddly diminished–an ignorant neophyte in the presence of a woman who had seen and suffered everything. Even when she spoke–and she was very gentle with me–there was a hieratic quality in her tone that diminished me still further.

'Do you know why Bruno sent you to me?'

'No, Madam.'

'We were lovers for a long time. Not happy lovers always, because I was famous and courted and Bruno was haunted by his own past: a mother who was a once famous courtesan, a father who lavished money on him, but was never prepared to acknowledge him. But the love was there. It is still there.'

'Even though you were taken; and he stayed.'

'We had parted long before. I went of my own free will. He stayed to fight against those who had taken me. He is still fighting.'

'How?'

'He is a strange man. He believes in forgiving. He does not believe in forgetting.'

'Is there a difference?'

'He thinks so.'

'You?'

'I accept what is: that I am alive and others are dead; that I cannot change it; that people must forget because they cannot bear to remember.'

'Can I trust Bruno Manzini?'

'To be what he is, yes.'

'What is he, Madam?'

'A man who has built himself, cell by cell, from nothing. . . . He is very strong, very faithful. What he promises he will do, however much it costs him. Each year, on the anniversary of the Black Sabbath, he sends me a card. In the right-hand drawer of the desk you will find a folder. Please pass it to me.'

The folder was of tooled leather made by a Florentine craftsman. On the cover, embossed in gold, was a Star of David. I handed it to her. She spread it open on her knees, took out the cards and handed them to me. The cards were identical with that which I had found in Pantaleone's bedroom. Only the inscriptions were different.

Hans Helmut Ziegler
Sao Paolo–3 January 1968

Emmanuele Salatri
London–18 August 1971

Franziskus Loeffler
Oberalp, Austria

'What do these mean, Madam?'

'They are the names of men connected, each in his own way, with what happened to me and to others in 1943. I have fifteen so far. There are nine to come. Bruno Manzini traced them all. A labour of years, because they were spread all over the world. When he traced them, he sent each man a card and a dossier on his past.'

'What do the dates mean?'

'The days on which they died.'

'Who killed them?'

'They killed themselves.'

'There is no date on this one.'

'He is still alive. . . .'

'The difference?'

'Bruno told me that this was the best gift of all—a man who had found a way to live honourably with himself. I was very content to know that.'

'Are you happy with Bruno Manzini—a man who plays God?'

'He does not see it that way.'

'How then?'

'He says that every man must be allowed to judge himself; but he must not be allowed to bury the evidence.'

'And you, Madam?'

'I agree with him, Colonel. I gave evidence at Nuremberg—for and against those in the dock. I hate no one now. I am afraid of nothing. But the terror has come again—in Vietnam, in Brazil, in Africa, here in Europe. Is not that why you have come to me; because you, too, are afraid?'

'Yes, Madam, I am very much afraid.'

'Then trust my Bruno, but not blindly, because then he would have no respect for you. Argue with him, fight him, friend to friend. You may not convince him; you may even end as adversaries; but he will never, never betray you. . . .'

'Thank you, Madam.'

'Thank you for coming. I wish peace on your house and in your heart.'

I was grateful for the blessing; but I walked out into the sunlight a very pensive man. A new conviction was crystallizing out of the murky fluid of my own thoughts. There was no cure for the human condition because every man read the present and plotted the future in the light of his own past. There was no such thing as a clean start, because no one truly forgave and no one wholly forgot. In the end, the folk memory betrayed us all. The wrongs of the fathers were revenged on the children. I understood Manzini and his cold conviction that, even in exile, the tyrants should not be allowed to flourish. I understood the Director and his willingness to settle for a balance, however precarious. I understood Leporello and his fanatic belief that order at any price was cheaper than chaos. The only person I did not understand was myself. . . .

On the way back to Stefanelli's, I stopped in a bar and made a telephone call to Manzini at the Grand Hotel. Our conversation was brief.

'Cavaliere, I have just spoken with Raquela Rabin.'

'And . . . ?'

'I am very glad we met. I should like to see you as soon as possible.'

'I leave for Bologna in half an hour. I am happy to receive you there at any time. When may I expect to see you?'

'In two or three days at the latest. Sooner if I can make it.'

'Good! What is your own situation?'

'Difficult. It may improve soon. I hope so, anyway.'

'Good luck then!'

His wish must have had some potency because when I called the Director, his aide told me he had been called to an urgent conference at the Ministry. Was there a message? None that I could deliver safely on an open line. He should tell the Director that there were new developments in my current investigation and that I would be out of contact for forty-eight hours. I was only putting off the bad day; but if I could get to Ponza and lay my hands on the rest of the Pantaleone files, I might still cheat the headsman.

I was faced now with a problem in space and time. The island of Ponza – which is not my favourite place in all the world – lies about sixty-five kilometres south-west of Gaeta. Legend says Pontius Pilate was born there. The Fascists used it as a place of exile for political prisoners. After the war, islands being scarce and getting scarcer in the twentieth century, people started to buy land and build villas on the slopes and around the shore line. The island is served by ferries from Anzio, Formia and Naples, but whichever way you choose, it still means a road journey from Rome and a three or four hour sea-trip, which in rough weather is a purgatory. At all costs I wanted to avoid using public transport, and to cut the time of the operation to a minimum. If the Director decided to send out a panic call for me, I would be as conspicuous as a wart on the Mona Lisa.

Besides, there was another and more sinister possibility. The papers, stolen from Bandinelli's office were now in the hands of persons unknown. By now it would be clear that the codex was incomplete. Conclusion: the hunters would be on the prowl again and by simple logic they must come back, sooner or later, to Lili Anders and to the villa which she had shared with Pantaleone. Postscript to the conclusion: I needed help in a hurry.

By the time I got back to Steffi's house, it was five-thirty. I put through a priority call to a certain Colonel Carl Malinowski at NATO headquarters in Naples. Malinowski is an agreeable American – sometimes too agreeable for his own good. Two years ago I managed to prise him out of an embarrassing situation which involved his Neapolitan girl-friend and a Russian agent operating in the naval dock areas. Malinowski owed me a favour. I needed it now, in the shape of the big Baglietto, which he used for drinking parties and seduction and which could do twenty-five knots in any reasonable sea.

Malinowski was happy to oblige. He could write himself a leave-pass. He also had a new girl-friend who would appreciate the outing. If we could be at Mergellina docks by first light, he would drive us to the island himself. Better still, if we care to come down to Naples tonight, he would feed us dinner and offer us a bed in his own apartment. The bed was matrimonial size. He presumed it would suit. If it wasn't that sort of party I could sleep on the divan and to hell with me. The rest was easy. I hired a Fiat 130 from a rental agency and by seven in the evening – to Steffi's infinite relief – we were out of Rome and heading south along the *autostrada* to Naples.

I enjoyed that drive; the sudden sense of relief as the city fell away behind us, the dusk gentling the hills of Lazio, the lights pricking out from the mountain farms, the processional sweep of the traffic along the highway, the rise of the yellow moon behind the crags of the Appennines, the brief but grateful privacy of man and woman in a small floating world.

Lili was tense at first, openly resenting my high-handed dealings with her person. I had leaned heavily on the dangers of her situation; but now, homeless and rootless she could see no hopeful future, and I was in no position to promise her one. She sat, stiff and withdrawn, as if she could not bear to be near me. I turned on the radio to a session of Neapolitan music, and affected to ignore her. After a while, she began to nod; and when I drew her towards me, she did not resist but laid her head on my shoulder and dozed, fitfully, until we passed Monte Cassino.

She was calmer then. She sat close and we talked, quietly and disjointedly, until the mood of the first evening came on us again.

'Know something, Dante Alighieri?'

'What?'

'At this moment we really are *noantri*. I can't go home. You don't know where you're going.'

'True, my love, true.'

'I like your Steffi.'

'Yes. . . . He's quite a character.'

'He's very fond of you.'

'We understand each other.'

'But he's afraid you'll make wrong decisions, isn't he?'

'I'm afraid too, *bambina*.'

'I hope you don't sell out–to anyone. Once you do, there's no way back. I know. . . .'

'Why did you come into the game, Lili?'

'Haven't you got that in your dossiers?'

'The how of it–not the real reason.'

'There's a whore in every woman, *caro*, and you know it. Come the low moment when she's lonely and unloved and the first crow's-feet are beginning to show, she'll sell, provided the price looks like a gift and the words are said gently, and tomorrow doesn't look too near. No excuses. No pity, thank you.'

'Suppose we get you out of the country, what then?'

'I'm a bachelor girl of modest means, in the market for a man.'

'What sort of man?'

'That's a private dream; and I won't have you laugh at it.'

'I wouldn't laugh.'

'What kind of a woman do you want, Dante Alighieri?'

'I've had all kinds, Lili–except the one I'd settle down with and make children.'

'Aren't you ever lonely?'

'Often. But it's a tolerable condition. At least it has been. . . .'

'Now?'

'I don't like the fellow who lives in my skin.'

'I like him–sometimes.'

'You don't know him very well, Lili.'

'Well enought to put a name to him.'

'What name?'

'*Bufalo Solitario*–the rogue male.'

'Paid to protect the herd.'

'From what? The Marxists, the Fascists, the Monarchists? I don't believe this "protection", neither do you. You're a political instrument. Any hand can lift you and use you for any work.'

'Let's talk about something else, eh?'

'If you like. What do you do when you can't bear to be alone. . . . ?

'I go out and play.'

'Like last night in Trastevere?'

'Like that. . . .'

'I wish we didn't have to go to Ponza.'

'So do I.'

'What happens when we come back?'

'It depends on what we find and how well I can hide it. . . . That's Capua over there where Spartacus raised the revolt of the slaves.'

'I know about Spartacus, *caro*. I just hope we have better luck than he did.'

Major Carl Malinowski of the United States Marines was a tonic for our jaded spirits. He was six feet tall, all brawn and muscle, with ham fists and a big laugh and a magnolia drawl which, although I speak tolerable English, was often hard for me to understand. He had an unshakeable conviction that the world was still a Garden of Eden, full of willing Eves and congenial serpents. His apartment, furnished in American style, was a bachelor's paradise, with a view across the Bay, from Vesuvius to Capo di Sorrento, a bewildering liquor cupboard and piped music in every room. His new girl was a Swede, culled from the summer crop of tourists and blooming after the transplant. He took one look at Lili and shouted his approval to the neighbourhood.

'*Bella! Bellissima!* Dante, my boy, your taste's improving. This is a real Southern-style woman! Honey, you be good to this man now. He's the best Eyetalian I known—all heart and sex-urge. Bright, too—though you wouldn't think it to look at him. Helga, why don't you take Lili and get her settled while Dante and I build some drinks.' He clamped an iron fist on my shoulder and steered me to the bar. 'Tell me now, Colonel, sir, is this business or pleasure?'

'Business, Carl.'

'So what do you want me to do?'

'Get us to Ponza, get us back fast.'

'In this weather it's three hours each way—more if the wind freshens. How long do you want to stay?'

'Two hours should do it.'

'We leave at six in the morning, we're back mid-afternoon. Suit you?'

'Fine.'

'Expecting trouble?'

'An outside chance.'

'What's with you and Lili-belle?'

'Some business, some pleasure. Too much of one, not enough of the other.'

'I read you, Colonel, sir. I read you loud and clear. So, tonight we drink Christ's tears, and have ourselves a love-in. Tomorrow we hit the beach at Ponza!'

It was a long night and a merry one. We dined like kings on caviar and beefsteak and Neapolitan ice-cream. We drank two litres of Lacrima Christi and half a bottle of Courvoisier, talked the world to rights and told bawdy stories and sprawled on the rug, drowsing to taped music. Sometime after midnight we paired off and went to bed, and I must tell you there is no bed in all the world more comfortable, more apt for love-making, than a big, brass Neapolitan *letto matrimoniale*.

It was a good night for both of us. We did what pleased us and we pleased each other. We were glad, we were grateful, and, for a while, not solitary. We slept deeply and we did not dream at all. We were awake and enjoying each other again when Malinowski hammered on the door and summoned us to breakfast.

I have told it badly; I might have used the same words for a dozen encounters; because I am–and I say it gratefully–a man who has been fortunate in most of his women. But this time there was a difference, a sense of consequence if not yet of commitment. There was another difference, too: I was disposed to be sentimental afterwards, while Lili would have none of it.

She told me so, bluntly, as we stood together on the after-deck of the Baglietto and watched the green cone of Ischia fade against the dawn.

'*Caro*, sometimes you treat me as if I had no brains at all. I know what's at stake. If the material at the villa is important, it puts power into your hands. You think it will also buy me a free passage out of Italy.'

'I hope it will.'

'And salve your conscience about me.'

'If you like to put it that way.'

'But you won't promise anything?'

'I can't.'

'Nonsense! I don't need you to get me out of Italy, Dante Alighieri.'

'You think you can run the frontier guards yourself? Don't try it, Lili.'

'I wouldn't have to do that. I could hire any fisherman on Ponza to run me into Corsica tomorrow.'

'What are you trying to say, Lili?'

'That you need me, like you need the Pantaleone records, as a bargaining card. Let me go and you rob yourself of power, you castrate yourself. I understand that. I accept it. But, you insult me when you try to dress the thing up like a confidence trick. Your friend Steffi was right. You always refuse to come to terms with yourself. . . . Now can we go inside please? I'm cold.'

It was cold. The wind was freshening from the north-west, whipping up an uncomfortable sea; and Malinowski was driving the boat hard, pitting his helmsman's skill against the yaw of the high-powered craft and the short, tricky chop. We settled ourselves in the saloon and I tried, with a kind of desperation, to salvage the argument and my own pride.

'Let's have it clear, Lili. I made a treaty with you. So far I've honoured it. So far, you're free and protected. Agreed?'

'Agreed.'

'Now you want to change it. You want me to turn a blind eye while you make a run for Corsica.'

'No! I want you to be sure what kind of treaty you are making with other people, and what it will do to you in the end.'

'And why the hell should you care?'

'Poor Dante Alighieri! So many women and you've learnt so little. What a waste!'

'At least I don't have any illusions.'

'Boh! Let's not argue then. You write the script; you say the words; you pull the strings; and when the play's over Lili, the puppet, is packed up in her box. Just so we know, my love.'

'And you said there'd be no blackmail! God!'

'Blackmail involves a threat, doesn't it? How can I threaten you? With the Pantaleone records? You will have those as soon as we reach the villa. With a night in bed? That's the custom of the trade isn't it? With your promise of protection? That's the trade, too—every little policeman plays the same trick at every interrogation. So . . . what frightens you, my brave Colonel, if not yourself?'

'If that's the way you read it—fine! Right or wrong, it doesn't change anything. . . . Let's go up on the bridge.'

'I'd like to be alone for a while.'

'This is business, Lili.'

'At your service, Colonel.'

Malinowski welcomed us with a blue-eyed smile, all health and innocence, and spread on the chart-table a small-scale map of Ponza. On this, Lili identified the site of the villa, a small promontory on the eastern shore of the island. The villa was noted in the Pilot as a landmark for mariners: '. . . a large square building of grey stone, due east of which the pillars and arches of a Roman ruin are clearly visible. In winds W to NW the southern inlet offers fair shelter to small vessels. The bottom is sand and rock with some weed.' I asked Lili:

'If we put in there, can we get to the villa from the beach?'

'Yes. There's a rough cart track that goes up to the ruins.'

Malinowski cut in with a sailor's question.

'If we anchor, we'll have to put down the dinghy and winch it up again. You'll have a wet and uncomfortable ride to the beach. Why don't we moor in the harbour itself and you take a taxi to the villa?'

'Strategy, Carl. In the port we'd be conspicuous. It's out of season. The locals would talk. I'd rather not have that.'

'Clear, Colonel, sir. We anchor.'

'The villa itself, Lili. Any servants?'

'No. Out of season it's closed up. A village family comes in once a week to clean it and turn on the heating for a few hours. But we don't have to go near the villa. What we want is there, in the ruins.'

'Why the ruins?'

'You will see when you get there.'

'Can you overlook the ruins from the house?'

'Only the top of them. Our domain is walled all the way round. The ruins are on Government land, part of the shoreline. The *demanio* line runs here.'

'Better still. Take a look at the chart, Carl. How close in can you anchor?'

'Let's see. . . . For safety, a cable's length.'

'Visible from the house?'

'On the approach, yes. When we're anchored, probably not. I don't understand your problem though. That's public terrain. Anyone can land from the sea. That's one piece of Italian law I do know.'

'I'm not worried about trespass, Carl. Lili owns the villa anyway. Let's say I'm concerned with hostile intruders.'

'Those, Colonel sir, we can take care of very nicely.' He opened the cupboard under the chart-table and brought out an automatic rifle. 'I carry this little baby in case the sharks chase one of my girls while she's swimming bare-ass. So, while you and Lili-belle go ashore, I stand deck watch for hostile intruders. . . . Satisfied?'

'No. I can't have an American officer involved in an Italian domestic drama. So, if you don't mind, I'll take the gun ashore with me.'

'Just as you like. Switch on the radio, will you? We should get the news in a minute and I'd like to catch the weather report afterwards.'

'If you don't want me any more,' said Lili, 'I think I'll lie down in the saloon. I'm feeling a little seasick.'

'You should have told me, Lili-belle. I've got just the thing to . . .'

'No, thank you, Carl. I'll be all right. Excuse me!'

When she left us, Carl grinned and fixed me with a knowing eye.

'Problems, brother? Need a little post-nuptial counselling?'

'As a matter of fact, I do.'

'Okay, tell Uncle Carl.'

'What would you say if I told you Lili was a double-agent working for me and for the Marxists?'

'I'd say half your luck–and forget you told me.'

'And if I told you I might have to toss her in gaol to satisfy my people?'

'I'd say you were in a nasty jam.'

'And if I then asked you to keep her on board and run her up to Corsica out of Italian jurisdiction, what would you say?'

'I would tell you, Colonel sir, that you are my very good friend, and I owe you a big favour which I am now repaying. But I would tell you also that I am a natural-born, dyed-in-the-wool Republican, that I have seen my buddies die in Korea and in Vietnam and I don't much like niggers, though I've learnt to live with 'em, but Commies of any sex or breed I can't abide. And so, if you asked me–and I'm sure you wouldn't–I would have to say no sir, no thanks, no way at all. You do read me, Colonel?'

I read him so clearly I couldn't believe it. For a moment I thought he was joking. He joked about most things. The shock was that he was in deadly earnest. I suppose I had never really believed that a great and vigorous people could survive on such simplistic formulas of faith. But then we Europeans had a much longer and bloodier experience and we were still not half as sceptical as we needed to be. . . . Carl Malinowski held out his hand.

'No hard feelings, eh, Dante?'

'No, Carl.'

'And I'm not saying you're a Red. You know that.'

'Of course.'

'And I'm not judging Lili-belle either. Just ducking the issue you might say.'

'I understand.'

'And I'm still with you against the hostile intruders.'

'Thanks.'

'Now, let's listen to the news, eh?'

The news, read in the bland, euphoric style of R.A.I., was the usual mixture: the tribal feuds of Africa, strikes in England, strikes in Italy, another piece from the Pope on the Italian divorce law, another Italian parliamentary squabble, this time over the allocation of provincial subsidies, and finally, a terse postscript: an Arab employee of the Libyan Embassy in Rome had been shot dead outside his house on the Aventine Hill. The victim was the Roman representative of the Palestine guerrilla organization, Al Fatah. The police were treating the murder as a political crime, probably organized by Israeli agents.

The item made the hair stand up on the nape of my neck. In the SID I was regarded as an expert on Arab-Israel terrorist activities. I had built up our first files on Palestinian guerrillas, resident or active in the Republic. I had good informants among the Jordanians and the Egyptians. I knew the director of the Jewish counter-terrorist organization, a cool-eyed Lett, who, in my view was one of the best intelligence men in the world. Once, in a very private gathering of experts, I had heard him discourse on the true nature of terror, both as a political weapon and a social infection.

'As a weapon, it is almost irresistible. In infuses fear and doubt. It destroys confidence in democratic procedures. It immobilizes police agencies. It polarizes factions: the young against the old; the have-nots against the haves; the ignorant against the knowing; the idealists against the pragmatists. As a social infection it is more deadly than the plague: it justifies the vilest of remedies, the suspension of human rights, preventive arrest, cruel and unusual punishment, subornation, torture and legal murder. The most moral of men, the sanest of governments, is not immune from the infection. Violence begets violence; blackmailers are paid from the public treasury; reprisals fall as heavily on the innocent as on the guilty. . . . You Italians made a hero of a man who hijacked an airliner. When we strike at an Arab who plants a bomb in Rome, we have to accept that we will waken all the latent anti-semites in Italy and give a scape-goat to the new Fascists. Every Marxist beaten in a police cell raises twenty recruits for the revolution. Every bomb thrown in the streets brings out a new brigade of riot-police with gas-guns and water-cannon. Every big city has its own university of terror. And the lessons are circulated from Ulster to the Udine, from Vietnam to Venezuela, from Rio to Athens to Rome. . . .'

For me, therefore, the murder on the Aventine was more than bad news, it was a personal disaster. Here I was cruising like a tourist between Naples and Ponza, in very mixed company, while the Director would be pressing panic buttons and combing the country for one delinquent expert on Semitic affairs. If I brought back the Pantaleone papers and Lili Anders, I might just escape the rack and thumb-screw. If I came back empty-handed, he would rend me limb from limb and feed me to the lions in the zoo.

For one panic moment I thought of trying to contact him by ship's radio, at least to report myself on duty. Then I realized that this would only compound the mistakes of the last two days and broadcast my business to the whole of the Western Mediterranean. To the devil with it then. He had given me a free hand. I would nail the brief to his door like Luther's articles; if he didn't like what he read he could eat it for supper. I rather hoped it might choke him.

We raised Ponza in a squall of wind and driving rain, and we had to coast slowly right under the lee of the island before we could make any positive identification of the promontory and Lili's villa. Even the Pilot book fell short of its promise. The shelter offered by the inlet was less than fair and the anchor-hold was dubious at best. There was one small profit. If there were any watchers in the villa, they would have no better visibility than we had. Lili and I draped ourselves in oilskins and scrambled into the bobbing dinghy. Carl handed me the rifle and after the customary struggle to start the outboard, we motored through a choppy surf to the beach.

The beach was deserted. On the promontory itself there was no sign of life. The track which led to the ruins was steep and greasy, and at one point we were scrambling on hands and knees, hauling ourselves upward by tussocks and the stalks of wild rosemary. By the time we reached the top, I was breathless and irritable. I was convinced that either Pantaleone was mad, or Lili had deliberately led me on a fool's errand. I could not, for the life of me, understand why, with a great fortress of a villa at his disposal, any man would hide valuable documents in a mouldering ruin, on land that didn't even belong to him. I said as much–and heatedly–to Lili, who burst out laughing.

'You look so silly–like a clown in a circus! And that little popgun. What are you going to shoot with it–seagulls?'

She took me by the hand and led me through an archway into the shelter of a vault which had, somehow, withstood the ravages of the centuries. The outer walls were of hewn stone, but the inner ones were of reticulated brickwork thrust upwards and inwards into a shallow dome. The floor was paved with slabs of marble, cracked, discoloured and sagging in places, but still mostly intact. The place smelt of stale droppings and seaspray. Lili threw back the hood of her oilskins and stood, hands on hips, surveying the shadowy interior.

'You think Massimo was crazy? So did I when he brought me here. But think again. The villa is left all winter. Servants poke into everything when the *padrone* is away. Look around. Go on, examine! What do you see?'

The brickwork of the walls revealed nothing. I walked the floor testing for hollow spaces beneath it. Again nothing. Lili stood there grinning at me in triumph.

'See, Dante Alighieri, you are not half so clever as you think you are. And Massimo was not always so stupid as he looked. Watch!'

She moved to a small sunken patch of floor, where the rain, driving in through the archway, had created a puddle, perhaps three or four centimetres deep. She knelt down and with her bare hands prised up a small triangular piece of marble. She held it up for my inspection. It was the size of my palm, coated on the underside with a thick wad of cement.

'Like a bath-plug, eh, Dante? You didn't walk in the puddle, but even if you had, the floor would have sounded solid.'

She plunged her fingers into the aperture and drew out a long aluminium tube such as architects use for plans and specifications. It was sealed at both ends with black adhesive tape. Immediately she removed the tube, the puddle emptied itself into the hole. Lili replaced the marble plug and handed the tube to me.

'It is exactly as we left it. The maps are rolled inside. The microfilms are in small capsules.'

'There's nothing else?'

'Nothing.'

'Let's go. You carry this.'

'Not even a thank you for puppet Lili?'

'Thank you, puppet Lili. Now you follow me until we come to the beach track. Then you go first.'

I released the safety catch on the rifle and made for the entrance to the vault. Half-way to the entrance I stopped to scan the narrow vista framed by the archway. All I could see was the rise of the land, covered with tussocks and boulders and stunted bushes and the lower courses of the wall surrounding the villa domain. So far, so good. I moved closer so that the vista widened and the upper courses of the wall became visible and then the top of it, a layer of cement stuck with fragments of broken glass. Then I heard a shout, amplified and distorted by a loud-hailer.

'You, in there! Come out with your hands up. This is the Carabinieri. I repeat–this is the Carabinieri.'

I turned back to Lili and snatched the tube from her.

'Now listen and understand. Stay close to me. Do nothing, say nothing, unless I tell you. Clear?'

'Clear.'

'We're going out now.'

I threw back the hood of my oilskins and then, holding the rifle and the tube high above my head, I walked through the archway with Lili at my heels. Twenty yards from the entrance, just outside my last field of vision, there were five men, two on one side, three on the other. Four were in uniform and armed with sub-machine guns. The fifth was in civilian clothes and carried the loud-hailer. I recognized him immediately: the freckle-faced red-head, aide to General Leporello. He recognized me, too, and the expression on his face gave me a singular pleasure.

The troops began to close in, guns cocked and ready. The young man followed, a little less confidently. I let them come to within five metres before I halted them in my best parade-ground style. They stopped, looking uncertainly from me to the red-head. Then I told them:

'I will identify myself in proper form. Whoever is in command will check my documents. I am Matucci, Dante Alighieri, Colonel in the Service of Defence Information. The person accompanying me is Anders, Lili, in my custody and assisting me in my investigations. Now, we shall lower our hands, and the officer in command will approach to complete the identification and explain this situation to me.'

The red-head found voice and courage at last. He approached, gave me a tentative salute and presented himself.

'Roditi, Matteo, Captain, aide to Major-General Leporello. May I see your papers please, sir?'

I fished them out from under the oilskins and handed them to him. He made a great play of reading them then handed them back.

'Thank you, sir. The situation, sir, is as follows. I am under orders from General Leporello to maintain surveillance of the Villa Pantaleone and its environs and to inhibit any attempt to remove papers or property of whatsoever kind from the premises. In pursuance of these orders I am empowered to call upon the assistance of local units. That explains the presence of this detachment.'

'May I see those orders please, Captain?'

'Certainly, sir.'

He handed them to me and I took a little longer than I needed to study them. Then I quizzed him, loud enough for the local boys to hear and take note.

'It would appear, Captain, that you have misread these orders.'

'Sir?'

'The orders refer specifically and exclusively to, and I quote, "the villa and the domain dependent thereon which is called the Villa Pantaleone". That's right, isn't it?'

'Yes, sir.'

'You will note that the land on which we are now standing, and the ruins at my back, are outside the domain of the Villa Pantaleone and are, in fact, public property delimited by the *demanio* markers on the land and the low water-mark on the shore. Correct?'

'Correct, sir.'

'Therefore you have exceeded your orders. You have impeded a senior officer of the Service of Defence Information in the discharge of highly secret duties. You have placed him and the person in his custody at considerable risk. One incautious move by any of your troops might have caused a fatal accident. You do see that?'

'Respectfully, I submit the danger was minimal.'

'No doubt that submission will be considered at the proper time and place. Anything else, Captain?'

'I should like a private word with you, sir.'

'Not possible at this moment, Captain. I suggest you return to your duties and leave me to carry out mine.'

'That vessel, sir, in the bay. . . .'

'Has been made available to me by courtesy of our friends and allies in NATO. Further questions?'

'No, sir.'

'My compliments to General Leporello. I shall telephone him on my return to Rome. Dismiss! Come, Miss Anders. Walk in front of me, please.'

It is hard to make a dignified exit with four guns at your back. It is harder still to make it down a slippery goat track in driving rain, carrying a rifle and a long tube of explosive documents. In point of fact, we slid the last thirty feet on our backsides and floundered into the dinghy like seals.

By the time we reached the Baglietto, we were both in shock. I was sweating from every pore and Lili was retching over the side of the dinghy. Helga hauled us inboard and made the dinghy fast. Carl–God bless the Marines!–had the anchor up and was charing seaward at twenty-five knots before I had poured our first brandy. Lili, grey and trembling, lay on the settee while I forced the liquor between her chattering teeth. She stared at me as if I were a stranger.

'Back there . . . they were going to kill us!'

'They didn't, Lili. And they can't touch us now.'

'Not now. But tomorrow, the day after. . . .'

'Finish your drink. Close your eyes. Try to sleep. . . .'

'Who was that man, Roditi . . . ?'

'You heard.'

'I heard. I didn't understand.'

'I'll explain later. Relax now. . . . Relax. . . .'

'I don't know you at all, Dante Alighieri. Your face changes all the time. I can't tell which one is yours.'

'I'm a bad actor. That's all. Trust me, *bambina*.'

'I have to . . . there's no one else.'

'Another drink?'

'I couldn't.'

'Close your eyes. . . . That's better. . . . *Lasci'andare, bambina* . . . let go. Let everything go.'

After a while, she lay quiet and the surge of the sea made her dozy. I poured myself another brandy, stripped the seals from the metal tube and examined the contents: a set of overlay maps on transparent paper, each labelled with the name of a city and references to standard ordnance maps, and half a dozen metal capsules, each containing a spool of microfilm. The maps were easy to interpret. They showed the positions of police posts, military installations, communication centres, traffic control points, military and civilian airfields. The microfilms were impossible to decipher without projection equipment. However, I borrowed the chart enlarger

from the bridge and was able to establish that they consisted of documents
and letters and nominal rolls, and lists of figures. I had no doubt at all that
they supplied the best possible motive for the murders in the Via Sicilia,
and were, in fact, the blue-prints of a *colpo di stato*. It would need a team of
experts to interpret them accurately, and a very wise statesman to decide
how to use them. I sealed them back in their container and went up on the
bridge to talk to Carl. I found him poring over his charts while Helga stood
wheel-watch. I asked him.

'How much fuel have you got, Carl?'

'Plenty. Why?'

'Enough to get us into Ostia?'

'Ostia! For Chrissake, that wasn't in the schedule at all!'

'I know, Carl. But could you get us there?'

'I could. Would you like to tell me why?'

'Because I've just identified a murderer and we could have been
murdered ourselves.'

'The Commies?'

'No, Carl. The other ones.'

'So, we go to Ostia. Take five while I lay me a course.'

'Can you give me an estimated time of arrival?'

'I'll give it to you firm, little brother.'

'Then I'd like to make a ship-to-shore radio call.'

'Can do. Sit tight now, while I play with my slide rule.'

While Carl was doing his arithmetic, I jotted down the coded message
which would convey to the Director my immediate needs: a car and an
armed escort to meet us at Ostia, an emergency conference immediately on
our arrival in Rome, safe lodgings and an agent to guard Lili Anders, until
her future was decided. Forty minutes later I had the Director's answer.

'Communication acknowledged. Arrangements agreed.'

We do have code-words for thanks and commendations. He didn't use
them. Under the circumstances I could hardly blame him.

In the event, the Director was extremely civil. He was a little frosty at first;
but he thawed like an ice-cube in whisky when I handed over the maps and
the microfilms and made my first verbal report. He approved, without
reserve, my concern for Lili Anders; in proof whereof he countermanded a
previous order and lodged her, in state, under a fictional name, at the Grand
Hotel. He even changed the guard for a more presentable type who would
not detract from the ambience.

He invited me to dinner at his apartment. He commended me for my
imagination, my finesse, my courage in risking my career and perhaps my
life to conclude an important investigation. He saw good sense in my
suspicions of Leporello, although he was not yet ready to pass judgment. He
sat with me through a private screening of the microfilms and was sedulous
to weigh my opinions of the documents and the personages named therein.
He read the maps with me and agreed the major points of my interpretation.
At the end of the session, which lasted until after midnight, he ordered fresh
coffee, brought out his best brandy and offered me the rewards of virtue.

'This Lili Anders ... I agree with your submission. She had done us a
service. She is no longer a security risk. She could be an embarrassment.
Let's get her out of the country—tomorrow.'

'Thank you, sir.'

'Now, let's talk about your own future. How much leave have you accumulated?'

'About four months.'

'I'd like you to take it, now. After you return from leave, I propose to detach you for extended studies with friendly agencies abroad. You will have the best possible introductions, a very flexible brief, and your pay and allowances will be supplemented by a generous grant from the funds of this Service. How does that sound?'

'Like an obituary notice.'

The Director smiled and spread his elegant hands in a gesture of depreciation.

'My dear Matucci! You and I live in an upside-down world. You will be buried for a while but you will not be dead, just enjoying yourself while you wait for resurrection day.'

'No alternatives?'

'There are always alternatives, my friend, but I do not think they would recommend themselves to an intelligent man. I could, for example, retain you on the Leporello investigation; in which case you would be at constant risk, an abrasive element, a prime target for assassination. I could, on the other hand, bow to the pressure which inevitably will be applied, to remove you from the Service altogether and return you to your own Corps of Carabinieri, where you would fall under the direct authority of Major-General Leporello. He knows you for a nuisance. He may consider you a threat.'

'I see what you mean.'

'You see everything except the core of the apple.'

'Which is?'

'You know too much. You lack the authority and—forgive me—the experience to make use of the knowledge.'

'And . . . ?'

'You would not be content as a passive instrument of a complicated and highly variable policy.'

'Also I would not submit to pressure by a murder suspect, however high he stood.'

'And you would be very unwilling to treat with political conspirators, however high they stood.'

'Exactly.'

'So, because I respect you and because I should like to be in a position to recall you at an appropriate moment, I immobilize you. I offer you as a propitiatory victim to the powerful people whose names we know. I buy myself time to deal with them by the classic formula: divide and rule. I told you once before, this is the only course I see as possible for Italy at this moment in history. You would polarize the factions, Matucci. You have already done it.'

'That, too, is a classic formula.'

'And like every formula it has limited application. I am not blaming you, Matucci. On the contrary, since I do not often choose to explain myself, I am paying you a compliment with I believe you merit. . . . Well?'

'I'd like to pay you a compliment, too, sir. I think you're a very civilized man. I couldn't ask for a more stylish funeral.'

'Excellent! More brandy?'

'Thank you.'

'Now, as to details. As from this moment you are officially on vacation for four months, and relieved of all duties and responsibilities in the Service–except one. You will escort Lili Anders to Zurich tomorrow morning. Your flight has been booked. A hotel reservation has been made for you at the Baur au Lac. I shall hand you the tickets and the necessary currency before you leave tonight. You will remain outside Italy for at least a month. After that, you may make whatever arrangements you choose for the rest of your vacation. If you choose to divert yourself with the lady–to whom obviously you have some attachment–that is your business. The Service has no further interest in her, provided she does not attempt to re-enter the Republic. It's all a little rushed I'm afraid, but I am sure you will find the financial arrangements more than generous. . . . Questions?'

'No. A minor worry. I'd hate to spend a long vacation waiting for a bullet in the back. I'd much rather stay on duty where there's a certain amount of protection.'

'I thought we had covered that. The whole purpose of the tactic is to demonstrate that you are no longer a threat to Leporello or anyone else and that action against you would violate what I might call your very useful neutrality. . . . There is a danger period, however: from the moment you leave this house until you take off for Zurich tomorrow.'

'I was wondering about that, too.'

'So I've assigned a two-man team to cover for all your movements. They've already packed your clothes and delivered the suitcases to the Grand Hotel. Your room adjoins that of Miss Lili Anders. You will leave the hotel together at eight-thirty. Much simpler from a security point of view.'

'Of course.'

'Now, . . . two air tickets, ten thousand Swiss francs in varying denominations and an order of the Union Bank in Zurich for another twenty thousand. That's a bonus with my personal thanks. Your salary will be credited in the normal way to your bank account in Rome. . . . That's all, I think. The car is waiting to take you to your hotel. I wish you a pleasant trip and a very restful vacation. *Sogni d'oro,* Matucci–golden dreams.'

We parted with a handshake, firm and fraternal. The Sicilian bodyguard escorted me to the ground floor and handed me into the care of two junior colleagues, who drove me like a visiting potentate to the Grand Hotel.

It was one-thirty in the morning. The foyer was deserted. They steered me past the reception desk and the concierge, rode up with me in the elevator and installed me in my bedroom. One of them checked cupboards and bathroom and even under the beds, while the other pointed out the beautiful job of packing, and how my suits had been pressed, and that if I wished to speak with the Signorina Anders the key was on my side of the communicating door. . . . As the Director had prescribed maximum precautions, I could sleep soundly. They bade me goodnight and retired like lackeys from the presence of a prince.

Perhaps they were right. I was the Prince's man, bought and endowed. His money was in my pocket. His gift was sleeping next door. His brand was on my forehead like slave-mark. Still, give the devil his due, he was a very rare specimen. He recognized merit. He enjoyed malice but never practised it wastefully. He had been scrupulously polite. He had exacted my consent with just the right amount of pressure and finesse. He was the king. I was the pawn. He had swept me off the board to wait for another game. Never once had he suggested that I was making a slave's bargain. He knew it, of course. So did I. Which is why, much as I wanted her, I could not turn the key and go to Lili, but, instead, lay dressed and wakeful until dawn, scheming revolt like Spartacus in Capua.

At dawn I abandoned the futile exercise and went to Lili Anders. With a very refined irony, the Director had kept her in ignorance of the arrangements, so that at six in the morning, sleepless and in need of loving, I was forced to explain the whole complicated play, step by step. When I explained that she was to be set at liberty in Switzerland, she was hysterically delighted. When I told her I would go with her, it was Christmas, Epiphany and all her birthdays rolled into one. After that I had no wish or heart to tell her the price. From the moment I left Italy I would be, in effect, an exile. From the moment I became an exile I would be subject to a clinical change which the Director had calculated to a nicety. For most Europeans, for all Anglo-Saxons and Americans, the word exile has an old-fashioned ring. Whatever crimes a man may commit he is never deprived of his citizenship or his primal relationship with his homeland. He may be imprisoned, he may be brutalized, but he is never robbed of that essential element of his identity, his contact with the mother earth.

For us Italians, however, for us whose identity depends upon a small terrain, a tribal group, a dialectal area, exile is a constant and sinister reality. We can still be legally transported and confined to a distant province, a depressed island, to a community whose tongue and customs and history are totally foreign to us, where we will be strangers until the day we die. We cannot move from it without permission from the police. We cannot flourish in it because we are an alien corn. We exist only by sufferance and under surveillance.

The personal consequences are as deep and as demoralizing as if we had been transported to Siberia or dumped like castaways in the dry Tortugas.

The terror begins subtly with a sense of disorientation and discontinuity. It can end with a trauma of impotence, when every act seems pointless, every step ends at a barred gate, every hope is proved an illusion.

The Director knew this because he had used it many times as a means of immobilizing men who were hostile to him. I knew it because my father had been in exile under the Fascists and I had seen him come home a broken man. But how could I explain it to Lili who had survived her own exile and was now breaking out into freedom. . . . Perhaps it was just as well, the loving would not have been half as sweet nor our exit from Italy half as impressive.

At eight twenty-five, our baggage was removed under the supervision of an agent. At eight-thirty, with no bills to pay, and as many bows as if we had paid them twice over, we were led from the foyer into an official limousine. At nine-fifteen, we were conducted into the V.I.P. lounge at Fiumicino and held in comfort and respect until fifteen minutes before take-off. Then, spurning the crush of common travellers, we were escorted to the aircraft and deposited in a pair of first-class seats. Our agent hovered over us until the moment before the doors were closed. Then, with a final salute on behalf of a grateful Republic, he left us. Five minutes later—this being a fair and strike-free day at Fiumicino—we were airborne in the care of the Swiss. We held hands. We made foolish jokes. We toasted each other in champagne. Then I fell asleep and did not wake until we were in the final approach to Kloten Airport in Zurich.

When we arrived at the Baur au Lac, we found that the Director had provided against all contingencies. We were accommodated in separate rooms, each communicating with a large salon, furnished already with flowers, fruit, liquor and a welcome note from the management. There was also a telegram from the Director: 'Second Samuel Seven One.' Zurich is a sound Calvinist town so I deciphered the joke from the Bible on my bedside table: 'The Lord gave him rest from all his enemies.'

Later in the day, a second telegram arrived, two words only: 'Tekel Stefanelli.' I didn't need a Bible for that one. I remembered the riddle from my religious youth: 'Tekel: Thou art weighed in the balance and found wanting!' I had to answer him and I did it with Deuteronomy one sixteen; 'Judge righteously between every man and his brother and the stranger that is with him.' By then the joke was stale and bitter. I had to make an end of it. I told Lili the truth.

The moment of telling had a curious quality about it. It was seven in the evening. We had decided to dine early in the suite, to relax after the alarms and excitements of the last few days. Lili, glowing from a visit to the hairdresser, the masseuse and the manicurist, was dressed in a house-coat she had bought to celebrate her new liberty. She had presented me with a silk shirt and a rather exotic cravat. I was mixing drinks like an amateur barman, feeling very domestic, very comfortable and yet somehow remote and passionless, as if I were recovering from a long illness. The story told itself in the same remote fashion and I heard myself speak it as if I were listening to a report from another man:

'. . . Everything the Director says is true and yet it all adds up to a lie, which you still cannot disprove. He is a very great actor. He conjures you into a world that doesn't exist and yet makes you believe that every leaf on every tree is real. He shows you another self—and makes you believe it is you. . . . "You lack authority, Matucci. You lack experience. You are an abrasive element. You polarize the fractions." All true, but true in an opposite way. . . . "You are not dead, just buried for a while." . . . But I knew, the moment I stepped on that plane, I was dead; because he has all my files and records now and he can reprocess history in any way he choose. He says he wants to divide and rule. But suppose he doesn't? Suppose he wants to unite and conquer, and then play Fouché to Leporello's Napoleon? I've given him the means to do it. . . . And he paid me for them: with you, with a long holiday, with a sinecure that half the men in the Service would give their eyes for. And he'll honour the payment, have no doubt of it, so long as I play the game according to his rules and wait on the word of the Lord. . . .'

'Why did you accept the payment, Dante Alighieri?' There was no reproach in the question. There was no compassion, either. She was calm and composed as an examining magistrate. 'Because I was part if it?'

'No. I believe that, even if I had fought him, he would still have let you go, if only to demonstrate that I was obstinate and unreasonable. He might even have worked to set you against me. . . . He spins webs so fine you cannot see the threads.'

'So, why did you consent? For me, this is freedom; for you, exile.'

'Strange, but at this moment I'm enjoying it.'

'If you could go on enjoying it, with me or without me, then it would be another story. Could you?'

'I don't know. . . . Yes, by God, I do know! Last night I dined with him and enjoyed him. After dinner we worked together on the documents and I

respected him—because he respected me. So, when he asked me to step out
of the picture, and gave me his reasons, I had to respect those, too. Then,
after I had agreed, he had to show me how clever he was, how he knew in
advance that I must consent. He was so certain that he had arranged
everything in advance—even to this liquor and the roses in your bedroom.
Suddenly, I was not a man any more, I was. . . .'

'A puppet, my love! A marionette, life-size and helpless, with no
manhood left at all. It's a bitter experience, isn't it?'

'I think it's funny, very funny!'

'Is it?'

'The joke of the century! Dante Alighieri Matucci, tenor castrato in the
puppet choir!'

'Why don't you laugh then?'

'I'm a clown puppet, Lili. I make other people laugh. That is his final
triumph, don't you see? He's spread the news all round the Service. How
else would Steffi know? Why else would he send me that telegram: 'weighed
in the balance and found wanting'. Mother of God! What a beautiful,
beautiful comedy!'

'I'd like to see the end of it.'

'This is the end, Lili. Don't you understand that?'

'It's the end he wrote. I think there's a better one.'

'I'd love to hear it.'

'The puppet becomes a man, scrapes off the clown's paint, and rides out
to confront his enemy.'

'It's a fairy-tale, Lili.'

'No! It's a truth—my truth. And now that we're quits, I can tell it. I know
you for a man, much more—and not just in bed, Dante Alighieri.'

'Thanks. That helps a little.'

'But not enough. Where's your wallet?'

'In the bedroom, why?'

'There's a card in it, remember? A salamander and an inscription: "One
fine tomorrow, brother!" A good motto, don't you think? And a very
appropriate device: the lizard that lives in the fire. Get the card, my love.
And find the telephone number of the Cavaliere Bruno Manzini. I think you
should call him in Bologna.'

The idea was seductive. But I was still gun-shy and suspicious of any new
entanglement. Bruno Manzini belonged to another world, with another set
of rules: the world of the *condottieri*, the free-booters, who had taken over
the ruins of a cardboard empire and built a new one of steel and concrete
and international gold. They dispensed enormous power; but the
dispensation was in another currency than that to which I was accustomed.
True, Bruno Manzini had invited me to trust him. Through Raquela
Rabin, he had offered me proof of good faith. But, if he betrayed me, then I
was lost beyond redemption; since the jurisdiction of money is universal
and its minions are devoid of pity.

I argued this with Lili—the new Lili who had flowered overnight into
another woman, serene, mature and wholly confident in herself. She
abolished my doubts with a simple challenge:

'What have you to lose? Nothing. What have you to gain? At best a
powerful friend. At least an alliance of interest that you can dissolve at will.
Most important of all, you will have begun to fight. Please! Telephone him
now!'

To make the call was easy. To speak to the Cavaliere was only less difficult than having a Sunday chat with the Pope. I was passed from a telephonist to a woman secretary, from the secretary to a male assistant, very efficient, very *alt'Italia*, who informed me that the Cavaliere was conducting an important conference and could in no wise be interrupted. I took a risk then and used the magical name of the Service, threatening all sorts of vague crises if the Cavaliere were not called immediately to the telephone. I waited another three minutes before he came on the line. I told him:

'Cavaliere, yesterday I recovered certain records from Ponza. I delivered them to my superior, our mutual friend. I am now on four months' leave and will later be transferred to other activities in the Service. I am under orders not to return to Italy for a month and I am lodged at the Baur au Lac in Zurich.'

There was a moment's silence, then a series of brusque questions:

'Have you yourself examined the records?'

'Yes.'

'Important?'

'As you suggested in Rome.'

'Do you know what will happen to them now?'

'Only what may happen. There are several possibilities.'

'Which you can no longer control.'

'Precisely.'

'Do you need assistance, financial or otherwise?'

'I need the man whom Raquela Rabin recommended to me, provided, of course, he is still available.'

'He is. He will be with you tomorrow evening. . . . By the way, how is our mutual friend?'

'Very pleased with himself.'

'No doubt. And you?'

'Happier. Now that I have spoken with you.'

'Are you in good health?'

'Our mutual friend assures me I have nothing to fear.'

'He would know, of course.'

'Yes. But he never tells all he knows.'

'Remember it, my friend. Walk close to the wall.'

'Thank you, Cavaliere. . . . Goodnight.'

When I put down the phone, I was trembling and the palms of my hands were wet. I was truly afraid, now. The old man's parting words had demolished the last frail illusion of security and revealed the full, refined malice of the Director's design. I was a stranger in a land stuffed with money and indifferent to the point of callousness. I was a member of a legal underworld, suspect everywhere and nowhere loved. I could be shot down on any street corner and the Swiss would have the blood hosed off and the traffic flowing before you could say John Calvin. I told you I am a Tuscan born. In that moment I tasted the full, Florentine flavour of the Director's revenge. Then, Lili came and put her arms around me and we held each other close while she whispered the words over and over like an incantation:

'One fine tomorrow, brother . . . one fine tomorrow. . . .'

Tomorrow was a gift of God: no wind, no cloud, the lake a-dazzle under the spring sun, snow on the uplands, the lower meadows ankle-deep in spring grass, the herdsmen moving the cattle up the slopes to a music of bells. I hired a car and we drove eastwards along the lake into the Grisons, aimless and happy as a honeymoon pair. Lili was in a rapture of contentment. She sang, she clowned, she played word-games and love-games and built dream-houses, furnished and demolished them, plucked children out of nowhere and blew them away like thistledown.

Me? I was happy, too. I had been a stranger too long to this kind of simplicity. My relationships with women had been too haunted by time, too frail and feverish to issue in any kind of peace. I hunted; they challenged; we joined, we parted, tomorrow was another day and another hunt, with a tip of the hat and *ciao, ciao bambina* at the end of it. I knew nothing of home-comings and kisses at the door and the daily loving absolution from all the sins of my trade. I was the *bufalo solitario*, always on the fringe of the herd, cutting out the errant females, leaving them for other males to breed and cherish. I used to boast of it, because this is our national pastime to prove that we are infinite in potency. But, today, humbled by fear, diminished with self-respect, I was, perhaps for the first time, truly grateful to a woman.

For the first time, too—and this may sound strange from a man who is trained to observe and fit every human being on to an anthropometric chart—I saw her to remember: the honey-colour of her hair, escaping from under the scarf, the high Slavic cheekbones flushed with the wind and the excitement, the little flecks of gold in her eyes, the half-smile that haunted the corners of her mouth, the lift of chin and shoulder and breast and the way she fluttered her hands when she spoke, even the first faint touch of time in the texture of her skin. She was no girl this Lili. She had lived too strangely for too long. But I was no boy either; and I was tired of baby-talk and lovers' lies and all the gossip of the model circuit.

We lunched in a mountain inn, perched high over the valley. We ate cheese soufflé and beef fondue and drank a thin petillant wine, much different from the rich vintage of my Tuscan hills. The girl who served was blonde and pink and white and dressed like a doll in dirndl and embroidered blouse. We sat in front of a big log fire and drank coffee and pear brandy; and we loved the solid, smug Swiss comfort of it all. We talked of the future and Lili assessed her own without resentment.

'. . . I am on file now. Any policeman who knows my record can harass me like a street-walker. So, I have to be careful. If I live modestly and soberly, the Swiss will give me a temporary sojourn. They will extend it grudgingly; but with a good lawyer in a small canton, I may be able to live in peace for a long while. If I married, it would be different. I would have a new civil status and a new life. So I have to think of that . . . but not yet. I have money here, enough for two years of simple living. I have the villa on Ponza which can be sold and will bring a good price. Massimo told me he had provided for me in his will; but that is stolen now. And, in any case, there is bound to be litigation and I base nothing on it . . . especially as I cannot return to Italy ever again. . . . Still, I am very lucky. Lucky in you, too, my love. . . . I did not believe you would have so much concern for me.'

'Boh! I didn't believe I would ever need a woman in this way. To be calm, to prove nothing, just to be glad that she is in the room. What would you say if I asked you to spend this month with me?'

'I would say yes. But I would also say, please leave me before you get bored; please let us have no quarrels and no bad words. Let it be as it is now, simple and easy, one hour, one day at a time.'

'One day at a time. Good. . . .'

'And when you go away–you must, I know that–and you find yourself lonely, come back again. We do not have to spell the words, you and I. We do not even have to say them. You must be very free now, free to risk or enjoy, as you choose. You have to begin to know the man who lives in your skin.'

'I'm afraid of him, Lili.'

'So, one day you must confront him in the mirror. After that, please God, you will be able to be happy.'

'I hope so. But there is something that must be said, Lili.'

'What?'

'If a day should come when you have to choose between me and yourself, consider your own interest first. I would want that.'

'I don't understand.'

'Listen, *bambina*! We are not here by accident. We are not lodged side by side in a beautiful hotel because people want us to be happy. This was arranged by the Director so that we would become tied to each other, the more closely the better. Then, a threat to one would be a pressure on the other. He has thought to buy me. Perhaps he is convinced he has bought me. But he is also buying insurance against a day when I may cheat on the contract. You see . . .?'

'I do. And I want you to cheat him. Tell me something.'

'What?'

'I have never heard you name this man. You speak of him only as the Director. Why?'

'A rule of the game that has become second nature. But, now that you ask, there is another reason. This is a very attractive man. He can seduce you, as he has seduced me, many times, with a smile, a handshake, a show of confidence and infinite good sense. He was born with that talent. It was bred into him through twenty generations. I envy it–God, how much! I am awed by it. I have grown more and more afraid of it. So, I force myself to think of him not as man, but as a function, like the Pope or the President. That way I can cope with him. I can obstruct, inhibit, redirect, as I have often done in the past. Strange! I've never admitted that to another living soul.'

'Perhaps one day will come when you will be able to name the two in one breath–the man who lives in your skin, and the other of whom you are still afraid.'

'Am I so great a coward, Lili?'

'There is one fear that makes each of us a coward!'

'And what is yours?'

'The little room, the light shining in my eyes, the faces I cannot see, the questions and the blows that come from nowhere. You saved me from that, and there is nothing I would not do to repay you.

'We're both rewarded, *cara* . . . the good day is enough.'

'And tonight your Cavaliere Manzini arrives. . . . Are you going to tell him about me?'

'I can hardly avoid it. Does it worry you?'

'No. But it's an odd situation. I was his brother's mistress. Now he finds me with you. I wonder what he will think or say.'

'Do you care?'

'Yes. I want him to be a friend to you.'

'He calls himself the Salamander. He must have paid his own price for survival. We start with the hope that he will understand ours. After that . . .

who knows? There are no signs in the sky and I cannot read a crystal ball. . . . We should go back now. It's an hour and a half to Zurich.'

At eight-thirty in the evening, the Cavaliere Bruno Manzini received me in his suite at the Dolder Grand. Once again, the setting was opulent: the vast salon, the vista of dark woodland and moonlit lake and the lights of the nestling city; yet the man, himself, was aloof, austere, so that you knew, if all the rest were swept away, he would still stand there, straight as a pillar, with his proud eyes and his patrician beak, and his hair like snow on a great alp. His greeting was warm and smiling; but, from the moment I entered he was reading me by stance and attitude and intonation. His first comment was characteristic:

'You are changed, Colonel.'

'How so, Cavaliere?'

'Every way. You wear your clothes as you enjoyed them. You are more loose, more forthcoming. I would guess that you had found yourself a satisfactory woman and a little more courage than you had yesterday.'

'Both true.'

'A drink?'

'Whisky, please.'

He served me himself and I noticed that he drank very lightly. He raised his glass in a toast:

'Health, money and love . . .'

'And time to enjoy them, Cavaliere.'

'That above all, Colonel. . . . I have ordered dinner to be served here in half an hour. I thought you would trust me to choose the menu.'

'Of course.'

'Now, tell me everything that has happened since we met in Rome.'

I told him. I recited all the facts without gloss or interpretation, up to, and including, my arrival in Zurich with Lili Anders, and the relationship which had begun to mature between us. During the whole narrative he did not utter a word, but his eyes never left my face and I knew that he was weighing every phrase and inflection. When I had finished, he sat a long time in silence and then began to question me. His tone was curt and inquisitorial.

'You are convinced that Major-General Leporello has allied himself with the neo-Fascists?'

'I am convinced that he was and is a candidate for such an alliance. I cannot prove he has concluded it.'

'You infer, therefore, that he ordered, or connived at, the murders in the Via Sicilia and the theft of the Pantaleone papers.'

'I state that there is a case to be investigated.'

'And the evidence in support?'

'Leporello knew, from me, where the papers were, and the steps that had been taken to guard them. If and when the papers came into his possession he would have known instantly that they were incomplete. He would—and in fact he did—take steps to trace the remainder, to wit the microfilms and the maps on Ponza. His aide was there, armed with an authority signed by Leporello.'

'And why would he be stupid enough to sign an order that would incriminate him and his aide?'

'The order would not necessarily incriminate him. He could justify it quite simply as an investigative measure under his own counter-insurgency programme. You know how our services and agencies are organized. Sometimes they run parallel, at others, they overlap; sometimes they run contrary to each other. There are rivalries between them and the ministries that control them.'

'There are also internal conflicts, yes?'

'Of course.'

'Conflicts of policy?'

'Always.'

'What is the ground of dispute between you and your Director?'

'There are several. I asked for an investigation of Leporello. He deferred it. I disobeyed a direct order and made contact with Leporello.'

'In effect you may be responsible for two murders and the theft of vital documents.'

'I believe I am responsible.'

'So your Director was perfectly justified in taking you off the investigation.'

'If he did it on disciplinary grounds, yes.'

'You suggest he had other reasons?'

'He stated them clearly: I lacked the authority and experience to deal with a complex political situation; I would polarize existing factions who would be better kept divided; I was a convenient victim who would buy him time.'

'Good reasons or bad?'

'Eminently sound.'

'And he has treated you very generously?'

'Very.'

'So what is your quarrel with him? Why do you object to the way he has acted?'

'I have no quarrel. I have no objection that I can validly sustain. But. . . .'

'But what, Colonel?'

'I said it to his face and I say it still. I do not trust him.'

'His answer?'

'I quote it verbatim: "I don't want dictatorship. I don't want Marxism. I'm sure the kind of democracy we have is too unstable to last. But, come one or the other, I'll try to make it as tolerable as I can."'

'A laudable ambition, surely?'

'That depends on the interpretation. He, himself, put a gloss on it: "I am king on the board and you are the pawn."'

'And you don't like being a pawn, Colonel?'

'No, I don't.'

'You would prefer to be king, no doubt?'

'Cavaliere, my father was an old line socialist, who spent five years of exile on Lipari under the Fascists. They let him come home to die.'

'I'm sorry, I didn't know that.'

'No reason why you should.'

'So, what would you like to be?'

'A servant of an open society.'

'But you joined a closed service, more subject than any to the corruption of secrecy. Why?'

'I was recommended, Cavaliere. I seized the opportunity.'

'Why?'

'I have a talent for investigation.'

'And intrigue?'

'That, too, if you like.'

'And a taste for influence without responsibility.'

'No. I like responsibility.'

'And you resent the fact that you can no longer exercise it?'

'Yes, I do.'

'And what do you resent most of all?'

'That one man can, at a whim, make me less than I am—and that the same man can if he choose, bury, manipulate or trade information that may determine the political future of this country. My country, Cavaliere . . . yours, too.'

'How much do you know about this country of ours, Colonel?'

'Too little. And too much from the wrong side. I know criminals, agitators, propagandists, policemen, politicians; but the people—eh!—there are times when I feel like a little green man from Mars, all brain and antennae but no heart at all.'

'Can you be bought, Colonel?'

'I was, Cavaliere, forty-eight hours ago.'

'Can you be frightened?'

'I am frightened now. I know too much. I'm isolated. I'm an easy target.'

'And who would want to eliminate you?'

'The Director for one. Leporello for another.'

'Or both, working together.'

'That's the real nightmare. And it could be true. Look what happened in Greece. And look how quickly the Colonels have become respectable. Pantaleone, your half-brother, had the first blue-prints for a military coup, and they are still very formidable. With Leporello and the Director acting in concert they could be twice as formidable, very quickly.'

'And when you called me yesterday, what did you think I could do about it?'

'I thought you might advise me how to stay alive and use the knowledge I have to prevent a *colpo di stato.*'

'What knowledge do you have, Matucci?'

'I know every name on the microfilms. I could reproduce every document. I could reconstruct every map. I have a photographic memory, Cavaliere. I'll back it for ninety per cent accuracy.'

'Does the Director know that?'

'Yes.'

'Then he told you the truth. You are a natural victim.'

'And you, Cavaliere?'

'I, too, told you the truth. We are natural allies. But you have to accept that it will be—what did you call it?—a lopsided league.'

'How will it be loaded?'

'Enormously in my favour. I will introduce you into a new world. You will have to learn its history, its language and its symbols. I have everything you lack: influence, money, friends or servants in every country of the world. Also I am old and obstinate. So I have to hold the advantage.'

'I understand that and accept it.'

'There is one more condition.'

'Yes?'

'This Lili Anders. . . . She is a danger to you, an embarrassment for me. Pay her off and forget her.'

'I can't do that, Cavaliere.'

'I insist on it, if we are to work together.'

'Cavaliere, thirty years ago I am sure you had many friends who gave you the same advice about Raquela Rabin. As a Jewish celebrity, she was a danger to you and a nuisance to them. What did you do?'

'I took their advice.'

'Raquela Rabin told me a different story.'

'I know, but mine is the true version.'

'And yet you ask me to do the same thing to another woman?'

'For a different reason.'

'The same reason, Cavaliere.'

'You are making a great mistake.'

'Probably. But you offer me the same stale bargain as the Director. Submit and be safe. I'm sorry. The market's closed. No deal.'

'Another whisky?'

'No thank you. And if you'll excuse me, I'll dispense myself from dinner.'

'You will not dispense yourself, Colonel. You will stay and humour me, if only because I'm thirty years older than you and I have some excuse for bad manners.'

'Cavaliere, I have excuses, too. I may be dead very soon. I should like to enjoy the time I have left.'

'Sit down, man, for God's sake! The game is over now.'

'I beg your pardon.'

'I offered you a shabby contract, my friend. Had you consented, I would have sold you myself to the assassins. . . . Now, ring the bell, please. I think we are ready to eat.'

The man who sat with me at dinner that night in the Dolder Grand was a phenomenon, different from any image I had formed of him. He was seventy years old, an age at which most men are content to lapse into comfort and idiosyncrasy. Not this one. He bubbled like champagne. He talked books, women, painting, money, oil, films, fashion, religion, game-parks, wine and the growing of roses. He was so various that he dazzled me, and yet, so complete in what he was and did that he shamed me with the waste of my own good years. It was not simply that he was eloquent or interested; he knew, and knew profoundly. He enjoyed. He savoured. He had made his own sense of the mad mathematics of creation. Above all, he still had respect for mystery and though he judged trenchantly, there was always a touch of reserve and compassion in the verdict. Between the fruit and the cheese, he opened a new line of talk:

'We are all inheritors, Matucci, and we can no more shed our past than we can slough off our skins. We are free only to make the best of what we have, in the now-time at our disposal. We send men to the moon and believe we have discovered tomorrow; but tomorrow is still growing out of all our yesterdays, and we decipher it in scraps and fragments like the arithmetic of the Incas. You and I, for instance, we have shared bread and salt and wine. We have begun a friendship. But you will never understand me unless you remember that I was born in an attic above a brothel, on the feast of the Assumption of the Virgin, the day the acrobats came to town. You are curious? . . . I'm glad. When you get to my age, Matucci, you will find there are few left with whom you can share your past. The old go away. The young have no interest. You are there, a broken pillar in a wheatfield, the triumphs you celebrate long forgotten, the hands that raised you, crumbled into dust and blow away. Let me tell you of my birthday. Most of it is true; some of it is uncertain; the rest, perhaps, I have dreamed into myself; but, none the less, it is part of me. Please pour yourself some wine. It may help you to be patient with my fairy-tale.'

And that is exactly how he told it, like a fairy-tale, in old-fashioned language, with ample gestures and quite obvious enjoyment. He was playing the *gigione*, the ham actor, and watching sidelong to see how I would react to his improvisation.

'. . . The time, my dear Matucci, was 1900. Victor Emmanuel III was king of Italy and Leo XIII was gloriously reigning as Pontiff of the Holy Roman Church. The place is the Piazza delle Zoccolette, the Square of the Little Wooden Shoes, in Rome. . . .

'I didn't see it, Matucci; but I can reconstruct it for you because I saw the acrobats many times in my childhood. . . . They came twirling and prancing and tumbling in their gaudy patchwork while the fifers tootled and the drummers made boom-boom-boom, rat-tat-tat and the mountebank tossed his ribboned staff and announced to one and all the wonders that would soon be enacted in the Piazza delle Zoccolette. . . . They set up a stage for the mummers and a booth to sell favours and cure-all potions . . . and a little theatre for Pulcinella. They hoisted poles and ladders and stretched a tight-wire so that the *funambolo* could do his death-defying walk high above the crowds from one corner of the Piazza to another. . . . They made a square of cords to hold back the crowds and laid down bright mats for the tumblers and rolled out the great bar-bells which only Carlo the Magnificent could lift . . . though he would pay a gold coin to any man who could match him. And, all the while, the mountebank strode about distributing handbills, crying the talents of his company and the virtue of his nostrums and the surpassing beauty of his female contortionists. . . .

'. . . In the old days, Matucci, there was a brothel in the Piazza called, by courtesy, a house of appointment, and run by a bawd called Zia Rosa. It wasn't the most fashionable place in town, yet again, it wasn't the seediest. I don't remember it but my old nurse Angela, who was Zia Rosa's sister, would sometimes tell stories about it to the goggling maidservants in my mother's house. . . . For Zia Rosa the feast day and the arrival of the acrobats spelt money in the cash box. The feast day meant eating and drinking and strolling by the river and afterwards every young fellow with red blood in his veins was ready for a bout in bed. The show meant crowds and a press of bodies in the Piazza; and the sight of the girl acrobats bouncing about in their tights, was enough to send St Anthony screaming for solace from his mid-summer lust. . . . I know, Matucci, I lusted after more than one myself in my salad days. . . .

'. . . On that day, Matucci, my mother was in labour in the attic of Zia Rosa's house. How she came there was simple enough; a pregnant girl, disgraced, with little money, found her way almost inevitably to Zia Rosa or to someone like her. Zia Rosa provided a double service. Her sister Angela was both midwife and abortionist. And afterwards she recruited the more likely girls for service in the house.

'I once overheard Angela describe my mother as she was then. She called her "an original", a *furbacchiona*, sideling and hard to read. She had pale skin and blue eyes and honey-coloured hair. She spoke Italian and English and Romanesco. Her clothes were good but a trifle too modest for someone who obviously knew more than her prayers. She had money in her pocket too—at least enough for Angela to attend her at the birth; for Angela would do nothing without cash in hand . . .

'. . . Even then apparently, my mother was arrogant and demanding, in spite of her swollen belly and her need of so mean a shelter. She wanted clean sheets and towels, and soap, and two good meals a day from the kitchen and a list of medicines from the pharmacy. She stated flatly that she would stay a week after the birth of the child and she would pay a maid to attend her during her convalescence. She was a tough one too. Most women by this time would have been screaming and tossing and clamouring to be spared the birth pangs. Not this one, said Angela. Every groan had to be wrenched out of her as if she were a martyr on the rack. As each spasm passed, she forced herself to talk in that cool matter-of-fact voice that made even Italian sound strange. What she said made little sense, especially from a woman sweating out her labour in the garret of a bawdy house. But then most women were a little mad at such a time so Angela humoured her until the pains came sharper and faster and she was compelled to cry continuously. . . . Does this sound strange to you, Matucci, that I should be reliving my own birth? There is a meaning at the end of it. At least I think there is.

'Down in the Piazza—and this I know, Matucci, because Angela was watching—Luca Salamandra, the wire-walker, was about to begin his pilgrimage across the sky. He was dressed all in black with plastered hair and curled moustaches. Half-way up the ladder he turned and saluted the cheering crowds. Then he climbed to the little platform on the top of the pole and stepped on to the wire. There was a gasp from the crowd as they saw it sag under his weight and watched him come perilously into balance. Then they fell silent. . . .

'. . . He moved slowly at first, testing the strength of the breeze and the tension of the cable under his footsoles. In the centre of the Piazza, he stopped and began bouncing himself on the wire. Then he flipped into a somersault and landed upright on the swaying cable. He was, perhaps, five metres from the end of the wire when he stopped, staring straight into Angela's eyes. She remembers him smiling at her, beginning to walk towards her. . . . At which precise moment, Matucci, my mother screamed and I poked my reluctant head into the world and Luca Salamandra toppled into eternity.

'Ten days later, a woman in deep mourning, with an elderly companion, presented herself at the General Registry Office to deposit a set of notarized documents. The first was a certificate of marriage, between Anne Mary Mackenzie, a spinster, of Great Britain, and Luca Salamandra, bachelor, acrobat. The second was the surgeon's certificate of the death of Luca Salamandra. The third was a notification of the birth of Massimo Luca Salamandra, male, infant, issue of Anna Maria Salamandra and Luca Salamandra, deceased.

'This extraordinary concatenation of documents was the result of a long discussion between Anne Mary Mackenzie and Zia Rosa, followed by three hours' hard bargaining between Angela, the midwife, Zia Rosa, the mountebank, and Aldo the Calligrapher, an elderly forger who lived in a lane behind the Piazza and specialized in the reproduction of historic manuscripts. The fact that the registry clerk accepted the documents without question was a tribute to his calligraphic skill.

'The result of the whole transaction was that Anne Mary Mackenzie became a respectable Roman widow, and I was endowed with a spurious legitimacy which would enable me to enter the service of the Crown or even to take Holy Orders, in the unlikely event that I should ever aspire to the priesthood. . . .

'Of course, I have never wanted to be a priest, Colonel, but I sometimes think I should have made a splendid Cardinal, under the Borgias, of course, when celibacy was less stringently demanded. . . . Shall I tell you what you are thinking at this moment? You are asking yourself what is the point of that long story; whether I am making fun of you or indulging myself with a captive listener. You are right on both counts. But I have also shown you a parable. I was sired by a nobleman, fathered by a dead acrobat. I am, and always have been, a contradiction. To treat with me you will need patience and as much faith as it takes to believe in the blood of San Gennaro. Now, you are the man on the tight-rope. You want to save yourself and serve a very divided country and a very contentious people. You will need steady nerves, because you, too, will see monsters borning, and if you slip once you are dead. . . . I hope you understand that.'

'I do. But where do we begin?'

'You are under orders not to return to Italy for a month. We use that month to establish an insurance. Tomorrow morning at nine, you and Lili Anders will check out of the Baur au Lac. A limousine will be waiting to drive you by a circuitous route into Liechtenstein, where you will be lodged in a house which belongs to one of my companies. It's actually a converted hunting lodge, quaint but comfortable. There you will record everything you know of the Pantaleone affair, the microfilms, the maps . . . everything. This material will be copied and the copies will be lodged in a series of banks inside and outside Italy. During this same month you will receive other material from me. You will study it, carefully, because it will prepare you for the next stage of the operation: your return to Italy. We shall, of course, remain in close personal contact. You will have two of my staff on constant call as guards and couriers.'

'And when I go back to Italy?'

'You will still be on leave, an underpaid career officer with specialist qualifications. I shall, to use a cant phrase, take you up, professionally and socially. I shall offer you substantial fees as a consultant on economic intelligence. This will be an open transaction, sanctioned by regrettable custom. Every public functionary in the country tries to supplement his income by private business. Of course, your Director will hear of it. In fact, I shall make it my business to secure his approval.'

'Are you sure he will give it?'

'Why not? It will give him another means of compromising you whenever he wishes. It will demonstrate that you are, what he hopes you are, a venal man, easily bought and silenced. Under cover of this situation, you will continue your investigations into the new Fascist movement and Leporello's connection with it. You will report your findings to me and we shall agree a course of action. Does that make sense to you?'

'With one reservation, Cavaliere.'

'Which is . . .?'

'The Director. . . . I have seen him write the script of similar comedies. I do not believe he will buy this one.'

'Nor I. But he will try to make us believe he has bought it—which is all we need. The real problem is rather different: we have to keep you alive.'

The hunting lodge was ten kilometres south of Triesen, where the peaks of the Rhatikon join with the Glarner Alps and the pine-forests climb, haunted and dark, towards the snow line. It was built at the neck of a high valley, accessible only by a single track of bitumen which ended at a massive gate of stout pine, tipped with steel spikes and slung between pillars of hewn stone. Inside the gate a paved driveway wound through tall trees to the lodge itself, a long, freestone building, raftered with logs, roofed with zinc on timber, standing squat and solid against the lift of the pines and the heave of the misty peaks.

Outside, it looked cold and unwelcoming, ready to withstand invasion or avalanche. Inside it was simple but warm, with firelight gleaming on panelled walls, and polished copper and peasant pottery. The house was kept by an elderly Tyrolese and his wife and there were two other staff: Heinz, a big taciturn fellow from the Grisons, and Domenico, a swarthy young Varese, who was garrulous in English, French, Italian and Switzerdeutsch. They were an odd, but formidable, pair; Heinz, a deadly shot with a rifle, Domenico, a circus athlete, who was also accomplished in pistol and karate. There were always one of them on duty patrolling the grounds, surveying the road, scanning the high defiles for herdsmen or climbers. Each morning, Heinz drove into Triesen to do the shopping and pick up mail. Each evening at sunset the gates were locked, a complicated series of alarms was set and the two men shared the night-watch.

There was a telephone in the house; but we were warned not to use it. We could walk freely in the confines of the estate, but always and only with Heinz and Domenico in attendance. For the rest, there was a typewriter, papers, carbons, a copying machine, and, if I needed anything else, I had only to ask for it and Heinz would procure it, even from as far away as Zurich.

For the first few days I felt caged and restless; but Lili was as carefree as a bird; and she scolded me into relaxation and a simple routine of work. We rose early and, after breakfast, I settled down to the task of reconstructing from memory the material in the microfilm. It was a tedious job, which depended on a whole series of mnemonic tricks, each of which triggered off a sequence of visual memories. With trained interlocutors and a stenographer to record the material immediately, I could have done the job in half the time. As it was, I had to interpose the mechanical labour of transcribing each sequence on a typewriter. I had therefore to reckon with a fatigue factor and stop work immediately it inserted itself into the memory equation. In effect, I could work only about four hours a day on the reconstruction. The rest of the time I spent sorting and annotating the despatches which arrived each day by mail from Bruno Manzini.

All the despatches were posted from Chiasso, which is the frontier town of the Swiss canton of Ticino. The information was beautifully codified and it covered a startling variety of subjects: the organization and control of labour unions, the location of Marxist cells, and the pattern of their activities; charts showing the financial and management structure of large companies, with dossiers on their principal directors; lists of contributors to political parties, matrimonial alliances among the great families; investment holdings by foreign organizations, credit reports, notes on the editorial policies of newspapers and publishing houses; the activities of foreign embassies; the names and private histories of prominent functionaries and a schedule of their visits to Greece and Spain; a whole set of illuminating documents on Vatican finances and the political activities of the Vatican Secretariat of State.

I had been in the intelligence trade a long time, but much of this material was new even to me, and it argued the existence of an enormous and expensive organization, not merely to gather the information, but to classify and process it for constant use. The more I read, the more I was in awe at the complexity of Italian life and the problem of maintaining even a semblance of order in a modern industrial nation. The tension was so high, the balance of forces so precarious that even the most sanguine could not ignore the daily threat of disaster.

I understood, vividly, the frustation of the revolutionary who wanted to sweep the whole mess out of existence and begin again. I understood the despair of the young, who wanted to drop out, like the Poverello of Assisi, and live in fraternal simplicity on cannabis and corn-bread. I understood the seductive illusion of dictatorship: that one messianic man, armed with plenary power, could impose order and unity with a wave of his sceptre. More slowly, I began to see the meaning of Bruno Manzini's belief that we were all prisoners of our genes and our history and that our future was written by scribes long perished.

There were days—bad ones—when memory was sluggish and reason balked, and I was oppressed by a sense of total futility. I was a vain fool, shouting down the avalanche. I was a prancing ape, crying to be a king of human-kind. What right had I to determine, however minutely or indirectly, the text of a single line of history? I found myself drawn with poignant yearning, back to the beliefs of my childhood: a personal God to whom not even the fallen bird was unimportant, who would, in one grand glorious judgment, redress and stabilize and make all things new. And then I knew that I had reasoned Him out of my universe and that He was forever beyond my appeal.

In those desert days, Lili was an oasis of comfort. She refused to be put out by my snappishness. She lavished tenderness on me. She coaxed me out of the house and walked with me through the pine-woods, forcing me to attend to every small wonder: the contour of fungus on a tree-bole, the music of mountain water, the texture of stone and bark, the play of sunlight on the high crags. Whatever was left of dreamer in my dried-out self, she woke and nurtured with extraordinary patience. She chided me, too, and shamed me back into sanity.

'. . . I know how you feel, my love. Everything passes. You and I will pass, too, and the horror of the world will still remain. But think of this while we are still fighting, we hold it back if only for a little while. If everyone gave up the fight, the barbarians would take over for another thousand years. Even if we are ignorant and misguided, the cause is still good. You must believe that, you must never let yourself forget it. Look . . . even I am one small triumph for you. No, please, hear me out. I cannot remember how long it is since I belonged to myself. Today I do. Even when I give myself to you, I give as a free woman. If you had not cared, even a little, I should be dead, or locked up with the prostitutes in the Maddalena. This is good, isn't it—this day, this place? We should not be enjoying it if you had not made your fight and your mistakes as well. . . . Now, why don't you take me home and make love to me. It's much too damp out here.'

The love-making was always good; but it was haunted, too, by the thought that all too soon it must end. We talked very little about that; I was a man without resources, too old to make another career in exile. She had to be reborn out of the dark womb of the trade into another existence. I was the cord that tied her to the past. The cord must be snapped before she could be wholly free. There was no hope for either of us in a day-dream future; but the thought of lonely tomorrows weighed heavily on us both and our nights were the more desperate and the more precious because of it.

We had been about two weeks at the lodge when Bruno Manzini came to visit us. It was a Sunday. He arrived just after lunch, tired and brusque. He took possession of my notes and retired to his bedroom and we did not see him again until he joined us for a drink at seven-thirty in the evening. He apologized for his ill-humour and made a special effort to set Lili at ease:

'You are good for this man, Lili Anders. I am sure you were good for Pantaleone. Please don't be embarrassed with me. Life is much too short to entertain ghosts at the dinner-table. . . . and I am old enough to value beautiful women. I've studied your notes, Matucci. Excellent! But very disturbing. Have you made any sense out of the stuff I've sent you?'

'Some, yes. I'd like to discuss it with you after dinner.'

'That's why I'm here. We will shut you out, young lady, but you are going to forgive me in advance; because the more you know, the more you are at risk, and our friend here has a singular concern for you. Have you told her, Matucci?'

'Told me what, Cavaliere?'

'That I ordered him to send you away and threatened to withdraw my help if he refused. He defied me. Meeting you now, I am glad he did.'

'Thank you, Cavaliere. He did not tell me.'

'Matucci, you're a fool.'

'That's old news. Let's not labour it, eh?'

He laughed, put his arm round Lili and toasted her with old-fashioned gallantry, then launched us into a cascade of small talk and reminiscences that swept us from soup to coffee without a noticeable pause. Afterwards, when we were alone, with the brandy warming in our hands, he told me:

'. . . Things are bad, Matucci, very bad. First we have this business of Bessarione. The police say he blew himself up while he was attempting to sabotage a power pylon. The Left say he was framed and assassinated by the Right. I knew the man: an eccentric if you like, a wealthy romantic, who was also a very good publisher. What's the truth? Who knows? But, at least, it should be open to public debate. What happens? A series of arrests of journalists and students. The charge? "Spreading news calculated to disturb public order." For God's sake! That's the old Fascist dragnet. I remember the day it was promulgated. Result? More division. More unrest. Tomorrow there will be another walk-out from Fiat. In Rome the garbage-collectors will be on strike and the city will be a dungheap in three days. After that, with Easter coming and the tourist season beginning, the hotel employees will walk out. In between we shall have a bomb or two and maybe a child hit by a police bullet. . . . You see how beautifully it works. The Fascists blame the Marxists, the Marxists blame the Fascists. Each provokes the other. Each blames the other for the consequences of violence. In the middle are the people: the students who cannot get an education because we do not build enough schools, the housewives who cannot get

home because the buses do not run; the sick, who are lined three-deep in our
hospital wards. Let me tell you something, Matucci. I am on notice to rush
deliveries of every piece of riot equipment I can fabricate. What I cannot
make, I am to buy, borrow or steal, and no limit on foreign valuta either.
The markets are beginning to panic, too. If I told how much money went
out of the country last week, it would make you weep. So, how does it add
up? The Marxists can, and maybe will, disrupt the country: but they are not
ready to run it. I am not sure they want to run it, at least not from the
Quirinal Hill. Their support is at the local level, in the cities and the
communes and the provinces. They can practise terror and intimidation
with urban guerrilla groups; but they cannot mount a military coup. The
Right could do that, as you know, provided they had enough tacit support
from the centre and from the confessional. As for outside encouragement,
they would have it from America, which has huge investments in the
country and the Sixth Fleet bottled in the Mediterranean playing cowboys
and Indians with the Russians. They would get it from Spain and Greece
and very probably from France. After that, who cares? ... Your notes
confirm all this, Matucci. But they tell more: my half-brother was less a fool
than I believed. He planned better than I knew. With certain modifications,
his strategy is still valid today or tomorrow. . . . I have kept the worst news
till last. Leporello has made his deal. He has stepped into Pantaleone's
shoes.'

'And the Director . . .?'

'Has joined him. . . . They met last weekend at a houseparty at the Villa
Baldassare.'

'How do you know this?'

'I was there, too. They wanted me to join the club.'

'And . . .?'

'I agreed, of course. A natural union when you come to think of it. Heavy
industry, textiles, newspapers, banking and a stable government pledged to
law and order.'

'Why had they never asked you before?'

'Because Pantaleone would never hear of it. And at that time, they needed
him more than me.'

'Why now?'

'Because, thanks to your investigation and to the information in my
brother's papers, the Director and General Leporello knew all about my
connection with my brother's death. So, the time was very ripe for a
civilized arrangement. Don't you think so?'

'I think, Cavaliere, that I am going quietly mad.'

'Not yet, please, Matucci. I need you very sane. I joined to be inside the
conspiracy. I want this precious junta broken and brought down. Between
us, I believe we can do it.'

'In God's name, how?'

'Convict Leporello of murder and the Director of conspiracy with a
murderer. Could you do it?'

'I'd be willing to try.'

'The dangers are doubled now.'

'I know.'

'Hesitations?'

'Some. I think we need a new script.'

'Let's discuss that in a moment. Do you have any conditions?'

'That I conduct the affair in my own way, without interference from anyone.'

'Agreed.'

'That I call on you for information, money and such other help as I need from time to time.'

'Agreed. What about financial arrangements?'

'No financial arrangements, thank you. I'm not a mercenary and I can hardly ask you to pay life insurance in advance. I have a request, that's all.'

'Name it.'

'From the moment we leave this place, I want Lili Anders protected. If I succeed in the job, I want a Presidential amnesty for her so that she can be free to re-enter Italy, if she chooses. Can you guarantee those things?'

'The first, yes. The second, no. But I would break my back to procure it.'

'That's all, then. Now, let's talk about the script.'

He sipped his brandy, slowly, set down his glass, then made a small cathedral with his fingertips and smiled at me across the roof of it. He said, placidly:

'My friend, I have already sold this script to the Director.'

Suddenly and unreasonably, I was angry. My gullet was sour with bile and my head full of buzzing wasps. I thrust myself out of the chair and stood over him, mouthing a vehement abuse.

'You are an arrogant old man. Arrogant and dangerous. This is my life, mine! . . . You can't play knuckle-bones with it! What you do is your own business. You're rich, protected. You can buy yourself advocates, bodyguards, diplomatic privileges, immunity from everything but cardiac arrest. I can't. I have to carry my own insurance—sole risk! So, you don't make arrangements that I haven't approved. You don't close sales that I haven't ratified. You haven't bought me, Cavaliere. Understand that. You haven't bought me! Oh, I know you're the Salamander and you've survived longer than I'm ever likely to do. But you wrote that history for yourself. I have to write mine, even if it's only two words: *Hic jacet!*'

Without thinking what I was doing, I slammed the brandy-glass into the fire, where it exploded in a rush of flame. The flames died in a few seconds and I turned to see Manzini still smiling at me over the tips of his fingers. Then, he stood up and faced me across the hearthrug, still bland and benign.

'My dear Colonel, truly you underrate me. Or perhaps I am too cryptic for a late evening. When we talked in Zurich two weeks ago, did we not agree on a strategy?'

'We did. But the circumstances are different. You are now inside the Club. That colours any public relationship I have with you.'

'May I suggest that the colours make a better camouflage than before?'

'You may suggest what you like. I need proof.'

'Let me try to give it to you, then. When I talked with your Director and with Leporello at the Villa Baldassare, your name was mentioned several times.'

'Who introduced it?'

'The Director first. Then Leporello. Naturally, I had comments to make, too.'

'What was said?'

'The Director, with his usual delicacy— said you were a nuisance. Leporello used the words, "grave risk"! The Director said you were immobilized. Leporello said he required the risk eliminated altogether.'

'And you, Cavaliere?'

'I pointed out that you were a very senior and very intelligent officer, and that if I were in your shoes I should have taken certain precautions, for example, by lodging documents in a bank, for publication in the event of your death. I offered the opinion that an untimely accident might demoralize your friends and colleagues in the Service. I then ventured a small fiction: that after your arrival in Switzerland you telephoned me and asked whether I could find a place for you in my organization. You told me that you had been badly treated and that you were thinking seriously of resigning your commission and seeking civil employment. I told the Director I had invited you here this weekend to discuss the matter. I thought it might be a good idea if I offered you temporary employment while he still retained you at the disposal and under the authority of the Service. In sum, I managed to persuade the Director that you were safer alive than dead, at least for the moment.'

'And Leporello?'

'Did not agree. The Director overrode him.'

'For how long, I wonder?'

'Good question. And I don't know the answer. However, as you see, the arrangement is not yet concluded because your consent is necessary. You may have changed your mind. You may still elect to conduct this operation in secret and without any overt connection with me. I would agree to that, too, if it left you more free and efficient. For the rest, I am often arrogant, though I do not wish to be so with you. I am also old, and I can be dangerous; but never to my friends, Matucci, believe that!'

'I do believe it, Cavaliere. I was rude. But I'm tired of people playing games with my life.'

'Do you often break out like that?'

'Not often.'

'I'm glad to hear it. That's expensive brandy. Have another.'

'Let's finish this discussion first. If I work underground, I am constantly on the run. I have to use false papers, perhaps two or three identities, and often unsuitable addresses. I've done it before. I can do it again; but I am handicapped. I should prefer to work in the open as your employee, but I may compromise your position and expose you to personal risk. So, it's your decision.'

'I've already taken it. You join me.'

'When?'

'I telephone the Director tomorrow, tell him I want to employ you on trial and ask his permission to bring you back to Italy with me.'

'So soon?'

'The answer's in your own notes. There is very little time.'

'I haven't finished the notes yet.'

'Finish them at my house. I'm lodging you there until you make other arrangements.'

'What do I tell Lili?'

'Whatever she needs to keep her happy. I'll instruct her on the security arrangements before we leave. You concentrate on the love passages.'

'Talking of love passages, Cavaliere. . . .'

'Yes?'

'What is your exact relationship with the Principessa Faubiani?'

It was his turn to be angry now. He flushed red as a cock's comb. His head jerked up and the nostrils of his patrician beak flared out. He snapped at me:

'And how the devil does that concern you?'

'I have to ask, Cavaliere. I've known several good men talked to death in bed.'

He stared at me for a long hostile moment. He gulped the last of his brandy and tossed the glass into the fire as I had done. Then he relaxed and smiled and the smile made him look twenty years younger.

'Let's say that I'm a wealthy patron who has visitor's privileges whenever I'm in Rome. But I do take your point, Matucci. The arrangement isn't exclusive and the lady does gossip. Perhaps I should introduce you and let you judge for yourself. Who knows? You might even find her useful. I also have other relationships, Matucci. Do you propose to intrude on them all?'

'If my life is involved, yes, Cavaliere.'

'*Dio*! We do snarl at each other, don't we? I don't mind. I need an argument occasionally to keep me honest. But let's not do it too often. I'll give you a thought to take to bed. Comes a moment when all you have left is sap for one good loving and courage for one good fight. Don't waste the loving on a whore, or the fight on a paper dragon. Goodnight, friend!'

It was an actor's exit; and I wondered, irritably, why he took the trouble to make it so obvious. He had nothing to prove. He commanded so much power, he had survived so many storms, that the teasing and the mystification only cheapened him. Then, I began to wonder whether he were not trying to cheapen me, to make me more pliant to his designs. I told the thought to Lili, as we lay together in the dark, spelling out the hours of our last night together. She disagreed, passionately.

'. . . You have to trust him, my love. I think he is a rather wonderful old man, so alert, so vigorous; but he resents the passing of time. He is lonely as he told you. So he preens himself to command your interest and respect. You can be a rough man, Dante Alighieri. You have lived an adventurous life. Manzini has been an adventurer, too. He sees you as a friend, but also as a rival. Indulge him a little. You will not lose in the end.'

I told her then the promises I had exacted to keep her safe and to claim an amnesty afterwards. To my surprise, she rejected the idea out of hand.

'No! You want to be kind. But this is not the way. Don't you see? You tie me to the past. You tie me to yourself in a way I do not want. When you come to me again–if you come–you will visit me in my house, you will drink my wine and eat at my table. I will not be empty-handed as I am now. I need that, my love. As for the risks, I do not care. We will arrange addresses where we can write to each other. There's another reason, too. You will be doing a dangerous work. You cannot do it with a divided mind. You will need other women. You must be free in the end to choose between them and me. I must be free, too. . . . Please, let's not be tense and desperate. Love me gently tonight, gently and slowly. I am so fond of you. . . .'

Somewhere, in the small dark hours, while we were sleeping in each other's arms, the alarm went off; a shattering noise of bells and sirens. I leapt out of bed and ran to the window. The grounds were lit with blazing floodlights, and I saw Heinz and Domenico loping across the open space towards the pine-woods. We threw on dressing gowns and hurried into the lounge where we found Manzini standing, erect and calm, at the window. It was impossible to speak. The noise went on and on, a vicious assault on the eardrums, until twenty minutes later, perhaps, Domenico came hurrying back, switched off the system and reset it. A few moments later he reported to Manzini.

'We got him, Cavaliere. Up on the northern boundary.'

'Alive or dead?'

'Dead. Heinz got him with the first shot.'

'Who was he?'

'Italian, I think. No one we know. No papers, no identifying marks. No labels in the clothes.'

'Armed?'

'Grenades, plastic explosive and fuses and a Walther pistol.'

'How did he get in?'

'He had to come over the mountain on foot. We might be able to trace his route when the sun comes up.'

'Not worth the trouble.'

'Do we call the police?'

'In Liechtenstein? No! Bury him.'

'With respect, Cavaliere, the alarm can be heard for miles.'

'So far as we know, a deer fouled one of the trip-wires.'

'As you say, Cavaliere.'

'Bury him deep, Domenico.'

'Leave it to me, Cavaliere. . . . Goodnight.'

When he had gone, Manzini poured three glasses of brandy and passed one to each of us. His hand was steady. He raised his glass in a kind of grim salute.

'Like the old days in the Partisans, Matucci, which you are too young to remember.'

He meant to proclaim it like an ancient battle-cry. To me it sounded like an epitaph.

PART II

The practice of politics in the East may be defined by one word: dissimulation.
Benjamin Disraeli: Contarini Fleming

We did not go directly into Italy, but drove by way of Salzburg, where Manzini wanted to discuss a lumber contract with an Austrian mill, and then down through the Brenner to Mestre where one of his companies was building a graving dock for small tankers. It was a tedious journey, because the weather closed in, with heavy snowfalls, north and south of the Alps, and the roads were a mess of churned snow and dangerous ice.

Manzini, however, was in high spirits, determined, as he put it, that we should divert ourselves before we stepped into the lions' cage. He had a taste for legend and for local history, and he understood the continuity of it all, and how the old feudal families were still mixed up in the omelette of modern Europe. He did not ramble as some old men do; but talked his themes through to a wholeness. He was a natural dramatist and even when he invented dialogues and situations, you were left with a sense of concordance and probability.

Time and again, he returned to his own childhood, as if his deepest need was to purge himself of old rancours and remember forgotten joys:

'I grew up in a spacious time, Matucci, in a tolerant and cynical city. I lived in a palace behind the Condotti; a house full of doting women, from which men were never absent. I had all the illusions I needed and no guilts at all. In this, I think, I was a very fortunate child. Strange as it may seem, I was most fortunate in my mother. There were so many of her, you see—a new one for every day.

'I remember her, naked in the bath, smooth and appetizing as a peeled peach, whistling and singing and sipping champagne from a glass perched on a stool beside the bath. I remember her in corset and camisole, all ribbons and laces, pirouetting before the mirror and chattering about my uncles. . . . No boy in all the world had as many uncles as I.

'There was Colonel Melchior, who had one hand made of wood, covered with a black leather glove, because he had lost his hand in Abyssinia at the slaughter of Adowa. There was Uncle Burckhardt, who wore a gold chain across his belly and huffed when he bowed and puffed when he talked and who bored my mother to distraction. There was Uncle Freddie, who bought me my first clockwork train and taught me to play chess. He was English and his name was ffolliot-Phillimore, and the servants called him the "pope's angel", because he had a high piping voice like the eunuch tenor in the papal choir. A lot of people hated him. Even Mamma hated him sometimes, because he could be very malicious. But I loved him. . . .

'He opened a new world to me. He took me down the Tiber in a row-boat. He read my first Latin and Greek with me. He showed me how to dig for shards and seals on Testaccio. He would sit with me on a tumbled pillar in the Forum and make me close my eyes and see the Vestals garlanded with flowers and the augurs telling the future from the flight of birds, and Petronius walking proud and elegant among the orators. . . . One day, he said to me; "When you grow up, young fellow, you must be an elegant man, else I shall be miserably disappointed in you. Look out there. That's your city. You must impose yourself on it as Petronius did, with brains and good taste and a talent for mockery. You must learn from it, too. Learn the art of survival and being reborn every day. When you have your first woman, let her be a Roman, all fire and fury, tears and tenderness. This is a rogue's city. Learn to be a rogue, too, if you must, but for God's sake be a rogue with style."

'Strange! I remember that as if it were yesterday. I didn't know anything about style, of course. So, I asked him what it was. He pointed up to the sky and said: "Look up there. See the swifts, how they fly, riding the wind as if they owned the whole heavens. Now, look over there. See that poor dumb donkey hauling the wine-cart. He's a useful creature. We couldn't live without him. But which would you rather be, the swift or the donkey? . . . The swift, of course! That's style, young fellow. That's style . . ."

'My father? Well, that's a hard one, Matucci. You see, I believed for a long time that my father was dead. I accepted it as children do, without question and truly without too much regret. Even after I had met him in the flesh, I was allowed for years to believe that he was just another kind uncle. That is one of the things I have found hardest to forgive. You told me I have too many enemies. I wonder sometimes if all the enemies are not one man: Massimo Count Pantaleone. I wonder if that is not why I hated my own brother, because he bore the name that should have been mine. And yet, given the custom of the time, given the laws of legitimacy and inheritance, I should not blame him too much.

'The first time I saw him, I was riding with Mamma on the Pincio. Uncle Melchior had bought me a pony and Mamma had given me a jacket and breeches in the English style and this was my first day out with her. You should have known the Pincio in those days. Matucci. It was the place where you would see the most stylish landaus and some of the best horses in Rome. The Cardinals would drive up in their carriages, and they would walk solemnly under the pines, while their retainers, all in livery, would gossip together. The nobles of Rome would ride and salute each other and flirt in the fashion of the time. Not everybody saluted Mamma. Most of the ladies held their heads high and looked through her as if she were a windowpane. I remember she used to toss her head and swear at them in Romanaccio: "Old farts! The only thing they can ever get under their skirts is a horse."

'Well, this morning, a gentleman reined up and fell into talk with Mamma. He was tall and bulky with a big eagle's beak—like mine, probably—and a shock of grey hair. He rode a black stallion with flaring nostrils and he looked like a giant statue come to life. Mamma was like a doll beside him, but she sat straight and smiling and held out her hand as if he were the humblest of men. They talked for a long time. Then suddenly he swept me off my pony and on to his saddle, and took me on a wild gallop through the woods. He rode the stallion into a lather and then dismounted in a small grove–long gone!–where there was a statue of Pan and a runnel of clear water. He put both his hands on my shoulders and looked at me, silent and frowning. Then he smiled and said: "Good boy. You have good manners and a stout heart–a trophy for any man in his autumn days. I wish I had the courage to claim you." . . . I didn't know what he meant, only that he was pleased with me. Then he took me back to Mamma. . . .

'Eh, Matucci! If you are bored, blame yourself. You wanted to know me. Here I am! Now, let's talk a little business. You will stay for a few days at my country place outside Bologna. Then I suggest you establish yourself in Milan. I have a furnished apartment, which I can place at your disposal, together with servants you can trust. You will need a bank account and credit facilities, and a cover-story for your activities in my employ; after that, good luck and a very active guardian angel.'

'More, Cavaliere. I need a list of safe houses and two or three sets of papers. The best forgeries.'

'Surely you know how to get those?'

'How and where and how much, but I cannot appear in the negotiations.'

'I know the best forger in the business.'

'I know him, too . . . Carlo Metaponte, pupil of Aldo the Calligrapher. He engraved your Salamander card. He's on our files.'

'Still usable?'

'If you can control him, yes.'

'I can control him. . . . Matucci, will you take a little advice from me?'

'Yes.'

'Please try to be generous with me. I'm old enough to be your father. Strange as it may seem, I still have a conscience; because I try to live by logic and conscience is the last term of a syllogism. I have tried to examine this conscience on our relationship. I conclude, rightly or wrongly, that what divides us is not principle but history . . . the class struggle, the class image. Your father was an old-line socialist, exiled to Lipari. Mine was an old-line aristocrat, who exploited the poor and broke his neck chasing women on the Pincio. But when you were thirteen years old, Matucci, I was making petrol bombs in a barn near Pedognana. When you were fourteen, I was hung by my thumbs in a Gestapo cell in Milan. What I fought for then, you are trying to preserve now, a liberty, however precarious and imperfect. I cannot risk what you risk; because I have only the tag-end of a life at my disposal. But it's still sweet and I savour every second of it. This is not a reproach, believe me. It is–how can I call it?–a plea that we should enjoy this fight. Go down, if we must; survive, if we can, singing and shouting. Can you understand that?'

'I can. I do. I'm grateful, Cavaliere.'

'Please! Not "cavaliere" anymore. I am Bruno. You are Dante Alighieri . . . *Bene?*'

'*Bene, grazie!*'

'And I want you to develop some style, my Dante. New uniforms for special occasions. A Colonel should look like a Colonel, not a conscript corporal. New suits, too, the best fashion, a modish cut. And don't be mean with money; spread it like sauce on spaghetti. . . . Good! That's the first time I've heard you laugh like a happy man!'

Then, because he must still play the conjuror, he hit me with a new surprise. We would stay, not in Mestre, which was a barbarous town, but across the water in Venice at the Gritti Palace–and the Director would join

us for dinner. After all the charm he had spent on me, I had to take it with
good grace. That pleased him almost as much as his own cleverness and he
explained the reason at length and in detail:

'. . . You would have to confront him sometime. Better with me than
alone. Better in his own city where he feels most a Prince. Across the water
he will see some of the enterprise that makes me what I am. He will see you,
too, in another light: a bought man enjoying the fruits of judicious
compromise. We are at home, now, where these subtleties matter. Not that
you will demean yourself. Never! You will be courteous, a little reserved,
but not insensible of his magnanimity. He will goad you, of course; but you
will still fight back, though not so strongly as before, because you have less
to lose. He will ask you about Lili Anders. You will shrug her off, a ripe
peach tasted and thrown away. When you think you have had enough, you
leave. You have to meet a woman in Harry's Bar. She will be there, too. Her
name is Gisela Pestalozzi. She will be on your list of safe houses. . . . The
barman will know her. You will say that the Salamander sent you. . . .
Clear?'

'Clear. Except how you manage it all.'

'It's a game, my Dante. One of the few I can still play well.'

We came to Venice in the early dark. There was mist on the canals, a thick
pestiferous haze, heavy with the fumes of sulphur and the exhalations of the
canals. Domenico parked the car and we took a gondola to the hotel because,
said Manzini, the gondoliers were all vultures, but even vultures had a right
to survive. At the Gritti we were welcomed like mediaeval Cardinals and
lodged in adjoining suites overlooking the Grand Canal. Not that there was
much to see, because the fog sat low on the water and the lights of the sparse
traffic made dull yellow blotches in the murk. I shaved and bathed at leisure,
while my clothes were pressed. I dressed with more care than usual and
managed to make my entrance just as Manzini and the Director were
settling themselves at the table. The Director received me like the prodigal
son.

'My dear Matucci! I'm delighted to see you. Filthy weather, isn't it?'

I agreed it was; but Venice was still Venice after all.

'You look well and rested. That's good. Did you have a good journey?'

'Brutal!' said Manzini, testily. 'Chains all the way! Still, it should bring
the skiers out. Did you invest in that little project I recommended at
Bolzano?'

'Regrettably, no. I bought a Picasso instead.'

'Rubbish! There's too much of him and more to come when he's dead.
You should have waited until the Pantaleone collection came on the market.
It has to, you know.'

'My dear Bruno! What's the use, if you can't export the stuff when you're
tired of it. Are you interested in painting, Matucci?'

'I am, sir; but I can't afford it. Not yet, anyway.'

'Take my advice. Start with the young ones. If you have a good eye, you
can't fail to pick at least one in ten. At that you'll still make a profit.
Wouldn't you say, Bruno?'

'I want him interested in my profits first. That's the quickest way he'll
make them for himself. Do you have any idea how many milliards of lire we
lose a year through pilfering, large-scale theft, industrial sabotage and bad
book-keeping? Matucci here, has made some intelligent suggestions. If he
can put them into action, I'll be prepared to bid very high for him.'

'Provided, my dear Bruno, that the Service is prepared to waive claims on his valuable talents. .... Still, I must say I'm glad to see him have this opportunity. He deserves it. I owe you some thanks, Matucci. You behaved very well in a difficult diplomatic situation. I don't blame you for feeling angry. I'm glad to see you had the enterprise to contact Bruno here. It's a situation that could work out very well for all of us, even for the Service; because, as you have often said, we are weak in the high industrial sector. Still, that's for another time. .... We've made a few changes at headquarters since you left.'

'Oh?'

'Gonzaga moves into the Middle-East section and Rampolla takes over the Balkan desk. The rest are minor, except that we've retired Stefanelli from Forensics. He was getting much too old and crotchety. .... Ah, the menu! What do you recommend, Bruno?'

'My dear fellow, you should know by now, I never recommend food, horses or women. It's the surest way to lose friends. Wine is another matter altogether. I believe you had a very good vintage last year.'

'One of our best in a decade. It's too early yet, but when it's ready, I'll reserve you a few cases.'

'Thank you. I'd appreciate it. By the way, have you recovered the Pantaleone will yet?'

'Not yet. Which reminds me, Matucci. We were lucky about Bandinelli. It appears the wife was having an affair with a young singer at San Carlo. She was only too pleased to consent to a quiet funeral with no embarrassing questions.'

'I'm delighted to know it, sir. I'm afraid I didn't handle that situation very well.'

'We all make mistakes. And you were under a big strain. Let's order shall we? I hate having waiters breathing down my neck.'

I was glad of the respite and the small talk that followed it: the talk of high men who played with power and people as if they were coloured counters on a gaming table. They were well matched these two: the Director so firmly entrenched in history that you had only to change his costume to set him back in the Council of the Ten; Manzini, the old technocrat, straddling the past and the present and the future like a colossus in a business suit. But the language was the same and the power was the same as in the days when one galley a day slid down the slips, and half the treasure of Byzantium poured into the Venice of the Doges. For a while they ignored me, and I was very content to listen and begin to learn the stylized language of this other world.

After a while, inevitably, the talk became spicy and scandalous: who was taking advantage of the new divorce law and who was not and why. Then, without warning, the Director tossed a question to me.

'By the way, Matucci, what happened to the Anders woman?'

'I took your advice, sir.'

'Oh, forgive me, Bruno, I forgot there was a family connection.'

'Please! I am not in the least concerned. I only hope Matucci enjoyed himself.'

'Did you, Matucci?'

'Briefly, sir.'

'Where is she now?'

'She was talking of going to Klosters for a while. I didn't inquire too closely. You know the way it is.'

'Do you think she'll go back to the trade?'

'Not our trade, sir. I think she has marriage in mind.'

'Any prospects?'

'Not with me, I assure you. Which reminds me, if you gentlemen will excuse me from coffee, I have an appointment with another lady.'

'By all means, unless Bruno here. . . .'

'No, no! Go ahead. Enjoy yourself while you can. You'll have little enough time later.'

'Oh, before you go, Matucci. . . .'

'Sir?'

'This dual employment of yours. I'm quite happy about it, of course. I'm glad to oblige my friend Bruno here. But you will be discreet about it, won't you? It's faintly illegal and I'd hate to raise discontent among your Service colleagues. You do understand?'

'Perfectly, sir. And I'm very grateful. Goodnight, gentlemen.'

'Good luck with the lady.'

'It's a dirty night,' said Bruno Manzini, with a grin. 'Don't fall into the canal.'

It was a fair warning and I took it seriously. I went up to my room, put on a top-coat and slipped a pistol into my pocket. I spent a moment at the desk in the lobby buying postage stamps from the concierge and then stepped out into the alley between the Palazzo Pisani and the Gritti. You know the place. The alley opens into a piazza in front of the Zobenigo. You turn right, cross over a small bridge and come into the Largo Ventidue Marzo, which brings you slap against the façade of the Basilica of San Moise. Even by day, it is a quiet route. There are few shops and nothing to see except the Basilica; and the stale backwater under the bridge is jammed with gondolas and barges. But at night, with choking fog, and every window shuttered, it was like a city of the dead.

I paused a moment under the light and heard a murmur of voices from the left; boatmen, probably, waiting to ferry some of the diners back home. I could not see them, but I could hear the boats bumping against the piles. I began to walk, not fast, but steadily, holding to the wall for direction, listening for the sound of other footfalls. Nothing, except the wash of the canal, and the sound of distant music and the wail of foghorns from the basin at Mestre. When I turned out of the Piazza Zobenigo, I stopped and listened again. This time I heard, or thought I heard, the faint slap-slap of rubber-soles, running tip-toe on the cobbles; but the sound was so vague, so muted by the mist that it could have been an illusion. I began to walk, faster now, towards the vague yellow glow that marked the hump of the bridge. Then, from behind me, I heard a long high whistle. I stopped, flattened myself against the wall, took the pistol from my pocket and slipped off the safety catch. The situation was clear now. Behind me was one man. Ahead, where the canal cut across the alley, there would be two, one at either corner of the *traghetto*. Before I reached the bridge they would close the trap and kill me inside it.

Backed against the wall, I began to ease myself slowly along it, feeling for a doorway or any projection of the wall that would give me the slightest shelter. I heard rubbershoes make a few swift, running steps. I saw a faint movement near the bridge, which might have been a man, but could just as easily have been a swirl of mist. Then my fingers slid off the rough surface of the wall and groped in emptiness. It was not a doorway. It was an open archway, low and narrow, leading back into the courtyard of a palace or a tenement. Thanks be to God! Now they would have to come for me. I slid down on one knee and peered out cautiously. It was, perhaps, ten seconds before they began to move, two hugging the wall on my side, the third moving down the opposite side of the alley. This was the one I must take first, if I could see clearly enough to hit him.

They moved irregularly, in a series of short runs, first one, then the others, never in the same sequence. I had to have them nearer. I dared not let them come too close, in case they were armed with grenades or a nail-bomb. Then, mercifully, the man on the opposite side made a run that brought him into range. I could not see him clearly. I had to guess him between a barred window and the deeper shadow of a doorway. I took careful aim and fired. In the narrow space the explosion was deafening. He did not fire back. He turned and ran. The others ran, too. I fired two more shots, wild into the mist. Then, because shutters were opening, and heads were showing at lighted windows, I, too, bolted down the alley and over the bridge. I did not stop running until I reached the shelter of Harry's Bar.

Mercifully, the bar was busy; so my breathless entrance attracted no attention at all. I ordered a large drink, carried it to the telephone booth and called Manzini at the hotel. They called him away from his coffee and I told him:

'Thanks for the warning. I nearly did fall into the canal.'

'What happened?'

'A well-laid trap. Three men. I fired shots. They got away.'

'Where are you now?'

'Where you sent me. I haven't met the lady yet.'

'Come to my room when you get back.'

'How's our mutual friend?'

'Smug as a cat. I think I'll stir him up a little. Until later, eh?'

I carried my drink back to the bar, nudged myself on to a stool and waited for a slack moment to chat to the barman. When I asked him about Gisela Pestalozzi, he grinned.

'Interested in a little fun, eh? Well, she's expensive, but she's got the best girls in town.'

'How expensive?'

'Sixty to a hundred thousand a night in season. At this time, maybe less; but you'll have to haggle. Still, they've all got their own apartments; and that's something in this weather. Where are you staying?'

'Friends of the family. Very stuffy people.'

'Eh! Then Gisela's your best bet.'

'How will I know her?'

'She sits over in the far corner. Big red-head in her middle forties. Wears lots of junk: bangles, neck-chains, big earrings, that sort of thing. You can't miss her. She's an old cow, but always good for a laugh. Give you a tip, though. Don't cross her. She's got lots of friends.'

'Police?'

'A few. More of the other kind.'

'Thanks. . . . And here's something for the service.'

'Thank you. Staying long in Venice?'

'I doubt it. Why?'

'Well, as I say, I wouldn't want to cross Gisela; but if you're interested, I have a few numbers of my own. . . .'

'Thanks. I'll remember. Pour me another drink and send it over to the corner.'

I spread myself over the banquette. The waiter brought the drink and I sipped it, slowly, while I thought about the Cavaliere Bruno Manzini, called the Salamander. Everything he said was magical but how much was true and how much was fairy-tale, I could not guess. Bruno Manzini, partisan hero, joined with the Fascists and then called on me, Colonel Nobody, to destroy them. I felt like a whirling dervish, dancing himself into oblivion to prove that God was God and all His works were a splendid inconsequence.

Then Gisela Pestalozzi came in, scattering greetings and perfume, and sat down beside me. She had rings on her fingers and dangling bells in her ears and enough chains to moor the *Galileo*. She had arms like a wrestler and bosoms bountiful enough to feed a continent. Her hair was titian red, her lips geranium and her voice was like pebbles in a gravel-grinder. She was sweating profusely and she fanned herself with a table napkin. She ignored me for a full half-minute, then she announced:

'This is my place, young man. You must be new here.'

'And you must be Gisela?'

'That's right. How did you know?'

'A friend told me.'

'What friend?'

'Can you lower your voice a little, please?'

'Why should I? It's my voice. It's my place. If you want to talk business, that's another thing.'

'I want to talk business.'

'Sixty thousand a night, dinner and drinks extra. Yes or no?'

'No. The Salamander sent me.'

'Eh!' She collapsed like a vast balloon and her voice dropped ten decibels. 'Why didn't you say so straight off? What do you need?'

'A safe house.'

'How long?'

'I don't know yet. Weeks, months.'

'With or without?'

'With or without what?'

'A woman, of course. What else?'

'Without.'

'Two rooms, kitchen and bath. Fully furnished, light, heat and telephone. Two hundred thousand a month. Suit you?'

'It's a murderous price.'

'It's a safe house. Private entrance. No porter and two other exits.'

'Where?'

'A hundred metres from San Marco.'

'Quality?'

'Well, it's not the Ca' d'Oro; but it's comfortable.'

'Where do I get the key?'

'From me. With a month in advance and a month's deposit.'

'I'll think about it. Where do I find you when you're not here?'

'The Salamander has my number.'

'Good. A drink?'

'What's your name?'

'I change it every day. Just call me lover.'

'Do you want a girl?'

'Not tonight.'

'Then move over, lover! This is working hours.'

'*Ciao*, Gisela! We'll be seeing each other.'

And that was it, pointless and purposeless as everything else that was happening to me. I left my drink unfinished on the table and paid a sleepy boatman one thousand lire to deliver me two hundred metres down the canal at the front door of the Gritti, which, being a civilized hotel, has a good telephone service and booths where you need not discuss your business with the world and his girl-friend. I ordered a call to Stefanelli in Rome and, two minutes later, I had him on the line. In ten seconds I knew that I was not a welcome caller.

'Steffi, this is Matucci.'

'I remember the name. Yes?'

'I'm in Venice, Steffi.'

'Happy you. Happy Venice.'

'Steffi, stop clowning for Christ's sake! This is serious.'

'I know. I am out of a job. Every *fascista* in the Service has jumped two grades and you are eating lobster in Venice. It can get more serious?'

'I want to see you.'

'I'm at home all the time–midnight to midnight.'

'Listen, please!'

'No! You listen. You sold out, little brother! You took a long leave and a lush sinecure and now you're on the payroll of private industry. You're a *stronzo*, Matucci. The worst I've ever known.'

'Where did you hear all this?'

'Does it matter?'

'Yes, it does. And if you hang up, Steffi, I'll spit on your grave. Now tell me!'

'I heard it from the great talking horse himself, our dear Director, on the day he retired me. I quote: "You are still active, Stefanelli. Why don't you emulate your colleague, Matucci, and direct your talents, your very considerable talents, to civilian occupation." I still quote: "The rewards are very great, as Matucci will tell you. We had our disagreements, but we were able to resolve them, and I venture to suggest that Matucci will end a very rich man." End of quote. Do you want to hear any more?'

'No, thanks. Did you get my telegram?'

'I got it.'

'But you didn't believe it?'

'No.'

'Will you do me one favour?'

'Flowers for your funeral maybe.'

'Save your money. It could be sooner than you think. Go talk to Raquela Rabin instead. Ask her what we discussed the day I went to see her.'

'And then?'

'I'll call once more. Then, if you want, you can call me all the names in the book. Goodnight, Steffi.'

After that I went upstairs to talk to Bruno Manzini. I was surprised to find that the Director was still with him; but the atmosphere had changed. They were tense with me and tense with each other. Manzini plunged straight into interrogation.

'Tell us what happened, Matucci.'

I told them. I drew a map on the hotel notepaper to make it clear. I made it even clearer that someone had set me up like a clay pigeon and I wasn't very happy about it. Manzini cut me off in the middle of this theme and said, flatly:

'I have already told your Director what happened at the lodge.'

'I see.'

'And I have conveyed to him your suspicion that both these attempts were officially inspired.'

'And I am shocked at the suggestion, Matucci.' He looked it, too. For the first time I caught a hint of unease under his sardonic mask. 'Did you really believe that, after we had settled an amicable arrangement, after I had agreed to your return to Italy and your private employment with my old friend, I would put out a contract for your life?'

'It had to be you or Leporello. You were kept constantly informed by the Cavaliere. You knew I had an appointment at his lodge. You knew I was coming to dinner here tonight. Knowing the trade as we both do, it's not too illogical is it?'

'From my point of view, Matucci, it's madness. I would stamp you out with no compunction at all if I had to; but, as things are, I have a vested interest in keeping you alive.'

'I will not work with fools,' said Bruno Manzini flatly. 'I will not tolerate threats against my staff. You will talk sense into that upstart Leporello.'

'Please!' said the Director softly. 'Please, Bruno. We're too old for tantrums. I will deal with it. . . . Sleep well, Matucci.'

When he had gone, Bruno Manzini lay back in his chair and surveyed me with ironic amusement.

'Well, my Dante, what did you make of that?'

'I think he's telling the truth.'

'I know he is. And I know he's worried. If he can't control Leporello now, he'll never be able to do it afterwards. . . . All profit, my Dante! When thieves fall out it's gold in the pockets of the godly.'

I laughed. What else could I do? I laughed until tears ran down my cheeks; while the old man sat chuckling in his chair like a spider who had just made a meal of a gad-fly.

There were lions at the gates, twin beasts of lichened stone, supporting beneath their upraised paws an illegible escutcheon. The gates were of black iron, scrolled and curlicued, twice the height of a man. The gate-keeper was a dwarfish manikin who came running to the door of the car to greet his master with a simian chatter of dialect. Beyond the gate a gravelled drive wound through an avenue of cypresses and opened into a geometer's fantasy of flowerbeds and miniature hedgerows, beyond which a stairway of white marble led to the villa, a small Palladian jewel, light and beautiful even under the grey sky and the steady drenching rain.

This was Pedognana, country seat of the Cavaliere Bruno Manzini, and he displayed it to me with child-like pride:

'Home, my Dante! The one place in all the world where I am truly myself. My mother bought it, in the good years, and sold it in the bad ones. When I made my first real money, I bought it again, and I have held it ever since. The arms over the gate are the ones my mother invented for herself. You can still make out the Salamander if you look closely enough. I defaced it in the partisan days, because this was my headquarters until the Germans arrested me and shoved me into gaol. There's everything here: orchards, farmland, mulberries for the silkworms, rice on the river flats, grapes and olives on the foothills. Something of the old life, too, as you will see for yourself. Come inside. . . .'

In the pillared entrance, under a dome resplendent with Tiepolo fantasies, the household was assembled: Gualtiero, the factor, six feet tall and solid as an oak-tree; Lanfranco, major-domo of the villa; Don Egidio, chaplain to the estate; Donna Edda, the housekeeper, a stout country-apple woman, full of flounce and fluster; and with them, a small hierarchy of maids, gardeners and grooms. Manzini saluted them all by name, and I had perforce to repeat the salutation, so that, by the time the ceremony was over, I was convinced that I had been translated into the nineteenth century.

The greetings over, I was consigned to the care of Donna Edda, who bustled me upstairs with such a fervour of welcome that I felt giddy. The splendour of the room overwhelmed me—the canopied bed, the vast buhl desk, the fire blazing behind the brass screen, the bookcase that climbed to the ceiling, full of leather-bound tomes. Suddenly, it was all too much; and I wondered irrationally whether this were not a tactic: to stifle me with grandeur and bind me like another serf to his service. However, he put himself at pains to explain himself and the scope of his design.

'. . . Try to understand, Dante Alighieri. I am a free man. I understand liberty in the Anglo-Saxon way, because my mother was a Scot and a free woman in her own right. She fought Pantaleone to establish an estate for me and he did it. She made a long nose at society; but she never complained when society looked down its nose at her. But freedom like this is a rare state of mind. People have to grow to it, be educated to it. And this country is still only half-educated, in parts not educated at all. Many prefer tyranny to freedom, because tyrants can be corrupted while liberty demands a drastic innocence, a daily battle like that of Sant' Antonio with the demons. . . . I am not innocent; neither are you; but we don't want to be whores all our lives. Remember Raquela Rabin? . . . Well, that's a story that says it all. We were lovers, as you know. We parted . . . each for the same reason. I bowed to social pressures. She found herself a more powerful protector—a vice-President of the Jewish Council, a man high in Fascist affairs. You are too young to remember, Dante Alighieri, but even the Jews believed in the *Duce* and trusted till the last that he would save them from the German holocausts. . . . In the end, we knew that we had both betrayed ourselves. Raquela went to Auschwitz—a willing victim. I went underground to fight. . . . Remember the Bible? "A man's enemies shall be those of his own household." It is like that still. So, I had to test you. I will go on testing you; because you have not yet been hung by the thumbs or been shocked with electrodes clipped to your testicles. . . . Forgive me. I am too vehement. I am still not as wise as I should like to be. . . .'

Later that evening, with maps and documents spread all over the table, we sketched the first plan of campaign. Once again I marvelled that so old a man could be so precise and ruthless in his designs.

'State the purpose of the exercise, Colonel.'

'To convict Major-General Leporello of conspiracy to murder Avvocato Bandinelli and Agent Calvi. To discredit the Director by showing him joined in the conspiracy.'

'And where do you begin?'

'With three facts: Leporello knew the location of the Pantaleone papers and my arrangements to guard them; his aide, Captain Roditi, appeared on Ponza with orders to claim the other documents; later, the Director joined Leporello in a plot to establish military rule.'

'Given those facts, where do you probe first?'

'At the weakest point. Captain Roditi.'

'Next?'

'Leporello.'

'Why not the Director? You know him better.'

'As he stands, he's almost impregnable. He can justify any action by the secret needs of the Service.'

'Come back to Leporello, then.'

'I've never seen his dossier. We can build one easily enough, but it will take time. Apart from that, we have two versions of him: his own and the Director's.'

'Quotes?'

'The Director: "A patriot, a devout Catholic, a Christian Democrat and financially independent. Doubt he could be bought or frightened."'

'His own?'

'Verbatim quote . . . "My loyalties were to the Crown. I never changed them–even when it might have been convenient to do so. I disliked the Fascists. I loathed the Germans; but even for that I could not make myself a turncoat soldier. Today I am able to be honest and proud." Quote ends.'

'*Dio mio*! A resolute virgin! I don't believe it.'

'Neither do I. What is your impression of him?'

'Cold, ambitious, more than a little paranoid. But put him on that balcony in the Piazza Venezia and many people would go mad for him. I'd like to examine him in social circumstances. I'll invite him to a suitable gathering in Milan. He's based there, so that's easy. He'll bring his aide, so that should give you a starting point, too. We'd better install you in the apartment as soon as possible. Which raises another question, Dante *mio*, . . . women!'

'Oh?'

'How do you propose to arrange yourself, for business and pleasure?'

'I'm organized for both.'

'I believe you. However, I suggest you take an interest in the marriage market as well.'

'You must be joking!'

'On the contrary. You're a bachelor, a full Colonel, with interesting prospects. So, you're a good candidate for any woman's guest list. Use that, my friend, especially here in the North where money talks and those who have it gossip like nuns. Now . . . since gossip is important, let's discuss your cover-story. You are appointed as my personal adviser on all aspects of industrial security. You enter at managerial level. You have free access to all plants and offices. You will be supplied with a company credit card and a car for your personal use. You will make as many friends as you can inside my companies and you will allay as far as possible any jealousies that may arise out of your privileged position. When I am absent from the country, as I am frequently, you will work at your own discretion and report to me in a code which I shall supply to you. My secretary will be instructed to inform you of my movements. If she does not know them–and they are sometimes secret–I shall inform you in advance. My banker arrives at ten tomorrow morning to open your account and establish a credit rating backed by me. Now, what else is on the list?'

'Personnel.'

'Employ whomever you wish. But check with me before you use any of my staff. Next?'

'You've written here: "The Church".'

'Oh yes. This is a delicate one, Matucci. Mother Church is up to her neck in Italian politics. We know that. She's a very old and very shrewd lady, and she has friends to the Left and Right as well as in the centre. Sometimes it's hard to distinguish them, because the cassock makes all priests look alike and everybody in the Vatican uses the same language—with very subtle overtones that make all the difference to the meaning. If you find you're treading on a cassock, tread lightly until you know who's wearing it. . . . Are you religious, by the way?'

'I was baptized, communicated and confirmed and the good brothers beat me into unbelief. Why the question?'

'It helps to know what a man thinks about dying—his own or another's.'

'I think about it as little as possible. I find that helps. You?'

'I'm old. It makes a difference.'

'I see that it might.'

'I've lived the discord, but I think I hear a harmony. I hear it plainest in the old words and the old signs of grace. Maybe it's an illusion, but I'd rather die with it than without it. . . . Still, each to his own. My God! I really must get you to a good tailor. That suit was cut by a pork-butcher.'

In the morning, the banker came, and in the afternoon, whirled from Milan, a tailor, who measured me for more clothes than my father had worn in a lifetime. In between, and late into the dusk, I played my memory game on the microfilms and sweated over the mountain of material from the data-bank. In the evening, with an odd feeling of trepidation, I called Stefanelli. This time, he was his old truculent self:

'So, I apologize Matucci; then what?'

'Then I say, don't mention it.'

'Then what?'

'Then I say, how would you like to work for me. Good salary, expenses, a little travel.'

'What sort of work?'

'Now, Steffi, if I were fool enough to tell you on an open line, you would be a fool to work for me.'

'Oh? That sort of work.'

'Yes, Steffi. What do you say?'

'I'll have to ask my wife.'

'You're a millstone round her neck and you know it. She can't wait to get you out of the house.'

'Now, that's a great truth, little brother. How soon?'

'A week. Ten days at most.'

'How long?'

'No idea.'

'How much?'

'Your Service salary.'

'You've bought me.'

'Good. I'll be in touch soon. And, Steffi, please. . . .'

'I know. Don't tell me. Once there were three wise monkeys. . . .'

'Steffi, you're a jewel.'

'I am also stark raving mad. But I'll be madder still if I stay in this house too long.'

'One more thing. Do I have any friends left?'

'Still a few. . . . Need something?'

'Yes. Roditi, Matteo, Captain of Carabinieri, aide to Major-General Leporello. Any background you can get.'

'Should be easy enough.'

'Thanks, Steffi. Soon, eh?'

'Shalom. . . .'

I felt happier after that. I sat down and typed a short note to Lili, who was staying at a small hotel in the Bernese Oberland. The note would be carried across the border by a courier and posted inside Switzerland. There is no official censorship of mails in Italy, but letters do get opened and a lot of private information finds its way into the files. I could not say very much because Lili might still be under surveillance and someone just might go through her things. And it's hard to be very passionate when you sign a letter 'Uncle Pavel'. Still she would know I was well and she would be able to answer through the accommodation address in Chiasso, provided by Manzini.

For the next week, I worked like a galley slave on notes and mnemonics, daily conferences with Manzini, broken only by sessions with the tailor who arrived every two days with a new batch of fittings, and who by some miracle of Italian industry would have everything ready for delivery the day I took possession of the apartment. I was inclined to be flippant about the tailor; but Manzini became quite testy and read me a five-minute lecture on the subject.   .

'This isn't a joke, Matucci. And don't let that Tuscan snobbery of yours cloud your judgment. We're talking about some of the most potent people in the world today—the image-makers, the dream merchants, the illusionists. Put eight hundred million people in black button-up tunics and what have you got—Mao's China, and the whole world goggle-eyed at the wonder of it. I make textiles, Matucci, and I know what the fashion business means. . . . Tourism is our second most important industry—and if you took the bikini off the travel posters, it would slump by half overnight. Have you read that batch of cuttings I put on your desk this morning?'

'Not yet. Why?'

'Because the image-makers are working on Leporello right at this moment. There are two picture stories, four excerpts from recent speeches on law and order, and twenty-three other references on various themes. It's the beginning of a campaign, Matucci. They're testing the market before they strike a line. There's a big agency behind it—Publitalia—and if you check your notes you'll find the name of the man who owns it. . . . Now, for God's sake, stop being coy and let's attend to business!'

He was a rough old pirate; but I was beginning to love him. He had so much talent, so much zest and drive that he made me feel sometimes like a country clod. No detail was too small for his attention; the names I should use on my false papers, the decoration of the apartment in Milan, the clubs at which he might present me, whether I should play tennis or take a few lessons in golf, and even the make of car I should drive. He instructed me in the workings of the bourse, so that I could talk stocks and bonds intelligently. He sketched the histories of the great families, the Torlonia, the Pallavicini, the Doria, the Orsini. He read me the careers of the modern merchant adventurers and the follies of their wives and offspring. He showed me where the American money was, and the German and the Swiss, and how the oil war was fought, and how the tentacles of the Honourable Society reached even into the North. Over and over again, he repeated the same lesson:

'. . . Think always in the frame of history, Dante. It takes more than a hundred and fifty years to build a nation and a national consciousness. Once Mussolini was toppled, we were back to the days of the warring dukedoms. Even the Marxists are split. Now we are looking for another point of focus; and that's the appeal of the new Fascism. What people don't see is that we have to grow out of disunity, not be bludgeoned out of it, by new blackshirts. If they try it . . . God! I hate to think of the consequences . . .!'

Then, abruptly, as always, he dropped the subject and took me out on a tour of the estate, reminiscing all the while about his youth and his relations with his father.

'. . . He was the perfect mirror of his time, Dante; an unblushing pragmatist who was convinced that money and a title could command anything, even immortality. He believed in God but found Him agreeably absent from most human transactions. He believed in the Church, as one of the more stable and useful human institutions. He believed in marriage as a social contract, but not as a solace for a normal man's desires. Diplomacy was an art for gentlemen, but politics was a trade for arrivistes and rogues. He was happy to profit from it but he refused to engage himself in it, being content with a public affirmation of loyalty to the Crown and a private manipulation of conflicting parties to the sole and singular interest of Pantaleone. . . .

'I see you smile, my friend. You're right. I'm very like him. He was a good business man, too. He invested in steel and electricity and shipbuilding and insurance and banks, and bought no stock at all in colonial adventures. As I told you, my mother fought him to make a settlement on me, and that was the foundation of what I have today. After that first meeting on the Pincio, he began to take an interest in me, and I accepted him as the best and most exciting of all my uncles. . . .

'Looking back now, I see his intentions very clearly. He wanted to get me out of the harem atmosphere of my mother's house and thrust me into a world of men. It was a wonderful world then, Matucci, especially if you didn't see the underside of it—and I was spared that for many years. Once each week, I would go to the *salle d'armes*, where Pantaleone practised sabre and épée with the master, Carducci. Sometimes, at first light, we would drive out along the Appia Antica to the stud at Tor Carbone where he bred racehorses from British and Irish stock. We would watch the morning gallops, make the rounds of the stables and then sit down to breakfast in the kitchen of the old farmhouse with the stud-master and the trainer. . . .

'On other days he would take me to visit the craftsmen who flourished under his patronage and that of his wealthy friends. They were wonderful men, Dante, all gone now. There was Ascoli, the antiquarian, a wizened old gnome who could take a handful of shards and rebuild them into an Etruscan urn, and read you a whole history from it. There was Haro, the Spaniard, a gunsmith who lived over on the Prati and whom even the British ranked with their own masters. He had a pistol range in his cellar and pigeon-traps and a line of butts in the fields where his gentlemen clients could test their skill. That was where I first learned to handle a gun and to care for it, too. . . . Eh, memory is a treacherous gift!'

'You look troubled. Something bothering you?'

'I've just recalled something. A lesson Pantaleone taught me. I hated him for it. Now—God knows why—it makes me want to weep.'

'Do you want to talk about it?'

'Why not? It's very short. One day at the gallops, I slipped and fell in the mud. A stable-boy laughed and I flew at him, clawing and punching and screaming in Romanaccio. Pantaleone hauled me away and cuffed me till my ears sang, and I was sobbing with pain. He was quite cold about it, brutal and deliberate. Then he told me: "You will never do that again. The boy did you no harm. You looked a fool and he laughed. He could not hit back because he is a poor peasant who depends on me for work. You are supposed to be a gentleman. You acted like an animal out of control. You will go now and apologize." I refused. He gave me a look of such contempt that I felt crushed. Then he walked away and left me. Later, I did apologize, but by then he was gone and the farm people had to drive me back to Rome in a wine-cart. I didn't see him for months afterwards. I thought he had rejected me because of my disobedience. I did not know until long afterwards that his wife had given him a legitimate son, and that I had been relegated to the shadows. . . . That's all.'

'Not quite all, I think.'

'What do you mean?'

'The lesson wasn't lost. I was talking to Gualtiero, your factor. He told me you've turned this place into a co-operative, so that your people can have tenure after your death.'

'Oh, that! Well, it's something, I suppose. I'm bowing to social necessity. Eh! Let's change the subject. Look at those blossoms, Dante. The whole hillside is in flower. You'll be gone soon. But I want you to know that you are welcome here whenever you choose to come. You're good for me.'

'And you for me, Bruno. I'll be sorry to leave this place.'

'Have you no land of your own?'

'None.'

'Then buy yourself a plot, however small. Plough and plant and love it a little. Every man needs one earth he can call his own.'

'Perhaps, after this is over. . . .'

The rest of the thought remained unspoken; but we both understood the big perhaps. If things went wrong, I should have all the earth I needed: two metres long, a metre and a half deep—a grave in the Campo Santo.

The apartment in Milan was the penthouse of a new block, built by Manzini, not far from the centre of the city. I had two bedrooms, two bathrooms, an American-style kitchen, a large salon, a dining-room and a study, as well as separate quarters for two servants. There was a terrace on three sides, planted with shrubs and spring flowers in urns. The only access was by private elevator whose entrance and interior could be scanned by closed-circuit televison from inside the apartment. The servants had one key to the elevator. I had another. The doors of the apartment were equipped with double locks and chain-bolts and the windows with steel shutters. There were two independent alarm systems, each connected by telephone circuit to the headquarters of the Mobile Squadron.

Everything in the place was new and designed for a rich and sociable bachelor: deep leather furniture, a well-stocked bar, a high-fidelity system, racks of records, a television set, bright modern canvases, books, new and old, for lonely nights. There was a typewriter, a Xerox copier, a tape machine, boxed notepaper with my name on it, two sets of visiting cards, one for civilian, the other for military occasions. Behind the bookshelves, concealed by a false panel, was a modern safe with an electronic locking device and an alarm connected to the central system. Even the telephone index on my desk was typed up to date with all the numbers I might need within Manzini's organization and with the addresses of tradesmen, doctor and dentist. Manzini made me free of it all with a smile of satisfaction.

'There, my dear Dante. All yours. Now you have nothing to do but to work and divert yourself profitably. Let me introduce you to the servants.'

There were two of them, twin brothers from Sardinia, small dark men, taciturn and dignified as grandees. They were named Pietro and Paolo, so that they could share the same feast-day. Pietro was cook and butler. Paolo was houseman and valet. There was always one of them on duty night and day. They had served Manzini for ten years, and, if first impressions meant anything, they would keep me like a filmstar. Within ten minutes of my arrival, my suits were ranged in the closet, my toilet things laid out, my soiled clothes whisked out of sight. They came from Nuoro, Manzini told me, and they had served a prison term for banditry. He had hired them for a season on his yacht and then offered them a permanence. They were fiercely loyal and so discreet that they would not give the time of day to a stranger.

We toasted the enterprise and blessed the house with a glass of champagne and then, before he left, Manzini did a touching thing. He put his hands on my shoulders and embraced me, cheek to cheek, as if we were brothers. Then he loosened his tie and took from round his neck a thin gold chain with a medallion. He slipped it over my head and said, quietly:

'It's a Saint Christopher. I had him all through the war. You don't have to believe. Just wear him for me, eh?'

An instant later he was his old ironic self, with a wave and a gibe as he walked out the door.

'Let's have some style now, Danto Alighieri. *Fregiamo i non-credenti!* Let's bugger the ungodly. Good luck!'

It was the first obscenity I had ever heard him use; but somehow it gave me courage and the will to be up and doing. I telephoned Steffi and told him to heave his backside out of the chair and get himself to Milan as soon as possible. He told me he had managed to pull a file on Captain Matteo Roditi, but there was nothing in it worth a second thought. Allora! I would have to start digging for myself.

There is a club in Milan called the Duca di Gallodoro. It was founded by an Englishman who sold it, under pressure, to some Milanese bandits and then, I am told, married an American widow and went to live in Boston. I never bothered to check the story; but I did use the club whenever I came to Milan, because it was one of the few surviving places where you could eat reasonably well, dance in comfort and not be beaten into insensibility by shouting oafs with a million-watt amplifier. The drinks were honest, the girls better than average, and the prices high enough to discourage the sweat-shirt brigade. It was also close enough to headquarters for the officers of the Carabinieri to drop in for a drink and see the kind of citizens they were paid to protect. I decided to go there, alone for once, so that I could drift and gossip and make my escape before I got bored or the girls got too eager.

It was about ten-thirty, when I arrived. The restaurant was full but the bar was slack, so I perched myself in my favourite corner and made small-talk with Gianni, the barman, who knew everybody and told everything in a thick Genovese accent. He was kind enough to notice my new clothes and pay me what he thought was a compliment.

'Eh! Beautiful! English cloth, virgin lambswool. And the cut—perfect! What is this, Colonel—a legacy or a rich widow?'

'My life's savings, Gianni, I'm on leave. I thought I owed myself a present. What's going on in town?'

'The same, only more so. Strikes every third day. Students marching. Police on every street corner. Takings are down, too. Twenty per cent last week. People are scared. They're buttoning their pockets and staying home to watch television. All this violence! There was another smash and grab raid this afternoon. Fabbri, the jeweller. Broad daylight and they got clean away. . . . Maybe we need a new *Duce* to pull things into line.'

'Maybe.'

'This new fellow's shaking things up though. What's his name? Lep-something. That's it—Leporello. I hear your boys talking about him. They say he doesn't care how many heads get broken, so long as we have a quiet city. And he's right! He doesn't sit on his backside either. He's out and about every night with the patrols. They tell me he's training new riot squads, like the French have. You know, slam-bam, clear the streets and no questions asked. You must know him, though. Big fellow. Looks like a German. The boys call him old Iron-jaw.'

'Good name. Do you know any of his staff?'

'Sure. Some of them come in here. Never on duty, though. He's stopped all that. One offence and out. That's the rule now they tell me. He even wants to know the kind of women they hang around with. Ask some of the girls. They'll tell you. . . . Hullo, isn't this a friend of yours?'

He sidled up to the bar, all two metres and a hundred and twenty kilograms of him: Giorgione, Big George, Major Marinello, on the official lists of the Corps. He looked like a great spaniel with sad eyes and dewlaps; but when he saw me, he brightened a little and raised a big fist in greeting.

'Hello, Matucci. Good to see you.'

'You too, Giorgione.'

'What are you doing in this town?'

'I'm on leave.'

'Chasing a woman, I'll bet.'

'Winding up to it. Let me buy you a drink.'

'Thanks, I need it. Old Iron-jaw's been snapping at my heels all day.'

'Big changes, eh?'

'Changes? God! He's ramming the whole United Nations down our necks. How the Greeks do it and the French and the Brazilians and the British and the Japanese. . . . *Salute!*'

'Chin-chin!'

'I tell you, Matucci, you should be glad you're seconded. This Leporello is a one-hundred-per-cent armour-plated bastard. And you should see the types he's getting around him. *Mamma mia!* He's bringing in brains, he says, computer boys and statisticians and, God help me, psychiatrists even! But that's not the end of it. He's building up a little private group of musclemen, for special duties! Something funny's going on. I wish I knew what it was. . . . He's got that Roditi fellow running round like a fart in a bottle. Do you know him?'

'I've met him. I don't know him.'

'You haven't lost anything. He's a real weird one. . . . God, I'm tired.'

'Have another drink.'

'Thanks.'

'How do you mean, weird?'

'Oh, you know: big front, big secrets, the General presents his compliments, sir . . . that sort of stuff. No friends, except among the new bunch. I wouldn't trust him very far.'

'Does he ever come here?'

'No, no! This is girl-territory, Matucci. You know that. I think our friend Roditi sits down to pee.'

'Any proof?'

'Proof? Hell, no! I'm running so fast these days, I can't tell whether I'm married or single.'

'Is Leporello that way, too?'

'I wouldn't say so. He's married, got two kids. Goes to lunch with the Cardinal Archbishop. Very proper!'

'Why Roditi then, and the other odd bunch?'

'I don't know. I think he just likes the idea of the elite guard and all that stuff. . . . Say, what's your interest anyway? You've got a nice sweet job with SID; why should you care what happens to us poor sweats? Hey, wait a minute. . . .' He set down his glass and swivelled himself round to face me. 'Come on, Matucci, give, eh?'

'How would you like to take a walk, Giorgione?'

'Where?'

'My place. It's quiet and the drinks are free. Come on, it's only half a dozen blocks; then you can put your feet up.'

'Well, all right. But don't think I'm letting you off the hook, Matucci. I want to know. . . .'

'Shup up, or I'll make you pay for the drinks.'

The walk gave me time to think. For all his vast bulk and his shambling ways, Giorgione was as cunning as a badger. He would never make promotion, but he was one of the mainstays of the division that dealt with fraud and corrupt practices. If I wanted his help, I had to give him enough of the truth to keep him happy and discreet. Strangely enough, the apartment helped. He smelt money and he smelt power and he had a healthy respect for both. Pietro helped, too. His cool wooden-faced service would have cowed a Cardinal. So, when I judged Giorgione ready and relaxed, I gave him the story.

'Facts for the record, Giorgione. You can tell these to the street-cleaner, if you like. I'm on leave. Four months. I'm working, all above board, for a big company, as security adviser. This apartment goes with the job. Everything else is off the record—and I mean so far off you can't see it with a telescope.'

'Listen, Matucci, I didn't mean to. . . .'

'I know you didn't, Giorgione; and you may be able to help me. First, I'm still with SID, active, you understand. All this is a cover; and I don't want the boys wandering up for a drink or a visit of inspection.'

'Understood.'

'Second. I'm on a job I can't tell you about. Maximum security and dangerous. That you don't even guess at. Check?'

'Check.'

'Third. We're interested in Roditi, too. I've been asked to check him out while I'm here and to do it without upsetting General Leporello. If he is a *finocchio*, we don't want him in a sensitive post. If he's a disruptive influence, that's another good reason for moving him out. So, I have to move carefully; but because of this other business, I can't waste time. If you can help me, fine! If not, there's no harm done, provided you sit quiet, as I know you will. That's the story, Giorgione. . . .'

'Well, thanks for telling me. I appreciate it. What do you want to know about this fellow?'

'The full sheet, Giorgione. Or as much of it as you can get.'

'You know I can't help you with eyewitness material. I'm too big and conspicuous.'

'You tell me where and when. I'll arrange the rest of it. Two main points: what's his relationship with Leporello, and what, if anything, does he have to do with the musclemen? Any immediate thoughts?'

'Some, yes. Roditi's a bit of a muscle-man himself. Cheer leader to the health and physical fitness squad. Works out every day in the gymnasium—weight-lifting, judo, karate. Anything that's going, he's in it. Pistol shoots, automatic weapons training. . . . How he gets time for it all, I don't know. Then he's doing some kind of recruiting job round the country, inside the Corps that is. From what I hear they're setting up some kind of commando group. It sounds like that French lot—what were they called?'

'The Barbouzes?'

'That's it. Real thugs from what I hear.'

'Where do they train?'

'Oh, that's one of the big secrets. Nobody seems to know and the boys themselves won't talk. Still, I'll smell around a bit and let you know.'

'Where does Roditi live?'

'I don't know that either, but it must be on file. I'll get Rita to dig it out. You remember Rita, don't you? Dark, gypsy type. Last time you were here, you and she. . . .'

'Let's not go into that, Giorgione. And for God's sake, don't tell her I'm in town. . . . Now, you think Roditi's a *finocchio*. Any evidence?'

'Well, no. But no girl-friends and all this body-building stuff. It points that way doesn't it?'

'It might. Any boy-friends at headquarters?'

'No. The women watch him like vixens at mating time. There are half a dozen who'd love to give him a tumble; but they haven't noticed anything.'

'How does Leporello treat him?'

'Oh, very formally, but—how shall I say it?—very much like a man of confidence. You know the sort of thing . . . "If you need any further direction, Captain Roditi will make himself available . . . Captain Roditi will call you to arrange a conference . . ." I know he visits Leporello's home.'

'Where's that?'

'On the road to Linate airport. Big villa with a high stone wall.'

'Does Leporello have any women working in his office?'

'Three. A senior secretary and two typists. Nothing for you there, Matucci. The secretary's a dragon and the two juniors are straight from the nunnery.'

'What about Leporello's wife?'

'Never seen her. I don't think she's ever come to headquarters. If she had, I'm sure we'd have heard of it.'

'When he made this study trip, did his wife travel with him?'

'No. . . . But Roditi did, by God! Yes he did.'

'It doesn't prove anything, Giorgione.'

'You're right. It doesn't.'

'What's the general feeling in the Corps about Leporello?'

'Well . . . I know I was sounding off about him at the bar. He is a bastard. He drives us like a slave-master. And it's easier to get milk from a chicken than it is to wring a word of praise out of him. . . . But he is good. He's very good. And a lot of the things he's done are real improvements. How do we feel about him? You know the Service, Matucci. You can cut it like a deck of cards. There's the big middle group who do their job and don't ask questions, and gripe about everything just to affirm their rights. There's the bottom group that I call the earth-brothers. They serve and serve willingly in country posts and small communes and outlying provinces. They're pretty good guardians of the peace. They're close to the people and, all in all, sympathetic with them. Then you've got the top group, the hard-nose boys, everything by the book, we serve the State, and it's three years' hard labour if you poke us in the nose when you're drunk. They like Leporello. The middle group are uneasy about him. The earth-brothers loathe him. Not always for the right reason, mark you, because some of them can be pretty sloppy as you know. But instinctively—did I say that right? I'm a little fuzzy—instinctively they mistrust him.'

'What about you, Giorgione?'

'Me? I just hate his tripes. But that's natural, too. I'm good enough at my job; but look at me! I'm no great ornament to the Service. And Leporello makes me feel it all the time. God! It's late! My wife will kill me! How soon do you want this stuff?'

'Yesterday, if possible.'

'How do I get it to you?'

'Phone me here. If I'm out, leave a message with the servants. Name a place and time and I'll meet you, or call you back if I can't make it. Thanks, Giorgione.'

'Don't mention it. Good to see you again. Oh, Matucci, if you change your mind about Rita . . .?'

'Do you think she fits this place, Giorgione?'

'Come to think of it, not quite. . . . Still, she's a nice girl. Take care now. There aren't too many of us good ones left.'

He shambled out, a great, kindly freak of a man who was beginning to find his Gulliver's world too complicated to live in. He left me both pleased and worried. Roditi, my first quarry, was an unpopular type with a dubious reputation. Leporello was a hard-nose with an unhappy staff. Therefore, the preliminary investigation could move quickly, and there would be plenty of enthusiastic helpers to dig up the dirt. On the other hand, the news about the new riot squads was very disquieting. It was a regressive step, a new threat to privacy and personal rights. It argued an official sanction for intimidation and police brutality.

Italian law was, in any case, heavily loaded in favour of the State and against the individual. Many of the old Fascist enactments were still on the books and could be invoked at will. We had never, God knows why, adopted the British system of *habeas corpus*. A man could be held almost indefinitely on a trumped-up charge; and a complaisant magistrate could delay inquiries and shuffle his documents till doomsday. Our judiciary was overworked, our documentation systems were hopelessly outdated. Our interrogation methods were brutal at the best of times, and our prison system a public shame. To compound all this, with an open or tacit brief of terror, and a deliberate exploitation of the Mediterranean vice of cruelty, was a leap back into the dark ages. I understood Manzini's anxious conviction that the twenty-third hour was past and the minute hand was climbing already to midnight.

I was restless now, itchy for company and action, so I flipped through my pocket-book in search of another contact among the night-owls. I settled on Patrizia Pompa, a Lesbian lady of singular beauty and metallic charm, who made a handsome living decorating the apartments of rich Milanese. To my certain knowledge, Patrizia never went to bed before three in the morning. In my salad days, I had tried to get her there, and I was raw from the experience for a long time afterwards. However, we understood each other in the end, and we had managed to maintain over the years a prickly kind of friendship. I called her. She answered in that deep, husky voice that promised all sorts of wild experience. She sounded faintly hostile.

'Who the hell is this?'

'Dante Alighieri Matucci, sweetheart. Did I interrupt something?'

'Nothing important. What do you want at this hour?'

'Information—and a little company.'

'You can have mine if you bring a bottle of whisky. . . . What sort of information?'

'Clubs for the gay boys. Know any?'

'A couple. Why?'

'I'm looking for a man.'

'I didn't think you'd be looking for a girl, lover. What sort of answer is that?'

'He's a nasty man. I think he killed a friend of mine.'

'Oh! Then try the Pavone and the Alcibiade. They're both open till four in the morning.'

'Do they admit girls?'

'Only nice girls, lover—like me.'

'Care to come along and hold my hand?'

'Why not? I am just bored enough to enjoy the sight of Matucci among the fennel-flowers.'

'You've got a dirty mind, sweetheart.'

'Don't say no till you've tried it, lover. I'll be ready in twenty minutes. Bring transport, eh? Where are you staying, by the way?'

'In a convent. Where else? See you!'

I picked her up in my own car, a red Mercedes sports model. She was dressed for the fray in a man-tailored suit with a white shirt and a flowing black cravat. When she saw my new rig, she chuckled.

'My God, Matucci, I believe you have passed over. You didn't do all this on a Colonel's salary. Who's keeping you?'

'Sweetheart, you embarrass me.'

'You'll be more embarrassed where you're going. Were you serious about . . .?'

'Yes, I was. So listen, darling, and get the story straight. I'm an old friend and you're showing me the town.'

'Suppose we meet someone you know.'

'Same story. And if you get any telephone calls afterwards, you stick to it. Don't play funny games. It could be dangerous.'

'With a friend like you, Matucci, I need extra life-insurance.'

'I'm the best insurance you've got, sweetheart. Who's going to touch you with a handsome youth like me around?'

It was a bad joke, and it got worse when we entered the Pavone—a smoky cellar-dive near the Duomo. The bouncers at the door set the tone of the place: two muscle-bound Adonises from the local athletic club, with tight jeans and studded belts and high-necked sweaters. They made a couple of cute remarks, collected four thousand lire by way of entertainment tax, and bowed us through. Inside there was more of the same, big boys and little boys, all in jeans and jumpers, and not a woman in sight. There was a fug you could cut with a knife, and just to help the atmosphere, a stuffed peacock with moulting tail-feathers, preening himself on a pedestal in the centre of the room. There was a piano-player and a pockmarked youth with an electric guitar pounding out a steady rock-beat and the talk was a low secretive chatter that stopped dead as we entered and made our way to the bar. Then there was a chorus of whistles and cat-calls, and Patrizia murmured in my ear:

'Somehow, lover, I think we've come to the wrong place.'

It was going to cost us two drinks anyway, so we ordered and sipped them slowly until the boys had finished their fun and settled back to their whispering. Then we turned to face the room and I peered through the murk to distinguish a familiar face. The barman tapped me on the shoulder with a soft, fat finger:

'Looking for someone, darling?'

'Yes, a friend.'

'What's he look like?'

'Big red-head with freckles. Looks like a German, but actually comes from Trento. Lovely boy. But I don't see him here.'

'Does he have a name?'

'He told me it was Matteo.'

'But not the rest of it.'

'No. . . .'

'You must miss him, darling.'

'I do.'

'How much do you miss him?'

I slid a ten-thousand-lire note across the counter and held it under my hand.

'That much . . . for a start.'

'Well, I think I've seen him in here a few times. Can't be sure, you know. There's a bunch that drops in every couple of weeks, three or four together. I never had much to do with them because they're too quiet . . . and they're interested in very rough trade. If I see him again, what would you like me to do?'

'Give me a call at this number.' I scribbled it on the back of a paper coaster and handed it to him. 'It's worth another ten if I make contact.'

'And when I ring, who do I ask for?'

'Just Dante. Like the poet, you know. My friend here is a poet. Aren't you, sweetheart?'

'I feel like a horse's arse,' said Patrizia, unhappily.

'You look like it too, darling,' said the barman, sweetly. 'Why don't you go where you belong and leave us girls to our knitting.'

The Alcibiade was a different proposition altogether, strictly plush, strictly for the carriage trade—and there was a great deal of it to be had, in both sexes. The place was designed in a complete circle, like the Pantheon, with a bar at one end of the diameter, and a curved stage at the other, and the tables ranged round a small dance floor at the centre. It was air-conditioned; which was a mercy, because there was a lot of smoking going on and not all of it tobacco. The decor was ingenious and furiously expensive. The walls were covered in black velvet, broken at regular intervals by illuminated niches in each of which was a white plaster figure, half-life and fully sexed, representing a classic male hero of antiquity. Woman was honoured only on the black dome, where a snow-white Leda was mounted by a very sinuous swan.

The clients were the most elegant bunch I had seen in a long time; mostly young, but with a sprinkling of grey-haired males and mannish dowagers, with short hair and long cigarette holders. This time our entrance attracted no attention at all. The stage was occupied by three youths in baggy gold pants and turned-up slippers. One of them was playing a sitar, the other was tootling soulfully on a pipe, while the third was executing some kind of slow dance which left me cold as Narcissus by his lily-pool.

The barman was a splendid boy, beautifully barbered and ineffably polite. The drinks cost an arm and a leg, but they were served in crystal goblets, with a fresh canapé to help the digestion. Patrizia purred with satisfaction.

'Lover, I'm glad you brought me. I think I've been out of circulation too long. If I strike it lucky, just pay the bill and leave me.'

'Anything you say, sweetheart.'

'Can you see your man?'

'Not yet. Wait till the act's over and the lights go up.'

We waited a small eternity before the last notes faded and the dancer sank like a tired petal to the floor, to a rather pallid applause. The lights were rather pallid, too, but they were bright enough to show me Captain Matteo Roditi, in a midnight blue jacket, seated with two other young men, at a table on the edge of the dance floor.

I turned back to the bar and whispered to Patrizia:

'I've seen him.'

'What do you want to do?'

'Talk to him . . . alone.'

'I'll wait for you.'

'Better you're not seen with me.'

'This is exciting.'

'It doesn't look it, but it's dangerous. Order another drink and make your own arrangements.'

I pressed some notes into her hand and then wandered down through the tables, like any other client surveying the local talent. Roditi and his friends were so busy with each other that they did not notice me until I stood over the table and offered my little greeting.

'Captain Roditi, isn't it?'

He didn't recognize me for a moment, then he leapt to his feet and stammered:

'Colonel Matucci! Forgive me, I didn't recognize you.'

'Relax, Captain, we're not on parade now.'

'What are you doing in Milan, sir?'

'Enjoying some leave.'

'Forgive me, but I heard you were retired from the Service.'

'It's under discussion. Nothing definite yet. I'm still on the active list. Won't you introduce me to your friends?'

'Oh, I'm sorry, sir. Franco Gozzoli, Giuseppe Balbo, Colonel Matucci.'

'Are you gentlemen in the Service, too?'

He was quick, but not quick enough, to intercept their swift looks of inquiry.

'No, sir, no. They're both in business here.'

'What sort of business?'

'Oh-er-architectural draughtsmen.'

'How very interesting. Please sit down, gentlemen. Do you come here often, Captain?'

'Occasionally. It's a change from the usual kind of club. You, sir?'

'Oh, I just dropped in for a drink–coasting you might say.'

'Indeed . . . ?' He reacted instantly to the familiar word, and a faint hint of conspiracy crept into his smile. 'Will you be staying long in Milan?'

'A few weeks, possibly. Why don't you come and have a drink with me one evening, Captain?'

'I'd like that, sir.'

'Good. I'll call you at headquarters. Please give my compliments to General Leporello. Tell him I hope to see him soon.'

'I'll do that, sir, with pleasure.'

'Goodnight, Roditi. Enjoy yourself.'

As I walked past the bar, I saw Patrizia Pompa deep in talk with a small doll-like blonde in a green pant-suit. She gave me a wink and a farewell twitch of the fingers. She didn't need me any more, she was back in circulation again.

It was three in the morning when I got back to the apartment. I was desperately tired; but I could not sleep until I had set down a summary of the evening's encounters. We were in profit on several heads. In Giorgione, I had a friend and a source of information. Roditi was vulnerable, by reason of his sexual interests. Leporello was unpopular with his staff, some of whom might be persuaded to inform against him. The debit column, however, was alarming. Leporello had in training an apparatus of terror which could operate at will inside or outside the law. Such a group attracted social delinquents and put enormous power into the hands of a political manipulator. If the manipulator achieved political success, the apparatus became an arm of government, self-perpetuating and self-justified. There was a debit against my personal account as well. If the murders in the Via Sicilia were the work of the apparatus, it would be difficult, if not impossible, to prove charges against Roditi and Leporello. If Leporello wanted me removed, he had a whole pack of well-trained bully-boys to stalk me into ambush.

It was a chill thought. It haunted me through a restless sleep, and was still with me when I woke, blear-eyed and irritable, at ten in the morning.

At midday, Steffi arrived, chirpy as a cricket. He brought me blessings from his wife, who, he claimed, was happy to be rid of him. He recited greetings from some of our colleagues in Rome and a litany of curses against the time-servers. He surveyed every inch of the apartment and concluded mournfully that only a whore could enjoy such luxury without a twinge of conscience. Purged at last of wisdom and bile, he listened in silence while I told him what had happened to me since our last meeting. Then, sober and subdued he gave me his own version of events in Rome:

'. . . We liberals are out of date, little brother. Every current flows against us. Every wind blows contrary. Just when we think we have a moment of quiet to water the flowers, the Arabs Hijack another airliner, or the Zionists knock off an agent, or some twenty-year-old idiots hold up a bank or the police fire on demonstrators in some depressed province. If it's not happening inside the country, it's just next door. Look, a simple thing! When I arrived at the airport this morning, the computer system had broken down. A little mechanical fault, but suddenly there was chaos. The booking clerks wouldn't handle the inquiries. The airline officials went into hiding. And five thousand passengers on domestic and international flights didn't know whether they were coming or going. We're not like the English. We don't form a queue and read *The Times*. We shout and scream just for the merry hell of it. But someone only had to scream too loud or jostle too hard this morning, and there could have been a riot. . . . For what? A blown fuse that cost maybe a hundred lire. . . . That's the terror of it, Matucci. Nobody blames the fuse. Everybody wants a scapegoat who can be kicked into a bloody mess because the plane's late. They're daubing slogans on the bridges of Rome now: "Death to the Fascists", "Down with the Marxists". And where I live, it's "Zionist pig!" . . . I wonder if you know what you're really fighting, my friend?'

'Do you?'

'Sometimes I wish I didn't. *Simia quam similis*. . . .'

'I don't know that one, Steffi.'

'The ape, the vilest of the beasts, how like to us! Cicero. . . . We haven't changed much since his time, have we?'

'No, except we've got computers to multiply the vileness. Steffi, understand something. This is a damn dangerous project. I don't want you too close to me. You work from the Europa Hotel. We meet in a variety of places.'

'What do you want me to do?'

'We're investigating murder. So, it's old-fashioned detective work, Steffi. On Leporello and Roditi first. I want to know what they eat for breakfast and what brand of toothpaste they use. If you've got any friendly colleagues at Milan Headquarters, use them; but for God's sake be careful.'

'I should give you the same advice, little brother. The Director doesn't love you any more.'

'But he has a vested interest in keeping me alive. His own words, Steffi!'

'He didn't tell you what the interest was, did he?'

'No.'

'So, let me give you more bad news. He has a man working full-time on your record.'

'Who told you this?'

'Rampolla. He was making a big joke of it. Some joke! You've sailed very close to the wind in your time, Matucci. You need a very sympathetic biographer to make you halfway respectable. At this moment, they're writing a Black Book on you.'

'I'm writing a Black Book of my own, Steffi.'

'The big question for the big money–who gets into print first? One more item. . . . Woodpecker has been under interrogation every day since you left Rome. He's sold out his whole network. And your girl-friend, Lili Anders, figures prominently in the transcript.'

'They can't touch her now. The Swiss don't extradite for political offences.'

'They do for criminal acts.'

'Oh, come on, Steffi. I know her dossier backwards. There's nothing like that against her.'

'There wasn't when you last looked at it. There may be now. If you're fond of the woman, it's a thing to think about. . . .'

'Steffi, you make me feel like Job on his dunghill.'

'So, bless the Lord for your afflictions, little brother, and pray loud and strong for His mercies. Also, don't underrate the Director. He wants you alive–but buried up to your neck in the same dunghill. . . . Do you have a drink in this bawdy-house?'

'For news like that, I should feed you cyanide.'

'Make it Scotch whisky and I'll give you a few good words for a change.'

'The words first, you old vulture.'

'Remember the letter-bomb that was posted in Lili Anders' flat?'

'Yes?'

'The police sent us a forensic report on it. The report came across my desk, together with a nice clear set of prints, matched from their files. I brought a copy with me, in case they might be useful.'

'And?'

'The prints belonged to Marco Vitucci, age twenty-eight, one-time steward with the Flotta Bernardo, wanted in Rome and Naples on several counts of larceny and robbery with violence.'

'Never heard of him.'

'Nor I. But it's a start–a link in the chain. The police are working actively to trace him. He is known to use two other names, for which he has false documents. The names are Turi Goldoni and Giuseppe Balbo. . . .'

'Say that last one again.'

'Giuseppe Balbo.'

'Steffi, you're a genius! You're a towering transcendental magician!'

'I know it; but since when have you discovered it?'

'Now . . . this minute! I told you I met Roditi last night at the Club Alcibiade. One of the boys with him was called Giuseppe Balbo.'

'If it's the same one, that's almost enough to nail Roditi as well.'

'Almost, but not quite. Not with the protection he's got. But it's a beautiful beginning and, since it's a police report, SID can't bury it. Steffi, the soup's beginning to cook . . . !'

'So, please may I have my whisky?'

We talked it upside down and roundabout, through lunch and into the afternoon. We arranged codes, meeting places, a schedule of telephone contacts; then Steffi left to rest his aged bones at the hotel and plot his own campaign of investigation. I had just finished transcribing the new information on to tape, when the telephone rang and Major-General Leporello came on the line. He was brisk, but surprisingly cordial:

'Welcome to Milan, Colonel.'

'Thank you, sir.'

'Captain Roditi delivered your message. I should be delighted to see you.'

'I simply wanted to pay my respects, sir. I know how busy you are.'

'Dinner on Thursday. How would that suit?'

'Yes, sir. I'm free on that night.'

'Good. My house at eight-thirty for nine. I'll send you a confirmation with directions how to get there. Strictly informal–a family foursome. Er–is there someone you would care to bring?'

'No, sir.'

'Leave it to my wife, then–she's the party girl. You and I can have a private chat over the coffee. By the way, have you ever thought about my offer?'

'Yes, sir, I have.'

'Let's talk about it again. Until Thursday then.'

'I look forward to it, General.'

I had expected some approach–drinks in the Mess perhaps, coffee at the Club–but this was out of all character and proportion. Two weeks ago he wanted me dead; now he wanted me to dinner. The two wishes were not necessarily in contradiction–there have been many notable treacheries at Italian dinner-tables–but they were certainly anomalous. I could hardly wear side-arms to a family foursome, but I had only forty-eight hours to find a very long spoon.

Steffi's news had disturbed me, profoundly, not because it was unexpected, but because, once again, I had lapsed into dangerous inattention, selecting only one issue and ignoring the whole complex of threats and problems behind it. The Black Book was an ingenious perversion, first designed by the Director as a training exercise and then refined into a technique of blackmail. The trick was to take a man's dossier and by editing, emphasis and interpretation, distort it into a criminal caricature. For 'bachelor' read 'not interested in women', for 'likes card games' read 'known gambler' and you have the art in a nutshell. It's a filthy game, but it works, because every man has some guilts, and the simple exhibition of the dossier to the victim is a crushing display of cynical power.

I knew the game, because I had played it often. I knew, too, that I was the easiest victim in the world, a secret agent working always on the outer margin of the law and sometimes a long way beyond it. Lili Anders was in a similar position, a known subversive, guest in a neutral country. It needed only a telephone call from the Director to his counterpart in Switzerland, and she, too, would be helpless as a leaf in a winter storm. I was still chewing on that sour thought when a courier arrived with two messages from Bruno Manzini.

The first was a note in which, apologizing for short notice, he requested me to dine with him this night at the Bankers' Club, in order, as he put it, 'to meet money and see whether it smells or not'. He suggested we meet in the card-room half an hour before dinner for a private briefing. The second was a letter from Lili:

> My dear,
>   It is so long since I have written to a man, that I hardly know how to begin. I would guess that you, my careful amorist, have never written letters to a woman at all. Uncle Pavel doesn't count, because he doesn't exist; but it was nice to hear from him just the same.
>   I am sitting on my balcony, bathed in sunshine, with a marvellous vista of green valley and snow-covered peaks, and farms that look like dolls' houses–all

mine to enjoy. And I am enjoying it, my dear, in a way I would never have thought possible. I do very little. I walk. I read. I have taken up petit point. I chat to the other guests. In the evenings, I play bridge. I am in bed by ten and I sleep until the maid brings my breakfast. It is all so simple, I wonder how I let it escape me for so long.

I worry sometimes, because I am still so transient and insecure; but my lawyer, Herr Neumann, reassures me. He is a little old man with white hair and gold pincenez. He calls me 'young woman'—which is always a help. He knows all about me now—except some very intimate things—and he says that perhaps I may be able to apply for political asylum. He has taken a lot of depositions and is seeking advice from colleagues in Zurich. I rather like the idea of asylum. It sounds almost like finding refuge in a church, where everything is confessed and everything is forgiven and you can begin again without fear.

The people here are simple folk, sober and kind. The guests are pleasant, too. There are a couple of elderly ladies, one of whom is my bridge partner. There is a honeymoon couple who make me envious sometimes; an American professor, rather elderly, who is writing a book on the Germanic migrations; and there is a very dashing fellow from Lugano, who talks to me in Italian and buys me a cocktail before dinner and keeps offering me whirlwind tours in his Maserati. I haven't accepted yet; but I may soon. He's attentive. He's not bad-looking and quite intelligent—an engineer or something on a construction project ten miles from here.

And you, my Dante Alighieri, how are you? I don't ask what you are doing because I know too much and can do nothing to help. I love you and I miss you; but I dare not let myself depend on the loving, and I must get used to the missing. I tell you only that I dream of you often and when I wake I half-expect to find you there beside me. As I write, I am jealous of every woman you meet or will meet. I wonder if you are jealous of my engineer. I'd like to think so.

Take care, my dear. Think gently of me as I do of you.

One fine tomorrow, perhaps I'll be

Yours Lili.

I read it three times, then tore it up and burned the shreds in the ashtray. I was jealous and I had no right to be. If I wasn't in love, then I was as near to it as I had ever been in my life. I couldn't risk the distraction. I couldn't afford the luxury. Forget it then! There were too many dangerous tomorrows to survive, and Lili's bright and shining day might never come.

The Bankers' Club in Milan is only a whit less venerable than the Chess Club in Rome. It is, however, much more impressive, because the focus of its power is clearer and all its members are fluent in a single, international language—money. It is a religious language reserved to priests and acolytes, like Church Latin or the time-symbols of the Incas. It is precise, flexible, subtle and quite unintelligible to the profane populace. It is proof of the cyclic nature of history: because the first banks in the world were the temples of Babylon, Greece and Rome, where you could raise loans, make deposits, arrange credit and have your coinage tested by assay under the vigilant eyes of the local deity.

If you ask why a fellow like me should know or care about such things, then I must remind you again that I am a Tuscan, and that I was bred to the history of the Bardi and the Frescobaldi and the Petruzzi, who were bankers to the English Crown in the fourteenth century and that my father was an old line socialist, who talked me blind about the need to nationalize the banks and put the speculators out of business. I like money. Who doesn't? I am also fascinated by its history, its forms, its potency why some men make it and most men lose it and even Charon, the ferry-man, demands a coin to row you across the Styx into eternity.

So, I found a certain propriety in the fact that my first entry into the world of Bruno Manzini should be made throught the portals of the Bankers' Club. I was also curious to know why he had chosen so sensitive and sacrosanct a place to present me. I put the question to him in so many words, as we sat over cocktails in the card-room, a privilege reserved to the most senior priesthood. He answered me, with a grin:

'It's an exercise in logic, my dear Dante. Here everyone has money. Money imposes discretion. Discretion conduces to free speech. Here, therefore, there is free speech—quite a lot of it, in fact. There are six of us who meet for dinner once a month. We talk about everything under the sun. Any member may bring a guest, provided he guarantees him as a safe man with a secret.'

'Thanks for the compliment.'

'I can pay you compliments anytime, my dear Dante. There are two men I want you to meet tonight. One is Ludovisi from the Banco Centrale, the other is Frantisek, from the Opera Pontificia at the Vatican. He's one of the shrewdest bankers in the business. The fact that he's an American and a Bishop is incidental. Both these men can be very useful to you.'

'How?'

'They can tell you, quicker than anybody, where the big money is going, and why. There's another reason, too. Ludovisi is the brother-in-law of your Director.' He chuckled and held up his hand. 'No, don't be alarmed. They love each other like cat and dog. Ludovisi is suing for divorce. He blames his wife's family for the failure of the marriage. He's very eloquent and very well briefed on the subject. Frantisek, on the other hand, is a very complex character. He looks like a football player, talks Italian with a Brooklyn accent, has a golf handicap of five, and stands in high favour with the reigning Pontiff. He helped to reorganize the Vatican's financial arrangements and negotiate the tax settlement with the Italian Government. He's not a very good theologian. His philosophy is pure pragmatism. His noblest virtue is a fanatical loyalty to the Holy See. Still, he does smell the wind, and if he likes you, he can be a very powerful friend. The rest? Well, they're agreeable and well-informed. One's a Liberal, the others are Christian Democrats of varying shades. Paolini's an out and out Fascist, but on a personal basis he's so agreeable you can almost forgive him.'

'And what do you expect me to do?'

'Whatever you like. Talk, listen, argue. If you make a gaffe, don't worry; it's the privilege of the Club. Now, tell me, what have you been doing?'

He heard me out in silence and then gave a long, low whistle of satisfaction.

'Good! Good! As you say the soup is beginning to cook. What do you propose to do now?'

'Wait until I have more evidence, much more. It's a risk. You must understand that. I may lose Giuseppe Balbo, who is our only link with what happened in Rome. But if I take him now, and hand him to the police, I may lose the big ones, Roditi and Leporello. You know the way things are. We need a brass-bound case before we open proceedings, and a notarized copy of every document in our own hands.'

He frowned over that for a long while and then, finally, nodded agreement.

'I hate the thought of losing a key witness; but the risk of premature action is even less palatable. These new riot squads worry me. It's only one step from those to the Brazilian *Esquadras de la Muerte* . . . police assassins. Let's take some soundings round the table tonight and see if there's any news floating around. I know Leporello is in high favour with the business men just now. He gave a talk here last week on the theme of Order and Progress. Very seductive, I hear. Very well received. I wonder why he's asked you to dinner, and who the fourth guest will be. Woman bait?'

'Possibly. Though it hardly seems his style.'

'If he's recruiting homosexual gymnasts and criminals, I shouldn't think he'd balk at simple seduction. Let's go in, shall we? The others should be here by now.'

We were eight people at a round table so that there was no question of precedence. Protocol was honoured by an opening grace from Bishop Frantisek, who, indeed, did look like a football player. His accent was appalling, but his grammar was faultless, his talk fluent and his manners affable. Ludovisi was the wit of the group, a lean, grey-eyed dandy, with a faun's grin and a fund of scandalous stories. The others, with the exception of Paolini, were typical of their breed, well-barbered, well-fed, eloquent about everything to do with money, agreeably cynical about any other human concern. Paolini I found an enigma. His manners were impeccable and he radiated charm, but his mind was closed to every logic but his own—which I must confess was hard to refute. His hobby-horse was multinational companies, the great concerns which spanned the frontiers of the world and operated in all jurisdictions, with no allegiance to any.

'. . . Four thousand companies making fifteen per cent of gross world product, that's what we're talking about. They control more assets than many of the countries in which they operate. Look at General Motors! Twenty-eight billion dollars in annual sales. Royal Dutch Shell, twelve and a half billion. . . . What single government can regulate enterprises like that? No democracy certainly. The lobby's too powerful, the leverage in employment and capital is too great, to say nothing of external pressures exercised through commerce and diplomacy. . . . And they're getting bigger all the time, like a fat man who can't stop eating. You fellows laugh at me and label me a Fascist, but show me any authority as strong and belligerent as a board of a giant company. De Gaulle saw it. The Labour unions see it, and it's the best argument they have for Marxism. . . . Even the Americans are seeing it now, as the Japanese apply the lesson and build multinationals of their own. . . .'

'So, what do you want?' Ludovisi cut in with a laugh. 'A junta that can be bought quicker than a parliament, because there's no one left to ask questions? Come now! Be realistic.'

'I am being realistic, my dear fellow. Look what happened in Greece. A few years ago you could hardly raise a dollar for investment. Now, they've got some law and order, the money's pouring in. Even expatriate capital is coming back. And the Government controls the terms. That's a much better situation than we've got at this moment.'

'Correction, old friend.' The Monsignore cut in with a tart reminder. 'The Colonels suspended law and imposed order.'

'It's a proper distinction,' said Bruno Manzini, mildly, 'but I wonder if it really makes any difference to the man in the street. We've got so many laws that we can't enforce them, and we end up with Government by regulation.

We've got so many parties that the people are not represented at all, only factional interests.'

Ludovisi gave him a quick questioning glance. Paolini applauded.

'Bravo! If Bruno here can see the light, why not the rest of you?'

'It's not the light,' said Manzini, with an impish grin. 'I think it may be a pillar of cloud with a very familiar demon inside it. Did anybody hear the speech General Leporello made here last week?'

'I did,' said Paolini. 'I thought he made excellent sense.'

There seemed to be a tepid agreement on that from everyone, except Ludovisi, who threw up his hands in despair and groaned aloud.

'My God! The fellow used every cliché in the handbook . . . "liberty is not licence; the desire of the people for a peaceful society; provocative elements; strong security measures" . . . Oh, dear, dear, dear! It sounded like my brother-in-law talking with his tongue in his cheek. Paolini, have you met this fellow personally?'

'I have. I think he's the kind of man we need, resolute, clear-headed, absolutely incorruptible.'

'I've yet to meet an incorruptible man. Has anyone else met this paragon?'

I saw, or thought I saw, a faint signal from Manzini, so I moved into the discussion.

'I know him.'

The Monsignore's eyebrows went up and he leaned his bulky body across the table to question me.

'And what's your opinion of him, Matucci?'

'I'd rather not make a judgment of him as a man. I will say he's embarked on a highly dangerous policy.'

'What policy is that?'

'Surely you gentlemen know. It's all over town. I'm new here, but I get it in every bar. He's recruiting special riot squads on the lines of the French Barbouzes. It's a secret operation and that worries me. I know where some of the recruits are coming from and that worries me even more.'

'Where do they come from, Matucci?'

'Resorts of known criminals and social delinquents.'

'That's a serious statement.' Paolini was visibly shocked.

'I know. I make it in the privacy of this gathering. I shall be presenting some evidence in support to Major-General Leporello himself next Thursday.'

'Perhaps he knows it already,' said Ludovisi, grimly. 'Have you thought of that? You mentioned the Barbouzes. You could also have mentioned the *Esquadras de la Muerte* in Brazil. It's a familiar pàttern: pull the rowdies off the streets and set them breaking heads under legal sanction. If your information is correct, Matucci, I'd say we were in for a very bloody mess.'

'I agree.'

'I think we're making a morbid pre-judgment.' Paolini was too bland and urbane to be true. 'Why don't we change the subject. No offence, Matucci, but you don't know my colleagues as well as I do. If you spread panic and alarm like that, you'll rattle the market for a month. Eh, Bruno?'

'I hope not.' Manzini chuckled like a happy child. 'I'm coming into the market myself tomorrow. The English have just come out with an electron welder that will join two plates of twenty centimetre steel in a single welding pass. I want to buy rights in it and finance a local manufacture. Any of you fellows interested, or do I have to go to the Vatican? You'll come in, won't you, Monsignore? Just what his Holiness needs to repair the rifts in the Church.'

They all laughed at that and the tension relaxed. As we moved from the dining-room to take coffee in the salon, Ludovisi laid a hand on my arm and steered me towards the men's room. He was sombre and preoccupied.

'That was bad news, Matucci. How sure are you?'

'Very sure.'

'Do you know where it's pointing?'

'Yes.'

'How do you know?'

'I work for SID, as well as for Manzini.'

'Then you know my brother-in-law.'

'Yes.'

'Where does he stand in this matter? Before you answer, it must be obvious that I don't like him. I think he's both devious and dangerous.'

'As a serving officer, I couldn't comment. As a guest in your Club, I would say that I agree with you. For the public record I would deny ever having made such a statement.'

'Thank you. Here's my card. If ever I can help, please call me.'

'Thank you, but I doubt you can help me with this mess.'

'You keep an open mind. I'll keep an open door. *D'accordo?*'

At eleven-thirty, the guests dispersed; but Manzini held me back for a final coffee in the card-room. He was obviously tired. There were dark circles under his eyes and his skin had a curious yellow tinge. Even his waspish wit had deserted him. When I asked if he were unwell, he shrugged wearily.

'That dinner tonight. . . . Truly, I could go out and cut my wrists in a bath-tub! You shoved a live grenade under their noses and only two had sense enough to see it. . . . The others didn't want to see it. . . . Have you never thought, friend, that if you die one night in a back street, you will be dying for men like these?'

'You must have thought about it, too.'

'I did, many times. Remember my telling you about my Uncle Freddie? I thought of him this evening when you were telling me about these types that Roditi is recruiting. Freddie could be vicious, too: mostly when he was short of money or frustrated in some affair, which happened more and more as he got older. He used to sponge on my mother, and if weeping didn't open her purse, he would try a little blackmail. . . . That's how I found out that Uncle Pantaleone was my father. I must have been—let me see—oh, about ten, I suppose. I had a new toy, a jack-in-the-box. I wanted to surprise Mamma with it. I crept into the salon where she was talking with Uncle Freddie and I hid behind the settee. I found myself in the middle of a bitter quarrel. Freddie wanted money. Mamma was refusing vehemently. Then Freddie threatened to spread the story of my parentage all over town. He must have been very desperate, because never before had he shown me anything but kindness. Finally, I couldn't stand it any longer. I burst out of my hiding-place and begged them to stop quarrelling. I don't remember what was said; but I do remember a long strange silence and how ill Freddie looked and how I had never seen Mamma so fierce and angry. . . . After that, I never saw Freddie again. . . . I know what happened to him. I could read by then. I saw it in a newspaper. One night, not long afterwards, he was wandering drunk and maudlin along Lungotuvere. He was accosted by a young sailor, who invited him on to a river barge. There he was bound, gagged and beaten until he died. A fowler discovered his body, ten days later, tangled in the reeds half-way to Ostia.... He wasn't very popular. Indeed, in his latter years, he was very disreputable. But he was well-connected in England, so the police were diligent in their inquiries and they made a voluminous report to the British Consul. It seems the people who killed him were paid for the job....'

'By whom?'

'Oh, I didn't know that for a long time. Not until my mother died and I had to go through her papers and possessions. I found Freddie's signet ring with a tiny label on it: "In memoriam . . . Pantaleone". My father was a very thorough man, you see; and like me, he had a taste for irony.... There's a sequel, my Dante. It may answer the question you've been too polite to ask. When the Gestapo had me in gaol—I'd been under interrogation for about a week, I think, and I wasn't in very good shape—my half-brother came to see me. He was Captain, then: very chic, very General Staff. He offered me a bargain. In return for the list of the Salamander network, the Gestapo would release me and I could live out the war in comfortable retirement at the Pantaleone Villa in Frascati.... I didn't spit in his eye, like a hero. I was too sick and tired. I told him the story I have just told you. I thought I was signing my death warrant, which would have suited me very well at that moment.... But my brother was only half the man my father was. I was handed back to the interrogators. They worked on me for another month. Then, one day, without warning, I was released into house arrest. I was put into a closed car and driven to Frascati. The servants at the Villa nursed me. My brother was away on army business. I couldn't leave the house. And, anyway, I was unwell and I had no place to go and no papers to take me. One day, my brother came to see me. He told me he had procured my release. He told me why: he wanted to discharge his father's obligations to me! I'm afraid I did spit in his eye then; though, looking back, I think he meant at least half of it. That was the half that took me to his funeral. The other half.... Well, you see what I mean about motives for martyrdom, don't you? Sometimes they're simple: and sometimes they're very confused....'

Early next morning, while I was still rubbing the sleep out of my eyes, Giorgione telephoned me from his home. He had good news. From a word dropped in the canteen and a few careful inquiries from Rita in the file room, he had discovered the location of a new camp. He thought it could be one of those used for the training of the riot squads. He gave me a name and a map reference: Camerata, a small Lombard town in the mountains north of Bergamo, about an hour's run from Milan. He told me I would have no difficulty finding the place, but I might have difficulty getting inside it. The location was classified as a maximum security area. He had other information, too. Captain Roditi lived, in some style, in a new apartment block not far from the Europa Hotel. The rents were higher than he could afford on a Captain's stipend. So, either he had private income, or someone was subsidizing him.

I called down blessings on Giorgione's tousled head and then sat down to a very meditative breakfast. After breakfast, I rang Roditi's office to set our appointment for drinks. His sergeant told me Roditi had left for Turin with General Leporello and would not be back until Thursday afternoon. At

nine, Stefanelli called in. I told him we were going for a run into the
country. I would pick him up at his hotel in thirty minutes. By ten, we were
out on the autostrada, cruising westward to the Bergamo exit.

My plan was simple but risky. As a serving officer of SID, I was still in
possession of my official identity document, which would procure me
entrance to any military or civilian installation, and access to all documents,
however classified. The risk was that the commanding officer could insist on
his right to check the document back to its origin before admitting me to his
area. I proposed, therefore, to drop Steffi off in Bergamo with instructions
to telephone Manzini if I were detained beyond a reasonable time. Steffi was
not enthusiastic.

'I think you're crazy, Matucci. If they do check your document, you're
up to your neck in trouble.'

'I know, Steffi; but the omens are good today. Leporello and Roditi are
out of town. I think I can bluff my way past any questions.'

'What's the reason for the visit—the official reason?'

'The best. I'm looking for a man named Marco Vitucci, wanted on
charges of subversion and murder. We feel he may have slipped through the
screening into a sensitive organization. I won't find Vitucci, of course. But if
I do find Giuseppe Balbo, then we're in big profit.'

'Enough to buy you a beautiful tombstone, little brother.'

'Relax, Steffi. It's a beautiful day. . . . I'll be back in a couple of hours and
I'll buy you the best lunch in Bergamo.'

'And what am I supposed to do for two hours in Bergamo?'

'Let's see . . . you could make a pilgrimage to the house of Papa Giovanni.
After all he did make the Jews respectable again, and a lot of people didn't
like him for it. . . . You could read some Tasso, you could listen to some
Donizetti or even dance the *bergamasca*, if you can find a girl old enough to
remember it.'

'Regular little tourist guide, aren't you, Matucci?'

'You wouldn't believe it, Steffi, but I was just that in my student
days—until I made an improper suggestion to one of the clients. She was
willing enough but her husband caught us holding hands in the Cappella
Colleoni and I lost my job. You might pay a little visit there, just for my
sake.'

'I've got a much better idea, little brother. Let's keep driving until we get
to Switzerland. You can settle down with your girl and I'll peddle cuckoo
clocks to the tourists. That way we both stay alive a little longer.'

From Bergamo the road wound upwards through the Brembo Valley,
curving along the flanks of the Lombard hills. I drove carefully, rehearsing
myself for the touchy moments of my first entry into the camp. At Camerata
I stopped to ask directions, and ran against the first security perimeter. The
three people I asked knew there was a camp somewhere, but had no idea
where is was. Finally, I had to call on the local police and produce my card
to the *brigadiere*, who drew me a map on a sheet of yellow paper. Even then,
I nearly missed the turn-off, a narrow corrugated defile enclosed at the end
of a stockade of logs surmounted by a watch-tower with a searchlight and a
machine gun.

There were guards at the gate as well, two husky fellows who halted me
ten yards from the entrance and demanded to know my business. I showed
them my card and told them I wanted to see the Commandant. One of them
took my card and went back to his box to telephone. I waited five minutes

and then they waved me through the gates and closed them behind me.

Inside, the place was grim and unwelcoming: twin rows of log huts with a broad parade-ground in between, and beyond, a vast basin, half-cleared, half still under timber, which was obviously the training area. I parked my car outside the Commandant's office and went inside. A desk sergeant took my card and disappeared into the next room. I waited another five minutes, before I was ushered into the presence of a slim bullet-headed Major, who looked as though he could straighten horse-shoes and tear telephone books with his bare hands. His desk was a mess of papers and he was quite self-conconscious about it. He fumbled with this sheet and that, as if he were still not sure what was written on it. His greeting was respectful, uneasy.

'Major Zenobio at your service, Colonel. I'm afraid I had no notice of your visit.'

'There were good reasons, Major.'

'Oh?'

'General Leporello left for Turin early this morning. I was still waiting on information from Rome, which came through just before ten o'clock. I left immediately. I am required to report to the General on his return. In fact, we're dining together tomorrow evening. If you feel the need to check that, please telephone his secretary immediately. I'd like to get down to business.'

He hesitated for a moment, took another look at my card, then closed it and handed it back to me. His tone was one degree less frigid.

'No, I don't think we'll need that, Colonel. Now, your business is . . . ?'

'Reserved to you and me at this stage, Major. I have to insist on that from the outset.'

'I understand.'

He fumbled with the papers again, tossing them about like confetti. For me, a man whose life depended on paper, it was a kind of sacrilege.

'Major, I'm looking for a man. The police want him for attempted murder. We want him because he is a known subversive, and we need to talk to him before anyone else.'

'And you hope to find him here, Colonel?'

'There's a certain logic in the idea that appeals to my people. These new groups of yours constitute a sensitive project, highly political. Your recruiting methods are, shall we say, unorthodox. To put it more bluntly, it has been decided, as a matter of high policy, that even social delinquents are acceptable, provided that they can be retrained to certain essential skills. Correct?'

'Correct.'

'Next. The project is secret, the requirements special. A man who wanted to go underground might well present himself for enlistment. If his dossier didn't look too disastrous, you would accept him.'

'A question, Colonel. The project is secret. How does your man know about it?'

'Ah, that's one of the matters I have to discuss with the General tomorrow night. It doesn't affect you, Major, but it does affect another officer who has been less than discreet. . . . However, that's confidential until the General gives clearance. Take it for granted that the man would know and could present himself. . . . Now, we're not interested in the police side of it at all. But a known subversive, an active Marxist agent, inside this kind of group—well! You do see my point?'

'Too clearly, Colonel. What's the name of your man?'

'Marco Vitucci.'

'Let's take a look at the nominal roll.'

'We'll come to that in a moment. What other records do you keep on your troops?'

'Each man has a record card, which contains his personal details and the reports of the training staff.'

'Photographs?'

'Each card carries a photograph, a thumbprint and a list of distinguishing marks. These are recorded also on the subject's identity document, which he carries at all times in addition to his civilian identification.'

'Good. Now, let's have a look at the nominal rolls.'

It took him three minutes to find them under the mess on his desk and in his trays. It took only a minute to establish that in a list of four hundred men in two training groups, there was no Marco Vitucci.

'Well, we do have one other alias.' I thumbed ostentatiously through my notebook. 'Here it is—Barone, Turi.' That landed me among the B's. There was no Barone either; but I did light on the name, Balbo, Giuseppe, and I pointed it out to the Major.

'Balbo, eh? Nothing to do with the case, of course. I was just wondering if he's any relation to General Balbo, who marched with the *Duce*?'

The Major smiled for the first time.

'I doubt it. But let's take a look, just for curiosity. Funny if it were though. Balbo was one of the first quadrumvirate of Fascism. We could be the new beginnings. . . . Here you are.'

He opened a filing cabinet, took out a card and handed it to me. I scanned it carefully. The identification was clear. This was the same man I had met with Roditi in the Club Alcibiade. If the thumbprint tallied with the one on the police files, then I had everything I needed. I handed the card back to the Major, who tossed it on to the littered desk, and then half-buried it under the nominal rolls.

'No connection, I'm afraid. The old General was a Ferrarese. This one comes from Gaeta. Well, it was a pleasant fantasy. That's all, I think, Major. Painless for you, disappointing for me. Still, we'll keep trying. I wonder if I could ask you one favour?'

'Anything, Colonel.'

'Could I have a cup of coffee?'

'Certainly.'

He yelled for the sergeant, and when there was no answer, he went through the door at a run and I could hear him shouting across the parade-ground. I slipped the Balbo card in my pocket and followed him out.

'Please, Major, don't disturb yourself. I'll be on my way. Just a reminder. This visit is strictly reserved.'

'Of course, Colonel. Have a good journey.'

He was glad to see me go; but not half so glad as I was to hear the gates of the stockade slam behind me. The moment I was out of sight of the watch-tower, I stepped hard on the accelerator and drove fast and dangerously all the way to Bergamo. I snatched a plaintive Steffi from the square of the High Town and drove straight back to Milan. The prints on the Balbo card matched those which Steffi had brought from Rome. We made four Xerox copies and locked the original in the safe. Then we rang for Pietro and ordered champagne and a gourmet meal to celebrate this first real rape of the ungodly.

It was one of those jubilant hours that only a professional can understand and share. It was like winning a lottery or having the prettiest girl in the room wilt into your arms. I was the shrewdest fellow in the world, as racy a gambler as ever bet his wife's virtue on the turn of a card. But—*post coitum triste, post vinum capitis dolor!* at four in the afternoon, sober but sleepy, we still did not know what to do with the Balbo document. Steffi, who had missed his siesta, summed it up irritably.

'*Ebbene!* We now have evidence to put one Giuseppe Balbo in prison for life. You don't want that. You want him here, in this room, singing like a love-bird, telling you all he knows about Roditi, and the letter-bomb, and the murders in the Via Sicilia. Then you want Roditi here, singing another song about General Leporello. Then, when you've copied down the whole melody, what are you going to do with it? Like the Rabbi who played golf on the Sabbath and got a hole-in-one, whom do you tell? And when you tell, who's going to want to believe you? And, much more important, who's going to do anything about it? Matucci, little brother, big wooden-head, you have to answer all those questions!'

'Give me time, Steffi, for God's sake!'

'You don't have time, little brother. Suppose your Major Zenobio has missed the card?'

'I'm hoping he hasn't. He's careless with papers.'

'Suppose he rings Leporello to check on you.'

'I'm gambling he won't.'

'Gambling, hoping! On a thread like that you could hang yourself.'

'I know, I know! Let's take it one step at a time. I want doubt, confusion and panic. . . . What's the time?'

'Three thirty. Why?'

'How far is it to Chiasso?'

'Less than fifty kilometres. Again, why?'

I grabbed the telephone and dialled Bruno Manzini's private number. When he came on the line, I told him what I wanted.

'. . . A courier, Bruno. I want him now. He's to drive to Chiasso and post some letters. They have to be delivered in Milan with tomorrow's mail. And I'd like to see you as soon as possible, here, at the apartment. I'm sorry to bother you, but it's very urgent.'

Crotchety he might be, but he always ran true to form. The courier would be with me in fifteen minutes. He, himself, would join me at six. Steffi was looking at me as if I were an amiable lunatic. I unlocked the safe, took out the Balbo document, rubbed it clean with a new handkerchief and laid it on the desk. Then, I rang for Paolo and asked him to bring me a pair of his clean white gloves. Finally, Steffi could bear it no longer:

'So, tell me, Matucci! Or do I just stand here and watch you make like Inspector Maigret?'

'Step one. We make two fresh copies of the Balbo document. This time without our fingerprints all over the copy-paper. Step two. We clip Balbo's thumbprint off each copy. Step three. I type two identical notes to accompany the thumbprints. Step four. The said notes and thumbprints are posted to catch tonight's mail from Southern Switzerland.'

'And what will be in the notes?'

'Two names: Bandinelli, Calvi. A place: Via Sicilia, Rome. And the date on which they died.'

'And who gets the notes?'

'Major-General Leporello and Captain Roditi—at their private addresses.'

'And how long does it take them to run the print through records?'

'Forty-eight hours at least.'

'And how long to tie everything back to you through a stolen card?'

'Another twenty-four. Those are inside limits. We might do better.'

'Then what, little brother?'

'Then there is the beautiful scene, Steffi. I think we'll get Fellini to film it. I, Dante Alighieri Matucci, am standing solitary and noble in the middle of the Olympic Stadium. All the stands are full. All the spectators look exactly like the Director. They all have guns and they're all pointing at me. . . . What happens after that, I'm not sure.'

'I'm sure, Matucci. I'm going home to mother.'

'Oh, no you're not. Not tonight anyway. At ten o'clock we are going to make a private visit to the apartment of Captain Matteo Roditi. How does that sound?'

'Like madness, little brother. Like old-fashioned dancing madness!'

Bruno Manzini arrived punctually at six. When he heard of my day's exploits, he was not amused. He gave me no tolerant elegies either. He was coldly and eloquently angry.

'. . . Matucci, you shock me! You do not lack talent. You have vast experience. You have at least a rudimentary sense of politics. So this children's game you have played today is an incredible and inexcusable folly.'

'Now, listen, Cavaliere. . . !'

'No! You hear me first! You have compromised yourself. You have compromised me. You have set in motion a whole train of events for which we are quite unprepared, and for which we have no time to prepare! Good God, man! Have you learnt nothing? This is high politics. We are talking of revolution, Matucci, barricades in the streets, gunfire and bombs! Yet, you behave like some fly-brained agent from a comic book! Truly I despair!'

'I think you despair too quickly, Cavaliere.'

'Do you, indeed. Then show me half a grain of sense in this crack-brained escapade and I'll die happy.'

'Then, here it is. Locked in that safe, there is a document, perhaps the only existing document which can tie Roditi and Leporello to a conspiracy of murder. I procured it by a risky act with awkward consequences, but. . . .'

'Awkward! Mother of God! Is that what you call it?'

'. . . But, Cavaliere, if you don't take risks in my business, you're left standing like a clown while people pour buckets of water over your head. Next point, we agreed on a policy of doubt and confusion. I have begun to create it. . . .'

'Prematurely. Without foresight!'

'With hindsight then. We are dealing with conjurors, Cavaliere: people who can make files disappear, people who can suborn witnesses and silence politicians and buy perjurers with straw in their shoes—if we give them enough time. I am trying, rightly or wrongly, to deny them time. I'm a fly-brained agent, because I don't have the luxury to be Lorenzo di Medici compassing the downfall of his enemies by slow and princely degrees. I'm

the opportunist, because I have to fight the skirmishes and the street-
battles, and if I lose those, your campaign is so much scrap-paper! . . . Eh!
This is madness! Let's drop it!'

He stared at me for a long moment, bleak-faced and hostile; then, he
nodded, slowly, as if assenting to some private proposition of his own.
Then, he set it down for me.

'*Ebbene!* You are right and I am right, and we are both equally wrong.
Let's start from there and see what we can salvage.'

'No, Cavaliere. Let's see what we can build.'

A small reluctant smile twitched at the corners of his mouth.

'You're a real wooden-head, Matucci. What am I to do with you?'

'Wear me, Cavaliere. Like a hairshirt, if you must, but wear me. And give
me some advice. We project from the evidence we have in hand. We
establish a case that involves Balbo as an assassin, and Roditi and Leporello
as conspirators. Where and how do we present our case? And how do we tie
the Director into it? You say we're not prepared. I know we're not. So I
need help against the high men, before they close ranks. Can you give it to
me?'

'It's the Director who bothers you, isn't it?'

'Yes. He's got a perfect position. He can excuse everything he has done on
the grounds that he was infiltrating a conspiracy that threatened the security
of the State. He knows so many secrets that everyone's afraid of him, even
his own Minister.'

'I'm not afraid of him, Dante.'

'That's hardly enough. You have to have the lever that will topple him.'

'We have the lever, my Dante. It's the fulcrum we need; and you, without
knowing, may have provided it.'

'I don't understand.'

'I know you don't. And that is what makes me angry with you. In the
fervour of a crusade, in the heat of a new situation, you slip out of gear. You
change from logician to opportunist. You chase the marsh-light and forget
the bale-fires burning on the hills behind you. Remember what happened at
the lodge? In Venice? The same thing is happening now. This is why you
are vulnerable to such a man as the Director. You have every talent he has,
and some he lacks, but you cannot or you will not focus them. So, always
until now, you have been a tool of other men's designs. . . . I'm sorry if I've
offended you; but I have so much regard for you that I cannot bear what you
do to yourself. . . . Let me show you what I mean. When you left my
brother's house on the morning after his death, you left an old servant
weeping into his liquor. You had asked him to record telephone calls for
you. He did that. You never went back to collect the messages. I did. I went
there to see to the wants of an old man who had known my father. Because
he was afraid, he told me that he had lied to you. He was not awake when my
brother came home from the Chess Club. He was drunk and snoring. He
lied because he thought he would be blamed, for not putting on the alarms.
They were off when he woke in the morning. . . . No, please don't interrupt.
Let me embarrass you a moment longer. The night after my brother's
funeral, I had his body removed from the vault. An autopsy was performed
in the mortuary of a private clinic. My brother did take barbiturates. He
probably took quite a large dose, but not enough to kill him. He was killed
by an injection of air into the femoral artery. The mark of the syringe was
clearly visible under the pubic hair. You see what happened, Dante? You

connived with the Director to hush up a suicide. You were made an accomplice in murder.'

'Why didn't you tell me this before?'

For a full minute he said absolutely nothing. His eyes were filmed over like those of a bird, so that he seemed not to be looking at me, but away and beyond into some immeasurable distance. He sat quite rigid, with his fingertips joined and laid against his thin pursed lips. When he spoke, his voice was frosty, remote, like the first chill wind of autumn.

'To teach you a lesson, Matucci. Trust no one. Not even me. Don't believe that the old Adam is dead until you've screwed down the coffin and seen the grave-digger stamp the last sod on top of him.'

He was right, of course. The old bastard was always right. We Latins are the most logical people in the world. We mistrust our mothers when they give us the teat. The only things we believe happily are unprovable propositions like weeping Madonnas, and flying houses and infallible Popes.

Our visit to Roditi's apartment began auspiciously. There was a party on the sixth floor; the foyer was busy with guests in evening-dress and the porter had lost count of the arrivals. Steffi and I rode with the party-goers as far as the fifth floor and stepped out on to a deserted landing. We rang the bell on Roditi's apartment; and, when there was no answer, I used a pick-lock and opened the door in thirty seconds. It was as simple as shelling green peas.

The interior of the apartment was a surprise. I had expected an epicene elegance or perhaps a feminine clutter. I found, instead, a place as aseptic and impersonal as a hotel room. The furniture was Danish modern. The pictures, arranged in a severe symmetry, were all of soldiers in historic costumes. There was a cabinet for drinks and a stereo-player with a collection of popular songs, film-scores and American musicals. The desk was bare, except for a blotting pad of tooled leather and a leather cup full of ball-point pens and freshly-sharpened pencils. The place was spotless and the teak furniture glowed with wax and recent polishing.

We began our search in the kitchen. We found coffee and bread and butter and cheese and a carton of milk. The dining-room was furnished with linen, cutlery and glassware for six persons. Everything was of good quality. None of it distinguished. In the liquor cabinet there was one spare bottle of each drink and perhaps a dozen assorted mineral waters. The books in the salon were innocuous: paperback novels, a few biographies. There was no pornography, no sign of sexy prints or photographs. The drawers of the desk were unlocked. They contained notepaper and envelopes and a few blocks of ruled drafting paper. The bathroom revealed nothing except that the Captain's toiletries were expensive, though not exotic.

The bedroom was more rewarding. Roditi had ten suits and four uniforms, all made by an expensive tailor. His shirts were handmade and monogrammed. He was prolific in shoes, ties, scarves and costly accessories. He was either a very tidy man, or he had a jewel of a maid, because his drawers were set with mathematical precision and his dressing-table was laid like a show-piece in a store.

In the right-hand drawer of the dressing-table, face-down, was a photograph in a silver frame. It was a portrait, obviously taken by a professional, of a woman in her early thirties, who bore a striking resemblance to Rafael's Donna Velata in the Pitti Gallery in Florence. There were the same dark eyes, large and lustrous, the same nose, a little large for perfect beauty, the same mouth, soft and enigmatic in repose. Even the hair-style was similar: dark, straight tresses drawn back over her ears and braided behind the head. The photograph was inscribed in a bold, round hand, 'To my dearest Matteo, for memory and for promise, Elena'.

Beside the photograph I found a bundle of letters, more than thirty, held together by a rubber band. They were written in the same hand, signed with the same name. I read them and passed them one by one to Steffi. They were love-letters, lyrical, tender, totally uninhibited in their celebration of the nights and days of a passionate affair. I have thumbed through many letters in my time, but these moved me deeply and I felt a sudden shame at my invasion of the privacy of this unknown woman. The letters were undated. There was no address. From the text and the references, it was clear that they had been written over a period of several years and that the last was written no more than a week ago. Elena was married, unhappily, to a husband older than herself. Roditi, whatever his other vices or virtues, was obviously a passionate and thoughtful lover. There was no reproach in any of the letters, only yearning and gratitude and a vivid, sensual poetry. Even old Steffi was awed. He handed the last note back to me and said, sombrely:

'Eh, Matucci! If you and I could move a woman like that. . . .'

'It doesn't make sense, Steffi. A fellow like Roditi. . . .'

'He makes sense to her, little brother, the most beautiful sense in the world.'

'A *finocchio* like that! Never.'

'Now hold it, Matucci. Maybe you're wrong from the beginning. You've seen him at the Alcibiade. You've heard—only heard, mark you—that someone like him chases rough trade at the Pavone. Giorgione told you he's a physical culture addict. That's all you've got. The rest is imagination and inference. This apartment now, does it smell of fennel-flowers? Not to me. Does the lady sound cheated? Not to me. Maybe you have to rethink this fellow. . . . Hand me that photograph a minute.'

He unfastened the clip at the back of the frame and slid out the photograph. On the back of it was the address of the photographer, together with a file number: A. Donati, Bologna, 673125. Steffi scribbled the notation in his notebook and put the photograph back in the frame.

'Tomorrow, Matucci, I should take a little trip to Bologna and trace that print, no?'

'Do that, Steffi. . . . Wait a minute though. There's something strange.'

'What?'

'We are looking at half a house, half a man. The place is incomplete, as though not enough important things have happened here yet. It's as neutral as a showroom.'

'But whichever way you read him, Roditi's not neuter.'

'Exactly.'

'So, why don't you take one of those letters from the middle of the bundle and let's haul our tails out of here. I feel like a criminal.'

'Which is exactly what you are, Steffi. But you bring me back the lady's name tomorrow and I'll pin a medal on you.'

We left the apartment pristine as we found it and rode down, innocent as babes, to the foyer. The porter was locked in his little booth watching television. We could have been trailing a bloodied corpse across the Garrara marble and he would not have blinked an eyelid.

It was still only a little after eleven. The night was balmy and the streets were still lively with strollers and traffic. Steffi was tired, so I dropped him at his hotel. I was too restless to sleep. Bruno Manzini had taught me a rough lesson. My thinking was confused. My judgments were hasty. My actions were precipitate and dangerous. The Director had judged me long before and made me a facile actor in his sardonic dramas. Even Lili knew my weakness, and would not commit to me until I had mastered it, if indeed I ever could.

The prospect of a solitary evening in the apartment daunted me, so I drove across town to the Duca di Gallodoro, where at least I could share my loneliness and have it set to music.

They gave me a table in a shadowy corner. I ordered a drink and sat watching the shuffle of the dancers and the drift of the drinkers around the bar. A couple of girls wandered past with hopeful smiles; but I waved them away. I was too morose to endure their inevitable small-talk and their constant thirst for bad champagne. I had been there for perhaps twenty minutes, when two men came in and sat three tables away on my right. One was a big sturdy fellow, with the lumpy battered face of a pugilist; the other was small, dark and dapper, with ferret eyes and a wide flashing smile.

The small one I knew. Everyone in the Corps knew him, at least by name and reputation. They called him the Surgeon, because, they said, he would cut the brain out of a living man and dissect it for the last morsel of information. They even had a proverb about him: Fall into the hands of God, not into the Surgeon's paws! The suspect, who had jumped or been pushed from the high window, had been under his studious care. The big fellow was obviously his bodyguard–and probably his assistant butcher. I sat back further into the shadows lest he see me and salute me and I be forced to acknowledge him.

A few moments later, the band stopped playing and the dancers drifted back to their tables. A microphone was set up in the middle of the floor and a master of ceremonies announced the presence of the eminent and well-beloved Patti Pavese, who would sing for us. Then all the lights went out and there were five seconds of darkness until a spot splashed in the centre of the dance floor and revealed the singer in a splendour of fishnet and sequins. She looked better than she sang, but the audience loved her and clapped handsomely. When she delivered her big number, *Una Manata d'Amore*, they went wild and called her back for two repeats of the chorus and sang the last one with her.

When the lights went up again, I glanced across at the Surgeon. He was lying slumped across the table in a welter of spilt liquor. His bodyguard was sprawled sideways on the banquette. They had both been shot in the head by a small-calibre pistol. I tossed a pair of notes on the table and made for the entrance. I was half-way to the door before I heard a woman's scream and the commotion that followed it.

The killing of the Surgeon made headlines in the morning press, and the foreign agencies made a big meal of it as well. The police announced a nation-wide hunt for the assassins and appealed for information from the public, especially from anyone who had left the Duca di Gallodoro before the arrival of the police.

Manzini, who had telephoned me at breakfast and bidden me on a tour of his factories in Milan, was gloomy and dispirited.

'. . . A fellow like that is better dead, but there are fifty others waiting to step into his shoes. So nothing is soled. The factions are polarized still more. The tyrants look so much more attractive to a scared and dispirited people. Watch, Dante! Watch and listen! Note the tension, the undercurrent of unrest and suspicion. You will see the groups of workers coalesce, each wary of the other, each on the look-out for spies and provocative agents. These are good people, Dante. We have fewer labour troubles than most, because we sign reasonable agreements and keep them. I am not hated as the *Androne*; I am even respected, I think. But as a man I am remote as the moon. I personify power. I am identified with all the excesses of power in this country. I had a telephone call from Rome this morning. The Government is considering a new regulation that will give the police even wider powers of search and arrest. They are talking of ninety-two hours preventive detention on mere suspicion. . . . Preventive detention! That's madness! It puts us back forty years. Your Surgeon is the symbol of the terror necessary to control the restless mass. In the old days he would have worn a mask and carried a headsman's axe. In part I am guilty of him, too. I have guards on my gates and plant detectives to stop pilfering. Forgive me, I am morbid today. We will have lunch with the managers and then I will show you something a little more cheerful.'

We drove ten miles outside the city towards Como and turned off the main road into a private parkland where twenty bungalows, all new, were grouped around a central building, which looked rather like a clubhouse, set about with lawns and flower-gardens. Manzini explained it to me with ironic deprecation.

'. . . A sop to my pirate's conscience, Dante. One of the things I hope may earn me a late reprieve from damnation. It's a home for mongoloid children who cannot be cared for within their own families. They tend to have a short life span, as you may know. If they are submitted to undue stress, for example, in an old-fashioned institution, some of them may become violent and anti-social. So, we've tried here to reproduce a family situation. Each house has six to ten children under the care of a married couple. The central building contains class-rooms, a clinic, a recreation hall and staff quarters. We're experimenting all the time and this place has become a prototype for others in different parts of Italy. In this country the Church used to be the fountain of charity; but too many of the old orders of monks and nuns have become sclerotic and outdated. As for the State institutions, the less said the better. I have seen orphanages, my friend, where children did not learn to speak until they were seven and eight years old, because no one ever talked to them. . . . Here, we are both teaching and learning, and every week there is some small revelation that makes it all worth while.'

To me, the greatest revelation of all was the old man himself. The staff adored him, men and women alike. Each one had something special to show him: a therapy project, a piece of recent equipment, a diet chart, a game that seemed to have a special fascination for their charges. With the children, he was like a happy grandfather. He fondled them, kissed them, squatted on the floor and played games with their blocks and models. He drew comic pictures on a black-board, and even pounded out a tune on the piano. He swung one tiny mite on his shoulders and carried him round the place, while half a dozen others tugged at his coat-tails for attention. There was nothing organized about the chanted chorus of welcome or farewell. He came and went as the patriarch of a frail family which without him would have remained ungathered and forgotten. The odd thing was that he needed to justify himself—and to me of all people.

'. . . There is a man in Rome, Dante, a priest I know, who deals only with monsters. I mean it, literally. Man still begets and women still throw monstrosities with one eye and three arms and half a brain and two hearts. Some of them survive. God only knows why and He never explains though I think He should if He wants us to believe in mercy and loving-kindness and all the rest! However, this man told me once, that he was, perhaps, the only one in all the world who could truly affirm miracles. Now, you have to understand, Dante, that the creatures we talk about are truly subhuman, beyond reason, beyond imagining, beyond even compassion. But this man told me that, sometimes at the strangest moments, he would feel, see, hear a response that shook the foundations of his sanity. These vegetables, these montrous nothings knew! They knew . . .! For how long, and how much? Eh! Impossible to say; but for one flash of time there was lightning on Tabor. This work I do is far easier than his. It costs me nothing but money. The rest is pure joy. I go back to the ant-hill changed, if only a little. I know that life is not all vendetta and woe to the vanquished. The mystery is that we still must fight, to hold room even for so small a loving. If we didn't, they would burn the monsters and sterilize those babies of mine and hand them over to the brutes of the world for anatomical experiment. . . . You are seeing Leporello tonight?'

'Yes.'

'Worried?'

'A little. If he opens a door, I have to walk through it, even if I'm not sure what's on the other side. You may not approve what I do.'

'Do you care whether I approve or not?'

'Yes, I care.'

'A warning, Dante Alighieri. Shut the door on today. Forget it until a calmer time. We are going back into the jungle. You cannot afford illusions.'

'What illusions, Bruno?'

'That the Salamander will always survive. That's a myth, a beautiful legend, like the Holy Grail and the Golden Apples of the Hesperides. I've had my warning, Dante. I have a mitral stenosis which will kill me—probably sooner than later. If I go before this is finished, you will be alone. What then?'

'Another test, Bruno?'

'No. A simple question.'

'Answer one: I finish my leave and go back to SID, an obedient servant. Answer two: I take the job which Leporello will offer me at dinner tonight.'

'Answer three?'

'I emigrate and live happily ever after, mining bauxite in Australia.'

'Is that all?'

'No. There's one more possibility. Write me into your will. Leave me the engraver's plate from which you print your cards. I'll set up in business as the Salamander. Who knows? I may write a new legend, before they hose me out from the ashes.'

It was a bad joke, but he laughed at it. I laughed, too—at the wondrous spectacle of Dante Alighieri Matucci, perched on his dunghill, flapping his

wings and crowing defiance at principalities and thrones and dominations
and all the dark powers of this sunlit Latin world.

I gave great thought to the manner in which I should dress for Leporello's
dinner. The suit should be sober, but not too sober lest I look like some
pettifogging clerk come to dine with the bank manager. Modish? Yes. The
ladies like a man who has a little colour about him, and the General would
not want another grey mouse on his staff. The shirt, white cambric, with
gold cufflinks, just for a hint of money. The General should know where
the bidding started. It was all *figura* . . . the thing we live by here in Italy.
The inwardness is something else. The women share it with their confessors. We males disclose it to our friends, or, given grace and time in our
advancing years, to God, who, by then may have lost interest in such trifling
matters.

My car was polished; Pietro had seen to that. There was no cloud on the
bright-work, no speck of dust in the interior. There was a basket of flowers
for my hostess and a bottle of brandy for my host, to honour my first footing
in their house. If my dinner companion proved willing, there was
champagne in the refrigerator and coffee on the stove and sweet music
would flood the place at the touch of a switch. All in all—saving the ravages
of time and middle age—the *figura* was not bad. Pietro flicked the last speck
of fluff from my lapels and swept me out into the night.

I drove carefully, because there were police at every intersection and
trucks full of carabinieri parked at strategic points. The murder of the
Surgeon was no small matter in this city of a million and a half people,
restive under the twin threats of violence and repression. I was stopped
twice on the way and a third time at the gates of Leporello's villa, where two
carabinieri checked my papers, waved me inside and closed the gates behind
me. Leporello was taking himself and his job very seriously. There were two
plain-clothes men inside the grounds. One of them opened the door of the
car and delivered me, unscathed, at the front door, where a maid took
charge of me and led me into the salon.

Leporello was alone. Even in civilian clothes he was still an impressive
figure, tall, straight and formal to the point of stiffness. Still, his greeting
was warm, his handshake firm and welcoming. He apologized for the ladies,
who were chatting upstairs. They would join us presently. A manservant
offered drinks, whisky or champagne. We toasted each other. Leporello
made a joking reference to the guards and the security men. I told him I
thought it wise and necessary to take precautions. I asked about his
investigation into the murder of the Surgeon. He frowned and shrugged:

'You know how it is, Colonel. The murder took place in a crowded night-
club, while the attention of the clients was focused on a popular performer.
Most of the place was in darkness. The assassins used silenced pistols, small
calibre, low velocity. Where do we begin?'

I was lavish with sympathy for his problem. I wished, fervently, that I
could offer some constructive suggestion. I was happy to be on leave and
dispensed from responsibility. He smiled, faintly, and said that we must
discuss that over the brandy. Then the ladies came—and it was as if the roof
had fallen on my unwary head. The woman in Roditi's photograph was the
wife of General Leporello.

I stammered God knows what by way of greeting and bent over her hand
in a panic of embarrassment. It is one thing to look into a woman's cleavage

when you know beyond all doubt that she has put it on show for you. It is quite another to look into her eyes when you have read all her secrets in a bundle of love-letters. You feel the small shameful triumph of the voyeur and you wonder that she cannot read it in your face. You feel a guilt that makes you withdraw from her touch, a fear that some unguarded word may expose the secret knowledge that you possess.

Fortunately, for me, my table-partner provided an adequate diversion. Laura Balestra was a lively *biondina*, with big, bedroom eyes and a little-girl smile and a talent for amusing chit-chat. She loved dressy men. She hated stuffy soldiers. She had an uncle in Bolivia who mined emeralds and lavished them on mistresses in six different countries. She had just come back from Austria where she had almost, but not quite, fallen in love with a ski-instructor. Didn't I love Elena's dress and wasn't this a beautiful villa? And why anyone would want to live in Milan, she couldn't imagine. She much preferred Florence, but then Mamma was ailing and she had to play duenna for Papa who was enjoying his second youth in a rather embarrassing fashion. . . . And dear, oh dear, she did carry on, didn't she?

She did, but I was so grateful I wanted to kiss her, and thought I would afterwards. Then, she turned to Leporello and left me to make my halting way with the lady of the love-letters.

I will say it once and be done with it: she was a beautiful woman; she wakened the old Adam in me the moment I set eyes on her. The photographer had flattered her a little because he had caught her in a moment of repose and contentment. I wondered how a ramrod like Leporello had managed to marry her. She was wondering about me, too. Her first question was a challenge.

'You're older than I expected, Colonel.'

'I try hard to conceal it, Madam.'

'I didn't mean that. My husband likes to surround himself with very young officers.'

'Oh? I've only met one member of the staff, Captain Roditi.'

'Do you know him well?'

'Hardly at all. We've met only three times and we've had very little to say to each other.'

'He's rather exceptional. He's been with my husband nearly seven years now. Are you married, Colonel?'

'No.'

'Not interested?'

'Very dubious—about marriage that is.'

'My husband tells me he's invited you to join his staff.'

'Yes.'

'You don't like the idea?'

'I have some reservations. I'll be discussing them with the General.'

'You're very tactful.'

'And you're very beautiful, Madam. Do you know the Veiled Lady?'

'I'm afraid not. Should I?'

'Rafael painted her. She's in the Pitti. You're her living image, even to the hairstyle.'

'Thank you for the compliment.'

'I'm sure you get many, from all those dashing young officers.'

'Very few, Colonel. I'm a respectable married woman with two children.'

'Girls or boys?'

'Twin girls. They'll be five this August.'

'Summer children! That's nice.'

'Summer or winter, does it make any difference?'

'Isn't there a proverb that says, "Spring loving's the brightest, but summer's the sweetest?"'

'I've never heard it. Is that your experience, Colonel?'

'Well, yes. I suppose it is.'

'You must tell me about it one day.'

'I'd be delighted; but I never tell names or write letters.'

'Very gallant–and very discreet.'

'In my business I have to be discreet.'

'Oh, yes, you're something in intelligence, aren't you?'

'That's right.'

'Do you like your work?'

'Not always. It destroys one's illusions too quickly.'

'Do you have any left, Colonel?'

'Some. . . . And you?'

'Ask me some other time.'

'I'll do that. It's a promise.'

Dinner was announced at that moment, so there was no chance to finish the gambit. But if I guessed my lady right, she was playing the old game of spite-my-husband, and playing it very recklessly indeed. Leporello, on the other hand, was punctiliously polite, though never casual or intimate. For a man, who was normally brusque and imperative, his attitude to his wife was surprisingly deferential. It was as if he had acquired the habit of stepping round arguments and avoiding the simplest discussions. I had the curious impression that he was afraid of her and that she, knowing it, was prepared to push him to the limit of endurance. At table, he concentrated his first attention on me. He was persuasive and complimentary. He wished most earnestly to have me on his staff. Men with my training and experience were precious. He hoped the women might persuade me if his own eloquence were not enough. Laura Balestra was on his side, teasing and inconsequent. Elena Leporello played her own game, flattering me and denigrating her husband in a dozen subtle ways. By the time we had finished the pasta, I was tired of their comedy. I began to devise one of my own.

'By the way, General, did you know someone tried to kill me in Venice?'

He was a very good actor. He choked on his wine and, as he set down the glass, he spilt the dregs on the tablecloth. The women were shocked and excited. Leporello silenced them with a gesture and demanded a full account of the affair. I shrugged it off.

'Well, I'd just had dinner with my Director and the Cavaliere Manzini. I was on my way to Harry's Bar to meet a girl. I was waylaid by three men who tried to bottle me up in an alley. I fired some shots. They ran away.'

'You reported the matter to the Director, of course?'

'Yes. . . . He told me he would make some inquiries and come back to me.'

'But you haven't heard from him yet?'

'Not yet.'

'This worries me, Colonel. It seems this kind of violence is becoming epidemic. You heard what happened here in Milan last night?'

'I was there, General.'

He was not acting now. He gaped at me, fish-eyed; I explained with elaborate discretion.

'You won't find my name in your reports because I slipped out before the panic started—to avoid embarrassing questions. I was sitting three tables away.'

'And you saw nothing?'

'Only the bodies, when the lights went up. It was obviously a professional job. I shouldn't think you'll get far with normal inquiries. Myself, I wouldn't be inclined to push them too hard.'

'That's an odd thing to say, Colonel?'

'Not really, General. Let's face it, both sides are in profit. The Left have their victim. You're rid of a discreditable nuisance.'

Elena Leporello was quick to see the point and turn it against us both.

'That sounds like a loaded proposition, Colonel.'

'Not at all. It's a statement of fact—unless you want me to say that your husband approved of sadism in police interrogations. However, I agree it's not the sort of thing one shouts about in public.'

Leporello brightened at that and nodded a vigorous approval.

'Very proper, Matucci.... Very proper. Our public image is very important at this time.'

'And what do you think of the image, Colonel?' Elena Leporello was a very persistent adversary. 'I get the impression it's rather tarnished just now.'

'In some respects, yes. On the other hand, your husband's reputation is growing.'

'His reputation for what, Colonel?'

'Firm policy, decisive action.... I was at the Bankers' Club the night before last. Your speech on Order and Progress made a big impression, General. I've heard other talk as I've been moving around. There's a great deal of popular support for your programme. These riot squads you are training....'

'Where did you hear about those, Colonel?'

'They're being talked about in every bar and club in town, General.'

'It's supposed to be a secret project.'

'I assure you it isn't any more.'

'Could you name me any places where you've heard this talk?'

'Certainly. The Duca di Gallodoro, the Hilton Bar, the Club Alcibiade....'

The mention of the Alcibiade produced a variety of reactions. Elena looked blank. The General developed a sudden interest in the strawberry flan. Laura Balestra quizzed me, pertly:

'The Club Alcibiade? And what were you doing there, Colonel?'

'Just looking.'

'Did you find what you were looking for?'

'Yes, I did, as a matter of fact. I found a man I've been chasing for weeks.'

'I didn't think you'd find a man within a kilometre of the place.'

'Indeed, yes. I was there. Captain Roditi was there....'

'Matteo?'

It was Elena who asked the question, and she addressed it, not to me, but to Leporello, who smiled over it as if it were the first real victory of the evening.

'Don't ask me, my dear. I wasn't there.... Now, if you don't mind, the Colonel and I will take coffee in the library. We'll join you when we've had our talk.'

No sooner were we settled and private than his manner changed, dramatically. He was every inch the soldier again: curt, decisive, dogmatic, as if he were addressing a staff conference.

'Matucci, the time has come for us to be frank with each other.'

'I'd welcome that, sir.'

'Your Director thinks you're a trouble-maker. I think you and I would get on well together. Why do you hesitate to join me?'

'Two reasons to begin with: I want to finish my leave. I want to test myself in civilian employment.'

'With Bruno Manzini.'

'Yes.'

'He's an old rogue–dangerous.'

'Dangerous?'

'He's a bad enemy. He has blackmailed a number of people into suicide. Before you leave this evening, I shall give you copies of two dossiers. I should like you to study them, carefully, and return them to me. I make no further comment. You will come to your own conclusions.'

'You seem sure they'll agree with yours.'

'We'll see. . . . If you decide to join me, you may finish your leave without curtailment.'

'That's very fair.'

'Now, as to the appointment itself. There is no establishment as yet, no title, no table of organization. You would be required to set up a completely new section, subject only to me and to my personal directives. You would model this section on the Service of Defence Information, with such variations as your experience dictated and we agreed together. Interested?'

'So far, very. What would be the purpose of this section?'

'Political intelligence, in the widest sense. If certain events take place, if certain projects mature, the scope of the work would be greatly enlarged, and your position would be one of considerable power.'

'Can you specify the events and the projects, General?'

'I can, but not yet.'

'May I ask why?'

'Because I must first be sure, Colonel, where your loyalties lie.'

'I should have thought that was obvious, General.'

'Indeed?'

'Yes, sir. We are both commissioned officers in the same Corps. We took the same oath of service. That specifies everything very clearly, I think.'

'Unfortunately, it doesn't. It does not specify, for instance, your political affiliation.'

'Am I required to have one?'

'For this post, yes.'

'Then you should nominate it, General.'

'I need a very conservative man.'

'That could be a contradiction in terms. Intelligence deals both with the actual and the possible. I could quote my Director at length on that subject.'

'Would it help if I told you that your Director has become a very conservative man.'

'I already know that, sir.'

'What do you know?'

'The meeting was held at the Villa Baldassare, was it not?'

'How the devil . . .?'

'I dined with the Director and with Bruno Manzini in Venice.'

'What did they tell you?'

'I could not depose that they told me anything. Let's say I became aware of certain situations and arrangements. For instance, there was a discussion as to whether I should be eliminated. There were two votes against, one for killing me–your vote, General. So you see, I'm rather puzzled by this offer of yours.'

I had thought to shake him. I was disappointed. Whatever he was as a husband, in his character of soldier and strategist, he was impregnable. He reproved me, quietly.

'Why? You know the trade. We're all at risk. I voted yes. Then, I changed my mind.'

'Why?'

'I have never trusted your Director. I have always regarded him as a useful but fickle ally. So, when I left the meeting at the Villa Baldassare, I thought very carefully. I concluded I had need of a rival and an ultimate substitute for the Director. . . . You, my dear Colonel. Simple, isn't it?'

'Too simple.'

'Why so?'

'Everyone carries life insurance, except me. Manzini has wealth and influence. The Director has a presidential appointment. You have general rank in the Carabinieri. Me? I'm out on the limb of the cherry-tree.'

'Join me and you will have my personal protection. Don't underrate that, Colonel.'

'I don't. But I was thinking of the Surgeon.'

'What about him?'

'He's dead.'

'I wasn't protecting him.'

'Oh, I see.'

'You said it yourself: the man was a discreditable nuisance. . . . More brandy?'

'Thank you. . . . Do you mind if I ask a few questions?'

'Please!'

'This aide of yours, Captain Roditi . . . explain him to me.'

I had touched him on the raw. His head jerked up. He was suddenly tense and threatening.

'I think you should explain yourself, Colonel.'

'*Ebbene!* You want me to join you. I am interested; but I am not prepared to walk blind into a new situation. I have studied you, General, as you have studied me. I hear that this Roditi is a court favourite. He is resented. Because of him, you are resented, too. I want to know why.'

He considered the question for a long time. He turned it over and over, as if it were a piece of putty from which he might mould an answer that would suit me. Finally, he said:

'Roditi is dispensable. You come, he goes, if that's what you want.'

'What was he doing at the Club Alcibiade?'

'He recruits there.'

'And at the Pavone?'

'Yes.'

'I'm curious to know why you're using these types.'

'We need men without ties, with no ambition beyond money and the companionship of their own kind. They, too, will be dispensable in time, like the Congo mercenaries.'

'General, if you were sitting in my chair, would you accept that answer?'

'If I were sitting in your chair, Matucci, I should not expect to have all the words spelt out for me.'

'Fair comment, General. . . . I accept it. However, you must be patient with me. You offer me patronage, protection. I have to know where the power lies, and the weakness, too.'

'I'm listening.'

'Your marriage is obviously unhappy.'

'Is it so obvious?'

'To me, yes. A man like you, with ambitions like yours, cannot afford an enemy in the house. You must be very lonely, General.'

'I am. I confess that these are desert days for me, Matucci. But I am prepared to endure them a while longer.'

'So, you lean on Roditi?'

'More than I should, perhaps. He's become like a son to me. But I need someone much stronger, much wiser. You, my friend.'

'But you're still not prepared to trust me. . . . Please, General, let's not play games. There's a dossier on you at SID. The Director knows what's in it. I don't, because he has always reserved it to himself. That's why you wouldn't move until you had him as an ally. You still don't trust him, and you want to set me up against him. I'm impotent, unless I know as much as he does. I can't protect you, unless I know what weapons he can use against you. . . . Now, why don't you think about that? If you still want me, we can meet again and discuss final questions. After that, we can sign transfer papers.'

'You might decide not to join me after all.'

'And you might decide to withdraw your protection. In which case, I could end like the Surgeon, with a bullet in the head. If that happened. . . .?'

'Yes, Colonel?'

'There is a data-bank in Switzerland, which would immediately circulate a lot of information to the Press and other interested parties.'

'Blackmail, Colonel?'

'No, General. That begins when I try to extort money or preferment. I have done neither. I have simply taken out insurance. But, talking of blackmail, are you sure you yourself are not a victim?'

'I told you once, Colonel, I tell you again. My life is an open book.'

'That's the public record, General. The secret one is what they hit you with on the day when you're proclaimed saviour of the country. . . . Look, I didn't ask for the job. You offered it. If you're unhappy with my terms, let's forget it.'

'Let's define them more clearly.'

'Full disclosure on both sides.'

'Very well. I'll be in touch with you again in a few days. Meantime, you can study the Manzini dossiers. . . . More brandy?'

'No, thank you. I should be getting home. It's been a long day.'

'Not too unprofitable, I hope?'

'Far from it, General. I think we've come a long way towards an understanding.'

'Good. . . . By the way, would you mind dropping Laura in town, otherwise I'll have to call a staff car. I don't like taxis calling at the house here.'

'No trouble at all. I'll be delighted.'

'I like her. She's a cheerful soul. A little stupid, perhaps, but rich in her own right—and still unattached. A word to the wise, eh?'

Cheerful she was, and more than a little drunk, and she chatted like a feather-brain; but stupid she wasn't. As we drove back to town, she gave me a zany but revealing commentary on the dinner-party.

'Meow-meow-meow! Talk about the cat in the pigeon-loft! You were very naughty tonight, Dante. You know you were. You've still got feathers all over your whiskers. You're the first man I've seen who was able to handle Elena in one of her moods. Eek! She really had her claws out for Marcantonio tonight. . . . Not that I blame her, really. He's no joy in bed and no fun anywhere else, as far as I can see. . . . You don't really want to work for him, do you? I can't see you fitting into the bunch of *finocchi* he's got around him. But then, I don't know you very well, do I? And you never did say what you were doing at the Alcibiade. And what was Matteo Roditi doing there? You didn't see Elena's face when you dropped that hot brick. I thought she was going to burst a gusset and pop that big bosom of hers in the gravy. You know they're lovers, of course? My dear man, everybody knows—even the General. If my arithmetic's right, Roditi has to be the father of the twins. . . . Why? Oh, come on, Matucci! Why do you think the old boy uses Matteo to do all his dirty work. . . . Me? I'm the little friend of all the world. But I am Elena's friend first. And I'll make a bet with you. If she doesn't call you in the next twenty-four hours, I'll give you a night in bed, myself. . . .'

'No bet. You're already invited.'

'I hate to be rushed.'

'No rush. There's champagne and caviar and soft music and. . . .'

'And Elena will hate me ever after.'

'Who's to tell, *bambina*?'

'That's right, who's to tell. She'll still ring you though. She's wild for you, Matucci. I know her.'

'You told me she was wild for Roditi.'

'Oh, that's special. The others—and there have been a lot of others—are her revenge on her husband. If you're going to join him, she'll get you to bed, if she has to scream rape and murder to do it.'

'She sounds like a candidate for the *manicomio*!'

'Wouldn't you be, if you were married to a middle-aged *finocchio* with delusions of grandeur.'

'God forbid!'

'Amen! Now, tell me about your love-life, Colonel. I'd like to know what I'm getting into before I have too much champagne.'

As it turned out, three glasses were more than enough. She passed out cold to the music of Henry Mancini. I undressed her, tucked her into the big double bed, hung up her clothes, stuck a get-well note to the bathroom mirror and closed the door on her.

It was now one in the morning in Milan; where, if her citizens are to be believed, money will buy you anything, day or night. My needs were essentially simple; an atomizer and a one-eyed notary, deaf and dumb, insomniac and avaricious. I record, as a matter of historic interest, that, even with my contacts, it took me an hour to find him, twenty minutes to haggle with him and a hundred thousand lire in cash to coax him out of the house.

I can be flippant about it now; but at that moment in time I was desperate. To explain: I wanted to take a legal deposition from a witness. I was prepared to exercise duress, threats, intimidation and physical violence, if necessary. So, I needed a notary, with a stack of *carta bollata* and a rubber stamp, and a flexible conscience.

At three-fifteen, armed and accompanied by the said notary, I presented myself at the apartment of Captain Matteo Roditi. The Captain was out, absent, abroad about the business of his master—or his mistress, as the case might be. I entered the apartment, closed the notary in the bedroom to doze awhile, made myself a cup of coffee in the kitchen and settled down to wait. At three-forty-five, red-eyed and almost sober, Roditi came home. I pushed him against the wall while I patted him for concealed weapons. Then I sat him in the Danish armchair and perched myself on the desk, with the pistol and the atomizer beside me. After that, I was able to talk to him like a country uncle.

'Captain, you don't know me very well. You may, therefore, be tempted to believe I am playing games. I am not. If you don't give me truthful answers, I'm going to kill you. I shall spray cyanic acid gas in your face and you will be dead in four seconds. If you co-operate, I may offer you a way out of the mess you're in now. Clear?'

'Yes.'

'In your bedroom there is the signed photograph of a woman, and a bundle of love-letters from a woman called Elena. Who is Elena?'

'She's the wife of General Leporello.'

'How long have you been lovers?'

'About six years.'

'Are you the father of her children?'

'I believe so.'

'Does the General know of your association?'

'Yes.'

'And condones it?'

'Yes.'

'Tell me why?'

'It gives him a hold over both of us.'

'Explain that.'

'He is the legal father of the children. His name is on the registration of birth. He could remove them from Elena's care and custody.'

'And what is his hold over you?'

'I have performed services for him which put me in legal jeopardy.'

'What services?'

'I have procured for him.'

'Inside or outside the Service?'

'Both. I have another apartment, near the Duomo. The lease is in my name. He uses that as a meeting place. I pay the people and make sure there's no trouble afterwards.'

'How do you do that?'

'Threats mostly. Action, if necessary.'

'You have people beaten up, that sort of thing?'

'Yes.'

'I'll need names and dates and places, but we'll come to that later. Do you know Major Zenobio, the Commandant of Camerata?'

'Yes.'

'Have you heard from him today?'

'There was a message to call him. I haven't done it yet.'

'Did you get a letter from Chiasso today?'

'Yes.'

'Did the General get one?'

'Yes.'

'What did you do about them?'

'I passed them to forensics to check the fingerprint and the typewritten sheet.'

'Have you had any answers yet?'

'No.'

'When would you expect the answers?'

'Tomorrow, or the next day.'

'Did you know whose print it was?'

'I had an idea. I wasn't sure.'

'Whose?'

'It could have belonged to Balbo.'

'Did he kill Bandinelli and Calvi?'

'Yes.'

'Did he plant a letter-bomb in the apartment of one Lili Anders?'

'Yes.'

'Who gave the orders?'

'I did.'

'Who gave you your orders?'

'The General.'

'Where are the Pantaleone papers?'

'I gave them to Leporello.'

'Where are they now?'

'I don't know. Possibly at his house.'

'Where is Giuseppe Balbo?'

'I think he's dead.'

'You think . . .!'

'I was told to take him to the Club Alcibiade tonight and make sure we left at two forty-five.'

'Who told you?'

'The General.'

'Because of the letter from Chiasso?'

'Yes.'

'Who was going to do the job?'

'I don't know. I wasn't told.'

'Any ideas?'

'Leporello talked of killing two birds with one shot—the Surgeon and Balbo.'

'Very neat. Did you ever think he might want to get rid of you one day?'

'Yes.'

'Did you never take out any insurance?'

'Yes, I did. I had the other apartment bugged. There are tapes and photographs.'

'Where are they?'

'Elena has one set. I have another in safe deposit at the Banco Centrale.'

'I'll need the key and an authorization of access.'

'Very well.'

'How do you feel about Elena now?'

'I love her, for God's sake! Why else do you think I've stayed in this rotten business?'

'Because you didn't want to get out. . . . When Leporello brought off his coup, you'd be a very big man.'

'What are you going to do now?'

'Not I, Roditi, you! You're going to write a deposition. There's a little man in your bedroom who will notarize the document. When that's done, we'll talk about the rest of it. . . . Now, there's the *carta bollata*, there's the pen. I'll dictate. You write.'

It took half an hour to compose the document and half a minute to stamp and notarize it. I sent the notary on his drowsy way, had Roditi write a letter to his bank, stuffed the documents into my breast pocket, and settled down to a more cosy chat. Roditi was utterly defeated, sallow and trembling, so I let him have a whisky to revive himself while I laid out the deal.

'. . . Your deposition buys you a life sentence, Roditi. A phone call from me to Leporello gets you killed before morning. So, you're going absent without leave. You'll pack a bag. I'll drive you to a safe place in the country and you'll stay there until I've built the last brick into my case against Leporello. You'll be interrogated. You'll make more depositions than you've ever dreamed of. But at least you won't be in gaol, and waiting for some cell-mate to put a skewer in your back. Then, before the case breaks, you'll have twenty-four hours to get out of the country with Elena and the children. . . . It's the best I can do. Take it or leave it.'

'It's no good. It won't work.'

'Why not?'

'It just won't, that's all.'

'Have you got a better idea?'

'Yes. Leave me free until you've finished your case. I can bluff it out. That's one thing I'm good at. I can feed you information–better information than you would get any other way. Things are starting to happen, Matucci, and they're going to happen very fast. . . .'

'What sort of things?'

'I can't tell you yet. But I will as soon as I know.'

'I'm sorry. I don't like it. Pack your bag, now.'

'I'm not going.'

'Then you're going to tell me why.'

'All right. You've been followed all the evening. While your car was at the General's house, they fixed a bleeper on it.'

'Which means they know where I am now?'

'Yes, yes.'

'And they're waiting for me, downstairs?'

'I don't know.'

'Then let's take a walk and find out. If they're not there, we'll take a little drive–to Balbo's place first, then over to the General's house. . . . If we have to finish it now, let's finish it. On your feet!'

'I'm not going. You can kill me here if you like, but I'm not going.'

'So, that's why it was all so easy, eh? They cut me down as I walk out the front door! Or they've taped the car with plastic and when I switch on the ignition, it blows me sky-high. Now, little man, which is it?'

'I don't know. I swear I don't know.'

'Then, let's find out.'

I fished out my pocket-book and found the number of the SID agency in Milan. I dialled it and spoke to the duty officer, quoting my identification number.

'. . . I am questioning a suspect. My car is parked outside the building. It's a red Mercedes with a Milan number plate. I know it has been bugged. It may have been planted with an explosive device. It is also possible there may be an attempt to assassinate me as I leave the building. The suspect is an officer of Carabiniéri, so I'd rather not have them brought in. Can you manage it by yourselves? And without making a fuss? I don't care about the car, you can deliver that for me when it's clean. But I'll need another vehicle at my disposal when I leave. When you're ready, send a man up to the apartment to let me know. Code-word "Dragon". . . . That's right— "Dragon". Don't let him forget it. He might get shot as he comes in. . . . Thanks. Hurry it up please. Oh, and just for safety, check me back on this number as soon as I hang up.'

He checked back and told me the boys would be with me in thirty minutes. It was a long time to wait and a lot could happen in that time. I switched off the lights and crossed to the window and parted the drapes. It was already happening. Three police cars were already parked outside the building, a third was turning into the street. Already the men were piling out of them and grouping themselves round the officer in command. The plot was very clear now. Arrest and search and ninety-two hours' detention on any charge in the book. I could think of two that would stick—breaking and entering and withholding information from the police on the killing of the Surgeon. By the time I got out, if I ever got out, the depositions would have disappeared into thin air. I hauled Roditi to his feet, thrust a wadded handkerchief into his mouth, poked my gun into his kidneys and hustled him out of the apartment.

There was no way down, except by the elevators, or the concrete stairs. Either way would land me in the arms of the Carabinieri. We went up. We climbed four flights until we came to a door that gave access to the roof and the watertanks on top of it. The door was locked. It took me a minute to pick the lock. I pushed Roditi out on to the roof and relocked the door from the outside. Then I leaned him, face against the door, and chopped him hard on the back of the skull. He went down like a sack. I dragged him into the shelter of the water-tanks and took the gag out of his mouth. I didn't want him to choke just yet. He had a lot more talking to do, if ever I could get out of this very neat trap.

I made a cautious circuit of the roof and found that the two adjoining buildings were similar in height and construction. It would be an easy matter to climb across the parapets and make my escape through the third building. It would be quite impossible if I had to take Roditi with me. I left him and a few minutes later I found myself in a deserted office block. I waited, frozen and disconsolate in a toilet, wondering what had happened to Roditi and why no one had bothered to check the rooftop. When the workers began to arrive in the morning, I walked out into the crowded, sunlit streets and took a taxi to Steffi's hotel.

For all his cavils and quirks, Steffi in crisis was a treasure. While I bathed and shaved, he strolled around to the Xerox offices and made copies of the deposition on a coin-in-the-slot machine. Then he went to the Milan office of his bank, cashed a cheque and deposited the original document for safekeeping against my signature or his own. After that, he surged, larger than life, into Manzini's office and demanded to see the old man. He presented my compliments, a photostat copy and a second-hand account of the night's events. The pair of them came back to the hotel for breakfast, chatting as if they had known each other all their lives.

Breakfast, however, was a sober meal. Manzini telephoned the editor of his newspaper and came back with three stories which would feature in the afternoon editions. The lead story dealt with a gun battle in which one, Guiseppe Balbo, a suspect in the murders at the Duca di Gallodoro, had been killed by police officers while resisting arrest. Also on the front page was the account of a mysterious occurrence in a fashionable apartment block. Answering an anonymous telephone call, the details of which could not yet be released, the police had visited an apartment on the fifth floor, occupied by Captain Matteo Roditi, personal aide to Major-General Leporello. The apartment was empty and in disorder. There was no sign of the Captain, who, at the time of going to press, was still missing. The police had already detained one man who was known to have visited the apartment in the early hours of the morning. They were also seeking to question a certain Dante Alighieri Matucci, member of a Government agency, whose car was parked outside the building and whose fingerprints were found in the apartment of the missing man. There was full and accurate description of me and a photograph obviously supplied by wire from the files of SID.

'. . . And that, gentlemen,' said Manzini, flatly, 'disposes of our case. Balbo is dead. Roditi is dead or in protective custody. Your notary is now under the lamps; and, by the time they have finished with him, he will sign whatever they want. Roditi's deposition is worthless, because they will produce a counter-deposition proving duress. You, my Dante, are now a man on the run. If they take you . . . *Buona notte!* It's the Matteotti affair all over again.'

'You're forgetting something, Bruno. I have a key and an authority that will open Roditi's safe-deposit at the Banca Centrale. If he was telling me the truth, there's enough material there to finish Leporello at one stroke.'

'There are three ifs in that proposition, Dante. If Roditi was telling the truth. . . . If Leporello hasn't already got a judical order to open the box. . . . If you could open it yourself. . . . Remember, you have to present identification. An hour from now, your description will be all over the streets of Milan. Which means also we have to get you out of here fast.'

'Let me answer first. I believe Roditi was telling the truth. I don't believe he would hand his last insurance to Leporello.'

'Not even if he were threatened with death? You broke him easily.'

'Only because he thought he was protected. If he sold out to Leporello, he would know he was leaving his woman and her children defenceless. I think he would cling to one last hope–that I, or someone else, might bring Leporello down.'

'I agree,' said Steffi, vehemently. 'One crumb of hope keeps a man going for a long time.'

'Access to the box, then.' Manzini was still gloomy. 'How do you manage that?'

'What does a banker need–not at the moment itself–but on his record after the customer is gone?'

'A signature and a note of the document of identification.'

'You have my document of identification. You have a very good calligrapher in Carlo Metaponte, who did your Salamander card. And you have your friend Ludovisi at the Banca Centrale who promised his help if ever we needed it. Well, Bruno . . .?'

'It depends on Ludovisi, doesn't it?'

'That's right.'

'I'll try him. Let me have your documents and the key. . . . Now, Matucci, what are we going to do with you?'

'I'll have to go underground. For that I'll need the false papers which are in the safe at the apartment.'

'I'll go there and get them. Meantime, where do we put you?'

'Where's your car?'

'Parked in front of the hotel. The doorman's been paid.'

'Could you get me out to Pedognana and keep me there for a couple of days?'

'Not in the house. I think we might have a visit from the Carabinieri. On the estate, certainly, if you don't mind a little peasant living. What about Stefanelli here?'

'I'll stay in town, Cavaliere. This big oaf needs me more than he admits.'

'I don't like it, Steffi. It's a very rough game now.'

'So, what do you need if not someone who understands the trade? Besides who cares about an old sorehead on a holiday he can't enjoy?'

'Thanks, Steffi. When I call, I'm Rabin. It should be a lucky name for us all.'

Manzini ignored the reference. He was still wrestling with a private problem. He asked, abruptly:

'Suppose Ludovisi won't play. What then?'

'There's one last hope. . . . Leporello's wife.'

'When she reads that report, she'll think you killed or kidnapped Roditi.'

'The report came from her husband. I don't think she'd believe him if he told her the day of the week.'

'It's an awful gamble.'

'I know a worse one.' said Steffi, sombrely. 'Leporello for *Duce* and the bully-boys keeping order with truncheons and castor oil.'

I spent four days at Pedognana, three of them lodged in the attic of the factor's house. The Carabinieri came once and spent an afternoon prowling the estate. I spent that same afternoon in a barn loft and emerged with a beautiful dose of hay fever. On the fourth day, Manzini arrived with my documents, and a suit-case of ready-to-wear clothes to fit my new identity as one Aldo Carnera. Thorough as ever, he had procured me a back-dated employment as a travelling salesman with one of his small off-shoot companies. I would never have to put in an appearance, but, if anyone checked back, my false name and personal details were on file.

He brought discouraging news, too. Ludovisi was in New York at a conference. He was flying from New York to Mexico City and thence to Buenos Aires. He was not expected back for ten days. Manzini was fretful. All his careful plans to introduce me into society, to elevate me to the status of a diplomatic agent, were now in ruins. I was back in the underworld from which he had taken me. I was, by presumption, disreputable and because of me, he, too, had fallen into some discredit with the Movement. He was excluded from its inner councils. The Director had sent him a caustic little note suggesting that, until his credit was restored, he might confine his activities to financial contribution, of which the Movement stood in constant need.

We dined together that night and I tried to coax him back into his anecdotal mood; but he refused to be drawn until I mentioned the two dossiers which Leporello had given to me, but which I had not had an opportunity to read. All I remembered were the names: Hans Helmut Ziegler and Emmanuele Salatri. He mused over them for a few moments and then threw up his hands, casting off ill-humour like a cloak.

'Eh! Why not? What is the past for, if not to renew our hope in the future. Hans Helmut Ziegler. . . . That one goes a long way back. It began, let me see, in nineteen-thirty. I was in Sao Paolo then, spending my first big money, making my first investment in the New World. In those days, my Dante, there were more Italians than Brazilians in Sao Paolo. Most of them were migrants, but some like myself were investors—in sugar and coffee land, in textiles and pharmaceuticals, small companies at first but immensely profitable. Those were wild days. I was coining money and spending it and coining more. . . . And the women, *Dio*! They dropped into your hands like ripe papayas.

'One night in a gambling club, I was standing next to a young fellow about my own age. He was Brazilian and he was playing higher than I was on roulette. I was having a run of luck. He was losing and chasing his losses. In the end, about midnight, he was cleaned out. He looked so disconsolate, so utterly despairing, I couldn't bear it. I put my hand on his sleeve and invited him to stay and share a stake with me—just for luck, my luck if not his. For a moment, I thought he was going to strike me. Then he laughed and said: "Why not? It's fools' money." Well, to cut it short, I put a big green chip on thirty-five. It won. We split the money and walked away from the table, arm in arm, friends for life. His name was Paolo Pereira Pinto and he is now one of the best bankers in Brazil. When he got his first directorship he sent me an emerald, five carats, square-cut, as a souvenir of that night. I had the emerald set in a brooch for Raquela Rabin.

'. . . That's the first part of the story. The second part is much later. Hans Helmut Ziegler was the Gestapo man who worked me over in prison. He loved his job and he was expert at it. A dialogue with him, in the interrogation cell, was like a confrontation with the evil one himself. Even now, old as I am, I remember him with terror and loathing. After the war, he disappeared, swallowed up in the chaos. In 1965 the daughter of my old friend, Pinto, was left a widow with two young children. A year later, she remarried and Pinto sent me the wedding photograph. The man she had married was Hans Helmut Ziegler. . . . It took two years' work and twenty-thousand dollars to build a dossier on him. I sent it to him with a Salamander card. He couldn't even manage a clean exit. He drove himself over a cliff at one hundred and fifty kilometres an hour. Old Pinto read the dossier and thought the Israelis had killed him. He was glad to be rid of Ziegler. He didn't want the Zionists operating in his bailiwick. He called in the police who sent the dossier to Interpol. Eventually, they found their way to me, by way of the Italian authorities—which is, I suppose, how the dossier came into Leporello's hands. You may not believe it, but Pinto and I are still friends. . . .

'That ought to be the end of the story, my Dante, but it isn't. In the days before the Black Sabbath, the Jews of Rome believed they had a deal with the Germans to ransom themselves. A fund was set up to which everyone contributed in gold and jewellery. Women even gave their wedding rings. All to no avail. The Germans took the gold and took the people as well. . . . However, one of the collectors was a man called Emmanuele Salatri. It was to him that Raquela gave the emerald brooch. Salatri never delivered what he had collected. He simply vanished with the loot. In 1969, there was an important auction of jewellery in Zurich. Among the pieces advertised in the catalogue, was that brooch. I was, therefore, in a position to trace its provenance. I traced it through two other owners to Emmanuele Salatri, who was then a prosperous gem-dealer in Hatton Garden in London. I sent him a dossier and a card. He blew his brains out. Once again, the dossier was traced back to me. Once again, nothing could be done about it because I had committed no crime. I gave the brooch back to Raquela. She would not accept it. There was blood on it, she said, and it would bring no joy to anyone. I sold it to Bulgari who broke it up and reset the stone.

'. . . Old history! Am I wrong to dig it up? I have thought so, many times, but always I have come back to the same question: why should the villains flourish while the victims still suffer the effects of their villainies? This is your question now, Matucci. It is one of the ironies of history that Leporello could wade through a whole ocean of crimes and still prove a potent and even a good ruler. But even if he did, should we still suffer him? Even if he came now in sackcloth with a halter round his neck, should we, in the same breath, forgive him and consecrate him to power? I cannot see it. I cannot. . . .

'There's one more story, my Dante; and then we must go to bed. Come over to the window. You see those far hills and the cluster of light at the top? . . . That's Vincolata. It's nothing much of anything, a little hill town with maybe five hundred people inside its old walls. In the Partisan days, I used it as an observation point, and sometimes I slept there in the house of a widow woman called Bassi.

'One day we ambushed a small German detachment a kilometre from the town, and killed two men. There were immediate reprisals. The Germans arrested twenty men, young and old, as hostages, and ordered them to be shot in the square of Vincolata. The officer in charge of the firing squad was a young Austrian Oberleutnant named Loeffler. . . . You can imagine the horror of such an event in a small place like Vincolata. Twenty men. . . . It is a loss and a trauma that can never be repaired. They were my people. They had suffered because of orders I had given. So, I promised, one day justice would be done.

'. . . Loeffler survived the war, went back to Austria and entered the pastoral priesthood. It takes us different ways you see. Me, it made an instrument of vengeance, him, it turned into an apostle. I had lost Loeffler by then and the more I came back here and saw the peace of this place, the less I wanted to disturb it.

'. . . Late in the sixties, I was in Austria, negotiating a contract for iron-ore. In the local press I read the news that the Right Reverend Franziskus Loeffler, parish priest of Oberalp, had been nominated to a Bishopric and would be consecrated in Rome by the Holy Father. I wasn't sure if it was the same man; so I went to see him. It was the same Franziskus Loeffler, and I didn't like him. I found him shallow, stubborn, vain, the kind of churchman I have always resented, half tyrant, half father-figure. I told him why I had come. I asked him whether he did not consider his elevation to a Bishopric an affront to his co-religionists in Vincolata.

'I could not come within a hand's touch of him. He was so secure in his conversion, it was as if he carried a private brief from the Almighty. I went away angry and bitter. I wrote to the Vatican. I incited a press campaign against the nomination, and suggested that Loeffler could and should be extradited to Italy to stand trial as a war criminal. Loeffler declined his nomination, resigned his parish and retired into obscurity.

'There is, however, an epilogue. About eighteen months ago, the parish priest of Vincolata came to see me, and asked as a special favour that I attend his Sunday Mass. Loeffler was there. He was dressed in clerical grey, with a white collar and a black tie and was kneeling in the front pew, by the nave. After the recitation of the Confiteor, he stood up, faced the congregation and announced very simply: "I am Franziskus Loeffler. I attended the execution of your relatives and friends during the war. I gave the firing order. I am here to beg your pardon if you feel you can give it. If not, I am prepared to offer myself for whatever retribution you may exact. I cannot bring back the dead. I wish I could. Please forgive me." He knelt down again and the Mass went on. Afterwards, I waited to see what the folk of Vincolata would do. . . . Nothing, my Dante! Absolutely nothing! They ignored him. They walked away and left him in what must have been the cruellest solitude of his life.

'. . . What could I do? I invited him home for lunch. I still didn't like him; but he was a bigger man than I, for whom the simplest apology is like drawing a tooth. Afterwards I thought he would probably have made a very good Bishop. . . . I'm sorry you won't meet him now. I'd have liked to know your opinion. . . . See you in the morning, my Dante. Sleep well!'

I didn't sleep. I sat up late, and, desperately lonely, wrote a letter to Lili; not from Uncle Pavel this time, but from Dante Alighieri Matucci, fugitive, who tomorrow must go back to the half-world of those who cannot conform or will not submit to the discipline of the ant-heap.

My dearest Lili,
   This letter is from your puppet-man who has discovered, late and painfully, how little he can control his own destiny.
   It is very late. The moon is full and high and all the land is silver. It is very still, so still that I can almost hear the mice breathing behind the panelling of my bedroom. The fire is almost dead and I am beginning to be cold; but I do not want to go to bed, because you will not be there and I cannot dream you back. I tore up your last letter because I wanted to put you out of my mind until all this business was finished. It was no use. I cannot forget you. I cannot bear the empty room in my heart. I am jealous that you may have found someone else to take my place in yours.
   I love you, Lili! There! Now! It is said. I love you. I have clowned the words before. I have lied them and have traded them. This is the first time there has ever been a truth in them. Will you marry me, Lili? If I call you one day, to some tiny place that is hardly a name on a map, will you come and join hands and lips and body with me for always and a day more than always? Don't answer until you are sure; because when you are sure and I am free, I shall follow you to the last frontiers and home again.
   Home? I have no home now, Lili. I am a man on the run. Things have gone badly for us, but there is still hope of a good outcome. Tomorrow I must leave this pleasant refuge and go back into the underworld, where the beggars plot against the tyrants and the tyrants use beggars for spies. I am looking for a legacy, left by a man I think is dead. If I find it, everything will be simple. If not, you may see me in Switzerland sooner than you expect.
   I am afraid, but not too afraid; because I am learning slowly, to live with the man who lives in my skin. I haven't seen him full-face yet. That, too, will come. The Salamander still flourishes; and I am learning from him, too, the arts of

survival. . . . You will smile; but I never thought I could survive so long without
a woman's company. Perhaps the truth is that my woman is never so far absent
that I am without her utterly.

Strange how the words come back: '*Quella che 'mparadisa la mia mente!*' . . .
she who makes my mind a paradise. My namesake wrote some very good things
in his day. A pity he didn't write more about the body. That's very lonely just
now.

Always yours,
Dante Alighieri . . .

I have the letter still, because it was returned to me in circumstances
which belong later in this record.

I came back to Milan in the early afternoon, and settled myself in a modest
pensione near the Ambrosian Library. It was clean, comfortable and
economical, the right sort of lodging for a travelling salesman whose only
visible possessions were a cardboard valise and a leather attaché case, with a
combination lock just to impress the customers.

After I had unpacked, I strolled out to look at the Sforza Castle, the vast
fortress of red brick built by Francesco, Fourth Duke of Milan and founder
of the Sforza dynasty. He began as a simple *condottiere* with a horse and a
sword and three pieces of advice from his father: never beat a servant, never
ride a horse with a hard mouth and never make love to another man's wife.
He made himself the sword-arm of Filippo Visconti, last of the line,
fathered twenty-two bastards, married Filippo's daughter, and, when the
Visconti died, rode into a starving city with all his men-at-arms festooned
with bread. He died of the dropsy in 1466; but the bastion he built is still the
pride of Milan.

They were wild men in those days; but their genius and their vices
perpetuate themselves in the Italians of today, and all who deal with us do
well to understand it. To the foreigner, we look like characters out of an
opera, exaggerated and larger than life. The reverse is true. The opera is
only a pale shadow of our history; and our history repeats itself in shorter
cycles than theirs. Filippo Visconti, for instance, was just like the Surgeon.
He, too, threw people out of windows. He conjured up plots and spies and
filled the city with soldiers of fortune to protect him. Galeazzo Maria was
murdered in the Church of St Stephen by three young men who went to
Mass first to tell St Stephen they were sorry for messing up his Church.
Where Leonardo wrote his Atlantic Codex, the Pirelli building stands, as a
monument to Leonardo's successors.

Aimless thoughts, perhaps, from a man too disengaged for safety, in a
city where every policeman had his name. And yet not aimless, not so
irrelevant. Major-General Leporello was vaulting higher than the Visconti
and the Sforza had even dreamed. They were content with duchies and
provinces. He wanted all Italy under his first. He had arms and communications beyond their imagining and he had no Emperor or Pope breathing
down his neck.

As I wandered through the galleries and corridors of the fortress, I
wondered how I should best approach Elena Leporello. She was my last
chance: the last filly in the last race. If I lost her I might just as well head for
the Alps. I could write her a note. Her husband or a household spy might
intercept it. I could accost her in the street. She might scream for the
nearest policeman. I could telephone. She might, and probably would, slam
down the receiver in my ear. I decided to telephone. I bribed a custodian to

let me use the telephone in his office. A maidservant answered. I asked:

'May I speak with the General please?'

'I regret. The General is not at home. I suggest you try headquarters.'

'This is headquarters. Is the Signora at home?'

I waited a very long moment, and when Elena Leporello came on the line, I talked fast and eloquently:

'Please, madam, whatever I say, do not hang up until I have finished. This is Dante Alighieri Matucci. There is an order out for my arrest. I have been in hiding for several days. I read the papers. I do not know whether Captain Roditi is alive, dead or going about his normal duties. Can you tell me, please?'

'I can't tell you, not at this moment.'

'The reports give the impression that I either kidnapped him or murdered him. Neither is true. If he is alive, I must find him. Are you willing to talk to me?'

'Yes.'

'When?'

'Any day between ten and six.'

'Thank you. Now listen, carefully. At ten-thirty tomorrow morning go to the Ambrosian Library. Ask to see Petrarch's Virgil. The librarian will bring it to you. He will stay with you while you inspect it. A friend of mine will contact you then and bring you to me. Is that clear?'

'Yes, thank you.'

'Are you being watched?'

'I don't know.'

'If you think you are, don't keep the appointment. The same arrangement will stand for three days. If we have not made contact in that time, I will telephone again and make other arrangements.'

'I understand.'

'My friend will give you a recognition signal. He will ask: "Are you Raquela Rabin?" You will answer, "Yes!" Then do whatever he asks. Expect to be out of town for four or five hours.'

'I understand that.'

'I want to ask you some other questions. Just give me yes or no. . . . Can I trust Laura Balestra?'

'No.'

'Can you trust your servants?'

'No.'

'Will you trust me?'

'Until we meet—yes.'

'Thank you. I will now repeat. The Ambrosian Library, ten-thirty for three days. Petrarch's Virgil. Are you Raquela Rabin?'

'Yes. Thank you. Goodbye.'

So far, so good; but how far is far when you are dealing with a woman practised in intrigue? I put another slug in the telephone and dialled the number of Steffi's hotel.

'Steffi? This is Rabin. Shalom.'

'And to you, too, old friend. How are you?'

'Surviving. Are you free for dinner?'

'When you get to my age, you're always free for dinner. Where?'

'Rent yourself a car. Pick me up at six at the entrance to the Sforza Castle.'

'Who dines at six o'clock?'

'Nobody. We're going for a drive first. Do you like red-headed women?'

'With green hair even.'

'Any news?'

'Only that I'm bored.'

'That's good news. *Sbrigati eh*! Move it! There's a long way to go and the traffic's heavy.'

It was six-thirty when he found me and another forty minutes before we were on the autostrada, bowling along at a hundred and twenty kilometres an hour in the direction of Venice. As we drove, through warm, soft air and a misty countryside of poplars and orchard trees, I told him of my conversation with Elena Leporello and what I proposed to do about it.

'. . . If Roditi was telling the truth—and we always come back to that—then Elena Leporello has films and tapes that will hang Leporello higher than Haman's gibbet.'

Steffi slewed himself round in the seat and regarded me with limpid, compassionate eyes. He smiled and nodded his head, vigorously, up and down, up and down, like one of those silly Chinese mandarins. He admonished me with doleful patience.

'Matucci, little brother, it is as plain and large as the nose on my face that you have never been married. What do you know about this woman? She writes beautiful love-letters to a frightened pimp who procures for her husband! She bitches her husband at a dinner-party. What wife doesn't? You should hear mine sometimes, when I spill sauce on my tie or make a remark about one of the pretty little tarts who work for her. And her girl-friend says she has fallen for you! Oy-oy-oy! How much is that to gamble your life on? The trouble with you bachelors is that you don't hear a word that's said between hullo and goodbye. Now, listen little brother. Keep your eyes on the road and hear what an old married man has to tell you. This woman is sick. Worse, she knows it and loves it. She needs a husband she can kick around and humiliate. If he's a big shot in his profession, so much the better. That's spice for the turkey. She needs a lover of the same kind. Sure, she writes him love-notes . . . better than Petrarch even! But she saddles him with two kids after a summer loving, and the poor bastard takes it; because he is a poor bastard and a rotten little pimp as well. . . .'

'I know all that, Steffi, but. . . .'

'But nothing, Matucci. Keep your eyes on the road and let me finish. Now, you come waltzing to her party all done up like a wedding-cake. You're new, you're male. Sure, she is interested. You're a challenge. She has to prove she can pat you down and make you eat out of her hand like the others. She's got something you want—no matter that it isn't what she'd like you to want—and she's going to make you sit up and beg for it. And beg, and beg. . . . And if you won't beg, she'll turn you in, just to show you who holds the whip. . . . So, you don't like it, you don't have to buy it; but that's how I read the story of Elena Leporello.'

'Even if you're right, Steffi, it still doesn't solve my problem. She has got something I want. How do I get it?'

'First question: where has she got it?'

'I don't know.'

'Second question: who shares it with her?'

'I don't understand.'

'A woman like that, with a wonderful dirty story and pictures to

ınatch. . . . You think she keeps it all to her lonely self? Never in a million
years! She has to tell it. Else, where's the fun?'

'Laura Balestra?'

'Possibly. Probably. What do you know about her?'

'Not much. I'm told she's rich. I know she's unmarried.'

'How old is she?'

'Oh, thirty . . . thirty-five.'

'What else?'

'She's amusing and she likes to flirt and I'd guess she likes to get drunk so
she doesn't have to say yes, and she can always blame the man when she
wakes up in the wrong bed. I'd say she's an almost girl: almost in love and
almost engaged and almost never likely to get married.'

'She sounds a likely candidate for the scandal session. . . . Matucci, do
you always drive like this? Please, I'm dyspeptic. Let me live to enjoy my
dinner.'

'So, Laura knows where the stuff is hidden. She tells me. What then?'

'Then, little brother, you have the whip. You threaten the lady. If she
doesn't hand over the material, you will tell her husband she has it.'

'It would never work, Steffi.'

'I told you. You'll never understand women . . . until you marry one and
then it's too late!'

'Let me think about it.'

'While you're thinking about it, here's a little bet. Ten thousand to a
thousand the lady doesn't show at the Ambrosiana tomorrow.'

'Done! Now what do you fancy for dinner?'

'First, I would like a Bacardi cocktail, in company with a red-headed
woman. . . .'

He got his Bacardi in Harry's Bar. He got his red-headed woman: but
Gisela Pestalozzi was too much even for Steffi's jaded palate. Her
appearance struck him dumb, her loud, bawdy talk reduced him to idiot
confusion, so that I expected him at any moment to go into fugue and retreat
under the table. However, the apartment she showed us was a little gem:
with a front entrance that gave on to a quiet alley, a rear one from which you
could step straight into a boat and an attic window from which you could
climb over the rooftops, as long as the tiles would hold. The heating was
more than adequate, the telephone worked, the furniture was worm-free
and the linen was fresh. At our first meeting she had called the price at two
hundred thousand a month. We settled on a hundred and fifty. There was
no lease; the Salamander's name was good enough on both sides. I paid two
months rent in cash. She handed me the key and some advice by way of a
bonus:

'If you want a boatman, call me. If you want to bribe a policeman, check
with me before you hand over any money. If you're in trouble, stay out of
Harry's Bar and use the phone. For false documents, there's a forty-eight-
hour service. It costs less if you can give me more time. No wild parties. No
brawls. You get resident's discount on my girls. . . . And you, old man, don't
be shy. I've had eighty-year-old cripples throw away their crutches. . . .'

She left us with a clatter of baubles and a toss of that extraordinary hair.
Steffi collapsed into a chair and spluttered:

'My God! She's straight out of the Wax Museum! . . . Safe house indeed!
With a man-eating monster like that, you'd be safer in a slaughter-yard. But
what do you want the place for?'

'Don't laugh, Steffi! After tomorrow you may be on the run yourself.'

Looking at him then, pop-eyed and speechless, I remembered one of the less useful facts of history. Pietro Aretino died in Venice. He was no mean pornographer himself; and he died of apoplexy, laughing at a dirty joke.

At ten o'clock the next morning, dressed in a mechanic's cap and overalls and smeared with engine oil, I was tinkering with a scrubby Fiat, sixty metres from the entrance of the Ambrosian Library. There was nothing wrong with the engine; but I was nervous and twitchy, half-hoping that Steffi would win his bet and I could call the whole thing off with a good conscience. At ten-fifteen, Steffi himself marched down the street, looking for all the world like an elderly professor, who could decipher fifteenth-century cursive or decide a disputed interpretation at the drop of his black fedora. He was whistling, 'The Hills are in Flower', which, if you could recognize the tune, was a sign that, so far at least, there were no *poliziotti* on the horizon.

At ten twenty-five Elena Leporello drove up in a white Lancia. She was alone, which was another good sign. She locked the car, put the keys in her handbag and, without a backward glance, walked into the library, calm and unflustered as any Milanese matron out for a morning's shopping. I straightened up, wiped my hands on the greaserag, lit a cigarette and surveyed the street, up and down, from the entrance. There was the usual passage of people. There were no suspicious loiterers; no convergence of cars or men that would indicate the imminent arrest of a dangerous character. *Ebbene!* There was nothing to do but wait and the waiting could be fairly long, because the inspection of Petrarch's Virgil is one of the most serious ceremonies at the Ambrosiana.

The volume is huge. The Chief Librarian, himself, must authorize the inspection. An attendant, reverent and watchful, must stand beside you as you turn the pages, illuminated by Simone Martini of Siena. If you cannot read the inscription, written in the poet's own hand, the attendant will translate it for you:

> Laura, with all her illustrious virtues and long celebrated in my poems, first appeared before my eyes, in my young manhood, on the sixth day of April, in the year of our Lord 1327 in the early morning, in the Church of St Claire in Avignon . . .

I have always had a sentiment for the ceremony. In my days as a tourist guide, I found a reading of Petrarch in the original worked wonders with impressionable young women. Now, impatient and sweating with nervousness, I cursed myself for an idiot. I tossed away my cigarette, closed the bonnet of the car and sat inside, watching the entrance through the rear-vision mirror.

At ten fifty-five, Steffi came out with Elena Leporello. They got into the Lancia and drove off. I followed far enough behind to see whether any shadow car had joined our cavalcade. In the howling chaos of Milan's traffic, it was difficult to be sure of anything, even my own sanity. I saw, or thought I saw, one or two likely followers, but they dropped away. When we came on to the autostrada, I hung well back, letting the cars build up between me and the Lancia; but by the time we passed the Verona exit, I was fairly confident that we were free of shadows. By Padua, I was sure of it; so, I let them drive far ahead of me all the way to Mestre. Steffi's instructions were to cross to Venice, buy the lady a sandwich in St Mark's Square and leave when I made my appearance. He would then go to the safe house and wait for me. Elena Leporello could drive back to Milan alone. I hoped the strategy might establish in her mind the fact that I had left Milan and was holed up somewhere in the city of the Doges.

I went straight to the house, washed and tidied myself, and then, dressed in slacks and a green pullover, walked round to St Mark's Square. Steffi saw me coming and left before I reached the table. Elena Leporello gave me a frosty welcome:

'I hope, Colonel, there is some sense in this sordid little drama.'

'I hope, madam, you will help me make sense of it. Have you heard from Captain Roditi?'

'Not a word.'

'Does your husband know where he is?'

'No. He has a team of investigators working night and day on the case. He says he knows what happened at Matteo's apartment. You forced him to write a false and incriminating document, then had him killed or kidnapped.'

'And how does he know that?'

'From the notary who witnessed the document in Matteo's apartment. He's been arrested and he has signed a confession.'

'Has your husband seen the document?'

'He hasn't said so.'

'Then how does he know it's false and incriminating?'

'Obviously the notary told him.'

'The notary didn't read the document. He simply stamped and signed it.'

'But a document does exist?'

'Yes.'

'Is it incriminating?'

'Yes . . . but not false. Would you like to see it?'

'Please.'

I handed her a photostat copy of Roditi's confession and watched her, closely, as she read it. The colour drained from her face. She trembled violently and I thought for a moment she was going to faint. I put out a hand to steady her, but she rejected me with a gesture and continued her reading. By the time she had finished, she was in control of herself again; and the sudden mastery of her emotions was frightening to see. She folded the document carefully and handed it back to me. Then she faced me, cold-eyed and contemptuous.

'That's a tissue of lies, Colonel—monstrous, horrible lies.'

'That is Roditi's handwriting.'

'But you dictated it; the notary heard you from the bedroom.'

'I dictated it after interrogation. Did he hear that, too?'

'He heard your threats, he must have heard the rest of it.'

'Are you sure, madam, that everything is false?'

'Everything!'

'Then you and Roditi were not lovers?'

'Of course not.'

'I read your letters, madam. I saw your signed photograph. Roditi kept them in the drawer of his dressing-table.'

'No, Colonel. There are no letters.'

'You mean they were removed on your husband's orders. Not all. I have

one in my pocket-now. I can tell you that the photograph was taken by
Donati in Bologna. He made an extra copy for me. ... Let me tell you
something else. Roditi, your lover, was a friend of Giuseppe Balbo who
was killed by the police a few nights ago. I met them together in the
Alcibiade. No, Madam. The statement doesn't lie. I'm not lying. You are.
Why? Are you afraid of your husband? Of what he may do to you or the
children?'

'No, Colonel.'

'Then, listen to me, please. Roditi told me you have material,
photographs and tapes which prove against your husband all the charges in
that document.'

'I have no such material, Colonel.'

'But, if your letters mean anything, you loved Roditi. He loved you. He
told me so.'

'Old love is cold comfort, Colonel.'

'He also told me that the tapes and photographs were your only insurance
against your husband.'

'I have no such material. And I need no insurance.'

'Why? Because Roditi's dead?'

'You said that, not I.'

'Or because his evidence is discredited and your husband's giving up his
little games for the time being? ... What about you? What sort of a woman
are you?'

'I'll tell you the sort of woman I am, Colonel. If my husband is clever
enough to handle this mess, then he's clever enough to climb right to the top
of the tree. I want to be there, too. If my husband can't make it ... Boh!
There's always another day for me.'

'You can settle that question now, madam. There's a policeman over
there, and two carabinieri at the entrance to St Mark's. Call them. Tell them
who I am and have me arrested.'

'No, my dear Colonel, I'm not quite sure yet how clever you are and
whether you're a match for my husband. It's a game, don't you see? I'm the
privileged spectator, I just sit back and enjoy it. I could even enjoy an hour
in bed with you, now, if you're interested, and your place isn't too far. ...
No? Another time, perhaps. I'm much better than Laura. ... By the way,
did you hear what happened to her?'

'What?'

'She drove her car into a tree last night. She drinks too much as you well
know. I've warned her many times; my husband has, too.'

'Is she badly hurt?'

'The doctors think she'll live, but she could end up as a vegetable. ...
Pity! She was such a pretty girl. Goodbye, Colonel.'

She offered me her hand. I could not take it. I would not even stand to
salute her going. I sat and watched her walk across the square, head high,
hips swinging, jaunty as any girl on the beat. The pigeons rose in clouds as
she passed and the waiter, counting my change, sighed, dolefully, at the
waste of so much woman. He was a Venetian, but he had forgotten the
cynical wisdom of his forebears. When they sent an ambassador abroad,
they let him take his cook. They made him leave his wife at home.

It was all defeat and disaster, and there seemed no way to mend it. Steffi
summed it up in a terse valediction.

'. . . Checkmate! You have no place to go, little brother. Your last hope—and that's a slim one—is the safe-deposit box. I wish I could help you. I can't. I'm going back to Rome. If there's something you need, call me. But take a little advice . . . cut out now and join your girl in Switzerland. Let Manzini handle the rest of it. Here, you're in a trap. Worse, you're in a vacuum, which is demoralizing. You know the system. They've immobilized you. All they have to do is wait. Sooner or later, you'll make a small mistake and they'll spring the trap. I'm fond of you, Matucci—God knows why, because you've given me grief and ulcers! I don't want to see you lopped before you've had a chance to grow up. . . .'

When he had gone, I called Manzini, who was equally gloomy. He told me he had been contemplating a press campaign to stir up the muddy waters; but that the risks were too great: risk of libel action, risk that old laws might be invoked to stop publication, risk that timid friends on the Quirinal might be lost by untimely action, risk of fomenting public disorder. He, too, suggested I move out to Switzerland. He sounded tired and spiritless and I wondered about the state of his health.

When I put down the phone, I found myself, suddenly, in the grip of a violent reaction. I cursed and swore and slammed about the apartment in a frenzy of frustration. It was incredible that with so much evidence, we could do nothing. It was monstrous that one man could manipulate an arm of the law to make it an instrument of crime. It shamed me that a bastard like Leporello could turn me into a fugitive while his bitch of a wife sat laughing and offering to go to bed with me. And, for a last straw, here I was, in an empty house, with no food or liquor, and suddenly afraid to poke my nose outside the door. To hell with it! I wasn't a criminal. Why should I behave like one? To hell with the whole rotten crew! I would stay!

. . . How I was going to stay was another matter. I needed to think that one out over a meal and a bottle of wine. I didn't bother to change. I strolled down the Calle dei Fabbri and found myself a simple place where the food smelt good and the waiter was friendly. The night was balmy, so I sat outside, where I could look at the girls of Venice, who are better in the flesh than Titian ever painted them. I ordered a risotto and a dish of sea-food and a bottle of Barolo and settled down like any honest citizen to enjoy my supper. It was a good meal and I relished every mouthful. I was relaxed and happy over my coffee, when two carabinieri picked me up like an orange from a basket and carted me off to the Questura.

They were very polite. They spared me all the usual routine and took me straight to the Commandant. The Commandant looked at my papers and asked me if I was the person therein described: Aldo Carnera, travelling salesman. I assured him I was. I asked whether I was charged with any offence. He assured me I was not. It was simply a question of the green pullover. Had I been in St Mark's Square that afternoon? I had. Ah! That explained everything.

It told me exactly nothing and I begged to know whether there was anything special about a green pullover. He admitted that he could see nothing special in it, except that he, himself, was not overly fond of green. However . . . at three in the afternoon, a woman, who declined to give her name, had telephoned the Questura with the information that she had identified a man wearing such a garment as one Dante Alighieri Matucci, wanted for questioning in Milan. She had seen his photograph in the papers.

Now, the Commandant had been informed of the Matucci affair, which was a highly political matter in which he did not wish to embroil himself. He understood that an agent of a secret service often carried a false identification. So, if in fact I was Colonel Matucci, the matter of the forged papers could be easily dealt with. Then, he brought out a photograph of me and a set of fingerprints from the SID files. I smiled and he smiled and we agreed that it was the luck of the game.

He offered me a cup of coffee. I asked whether I might make a telephone call. He smiled again and produced an order stating that, when and if Dante Alighieri Matucci were apprehended, he should be held *incommunicado*, pending instructions from Milan Headquarters. He was going to telephone Milan now. He hated to do this to a senior colleague in the Service. He hoped I understood that there was nothing personal. He begged me to make myself comfortable until he returned.

A wink being as good as a nod to a blind elephant, I used the telephone on his desk, asked for an outside line and dialled an interurban call to Manzini's Milan apartment. The old man was out. His manservant took the message. It was a disappointment, but at least Manzini would know what had happened to me. There was one other crumb of comfort. The Surgeon was dead and I should be spared his tender attentions.

The Commandant was gone a long time. He came back looking grave and preoccupied. He told me that I was now formally under arrest and that I should surrender all my personal belongings, for which he would issue a receipt. His orders were to detain me overnight at the Questura, and send me, in the morning, to Milan.

A *brigadiere* escorted me to the detention cell. A turn-key locked me in. About fifteen minutes later the *brigadiere* returned accompanied by a guard and a man in a white coat carrying a kidney-dish covered with a towel. He introduced himself as the police surgeon and asked me to roll up my sleeve. He told me he wanted to give me a sedative. I protested, vigorously, against this invasion of my rights and my person. The surgeon suggested it would be simpler if I complied, otherwise he would be forced to put me under restraint. I did as I was told. I rolled up my sleeve and twisted it into a tourniquet. I made a fist and presented my arm for the injection. I winced at the prick of the needle and began counting one-two-three. . . .

Then all the lights went out.

PART III

We have changed all that.

Molière: *Le Médecin malgré lui*

I woke–or dreamed I woke–in absolute darkness and absolute silence. I was–or dreamed I was–floating in undetermined space in a timeless continuum. I was not sad; I was not happy; I was not in pain; I simply was. At first, that was enough: the floating and the dreaming and the simply being. Then I began to be uneasy, faintly at first, then more and more acutely. Something was absent. I could not define what it was. I could not define anything. My mind was a swirl of mist. I was groping, without hands, into nowhere.

The mist dispersed slowly in drifts and eddies. Slowly and intermittently, I began to collect the scattered parts of myself. My thumb encountered my fingertips. My tongue met my palate. My eyelids blinked. Somewhere out in the fog my feet brushed, one against the other. Then the parts became a whole and I was aware that my body and I were still together. I was able to lift my hand–both my hands–and run them over my face and shoulders and breast and belly and genitals. I was there, naked and lying on a hard flat surface, warm to the touch.

Then, panic engulfed me. I was buried alive. I was blind. I was deaf. I was dumb. When I cried out, no sound would issue from my parched constricted throat. I broke out into a sweat of terror and curled myself into a foetal ball, huddling away from the horror of nothingness. The panic rose and fell, endlessly, like waves on a beach, but slowly, slowly, it subsided to a ripple, constant, threatening, but, mercifully, no longer a madness. The mist about my mind was tendrils now and cobwebs, but at least I knew I had a mind, and must, somehow, begin to use it.

First I directed my body to uncurl itself; and, reluctantly, my body obeyed. Then I asked my fingers to explore my immediate ambience. The slab on which I lay felt like marble or smooth stone. It terminated a few centimetres either side of my body; and above it and all around there was empty space. Below it, my fingers encountered a floor, not paved, but rough to the touch. The floor was colder than my slab. How far it stretched, I did not know. Enough that I had found a foot-hold in reality.

Now I must make a search of my inward self, testing for time-holds and memory-pegs. This was more difficult. Inside my skull was a kaleidoscope that made patterns, fragmented them, rearranged them, dissolved them into monochrome fluid. I was lifted on a wave of panic, dropped into despair, **tumbled over and over in an undertow, floated free again.**

At last one picture held, one peg was firm; a woman walking through a cloud of pigeons, a man in a green pullover sitting at a table watching her. I could go forward from that. I could go back from it. I found myself weeping quietly in the dark. The tears were good. They fell like oil on the panic waters. When they were spent, I knew that I was still a man. I knew, and I knew that I knew, what had happened to me and what would happen very soon.

If you walk through the museums of the world you will find a variety of instruments of torture: racks, thumbscrews, barbed whips, iron maidens, pincers, branding irons, machines for electric shocks. The most potent instruments of all you will never see. They are darkness and silence. Each is an absence, a negation. Darkness is a negation of light. Silence is a negation of sound. Evil, said Thomas Aquinas, is an absence of good. My namesake, Dante Alighieri, wrote a poem about hell which has become one of the world's classics. I stand now to witness that he did not know what he was talking about. Hell is nothing but a dark and silent room. Damnation means to be locked inside it—alone.

Please let me explain. It is necessary to me. Come the day of the tyrants, it may be necessary for you, too, to understand it. Do you know the word 'parameter'? Many people use it, too few understand its meaning or its importance. The dictionary defines it as 'a quantity constant in the case considered, but varying in different cases'. Admit is now: the definition means little, if anything, to you. But suppose one night, you went to sleep and when you woke in the morning the campanile or the oak-tree that was always framed in your window was not there. Suppose you opened the door to your kitchen and found instead a rose garden. The constant quantities in your life would be gone. You would be lost. You would say: I do not know where I am. If the changes continued, day after day, you would become a victim of their inconstancy. You would say in the end: I do not know who I am.

But suppose.... Suppose, suddenly, all the constants are gone: the steeple and the kitchen and the sunrise and the sunset and the sun and the moon and the stars and even the light . . .? Suppose the inconstants, too, are taken away; the cars in the street, the doves in the cabbage garden, the dripping tap, the passing clouds, the wind, the sound of rain, the vagrant human voices . . .? Then you are damned beyond redemption.

This is what happens when you close a man inside a dark and silent room and leave him. He has nothing against which he can measure himself, except the confines of the floor, and the monotony of that measurement helps to drive him mad. He has no sense of height, no sense of time. He is cut off from his past. He has no expectation of the future. His present is darkness and silence. He cannot divert himself with the minutest things—a fly buzzing against a windowpane, an ant crawling across the floor, dustmotes in a sunbeam. His only points of reference are the contours of his body, the fixed contours of the walls and the floor and his sleeping-place, and the little world of memory inside his own skull-case. And there are less, much less, than enough to keep him sane.

I can tell you what happens, because it happened to me. It was planned to happen. It was contrived, inflicted, as the subtlest vengeance any man could contrive against another. . . . You are alone in this dark and silent nowhere. You say to yourself: I know who I am. I know what they are trying to do to me. I will not let them do it. I will retreat into my skull-case and live there, feeding on memory and hope and faith and love, the whole capital of a lifetime. I will hold fast to the facts I know: that this nowhere is, in truth, a somewhere; that outside there are humans and animals and solid, tangible things. I know that they will have to feed me, or at least give me something to drink. This perpetual non-motion is as impossible as perpetual motion. Something has to break, sometime; else why would they take all this trouble to torment me. Someone will come, if only to gloat. Otherwise, it would have been simpler to put a bullet in my head and toss me in a ditch.

... Eh-eh-eh! It is an illusion. Nobody comes. The silence and the darkness remain unbroken. You discover, in your first circuit of the walls that they have left three plastic demi-johns of water, enough to keep you alive for a long, long time. You discover other things, too. The world inside your skull-case becomes quickly confused. You grasp for one memory and find another. Pictures flash by and you cannot hold them in focus. You lean on hope and collapse into weeping despair. You try to pray and find yourself cursing. You recite poems and hear yourself babbling nonsense. After three days, though you have long since forgotten time, you are hallucinating constantly; and, even if anybody came, you would not know whether they were real or not.

This is the trick of it, you see. They do come, but you do not know. They scoop you up from the floor and pump barbiturates into you to continue the hallucination. They drip enough glucose into your veins to keep you alive; and they feed you with new fears to drive you closer and closer to the cliff-edge of permanent derangement. I learned later that I was there fifteen days. When they brought me out, I was blind for a while, and dumb and ataxic, shambling like an animal, bearded and filthy from my own droppings. They put me under deep sedation for forty-eight hours, and when I came out of it, I was sure I had died and arrived, by some cosmic mistake, in Paradise.

There was so much light, I could only bear it for the shortest while and then must close my eyes and shut it out. There were flowers on a table. I remember that they were iris, blue and yellow and plum purple. Always, when I opened my eyes, there was a pretty nurse in the room, sometimes close to the bed, sometimes sitting in the armchair, reading. For a time I thought she was Lili; but later, when I could concentrate a little, she told me her name was Claudia and that I had been very ill, but now I was getting better.

Whenever the light began to fade, I would become restless and fretful, scared that it would go out altogether. But it never did. Always another nurse came in and turned on the lamps; and even when I slept there was always a small light burning. The night nurse was not so pretty as Claudia, but she was very gentle and solicitous. She was very patient, too. Sometimes I talked and talked until I couldn't stop myself. At others, I was morose and silent, staring at the small circle of light on the ceiling, hating myself, hating everything, unable to change the fixed and horrible trend of my thoughts. When I talked, she listened. When I was silent, she talked, a steady stream of soothing meaningless gossip that lulled me at last into a doze.

Every day the doctor came and examined me and chatted for a little while about my illness, which he said was a psychic dysfunction induced by my experience in confinement. It would cure itself, he told me. All it needed was time and patience, a little sedation and the simple therapy of human communication. A couple more days of complete rest and he would let me walk in the garden. When I asked him where I was, he told me I was in his clinic and left it at that.

I told him I was troubled with nightmares. He nodded sagely, and said that this, too, was a curative process: the subconscious mind working on the intolerable to make it tolerable. I told him that I had difficulty in remembering; that I could not concentrate even on a page of print; and that to reason through the simplest proposition was an enormous effort. He explained that this was the natural response of an organism taxed beyond endurance. It simply refused to function until it was rested and ready. When I asked whether I was still under arrest, he smiled and told me that I was free; but that I needed to be prepared if I were to enjoy the freedom I had.

It was all pleasantly vague; but gradually, one by one, new parameters were established and I began to take a more confident hold on the realities around me. The distant realities were still vague. I thought often about Lili and Manzani and Steffi; but I could not grasp them as present or regret them too much as absent. They would come, or I would go to them, in some near future, which I did not need, as yet, to determine by days or weeks. My whole concept of time was still rather uncertain. I never once asked the date or the time of day. The inimical realities, Leporello, his wife, the Director, were so vague as to be almost irrelevant. In some fashion, which I could not yet describe, I had survived them. I had walked through them as if they were a paper wall and come out on the other side. When I looked back I saw only tattered images blown by the wind.

When they allowed me out of bed for the first time, I was astonished to find how weak and insecure I was. My sense of balance had been impaired and I felt as though I were listing, now to one side then to the other. If I turned my head too suddenly, I became dizzy. And the first short walk to the window, left me weak and trembling. Even the view outside proved a shock. I saw it first in a single dimension. Then, quite suddenly, it solidified and fell into perspective.

There was a belvedere, set with cane-chairs and bright umbrellas. Beyond the belvedere was a lawn, broken by flower-gardens, and then an unbroken wall of cypresses, dark against a limpid sky. It was pleasant to look at, but it told me nothing. There were no people, no landmarks. After a few moments, I was bored with it and glad to go back to bed. Claudia sponged my damp forehead and smoothed my pillows and closed my eyes with the tips of her fingers and told me to go to sleep.

When I woke, the night-light was burning and Bruno Manzini was standing at the foot of my bed. He came to me and took my hands between his own and held them a long time in a wordless greeting. Suddenly, and without reason, I was weeping. Manzini took the handkerchief from his breast-pocket and wiped the tears from my cheeks. Then, he perched himself on the edge of the bed and talked me back to composure.

'. . . Eh! It's been a rough road, hasn't it, my Dante. But you've survived it. Another ten days will see you out of here. Then I'm taking you home with me to Pedognana. You'd like that, wouldn't you?'

'Yes, I would. I feel so weak and lost. I don't know what's the matter with me.'

'You've had your season in hell, my friend. It takes time to recover from that.'

'I suppose so. Where is this place?'

'Near Como. It's a small psychiatric clinic. I finance it. . . . Oh, don't worry, you're quite sane; but you wouldn't have been if they'd held you much longer.'

'How did I get here?'

'I brought you. It took me ten days and a lot of bribery to find where they were holding you. Then I had to get a judicial order for your release. That was harder; but we managed it. You're on provisional liberty, of course. Charges still lie against you.'

'I can't imagine why Leporello let me go.'

'He was convinced you were broken beyond repair. And the Movement would have lost a large cheque from me. He may still get you into court. Fortunately, we now have medicial evidence of the treatment to which you were submitted; and I don't think he wants that revealed just yet.'

'You've no idea what it's like . . . no idea. . . .'

'It's over now—finished. I am proud of you, my Dante.'

'Everything's in pieces. I—I can't put them together.'

'You put it all together before this happened. We have everything in our hands. Your notes on the microfilms, the tapes and the photographs from the bank. We can break Leporello now—and the Director after him.'

'Do you know what happened to Roditi?'

'Oh, yes. He's on indefinite sick leave. They put him through the treatment, too. He's no danger to Leporello now and no use to anyone else.'

'I'm afraid I'm not going to be much use to you, either.'

'Listen to me, my Dante, and listen well. . . . You are a lucky man, too lucky to have pity for yourself. You cannot surrender now. You will not; because if you do, you hand the victory to Leporello and all you have suffered will be useless. Also you have cost me an enormous sum of money. . . . Come, man! I have been where you are now. I have climbed the dark mountain and come down into sunlight on the other side. You will, too. . . .'

'I'm so tired. . . .'

'Try a little hating, my friend. It's the best stimulant in the world.'

'It's all too big and complicated. I just want to drop it and get out.'

'Easy now, relax. We'll talk about it another time. I'll see you again in a few days.'

I was glad to see him go. I wanted to feel sorry for myself. I deserved a little pity and this terrible old man had none. I would put him out of my mind. Later, when I was well, I would shut him out of my life.

Next day, I was stronger and I sat for an hour on the terrace looking at the pictures in the scandal magazines. The day after, I made my first circuit of the garden with Claudia and found that I could walk without staggering and talk without confusion and fatigue. In the evening I watched a cabaret show on television and found myself laughing at the comedian and beating time to the music and wondering why my nurse wasn't there to share the pleasure with me.

My sedatives were withdrawn that night for the first time, and I was swirled through a series of disconnected dreams; so that I woke, red-eyed and irritable, but aware that I had gained much ground on the climb up the dark mountain. After that I walked in the garden every morning, ambling like a monk in meditation, from one end of the lawn to the other, soaking up the sun and the colour of the flowers, knowing that the parameters were holding firm, and I was beginning to be a man again. I was reading print now, colour magazines and light novels, which I never finished, because my concentration still waned after an hour. The newspapers were brought to me, but I did not open them. Newspapers were today. Newspapers were a responsibility which I was not yet ready to shoulder.

Then Manzini came to see me again. He brought a bottle of champagne and a pot of fresh caviar and we made a picnic on the terrace, and afterwards strolled around the garden. He approved the change in me; but I was wary of him. I did not want him to disturb my still precarious comfort. He did not disturb it. He shattered it with a single stroke.

'I have bad news for you, my Dante. Lili Anders is back in Italy. She is in prison in the Maddalena in Rome.'

'No . . . it can't be true.'

'It is. Your Director called me yesterday to announce the good news. He asked me to pass it on to you.'

'But why? How? Did the Swiss deport her?'

'She came back of her own accord. She entered the country by way of the Brenner and was arrested by the border police.'

'But that's madness! I don't understand it!'

'It seems you called her back, by telegram.'

'How could I? I've been out of action for nearly four weeks.'

'That's the way the Director tells it. Your telegram said she was free to return. You would meet her in Bolzano and you would make immediate arrangements to get married. She was carrying the telegram in her handbag. She produced it when the frontier police looked her up in the black-book and questioned her.'

'It was a trap!'

'Of course. But she walked into it.'

'We've got to get her out.'

'How, my Dante? You collected the evidence against her. You prepared her dossier. You broke her network, and gaoled her master, the Woodpecker. You can hardly refute your own testimony, can you?'

'But the Director promised to let her go.'

'He did. She came back. Illegal entry for a start.'

'Mother of God! What a stinking filthy mess! I've got to get out of here, Bruno!'

'I'm not sure that's wise.'

'I don't give a curse whether it's wise or not. I can discharge myself. Let's go back. I'll do it now.'

'If that's what you want, so be it.'

We were half-way back across the lawn, when a sudden thought stopped me dead in my tracks. I caught his arm, and heedless of his age and his infirmity, swung him round to face me. I challenged him, brutally:

'Did you arrange this, Bruno?'

There was not a tremor in him. He stood straight and firm as a pine-tree, staring me down. His eyes were cold. His mouth, under that great eagle's beak, was tight as a trap.

'Do you think me capable of it?'

'Yes, I do.'

'Good. Then you have learned something.'

'Did you do it?'

'I might have—if I had thought it useful. In fact, I did not. I think you did, sometime in that fifteen days of dysfunction and hallucination. I know that you told things about me; because I had to lie about them later. I know we nearly missed the safe-deposit box, because Leporello did get a judicial order to open it the day after we had extracted the contents.'

'Oh Christ, I'm sorry.'

'Don't be sorry. Think about those who made a traitor out of you against your will.'

'I'll kill the bastards.'

'They'll expect you to try. They'll be waiting for you. And if they take you a second time, there'll be no escape. . . . No, Dante, this time we'll do it my way. . . . Now, let's talk to the doctor. You're not setting foot outside the gate until he tells me you're ready.'

'The doctor was hesitant and very dubious. He was prepared to let me go only on condition that I understood the risks. I was still convalescent. There were still dysfunctions which would become acute again under stress. My memory would play tricks. My concentration would be limited for a long time. I would be subject to fits of depression and anxiety. I should not throw away too quickly the crutch of sedatives and tranquillizers. For the rest, I should trust to nature and not to try to force myself too fast along the road.

It was easy to say, impossible to do, with the guilt of Lili's betrayal nagging at me like an aching tooth. The moment we drove out the gates of the clinic and into the sunny countryside of Lombardy, I lapsed into deep despondency. It was Lili who should be at liberty and not I. It was Lili who should be travelling in luxury with the sun on her face and all the world smiling back at her. Instead, she was penned with thieves and prostitutes and child-slayers in a mediaeval hell-hole on the banks of the Tiber. Manzini let me brood awhile, and then faced me with a blunt question:

'How serious are you about this woman of yours?'

'I love her.'

'Enough to marry her?'

'I've already asked her.'

'When?'

'I wrote her just before I left Pedognana last time. I gave you the letter to mail through Chiasso.'

'I thought you were supposed to be her Uncle Pavel.'

'I wasn't when I wrote the letter.'

'Wasn't that rather foolish?'

'On the face of it, yes.'

'So, you don't know whether she wants to marry you or not?'

'No. . . . Why?'

'A vague thought. Let me play with it awhile. . . . There's something else more important. I think we know the date of the *colpo di stato*.'

'When?'

'October thirty-first, mid-autumn. The tourists have gone home. Diplomats have returned from the summer holidays. Training programmes have been completed. Transport still functions freely, which it doesn't in mid-winter. More importantly, the word is being whispered among the initiates . . . and it checks with dates mentioned in your notes on the microfilms.'

'That's five months ahead.'

'Never count on time, Dante. It runs away too quickly. Opinion is hardening on both sides. Leporello is a splendid organizer; and you are not the only one he has eliminated or immobilized. The Milan bomb cases have not been brought to trial. Several important witnesses have disappeared; others have been systematically intimidated. No, we have to move before summer.'

'What do you want me to do?'

'For the moment, exactly what the doctor has ordered—rest and recuperate. However, there is one thing which you can do without prejudice to your health.'

'What's that?'

'Entertain your friends. I presume you do have friends of your own rank and standing in the Corps?'

'Some, yes. But they're scattered up and down the country. I'm a bad correspondent. It's hard to keep in touch.'

'Now you will have time. Write a few letters. Make some direct calls. You've been ill. You've been in personal strife. You would like to see them sometime at Pedognana. We have plenty of guest-rooms. There is riding and shooting. . . . They'll come.'

'What are you looking for now, Bruno?'

'A pretorian guard. Ten men would be enough, so long as they were resolute and understood what was at stake. On your own showing, there's quite a large amount of disaffection from Leporello and his policies.'

'If you're asking me to stage a revolt of the armed forces, Bruno, forget it. I'm not very bright at this moment; but that's mystical madness.'

'Who said anything about revolt? On the contrary, we need men proud of the traditions of the Corps, jealous of its honour and its oath; old-fashioned patriots, who don't like seeing their fellow-citizens kicked in the teeth and justice denied by perjured witness.'

'Buy me a tub and a lamp, Bruno. I might have a better chance.'

'We're bitter today, aren't we, my Dante? But I agree. Go play Diogenes. But find me ten good men willing to put their heads on the block for one night. . . . Oh, by the way, I brought your clothes back from the apartment. You've lost some weight, but they'll still fit. I can't bear that rubbish you're wearing now.'

He would not tell me any more and I was too tired to press him. I lay back in the seat and dozed fitfully until we drove through the gates of Pedognana.

At cocktails that evening, I discovered there was another guest at the Villa: the Principessa Pia Faubiani, prima donna of Roman fashion, mistress of Bruno Manzini. She was slim, dark, leggy, flat-busted and, if you favour the pinched and glacial modella, very attractive. At first meeting, I did not favour her at all. I was edgy, jealous of my privacy and in no mood to lavish on her the attention which she very obviously demanded. I was also mistrustful, because of Manzini's equivocal description of his relations with her. However, this was his house and he could open it to whom he liked. The least I could do was to exert myself to be agreeable.

I was amply rewarded for my pains. Pia Faubiani was a witty and intelligent woman with enough malice to survive in the rough world she exploited, and more than enough affection and good humour to spend on her friends. I was glad I wasn't married to her; her claws were too sharp for comfort; but for playmate and boon companion . . . yes, without a second thought. She was wearing the salamander pin from Fosco's exhibition, and when I commented on it, she announced, cheerfully:

'It's a parting gift. This is my first and last season with Bruno.'

Manzini chuckled and held up his glass in a toast.

'You're too young and I'm too old, my love; and I hate to be second-best at anything. Besides, the way you're going, you'll need a bank of your own, just to pay the interest bills. This woman, Dante, is the best designer and the worst accountant in the business. I keep telling her she'll either marry a gold-mine or end in debtor's prison.'

'I was thinking of a convent, darling; now that you've deserted me.'

'I've never deserted a woman in my life and you know it. I've just retired from the field—with honour.'

'With honour! Listen to the man! You're an old fox, Bruno! *Buon giorno—buona notte, ciao bambina*—and you're over the hills and far away licking your chops as you go. This man, Dante, has had many mistresses as I've had birthdays, and I don't think he's ever been in love in his life. . . . Have you ever been in love, Dante?'

'Handle him gently, Pia. He's in love and his woman's in gaol.'

'Oh, I'm sorry. . . .'

'So, you're going to cheer him up for me.'

It was obviously as much of a shock to her as it was to me. She sat, with a morsel of cream-cake poised precariously on the end of her fork, and gaped at Manzini.

'I am? I'm glad you told me, darling.'

'If you drop that cake, you'll spoil a very expensive dress. Put it in your mouth, like a good girl. . . . No wonder God gets bored, Dante. Nobody ever gives him any surprises. Now, where was I? Oh, yes: what you, my Pia, are going to do for me. When do you open your show in Bologna?'

'Next Wednesday.'

'And in Milan and Turin?'

'Each one ten days after the other?'

After that, you're free.'

'Well, not exactly free, darling. I have to go back to Rome and. . . .'

'I know, but you'd come for at least a couple of says, wouldn't you? For last season's sake?'

'Of course, but why?'

'I want you to hostess a party for me, here, at Pedognana. I've been promising to introduce Dante to people ever since he came to Milan. He's had a rough time, as I told you, and I think he needs some diversion.'

'Please, Bruno! A party's the last thing I need.'

'It may be the last one you'll get, if you go to trial. Besides, there's a month yet to get used to the idea. Enjoy, man! Enjoy! They'll be toasting our funerals soon enough. . . . You'll do it for me, won't you, Pia?'

'You know I will.'

'And if you see this fellow moping around like a barnyard owl, take him out, introduce him to your girls, seduce him yourself if you like. . . . But bounce him out of his miseries, understand?'

'Your servant, Cavaliere.'

'I wish you were, my love. I think we'd have lasted longer. Still, it's been fun hasn't it . . .?'

She laid a hand on his and said, gently:

'It's been fun, *caro*. And I'm sorry about . . .'

'Enough, please! I've had a good life and I'm very grateful for it. Also I'm tougher than they think. . . . And I'll tell you something, my Pia. I have been in love, twice, in my life. That's more than enough for any man.'

'I know about Raquela, darling. That's something even I wouldn't joke about. But who was the other one?'

'My wife.'

We both stared at him then. He gave us an odd, embarrassed, little smile and a shrug of apology.

'I'm sorry. I wasn't trying to surprise you this time. I've been thinking a lot about her lately, wondering if we'll meet again, and if we do will we recognize each other. . . . I married her in Paris in 1934. She was nineteen years old. I was thirty-five. I had travelled all over the world and I thought she was the most beautiful creature in it. I brought her back here to Pedognana and she fell in love with the place at first sight. Ask some of the old ones and you'll find they still remember her riding the rounds with the factor, kneeling in the chapel on Sunday, with all the children about her.

'She was born to the land. Her people farmed a big estate near Poitiers. This place flowered under her hand in those two strange years. . . . You're too young to remember it, my Pia, but they were very strange. We had an empire then. We took Addis Ababa and annexed Ethiopia. Ciano became Foreign Minister, Farouk became King of Egypt and Germany occupied the Rhineland, and Charlie Chaplin made *Modern Times*. . . . But, here at Pedognana, we were almost able to forget the madness that was going on around us. We were ludicrously happy. My affairs were prospering. If things went wrong in Europe, I had capital planted and growing abroad, and, best of all, Marie Claire became pregnant. For a man like me, who had never known a family life, this was like the announcement of the Second Coming. I was out of my mind with delight. I was bubbling with wild plans for my son's future—because, of course, it had to be a son.

'In the fourth month of her pregnancy, Marie Claire fell sick and died within a week, of cerebro-spinal meningitis. . . . She's buried in the chapel here on the estate. I know you're not a praying man, Dante, but you'd have seen the inscription if you'd bent that stubborn neck of yours. Marie Claire, beloved wife of Bruno Manzini. Born Paris, April 20, 1915. Died Pedognana, June 17, 1936. Requiescat . . . Boh! Long ago and far away. Let's have coffee in the study. It's cosier there.'

When the coffee was brought, he refused it and announced, abruptly, that he was going to bed. Pia Faubiani made a move to go with him, but he pushed her gently back into the chair and bent to kiss her on the forehead. His tone was very tender.

'Stay here, my love. I'm very tired tonight.'

'But, darling. . . .'

'Don't worry. I'll sleep. Tomorrow we'll talk about the party. . . . Goodnight, my Dante. Think about the pretorian guard, won't you? It's very important. Golden dreams to you both.'

When he had gone, Pia Faubiani kicked off her shoes, curled herself in the armchair and gave a deep sigh of relaxation and contentment.

'*Dio!* I'm so glad it's ended like this! He's one man in the world I wouldn't want to hurt. I never thought I'd let any man dismiss me; but that one—God bless him—is very particular.'

'I know what you mean.'

'You're rather particular, too, Dante Alighieri. I can't quite read you yet.'

'Don't try, Pia. I'm a mess just now. You'd get the wrong reading anyway.'

'Bruno loves you.'

'I know. He's told me.'

'How do you feel about him?'

'I don't know. I admire him very much. I wish sometimes I could be like him. I fight him often. I never quite understand him. . . . How sick is he?'

'He's not sick at all, really. He's an old man. His heart's tired and wearing itself out. He could go quickly and he knows it. I think he's more afraid of lingering too long. His big regret is that he doesn't have a son. . . . Wasn't that a sad little story about his wife?'

'Very. It's the shortest story I've ever heard him tell. . . . What are you going to do now?'

'Me? The same, with someone else's money. I'm a pretty hardy plant, you know. Give me a little sun and I can grow anywhere. Tell me about yourself.'

'What's to tell? I am an intelligence man who thought he could break the system. Instead the system broke me.'

'You don't believe that.'

'I do. Look at my hands. I can't hold a glass steady. Do you know why? I'm scared to go to bed and switch off the light. I know it will pass: but I'm still scared.'

'Did they hurt you in prison?'

'No. Nobody touched me. Would you like another brandy?'

'Yes, please. I don't want to go to bed either.'

'What are you afraid of?'

'If I told you, you wouldn't believe me.'

'Try me.'

'Getting old and raddled like Coco Chanel and having some bright boy write a musical about me.'

'I promise you, Pia *mia*, it will never happen.'

'Can you swear that?'

'On the bones of my ancestors.'

'Then I'll make you a promise, too, Dante. You'll sleep well tonight.'

And I did sleep well. I had no nightmares either. In the morning across the breakfast table, Bruno Manzini blessed us with a grin and a Venetian proverb: '*El leto xe' una medicina* . . . Bed is a medicine'. As usual the old monster was right.

I found I could not write letters; so I made telephone calls from one end of the country to the other. I talked to men who had once been friends and were no longer. I talked to friends who were no longer. I talked to friends who were delighted to gossip but were always too busy to make a train journey to a place so outlandish as Pedognana. There were others who said they would be delighted to come, but found it hard to set a date. There were a few, six only, who expressed a care for an old friend, and a concern about what they heard had been done to him. These would give up their leave and come on various days to have a meal and a chat with me. I wondered, with growing disillusion, why there were so few of them. As we sat in the study, examining papers and photographs and tapes, Manzini gave me his own answer:

'Cattle smell the wind, my Dante. They turn their tails to it and wait for it to pass. Reeds bend with the wind, and sing whatever music it plays on them. Chaff blows away in the gusts and only the good grain settles. Be grateful, however small the harvest. I talked to Frantisek at the Vatican today. If you want, he will visit your Lili in the Maddalena. If she wants to marry you, we can, perhaps, arrange for you to visit her so that you can become betrothed in the prison. The regulations provide for that, but you must be very sure what you want. You cannot live a lifetime on guilt and pity. Besides, you have to face the fact that we may not get her out. The law in this country is a madness out of the Dark Ages. People can rot in prison for years without a trial. And there is nothing so destructive as a disappointed hope. So, think carefully before you lay new burdens on the girl. . . .'

I knew I must. I knew equally that I could not determine myself to a lifetime of lonely fidelity. I was not proud to admit it—God help me!—but the fact was there, brutal and inescapable. I tried to put it out of my mind and concentrate on the work in hand, which was the collation of all the material at our disposal to see if it added up to a case which would unseat Leporello and the Director.

There were two problems. My notes on the microfilms from Ponza were third-hand material collated from memory. Even the originals had belonged to Pantaleone and represented his plans for a military coup, not those of Leporello. From an intelligence point of view, my material was valuable. From a judicial one, it was quite invalid. All we had left, therefore, were the photographs and tapes of Leporello's sexual activities in Roditi's apartment in Milan. With these, we could make a scandal; but, in Italy at least, the scandal could be suppressed, because the law forbids the publication of obscene material. We could publish the material outside the country, but then we would be open to suspicion of forgery and the accusation of political chicanery. However, we might yet be forced to take that risk.

Whether we could make a case out of the obscene material was even more problematic. Photographs can be forged very easily. Roditi could testify to their authenticity, but Roditi had succumbed to the brain-washing and was no longer a competent witness. The tapes were even more dubious evidence. Leporello could be identified by a voice print, but the defence could claim that the tapes themselves had been edited and thus constituted a forgery.

There was another problem, too. Sexual misdemeanour is the commonest human aberration; and while everyone loves scandal, public sympathy is generally on the side of the offender—unless children are involved, which in this case they were not. If we could identify Leporello's partners as junior members of his own service, then we would have a case, and a strong one, to have him cashiered. . . . But, as Manzini pointed out, this was a long way from murder and political conspiracy and the high men, including the Director, would still go untouched. Roditi could have proved murder. Balbo had committed it. But Balbo was dead and Roditi lost to us.

At the end of an hour's discussion, we decided to concentrate our case on the photographs. I borrowed a magnifying glass from Manzini and settled down to study them minutely. There were more than thirty in all, some of them clear, some of them out of focus, some so contorted in their poses that it was impossible to identify the participants. We had Leporello. There was no doubt of that. I was concerned to see if I could identify any of his partners. The problem was that we had only contact prints of thirty-five-millimetre size and each one had to be examined minutely. It would have been easier in a studio, with full equipment available, but the material was so explosive we dared not yet commit it to other hands.

Finally, I was lucky. In one frame there was a man whom I could almost certainly identify–Giuseppe Balbo. In another there was a face which, though less clear, was very familiar to me. I groped vainly for the name, but my memory, jolted and jarred by my experience, failed me every time. I called Manzani and showed him what I had found. He was jubilant.

'If that's Balbo, then we have all we need. A known criminal, probably a murderer, whom we can identify from a thumbprint and your testimony, and who was killed by Leporello's men in Leporello's zone of command. Yes, that would do it! The other one. . . . Well, he'll come back to you. . . . Now, listen! We can't afford to let this stuff out of our hands. We'll have to bring all the equipment we need into the villa. Can you do the job?'

'No, only the basics. This needs an expert. One we can trust.'

'Then let's bring one in from outside. I'll call my people in Zurich and they can find a man and fly him down. We're coming closer, my Dante . . . two steps closer. Maybe your party will be a victory celebration after all. I'll call Zurich now. You lock that stuff away. We mustn't scandalize the servants.'

It was still an hour to lunch-time, so I walked out on to the terrace and paced up and down, trying to reason, calmly, about Lili's situation. Wherever I looked, there was no way out for her. Escape was impossible. Acquittal was unthinkable. There was enough material in my dossiers alone to convict her twenty times over. The Director could recommend deportation or exchange if he saw a political advantage in either. All his advantage lay in keeping her in Italy.

The afterthought was even less comforting. Lili knew her own plight better than I. The thing she feared most was now a present reality: the small room, the lights, the questions that came from nowhere. She could not bargain even for a respite. I had robbed her of the last face cards in the pack. Having once tasted liberty and hope, how would she tolerate despair?

Manzini came out to join me, rubbing his hands with satisfaction. The equipment we needed was already being packed in Milan. His expert would fly in from Zurich tomorrow. When the news failed to cheer me, he frowned and snapped at me:

'Matucci, stop it! I refuse to spoon-feed you any more. Your Lili is no child. She will survive if she wishes. So long as she survives, there is hope. You do her no service with self-torment or self-denial either! Now, have you put a name to that face in the photograph?'

'Not yet.'

'Keep trying. I have set the date of the party for four weeks from now. My secretary is working on the guest list and the invitations. It will be a gala affair. This old place needs some life put into it. So do I, for that matter–and you.'

'Truly, Bruno, I don't see. . . .'

'You don't see the nose on your own face, Dante Alighieri! That's your problem. Look! You think you can go back to the Service again? Never– even if they wash you in the blood of the lamb and give you a new baptismal robe. So, you have to start again. Where do you start? As a *spazzolino*, sweeping up rubbish on the streets? Of course not. You want to begin as far up the ladder as you can. For that you need friends and recommendations. Hence the party. . . . And, because it's my party too, it must be something everyone will want to attend and everyone will remember. "*Che vale petere . . . e poi culo stringere*. . . . If you're going to fart don't tighten up. It strains the arse." I've left a book in your bedroom, you might find it instructive. . . .'

The book was the *Ricordi of Francesco Guicciardini*, and I read it after dinner in the study, because Bruno retired early and Pia Faubiani was not returned from Bologna. My father was a great reader, and I had learned the habit from him; though latterly, between chasing information and chasing women, I had fallen out of it. Now, like sick Satan, I was disposed to be contemplative, and I found the experience rather pleasant. I also found that Messer Francesco Guicciardini was very entertaining company.

Like me, he was a Tuscan born, a Florentine, who at twenty-nine was named by the Republic as ambassador to the King of Spain. Pope Leo X, Medici of the Medici, made him Governor of Reggio and Modena and Parma, and Pope Clement VII made him Lieutenant General of the Papal armies. He was utterly without mercy, but he knew how to govern and he loved women of all kinds and ages and conditions. The only man who could handle him was Cosimo de Medici, who climbed to power on his shoulders and then kicked him into retirement. But Guicciardini was a natural survivor. He retired gracefully, grew vines, wrote books and died peacefully of a stroke at fifty-eight.

The *Ricordi* were his secret memorials, a kind of diary of opinion and experience, which he was wise enough never to expose in his lifetime, and which were published centuries after his demise. Manzini had marked several passages and annotated them in his precise script:

'To be open and frank is a noble and generous thing, but often harmful. On the other hand, it is useful and often indispensable to dissemble and deceive, because men are evil by nature.' (So smile, my Dante. Show them you are a man who has no care in the world, because you have aces in your sleeve!)

'I do not blame those who, on fire with love of country, confront dangers to establish liberty . . . though I think that what they do is very risky. Few revolutions succeed and, even if they do, you find very often they didn't win what you hoped. . .' (Which is why I draw back from public disorder and seek rather to seduce the ungodly in secret.)

'Nearly all men are more concerned for their own interest than for glory and honour.' (Remember this when you come to confront the Director, who is a quite unbearable patriot.)

'I believe that a good citizen . . . should maintain friendly relations with the tyrant, not only for his own security, but also for everyone else's good.' (Which is why I pay money to the Movement and dine the Director, and plot with you to bring them down. You have wondered, and I know it!)

'Do not take people too seriously when they prate the advantages of freedom. . . . If they could find a good job in a tyrannical state, they would rush to take it.' (I would go further. If they could be tyrants themselves, they would climb over a mountain of skulls to arrive.)

'My position under several Pontiffs has forced me to seek their glorification for my own profit.' (I wonder if the Director had this in mind when he cast his vote in favour of Leporello. Think about this as a motive for murder. Old Guicciardini had a lot of people executed in his time.)

'The past illuminates the future; the world has always been the same. . . . The same things come back with different names under different colours. . .' (You and I, my Dante, are trying to change the course of history. But let's not expect too much. The river is still the same.)

'Nobody knows his subjects as little as their ruler.' (This is what we are betting on, you and I. They think they have bought me. They know they have frightened you. They do not understand we have not yet begun to fight back.

It was, at that point, that I laid down the book and went upstairs to bed. I still could not turn out the light; but lay a long time, wakeful, staring at the ceiling, until Pia Faubiani came home from Bologna.

Next day, a variety of things began to happen at Pedognana. The artisans of the estate marched in force to the villa, and in the space of a few hours converted an attic suite into a very passable photographic studio. The expert arrived from Zurich, was briefed, sworn to secrecy, and set to work installing the new equipment which had arrived from Milan. Early in the evening Corrado Buoncompagni, the editor of Manzini's newspaper, arrived in company with a tubby little Torinese, whom he presented as Milo de Salis, the noted film director.

We were five at dinner that night—Manzini, Pia, Milo de Salis, Buoncompagni and myself. The photographer dined alone in his suite and continued working into the night. The meal turned into a council of war, at which Manzini exposed, for the first time, the scope of his design. I had seen him in many moods and acting out many roles, but I had never quite grasped him as the director of giant enterprises, a strategist of great and risky campaigns. Now, at last, I saw him plain, and was amazed at the subtlety and the audacity of his genius. He was calm, dispassionate, unhurried and yet he held us as no orator could have done.

'. . . I ask no oaths of you, my friends. From this moment, we are all conspirators. We are all at risk. All of you understand the nature of the risk. We shall have to use other people. That is unavoidable. We give them only the information they need to carry out their tasks. For the rest, we lie, conceal, confuse and obfuscate, so that the true issue is clear only to us, inside this room.

'I will define that issue. We are attempting to discredit and remove from power men who wish to impose by force, or threat of force, a government by dictation. We believe that this form of government is unacceptable to the vast majority of the people. We know, however, that it can be imposed, as it has been in the past, and that with all the modern mechanisms of control, it could be held in power for a very long time. Therefore, we must abort the *colpo di stato*, which we know is already planned.

'The means at our disposal are limited. They are limited by considerations of humanity and common prudence, and by the nature of the democratic process itself. We have in our hands, explosive information, which, if improperly handled, would confuse the public mind and lead to civil disorders, which themselves would provide the best excuse in the world for an imposed order. We cannot appeal directly to the people who are already torn between the factions. We must appeal to those in power on the basis of their own self-interest, whether that interest be blind or enlightened. In other words, we work within the context of the history of this country, and not of any other. Here the people speak, but are not heard. Therefore, we do not attempt to manipulate the many-headed monster. Instead we threaten those who are afraid of the monster: ministers of state, big public functionaries, members of the elected assembly, industrialists like myself, all who have a vested interest in order and public security.

'The threat will not be overt, but implicit. It will not be protracted, but sudden and surprising. It will call for immediate action. The action must be such as to command the approval of all those who see themselves endangered. We must be prepared to take it.

'The preparations begin now. Corrado, commencing with Thursday's edition, you will reverse the editorial and news policy of the paper. We are no longer Centrists, we are swinging very rapidly to the Right. I know you don't like it. I know the staff won't. It's your job to keep them happy, with the best lies you can tell. I don't think they'll go as far as a strike; but, even if they do, it may help us. I want editorials that my Fascist friends will read and applaud. I want a big feature on the work of Major-General Leporello. Let's call it an accolade, modified by stringent and critical recommendations. In other words, let us not be cretinous or fulsome. I don't want to lose staff or circulation, but I want it known that I am prepared to support the Right under conditions. I want them to call me and invite me to lunch. Then I can invite them here instead.

'Milo, your job is more difficult, because of the time and the technical problems involved. Upstairs, we have a mass of documents and notes collated by Matucci, of which the most important are the military maps and the campaign plans. In addition, we have a collection of obscene photographs and sound tapes. You have access to certain other material from film files and newreels. You have three weeks in which to write, film and edit a ten minute film based on all that material. The film will say that Major-General Leporello is a pederast with his own troops, a murderer and a conspirator against the security of the State. Matucci, here, will edit the film with you. He will also appear as commentator and final accuser. As an actor, he needs much direction. I trust you will succeed where I have failed.

'Matucci, you will work with Milo on the film. You will recruit and have at my disposal within the same three weeks, a pretorian guard of senior officers, who will agree to attend with you at an official function and act with you if a certain expected crisis should arise. Now, this is the riskiest point of the plan, because it involves a nice consideration of how and when the nature of the crisis is to be revealed to them. I do not know your friends. I cannot pretend to decide how you will treat with them. I can tell you only this: if they fail us at the last moment, we may all be brought low, and the ungodly may survive, stronger than ever.

'Now, let me describe the moment at which our plan comes to fruition or disaster. I have just completed plans for one of the biggest ventures of my career, a chain of tourist hotels and marina developments around the southern coastline of the peninsula. This enterprise will bring a flow of tourists and dependent tourist industries into the depressed South. It is, therefore, of major interest to the Government. I am now able to announce that a consortium of Italian and foreign banks has agreed to finance the whole project. I propose to make that announcement at a gathering in this house a little over three weeks from now. The party will be private. No Press will be invited, but Corrado will attend as my personal guest, and as pipeline to the communications media. If we fail here, we shall, for our own protection, publish all the material we have.

'The guest list is already prepared. It includes senior ministers and functionaries—all the people of whom I have already spoken. Major-General Leporello and his wife are on that list, as also is the Director of SID. I believe that the tone of our new editorials and features will encourage them both to attend. . . .

'I am still not decided what will happen on that night. We shall have to wait until acceptances have been received, before we can arrange a protocol and an order of ceremonies. I will consult with all from time to time before decisions are made. However, let me make one thing clear to all of you. If we win, no one will thank us. If we lose. . . . Eh! We'd better take the next plane to Rio!'

The next day, I identified the second man in the Leporello photographs. It was Captain Girolamo Carpi, one-time aide to Pantaleone. This was a stunning surprise. It established a direct link between Leporello and Pantaleone. It also revealed a yawning hiatus in my own information on Carpi, since there was no hint of any deviate practices in his army dossier. I had hired him. I had dismissed him and arranged for his safe exile to a training base in Sardinia. Now I had to rethink, and, if possible, arrange for his return to the mainland. Neither was going to be easy. I was no longer on active duty. Therefore, I had no access to files and could not make any formal requests to Army authorities.

I took the news and the problem to Bruno Manzini. He frowned over it for a long while and then announced:

'Dante, this man could be the most important witness we have. We must get him here, question him, break him and, if possible, get him on the film in time for our function. How do we do that, without showing our cards to the Army?'

'I go to Sardinia with the photograph in my pocket and frighten him into talking.'

'No, Dante. I can't risk you outside the gates of Pedognana.'

'If we could get Carpi posted to Bologna, we could arrange access easily enough. You must have friends in the Army high enough to swing a transfer.'

'I have. The problem is how far I can trust any of them at a time like this. . . . Leave this with me, Dante. I need to think about it quietly. What about your pretorians?'

'One is coming tomorrow, two more over the weekend, the others during the following week.'

'Have you decided what you're going to tell them?'

'I can't decide that until I've talked to them. How important is the number?'

'Less important than the security. Ten field officers in full uniform would be very impressive, but I would rather have three, primed and resolute, than risk a single waverer.'

'I'll report back to you after I've talked with each one.'

'Let me ask you something else about Carpi. How did you come to use him in the first place?'

'Let me see now. . . . He was appointed as aide to your brother about eighteen months ago. About six months after that, the Director called me and suggested we enlist Carpi as a domestic spy. He gave me Carpi's dossier, which showed that he was living beyond his means and was heavily in debt to a money-lender in Rome. I approached him with the proposition that if he worked for SID, we would pay his debts and give him a monthly stipend as well. He leaped at the offer. . . .'

'But his dossier was given to you by the Director. You didn't call for it yourself from the Army?'

'No.'

'And knowing the Director's way with dossiers, what does that suggest to you?'

'It could have been doctored before I saw it.'

'Exactly. Now I will tell you something else, my Dante. The Director knew my half-brother quite well. You remember he was selling his art collection?'

'Yes. He was in correspondence with Del Giudice.'

'And your Director was bidding against me for certain items.'

'I thought he wasn't interested in old masters.'

'He isn't—except as negotiable currency. He buys them as non-exportable commodities. He sells at a big profit to another dealer, not as honest as Del Giudice. This dealer has them copied by an expert, gets an export licence for the copy and sends the original out of the country. Three of my father's paintings have gone on this route. This was the substance of my talk with Pantaleone on the night of his death.'

'Can you prove that?'

'Yes. But don't delude yourself, Dante. It's a good point for a dossier. It is not enough to bring down the Director, who is in a strictly legal position. We have to prove murder.'

'For what motive?'

'Profit—on every level. Pantaleone dies. Leporello replaces him as military leader. Since Leporello has organized the murder, the Director moves in as head of State, just to keep the record pure. Don't you see? It's the classic method. They are like bull-leapers, vaulting over the horns. The one who vaults the last beast and gives it the last pat on the rump is champion. Yes, we need your Captain Carpi. Somehow I will get him here. . . . Tell me, how are you feeling?'

'Better. You were right. Bed is a good medicine; and hate's a better one. What are our chances?'

'*Cosi-cosi* . . . fifty-fifty. It all depends on the mood of the gathering. If they walk out, we are sunk. If they stay, we shall win. It's an opera, my Dante, staged for an operatic people. Everyone knows the score backwards. It's a question of how well it is staged and sung. . . . I know this is positively my last performance. I hope I can hit the high note and hold it till the last chord and take the final bow. I hope . . . that's all. But if you see me wilting, prop me up until the curtain comes down. . . . Dante, even if I can get Carpi here, there will be no time for a full inquiry. You may have to bluff with him.'

'I don't relish that. Let's wait and see whether you can get him and what I can do with him. . . . There's something that's bothering me, Bruno.'

'Oh, what's that?'

'You're going to have a hundred, a hundred and fifty, highly sophisticated men and women who come to your house for a celebration party. How are you going to get them to sit for ten minutes through a very sordid film, which impugns some of their fellow-guests, casts suspicion on others and makes them all feel very uncomfortable?'

'Would you believe, my Dante, I have been so bothered by that same question I have a certain Professor Mueller flying in tomorrow from Munich. He is an acknowledged expert on mass psychology and group manipulation. I want to pose the problem to him in the most precise terms, and in the ambience where it will arise. I should have preferred someone more familiar with our own Latin character, but I dare not use any of our own people. The old story, my friend: "A man's enemies shall be those of his own household." Sad, isn't it?'

'That's strange . . .'

'What?'

'Pantaleone used the same words to Lili Anders.'

'In what connection?'

'Let me think now. . . . I want to get it right, and my memory still plays tricks. Oh, yes. Apparently Pantaleone had a habit of making cryptic remarks and then refusing to explain them. Lili linked two such remarks: "There is no simple future for me, because my past is too complicated" and the words you have just used.'

'In what connection were these remarks made?'

'As I understood it, in connection with the Salamander.'

'Could he have been referring to Carpi, who was a domestic spy?'

'Very possibly.'

'Think about it, Dante. Think of Carpi as an intimate of Leporello, as an emissary of the Director, as a man with free access to the Pantaleone apartment . . . as the man who killed my half-brother.'

'And myself, as the man who employed him. That's very pretty!'

'I'm glad you've seen the point. You told me the Director was preparing a Black Book on you. If we indict Carpi, you could be in bother, too.'

'Bruno, let's face it now. You can stay me with apples and pomegranates, you can surround me with angelic choirs. I'm still up to my neck in the *merda*. I'm the man who started all this. I'm the man who must finish it. That's the way I'm constructing the film with Milo. If things go wrong, you must walk away from me.'

He lifted his white head and gave me a small enigmatic smile.

'Dante, son of my heart, never underscore the obvious. If we lose I can't afford you. If we win–touch wood!–we shall both be very busy men. Too busy for dramatic gestures. . . .'

The next three weeks were a period of mounting panic, suppressed only by the calm generalship of Manzini. The ballroom of the villa was invaded by an army of painters, decorators and electricians. A barn was transformed into a studio, offices and cutting room for Milo and his crew. Manzini worked, sometimes at home with a battery of secretaries, sometimes in Milan, from whence he would return, grey-faced and tired, but always with some new word of encouragement. His guest list was filling up. His press campaign had been well received by the Right. Leporello and the Director had consented to come. This minister or that had sent him words of personal greeting.

Milo and I quarrelled our way through the film, he concerned with the visual impact of his work, I troubled always by the legal logic of the case we must present. My friends came, one by one, to visit me and I probed them like a confessor before I dared a single hint of the project on which we were embarked. All of them were troubled by the situation of the Republic and the divisions within the armed forces. They, themselves, were divided on the remedies. In the end, there were only four of whom I felt I could commit with any real confidence. To these, I proposed as follows:

'You will be invited as guests to an official ceremony, here at the villa. It's a big occasion and you will wear formal mess uniform. I guarantee you each a pretty girl as escort. Now, here's the reason. The place is going to be full of important people, ministers, functionaries, that sort of thing. There'll be the usual contingent of security men in attendance, but we don't want them inside the dining-room. That's why I want you there, looking like happy guests. . . . We've been told something may happen on that night. I can't tell you what it is. I don't want you to ask. I want you to trust me and come for friendship's sake . . . and maybe for the sake of all the things we've talked about. You are committed to nothing beyond attendance. You will receive the same invitation card as every other guest. Now, can you accept that or not? If you can, will you accept one other condition? This is a State secret and you'll have to keep it like that.'

They accepted and I believed them. They were friends of the heart, close as family, which is the one thing on which you can depend in this troubled disparate land of mine. When I told Manzini, he nodded a curt agreement and dimissed the matter. This was my province. I was on my own responsibility. When I asked him about Carpi, he frowned and shook his head:

'Nothing yet. Tomorrow I am flying to Rome to see a friend of mine in the Ministry of Defence. There is a risk involved and some very devious staff work. But I hope we shall get him here in time.'

In the event, he was disappointed. The last week passed in a flurry of frantic activity. On the day of the dinner party, Captain Carpi had still not arrived.

At the final council of war, which was held at three o'clock in the afternoon, it was decided that I should not attend the function at all, but should present myself only in its closing moments. The reason was simple and perfectly valid. My presence could prove an embarrassment to Leporello and the Director and introduce a dangerous note of uneasiness into a gathering whose success depended upon a careful contrivance of atmosphere.

After the meeting, Manzini walked us round on a final tour of inspection. In the foyer, the guests would be received by four of Pia's girls, and led to the first reception room, to be presented to Manzini and Pia and circulate for cocktails round a huge illuminated projection of the development—a large scale-relief map of the boot of Italy, showing the tourists arteries and the location of the development sites, and a series of models showing the completed installations.

After cocktails, they would proceed to the ball-room, which had been converted into a dining-room for the occasion. The place was ablaze with flowers and the lighting was contrived to flatter the least beautiful of women. The seating was unusual for such a function: a series of small rectangular tables, each seating three persons a side, so that the guests faced each other in a small closed community. At one end of each table was a silver bucket in which were six flat rectangular packages wrapped in gold paper and tied with ribbon—party favours for each guest. At the other end of each table was a small television set of the most advanced design, connected by closed circuit to a central control in an adjoining room. The host's table at the far end of the room was arranged as a horseshoe, with the television receiver placed between the points of the shoe.

Each guest was supplied with a programme card, illuminated by Carlo Metaponte, and, for a final impudent irony, the place-cards were set in small silver mounts in the shape of a salamander. The programme was simple: a toast to the President and the Republic, an opening address by the Minister for Tourism, a reply by Bruno Manzini and the showing of a short television film on the new development, produced and directed by Milo de Salis.

There were other refinements, too: three television scanners were placed at various points of the room. Two were focused on the tables where Leporello and the Director were to be seated. The third covered the room, so that all the proceedings could be monitored and recorded on tape for later evidence. Leporello and the Director were seated at opposite sides of the room, out of each other's line of vision. One of my pretorians was seated at each of their tables, with another at the table next in line. What Manzini had spent in terms of money was staggering. What he had spent of imagination and ingenuity were unbelievable from a man of his years. When the tour was over, he took me back to his study, poured brandy for both of us and made a last toast to the venture.

'. . . I will not say, good luck, my Dante. What has brought us to this point is believing and working and daring. What happens tonight will depend on how nicely we have calculated the interaction of small groups of people submitted to a sudden and shocking experience. According to Mueller, we are gambling that their curiosity will overcome their repugnance and hold them seated until the end. However, he does say there will be a crisis point at which either Leporello or the Director may attempt to leave, calculating that a sudden move may upset the audience. You must prevent that at all costs. You will be armed, of course, but for a threat only. There must be no violence. What happens at the end, of course, is in the hands of God . . . and though you may not believe it, Dante, He has to have an interest in tonight's affair. . . . Perhaps that should be my toast, I pray that He may hold you safe, my Dante, and bring you to a quiet harbour.'

I said amen to that and it was the closest I had come to praying for a long time. We drank and set down our glasses. Then Manzini sprang his last surprise.

'Dante, my friend, have you thought about tomorrow?'

'Tomorrow?'

'Yes. It will come, you know–unless we both die in our sleep.'

'So?'

'So if our strategy succeeds you will have the Director and Leporello under arrest on a variety of charges. How will you proceed from that point?'

'According to the book. Deposition by the arresting officer, desposition by the accused. Documents forwarded to the magistrate. Examination by the magistrate, indictment, submission of pleas by the defence and public trial.'

'Which will of course make an international scandal?'

'Yes.'

'And have profound political consequences?'

'Inevitably.'

'Consequences for which neither the Government nor the country are as yet prepared.'

'True.'

'Read me the consequences as you see them.'

'We shall have aborted a Fascist coup. We shall have damaged public faith in the senior bureaucracy. We shall have given vast new strength to the Left. . . . On the other hand we shall have affirmed that the State is capable of purging and regulating itself to the benefit of the people.'

'And the final outcome?'

'Potentially healthy.'

'Potentially?'

'That's my best estimate.'

'Which leaves us still at risk—grave risk.'

'Yes.'

'The first risk is yours. You have passed the film. You will make the arrest, you will prefer the charges. You must file the indictment. Is the case complete?'

'Against Leporello, yes. Against the Director, no. A good laywer could win it for him.'

'And then you would go to the wall.'

'Obviously.'

'Are you ready for that?'

'I hope so.'

'You could avoid it.'

'How?'

'Accidents happen—fortunate accidents.'

'I know. . . . "The prisoner was shot while attempting to escape. The prisoner suffered a cardiac seizure while under normal interrogation and the police surgeon deposed to a long-standing mitral defect. The suspect was granted provisional liberty on the instance of his attorneys and failed to appear at the court hearing. . . ." No, Bruno! Not this time! Not for me. Not for you. Not for the Minister or the President himself.'

'Not for the people either? Your people, my Dante.'

'The people belong to themselves. I am the only man who belongs to me. You taught me that lesson, Bruno. I can't unlearn it now.'

He gave me a long, quizzical look, grinned and dismissed the matter with a shrug. Then he went to his desk, unlocked a drawer and brought out a small velvet box. He handed it to me and said simply:

'It's a gift. I hope you like it.'

I opened the box and found, slotted in the velvet bed, a gold signet ring. The symbol engraved on the seal was a crowned salamander.

My emotions were still unsteady; and I was deeply moved. Manzini, however, would not indulge me in any expressions of gratitude. He stood towering over me, like a sardonic sage, and read me his last cautionary tale.

'. . . We are the victims of those who love us, my Dante. They dream our destinies and plunge us into nightmares. They plot fabulous voyages and blame us when the voyages end in shipwreck. Yet, we have no recourse, because we, too, are born dreamers and conspirators. . . . My father robbed me of his name and the inheritance of his history and thought to recompense me with the foundations of the fortune which I have today. Your father dreamed his noble dreams of a new world, and his family suffered for them. In the end, you, my Dante, came to wear the uniform of the men who arrested him.

'Yet, each of us learned the same lesson: there are no guarantees; there is no permanence; life is a riddle propounded by a Divine comedian, whose answer is so simple, we never see it until it is too late. I have never told you this, but after the war when we were, for a long while, a nation of beggars, subsisting on reconstruction funds from America, making all sorts of shabby bargains which today we are trying to undo, I toyed with the idea of quitting Europe altogether and investing what remained of my life and my fortune in the New World. Here I was entangled by history, caught like a lamb in a bramble-bush, torn and scarred and totally confused. There, I felt I could be another man, a builder looking only to the future. . . .

'I came back here to Pedognana. One evening, I walked down to the chapel and sat a long time looking at the slab which covered Marie Claire's grave. I tried to talk to her. There was no answer; because that is the nature of the Divine riddle: the eloquence of those who do not understand it, the silence of those who have solved it at last. I wept then, the last tears I have ever shed. Old Don Egidio came in. You've met him. He's the typical peasant priest, not very learned, slipshod and cross-grained, something of a tippler too, but, with it all, very shrewd.

'He did not try to comfort me. He knew me too well for that. He knew that I should have rejected him as a man too ignorant to understand the complexity of my condition. He sat down beside me, and told me the tale of the puppy with the straw tail. . . . You have never heard it? It's very simple. There was once a puppy who was born with a short tail. He was very ashamed of this defect, so he made himself a long and beautiful tail of golden straw. He was proud of himself then. He wagged his tail twice as vigorously as any dog in the village. He strutted and preened himself and was courted by all the bitches. Then, one day, as he lay by the fire in his master's cottage, his tail caught fire. . . . He couldn't get rid of it, of course. He ran around yelping until his master tossed him in the pond to put out the flames.

After that, he had another problem. His real tail was still shorter and now his rump was scarred and all the other dogs laughed at him. What did he do? He had been very happy with his straw tail, so he made himself another one; but ever afterwards he was careful to stay away from the fire. . . . He could, of course, have made another choice. He could have shed his false tail, and worn his scars and slept comfortably through the winter, close as he wanted, to the fire.

'. . . The moral, you would think, was obvious. Not to Don Egidio. His conclusion was quite different: man is not a puppy dog; he embraces all elements and is embraced by all and can survive them all: he can write his own bargain with life; the only thing he cannot haggle over is the final price: death and solitude. . . . You will be lonely tonight, my Dante. You will be lonely afterwards; because there is no credit for anyone in the company of the public executioner. The ring I have given you is a symbol, not a talisman. The only magical thing about it, is the love that goes with the giving. Remember that, when I leave you, as I shall, as I must. . . .'

I had a long wait ahead of me. The guests would not arrive until eight-thirty. They would not sit down to dinner until nine-thirty, when I would go down to the control room and follow the proceedings on closed circuit with Milo and his crew. The moment Manzini finished his speech, the lights would be extinguished and the television screens illuminated. I would move immediately to the ball-room, take up my post inside and lock the door. If anyone tried to leave, unless it were a woman, I would detain them until the end of the screening. It still lacked twenty minutes to six. I went to my room, set the alarm for eight, read a few pages of Guicciardini and lapsed into a deep and dreamless sleep.

I woke refreshed and strangely calm. I shaved, carefully, bathed and put on my new uniform. When I looked at myself in the mirror, I saw a man I hardly recognized: a serving officer of a Corps whose oath still had a ring of royalty about it, whose tradition of service, however besmirched by individuals, still carried a blazon of honour. The badges of rank I had earned myself. I, the son of a political exile, could claim some service to the country for which he, in his own way, had sacrificed himself. For all the sordid shifts of my trade, I could still feel some pride, and a small, hesitant affection for the man inside my skin. Enough! It was time to go.

As I walked down the stairs into the empty foyer, the major-domo opened the front door and let in Captain Carpi. For a moment, he did not recognize me; and when he did, he was non-plussed. He told me that he had been sent from Sardinia with urgent despatches to be delivered personally into the hands of Major-General Leporello. His plane had been delayed at Cagliari, and he had been forced to hire a car to bring him out to Pedognana. I told him the General was at dinner, but that I would take him in as soon as the function was over. He asked me what I was doing. I told him I was on special duty. That seemed to satisfy him. He was quite in the dark about the whole affair. All he knew was that his commanding officer had called him, told him he was to act as courier on a special mission and sent him on his puzzled way. I wondered what devious staff work had gone into that manoeuvre. I took him into the control room, fed him a glass of champagne and a canapé and drew Milo aside to warn him not to make any indiscreet comment. Then we settled down to watch the show, while I tried frantically to figure how I should make use of this very untimely arrival. By the time Manzini stood up to announce the Presidential toast, I had made my decision.

The Minister of Tourism made an elegant and witty speech, a little long, perhaps, but then he had important people to impress: his colleague, the Minister for the Interior among them. He noted the variety and the magnitude of Manzini's enterprises. He praised the boldness of his vision, which he said made a lot of people blink, and others close their eyes and wait for the thunderclap. He complimented the bankers on their foresight and their confidence in the economy of the country, and its political stability. He was grateful for the lavish welcome extended by the Cavaliere to his guests. He saw it as the symbol of the welcome extended by Italy to the millions who came visiting each year. He wished the project well, assured all the participants of the benevolence of the Government, added a flourish or two of metaphor and sat down to polite applause.

Then Bruno Manzini stood up and began his own speech.

'I thank the Minister for his kind words. I thank him for his confidence in our enterprise, which is, itself, an act of faith in the future of this beloved country of ours. This act of faith is the more sincere, because my colleagues and I have committed huge sums of money to Italian development at a time when, despite the optimism of my good friend, the country is divided on many issues. I can say this here, in this gathering, because there are no Press to report my remarks, and you are intelligent men and women concerned as I am for the future of this country and its children. The divisions of which I speak, are very deep. Some of them are historic; some of them are political; some are social. We are one people under one flag, but we are also many peoples with many different histories. We have too many parties and too little consensus to achieve easily a government for the people and by the people. Too much wealth is concentrated in too few hands, my own among them. However, to attempt to reconcile these differences, as some seek to do, by violent and sinister means, is a dangerous folly; so dangerous, indeed, that it could negate at one stroke all that we have achieved since the war, all that we hope to build in the coming years. . . .'

They applauded him then. It was a proposition they could all accept; because they didn't have to examine it too closely. Divisions they knew, and violence they knew; and they all had sinister symbolic scapegoats to carry their sins into the wilderness of forgetting. Manzini hushed them, slowly, with a smile and a gesture. His manner changed. He was happy now, and teasing.

'. . . Have you ever thought of this, my friends: right through our history, dinners have been important occasions. That's strange, because we are not gross feeders, like the Germans, nor big drinkers like the French. We enjoy the food and we enjoy the wine and we enjoy the company of beautiful women, of whom there are so many here tonight. But the fact is, we do make history at meal-times. There was Trimalchio's supper. You all remember that: very gross, very disgusting, even when dignified by the art of the great Petronius. Then, there was the fatal supper of the Tolomei and the Salimbeni, which those of you here who are privileged to be Tuscans will remember. That one ended in murder. But I assure you all, dear friends, there will be no murder here, tonight. Then, there were the *canacoli* of the Blessed Catherine of Siena, where souls were elevated by spiritual discourse and bodies were mortified by a very restricted diet. Saving the reverence of Monsignor Frantisek, who is here with us tonight as unofficial representative of the Holy Father, I regret we have not attained to this degree of spiritual perfection. However, I dare to think that this is an historic occasion.

'. . . In the silver buckets at the end of each table, you will find a number of packages. If the gentlemen will pass them round the tables, please . . . No, no, don't open them yet. They will make no sense until you have seen the film—which is not, I must tell you, the one promised on your programme. . . . This one is a privileged document. The Press does not know of its existence. The public will never see it—only you, my friends and compatriots. You will find it a strange experience. Some of you, especially the ladies, may be discomfited and embarrassed. I beg you to be patient and tolerant until the film justifies itself. . . . Now, if you will turn your chairs a little you should all have a comfortable view of the television screens at the end of each table.'

This was the cue. In the movement that followed, two of my pretorians stood up and leaned casually against the wall, so that a single pace would bring them to Leporello and Baldassare. The other men did the same, so that the whole thing had the air of a casual and comfortable reshuffle. Manzini went on:

'If anyone of you hesitates to share this experience with us, I beg him or her to leave now. . . . You are all resolved? Good! In a moment the television screens will light up: and this room will be plunged into darkness. I think you will agree with me that secrets should be told in the dark and enjoyed in the light.'

That was my signal. I hurried Carpi out of the control room and we reached the dining-room just as the lights went down and the television screens lit up. I locked the door, put the key in my breast pocket and focused on the nearest screen.

Milo de Salis had settled on a film method that was as simple as a child's primer and as devastating as a death sentence. It consisted of a series of direct and unqualified statements, in image and commentary. The image was too distant for comfort, but I knew the commentary by heart.

'. . . This is a photograph of Major-General Massimo Pantaleone, who died in Rome this year, on Carnival night.

'This is the death certificate which states that he died of natural causes. . . . In fact, he died of an injection of air into his femoral artery. He was murdered. . . .'

There was a gasp of surprise, a rustle of movement, a flurry of whispers, then silence, as the commentary began again.

'This is a photograph of the later autopsy report, signed by three very reputable physicians.

'This is a photograph of an office block in the Via Sicilia, where the General's papers were stored after his death. The papers were stolen and two men were murdered–Avvocato Bandinelli and Agent Calvi of the Service of Defence Information. . . .

'This is the identity card of the man who murdered them: Giuseppe Balbo, a criminal who used a number of aliases.

'Among the General's papers were these maps: Turin . . . Milan . . . Rome . . . Naples . . . Taranto . . . These are military maps which have since been altered in detail but not in substance. They show how, on the thirty-first of October of this year a military junta plan to overthrow the legitimate Government of Italy and establish a government by dictation.

'The moving arrows illustrate how the plan would operate.

'The maps and plans you have just seen are in the possession of this next man, Major-General Leporello, who is a guest here tonight.'

Once again there was a stir as all heads were turned to identify Leporello. They could not see him in the dim light, so once again the image and the commentary commanded their attention.

'This is a recent photograph of General Leporello's aide, Captain Matteo Roditi. He is at present under psychiatric care because he was tortured into insanity to prevent his giving testimony in court.

'This is another photograph of Giuseppe Balbo, murderer, who was shot down while resisting arrest by General Leporello's men.

'This is the Club Alcibiade, a resort of deviates, where Captain Roditi met often with Giuseppe Balbo, who was, strange to say, an enlisted member of the Carabinieri, under General Leporello's own command.

'This woman, shopping with her children in Milan, is the wife of the Major-General Leporello.

'This is a love-letter, one of thirty, which she wrote to Captain Roditi, her husband's aide and true father of her children. Their love-affair was condoned by the General, for good reason.'

This was the crisis point which Mueller had predicted. Leporello could not defend himself, he would and must defend his wife. Instantly he was on his feet, his tall frame monstrous in the half-dark. He shouted: 'This is an outrage against an innocent woman. I demand. . . .'

He demanded nothing. My pretorian was at his side with a pistol rammed into his ribs. Manzini's voice rang like a trumpet blast from the rostrum:

'Sit down, General. Ladies and Gentlemen, I beg that you control yourselves. We are not here to insult a woman, but to prevent an imminent bloodshed.'

There was a gasp of horror which I could feel physically. They did not settle immediately. They watched and waited until Leporello subsided into his chair then, lost and leaderless, they submitted in silence to the last brutal revelations.

'These next photographs will distress you, but I beg you to look at them carefully. This one shows Major-General Leporello engaged in a sexual act with Giuseppe Balbo, murderer.

'This one shows him in another act with the man identified as the personal aide, and probable murderer, of the late Major-General Pantaleone. His name is Captain Girolamo Carpi.

'This man, Major-General Leporello, ladies and gentlemen, was chosen to lead the *colpo di stato*. He, himself, however, would never have assumed power. There was another man behind him. . . .

'. . . This man–Prince Filippo Baldassare, Director of the Service of the Defence Information. This man plotted the death of Pantaleone, hired Carpi to kill him, and then arranged for Leporello to replace him.'

Again the audience slewed round in the darkness to identify Baldassare. I was one of the few who could see him. He sat calm and unmoved, sipping brandy from a crystal goblet.

'Who am I? I am Colonel Dante Alighieri Matucci of the same service. I collected this information. I too was imprisoned and submitted to psychological torture to prevent my revealing it. I take full responsibility for the substance and presentation of this film. I depose it as true and I shall offer to the appropriate authorities documents in support.'

The screens went dark. The lights went up and a hundred and fifty people sat there, dumb and ashamed to look at each other. I moved forward into the silent room with Carpi, like a sleepwalker, at my side. I had one moment of blind panic. Then I found the words.

'The officers present will place the General and Prince Baldassare under arrest.'

I did pray then. I said, 'Dear Christ, please make them move, please!'. . . . They moved. They placed their hands on the shoulders of the two men. The act was final and complete. Now I had to speak again. I heard myself say:

'Cavaliere, Ladies and Gentlemen, I have with me, under arrest, Captain Girolamo Carpi who will testify in the proper place to his part in this affair.'

Then, from his own table, Bruno Manzini took command:

'My countrymen! You have been insulted tonight. You have been shocked and shamed. You may choose never to pardon me for the pain I have inflicted upon you. I will not apologize. I tell you only that it is a small price to pay to prevent the bloodshed and the misery of a civil uprising and the oppression of a new tyranny. . . . Now, may I ask you to retire to the salon where coffee and liqueurs will be served.'

They got up, slowly, and moved away blank-faced, like automatons, each carrying the supper gift, a dossier of the damned, with a complimentary card from the Salamander. Elena Leporello left too, and she passed me without a glance of recognition. Finally, there was no-one left but the pretorians and the accused and Manzini and the Minister for the Interior and myself.

Manzini and the Minister stepped from the high table and walked slowly down the room towards me. They stopped. They faced me, bleak and expressionless. The Minister said:

'Thank you, Colonel. You will do what has to be done with these gentlemen. I shall wait here. You will report to me before you leave.'

Bruno Manzini said nothing. He did exactly as he had promised. He walked away.

It was an eerie moment. Three prisoners, three gaolers, silent among the debris of a rich man's feast. We were like actors, frozen on an empty stage, waiting for the Director to move us. Then, I understood that I was the Director and that, without me, the play would neither continue nor conclude. I must move. I must speak. I must decide. I heard the words as if they issued from the mouth of another man.

'Prince Baldassare, General Leporello, will you please remain seated. You other gentlemen, will you please conduct Captain Carpi to the monitor room and wait there till I call you.'

Two pretorians linked arms with Captain Carpi and led him mute and unprotesting from the room. Those standing guard over the Director and Leporello left their posts and walked out. If I read their looks aright they were very glad to be gone. When the door closed behind them I was, at last, alone with my enemies. I felt no triumph, only a strange sense of disillusion and of loss, and a vague humiliation as though my best-told joke had fallen flat. Both men sat bolt-upright in their chairs, hands flat upon the tables, their faces averted from me. They were so far apart that unless I stood far away like a ring-master or a theatrical tyrant I could not address them together, nor even compass them with a single glance. I had to confront them, one by one, face to human face. I went to Leporello first. I straddled a chair in front of him and found myself staring into a death mask. I told him:

'General, it is your privilege to be held under arrest, in barracks under custody of service officers, and you may elect to be tried under military law. If you waive this privilege you become immediately subject to civil process. Which do you choose?'

He did not answer. He sat like a stone man, cold and motionless. I tried again.

'General, there are formalities. I want to make them as simple and easy as possible. If you would like to speak to your wife, I can have her brought to you. Afterwards, as you know, it will not be so easy. If you are unwell, I can call a doctor. For your own sake, General, I advise you to answer me.'

He had not even heard me. His lips were locked: his eyes blank as pebbles. I stretched out a hand and laid it on his wrist. There was pulse, but nothing more. The muscles were rigid as iron, there was no twitch of recognition or aversion. Then I heard the Director's voice, cool and ironic as always:

'Classic fugue, Matucci. Total withdrawal. You'll get nothing out of him tonight—if ever. To cover yourself I'd call a doctor and have the wife present when he makes his diagnosis.'

I swung round to see him, calm and smiling, sipping a glass of brandy and puffing a cigar. He raised the glass in a toast:

'My compliments, Matucci. . . . Trial by television! I wonder why I never thought of that. It's hardly a democratic process, but it's very effective.'

He poured a goblet of wine and pushed it across the table towards me.

'Sit down! Relax. I'm a co-operative witness. You can afford to be pleasant to me. I imagine you've had rather a tense evening. Still, you must be very satisfied. You've got everything now; except the fellow singing "Sic transit" and burning flax under your nose. What's the next move?'

'You know the code as well as I do, sir.'

'And I know the trade better, Matucci. You made your case against Leporello—though I doubt he'll ever stand to answer it. The man was always a psychotic, in full flight from reality. Tonight you pushed him over the edge and I doubt he'll ever come back. Even if he does, a good lawyer will plead him unfit and the State will, in its own interest, concur. Against me, what have you got? Carpi, a man with straw in his shoes, who will be frightened, suborned or eliminated before you get a line of decent testimony out of him. Still, it's your case, and you must make it, win or lose. Unless of course. . . .'

'What?'

'Unless you are open to a little lesson in statecraft. You were always weak in that discipline, as I told you. That's what held you back in your career.'

'If you're proposing a deal, the answer's no.'

'My dear Matucci! Why do you always underrate me? Do you think I would be so naïve as to propose a deal to a man both righteous and triumphant? On the contrary, I invite you to a mature consideration of realities. . . . Statecraft has nothing to do with morals, has nothing to do with justice relative or absolute. It is the art and craft of controlling large masses of people, of holding them in precarious equilibrium with one another and with their neighbours. All means are open to the statesman and he must be prepared to use them all in their seasons from the headsman's axe to the circus holiday. He must never overrate his triumph nor lose courage in temporary adversity. From time to time he needs a victim, if he is to avoid a holocaust. Clemency for him is not a virtue but a strategy. . . . Only the aim is constant, to hold the many-headed monster in control, to calm him when he growls, to curb him when he gets too playful, to wonder at his visions but sedate him before they turn into nightmares. . . . You, Matucci, are still a servant of the state. . . . You are not yet a statesman. Tonight you have the opportunity to become one.' He broke off, sipped his brandy, drew on his cigar and smiled at me though the eddies of fragrant smoke. I said nothing and after a while, he began on a new tack.

'At this moment, Matucci, you are in a position of great strength. You have forestalled a military coup. You have discredited the authors of it. You have two important victims to toss to the lions, Leporello and myself. In Manzini you have a powerful friend. In the Minister you have an important patron who is waiting only for you to give him the right advice. . . . Think about the Minister, Matucci. He is a politician–a thinking reed, blown by every gust of popular vociferation, by every whisper in the corridors of the Assembly. What does he want? What would you want if you were in his shoes? A discreet and well-managed triumph or a platter full of bleeding heads . . .? One head is useful. You can stick it on a pike and display it for a warning to the populace. More than one is a carnage. . . . Which head would you select for the pike? In my view–which I admit could be prejudiced–the one with the fewest brains. You've got it, over there. . . . Mine is worth much more to you and the Minister if you leave it on my shoulders. I am discredited; so I can't do any harm unless you bring me to trial–when, my dear Matucci, I can promise you scandals that will be shouted from Moscow to the Golden Gate. On the other hand, if clemency were offered, I should respond to it gratefully. I would remove myself from the scene and leave a rich legacy of information to my successor. . . . Do I make myself clear?'

I was ashamed for him then. For a moment he had been eloquent. Now he was merely plausible. I told him bluntly: 'I must be equally clear. I have no authority to offer clemency.'

'My dear fellow, I know that. I will go further. It would be useless and dangerous for you to treat with me at all. You should and you must treat only with the Minister.'

'What are you asking of me then?'

'I want to speak to the Minister privately, now.'

'He may not want to speak to you.'

'He will. And afterwards he will ask to see you.'

'And?'

'All I ask is that you give him an honest professional answer to any questions he asks you.'

'Can you be sure I'll do that?'

'No. I hope you will. You have no reason to love me. I would not blame you if you pressed to the limit the advantage that you have now. In fact I'd be rather surprised if you didn't. However, I've read you the lesson; make what you like of it. Will you convey my request to the Minister?'

'Give me a hand with Leporello, we'll get him to a bedroom. I'll call a doctor and then I'll see the Minister.'

The interview between Prince Baldassare and the Minister lasted more than three hours. I was not present. I was closeted with Professor Malpensa of the Army Psychiatric Unit in Bologna who had been roused from his bed and brought by helicopter to Pedognana. With him was Doctor Lambrusco, a guest at the party and Manzini's personal physician. I had asked them to examine Leporello separately and in concert, and then render me a joint diagnosis. They expressed in in writing: '. . . a catatonic or pseudo-catatonic state, expressive of a profound fugal impulse induced by guilt and shock. It is our joint recommendation that the patient by institutionalized for clinical observation. It is our opinion that the patient is at present incapable of rational communication, and that to submit him to interrogation or confinement would be pointless and dangerous. Prognosis, doubtful.'

I accepted the document, signed the General into the hands of Professor Malpensa, who flew him back to Bologna. Then I went in search of Manzini. His guests had gone, long since and he was sitting alone in the drawing-room. He was grey about the gills but still alert and cheerful. He greeted me with a smile and a grim, dry chuckle: 'Well, Matucci, we did it!'

'Yes. . . . It's very quiet now.'

'What did you expect? Garlands and a triumph?'

'Blessed is he who expects nothing; because he is sure to get it. . . . I think I'd like a brandy.'

'Help yourself.' He gestured in the direction of the study. 'Our friend Baldassare is trying to strike a bargain with the Minister.'

'I know.'

'Would it surprise you to know that I have recommended it?'

'In what terms, Bruno?'

'I have represented that without the co-operation and connivance of the Director we should never have been able to stage this evening's drama.'

'That's not true.'

'I know it. You know it. The Minister knows it. But it happens to be a fiction that fits the moment. Objections?'

'None.'

'You approve?'

'I don't approve. I think it's expedient.'

'You're learning, my Dante.'

'The hard way. How much of tonight's affair will reach the Press?'

'By direct report, nothing. By leaks and gossip, quite a lot. It's unfortunate, but inevitable.'

'Could you reach your editor now?'

'Of course. Why?'

'I'd like him ready to file a report to the wire services. We've missed the morning editions; but we'll make the evening papers and the international correspondents will have it on the teletype when the bureaux open in the morning.'

'What do you have in mind?'

'I can't tell you, until I've spoken with the Minister.'

He gave me a swift appraising glance and then a nod of satisfaction.

'*Bene*! At last I can approve you, Dante Alighieri. For a long time, I wondered. . . .'

'Wondered what?'

'How much of you was man and how much a confection of circumstance. Forgive me! How does one know whether a nut is sound until one cracks the shell? You are a man full of contradictions, my Dante. You are coward and hero. You are wise and foolish. You are soft as putty and hard as iron. A friend can buy you with a smile. A purse of gold will not corrupt you. How you will end, God knows; but I am happy to know I have not wasted myself on you. . . . Excuse me, I'll call my editor.'

He was gone perhaps three minutes, when the door of the study opened and the Minister came out. When he saw I was alone, he announced brusquely:

'I have some questions to ask you, Colonel.'

'At your service, sir.'

'I need direct answers: yes or no.'

'I understand, sir.'

'The charges which you made public tonight, are they true?'

'Yes.'

'Can you sustain them in court?'

'I can sustain those against General Leporello. Those against Prince Baldassare will be more difficult to prove.'

'Could you guarantee a conviction in his case?'

'Guarantee, no.'

'But you would be willing to proceed?'

'As an officer of Public Security, yes.'

'You have qualified that statement. Why?'

I handed him the medical report on Leporello and waited in silence while he read it. He folded it and handed it back to me.

'I repeat the question, Colonel. Why did you qualify your last statement?'

'Because, sir, I am commissioned to act and advise as an officer of Public Security. I have not been asked to tender an opinion of a political nature.'

'I take your point. I now ask you to offer, without prejudice, a political opinion. We have, thanks to your efforts, averted a national crisis. How should we act to avoid a national scandal?'

'We have two important men under arrest, sir. One is clearly incompetent by reason of a psychotic condition. The case against the other is incomplete; and even if we could complete it we should risk embarrassing revelations prejudicial to public security. We should risk also deep and divisive enmities in the Republic and between the Republic and her allies. I would advise, with deference and respect, that Prince Baldassare be permitted to retire from public life and remove himself within twelve hours from the confines of the Republic.'

'Could that be done without raising a public outcry?'

'There would be hostile comment, a great deal of it. There would be political embarrassment. In my view that would be a lesser evil than a celebrated and scandalous trial.'

'What are your personal feelings about Prince Baldassare?'

'I admire his talent greatly. I have learnt much from him. I disapprove his politics and his personal ambitions. I have very private reasons for wishing to see him brought down.'

'What are those reasons?'

'He has imprisoned a woman, once a foreign agent, with whom I am in love. He has damaged my career. He has conspired to submit me to psychological torture from which I am only recently recovered.'

'But you would still recommend his release?'

'As a political expedient, yes.'

'Would you arrange it and supervise it?'

'What you mean, sir, is will I accept personal responsibility for it?'

'Yes.'

'And will I, by consequence, absolve the Ministry and the Government and place myself in jeopardy?'

'You express it very accurately, Colonel.'

'We could of course do it another way, sir.'

'How?'

'You give me a ministerial directive. I execute it. Very simple.'

'Too simple, Colonel, and you know it. A politician cannot afford to be a patriot. The moment he is elected, he abjures the luxury. I know it's a difficult decision. Would you like a little time to think about it?'

'There is no time, sir.'

'A condition then? A gift to sweeten the risk?'

'No, sir. I'm not for sale—not any more. I'll do it. I'll get him across the border tonight. The Cavaliere Manzini will help me to handle the Press.'

'Thank you, Colonel.'

'Is there anything else?'

'One other matter. I should like you to report to me as soon as possible in Rome. We have to begin cleaning house.'

'May I remind you, sir, that I am still on provisional liberty, under charges laid by General Leporello.'

'The charges will be withdrawn. As of this moment you are restored to active duty.'

'Answerable to whom?'

'To me, Colonel. By the time you return to Rome I trust to be able to confirm your appointment as Director.'

He meant it as an accolade—manna in the hungry desert of a bureaucrat's career. Instead it tasted like Dead Sea fruit, dust and ashes on the tongue. For a moment I had felt like a patriot; then, for reward, he had made me a whore again. Still, that was the rule of the game. I had no choice but to play it or toss the cards back on to the table. I bowed and smiled and said: 'Thank you, sir. You do me a great honour.'

'Thank you, Colonel. Goodnight.'

It was strange sitting in the Director's chair. For a man so elegant, he kept a
very dingy office. There were no ornaments, no pictures, no photographs,
not even a lictor's axe. The only symbols of power were the grey filing
cabinets and the scrambler telephone and the intercom switchboard, which
would bring twenty people running to attend me. Old Steffi sat on the other
side of the desk, cocked his parrot head at me and cackled:

'Eh-eh-eh! So, you've arrived, Matucci! How does it feel? Does your
backside fit the seat of the mighty? And what now, little brother? What's the
policy? Left, Right or Centre?'

'Middle of the road, Steffi. *Toleranza.* I think we all need to breathe a
little.'

'Same as before, eh? Until somebody tosses a bomb in Turin, or the
police fire on rioters in Catanzaro and the boys up top get panicky and
scream for action. I wonder how tolerant you'll be then! . . . Well, *speriamo
bene*! Here's hoping!'

'Come on, Steffi, give me time!'

'I can give you time. All the time you want. But what about them? . . .
What about you?'

'Please, old friend . . .!'

'So, I'm still without a job and my nose is twisted out of joint. I'm sorry.
What do you want me to do?'

'I've called the Commandant at the Maddalena. He's expecting you. You
present the Minister's letter and mine. Lili is released to you. You deliver
her to her apartment. I'll be there when you arrive.'

He stared at me as if I were some curious animal, kicked up from under a
stone. There was contempt in his eyes and a kind of wondering sorrow.

'My God! What kind of a man are you, Matucci? She's your woman, why
don't you fetch her yourself? What have you got in those veins of yours,
icewater?'

I was angry then, bitterly and desperately angry. I poured out on him all
the pent-up fury of the last months.

'I'll tell you what kind of a man I am, Steffi. I bleed like everyone else. I
bruise like everyone else. I'm sick and tired of being pushed and shoved and
used and mis-used and mis-judged and mis-read by every clot who thinks
he knows the secrets of the universe. I'm sick of all the smug bastards like
yourself who think they can sum me up in a line and pay me off like a whore
after an hour in bed. I'm sick of friends who make like Father Confessors
and expect me to walk round ever afterwards in sackcloth and ashes. You
want to know why I'm not going to the prison? I'll tell you! Because the first
time Lili sees me I'll be in company with the Commandant and a notary
and a turnkey with a pistol at his belt. I'll look exactly the way they do
and I don't want her to see me like that; because that's not the kind of man I
am . . . at least not to her. I'll want to take her in my arms and kiss her and
comfort her and I won't be able to do that while every whore and pickpocket
in the gallery makes a dirty joke of it and every little jack-in-office smiles
behind his hand. . . . I won't submit her to that. I asked you to go because I
thought you were my friend. Instead you sit there and insult me and make
lousy ghetto jokes as if God gave you the right to be the conscience of the
world. Now get the hell out of here! I'll find someone else.'

He did not move. He sat there, downcast, his lips working as if he could
not frame coherent words. Finally, he faced me and there was compassion in
his look and a new kind of respect. He said quietly:

'I'm an old fool with a bird's brain and a frog's mouth. I'm sorry. I'll be glad to do it for you.'

'Thank you.'

'You're scared, aren't you?'

'Yes, Steffi, I'm scared.'

'*Piano, piano*, eh! . . . Take it very easy!'

Even for a Director, formalities are long in Rome. Functionaries come and go, but the great paper machine goes round and round, churning out hundreds and thousands and millions of reams of *carta bollata*, signed and countersigned and stamped and sealed and stuffed into pigeon-holes and dumped into subterranean repositories, until one fine or cloudy day, some poor devil goes to gaol and stays there while they dig, or say they dig, for the one line of evidence that may prove him innocent.

I filled the apartment with baskets of flowers. I had champagne cooling in a bucket, and canapés on a silver tray and a whole refrigerator full of food. I had documents from the *Comune* to put up the marriage banns on Capitol Hill. I had even an emerald betrothal ring, especially designed by Bulgari. I still had to wait an hour and a half before Lili came home.

The ring at the door was like camel-bells in the desert. When I opened it, she was standing alone and very still. I swept her into my arms and was astonished at how light she was. I kissed her and hugged her, and wondered where all the passion had gone. I sat her in the armchair and served her like a princess. And then I looked at her. . . . She was so pale, she was almost transparent. She had shrunk to skin and bone. Her clothes hung on her like scarecrow garments. Her mouth was pinched, her hands fluttered nervously. Her eyes, those eloquent eyes, were glazed and dull as pebbles. She ate and drank, not hungrily, but mechanically, and when I laid my hands on her brow and her cheeks, she submitted but did not respond. I knelt beside her and begged.

'Tell me, Lili, what happened. What did they do to you?'

'Not much. Sometimes they questioned me. Most times they left me alone.'

'Lili, you know I didn't send the telegram. . . .'

She stared at me, blankly:

'What telegram?'

'I was told you came back because of a telegram from me?'

'There was no telegram.'

'Then why did you come back?'

'I got your letter. I used to read it every night before I went to bed. One night it wasn't there. I thought I had mislaid it. The next day, I was out walking. My friend from Lugano stopped and offered me a lift in his car. I got in. Someone put a pad over my face. The next thing I remember we were in Italy, near Bolzano. Then two other men took over and drove me here to Rome. That's all. Except they told me you were in prison, too.'

'Oh, darling, darling. . . . I'm so sorry.'

'It doesn't matter.'

'Listen, sweetheart. This is what's going to happen. I'm going to move in here with you. I'm going to nurse you and get you well and we're going to be married. The notice goes up on Capitol Hill tomorrow. After that, no problems! You're my wife. You're under the personal protection of the Director of SID, for ever and ever, amen. . . . How does that sound?'

'It sounds the most beautiful thing in the world, Dante Alighieri. But I don't want it.'

As I stared at her, not understanding, I saw the first flush of life in her cheeks, the first dawning of emotion in her eyes. She put out her hands, not soft now, but thin and creped like raw silk, and cupped them round my face. Then she told me, very gently:

'Dante, I know you love me. Your letter was the most touching compliment I have ever read in my life; but I'm going to give it back to you. I couldn't bear to keep it. I don't want to destroy it.'

'But you said the letter was gone.'

'They gave it back to me in prison. I don't know why, but they did. They do strange things, cruel and kind; and you never know which will be next. I love you, too, Dante. I suppose I'll always love you . . . but not to marry, not to live with for ever and ever.'

'Lili, please. . . .'

'No, listen to me, Dante! You have to know . . .! I don't understand you Italians any more. You are so warm and kind; then, suddenly, you are devious and cold and so cruel, it makes my blood run cold. You smile at each other in the morning, and plot against each other at night. You have no loyalties, Dante—only to the family and to today. Outside the family, after today, everything is doubt and calculation. Oh, Dante Alighieri, I hate to hurt you, but I have to say it. You're the people who always survive, no matter what happens to you. That's a wonderful, a hopeful thing. But it is also very terrible, because you will trample each other down to get the last drop of water in the world. . . . Even you, my Dante, even your Bruno! I can't face that any more. I want to live secure, with a little book that tells me what to do. I want to be sure that if I keep the rules, the rules will keep me safe—safer than marriage, Dante Alighieri, safer than promises, safer even than loving. In Switzerland, I can do that. Not here . . . I cannot risk you any more.'

What could I say? It was all true. The ring on my finger symbolized it: the fabulous beast that survived the hottest fire. And yet, it wasn't true. Not the way she said it. The book of rules wasn't the answer. Not for us, the sun-people. The light was too clear. It showed the cross-wise writing on the palimpsest. How could we believe in permanence, who walked to the office over the bones of dead emperors? We couldn't trust tomorrow; we could only make do with today. I knelt there a long time, face buried in her hands, whose pores still exuded the stale smell of prison. I pitied her. I loved her. I could find no words to comfort her or myself. Then, I heard her say:

'Will you help me to pack, please, Dante; and see if you can get me a flight to Zurich. I'd like to leave as soon as I can.'

It was then I discovered how important it was to be the Director. I was able to command a first-class seat on an over-booked aircraft. I was able to park the car in a prohibited zone at Fiumicino. I was offered free drinks in the distinguished visitors' lounge. I was able to walk Lili all the way to the aircraft and settle her in the seat and commend her to the good offices of the Chief Steward. All that came out of a small piece of card in a black leather folder, stamped with the Arms of the Republic.

I didn't wait for the take-off. I drove back to Rome and telephoned Pia Faubiani. She wasn't at home; she had gone to Venice to open her show there. I called an agency and commissioned them to find me a larger apartment in a more fashionable district. I needed a better *figura*, no that I should be dealing with high men and large affairs. I dined at my old place in Trastevere; but found it suddenly cramped and provincial. Even the musician seemed to have lost his touch. I went home early and tried to read a little of my namesake before I went to bed. I was too sleepy to concentrate on his ponderous imagery–and besides, I didn't believe a word of him. . . . No, that's not true. There were three lines I had to believe:

> *E quella a me, 'Nessun maggior dolore*
> *Che ricordarsi del tempo felice*
> *Nella miseria; e cio sa 'l tuo dottore.'*
> And she said to me: 'There is no greater grief
> Than to remember happy times, in misery;
> And your teacher knows it, too.'